Stendhal (a pseudonym for Marie-Henri Beyle) (1783–1842) was a prolific diarist who made detailed notes on his thoughts, travels, and many love affairs. These elaborate journals, his great interest in psychology, and his experiences as an officer under Napoleon served him well when he decided to write. His first novel, *Armance* (1827), was notable for its artistic skill and psychological insights, but was virtually ignored by the public. His second novel, however, *The Red and the Black* (1830), created a sensation and brought him fame. But adverse criticism of this book probably cost Stendhal any further promotions with the diplomatic service, his profession at the time. His last years were spent mainly as consul general in a small Italian town. Aging, bored, and in ill health, he found solace only in his artistic endeavors. Among his last works were an autobiography, several travel books, and *The Charterhouse of Parma* (1839), a novel of political corruption that many critics consider his masterpiece.

Jonathan Keates is a prizewinning biographer, travel writer, novelist, and critic, with a special interest in the history and culture of nineteenth-century Europe. Among his recent books are *The Siege of Venice* and *Stendhal*, a *New York Times* Notable Book. A Fellow of the Royal Society of Literature, he lives in London.

THE RED AND THE BLACK

A Chronicle
of the Nineteenth Century

STENDHAL

———

Translated by
LLOYD C. PARKS

With a New Introduction by
JONATHAN KEATES

and an Afterword by
DONALD M. FRAME

SIGNET CLASSICS

For Teck and Jean Guiguet, this translation

SIGNET CLASSICS
Published by New American Library, a division of
Penguin Group (USA) Inc., 375 Hudson Street,
New York, New York 10014, USA
Penguin Group (Canada), 90 Eglinton Avenue East, Suite 700, Toronto,
Ontario M4P 2Y3, Canada (a division of Pearson Penguin Canada Inc.)
Penguin Books Ltd., 80 Strand, London WC2R 0RL, England
Penguin Ireland, 25 St. Stephen's Green, Dublin 2,
Ireland (a division of Penguin Books Ltd.)
Penguin Group (Australia), 250 Camberwell Road, Camberwell, Victoria 3124,
Australia (a division of Pearson Australia Group Pty. Ltd.)
Penguin Books India Pvt. Ltd., 11 Community Centre, Panchsheel Park,
New Delhi - 110 017, India
Penguin Group (NZ), cnr Airborne and Rosedale Roads, Albany,
Auckland 1310, New Zealand (a division of Pearson New Zealand Ltd.)
Penguin Books (South Africa) (Pty.) Ltd., 24 Sturdee Avenue,
Rosebank, Johannesburg 2196, South Africa

Penguin Books Ltd., Registered Offices:
80 Strand, London WC2R 0RL, England

Published by Signet Classics, an imprint of New American Library,
a division of Penguin Group (USA) Inc.

First Signet Classic Printing, July 1970
First Signet Classics Printing (Keates Introduction), June 2006
10 9 8 7 6 5 4 3 2

Translation copyright © Lloyd C. Parks, 1970
Introduction copyright © Jonathan Keates, 2006
Afterword copyright © Penguin Group (USA) Inc., 1970
All rights reserved

 REGISTERED TRADEMARK—MARCA REGISTRADA

Printed in the United States of America

INTRODUCTION

Stendhal, a writer by pure instinct, became a novelist by accident. When *Le Rouge et le Noir—The Red and the Black*—was published in 1830, he had only one novel to his name. *Armance*, subtitled *Some Scenes from a Parisian Salon*, had appeared four years earlier. Its readers were baffled by its curiously terse narrative style and by the author's reluctance to disclose the nature of the profound secret that prevents his hero and heroine from consummating their love affair. Had Stendhal not later revealed this, in a letter to his friend Prosper Merimee, as sexual impotence, we should probably still be in the dark.

Otherwise such literary fame as he had so far achieved was based on anything but fiction. As Marie-Henri Beyle, born in the French city of Grenoble in 1783, he had yearned to make his name as a dramatist. When his successful career in civic administration under the empire of Napoleon Bonaparte ended with the Emperor's defeat at Waterloo, he embarked on a memoir of the great man's earliest victories as commander of a French army invading northern Italy. Under the pen name Stendhal, derived from a small German town he had visited in 1806, he tried his hand as an art critic with a history of Italian painting, indulged his passion for opera with a biographical study of Gioacchino Rossini, composer of *The Barber of Seville*, issued a clever little handbook to Romanticism and published a travel journal entitled *Rome, Naples and Florence*—misleadingly, since most of it deals with Milan.

Meanwhile Stendhal had started to make his living as a journalist for British magazines. Copy filed from Paris to translators in London included waspish book reviews, articles on new plays and items of literary gossip picked up from his weekly trawl of fashionable salons. In one of these Parisian dispatches, dated 1826, he urged English visitors to France to read the *Gazette des Tribunaux*, a daily account of proceedings in the law courts throughout the nation. A mine of detail and absorbing narrative, this report, according to Stendhal, provided an essential guide to contemporary French society, its manners, foibles and aspirations. It was among the columns of the *Gazette*, indeed, that he found his earliest inspiration for the novel that became *The Red and the Black*.

In France the word *affaire* is used when discussing crimes and criminal trials, and *"l'affaire Berthet"* was one of the most-talked-about cases of 1827. It involved a handsome young blacksmith's son, Antoine Berthet, from Stendhal's native town Grenoble, who had trained for the priesthood before entering the household of the Michoud family as a tutor to the children. Dismissed for reasons never made clear, Berthet had tried to blackmail Madame Michoud by accusing her of carrying on a liaison with his successor. When her husband sought to prevent further scandal by finding Berthet a job with a different family, Madame Michoud was quick to denounce the young man to his prospective employers. Some days later, after issuing a death threat, Berthet burst into the church where she was attending mass, pulled out a pistol and severely wounded her. Turning the gun on himself, he merely succeeded in breaking his jaw, and was executed after a trial, during which his good looks and noble bearing had excited considerable sympathy in court.

Another case in the *Gazette des Tribunaux* had been used by Stendhal to pad out a decidedly eccentric travel guide to Rome he produced in 1828. On this occasion a youthful cabinetmaker named Adrien Lafargue, having found his mistress in bed with one of her former lovers, fired two shots at her before cutting her throat. Despite a guilty verdict, he was awarded a fairly brief prison sentence (French law acknowledged the mitigating circumstances surrounding a crime of passion). Stendhal plainly admired the single-mindedness with which Lafargue had carried out his revenge, and read a lesson in the whole affair as to the contrast between the feebleness of France's aristocratic governing echelons and the fervor and imagination of the young working-class murderer.

Out of these two episodes sprang the concept of a novel, provisionally titled "Julien," which portrayed the career of an ambitious young man emerging from humble origins in a provincial town. His career, whether as lover, politician or social adventurer, would end in tragedy with the attempted murder of his mistress and his own execution. As work on the book continued, Stendhal inevitably seized the chance

vi

to broaden its perspectives, creating in the process a story both rich in contemporary resonances and self-consciously historical in certain aspects of the plot. Context is all important. Characters such as the dandy Charles de Beauvoisis, preoccupied with the cut of Julien Sorel's coat, or the lethally imperturbable Maréchale de Fervaques, who considers the merest hint of sensibility to be "a species of moral drunkenness," are molded by their fallible humanity, but Stendhal never underestimates the influence on each of that patrician world whose assumptions his hero deliberately sets out to challenge.

How heroic, in fact, is Julien? An essential feature of Stendhal's creative personality was his enduring self-absorption. A massive egoism informs everything from his collection of novellas known as *Italian Chronicles* to an essay on Michelangelo in his *History of Painting*, which he suddenly interrupts with a digression on his experiences during Napoleon's 1812 retreat from Moscow. Yet it would be wrong to see Julien simply as an alter ego of his creator. In various ways, Stendhal carefully sought to distance himself from his protagonist, making use of a narrative idiom that, while less curt and more subtly urbane than the style he had exercised in *Armance*, presented a calculatedly detached view of the young man's motives and strategies.

On the surface, then, Julien seems too embittered, callous and vengeful, too eaten up by ambition to endear himself to us even as an antihero. His seduction of Madame de Rênal, for example, is based as much on the need to assert his strength of character and social equality as on the force of an authentic passion. At various moments in the novel, he sees himself as a monster, less in the grotesque or destructive sense than as someone whose process of reinvention involves a continuous sequence of transgressive acts and the sacrifice of anything like the traditional morality with which social conditioning has tried to imbue him. As such, "the little abbé" is a singularly charismatic figure, self-empowered and coming from nowhere, as it seems, to captivate the reader in ways denied to more conventionally glamorous heroes.

This quality of uniqueness matches the novel's own individuality as a work of art. Unlike *Armance*, which was heavily influenced by the "silver fork" tales of high life popular in England during the 1820s, *The Red and the Black* has no obvious predecessors. True, a great many influences feed into the book from Stendhal's own astonishingly wide and eclectic reading. The ending, for instance, centered upon Mathilde de La Mole's bizarre transformation of her lover's head into a cult object, which she buries with her own hands beside his decapitated body in a candlelit mountain cave, is modeled on medieval romances and an episode in sixteenth-century French history. The firm location of the rest of the story in a recognizably contemporary France and the presence of a historical dimension as a determinant factor in its characters' lives reveal Stendhal's indebtedness to Sir Walter Scott, a novelist whose reactionary politics he despised as profoundly as he admired the older writer's achievement in widening the scope of fiction as a serious international art form.

Lacking any immediate fictional models, *Le Rouge et le Noir* asserts its originality above all in a sympathetic treatment of its female protagonists. Stendhal, almost perpetually in love or at any rate believing himself to be so, used the idea of sexual availability as the springboard for a whole series of deeply significant friendships with women. Even if, as often happened, they rejected sex as the prelude to a close relationship, it was more often with rueful amusement than prudish outrage. Thereafter Stendhal would treasure their companionship as equals, making them his confidantes and correspondents, occasionally giving them male nicknames and canvassing their opinions on art, literature and politics.

Such an attitude, reflected most strikingly in his unfinished story *Lamiel* (1839), whose heroine ends up as a kind of free-spirited urban guerrilla, is without parallel in the French novel until the appearance of Marcel Proust's *À la recherche du temps perdu* in the early decades of the twentieth century. A hundred years or so after Stendhal's death, no less a figure than Simone de Beauvoir could hail "this tender friend of women" as a protofeminist, loving the whole sex for itself rather than for some idealized notion of the eternal feminine. She singled out Madame de Rênal for her spiritual independence, her delicacy and lack of falsehood or vulgarity, and praised Mathilde de La Mole for her deliberate efforts to distance herself from the banal limitations of birth and status.

The ladder Julien uses to clamber up to Mathilde's window becomes, in de Beauvoir's reading, a symbol both of his destiny and of Mathilde's growing courage, which achieves its consummation on the novel's final page. Stendhal seems absolutely determined that such women should triumph over a society that tries incessantly to curb their nobler impulses. Their refusal to compromise—in Madame de Rênal's case her death from a broken heart is tantamount to rejection of a world without her lover—compares significantly with Julien's readiness to accommodate himself to a despised value system for the sake of advancement and prosperity.

Built into *The Red and the Black* is a prophetic awareness that the world it describes, whether in the small town of Verrières or the Parisian Hotel de La Mole, must soon implode, with its more preposterous denizens, like the anonymous duke who dresses like a dandy, walks on springs and contrives to look simultaneously noble and insignificant will vanish in smoke. This was indeed what happened as the first volume went to press in the summer of 1830. The Bourbon monarchy restored after Napoleon's fall had become increasingly unpopular, and when King Charles X sought to abolish the trappings of bicameral government, limiting the franchise and muzzling the press, Paris took to the streets. At the printers where the book had entered its proof stage, the compositors took up tools and joined the revolution. By the time the second volume was published in November, a new regime, under the rule of Charles's cousin the "citizen king" Louis-Philippe, was in place, and Stendhal had been named as His Majesty's consul in Trieste.

The critical reception of the novel was neither better nor worse than those accorded to Stendhal's earlier books. For the *Revue de Paris*, it was spoiled by too great a sense of effort in the writing, the *Gazette de France* judged it time for the author to change both his pen name and his style, and the *Revue encyclopedique* rather oddly dismissed the work as "aristocratic and hence ephemeral." One reviewer was convinced that "M. de Stendhal will write a much better book when he really wants to do so," while another, damning with faint praise, declared, "A volume as carefully considered as this one is bound to be successful, but never, never shall we learn to love its author."

What puzzled everybody, as it has mystified readers ever since, was the title. How precisely are we meant to interpret those two colors, red and black? The name "Julien" was only dropped from the title page at the last moment, according to Roman Colomb, Stendhal's friend and executor, but there was no obvious pointer in the printed text to the new title's real significance. A popular interpretation relates red to the military uniform Julien desires to wear (even though this was the color of the British army rather than the French) and black to the priestly soutane he dons during his period at the seminary. Equally plausible is the notion of black representing gloomy political reaction, as opposed to the lurid scarlet of liberal opposition. Dismissing the suggestion that the story is nothing more than a literary version of the popular gambling game *rouge-et-noir*, with Julien bouncing about on a wheel of destiny, Claude Roy, one of Stendhal's most distinguished modern commentators, proposes the wisest solution of all. In his reading, both colors prefigure the book's absorption with death. Balancing Julien's somber clothes and Mathilde's mourning is the blood flowing from the wound in Madame de Rênal's shoulder following her bungled murder during mass. This sanguinary effect is strikingly foreshadowed earlier by Julien's idea that the contents of the holy water stoups have somehow turned into blood.

Just as strange to many of his contemporaries was the narrative mode employed by the author. Other novelists of Stendhal's era dealt punctiliously with scene setting, used paragraphs of conventional length and declined to interfere with the story once set in motion. The author of *Le Rouge et le Noir*, on the other hand, treated paragraphing as the most perfunctory of considerations and bundled the reader unceremoniously through a sequence of breathless chapter openings: "He hurried to brush his coat," "Julien read over his letters," "The children adored him, he cared nothing for them," et cetera. Worse still, he had the nerve to pause the action so as to predict our likely response to the events described. More than a few brows must have been furrowed in anger or perplexity when, in Book II Chapter XIX, Stendhal presents his famous comparison of a novel to a mirror on a journey down the high road, sometimes reflecting the sky and sometimes the mud in the puddles.

No wonder Stendhal came to believe that his true audience would emerge in the twentieth century rather than from the nineteenth. In a post-Freudian age, readings of *The Red and the Black* have focused increasingly on the emblematic relationship of certain elements in the story to Stendhal's deepest personal obsessions. The cave in the Jura for example, where Mathilde buries Julien's head, has been labeled a symbolic womb, linked to the submerged memory of the writer's prematurely dead mother. Rather more convincingly, an entire pattern of surrogate fatherhood has been traced from end to end of the novel, relating to Stendhal's enduring wish not to have been the son of the dull and unprepossessing Cherubin Beyle.

As for the book's political stance, reverent toward the officially discredited figure of Napoleon, chilly in its scrutiny of the royalist establishment represented by the nobles and the church, Paul Bourget, a later French novelist, rightly observed that Stendhal would only begin to receive his due when France grew more wholehearted in its acceptance of democracy. For Prosper Merimee the problem from the outset lay with the writer's all-or-nothing relationship with fiction as a mediator of absolute truth. "One of your crimes," he wrote to Stendhal, only half in jest, "has been to lay bare, in the harsh light of day, certain wounds in the human heart too foul to be acknowledged. In the character of Julien there are several atrocious aspects, which we all know to be true, but which horrify us nevertheless. The purpose of art does not lie in disclosing this side of human nature."

Stendhal's triumph lay in proving Merimee's scruples wrong. It is surely a mistake to see *The Red and the Black* as an early adventure in realism, prefiguring the work of Émile Zola, who would call it "our greatest novel." Its concern is not with establishing accuracy of perception through atmospheric detail. Passages of extended description in *The Red and the Black* are notably few, and Stendhal always hated the notion that a novelist should be duty bound to fill out the background for its own sake. His interest lay instead with an absolute exactness in the registers of feeling, expression and perception. What his characters were capable of understanding, their intuitive and interpretative faculties, measured the realities of a given situation and gave the novel's various phases their essential momentum.

Above all else, even the passion he sought to analyze and codify in his treatise on love, *De l'Amour*, Stendhal respected intelligence. Friends indeed sometimes found his obsession with what he loosely termed "logic"—meaning rational discourse based on commonsense observation—rather tiresome. In an age of romantic surrender to the imperatives of raw emotion, it seemed dry and old-fashioned, an inheritance from the age of Voltaire, Diderot, the "philosophes" and "encyclopedistes," when the novelist himself was born. It is this very same respect he demands for his hero, Julien Sorel, whose death, as Mathilde implicitly grasps when taking possession of his head, amounts to the pointless waste of a great, restless, eternally entrancing intellect.

The Red and the Black was a book that demanded to be written. There is no evidence, among Stendhal's papers, of hesitation, uncertainty or vagueness of intention in his work on the project, and the gaze it turns upon us is serene and determined. Throughout his life he was distinguished for an extraordinary fearlessness, shown in the various duels he fought and his bravery under fire during Napoleon's battles in Austria and Russia. It is this same refusal to look over his shoulder—courage, in short—that underpins the novel's compelling grip on our imagination.

—Jonathan Keates

Editor's Note: *This work was ready for publication when the crucial events of July occurred and gave everyone a turn of mind that was hardly conducive to a free play of the imagination. We have reason to believe that the following pages were written in 1827.**

---

* Stendhal is the author of this "Editor's Note." Here, as elsewhere in his writings, he is trying to disassociate himself from the July revolution of 1830, which brought down Charles X's Government. *The Red and the Black* was, in fact, composed between 1829 and 1830.

CONTENTS

Book I

CHAPTER

Book II

TO THE HAPPY FEW

BOOK ONE

> The truth, the bitter truth.
> —DANTON*

*Most of the epigraphs in *The Red and the Black* are imaginary, and so are their ascriptions. They serve chiefly to supply a thematic gloss for each chapter. Therefore, I have annotated only those that are genuine quotations and whose authors may be obscure to the modern reader, and those not translated on the page on which they appear.

Chapter I

A Small Town

> Put thousands together
> Less bad,
> But the cage less gay.
> ——HOBBES

Verrières* is no doubt one of the prettiest small towns
in Franche-Comté.* Its white houses with their steep
red-tiled roofs are spread out over a hillside, the slightest
contours of which are marked by clumps of hardy chestnuts. The Doubs* flows a few hundred feet below the
town's fortifications, built long ago by the Spanish and
now in ruins.

Verrières is sheltered on the north by a high mountain
chain, a spur of the Jura. The Verra's jagged peaks* are
covered with snow from the first cold days in October. A
torrent that gushes from the mountain runs through Verrières before plunging into the Doubs and supplies the
power for the numerous sawmills; a simple industry, this
provides a measure of well-being for the majority of
inhabitants, more peasant than burgher. It was not, however, sawmills that made this town rich. It is to the
manufacture of calico, so-called Mulhouse cloth, that it
owes the general affluence which, since Napoleon's fall,
has put a new facade on nearly every house in Verrières.

As soon as you enter the town, you are stunned by the
racket from a noisy machine, an awful-looking thing.
Twenty heavy hammers, falling with a noise that shakes
the pavement, are lifted by a water wheel set in motion by
the torrent. Each of these hammers turns out daily I don't
know how many thousands of nails. Fresh and pretty girls
present to the blows of these enormous hammers the little

13

iron scraps that are quickly turned into nails. This work, apparently so hard, is one of the occupations that most impress the traveler who ventures for the first time into the mountains separating France from Switzerland. If, on coming into Verrières, the traveler inquires as to who owns the fine nail factory that deafens everyone who passes up the main street, he will be told in a drawling accent: "Eh! it belongs to the mayor."

Though the traveler stop for only a few minutes on the main street of Verrières, which runs from the bank of the Doubs nearly to the top of the hill, it is a hundred to one he will see a tall man, looking busy and important, make his appearance.

At the sight of him all hats are quickly raised. His hair is graying and he is dressed in gray. He is a knight of several orders. He has a high forehead, an aquiline nose and, on the whole, his face is rather well proportioned; on first impression, it even seems to combine the dignity of a small-town mayor with the kind of charm that one may still find in a man of forty-eight or fifty. But the visitor from Paris is soon taken aback by his smug and conceited air, compounded with a hint of narrowness and lack of imagination. One senses before long that this man's chief talent is to make his debtors pay him exactly on time and to pay his own debts as late as possible.

Such is the mayor of Verrières, M. de Rênal. After crossing the street at a solemn pace, he goes into the town hall and passes from the traveler's sight. But if the latter continues his stroll a hundred yards up the hill, he will see a fine house, and through the adjoining wrought-iron gates, its magnificent gardens. Beyond lie the hills of Burgundy, which mark the horizon and seem to have been created for the sole purpose of pleasing the eye. This view helps our traveler to forget the town's foul atmosphere of petty concern about money, which has begun to stifle him.

He is told that this house belongs to M. de Rênal. It is to the profits from his big nail factory that the mayor is indebted for this handsome freestone residence, which he has just finished building. His family, they say, is Spanish, very old, and, so they say, was settled in the region long before Louis XIV conquered it.

Since 1815* he has been ashamed of being a factory owner; 1815 made him mayor of Verrières. The retaining walls that support the various levels of the magnificent garden which, terrace by terrace, runs down to the Doubs, are also a reward for M. de Rênal's skill in the iron business.

14

Do not for a moment expect to find in France those picturesque gardens that surround the factory towns of Germany—Leipzig, Frankfort, Nuremberg, etc. In Franche-Comté, the more walls a man builds, the more his property bristles with stones piled one on top of the other, the greater the right he will have to his neighbor's respect. M. de Rênal's gardens, though full of walls, are admired even more because he bought, for their weight in gold, certain small patches of the land they cover. For instance, that sawmill whose odd location on the bank of the Doubs struck you as you came into Verrières, and above which you noticed the name "SOREL" written in gigantic letters on a sign that rises above the roof—six years ago it occupied the site on which they are now raising the wall for the fourth terrace of M. de Rênal's garden.

His pride notwithstanding, the mayor was obliged to make many overtures to the hard, stubborn old peasant; he had to count out many a fine gold louis before Sorel would agree to move his mill elsewhere. As for the "public" stream that operated the saw, M. de Rênal, by using the influence he enjoys in Paris, managed to have its course changed. He was granted this favor after the election of 182—.

For one acre he gave Sorel four, five hundred yards lower down on the bank of the Doubs. And though this location was much better suited to the manufacture of pine board, Père Sorel, as they call him now that he is rich, found the way to extort an additional six thousand francs from the impatience and *mania for owning property* that goaded his neighbor.

True, the deal was criticized by all the local wiseacres. Once—it happened on a Sunday, four years ago—as M. de Rênal was returning home from church, dressed in his garb of office, he caught sight of old Sorel at a distance, flanked by his three sons and watching him with a smile on his face. That smile shone a deadly light into the mayor's soul; he began to think he could have made a better bargain.

In order to win public esteem in Verrières, the essential is never to adopt, though you build ever so many walls, any design brought from Italy by those masons who in springtime come through the passes of the Jura on their way to Paris. Such an innovation would give the rash builder an undying reputation for *wrongheadedness*, and he would be ruined forever in those circles of solid and conservative citizens who grant respectability in Franche-Comté.

15

The influence of the solid citizen there is, in fact, one of the most irksome kinds of *despotism* imaginable. Because of this wretched word, life in a small town is unbearable for anyone who has lived in that great republic we call Paris. The tyranny of opinion (and what an opinion!) is just as *stupid* in the small towns of France as it is in the United States of America.

Chapter II

A Mayor

> Social importance! Sir, do you
> think it counts for nothing? It earns
> the respect of fools, the amazement
> of children, the rich man's envy, the
> philosopher's scorn.
>
> —BARNAVE

Happily for M. de Rênal's reputation as an administrator, a huge supporting wall was needed for the public promenade which rounds the hill a hundred feet or so above the course of the Doubs. Thanks to this wonderful site, it affords one of the most picturesque views in France. But, every spring, rainwater cut channels across the avenue, hollowed out gullies, and made it unusable. This inconvenience, suffered by everyone, lay M. de Rênal under the happy obligation of immortalizing his name by means of a wall twenty feet high and sixty or eighty yards long.

The wall's parapet—on account of which M. de Rênal had to make three trips to Paris, since the next-to-last Minister of the Interior had declared himself the mortal enemy of Verrières, promenade—now rises four feet above the ground. And, as if in defiance of all ministers, past and present, it is at this moment being topped with slabs of hewn stone.

How often, as I leaned over those great stone blocks of a beautiful blue-gray, dreaming about the ballrooms of Paris which I had abandoned only the night before—how often my gaze had plunged into the valley of the Doubs! Beyond it, on the left bank, there are five or six winding valleys, in the depths of which the eye may easily discern

17

a number of small streams. After having coursed from waterfall to waterfall, they may be seen pouring into the Doubs. The sun is hot in these mountains; when it stands directly overhead, the traveler's meditation is shielded on this terrace by a stand of magnificent sycamores. Their rapid growth and their handsome bluish foliage are both due to the topsoil his Honor the Mayor had brought in and piled up behind his immense retaining wall; for despite the town council's opposition, he widened the promenade by more than six feet (even though he is ultraconservative and I am a Liberal, I give him credit for it). That is why, in his opinion and in that of M. Valenod, the happy director of Verrières' workhouse, this terrace will bear comparison with the one at St. Germain-en-Laye.*

Personally, I have only one thing to find fault with in Fidelity Drive (you see the official name in fifteen or twenty different places, on marble plaques that have won M. de Rênal still another cross). What I object to about Fidelity Drive is the barbaric way the authorities have those hardy sycamores clipped and trimmed down to the quick. Instead of looking like the most vulgar plant in the vegetable patch, with their low, round, flattened heads, all they ask is to be left to grow into those magnificent shapes they assume in England. But the mayor's will is despotic, and twice a year all the trees belonging to the commune are mercilessly lopped. The Liberals of the place claim— they exaggerate, of course—that the official gardener's hand has grown much heavier since the Vicar Maslon took the habit of appropriating the clippings.

This young cleric was sent down from Besançon, some time ago, to keep an eye on Father Chélan and other priests in the vicinity. An old surgeon major, who had served in Italy,* retired to Verrières, and who in his days had been, according to the mayor, Jacobin* and Bonapartist at the same time, dared complain to him one day about the periodic mutilation of those fine trees.

"I like shade," replied M. de Rênal, with the hint of arrogance that is appropriate when one is speaking to a surgeon, member of the Legion of Honor. "I like shade. I have *my* trees clipped so they will give shade. And I cannot imagine what else a tree was made for if, unlike the useful walnut, it doesn't *bring in anything.*"

There you have the catchword that settles everything in Verrières: BRING IN SOMETHING. It sums up the thinking of three quarters of the population.

Bring in something is the logic that determines every

18

move in this small town, which struck you as being so pretty. The stranger who comes here, charmed by the deep, cool valleys that surround it, imagines at first that the inhabitants must be sensitive to the *beautiful*. How they go on about the beauty of their province! There's no denying that they think a great deal of it, but only because it attracts a number of tourists whose money enriches the innkeepers, and so, through the machinery of the tax system, *brings in something for the town.*

It was a fine autumn day, and M. de Rênal was out for a walk on Fidelity Drive with his wife on his arm. While she listened to her husband, who spoke with a grave air, Mme. de Rênal was anxiously following the movements of three small boys out of the corner of her eye. The eldest, who might be eleven, kept going over to the parapet as though he meant to climb up on it. A gentle voice would pronounce the name "Adolph," and the child would give over his ambitious project. Mme. de Rênal appeared to be about thirty, but still very pretty.

"That fine gentleman from Paris may well live to regret it," M. de Rênal was saying with an offended air, his cheeks even paler than usual. "I still have a few friends at the Château. . . ."*

But, though it is my intention to tell you about life in the provinces for some two hundred pages, I will not be so barbarous as to inflict on you the long-windedness and "witty turns" of a provincial dialogue.

That fine gentleman from Paris, so obnoxious to the mayor of Verrières, was none other than M. Appert,* who two days before had found a way of getting into not only the prison and the workhouse of Verrières, but the hospital as well, which was directed gratis by the mayor and the chief property owners of the vicinity.

"But," said Mme. de Rênal timidly, "what harm can this gentleman from Paris do you, since you administer the poor fund with the most scrupulous honesty?"

"He has come for the sole purpose of *finding* fault; afterwards he will write articles for the Liberal newspapers."

"You never read them, my dear."

"But people tell us about those Jacobin articles: all that distracts us and *keeps us from doing good.** As for myself, I will never forgive the curé."

19

Chapter III

The Welfare of the Poor

> A virtuous priest who does not
> meddle is a godsend for a village.
>
> ——FLEURY

It must be explained that the curé of Verrières, a man
eighty years old who, thanks to our bracing mountain air,
possessed an iron constitution and character, had a right
to visit the prison, the hospital, and even the workhouse at
any hour. M. Appert, who came to the curé with a letter
of recommendation from Paris, had had the foresight to
arrive in a meddlesome little town at precisely six o'clock
in the morning. He went at once to the rectory.

As he read the letter from the Marquis de La Mole, a
peer of France and the wealthiest landowner in the province, Father Chélan paused thoughtfully.

"I am old and well liked here," he whispered to himself
at length. "They wouldn't dare!" His eyes shining, despite
extreme old age, with a sacred fire that declared his
delight in doing a fine deed involving some risk, he then
turned to the gentleman from Paris: "Come with me, sir,
but please be so good as not to make any comment in the
presence of the turnkey and especially of the workhouse
supervisors about anything we see."

M. Appert realized that he had to do with a man of
heart. Following the venerable curé, he visited the prison,
the clinic, and the workhouse, asked many questions, and
notwithstanding some odd answers, never showed the least
sign of disapproval.

The visit lasted several hours. The curé invited M.
Appert to dine, but the latter excused himself on grounds
that he had letters to write; he had no wish to compromise

his generous friend any further. Around three o'clock the gentlemen went to complete their inspection of the work-house and afterward returned to the prison. There at the door they found the jailer, a bowlegged giant six feet tall whose ignoble countenance had grown hideous from the effects of terror.

"Ah! sir," he said to the curé, as soon as he caught sight of him, "that gentleman I see there with you, isn't he M. Appert?"

"What if he is?"

"Since yesterday I have the strictest orders, and the prefect sent a gendarme who must have ridden all night, not to allow M. Appert in the prison."

"I assure you, Monsieur Noiroud," said the curé, "that the traveler with me is, indeed, M. Appert. And do you acknowledge my right to enter the prison at any hour of the day or night, and to bring with me anyone I please?"

"Yes, Monsieur le Curé," said the jailer in a subdued voice, lowering his head like a bulldog that obeys unwillingly for fear of the stick. "Only, Monsieur le Curé, I have a wife and children; if I am reported they will fire me; I have nothing to live on except my job."

"I should be just as sorry to lose mine," replied the good father, his voice growing more and more agitated.

"It's not the same thing," the jailer answered hotly. "You, Monsieur le Curé, everyone knows you have an income of eight hundred francs, from good landed property. . . ."

Such are the facts which, commented on, distorted in twenty different ways, had been stirring up all the hateful passions of the town of Verrières for the past two days. At the moment, they served as the subject for a little discussion M. de Rênal was having with his wife. That morning, followed by M. Valenod, the director of the workhouse, he had been to see the curé in order to express his most lively displeasure. M. Chélan had no one to protect him; he felt the full weight of everything they said.

"Very well, gentlemen! I will be the third priest eighty years old to have been dismissed in this region. I have been here for fifty-six years; I have baptized most of the people in the town—which was only a village when I first came. Every day I marry our young people, whose grand-parents I married a long time ago. Verrières is my family, but the fear of leaving it will not make me compromise with my conscience nor accept any other guide for my conduct. I said to myself when I saw the stranger: 'This man who has come from Paris may well be a Liberal, there are only too many of them, but what harm can he do our poor and our prisoners?' "

M. de Rênal's reproaches, and especially those of M. Valenod, director of the workhouse, becoming more and more biting, the old priest cried out in a trembling voice: "Very well, gentlemen! Have me dismissed. That won't keep me from staying on here. As everyone knows, I inherited a field forty-eight years ago which brings me eight hundred francs a year. I will live on that income. I, sirs, have not used my position to line my pockets; perhaps that is why I am not so frightened as some when there is talk of taking it away from me."

M. de Rênal got along very well with his wife, but not knowing how to reply to her notion, which she repeated timidly—"What harm can that gentleman from Paris do the prisoners?"—he was on the point of losing his temper, when she let out a scream. Her second eldest son had just climbed up onto the parapet of the terrace wall and was running along it, even though this wall rose more than twenty feet above the vineyard on the other side. The fear of frightening her son and causing him to fall stopped her from speaking to him. In time the child, laughing at his own prowess, looked toward his mother, and seeing how pale she was, jumped down to the promenade and ran to her. He was thoroughly scolded.

This little incident changed the course of the conversation.

"I am set on taking Sorel into my service—the carpenter's son," said M. de Rênal. "He will look after the children, who are getting too devilish for us. He's a young priest, or almost, a good Latinist, and he will make the children learn their lessons; for he has a strong character, the curé says. I will give him three hundred francs and board. I had some doubt about his morals, since he was the pet of that old surgeon, the member of the Legion of Honor who, claiming to be their cousin, took his room and board at the Sorels'. That man might very well have been a secret agent for the Liberals. He said our mountain air helped his asthma, but that has never been proved. He had been on all of *Buonaparte*'s campaigns* in Italy and had even, they say, voted *no* to the Empire in the old days. That Liberal taught the Sorel boy his Latin and left him the pile of books he brought with him. For that reason, I would never have dreamed of putting the carpenter's son in charge of our children; but the curé, just the night before the scene that has made us enemies for life, told me that Sorel has been studying theology for the past three years with the intention of going into the seminary; so he is not a Liberal, and he is a Latinist.

"This arrangement suits me in more ways than one," M. de Rênal continued, looking at his wife with the air of a diplomat. "Valenod is proud as he can be of the two fine Normans he just bought for his calash. But his children have no tutor."

"He might take this one away from us."

"You approve of my plan, then?" said M. de Rênal, thanking his wife with a smile for the wise observation she had just made. "There, it's all settled."

"Heavens! my dear, how quickly you made up your mind!"

"That's because I have character, as the curé has good reason to know. There's no denying it; we're surrounded here by Liberals. All those cloth dealers envy me; I'm certain of it. Two or three are on the way to being millionaires. Well! I should rather like them to see M. de Rênal's children passing by, out for a walk in the care of *their tutor*. It will make an impression. My grandfather used often to tell us how, when he was young, he had a tutor. It could cost me a hundred écus, but we should put it down as an expense necessary to keep up our position."

This sudden decision left Mme. de Rênal deeply thoughtful. She was a tall, shapely woman who had been the belle of the province, as they say in the mountains. She had a certain air of simplicity about her and a girlish walk. Her artless grace, so full of innocence and vivacity, might well set a Parisian to dreaming of a gentle passion. If she knew she had this kind of success, Mme. de Rênal would have been thoroughly ashamed. Neither coquetry nor affectation had ever found a way into that heart. M. Valenod, the wealthy director of the workhouse, was said to have courted her, but unsuccessfully; this cast an extraordinary luster over her virtue. For this M. Valenod, a tall, rough-hewn young man with a florid complexion and big black sideburns, was one of those coarse, bold, and loud fellows who in the provinces are called fine men. Extremely shy and apparently very unstable, Mme. de Rênal was especially offended by M. Valenod's loud voice and his continual moving around. Her aversion for what in Verrières is called a good time had earned her a reputation for being proud of her birth. She never gave it a thought but had been more than glad to see the townsmen paying her fewer calls. We will not hide the fact that she passed for a simpleton in the eyes of *their* ladies because, not knowing how to manage her husband, she let slip all the best opportunities to make him buy her some of the fine hats from Paris or from Besançon. Provided she was left alone to wander in her beautiful garden, she never complained.

She was a naïve soul who had never presumed so far as to judge her husband, or admit to herself that he bored her. She supposed, without saying so, that there could be no tenderer relationship between husband and wife. She especially liked M. de Rênal when he told her about his plans for their children, one of whom he had slated for the army, the second for the bench, and the third for the church. In short, she found M. de Rênal far less tiresome than all the other men of her acquaintance.

This wifely esteem was not unwarranted. The mayor of Verrières owed his reputation for wit and above all for good tone to half a dozen amusing stories he had inherited from an uncle. The old Captain de Rênal had served in the Duke of Orléans' infantry regiment before the Revolution, and whenever he went to Paris, he was admitted to the prince's drawing rooms. There he had seen Mme. de Montesson, the famous Mme. de Genlis, M. Ducrest, the inventor of the Palais-Royal.* These characters turned up only too often in M. de Rênal's anecdotes. But little by little, the effort of recalling things so tricky to recount had become a labor for him, and for some time he had been in the habit of repeating his anecdotes relative to the house of Orléans only on important occasions. Since he was, moreover, very polite, except when money was being discussed, he passed, and rightly so, for the most aristocratic of Verrières' notables.

24

Chapter IV

Father and Son

E sarà mia colpa se così è?
—MACHIAVELLI*

"My wife really has a head on her shoulders!" the mayor of Verrières remarked to himself the next day, at six in the morning, as he walked down to Père Sorel's mill. "Though I told her it would be a way of keeping up my social position, still it never occurred to me that if I don't hire this little Abbé* Sorel, who they say knows his Latin like an angel, the director of the workhouse, meddler that he is, might very well think of it himself and snatch him away. What airs he would put on when he talked about his children's tutor! Once he is mine, will this tutor wear a cassock?"

M. de Rênal was mulling over this question when, from a distance, he saw a peasant, a man close to six feet tall, who seemed to have been busy from the crack of dawn measuring the lengths of timber that had been dumped beside the Doubs, along the towpath. The peasant did not look very happy to see the mayor approaching, since his pieces of wood obstructed the path and had been dumped there in violation of the law.

Père Sorel, for it was he, was very surprised and even more pleased by the odd proposition M. de Rênal made him with regard to his son Julien. He listened to it, nonetheless, with the same air of sad discontent and indifference by which the inhabitants of those mountains know so well how to hide their cunning. Slaves in the time of the Spanish domination, they have retained this trait of the Egyptian fellah's character.

Sorel's answer was at first nothing but a long recitation

25

of all the formulas of respect he knew by heart. During the whole time he kept repeating such idle phrases, with an awkward smile that heightened the air of falseness, almost roguishness, that was natural to his features, the old peasant's active mind was trying to discover the reason which could induce such an important man to take his good-for-nothing son into his house. He was thoroughly dissatisfied with Julien, and it was for Julien that M. de Rênal was offering him the unhoped-for wage of three hundred francs a year, with board and even clothing. This last condition, which Père Sorel had had the genius to put forward suddenly, had been just as quickly agreed to by M. de Rênal.

The mayor was impressed by this demand. "Since Sorel is not delighted and overwhelmed by my proposition, as he naturally should be, it is clear," he surmised, "that he has had an offer from another party, but from whom, if not Valenod?" To no avail, M. de Rênal pushed Sorel to close the deal on the spot; the wily old peasant stubbornly refused; he wanted, he said, to talk it over with his son. As though, in the provinces, a rich father ever consulted a penniless son about anything, except as a matter of form.

A water-powered sawmill consists of a shed at the edge of a stream. The roof is supported by a framework that rests on four big wooden pillars. One may observe the saw itself in the middle of the shed, some eight or ten feet in the air, going up and down, while another very simple device pushes a length of wood against it. A wheel set in motion by the stream drives this dual mechanism: the saw which moves up and down, and the device that gently nudges the log toward the saw, which cuts it into boards.

As he went over to his mill Père Sorel called out to Julien in a stentorian voice; there was no answer. He saw only his elder sons, young giants, who were using heavy axes to square the fir trunks they would later carry over to the saw. They were deeply engrossed in trying to keep exactly to the black marks traced on the timber. At every blow of the axe, they would cut off enormous chips. They didn't hear their father. The latter headed toward the mill. On entering it, he looked in vain for Julien at the spot where he was supposed to be, beside the saw. He caught sight of him five or six feet higher up, astride one of the beams. Instead of tending carefully to the operation of the machine, Julien was reading. Nothing could have been more distasteful to old Sorel. He might have forgiven him his slender build, not much good for hard work and so different from that of his brothers'; but this mania for

26

reading was positively hateful to him. He himself couldn't read.

He called to Julien three or four times without result. The young man's concentration on his book, even more than the noisy saw, prevented him from hearing his father's terrible voice. Finally, in spite of his age, the latter jumped up nimbly onto the log being put through the saw, and from there onto the crossbeam that supported the roof. A violent blow sent the book Julien held flying into the stream. Another blow, just as violent, a cuff laid against his head, knocked him off-balance. He was about to drop twelve or fifteen feet into the moving gears of the machine, which would have crushed him; but as he fell his father caught him with his left hand.

"So, good-for-nothing! you will keep on reading your damned books when you're supposed to be watching the saw? Read in the evening, when you go and waste your time at the curé's house . . . a fine thing!"

Julien, though dazed by the blow and all bloody, moved over to his official post by the saw. He had tears in his eyes, less from physical pain than for the loss of his book, which he adored.

"Come down, animal. I want to talk to you." Again the noise of the machine kept Julien from hearing the order. His father, having descended, and unwilling to go to the trouble of climbing up on the machine again, found a long pole used for knocking down walnuts and struck him on the shoulder with it. Julien was hardly on the ground when old Sorel, pushing him roughly before him, drove him toward the house. "God knows what he'll do to me!" the young man said to himself. As he passed it, he looked sadly into the stream where his book had fallen. Of all his books, it was the one he prized most—the *Mémorial de Sainte-Hélène.**

His cheeks were crimson, his eyes downcast. He was a small, weak-looking young man between eighteen and nineteen, with irregular but delicate features and an aquiline nose. His big dark eyes, which in quiet moments revealed a reflective and passionate nature, were at the moment animated by an expression of the fiercest hatred. Dark brown hair, growing very low, gave him a narrow forehead, and in moments of anger, a wicked look. Among the countless variations of the human physiognomy, there is probably none distinguished by a more striking particularity. A slim but well-proportioned body suggested agility rather than strength. When he was a child, his extremely pensive air and extraordinary pallor made

27

his father think he would not survive, or live only to be a burden to his family. Looked down upon by everyone in the house, he hated his brothers and his father. At the Sunday games on the public square he was always beaten.

It was less than a year since his good looks had begun to win him a few partisan voices among the girls. Despised by everyone as a weakling, Julien had worshiped the old surgeon major who had dared to speak to the mayor about the sycamores.

From time to time, this surgeon used to pay Père Sorel a day's wages for his son and teach him Latin and history; that is to say, the history he knew, the campaign of 1796 in Italy. When he was dying, he willed him his Legion of Honor cross, the arrears of his half-pension, and thirty or forty volumes, the most precious of which had just plunged into the "public stream"—diverted by the mayor's influence.

Barely inside the house, Julien was stopped short by his father's powerful hand on his shoulder; he trembled, waiting for the blows to fall.

"Answer me without lying," the hard-voiced old peasant shouted into his ear, as he turned him around with his hand as a child turns a lead soldier. Julien's great dark eyes filled with tears confronted the small, mean gray eyes of the old carpenter, who looked as though he meant to read the very depths of his soul.

Chapter V

A Bargain

Cunctando restituit rem.
—ENNIUS*

"Answer me without lying if you can, worthless book-worm! How come you know Mme. de Rênal; when did you speak to her?"

"I have never spoken to her," answered Julien. "I have never seen the lady, except at church."

"You must have looked at her, then, brazen scoundrel?"

"Never! You know that in church I see none but God," replied Julien with a hypocritical little air, just right, so he thought, to keep off another cuffing.

"Just the same, there's something behind all this," replied the sharp peasant, and he was silent awhile. "But I'll never find out anything from you, damned sneak. As a matter of fact, I'm going to be rid of you, and my saw will work all the better for it. You've won over the curé, or someone else, who has found a good job for you. Pack up and I'll take you to M. de Rênal's house, where you are to be the tutor for his children."

"What will I get for that?"

"Board, clothes, and three hundred francs wages."

"I won't be a servant."

"Animal, who said anything about being a servant; would I want my son to be a servant?"

"But with whom shall I eat?"

This question caught old Sorel off guard; he sensed that if he went on talking he might say something ill-advised; he lost his temper and heaped Julien with abuse, accusing him of greediness, then left to consult his other sons.

Julien saw them soon afterward, each leaning on his axe

29

and giving counsel. After having watched them for a long while without being able to make out anything they said, Julien stationed himself on the other side of the mill, to avoid being surprised. He wanted to think over the unexpected announcement that had changed his fate, but he felt incapable of solid reasoning; his imagination was too busy picturing what he would see in M. de Rênal's fine house.

"I will give up all that," he thought, "rather than lower myself to eating with the servants. My father will try to force me; I'd sooner die. I have fifteen francs, eight sous, saved up; I'll run away tonight. In two days on the side roads, where I won't have to worry about police, I'll be in Besançon. There I'll enlist as a soldier, and if I have to I'll cross over into Switzerland. But if that's the case, no hope for advancement, an end to my ambition, no hope for the priesthood either . . . a fine profession that can open any door."

This horror of eating with the servants was not instinctive with Julien; in order to make his fortune, he would have done far more disagreeable things than that. He had borrowed this aversion from Rousseau's *Confessions*. It was the only book by which his imagination had formed any idea of society. A collection of the bulletins of the Grand Army and the *Mémorial de Sainte-Hélène* completed his Koran. He would have died for those three works. He had no faith in any other. Following the old surgeon major's lead, he regarded all the other books in the world as lies, written by cheats for the sake of getting ahead. Besides a fiery soul, Julien had one of those amazing memories that so often go hand in hand with foolishness. To win over old Father Chélan, on whom he saw clearly that his whole future depended, he had memorized the whole New Testament in Latin. He also knew the book *Du Pape*, by M. de Maistre,* and believed as little in the one as in the other.

As if by mutual consent, Sorel and his son avoided speaking to one another that day. Toward nightfall, Julien went to the curé's house for his lesson in theology, but he judged it would be wise not to tell him anything about the odd proposition someone had made his father. "It may be a trap; I should pretend to have forgotten all about it."

Early the next morning M. de Rênal sent for old Sorel, who, after making him wait for an hour or two, finally showed up, and beginning at the door made a hundred excuses interspersed with as many bows. By dint of working through all kinds of objections, Sorel reached an understanding that his son was to eat with the master and the mistress of the house, and on days when there was company, in a room apart with the children. Always more disposed to cavil in proportion as he detected a genuine eagerness on the mayor's part, and otherwise full of suspicion and awe, Sorel asked to see the room where his son would sleep. It was a large room and very decently furnished; the servants were already busy moving the three children's beds into it.

After this visit the old peasant saw things in a different light; reassured, he asked at once to see the outfit his son would be given. M. de Rênal opened his desk and took out one hundred francs.

"With this money, your son will go to M. Durand, the draper, and pick up a black suit."

"And even if I should decide to take him back home again," said the old peasant suddenly, forgetting all his ceremonious forms of respect, "will he keep this black suit?"

"Of course."

"Fine, fine," said old Sorel in a drawling voice. "Then there's only one thing left to settle: the money you mean to pay him."

"What!" shouted M. de Rênal indignantly. "We agreed on that yesterday; I will give three hundred francs. I think that's a great deal, perhaps too much."

"That was your offer. I won't deny it," said old Sorel, speaking even more slowly; then, with the inspiration of genius—something that will astonish only those who do not know the peasants of Franche-Comté—he added, looking M. de Rênal straight in the eye: "We can do better."

At these words the mayor's face dropped. He recovered himself, however, and after a weighty conversation, two good hours long, in which not a word was left to chance, the peasant's shrewdness won out over that of a rich man, who had no need of it to live. All the numerous articles that were to regulate Julien's new life had been given final shape; not only was his salary set at four hundred francs, but it was to be paid in advance, on the first of each month.

"Very well! I will advance him thirty-five francs," said M. de Rênal.

"Surely a rich and generous man like our mayor," said the peasant in a wheedling tone, "will make it thirty-six francs,* just to round off the sum."

31

"Agreed," said M. de Rênal, "but let that be the end of it." For the moment anger lent firmness to his tone. The peasant saw it was time to stop taking the lead; then M. de Rênal made progress. Under no circumstances was he willing to hand over the first month's pay of thirty-six francs to old Sorel, more than willing to accept it for his son. M. de Rênal happened to think that he would be obliged to tell his wife all about the role he had played in this transaction.

"Give me back the hundred francs I handed you," he said testily. "M. Durand owes me something. I will go with your son to pick out the black cloth."

After this show of energy, Sorel beat a prudent retreat to his formulas of respect; they took up a quarter of an hour. Eventually, seeing that there was really nothing more to be gained, he withdrew. His last bow ended on these words: "I'll send my son up to the château." Those who lived under the mayor's administration referred thus to his house when they wanted to please him.

When he returned to his mill, Sorel looked for his son in vain. Wary of what might happen, Julien had gone out in the middle of the night. He wanted to put his books and Legion of Honor cross in a safe place. He had moved everything to the house of his friend Fouqué, a young wood dealer who lived on the high mountain that overlooks Verrières.

When he turned up again, his father said to him, "God knows, damned good-for-nothing, if you will have enough sense of honor to repay me the price of your board, which I have been advancing these many years. Take your rags and go on over to the mayor's house."

Astonished not to get a beating, Julien left in a hurry. But hardly out of sight of his terrible father, he slackened his pace. He judged that it would further the ends of his hypocrisy to stop for a while at the church.

The word surprises you? Before coming to this horrible word, the young peasant's soul had had to cover a lot of ground.

When he was still a child, the sight of some dragoons from the Sixth in long white cloaks and helmets topped with long black crests made of horsehair, on their way back from Italy and whom he saw tying up their horses at the grated window of his father's house, had driven Julien wild for a military career. Later on he would listen enraptured to the accounts the old surgeon major gave him of the battles of the bridge of Lodi, of Arcole, of Rivoli. He noted the fiery look in the old man's eyes when he glanced down at his cross.

But when Julien was fourteen, they started to build a church in Verrières, one that might be called magnificent for such a small town. Most noteworthy were its four marble columns, the sight of which made a strong impression on him. They became famous in the region for the deadly hatred they caused between the justice of the peace and the young vicar sent down from Besançon, who was thought to be a spy for the *Congrégation*.* The justice of the peace was on the point of losing his office, at least such was the general opinion. Hadn't he dared to disagree with a priest who went to Besançon almost once every two weeks, where he visited, so it was said, Monseigneur the Bishop?

About that time the justice of the peace, father of a large family, handed down several decisions that seemed unjust; all of them went against citizens who were readers of the *Constitutional*.* The Ultras triumphed. True, nothing but small sums were involved, of three to five francs; but one of these little fines had to be paid by a nail dealer, Julien's godfather. In his wrath, the man cried out: "What a change! and to think that for more than twenty years the justice of the peace passed for an honest man!" Julien's friend the surgeon major was dead.

One fine day Julien stopped talking about Napoleon; he announced his intention of becoming a priest and was to be seen constantly in his father's sawmill, busy memorizing the Latin Bible the curé had loaned him. That good old man, marveling at his progress, spent whole evenings teaching him theology. In his presence Julien evinced nothing but pious sentiments. Who could have guessed that behind his girlish face, so pale and gentle, lay hidden the most unshakable resolution to expose himself to a thousand deaths rather than fail to make his fortune!

For Julien, making his fortune meant first of all getting out of Verrières; he loathed his birthplace. Everything he saw there froze his imagination.

From his earliest childhood on, he had had moments of exaltation. At such times he would have delightful visions of himself being one day introduced to the beautiful women of Paris; he would attract their attention by some glamorous feat. Why shouldn't he be loved by one of them, as Bonaparte, still a poor man then, had been loved by the dazzling Mme. de Beauharnais?* For many years now, scarcely an hour of Julien's life had gone by without his telling himself that Bonaparte, an unknown and penniless lieutenant, had made himself master of the world by his sword. This idea comforted Julien in his misfortunes, which he considered very great, and doubled his joy when joy came to him.

The building of the church and the justice of the peace's decisions suddenly made things clear to him. A notion came to his mind that drove him almost crazy for weeks, and finally took hold of him with the overwhelming force of the first idea that a passionate soul imagines it has discovered.

"When people began to talk about Bonaparte, France was afraid of being invaded; military talent was badly needed and in fashion. But today, you see priests at forty with incomes of one hundred thousand francs; that is, getting three times as much as the most famous generals in Napoleon's divisions. They all have someone behind them. Look at that justice of the peace, such a good mind, such an honest man up to now . . . so old and disgracing himself for fear of offending a young vicar of thirty. The priesthood's the thing."

Once, in the midst of his newfound piety—he had already studied divinity for two years—he was betrayed by a sudden irruption of the fire that was devouring his soul. It happened in M. Chélan's house at a dinner for priests, to whom the good curé had introduced Julien as a prodigy of learning. He found himself praising Napoleon in a kind of fury. He bound his right arm against his chest, claimed to have dislocated it while moving a fir log, and carried it in this uncomfortable position for two months. After this corporeal punishment, he pardoned himself.

Here then is our young man, nineteen years old, yet so delicate in appearance that one would take him for seventeen at the most, and who, carrying a little bundle under his arm, has entered Verrières' magnificent church.

He found it dark and empty. In honor of some feast day, all the windows of the edifice had been draped with crimson cloth. The result, with the sun shining through, was an effect of dazzling light—most impressive and most religious. All alone in the church, he settled down on the handsomest pew. It bore M. de Rênal's coat of arms. On the kneeling chair, Julien noticed a scrap of printed paper, placed there as if to be read. He glanced at it and saw: *"Details of the last minutes and execution of Louis Jenrel, executed at Besançon, the—"*

The paper was torn. On the other side, he read the first two words of a line, *"The first step—"*

34

"Who could have put the paper there," Julien wondered. "Poor beggar," he added with a sigh, "his name ends like mine. . . ." And he crumpled the paper.

On his way out, Julien thought he saw blood near the stoup; it was holy water that had been spilled; the reflection of the red curtains over the windows made it look like blood. Eventually he grew ashamed of his secret terror. "Shall I be a coward?" he asked himself. "To arms!"

This phrase, repeated so often in the old surgeon's accounts of battles, had a heroic ring for Julien. He got up and walked rapidly toward M. de Rênal's house.

Despite his fine resolutions, he was seized by an uncontrollable shyness when he caught sight of it some twenty yards away. The wrought-iron gate was open; it seemed magnificent to him; he would have to go through it.

Julien was not the only one whose heart was troubled by his arrival at that house. Extremely shy herself, Mme. de Rênal was disconcerted by the idea of a stranger who, in the course of his duty, would come constantly between her and her children. She was accustomed to having her sons sleep in her bedroom. Many a tear had flowed that morning when she saw their little beds being carried into the apartment set aside for the tutor. It was to no avail that she asked her husband to have the bed of Stanislas-Xavier, the youngest, brought back into her room.

In Mme. de Rênal's nature, feminine sensibility was developed to the point of excess. In her imagination she had formed the most disagreeable picture of a coarse and ill-kempt creature, whose duty it would be to scold her children, simply because he knew Latin—a barbaric language on account of which her sons were to be whipped.

Chapter VI

Boredom

Non so più cosa son,/Cosa facio.
—MOZART (*Figaro*)*

With the vivacity and grace natural to her whenever she
was far from the sight of men, Mme. de Rênal was leaving
the drawing room by the French window which opened
onto the garden, when near the front door she caught
sight of the face of a young peasant; little more than a
boy, he was extremely pale, and had lately been weeping.
He had on a spotless white shirt and carried a very clean
purple frieze jacket under his arm.

The little peasant's complexion was so white, his eyes so
gentle, that it first occurred to Mme. de Rênal's rather
romantic imagination that this might be a girl in disguise,
coming to ask the mayor for some favor. She pitied the
poor creature standing at the front door and obviously not
daring to raise a hand to ring the bell. Distracted for the
moment from the bitter sorrow caused her by the tutor's
coming, Mme. de Rênal went over to Julien. Facing the
door, he did not see her approach. He shivered when a
soft voice very close to his ear said:

"What do you want here, my child?"

Julien turned sharply, and struck by Mme. de Rênal's
gracious expression, forgot some of his shyness. Amazed
at her beauty, he soon forgot everything, even what he
had come for. Mme. de Rênal had repeated her question.

"I've come to be the tutor, madam," he said to her
eventually, ashamed of his tears, which he was wiping
away as best he could.

Mme. de Rênal was dumbfounded; they stood very close
looking at one another. Julien had never known anyone
so well dressed, especially a woman with such a dazzling

complexion, to speak to him gently. Mme. de Rênal looked at the big tears standing on the young peasant's cheeks, so pale at first and now so pink. Then she began to laugh with the wild abandon of a girl. She was laughing at herself and could hardly believe in her own happiness. What, this was the tutor she had pictured as a dirty and ill-clad priest who was coming to scold and whip her children!

"Sir," she said to him after a while, "do you really know Latin?"

The word "sir" so astonished Julien that he reflected for a moment.

"Yes, madam," he answered shyly.

Mme. de Rênal was so happy that she dared to ask him: "You won't scold those poor children too much, will you?"

"I, scold them?" said Julien, astonished. "Why?"

"You will be kind to them, won't you, sir," she added after a short silence, her voice becoming more and more emotional. "You promise me?"

To hear himself addressed again as "sir," in all seriousness and by such a well-dressed lady, was beyond anything Julien had foreseen; in all the wildest dreams of his boyhood, he kept telling himself that no real lady would ever bother to speak to him until he had a fine uniform. Mme. de Rênal, on the other hand, was completely taken in by Julien's beautiful complexion, his great black eyes, and his pretty hair, which curled more than usual because he had dipped his head in the public fountain a while before to cool off. To her great joy, she discovered that this fell tutor, whose harshness and surly humor she had so much dreaded for her children's sake, was bashful as a girl. For Mme. de Rênal's peace-loving soul, the contrast between her fears and what she saw before her was a great event. At length she recovered from her surprise. She was astonished to find herself thus at the door of her house with this young man, almost in shirt-sleeves, and so close to him.

"Shall we go in, sir," she said with some embarrassment.

In all her life, no purely enjoyable sensation had ever moved Mme. de Rênal so deeply; never had so charming an apparition followed upon more disquieting fears. Those darling children, whom she tended so carefully, were not, then, to fall into the hands of a cross and dirty priest. She had just entered the hall when she turned to Julien, who was following her shyly. His awe at the sight of such a fine house was another charm in Mme. de Rênal's opinion. She couldn't believe her eyes; what struck her especially was that the tutor ought to be wearing a black suit.

"But is it true, sir," she said, stopping again, deathly afraid she might be mistaken, having been so happy in what she believed, "do you really know Latin?"

This question offended Julien's pride and broke the spell under which he had been living for the past quarter of an hour.

"Yes, madam," he said, trying to assume a chilly manner. "I know Latin as well as the curé, and sometimes he is so kind as to say I know it better."

Mme. de Rênal thought Julien looked very wicked at the moment; he had halted two steps from her. She went up to him and said in a low voice: "You won't take the whip to my children during the first few days, will you, even when they don't know their lessons?"

The gentle and almost pleading tone of such a beautiful lady suddenly made Julien forget what he owed to his reputation as a Latinist. Mme. de Rênal's face was close to his; he smelled the perfume of a woman's summer dress, an astounding thing for a poor peasant. Julien blushed scarlet and said with a sigh, in a faltering voice, "Never fear, madam, I will obey you in every respect."

It was only at that moment, after her anxiety about her children had been completely dispelled, that Mme. de Rênal was struck by Julien's extraordinary good looks. The almost feminine cast of his features and his embarrassment did not seem ridiculous to a woman who was extremely shy herself. The male look which is commonly thought to be essential to masculine beauty would have frightened her.

"How old are you, sir?" she asked Julien.

"I will soon be nineteen."

"My eldest son is eleven," replied Mme. de Rênal, totally reassured, "almost old enough to be a companion for you. You will talk sense to him. His father tried to give him a beating once and the child was sick for a whole week, and yet he hardly touched him."

"How different from my case," Julien thought. "My father thrashed me again yesterday. How happy these rich people are!"

Mme. de Rênal was already at the stage where she could detect the slightest change in what was going on in the tutor's mind. She mistook his sudden fit of gloom for shyness and wanted to encourage him.

"What is your name, sir?" she said in her graceful

accent, all the charm of which Julien felt without being able to account for it.

"My name is Julien Sorel, madam; it frightens me to enter a strange household for the first time in my life; I need your protection and hope you will excuse all the mistakes I will make in the first few days. I never went to high school; I was too poor. I have never talked with any men except my cousin the surgeon major, member of the Legion of Honor, and the curé, Father Chélan. He will give me a good recommendation. My brothers have always beaten me; don't believe them if they tell you bad things about me. Pardon my mistakes, madam; I shall always mean well."

Julien was overcoming his fears during this long speech; he was studying Mme. de Rênal. Such is the effect of perfect grace, when it is natural, and especially when the person whom it adorns is totally unaware of being graceful, that Julien, something of an expert in feminine beauty, would have sworn at the moment that she was no more than twenty years old. Suddenly he had the bold notion to kiss her hand. Before long he was frightened at his boldness. A second later he told himself: "It would be cowardly of me not to carry out an action that may be useful to me and lessen the contempt this fine lady must feel for a workingman who's just been torn away from his saw." Perhaps Julien was a bit heartened by the remark "good-looking boy" which he had been hearing the girls repeat every Sunday for the past six months. While this inner debate was in progress, Mme. de Rênal gave him a few instructions as to how to begin with the children. Julien's violent effort to control himself made him turn very pale again; he said in a constrained voice: "Madam, I will never beat your children; I swear it before God."

As he spoke these words he ventured to take Mme. de Rênal's hand and raise it to his lips. She was amazed at this gesture, and on reflection, shocked. Since it was very warm, her whole arm was bare under her shawl, and the motion Julien made in conveying it to his lips had uncovered it entirely. After a few moments she scolded herself; it seemed to her that she had not been quick enough to take offense.

M. de Rênal, who had heard voices, came out of his office. With the same majestic and paternal air he assumed when he performed marriages at the town hall, he said to Julien: "It is essential that I have a word with you before the children see you."

He showed Julien into a study and detained his wife,

who had meant to leave them together. When the door was closed, M. de Rênal sat down solemnly.

"The curé tells me that you are a steady fellow; here, everyone will treat you with respect; and if I am satisfied, I will help you in time to set up a little business. I don't want you to see any more of your parents or your friends; their tone would not suit my children. Here are thirty-six francs, your first month's salary; but you must promise on your word not to give a sou of this money to your father."

M. de Rênal was irritated with the old man, who, in this part of the bargain, had been sharper than he.

"Now, sir—for by my order everyone here is to address you as 'sir,' and you will appreciate the advantage of joining a household where people are well-bred—now, sir, it is not proper for the children to see you in your jacket. Have the servants had a look at him?" M. de Rênal asked his wife.

"No, my dear," she answered in a deeply thoughtful manner.

"So much the better. Put this on," he said to the surprised young man, handing him one of his own frock coats. "Now we will go and see M. Durand, the clothier."

More than an hour later, when M. de Rênal returned with the new tutor all dressed in black, he found his wife sitting in the same place. Julien's presence soothed her; as she looked him over, she forgot to be afraid of him. Julien didn't give her a second thought; despite his suspicion of destiny and of men, his feelings at that moment were those of a child; it seemed to him that he had lived years since the time, three hours before, he had stood trembling in the church. He noted Mme. de Rênal's icy look; he supposed she was angry because he had dared to kiss her hand. But the pride he felt at the contact of clothes so different from what he was used to wearing excited him so, and he wanted so much to hide his joy, that there was something brusque and foolish about every movement he made. Mme. de Rênal watched him with astonishment in her eyes.

"Be grave, sir," M. de Rênal said to him, "if you want the respect of my children and of my servants."

"Sir," answered Julien, "I feel strange in these new clothes; poor peasant that I am, I've never worn anything but jackets; with your permission, I will go to my room."

"What do you think of our new acquisition?" M. de Rênal asked his wife.

Almost instinctively, and certainly without being aware

of it, Mme. de Rênal hid the truth from her husband. "I am not so wild about this little peasant as you are; your kindness will make him impudent, and before the month is out, you'll be obliged to dismiss him."

"Very well! we'll dismiss him. He may cost me a good hundred francs, but Verrières will have got used to seeing a tutor with M. de Rênal's children. That goal could never have been reached had I left Julien in his workman's getup. When I dismiss him, I will, of course, keep the black suit I just had cut at the draper's. He will keep nothing but the ready-made clothes I found at the tailor's, which I just put on his back."

The hour Julien spent in his room seemed a minute to Mme. de Rênal. The children, who had been told about the new tutor, wore their mother out with questions. At last Julien appeared. He was another man. It would be putting it mildly to say he was grave; he was gravity incarnate. He was introduced to the children, and his way of speaking to them astonished even M. de Rênal.

"I am here, sirs," he told them as he brought his allocution to a close, "to teach you Latin. You know what it means to recite a lesson. Here is the Holy Bible," he said, showing them a small volume in 32mo, bound in black. "This is, to be precise, the history of our Lord Jesus Christ; it is the part called the New Testament. I shall ask you to recite your lessons often; ask me to recite mine."

Adolph, the eldest child, had taken the book.

"Open it at random," Julien continued, "and tell me the first three words of a paragraph. I will recite the Holy Book, the golden rule for us all, by heart, until you stop me."

Adolph opened the book, read three words, and Julien recited the whole page as easily as if he were speaking French. M. de Rênal beamed at his wife triumphantly. The children, seeing their parents' astonishment, opened their eyes wide. A servant came to the drawing-room door; Julien went on speaking Latin. At first the servant stood there motionless, then disappeared. Soon Madam's chambermaid and the cook came and stood close to the doorway. By that time Adolph had already opened the book at eight places, and Julien was still reciting with the same ease.

"Oh, Lord! The darling little priest," the cook, a good-natured and very pious girl, said out loud.

M. de Rênal's vanity was piqued; far from having any thoughts of examining the tutor himself, he was busy racking his memory for a few words in Latin; he managed eventually to quote a line from Horace. All the Latin Julien knew was his Bible. He answered with a frown, "The sacred ministry to which I will dedicate myself forbids me to read such a profane poet."

M. de Rênal recited quite a number of supposed verses from Horace. He explained to his children who Horace was; but the children, smitten with admiration, paid scant attention to what he said. There were watching Julien.

Since the servants were still in the doorway, Julien felt he ought to prolong the demonstration. "Now," he said to the youngest child, "it is time M. Stanislas-Xavier also picked out a passage for me in the Holy Book."

Proud as he could be, little Stanislas read the first few words of a verse aloud as well as he might, and Julien recited the whole page.

So that nothing should be wanting to M. de Rênal's triumph, M. Valenod, the owner of the fine Norman horses, and M. Charcot de Maugiron, subprefect of the district, entered the room while Julien was reciting. This scene earned Julien the title of "Sir" which not even the servants dared to deny him.

That evening, all of Verrières' high society flocked to M. de Rênal's house to see the wonder. Julien answered them all with a gloomy look that kept them at a distance. His fame spread through the town so quickly that a few days later M. de Rênal, for fear someone might snatch him away, proposed to Julien that he sign a contract for two years.

"No, sir," Julien replied coldly, "if you dismissed me, I should have to go. A contract that binds me without obligating you in any way is not equable; I refuse."

Julien acquitted himself so well that less than a month after his coming into the house, even M. de Rênal respected him. Since the curé had fallen out with MM. de Rênal and Valenod, there was no one to give away Julien's old passion for Napoleon. He never mentioned him except in horror.

Chapter VII

Elective Affinities

> They cannot touch the heart without crushing it.
>
> —A MODERN

The children adored him, he felt nothing for them; his thoughts were elsewhere. No matter what those brats might do, he never lost patience. Cold, just, impassive, and yet beloved, for his arrival had, so to speak, driven boredom from the house, he was a good tutor. For his part, he felt only loathing for and a horror of the high society into which he had been admitted—at the lower end of the table, to be sure, which explains, perhaps, the loathing and the horror. There were certain formal dinners during which he had a hard time containing his hatred for everything around him. One St. Louis' day in particular, when M. Valenod was holding forth at M. de Rênal's house, Julien came close to tipping his hand; he ran out into the garden under the pretext of seeing about the children. "Such high praise for honesty!" he cried out. "You'd think it was the only virtue in the world; and for all that, what a high regard, what servile respect they show a man who has obviously doubled or tripled his fortune since he has been in charge of the poor fund! I'll bet he makes something even on the money set aside for the foundlings, those poor creatures whose want is still more sacred than anybody else's! Ah! monsters! monsters! Hated by my father, by my brothers, by my whole family, I, too, am a kind of foundling."

A few days earlier, while he was walking alone and saying his breviary in a small wood called the Belvedere, which overlooks Fidelity Drive, Julien had tried in vain to avoid his two brothers, whom he saw from afar coming down an isolated path. Their brother's fine clothes, his extremely neat appearance, and his heartfelt contempt for them had so provoked the jealousy of these rough workingmen that they beat him and left him unconscious and all bloody. Mme. de Rênal, out for a stroll with M. Valenod and the subprefect, happened to turn into the small wood; she saw Julien stretched out on the ground and thought he was dead. Her shock was such as to make M. Valenod jealous.

He was too quick to take alarm. Julien thought Mme. de Rênal very beautiful but hated her for her beauty; it was a reef, the first, on which he had almost wrecked his career. He spoke with her as little as possible, hoping to make her forget the rapture which, on the first day, had moved him to kiss her hand.

Elisa, Mme. de Rênal's chambermaid, had not failed to be smitten by the young tutor; she talked to her mistress about him often. Mlle. Elisa's love had earned Julien the hatred of one of the valets. One day he overheard the man saying to Elisa, "You won't talk to me anymore since that filthy tutor came into the house." Julien didn't deserve this abuse, but with the instinct of a good-looking boy, he paid more attention to his person than ever. M. Valenod's hatred grew proportionately. He said publicly that such fastidiousness was unbecoming in a young priest. Except the cassock, Julien was now dressed as such.

Mme. de Rênal noted that he was speaking more often than usual with Mlle. Elisa; she learned that these conversations were prompted by the shortages in Julien's scanty wardrobe. He was so short of linen that he was obliged to send it out frequently to be laundered, and in such small matters Elisa was useful to him. Mme. de Rênal was touched by his extreme poverty, which she had not suspected. She would have liked to make him a few presents, but she didn't dare. This instinctive reluctance was the first painful feeling she had had about Julien. Up to then, the name Julien and a sentiment of pure and wholly intellectual joy were synonymous for her. Tormented by the idea of Julien's poverty, Mme. de Rênal spoke to her husband about making him a gift of some linen.

"What foolishness!" he answered. "What! make presents to a man with whom we are perfectly satisfied, and who serves us well? It's only in case he becomes slovenly that we should try to stimulate his zeal."

Mme. de Rênal felt humiliated by this way of seeing things; before Julien's arrival she wouldn't have noticed it.

She never remarked the extreme neatness of the young abbé's dress, which was also very simple, without saying to herself: "The poor boy, how does he do it?"

Little by little she began to pity Julien for his shortcomings instead of being offended by them.

Mme. de Rênal was one of those provincial women whom you might very well take for a simpleton during the first two weeks you knew her. She had no experience of the world and no taste for conversation. Because she was endowed with a sensitive and disdainful nature, the instinct for happiness, which is common to every human being, caused her, most of the time, to ignore the conduct of the coarse company into whose midst chance had thrown her.

She might have attracted attention by the naturalness and liveliness of her mind had she received the meagerest education. But as a prospective heiress, she had been raised by the passionately devout nuns of the Sacred Heart of Jesus, who bore a violent hatred against all the French who were enemies of the Jesuits. Mme. de Rênal had sense enough to dismiss afterward, as absurd, everything she had learned in the convent; but she put nothing in its place and ended up by knowing nothing. The untimely flattery to which she had been subjected as heiress to a great fortune, and a decided inclination to fervent piety, had caused her to live entirely within herself. Despite an appearance of the most gracious compliance and submission, which husbands in Verrières held up to their wives as exemplary, and which were a constant source of pride for M. de Rênal, her inner life was, in fact, generally motivated by the loftiest kind of temperament. Such and such a princess, noted for her arrogance, pays infinitely more attention to what the gentlemen in her retinue are doing than this woman, who seemed so meek and modest, paid to anything her husband said or did. Until Julien came, she had shown no real interest in anyone except her children. Their little sicknesses, their sorrows, their small joys, preempted all the tenderness of this soul who had never in her lifetime adored anyone but God, when she was at the Sacred Heart of Besançon.

Although she scorned to tell anyone, a bout of fever in any of her sons would reduce her to almost the same state as if the child had died. A burst of coarse laughter, a shrug of the shoulders accompanied by some trivial maxim about woman's folly, had invariably greeted her confidences about such anxieties, which the need to pour out her heart had led her to make to her husband in the early years of their marriage. This kind of raillery, especially when it had to do with her children's illnesses, twisted the dagger in Mme. de Rênal's heart. And that is what she found instead of the eager and honeyed flattery she had known at the Jesuit convent where she spent her girlhood. She had been schooled by suffering. Too proud to discuss such afflictions, even with her friend Mme. Derville, she imagined that all men were like her husband, M. Valenod, and the subprefect Charcot de Maugiron. Coarseness and the most brutal indifference about any question that did not involve money, precedence, or a cross, and a blind hatred for every argument that opposed their interests, these things seemed to her as natural in the male sex as wearing boots and a felt hat.

After many long years, Mme. de Rênal was still not used to the moneygrubbers among whom she was obliged to live.

Thence, the little peasant Julien's success. She found a sweet pleasure, all shining with the charm of novelty, in the sympathy of that proud and noble soul. Mme. de Rênal soon excused him for his very great ignorance, which was an additional charm, and for his rough manners, which she succeeded in correcting. She discovered that it was worth her while to listen to him, even when they talked about the most commonplace things, even about a poor dog being run over, as it was crossing the street, by a peasant's cart going at a trot. The spectacle of its suffering had set off her husband's big laugh; whereas she saw Julien knit his handsome black and finely arched brows. By degrees it began to seem to her that generosity, noble character, humanity, were to be found nowhere but in this little priest. For him alone she felt the sympathy and even admiration which those virtues will arouse in a wellborn nature.

In Paris, Julien's relationship with Mme. de Rênal would have been simplified very quickly; but in Paris, love is the child of fiction. The young tutor and his timid mistress would have found their position clarified for them in three or four novels, even in the couplets sung at the *Gymnase*.* The novels would have outlined the parts they should play, have shown the model to be imitated; and sooner or later, vanity would have compelled Julien to imitate this model, although with no pleasure and perhaps boggling.

In a small town in the Aveyron or in the Pyrenees, the slightest incident would have been made decisive by the torrid climate. But as matters stand, under our duller skies, a poor young man, ambitious only because his refined nature requires some of the pleasures money can buy, is coming into daily contact with a thirty-year-old woman, one who is sincerely virtuous, occupied with her children, and who does not take the novels for a model of conduct in any respect. Things go slowly; things happen gradually in the provinces; people are more natural there.

When she thought about the young tutor's poverty, Mme. de Rênal was often moved to tears. One day Julien came upon her weeping outright.

"Eh! Madam, have you had some bad news?"

"No, my friend," she answered. "Call the children; we will go for a walk."

She took his arm, and the way she leaned on it seemed peculiar to him. It was the first time she had called him "my friend." Toward the end of the stroll, Julien noted that she was blushing a good deal. She slowed her pace.

"They must have told you," she said without looking at him, "that I am the sole heir of a very rich aunt who lives in Besançon. She loads me with presents. . . . My sons are making . . . such wonderful progress . . . that I would like to ask you, please, to accept a little gift as a token of my gratitude. It's only a matter of a few louis to get you some linen. But . . ." she added, blushing still more, and stopped speaking.

"What, madam?" asked Julien.

"There is no need," she continued, bending her head, "to mention this to my husband."

"I am humble, madam, but I am not low," Julien replied, stopping in his tracks, eyes aglow with anger, and drawing himself up to his full height. "That is something you have not allowed for. I'd be worse than a lackey if I put myself in the position of having to hide anything whatsoever from M. de Rênal that had to do with *my money*."

Mme. de Rênal was bowled over.

"The mayor," Julien continued, "has paid me thirty-six francs five times since I've been living in his house. I am prepared to show my account book to M. de Rênal or to anyone else, even to M. Valenod, who hates me."

After this outburst, Mme. de Rênal remained pale and trembling, and the walk came to an end without either of them being able to find a pretext to renew their dialogue. Love for Mme. de Rênal became less and less a possibility in Julien's proud heart; as for her, she respected him, she admired him; she had been scolded by him. On the pretext of making amends for the humiliation she had unwittingly

47

caused, she permitted herself to show him the most delicate attentions. The novelty of such behavior delighted Mme. de Rênal for a week. Its effect was to appease Julien's wrath in part; he was far from seeing anything in it that might be taken for a personal inclination.

"That's the rich for you," he told himself. "They humiliate you, and then they think they can make up for it with a lot of fuss!"

Mme. de Rênal's heart was too full, and still too innocent, for her, in spite of resolutions to the contrary, not to tell her husband about the offer she had made Julien and how it had been rejected.

"What," replied M. de Rênal, sharply annoyed, "how could you tolerate a refusal on the part of a *servant*?"

And because Mme. de Rênal protested against this word, he told her, "I use the term, madam, in the manner of the late Prince de Condé, when he presented his chamberlains to his new wife: 'These people,' he told her, 'are all our servants.' I've read you that passage in the *Mémoires de Besenval* . . . indispensable in matters of precedence. A man who lives at your house, who is not a gentleman, and who receives a salary, is your servant. I'm going to have a few words with M. Julien, and give him a hundred francs."

"Ah! my dear," said Mme. de Rênal, trembling, "at least not in front of the servants, please!"

"Yes, they might be jealous, and with good reason," said her husband as he went out, thinking about the size of the sum.

Mme. de Rênal fell into a chair, almost in a swoon from suffering. "He will humiliate Julien, and it's my fault." She loathed her husband and buried her face in her hands. She promised herself never to confide in anyone again.

The next time she saw Julien she was trembling all over; her chest felt so constricted that she couldn't get out a single word. In her embarrassment she took his hands and squeezed them.

"Well! my friend," she said to him at last, "are you satisfied with my husband?"

"Why shouldn't I be?" answered Julien, smiling bitterly. "He gave me a hundred francs."

Mme. de Rênal gazed at him as though uncertain.

"Give me your arm," she said after a while, in her voice a note of courage that Julien had never heard before.

She made so bold as to go to Verrières' bookstore, despite the owner's awful reputation for Liberalism.

There, she chose ten louis' worth of books, which she handed to her sons. But these were books she knew Julien wanted. She insisted that there, in the bookstore, each child write his name in the books that had fallen to his lot. While Mme. de Rênal was rejoicing over the kind of reparation she had had the audacity to make to Julien, the latter was staring in amazement at the quantity of books he saw in the shop. Never before had he dared to enter such a den; his heart was beating fast. Far from trying to guess what might be going on in Mme. de Rênal's heart, he was lost in thought, trying to find a means whereby a young divinity student might procure a few of those books for himself. Eventually the idea came to him that it might be possible, if one went about it the right way, to convince M. de Rênal, that his sons ought to be given the history of famous gentlemen born in the province as the subject of a theme.

After a month's careful preparation Julien saw his idea catch on, and to such an extent that not long afterward, while talking with M. de Rênal, he risked mentioning the next step, which was far more painful to the noble mayor; it involved taking out a subscription at the bookseller's and thereby contributing to the welfare of a Liberal. M. de Rênal fully agreed that it would be wise to give his eldest son a *de visu* idea of several works he would hear mentioned in conversation when he went to the military academy; but Julien saw that the mayor was doggedly determined not to go any further. He suspected a secret reason but could not guess what it was.

"I was thinking, sir," he said to him one day, "that it would be highly improper for a fine gentleman's name, like Rênal, to appear on the bookseller's dirty ledger."

M. de Rênal's face lit up.

"It would also be a black mark," Julien went on in a humbler vein, "against a poor divinity student, if it could one day be shown that his name appeared on the ledger of a bookseller who keeps a rental library. The Liberals might accuse me of asking for the most infamous works; who knows but they might even go so far as to write the title of those perverse books after my name."

But Julien was getting off the track. He saw the mayor's countenance resume its expression of embarrassment and annoyance. Julien stopped talking. "I have my man," he told himself.

A few days later, when the eldest boy asked Julien about a book advertised in *The Daily*,* in M. de Rênal's presence, the young tutor said: "So as to avoid playing

49

into the Jacobins' hands, and still provide myself with the means to answer M. Adolph's question, wouldn't it be possible to have a subscription taken out at the bookseller's by the lowliest of your servants?"

"That's not a bad idea," said M. de Rênal, obviously overjoyed.

"All the same, one should specify," said Julien with the grave and unhappy air that fits some people so well when the long-desired and successful end of a transaction is in sight, "one ought to specify that the servant not be allowed to take out any novels. Once in the house, such dangerous books might corrupt Madam's maids, and the servant himself."

"You're forgetting the political pamphlets," added M. de Rênal haughtily. He wished to conceal his admiration for the wise middle course his children's tutor had devised.

Julien's life was thus composed of a series of small negotiations, and he was far more concerned about their success than about any marked feeling of preference that it depended only upon himself to read in Mme. de Rênal's heart.

The position in which he had found himself all of his life was duplicated at the mayor of Verrières' fine house. There, as at his father's sawmill, he utterly despised the people with whom he lived, and was hated by them. Day after day he saw from the subprefect's accounts, from M. Valenod's, from those of other friends of the house, made on the occasion of events that had just occurred under their noses, how little their ideas corresponded to reality. If an action seemed praiseworthy to Julien, it was sure to be the one everybody censured. His comment to himself was always, What monsters, or What fools! The funny thing was that, for all his pride, he often understood nothing of what was being discussed.

He had never in his whole life spoken frankly with anyone except the old surgeon major; the few ideas he had were related to Bonaparte's campaigns in Italy, or surgery. In his young courage, he had delighted in detailed accounts of the most painful operations. He would tell himself: "I wouldn't have batted an eyelash."

The first time Mme. de Rênal tried to hold a conversation with him about something other than the children's education, he began talking about surgical operations; she turned pale and begged him to desist.

He had no other subject. Consequently, as he passed his days with Mme. de Rênal, the most peculiar silence would set in as soon as they were alone. In the drawing room, however humble his bearing might be, she read in his eyes an attitude of intellectual superiority toward all who came to her house. If she happened to be alone with him for a minute, she saw him grow visibly embarrassed. She was uneasy about this, for her feminine intuition told her that his embarrassment had nothing tender about it.

Following I don't know what notion, derived from some account of high society, such as the old surgeon major had seen it, wherever Julien happened to be with a woman, he felt humiliated as soon as there was silence, as though it were his own particular fault. This sensation was a hundred times more painful during a tête-à-tête. Filled with the most exaggerated and Spanish ideas about what a man ought to say when alone with a woman, his imagination had nothing to offer him in his perplexity but inadmissible ideas. His head was in the clouds, and yet he could not find a way out of the most humiliating silence. Thus, the stern look he wore during his long walks with Mme. de Rênal and the children was accentuated by the cruelest suffering. He despised himself horribly. If unfortunately he made himself speak, it occurred to him to say the most ridiculous things. To crown his misery, he was aware and had an exaggerated idea of his own absurdity. But what he couldn't see was the expression in his eyes. They were so handsome and revealed such a fiery soul that, like good actors, they sometimes gave a charming import to words that had none at all. Mme. de Rênal observed that, if alone with her, he never said anything well, excepting when, distracted by some unforeseen occurrence, he was not thinking about how to turn a compliment. Since the friends of the house did not exactly spoil her with new and brilliant ideas, she took great delight in Julien's flashes of wit.

Since Napoleon's downfall, every hint of gallantry has been rigidly excluded from provincial manners. Everyone is afraid of losing his position. The crook looks to the *Congrégation* for support; and hypocrisy has made the most wonderful progress, even among the Liberals. Boredom is on the increase. The only pleasures left are reading and agriculture.

Mme. de Rênal, wealthy heiress of a pious aunt and married at sixteen to a fine gentleman, had never experienced or seen anything that bore the least resemblance to love. Scarcely anyone had ever spoken to her about love except good Father Chélan, and then only in connection with Valenod's advances; yet he had painted such a disgusting picture of it that to her mind the word stood for nothing but debauchery of the lowest sort. She regarded love, such as she had found it in the few novels chance had put in her way, as exceptional, or even extra-natural. Thanks to her ignorance, Mme. de Rênal was perfectly happy, incessantly concerned about Julien, and far from blaming herself the least bit.

Chapter VIII

Minor Events

> Then there were sighs, the deeper
> for suppression,
> And stolen glances, sweeter for
> the theft,
> And burning blushes, though for no
> transgression.
> —*Don Juan*, C. I, st. 74

Mme. de Rênal's angelical sweetness, due as much to her character as to her present happiness, altered slightly only when she happened to think of her chambermaid Elisa. That girl had come into an inheritance, gone to Father Chélan to confess herself, and told him about her plans for marrying Julien. The curé was truly delighted at his friend's good luck, but he was extremely surprised when Julien told him with a resolute air that Mlle. Elisa's offer would not do.

"Beware, my child, of what is going on in your heart," said the curé with a frown. "I congratulate you on your vocation if it is that alone to which you owe your contempt for a more than adequate income. I have been the curé of Verrières for fifty-six years all told, and yet, to judge from the way things look, I am about to be dismissed. This grieves me. However, I have a private income of eight hundred francs. I mention this detail so you will have no illusions about what to expect when you enter the priesthood. If you have any thought of currying favor with men in power, your eternal damnation is assured. You may make your fortune, but you will be obliged to do it at the expense of the indigent, flatter the subprefect, the mayor, the man of consequence, and serve his interests. This course, which is called *knowing how to get along in the world,* may not be absolutely incompatible with salvation for a layman, but in our profession one is forced to make a choice: either to lay up treasure in this world or the next. There is no middle way. Go now, my dear friend; think it over, and come back in three days with your final answer. To my sorrow, I have caught a glimpse in the depths of your character of a dark passion, which does not promise the moderation and complete abnegation of things worldly that are essential in a priest; I predict good things of your mind, but, if you will allow me to say so," added the good father, with tears in his eyes, "once you became a priest, I would tremble for your salvation."

Julien was ashamed of his feelings; for the first time in his life he saw that he was loved; he wept for joy and went to the great woods above Verrières to hide his tears.

"Why am I in such a state?" he asked himself eventually. "I feel I could lay down my life a hundred times over for good Father Chélan, and yet he has just proved that I am a blockhead. It was more important to deceive him than anyone else, and he has found me out. That secret passion he was talking about is my plan to make a fortune. He has concluded that I am unworthy to be a priest, and just when I figured that sacrificing an income of fifty louis would give him the highest opinion of my piety and of my vocation.

"In the future," Julien went on, "I will rely solely on those sides of my character that I have tested. Who could have told me that I would enjoy shedding tears! That I would love the one person who has proved to me that I am a fool."

Three days later, Julien found the pretext with which he should have armed himself the very first day; it was a slander, but what of it? With a great deal of hesitation, he confessed to the curé that a reason which he could not divulge, because it would injure a third party, had dissuaded him from the proposed union right at the start. It was a way of casting blame on Elisa's conduct. M. Chélan found an altogether mundane heat in his manner, very different from the kind that ought to have stirred a young Levite.

"My friend," he told him again, "be a good country squire—learned and well thought of—rather than a priest without a calling."

To this latest remonstrance, Julien replied very satisfactorily, in point of language; he found the words a fervent young seminarist might have used; but the tone in which he pronounced them, and the ill-concealed fire that flashed from his eyes, alarmed M. Chélan.

Yet one should not augur too ill of Julien's future; he hit upon the right phrases of a mealy-mouthed and cautious hypocrisy. That's not bad at his age. As for his tone and gestures—he had lived among country people; he had been deprived of the great models. Later on, when he had been given the opportunity to approach those gentlemen, he became as admirable in gesture as in speech.

Mme. de Rênal was surprised that her maid's newfound wealth did not make the girl any happier; she saw her set out for the curé's house time after time and come back with tears in her eyes; finally Elisa spoke to her about her plans for marriage.

Mme. de Rênal thought she herself must be ill; a kind of fever kept her from falling asleep; she felt half dead when her maid or Julien was not in sight. She could think of nothing but them and of the happiness they would find in their own home. The poverty of the little house in which they would have to live on fifty louis a year appeared to her imagination in ravishing colors. Julien might very well become a lawyer in Bray, where the subprefecture was, two leagues from Verrières; in that case she would see him once in a while.

Mme. de Rênal really thought she was going insane; she said so to her husband and, in fact, took sick. The same night, while her chambermaid was waiting on her, she noticed that the girl was crying. She couldn't bear Elisa at that moment and was short with her; she begged her pardon. Elisa's tears flowed twice as fast; she said that with her mistress's permission she would tell her all about her unhappiness.

"Speak," answered Mme. de Rênal.

"Very well, madam, he won't have me; wicked people must have said nasty things about me; he believes them."

"Who won't have you?" said Mme. de Rênal, scarcely breathing.

"Who else, madam, but M. Julien," answered the maid, sobbing. "The curé couldn't break down his resistance; for the curé thinks he ought not to refuse an honest girl just because she's been a chambermaid. After all, M. Julien's father is nothing but a carpenter; and how did he make a living himself before he came to Madam's house?"

Mme. de Rênal was no longer listening; intense happiness made it almost impossible for her to think. She had the girl repeat to her several times her conviction that

Julien had refused so categorically as to make it impossible for him to come around to a more reasonable position.

"I mean to make one last effort," she said to her chambermaid. "I will speak to M. Julien."

The next day, after lunch, Mme. de Rênal allowed herself the exquisite pleasure of pleading her rival's cause, and of seeing Elisa's hand and fortune steadfastly declined during the course of an hour.

Little by little Julien came out from behind his stiffness and ended by replying to Mme. de Rênal's wise remonstrances with some spirit. She couldn't bear up against the torrent of happiness that came flooding into her heart after so many days of despair. She fainted dead away. When she came to and was settled in her room, she sent everyone out. She was amazed.

"Could I be in love with Julien?" she asked herself eventually.

This discovery, which at any other time would have upset her deeply and plunged her into remorse, now seemed to her little more than a curious spectacle that somehow did not touch her. Exhausted by everything she had just been through, her heart no longer had any feeling left for the use of the passions.

Mme. de Rênal intended to do some work but fell into a deep sleep; when she woke, she was not so alarmed as she should have been. She was too happy to think ill of anything. Artless and innocent, this good provincial woman had never tortured her soul with trying to squeeze a bit of sensibility from it for some novel shade of feeling or of distress. Entirely occupied, before Julien's arrival, with that pile of work which is the lot of any good mother when she lives far from Paris, Mme. de Rênal had the same opinion of the passions that we have of the lottery: a cheat certainly and a happiness pursued only by fools.

The dinner bell rang; Mme. de Rênal blushed a great deal when she heard Julien bringing back the children. A bit more resourceful now that she was in love, she complained of a terrible headache to explain away her flushed face.

"Just like a woman," M. de Rênal answered her with his big laugh. "Something's always going wrong with those machines!"

Although accustomed to his kind of wit, Mme. de Rênal was shocked by his tone of voice. To take her mind off it, she gazed at Julien's features. Had he been the ugliest man in the world, at that moment he would have appealed to her.

Prompt to copy the ways of court society, M. de Rênal took up his residence in Vergy* during the first fine days of spring; it is the village made famous by Gabriella's tragic love affair. A few hundred yards from the picturesque ruins of the ancient Gothic church, M. de Rênal owned an old château with four towers and a garden laid out like that of the Tuileries, including many a box hedge and walk lined with chestnut trees, trimmed twice a year. An adjacent field planted in apple trees served as a promenade. Eight or ten magnificent walnut trees stood at the end of this orchard; their massive foliage rose to a height of some eighty feet.

"Each of those damned walnuts," M. de Rênal would say, whenever his wife admired them, "costs me the yield of half an acre; wheat won't grow in their shade."

The sight of the countryside seemed new to Mme. de Rênal; her admiration bordered on rapture. The emotion that had quickened her pulse also sharpened her wits and made her resolute. Just two days after their arrival at Vergy, M. de Rênal having been called back to town by his duties as mayor, Mme. de Rênal hired some workmen at her own expense. Julien had given her the idea for a little graveled path which was to run through the orchard and under the great walnut trees, and which would allow the children to go for walks in the early morning without getting their shoes soaked with dew. This idea was carried out less than twenty-four hours after its conception. Mme. de Rênal spent the whole day with Julien, gaily supervising the workmen.

When the mayor of Verrières came back from town, he was surprised indeed to find the finished path. Mme. de Rênal was also surprised by his arrival; she had forgotten his existence. For two months after, he spoke ill-humoredly about how bold she had been to make such an important "repair" without consulting him; but Mme. de Rênal had undertaken it at her own cost, which consoled him to a certain extent.

She spent her days running in the orchard with the children, and in chasing butterflies. They had made big hoods out of gauze, with which they caught the poor *lepidoptera*. That was the unlikely name Julien taught Mme. de Rênal. For she had sent to Besançon for M. Godart's handsome volume, and Julien told her all about the odd habits of those insects.

They pricked them mercilessly with pins and arranged

them in a big pasteboard frame, likewise constructed by Julien. At last Mme. de Rênal and Julien had a subject of conversation; he was no longer exposed to the awful torture that their lapses into silence used to cause him. They talked incessantly, and with great interest, though always about very innocent things.

Active, busy, and gay, this life was to everyone's taste, save that of Mlle. Elisa, who considered herself overworked. "Not even at carnival time," she would say, "when there is a ball in Verrières, has Madam ever spent so much time at her dressing table; she changes her gown two or three times a day."

Since it is our intention not to flatter anyone, we will certainly not deny that Mme. de Rênal, who had a superb skin, had some of her dresses altered in such a way as to leave her arms and bosom very much uncovered. She was shapely, and this manner of dress studied her wonderfully well.

"*You have never been so young,* madam," her friends from Verrières would say when they came to dine at Vergy. (That is an expression used in the province.)

A curious thing, which few of my readers will credit, is that Mme. de Rênal went to all this trouble with no specific purpose in mind. She took pleasure in doing so. And not giving the matter any further thought, the time she wasn't chasing butterflies with her children and Julien, she worked with Elisa at basting dresses. Her only trip into Verrières was prompted by a desire to buy some of the new summer frocks that had just come in from Mulhouse.

She brought a young woman back to Vergy, one of her relatives. After her marriage, Mme. de Rênal had gradually become attached to Mme. Derville, who had been her schoolmate at the Sacred Heart.

Mme. Derville used to laugh a great deal over what she called her cousin's crazy notions: "I never think of such things myself," she would say. Though these unexpected thoughts might have been called sallies in Paris, whenever she was with her husband, Mme. de Rênal felt ashamed of them, as of a foolish remark. But Mme. Derville's presence gave her heart. At first she would reveal her thoughts to her in a timid voice; but when these ladies were left together for a long while, Mme. de Rênal's wit would grow more and more lively, and the long, solitary morning would pass like an instant, leaving the two friends very gay. On this visit, the sensible Mme. Derville found her cousin far less gay and a good deal happier. As for

Julien, he had been living like a veritable child since the beginning of his stay in the country and was as happy as his pupils to be chasing butterflies. Alone, far from the sight of men, and by instinct totally unafraid of Mme. de Rênal, Julien, after so much constraint and clever diplomacy, had given in to the pleasure of being alive— so keen at that age—amidst the most beautiful mountains in the world.

As soon as Mme. Derville arrived, it seemed to Julien that she was his friend. He hurried to show her the view to be had at the end of the new path that ran beneath the great walnut trees; it was, in fact, equal if not superior to the finest that Switzerland and the Italian lakes can offer. If you continue on up the steep hillside which begins a few feet from that point, you soon come to the top of a high cliff, tufted with an oak wood that almost hangs out over the river. It was out onto the summits of these rocks, cut to a sheer drop, that Julien, happy, free, and, what's more, lord of the manor, led the two friends and delighted in their wonder at the sublime prospect.

"For me it is like Mozart's music," Mme. Derville was saying.

His brothers' jealousy, the presence of a despotic father always in a bad temper, had spoiled the scenery around Verrières for Julien. At Vergy he found nothing like those bitter memories; for the first time in his life he saw no enemy. When M. de Rênal was in town, which happened often, he took the liberty of reading. Before long, instead of reading at night, and only then by being careful to hide his lamp with an inverted flower vase, he could indulge himself in sleep; by day, in the interval between the children's lessons, he came to these rocks with the book that was his sole rule of conduct and object of his rapture. In it he found at once happiness, ecstasy, and comfort in his moments of discouragement.

Some of the things Napoleon says about women, several discussions about the merits of novels that were fashionable during his reign, gave Julien, for the first time in his life, a few of the notions any other young man of his age would have come by long before then.

The hot weather set in. They took the habit of spending their evenings under a huge lime tree several yards from the house. The night was very dark there. One night Julien was talking forcefully; he was reveling in the pleasure of speaking well to two young women; as he gesticulated, he happened to touch Mme. de Rênal's hand, which was lying along the back of one of those painted wooden chairs which are set out in gardens.

The hand was pulled back very quickly, but Julien considered it part of his *duty* to see to it that this hand should not be withdrawn the next time he touched it. The idea of a duty to be performed, and the ridicule, or rather, the feeling of inferiority to be incurred if he should fail, suddenly drove every pleasurable sensation out of his heart.

Chapter IX

An Evening in the Country

—M. Guérin's *Dido*, a charming
sketch!—

—STROMBECK*

When he saw Mme. de Rênal again, the next morning,
he had a peculiar look in his eye; he watched her as if she
were an enemy with whom he would soon have to do
battle. His expression, so different from that of the night
before, threw her into a state of confusion; she had been
so good to him and he seemed angry. She could not take
her eyes off his.

Mme. Derville's presence allowed Julien to talk less and
give more attention to what was on his mind. His only
real concern, all that day, was to fortify himself by reading in the inspired book which tempered his soul anew.

He cut the children's lessons very short, and later on,
when Mme. de Rênal's presence reminded him to look to
his own glory, decided it was absolutely essential that
tonight she allow her hand to remain in his. The sun
setting, bringing the decisive moment closer and closer,
made his heart beat strangely. Night came. He observed
joyfully, relieved of the immense weight on his chest, that
it was very dark. The sky, heavy with big clouds driven by
a hot breeze, seemed to forecast a storm. The two cousins
were out walking very late. To Julien, everything they did
this evening seemed out of the ordinary. They delighted in
such weather, the kind which, for certain delicate sensibili-
ties, seems to enhance the pleasure of being in love.

Finally they sat down: Mme. de Rênal beside Julien
and Mme. Derville next to her cousin. Preoccupied with
the attempt he was about to make, Julien could find
nothing to say. The conversation flagged.

61

"Will I shake like this and feel so wretched the first time I have to fight a duel?" Julien wondered; for he was too mistrustful of himself and of others not to realize the state he was in.

In his mortal agony, any other danger would have seemed preferable. How many times had he wished that something unexpected would come up and oblige Mme. de Rênal to go back into the house, and leave the garden! The violence Julien was obliged to do his feelings was too great for his voice not to be markedly altered. Soon Mme. de Rênal's voice was trembling too, but Julien didn't notice it. The frightful combat going on in his breast, waged by duty against timidity, was so painful that he was in no condition to observe anything outside himself. A quarter to ten had just sounded in the clock tower, without his having yet dared anything. Shocked at his own cowardice, Julien told himself: "At the exact moment the clock strikes ten, I will act on the plan I have been promising myself all day that I would execute tonight, or go to my room and blow out my brains."

After one last minute of waiting and anxiety, during which the excess of his emotion almost drove Julien out of his mind, ten o'clock sounded from the tower over his head. Each stroke of the fatal bell echoed in his chest, causing there a sort of physical impulsion.

Finally, while the last stroke of ten was still vibrating, he reached out and took the hand of Mme. de Rênal, who pulled it away at once. Hardly aware of what he was doing, Julien seized it again. Though deeply agitated himself, he was struck by the icy coldness of the hand in his grasp; he squeezed it convulsively. A last effort was made to wrest it from him, but in the end the hand was his.

His heart flooded with happiness, not because he loved Mme. de Rênal but because a horrible torture had come to an end. He felt obliged to speak, so that Mme. Derville would not notice anything; this time his voice was strong and resonant. Mme. de Rênal's, on the contrary, betrayed so much emotion, her friend thought she must be ill and suggested going indoors. Julien saw his danger: "If Mme. de Rênal goes into the drawing room now, I will be back in the same horrible position I've been in all day. I've held this hand too short a time to claim a decided victory."

When Mme. Derville repeated her suggestion that they return to the drawing room, Julien gave the hand that had been abandoned to him a hard squeeze.

Mme. de Rênal, who was already getting up, sat down

again and said in a dying voice, "To tell the truth, I don't feel very well . . . but the fresh air is doing me good."

These words confirmed Julien's happiness, which, for the moment, was immense. He talked; he forgot to feign; to the two friends who were listening, he seemed the most charming of men. And yet, in this sudden flow of eloquence, there was still some want of courage, an apprehension. He was deathly afraid that Mme. Derville, tired by the rising wind that preceded the storm, might decide to go back to the drawing room by herself. Then he would be left in a tête-à-tête with Mme. de Rênal. Almost by chance, he had found the blind courage it takes for action; but he felt it was beyond his power to utter the simplest word to Mme. de Rênal. However inconsequential her reproaches might be, he must be beaten, and the advantage he had just won would be wiped out.

Luckily for him, his speech, high-flown and affecting that night, won over Mme. Derville, who as a rule found him awkward as a schoolboy and by no means entertaining. As for Mme. de Rênal, her hand in Julien's, she hadn't a thought in the world; she was letting herself live. For her the hours they spent beneath that great lime tree, which, as local tradition would have it, had been planted by Charles the Bold,* were a time of bliss. She listened delightedly to the wind moaning in the tree's thick foliage and to the sound of the first few scattered drops that were beginning to fall on its lowest leaves. Julien failed to remark one detail that might well have reassured him; Mme. de Rênal, who had been forced to take her hand out of his so she could get up to help her cousin right a pot of flowers the wind had knocked over at their feet, was scarcely seated again when she gave him back her hand with almost no fuss, as if it were already a thing understood between them.

Midnight had struck long ago; it was high time to leave the garden; they separated. Mme. de Rênal, transported by the joys of love, was so ignorant that she hardly blamed herself at all. Happiness robbed her of sleep. Julien, tired to death by the pitched battle between timidity and pride that had been raging in his heart all day long, was carried off by a leaden sleep.

The next morning he was awakened at five o'clock, and though Mme. de Rênal would have suffered cruelly had she known it, he barely gave her a thought. He had done *his duty, a heroic duty.* Filled with joy by this sentiment, he locked the door to his room, and with an entirely new pleasure, gave himself over to reading about the exploits of his hero.

By the time the bell for lunch was rung, he had forgotten, while reading the reports of the Grand Army, all the advantages he had won the night before. He said to himself offhandedly, as he went down to the drawing room: "I must tell this woman I love her."

Instead of the passionate gaze he was expecting to meet, he found the stern face of M. de Rênal, who, having arrived from Verrières two hours before, took no pains to hide his displeasure at Julien's having spent the entire morning without a thought to his children. Nothing could be uglier than this important man in a bad temper and sure of his right to show it.

Every one of her husband's harsh remarks pierced Mme. de Rênal to the heart. Julien, on the other hand, was still so deeply immersed in his ecstasy, so full of the great events which, for the past several hours, had been taking place before his eyes, that at first he was hardly able to lower his attention enough to listen to the hard language M. de Rênal was directing at him. At length he told him, sharply enough, "I was sick."

The tone of his reply might have nettled a man far less touchy than the mayor of Verrières. The thought crossed his mind to answer Julien by turning him out, then and there. He was restrained only by the rule he had laid down for himself: Never be hasty in business matters.

"The young fool," he soon concluded, "has made a sort of reputation for himself in my house. If I dismiss him, Valenod may take him on, or else he will marry Elisa; in either case, he will be able to laugh in his sleeve at me."

Despite the wisdom of these reflections, M. de Rênal's annoyance erupted in a series of coarse expressions which, little by little, succeeded in irritating Julien. Mme. de Rênal was on the point of tears. Lunch barely over, she asked Julien to give her his arm for the walk. She leaned on it in a friendly manner. To everything Mme. de Rênal said to him, Julien would only mutter, "That's the rich for you."

M. de Rênal was walking close by them; his presence increased Julien's wrath. Suddenly he became aware that Mme. de Rênal was leaning on his arm in an obvious way. Horrified by this gesture, he pushed her off and freed his arm.

Fortunately, M. de Rênal did not see this fresh bit of impertinence; only Mme. Derville noticed it. Her friend burst into tears. At this moment M. de Rênal began throwing stones at a little peasant girl who was taking a shortcut across the corner of his orchard.

"Monsieur Julien, for heaven's sake, control yourself. Remember that we all lose our temper at times," said Mme. Derville quickly.

Julien gave her a cold look, his face a picture of the most sovereign contempt.

His look astonished Mme. Derville and would have surprised her even more could she have guessed its full import. In it she she might have read a vague hope for the most atrocious kind of vengeance. It is, no doubt, such moments of humiliation that have produced our Robespierres.

"Your Julien is a violent man; he frightens me," Mme. Derville whispered to her friend.

"He has a right to be angry," replied the latter. "After the amazing progress the children have made with him, what difference does it make if he goes for one morning without speaking to them? You must admit that men are very hard." For the first time in her life, Mme. de Rênal felt a sort of desire to be revenged against her husband.

The intense hatred Julien bore the rich was going to burst out before long. Luckily, M. de Rênal summoned his gardener and stayed behind to help him set up a barrier of thorn branches across the illegal path through his orchard. During the rest of the stroll, Julien did not respond by so much as a word to all the little attentions that were shown him. No sooner had M. de Rênal left than the two ladies, on the pretext of being tired, asked him each for an arm.

Between these two women, both deeply disturbed and whose cheeks were flushed with embarrassment, Julien's haughty pallor, his determined and somber air, made a strange contrast. He despised these ladies and all tender feelings.

"What!" he said to himself, "not even five hundred francs a year to finish my education! Ah! how I'd love to tell him off!"

Absorbed in these hard thoughts, the little he condescended to take in of the two friends' well-intended remarks displeased him as void of sense, silly, weak—in a word, *feminine*.

By dint of talking for the sake of talking, to keep the conversation from dying, Mme. de Rênal happened to mention that her husband had come out from Verrières because he had made a bargain with one of his tenant farmers for some corn husks. (In that region they use husks to fill their mattresses.)

65

"My husband will not rejoin us," added Mme. de Rênal. "He is going with his gardener and valet to see to it that the rest of the mattresses in the house are changed. This morning he put fresh husks in all the beds on the second floor; now he is on the third."

Julien changed color; he gave Mme. de Rênal an odd look and shortly afterward took her aside, so to speak, by doubling his pace. Mme. Derville let them go on.

"Save my life," Julien said to Mme. de Rênal. "Only you can do it. For you know that the valet hates the sight of me. I must confess, madam, that I have a portrait; I've hidden it in the mattress on my bed."

At this information, Mme. de Rênal also turned pale.

"You alone, madam, can go into my room right now. Feel, without letting anyone see you, in the corner of the mattress nearest the window; there you will find a small, shiny black cardboard box."

"It contains a portrait!" said Mme. de Rênal, hardly able to stand.

Her disheartened air did not escape Julien, who was quick to take advantage of it.

"I have a second favor to ask of you, madam: I beg you not to look at that portrait. It is my secret."

"It is a secret," repeated Mme. de Rênal in a barely audible voice.

Although she had been brought up among people who were proud of their fortunes and sensitive to money matters alone, love had already introduced some notion of generosity into her soul. Though cruelly wounded, it was with an air of the simplest devotion that Mme. de Rênal asked Julien the questions she had to, if she was to do his errand properly.

"So," she said to him as she was leaving, "a small round box, made of black cardboard . . . shiny."

"Yes, madam," replied Julien, with that hard look danger imparts to men.

She climbed to the third floor of the château, pale as if she were going to her death. To crown her misery, she felt as if she were about to faint, but the necessity of doing a good turn for Julien restored her strength.

"I must have that box," she said, quickening her step. She heard her husband speaking to his valet, in Julien's room itself. As luck would have it, they moved on to the children's bedroom. She raised the mattress and thrust her hand into the stuffing so violently that she skinned her fingers. But, though very sensitive to little hurts of that kind, she was unconscious of this one, for almost simultaneously she felt the slick surface of the cardboard box. She seized it and disappeared.

No sooner was she delivered from her dread of being discovered by her husband than the horror inspired by that box made her feel that she was definitely on the point of fainting.

"So Julien is in love, and I have here a portrait of the woman he loves!"

Seated on a chair in the anteroom of the apartment, Mme. de Rênal became a prey to all the torments of jealousy, but her extreme ignorance was again useful to her at this juncture; astonishment tempered her suffering. Julien appeared, grabbed the box without thanking her, without saying a word, and ran into his bedroom, where he made a fire and burned it in a minute. He was pale, wrung out; he exaggerated the extent of the risk he had just run.

"Imagine," he said to himself, shaking his head, "Napoleon's portrait found hidden in the room of a man who professes nothing but hatred for the usurper! found by M. de Rênal, so *Ultra* and so irritated! And—the height of recklessness—on its white cardboard backing, lines written in my own hand which can leave no doubt about the warmth of my admiration! And each of those raptures of love is dated! . . . one from the day before yesterday.

"My whole reputation ruined, wrecked in a moment!" thought Julien as he watched the box burn up. "And my reputation is all I have; my living depends on it . . . and what a living at that! good God!"

Weariness and self-pity inclined him an hour later to tenderness. Coming across Mme. de Rênal, he took her hand and kissed it with more sincerity than he had ever felt before. She blushed with delight, but almost instantly pushed Julien away in a jealous rage. His pride, so recently wounded, made a fool of him in that moment. All Julien could see in Mme. de Rênal was the rich woman; letting her hand drop disdainfully, he walked away. He went out for a thoughtful stroll in the garden. Before long a bitter smile appeared on his lips.

"Here I am, taking a walk, at my ease, like a man who is master of his own time! I am neglecting the children! I am exposing myself to M. de Rênal's humiliating criticism—and he will have good reason!" He ran to the children's room.

The affection of the youngest boy, of whom he was very fond, did much to calm his searing pain.

"This one doesn't despise me yet," thought Julien. But he was soon reproaching himself for this diminution of his pain, as for a new weakness. "These children hug me just as they would hug the hound puppy their father bought yesterday."

Chapter X

A Big Heart and a Small Fortune

> But passion most dissembles, yet
> betrays,
> Even by its darkness; as the
> blackest sky
> Foretells the heaviest tempest.
> —*Don Juan,* C. I, st. 73

M. de Rênal, who was visiting all the bedrooms in the château, returned to the children's with the servants, who were bringing back the mattresses. For Julien this man's sudden entrance was the last straw.

Paler, gloomier than usual, he rushed toward him. M. de Rênal halted and looked at his servants.

"Sir," Julien said, "do you think your children would have made the same progress with any other tutor? If your answer is no," Julien went on, not giving M. de Rênal time to speak, "how dare you accuse me of neglecting them?"

Barely recovered from his fright, M. de Rênal concluded from the strange tone he noticed the little peasant assume that he had some advantageous offer in his pocket and was about to leave him.

Julien's anger increased as he spoke. "I can make a living without you, sir," he added.

"I am truly sorry to see you so upset," answered M. de Rênal, stammering a bit. The servants were just ten feet away, busy making up the beds.

"It will take more than that to put things right, sir," answered Julien, beside himself. "Think of the shameful things you said to me, and in front of women, too."

M. de Rênal understood only too well what Julien was after, and his soul was torn by a painful conflict. Julien, really mad with rage, happened to cry out, "I know where to go, sir, when I leave you."

With these words, M. de Rênal saw Julien installed in M. Valenod's house.

"Very well! Sir," he said to him at length with a sigh, and looking as though he had just called in a surgeon for the most painful operation, "I accede to your demand. Starting the day after tomorrow, which is the first, I will give you fifty francs a month."

Julien felt like laughing but stood there stupefied; all his anger had vanished.

"I couldn't despise him more, the dog," Julien said to himself. "That is, no doubt, the finest apology such a low-minded fellow can make."

The children, who had been listening open-mouthed to this scene, ran into the garden to tell their mother that M. Julien was very angry, and that he was going to have fifty francs a month.

Julien followed them out of habit, without even looking at M. de Rênal, whom he left deeply irritated. "There's a hundred and sixty-eight francs," said the mayor to himself, "that M. Valenod has cost me. I must absolutely have a word with him about his contract for supplying the foundling home."

A few minutes later Julien returned to face M. de Rênal again. "I must speak with M. Chélan about a matter of conscience; I have the honor to inform you that I will be absent for several hours."

"Why, my dear Julien!" said M. de Rênal with the falsest kind of laugh, "all day long, if you wish, all day tomorrow too, my good friend. Take the gardener's horse to go to Verrières."

"There he goes," M. de Rênal said to himself, "on his way to give Valenod an answer; he hasn't promised me anything, but we must give this young hothead time to cool off."

Julien got away quickly and climbed up into the great woods, through which one can go from Vergy to Verrières. He was in no hurry to reach M. Chélan's house. Far from wishing to subject himself to a new scene of hypocrisy, he felt a need to look clearly into his soul and give a hearing to the crowd of feelings that were troubling him.

"I have won a battle," he told himself, as soon as he

saw he was in the woods and far from the sight of men, "yes, I have won a battle!"

This phrase summed up his position in glowing colors and restored some measure of peace to his soul.

"Here I am with a salary of fifty francs a month: M. de Rênal must have had a good scare. But of what?"

His speculations about what could have frightened the happy, powerful man on whose account he had been boiling with rage an hour before restored all of Julien's equanimity. For a moment he was almost alive to the ravishing beauty of the woods through which he was walking. Long ago immense boulders had tumbled down the mountainside into the middle of the forest. Great beeches rose almost as high as those rocks, whose shade gave off a delightful coolness three feet from spots where the heat of the sun made it impossible to linger.

Julien caught his breath for a while in the shadow of the great rocks, and then started climbing again. Before long, by following a narrow and barely visible path used only by goatherds, he found himself standing upon an immense rock and certain of his isolation from all mankind. The thought of his physical position made him smile; to him it represented the moral position he was burning to attain. The pure air of those lofty mountains conveyed its serenity and even its joy to his heart. To be sure, the mayor of Verrières was still, in his opinion, the type of all the rich and insolent men on earth; but Julien realized that the hatred which had shaken him awhile ago, despite its violence, had nothing personal in it. If he had stopped seeing M. de Rênal, he would have forgotten the man, his château, his dogs, his children, and his whole family in a week. "I forced him, I don't know how, to make the greatest sacrifice. Think of it! more than fifty écus a year! A few minutes before that, I escaped from the greatest danger. That's two victories in one day. The second does me no credit; the important thing is to guess the reason for it. But tomorrow's soon enough for a careful inquiry."

Julien, standing on his huge rock, looked up at the sky, set ablaze by an August sun. Cicadas were singing in the field below the rock; when they paused, there was total silence. At his feet he could see twenty leagues of countryside. From time to time he caught sight of a sparrow hawk that, starting from the huge rocks above his head, was soaring noiselessly in vast circles. Julien's eye followed

71

the bird of prey instinctively. Its calm and powerful movements impressed him; he envied its strength; he envied its isolation.

Such was Napoleon's destiny; would it one day be his?

Chapter XI

An Evening Party

> Yet Julia's very coldness still was
>   kind,
>   And tremulously gentle her small
>   hand
> Withdrew itself from his, but left
>   behind
>   A little pressure, thrilling, and so
>   bland
> And slight, so very slight that to the
>   mind
>   'Twas but a doubt.
>   —*Don Juan*, C. I, st. 71

In any case, he still had to make sure he was seen in Verrières. Coming out of the rectory, he had the good luck to run into M. Valenod, whom he hastened to inform of the increase in his salary.

Once back at Vergy, Julien did not go down into the garden until nightfall. His heart was exhausted from the great number of powerful emotions that had been assailing it all day long. "What shall I say to them?" he asked himself anxiously, thinking about the ladies. He was far from seeing that his mind was precisely on a level with those trivial events which usually occupy a woman's whole interest. To Mme. Derville and even to her friend, Julien was often unintelligible, while he in turn would only half understand what they were saying to him. Such was the effect of the strength and, if I dare say so, the grandeur of the passionate impulses that were playing havoc with this

73

ambitious young man's soul. For this strange fellow, it was stormy almost every day.

When he entered the garden that night, Julien felt disposed to take an interest in the pretty cousins' ideas. They were waiting impatiently for him. He took his usual seat beside Mme. de Rênal. It soon grew very dark. He tried to take the white hand which for a long while he had seen resting on the back of a chair close by him. There was some indecision, but in the end it was withdrawn from his in such a way as to indicate annoyance. Julien was inclined to accept this as final and continue the conversation cheerfully, when he heard M. de Rênal approach.

His offensive language of the morning still rang in Julien's ears. He asked himself, "Wouldn't it be a good way to get even with this creature, on whom fortune has heaped every advantage, by taking hold of his wife's hand right under his nose? Yes, I'll do it—I, the man for whom he has shown such contempt."

At that moment his peace of mind, so alien to Julien's character in any case, promptly deserted him; he anxiously wished, and was unable to think about anything else, that Mme. de Rênal would leave her hand in his.

M. de Rênal was talking politics angrily; two or three of Verrières' industrialists had become decidedly richer than he and meant to oppose him in the elections. Mme. Derville was listening. Julien, irritated by this oration, edged his chair closer to Mme. de Rênal's. Darkness covered all his movements. He risked placing his hand very close to the pretty arm left bare by her dress. He grew confused; he lost all control over his thoughts. He laid his cheek against that lovely arm; he dared to press his lips to it.

Mme. de Rênal shivered. Her husband was just a few feet away. She hastened to give Julien her hand and at the same time push him off a bit. Since M. de Rênal persisted in heaping abuse on the have-nots and Jacobins who get rich, Julien covered the hand that had been relinquished to him with passionate kisses, or so they seemed to Mme. de Rênal. Nevertheless, the poor woman had had proof, on this same fateful day, that the man she adored without admitting it to herself loved elsewhere! All during Julien's absence, she had been a prey to utter wretchedness, which had caused her to reflect.

"What! can this be love!" she kept asking herself, "could I have fallen in love! I, a married woman, in love! But," she said to herself, "I have never felt this somber

74

passion for my husband that makes it impossible for me to take my mind off Julien. Really, he's nothing but a child full of respect for me! This madness will pass. Whatever my feelings about this young man may be, what difference does it make to my husband! M. de Rênal would be bored with the conversations I have with Julien about things of the imagination. He has nothing on his mind but business. I'm not taking anything from him to give to Julien."

No hypocritical thought came to debase the purity of this simple soul, led astray by a passion it had never known before. She was deluding herself, though unawares, and yet a virtuous instinct had been startled. Such was the conflict that was troubling her when Julien appeared in the garden. She heard him speak and, in almost the same instant, saw him sit down beside her. Her heart was, as it were, carried away by the bewitching happiness that for the past two weeks had amazed even more than beguiled her. For her, everything was unexpected. However, after a little while, she asked herself: "Is Julien's presence enough, then, to make me forget all the wrong he has done?" She was frightened; it was at this juncture that she withdrew her hand from his.

His passionate kisses, the like of which she had never received, made her forget suddenly that he perhaps loved another woman. Soon he was no longer guilty in her eyes. The end of her keen suffering, daughter of suspicion, a present happiness of which she had never dreamed, sent her into raptures of love and wild gaiety. It was a charming evening for everyone except the mayor of Verrières, who couldn't take his mind off the newly rich industrialists. Julien gave no further thought to his dark ambition, or to his scheme, so difficult of execution. For the first time in his life, he was swept away by the power of beauty. Lost in a vague and gentle reverie, so foreign to his character, and gently pressing a hand that struck him as perfectly lovely, he half listened to the rustling of the lime-tree foliage and the dogs at the mill of the Doubs, barking in the distance.

But this emotion was pleasure and not passion. On the way back to his room, he had but one delight in mind, that of returning to his favorite book; at twenty, one's idea of the world and the impression one intends to make on it prevail over everything else.

In a short while, however, he put down the book. By dint of pondering over Napoleon's victories, he had a new insight into his own. "Yes, I have won a battle," he told himself, "but I must profit by it. I must crush that conceited gentleman's pride while he is still in retreat. That was the heart of Napoleon's strategy. He accuses me of neglecting his children. I must ask for a three-day leave to go and see my friend Fouqué. If he refuses, I will force his hand again, but he will give in."

Mme. de Rênal couldn't sleep a wink. It seemed to her that up to then she had never lived. She couldn't take her mind off the happiness of feeling Julien cover her hand with flaming kisses.

All of a sudden the dreadful word "adultress" occurred to her. Everything disgusting that the vilest lewdness might impart to the idea of sensual love came crowding into her imagination. Ideas of this sort were doing their worst to tarnish the tender and divine image she had made of Julien and of her happiness in loving him. The future loomed before her in terrible shapes. She saw herself as a despicable woman.

It was a ghastly moment; her soul had crossed into alien territory. That evening she had tasted a happiness unknown to her; now she was plunged into the most atrocious agony. She had no idea of such suffering; it affected her reason. For an instant she thought of confessing to her husband that she was afraid of falling in love with Julien. It would give her a chance to talk about him. Fortunately, she happened to remember a precept her aunt had once given her, on the eve of her marriage. It had to do with the dangers of confiding in a husband, who is, after all, one's master. Out of unbearable suffering, she kept wringing her hands.

She was being dragged this way and that by painful and conflicting visions. One minute she was afraid of not being loved; the next minute, the horrible idea of crime tormented her as much as if she were slated to be pilloried the next day in the public square with a placard around her neck proclaiming adultery to the whole populace.

Mme. de Rênal had no experience of life; even fully awake and in full possession of her faculties, she would not have seen any real distinction between being guilty in the sight of God and in being publicly harassed by the noisiest manifestation of popular scorn.

When the hideous idea of adultery and all the shame that, in her opinion, the crime carries with it left her a moment's peace, and while she was dreaming of how sweet it would be to live with Julien innocently, as in the past, she found herself driven to face the horrible thought that he loved another woman. She could still see how pale he had been when he was worried about losing that woman's portrait, or of compromising her by letting it be seen. For the first time she had caught a glimpse of fear in his countenance, otherwise so calm and so noble. Never had she seen him disturbed to such a degree, either on her account or her children's. This surplus of pain brought her to the most intense pitch of suffering the human soul can bear. Unconsciously, Mme. de Rênal cried out in the night and wakened her chambermaid. All of a sudden she saw a light appear at her bedside and recognized Elisa.

"Is it you he loves?" she cried out in her derangement.

Fortunately the chambermaid, astonished at the frightfully disordered state in which she had come upon her mistress, paid no attention to her odd question. Mme. de Rênal realized her indiscretion: "I have a fever," she told her, "and a bit of delirium, I think. Stay with me." Completely wakened by the need to restrain herself, she felt less miserable; reason recovered the authority of which her half-somnolent state had deprived it. To rid herself of her maid's intent stare, she ordered her to read the newspaper, and it was to the montonous sound of this girl's voice, reading a long article out of *The Daily*, that Mme. de Rênal made the virtuous resolution to treat Julien with perfect coldness the next time she saw him.

Chapter XII

A Trip

> In Paris one finds elegant people;
> in the provinces there may be peo-
> ple with character.
>
> —SIÉYÈS

By five o'clock the next morning, before Mme. de
Rênal was up and about, Julien had obtained a three days'
leave from her husband. Contrary to his expectations, he
felt a desire to see her again; he kept thinking about her
pretty hand. He went down into the garden; Mme. de
Rênal made him wait a long time. But if Julien had been
in love with her he would have noticed, behind the half-
closed shutters on the second floor, her forehead pressed
against the windowpane. She was watching him. In the
end, despite her resolutions, she decided to make an appearance in the garden. Her usual pallor had given way to
the liveliest coloring. This artless woman was obviously
troubled: a feeling of constraint, even of anger, altered
her expression of deep serenity and, so it seemed, of
superiority to all the common concerns of life . . . an expression which had lent such charm to that heavenly face.

Julien went over to her eagerly; he admired those
beautiful arms, which a shawl thrown on hastily had left
uncovered. The coolness of the morning air seemed to
heighten still further the radiance of a complexion that the
commotion of the night before had but rendered all the
more sensitive to every kind of impression. It seemed to
Julien that this woman's beauty, modest and touching, yet
so thoughtful, a kind not to be found among the lower
classes at all, revealed to him a faculty of his own soul
that he had never suspected. Lost in admiration of the

charms his avid gaze had chanced upon, he completely forgot about the friendly welcome he had been expecting. He was all the more astonished then by the icy coldness she kept trying to show him, and through which he believed he could make out an intention to put him in his place.

The smile of pleasure died on his lips; he remembered the position he occupied in society, and especially in the eyes of a rich and noble heiress. In a moment there was nothing to be seen in his features but haughtiness and anger with himself. He felt a violent spite against himself for having been foolish enough to put off his departure by more than an hour, only to be given such a humiliating reception.

"Only a fool," he told himself, "gets angry with others: a stone falls because it is heavy. Will I always behave like a child? When will I ever acquire the good habit of giving those people only as much of my heart as they pay for? If I want to be esteemed by them as well as by myself, I will have to show them that though my poverty may do business with their wealth, my heart is a thousand leagues removed from their insolence, and set in too high a sphere to be reached by their petty marks of disdain or favor."

While such sentiments were crowding into the young tutor's soul, his mobile countenance took on an expression of outraged pride and ferocity. It troubled Mme. de Rênal no end. The virtuous chill she had meant to inject into her welcome gave way to an expression of interest, and of an interest quickened by all her surprise at the sudden change she had just witnessed. The empty remarks people make to one another in the morning about their health, about the beauty of the day, gave out for both of them at the same time. Julien, whose judgment was not disturbed by any passion, soon found a way of letting Mme. de Rênal know how far he was from considering himself on a friendly footing with her; saying nothing about the little trip he was about to take, he bowed and left.

While she watched him go, dismayed at the sullen haughtiness she had seen in his look, so friendly the night before, her eldest son came running from the end of the garden, and said as he kissed her, "We have a holiday; M. Julien is going on a trip."

At these words Mme. de Rênal felt stricken with a mortal chill; she was wretched because of her virtue, and even more wretched because of her weakness.

This latest event engrossed her whole imagination; she

was carried well beyond those wise resolutions for which she was indebted to the terrible night she had just passed. It was no longer a question of whether to resist this charming lover, but of losing him forever.

She had to sit through lunch. To crown her suffering, M. de Rênal and Mme. Derville spoke of nothing but Julien's departure. The mayor of Verrières had noticed something unusual about the firm tone in which he had asked for a leave.

"There's no doubt but the little peasant has an offer from someone in his pocket. But that someone, even if it's M. Valenod, must feel a bit discouraged by the sum of six hundred francs to which he is now obliged to raise the annual outlay. Yesterday, in Verrières, he must have asked that person for three days' time to think it over; and this morning, to avoid my questions, the little gentleman goes off to the mountains. Imagine having to reckon with a miserable workman who's grown insolent, and yet that's what we've come to!"

"Since my husband, who doesn't realize how deeply he has wounded Julien, thinks he will leave us, what am I to believe?" Mme. de Rênal asked herself. "Ah! it's all decided!"

So that she might at least weep freely, and not have to answer Mme. Derville's questions, she said something about a frightful headache and went to bed.

"That's a woman for you," repeated M. de Rênal. "Something's always going wrong with those complicated machines." And he went away scoffing.

While Mme. de Rênal was being preyed upon by the cruelest torments of the terrible passion in which chance had involved her, Julien was gaily making his way through some of the most beautiful scenery mountains can afford. He had to cross over the high range to the north of Vergy. Rising by degrees in the midst of a great beech wood, the path he was following zigzagged endlessly up the high mountain slope that walls in the valley of the Doubs on the north. Before long our traveler's gaze, after having passed over and beyond the smaller slopes that channel the course of the Doubs toward the south, extended as far as the fertile plains of Burgundy and of Beaujolais. However indifferent the ambitious young man's soul might be to beauty of this sort, he couldn't help but stop from time to time and gaze at a spectacle so vast and awe-inspiring.

Eventually he attained the great mountain's summit, close to which he would have to pass in order, by this shortcut, to reach the isolated valley where his friend Fouqué, the young wood dealer, lived. Julien was in no hurry to see him, or any other human being. Hidden like a bird of prey among the barren rocks that crown the great mountain, he could spot anyone coming toward him from a long way off. He discovered a small cave halfway up the almost vertical slope of one of the rocks. He took it at a run and was soon holed up in this retreat. "Here," he told himself, his eyes shining with joy, "men cannot harm me." He thought he might allow himself the pleasure of writing out his thoughts, a dangerous thing to do anywhere else. A flat stone served as a desk. His pen flew; he was completely oblivious to his surroundings. He noted eventually that the sun was going down behind the distant mountains of Beaujolais.

"Why shouldn't I spend the evening here?" he asked himself. "I have bread and I am *free!*" At the sound of that great word, his soul exulted; his hypocrisy was such that he couldn't feel free even in Fouqué's house. Supporting his head in both hands, stirred by his dreams and his happiness over this newfound freedom, Julien sat in his cave looking out over the plain, and was happier than he had ever been in his whole life. Without paying any attention, he watched the twilight rays fade out one by one. In the midst of this vast darkness, his soul was lost in contemplation of what he imagined he would one day meet with in Paris. First of all there would be a woman, far more beautiful, more intelligent by far, than any he had ever seen in the country. He would love her passionately; he would be loved in return. If he should tear himself away from her for a while, it would be only to cover himself with glory and deserve to be loved still more.

Even supposing he had Julien's imagination, any young man who had grown up among the sad realities of Parisian society would have been roused from his fiction at this point by the cold irony of life: his dream of great deeds would have vanished with the hope of a chance to perform them and would have made way for the well-known maxim: Leave your mistress behind and you run the risk, alas! of being cheated three or four times a day. But this young peasant saw nothing standing between him and the most heroic deeds but a want of opportunity.

Pitch-darkness had replaced daylight, and he still had two leagues of downhill climbing ahead of him to reach the hamlet where Fouqué lived. Before he left the small cave, Julien lit a fire and carefully burned everything he had written.

It was a big surprise for his friend when he knocked on his door at one in the morning. He found Fouqué busy keeping his accounts. He was a tall young man, rather badly built, with big, hard features, an endless nose, and a great deal of good-naturedness lurking beneath this repulsive exterior.

"Have you had a falling-out with your M. de Rênal, then; is that what brings you here so unexpectedly?"

Julien related to him (with appropriate omissions) what had happened the day before.

"Stay with me," Fouqué said to him. "I can see that you know M. de Rênal, M. Valenod, Maugiron the subprefect, and Father Chélan; you know all their tricks, you're ready to go to cautions and bid. You are better at arithmetic than I am; you can keep my accounts. I make a lot of money in my business. But because I can't do everything myself, and because I'm afraid of running into a crook in any man I asked to be my partner, I'm forced to turn down some fine deals every day. Less than a month ago, I let Michaud de Saint-Amand make six thousand francs. I hadn't seen him for six years and happened to run across him at the timber sale in Pontarlier. Why shouldn't you have made those six thousand francs, or at least three thousand? If I'd had you along with me that day, I would have raised the bid on that cutting, and in no time all the others would have left it to me. Be my partner."

This offer put Julien in a bad mood; it interfered with his mania. During the supper, which the two friends prepared themselves, like Homer's heroes, since Fouqué lived alone, he showed Julien his ledgers and proved to him how many advantages his lumber business had to offer. Fouqué had the highest regard for Julien's intelligence and character.

When the latter was finally alone in his small room made of fir boards, he remarked to himself, "It's true, I could make a few thousand francs here, and then, with that advantage, take up a military career or go into the priesthood, depending on whichever was fashionable in France at the time. The little purse I would have got together would spare me any worries about finances. Isolated in the mountains, I would have a chance to dispel a little of my frightful ignorance about so many things gentlemen discuss in drawing rooms. But Fouqué has given up the idea of marriage, and he keeps telling me that solitude depresses him. It's obvious that if he's willing to take on a partner who has no capital to put into his business, he hopes to find a companion who will never leave him.

"Shall I play false to my friend?" Julien cried out angrily. This individual, for whom hypocrisy and a total lack of human sympathy were the usual means of self-preservation, could not, in this instance, bear the thought of the slightest dishonesty with regard to a man who loved him.

But all of a sudden Julien was glad; he had found a reason for refusing. "What! am I to waste seven or eight years in such a fainthearted way! That would bring me to my twenty-eighth birthday; by that time Bonaparte's greatest achievements were behind him. And after I had humbly earned a bit of money by running to all these timber sales and by currying favor with a few crooked subalterns, who can say whether I would still have the sacred fire by which one makes a name?"

The next morning Julien very coolly gave the good Fouqué, who considered their partnership a forgone conclusion, his answer, to the effect that a call to sacred orders would not allow him to accept. Fouqué couldn't get over it.

"But do you realize that I'm offering you a partnership, or if you prefer, to pay you four thousand francs a year? And you want to go back to your M. de Rênal, a man who despises you like the mud on his shoes! When you are two hundred louis ahead, what's to keep you from going into the seminary? Better than that, I'll see to it that you get the best parish in the department. For," added Fouqué, lowering his voice, "I supply firewood to the ———, and the ———, and M. ———. I deliver them top-grade oak, for which they pay me the price of deal, but money was never better invested."

Nothing could prevail against Julien's calling. In the end Fouqué decided that he was a bit mad. Early the third morning, Julien left his friend to spend the day among the rocks on the great mountain. He located his little cave again but had lost his peace of mind; his friend's offer had deprived him of it. Like Hercules, he found himself caught, not between vice and virtue, but between mediocrity leading to guaranteed security and all the heroic dreams of his youth. "So there is no real firmness of purpose in me," he said to himself. This was the doubt that hurt him most. "I am not cut from the same stuff out of which great men are made, since I am afraid that eight years spent getting my bread will rob me of the sublime energy it takes to do extraordinary things."

Chapter XIII

Openwork Stockings

> The novel: it's a mirror one carries
> down a road.
>
> —SAINT-RÉAL

When Julien caught sight of the picturesque ruins of Vergy's ancient church, he noted that for the last couple of days he hadn't once thought about Mme. de Rênal. "As I was taking my leave the other day, that woman reminded me of the infinite distance that separates us; she treated me like a workman's son. Doubtless, she meant to make it clear how much she regretted letting me hold her hand the night before. . . . All the same, it's a mighty pretty hand! What charm, what nobility in that woman's glance!"

The possibility of making his fortune with Fouqué lent a certain facility to Julien's efforts at thinking things through; they were not so often spoiled by irritation and by a keen sense of his poverty and his insignificance in the eyes of the world. As though standing on a high promontory, he was able to judge and, so to speak, look down on both extreme poverty and easy circumstances, which he still called wealth. He was far from judging his position philosophically, but he was clearsighted enough to feel that he was *different* after his little trip into the mountains.

He was struck by the extreme nervousness with which Mme. de Rênal listened to his short account of his trip, for which she had asked.

Fouqué had had plans for marriage, and unhappy love affairs; the two friends' conversations had been filled with lengthy confidences about these subjects. After having found happiness too soon, Fouqué had become aware that he was not the only one to enjoy his mistress's favors. These various revelations had amazed Julien; he learned many new things. His solitary life, compounded of imagination and suspicion, had kept him away from any experience that might have enlightened him.

During his absence, life for Mme. de Rênal had been nothing but a succession of different tortures, all unbearable; she was really ill.

"Above all," Mme. Derville said to her, when she saw Julien arrive, "ailing as you are, you must not go down into the garden tonight; the damp air will only aggravate your condition."

Mme. Derville noted with astonishment that her friend, whom M. de Rênal was always scolding for the extreme simplicity of her dress, had just put on openwork stockings and a pair of charming little shoes from Paris. For the last three days, Mme. de Rênal's only distraction had been to cut a summer dress out of a pretty little fabric that was all the style, and to have Elisa sew it as fast as she could. It was impossible to finish the dress until a few minutes after Julien's arrival; Mme. de Rênal put it on at once. Her friend no longer had any doubts. "She's in love, poor thing!" said Mme. Derville to herself. She understood all the odd symptons of her illness.

She saw her talking with Julien. The most vivid redness gave way to a pallor. Anxiety was depicted in her eyes, which were fastened on the young tutor's. Mme. de Rênal was expecting him at any moment to make clear his intentions and announce that he was leaving the house, or staying. Julien wasn't trying to avoid the subject; it hadn't entered his thoughts. After a frightful struggle, and in a trembling voice that revealed all her passion, Mme. de Rênal finally dared to ask him:

"Are you going to leave your pupils to take a position somewhere else?"

Julien was struck by Mme. de Rênal's uncertain voice and by her look. "That woman's in love with me," he told himself. "But after this passing weakness, for which her pride is reproaching her now, and as soon as she no longer has my departure to fear, she will revert to her haughty ways again." Julien made this review of their relative positions in a flash. He answered hesitantly, "It would pain me deeply to leave such likable and *such wellborn* children, but it may be necessary to do so. One has obligations to oneself as well."

As he pronounced the words *"such wellborn"* (it was one of those aristocratic expressions Julien had learned a short time before, he was moved by a strong feeling of alienation.

"In this woman's opinion," he thought, "I am not *well-born*."

As she listened to him, Mme. de Rênal admired his intelligence, his beauty, her heart transfixed by the possibility of his departure, at which he had hinted. All her friends from Verrières who had been to dine at Vergy during Julien's absence seemed to vie with one another in congratulating her on the astonishing man her husband had had the good luck to dig up. This does not mean that anyone was in the least aware of how much progress the children had made. The feat of learning his Bible by heart, and what's more in Latin, evoked a feeling of admiration in Verrières' citizens that will probably last for a century.

Julien, who never talked with anyone, knew nothing of this. If Mme. de Rênal had had the least presence of mind, she would have complimented him on the reputation he had acquired for himself; and once his pride was set at ease, he would have been gentle and kind to her, all the more so because he thought her new dress charming. Mme. de Rênal, also pleased with her pretty dress, and with what Julien said about it, suggested a little stroll around the garden; in a short while she confessed that she was unable to walk. She had taken the traveler's arm, but far from giving her strength, contact with that arm had robbed her of the little she had.

It was night; they had no more than sat down when Julien, exercising his old privilege, dared apply his lips to his pretty neighbor's arm and take her hand. He was thinking about how forward Fouqué had been with his mistresses and not about Mme. de Rênal. The word *well-born* still weighed on his heart. He felt his hand being squeezed, and this gave him no pleasure. Far from being proud of, or at least grateful for, the feelings Mme. de Rênal betrayed that night by too-obvious signs, he was all but indifferent to her beauty, her elegance, her freshness. There is no doubt that purity of soul and the absence of every hateful emotion prolong the term of youth. It is the physiognomy that ages first in most pretty women.

Julien sulked all evening; up to that time he had been angry with chance and society alone; now that Fouqué had offered him an ignoble way to affluence, he was irritated with himself. Though he spoke a few words to the ladies from time to time, Julien, all wrapped up in his thoughts, ended by letting go of Mme. de Rênal's hand

87

without noticing what he had done. His gesture completely unsettled the poor woman; in it she saw a premonition of her fate.

Certain of Julien's affection, her virtue might have found the strength to resist him. Fearful of losing him forever, she was led so far astray by her passion as to clasp Julien's hand again, which he had absentmindedly left lying on the back of the chair. This action roused the ambitious youth; he wished it could be witnessed by all those proud nobles who, at table, when he was sitting at the lower end with the children, would look at him with such a patronizing smile. "This woman is no longer capable of looking down on me; in which case," he told himself, "I ought to be susceptible to her beauty; I owe it to myself to become her lover." Such an idea would never have entered his mind before he heard his friend's naïve confidences.

The sudden decision he had just taken provided him with a pleasant diversion. He said to himself, "I must have one of these two women." He realized that he would have much preferred to court Mme. Derville; not that she was better company, but because she had always known him as a tutor, honored for his learning, and not as a journeyman carpenter with a rateen coat folded up under his arm, as he had appeared to Mme. de Rênal.

It was precisely as a young workman, blushing to the roots of his hair, standing at the front door to her house and not daring to ring, that Mme. de Rênal pictured him most charmingly. This woman, whom the bourgeoisie of the district claimed to be so haughty, rarely thought about class, and the slightest proof of character easily won out in her mind over anything promised by a man's rank. A carter who had shown courage was more courageous to her way of thinking than any terrible captain of the Hussars adorned with mustache and pipe. She believed that Julien had a nobler soul than any of her cousins, all gentlemen-born and several among them titled.

As he went on reviewing his position, Julien saw that he must give up the idea of making a conquest of Mme. Derville, who was probably aware of the marked preference Mme. de Rênal kept showing him.

Thrown back on the latter, Julien asked himself, "What do I know about this woman's character? Only this: Before my trip I used to take her hand; she kept pulling it away. Today I pulled my hand away; she took it and squeezed it. A good chance to pay her back for looking down her nose at me! God knows how many lovers she's had! Perhaps she decided in my favor only because it's easy for us to see one another."

Such is, alas! the unhappy consequence of too much civilization! At twenty a young man's heart, if he has any breeding, is a thousand leagues removed from that casualness without which love is often no more than the most tedious of duties.

"I owe it to myself to succeed with this woman," Julien's petty vanity went on, "especially because it will allow me, if ever I make my fortune and someone should criticize me for having done such lowly work as tutoring, to imply that love brought me to such a pass."

Once more Julien withdrew his hand from Mme. de Rênal's, then took it again with a squeeze. As they were returning to the drawing room around midnight, Mme. de Rênal asked in a whisper, "Are you leaving us, are you going away?"

Julien answered with a sigh, "I must go, for I love you passionately; that is a sin . . . and what a sin for a young priest!"

Mme. de Rênal leaned on Julien's arm, but with such abandon that her cheek could feel the warmth of his.

Nights were very different for these two persons. Mme. de Rênal was exalted by raptures of the loftiest moral passion. The flirtatious girl who comes to know love early in life grows used to its ups and downs; by the time she reaches the age of true passion, the charm of novelty has worn off. Since Mme. de Rênal had never read any novels, every shade of her happiness was new to her. No sad truth had come to chill it, not even the specter of the future. She saw herself just as happy in ten years as she was at that moment. Even the thought of the vow of chastity and fidelity she had sworn to M. de Rênal, which had troubled her a few days before, presented itself in vain; she sent it on its way like an unwelcome guest. "I will never give in to him the least little bit," said Mme. de Rênal; "we will live in the future just as we have lived during the past month. He will be a friend."

Chapter XIV

English Scissors

> A young girl of sixteen had a skin
> like a rose, and she put on rouge.
> —POLIDORI

As for Julien, Fouqué's offer had, in effect, driven all his happiness away; he couldn't settle on any course of action.

"Alas! it must be that I lack character; I would have made a poor soldier for Napoleon. At least," he added, "my little affair with the mistress of the house will give me something to do for a while."

Fortunately for him, even in this minor incident, his deepest feelings were at variance with his cavalier language. He was afraid of Mme. de Rênal because of her very pretty dress. In his eyes this dress was the avant-garde of Paris. His pride would not allow him to leave anything to chance or to the inspiration of the moment. Drawing on Fouqué's confidences and the little he had read about love in the Bible, he planned a detailed offensive. Since, without admitting it to himself, he was very nervous, he wrote out his plan.

The next morning Mme. de Rênal was alone with him in the drawing room for a few minutes. She asked, "Have you no other name but Julien?"

Our hero didn't know how to answer this very flattering question. Such an eventuality had not been allowed for in his plan. But for this foolish business of making a plan, Julien's quick wit would have served him well; surprise would simply have added to the sharpness of his observations.

He was awkward and thought himself more awkward than he was. Mme. de Rênal readily pardoned this in him.

90

She saw it as an effect of a charming candor. And what precisely, in her opinion, had been lacking in this man, whom everyone found so intelligent, was an air of candor.

"I don't trust your little tutor," Mme. Derville would say to her now and then. "He gives me the impression that he thinks all the time and never acts without a motive. He's a sly one."

Julien went on feeling mortified by the disaster of his not having known how to answer Mme. de Rênal.

"A man like me owes it to himself to make up for this reverse"; and seizing on the moment when they were passing from one room into another, he judged it his duty to give Mme. de Rênal a kiss.

Nothing could have been less prepared for, nothing more unpleasant for him as well as for her, nothing more risky. It's a wonder they weren't seen. Mme. de Rênal thought he was crazy. She was frightened and, above all, shocked. This blunder reminded her of M. Valenod. "What would happen to me," she asked herself, "if I were alone with him?" All her virtue returned, for her love had vanished. She arranged to have one of the children near her at all times.

It was a tedious day for Julien; he spent all of it clumsily executing his plan of seduction. He did not once look at Mme. de Rênal without there being a reason for that look; nevertheless, he was not so foolish as to miss the fact that he was not succeeding at all in being amiable, much less seductive.

Mme. de Rênal couldn't get over her astonishment at finding him so awkward and at the same time so bold. "This is the man of parts made shy by love!" She told herself eventually with inexpressible joy. "Is it possible that my rival has never returned his love!"

After lunch, Mme. de Rênal went back to the drawing room to receive a call from M. Charcot de Maugiron, the subprefect of Bray. She set to work at a little tapestry loom on a tall stand. Mme. Derville was at her side. It was in this position, and in broadest daylight, that our hero thought fit to advance his boot and press the pretty foot of Mme. de Rênal, whose openwork stocking and charming shoe from Paris were obviously catching the gallant subprefect's eye.

Mme. de Rênal had an awful fright; she let drop her scissors, her skein of wool, and her needles so that Julien's action might pass for an awkward attempt to catch the falling scissors, which he had seen slipping. Luckily, these little scissors made of English steel broke, and Mme. de

Rênal went on and on about how sorry she was Julien hadn't been sitting closer to her.

"You saw them fall before I did . . . you might have caught them. Instead of that, your eagerness has led to nothing but a good hard kick for me."

The subprefect was taken in, but not Mme. Derville. "This pretty boy behaves like a fool!" she thought; the decorum of a provincial capital never pardons breaches of that sort.

Mme. de Rênal found the right moment to tell Julien, "Be careful; that is an order."

Julien saw his clumsiness; he was annoyed. He deliberated for a long time as to whether he ought to take offense at the words: *that is an order.* He was simpleminded enough to think: "She has a right to tell me *that is an order* if it has to do with the children's education, but in responding to my love, she implies that we are equals. Love without equality is impossible. . . ."; and he racked his brains for commonplaces about equality. He kept repeating to himself wrathfully a line from Corneille that Mme. Derville had taught him a few days before: "Love creates equalities and does not seek them."

Julien, who had never had a mistress in his life, persisted in playing the role of a Don Juan and kept making an ass of himself all day long. He had only one decent idea. Bored with himself and Mme. de Rênal, he noted with terror that evening was drawing near, when he would be seated beside her in the garden in the dark. He told M. de Rênal that he was going to Verrières to see the curé. He left after dinner and did not return until late that night.

In Verrières, Julien found M. Chélan busy moving. He had finally been dismissed; he was being replaced by the Vicar Maslon. Julien gave the good curé a hand, and it occurred to him to write Fouqué that the irresistible calling he felt for the holy priesthood had at first kept him from accepting his kind offer, but that he had just seen such a flagrant example of injustice that it would perhaps be better for his own salvation if he did not go into sacred orders.

Julien congratulated himself for being shrewd enough to take advantage of the curé's dismissal to leave a door open for himself so he could go into business, if in his spirit dreary prudence should ever get the best of heroism.

Chapter XV

Cock's Crow

Amour en latin faict amor;
Or donc provient d'amour la mort,
Et, par avant, soulcy qui mord,
Deuil, plours, pieges, forfaitz,
remords.
—*Blason d'amour**

If Julien had had a little of that cleverness he imputed to himself so freely, he might have congratulated himself the next day on the effect produced by his trip to Verrières. Absence caused the ladies to forget his bungling. All that day, too, he was sullen; toward evening an absurd idea crossed his mind, and he communicated it to Mme. de Rênal with rare intrepidity.

They were no more than seated in the garden when Julien, not waiting until it was dark enough, put his mouth to Mme. de Rênal's ear, and at the risk of compromising her horribly, said:

"Madam, tonight at two o'clock I am coming to your room; there's something I must tell you."

Julien trembled for fear that his request might be granted; the role of seducer weighed on his mind so heavily that had he been free to follow his own inclination, he would have retired to his room for several days, never to see those ladies again. He realized that yesterday's subtle tactics had spoiled the fine impression he had made the day before, and really he didn't know which way to turn.

Mme. de Rênal responded with a real and by no means exaggerated indignation to the impertinent announcement Julien had had the audacity to make. He thought he detected scorn in her curt answer. It's certain that in this reply, spoken in a whisper, the words *"for shame"* had occurred. Under the pretext of having something to tell the children, Julien went to their bedroom, and on his return sat down beside Mme. Derville, a good distance from Mme. de Rênal. Thus he removed any possibility of taking her hand. The conversation was serious, and Julien held up his own end of it very well, if we except a few moments of silence during which he was racking his brains. "Why," he was asking himself, "can't I think up some fine maneuver and force Mme. de Rênal once more into showing me those unmistakable signs of affection that led me three days ago to believe she was mine!"

Julien was dismayed at the almost desperate state of affairs into which he had got himself. Yet nothing would have embarrassed him more than success.

When the company parted at midnight, his pessimism made him believe that he enjoyed Mme. Derville's contempt, and that he was probably not on much better terms with Mme. de Rênal. Humiliated and in a foul temper, Julien didn't sleep. Yet he was a thousand miles away from any thought of forswearing all sham, all his schemes, and of living with Mme. de Rênal on a day-to-day basis, contenting himself like a child with the happiness each day would bring.

He wearied his brain trying to think up expert maneuvers; a moment later they would all seem ridiculous. He was, in short, thoroughly miserable when the château clock struck two.

This sound roused him, just as the cock's crow roused St. Peter. In that instant he saw himself at the most painful juncture of his life. He hadn't given another thought to his impudent proposition since he made it; it had been so poorly received!

"I told her I would go to her room at two o'clock," he said to himself as he got up. "I am as inexperienced and boorish as a peasant's son should be. Mme. Derville made that clear enough; but at least I won't be weak."

Julien had reason to think highly of his courage; he had never forced himself to do anything more painful. When he opened his door, he was shaking so that his knees gave way beneath him, and he was obliged to lean against the wall.

He was barefoot. He went to listen at M. de Rênal's door; he could make out his snoring. He was sorry indeed. So there was no longer any excuse for not going to her room. But good God! what would he do there? He had no plan, and even if he had one, he felt so upset that he would have been in no condition to follow it through. At last, suffering a thousand times more than if he were walking to his death, he stepped into the short corridor just off Mme. de Rênal's room. With a trembling hand and making a frightful racket, he opened her door.

There was light; a night-light was burning in the fireplace; he was not prepared for this fresh calamity. On seeing him enter, Mme. de Rênal jumped out of bed. "Wretch!" she cried. There was a moment's confusion. Julien forgot his useless plan and reverted to his natural self. Not to find favor in the eyes of such a lovely woman seemed to him the worst of misfortunes. His only answer to her reproaches was to throw himself at her feet and clasp her knees. Since she said some very harsh things to him, he burst into tears.

When Julien left Mme. de Rênal's bedroom some hours later, it might be said, in the style of the novel, that he had nothing more to desire. He was, in fact, obliged to the love he had inspired, and to the unexpected impression her seductive charms had made on him, for a conquest that all his clumsy maneuvering could never have brought off.

Yet, victim of a bizarre pride, even in the sweetest moments he still aspired to the role of a man who is used to subjugating women. He applied himself with incredible effort to spoil whatever was likable about him. Instead of being attentive to the raptures he had awakened and to the remorse that only heightened their intensity, he could think of nothing but his *duty*. He dreaded the terrible regret and sense of everlasting ridicule that must follow, should he lose sight of the model he had proposed for himself.

In a word, what made Julien a superior person was precisely what kept him from relishing the happiness that lay at his feet. He was like the sixteen-year-old girl with a lovely complexion who, when she goes to a ball, has the crazy notion of putting rouge on her face.

At first mortally terrified by Julien's appearance, Mme. de Rênal was soon a prey to the most agonizing fears. Julien's despair and his tears troubled her profoundly.

Even when she had nothing left to refuse him, she kept pushing Julien away out of real indignation, and would then fling herself into his arms. There was no design apparent in this behavior. She believed she was damned beyond remission, and kept trying to hide from her vision of hell by covering Julien with the most passionate kisses. In short, nothing would have been wanting to our hero's happiness, not even a burning tenderness in the woman he had just swept off her feet, had he but known how to enjoy it. Julien's departure did not put an end to the raptures that kept surging through her in spite of herself, or her struggles against a feeling of remorse that was tearing her apart.

"My God! to be happy, to be loved, is that all there is to it?" Such was Julien's first thought when he got back to his room. He was in that state of astonishment and uneasiness into which a man who has just obtained what he has long desired may lapse. He is used to desiring, has nothing more to desire, and hasn't, as yet, any memories. Like the soldier who comes back from a parade, Julien was busy reviewing every detail of his conduct.

"Have I failed in any way with respect to what I owe myself? Have I played my part well?"

Which part? That of a man who is used to having his way with women.

Chapter XVI

Next Day

> He turn'd his lip to hers, and with
> his hand
> Call'd back the tangles of her wan-
> dering hair.
> —*Don Juan*, C. I, st. 170

Luckily for Julien's self-esteem, Mme. de Rênal had been too agitated, too astonished, to see the foolishness of the man who in a moment had become all the world to her.

While she was urging him to leave, seeing that day was breaking, she said, "Oh, my God! if my husband has heard any noise, I am lost."

Julien, who still had time for a few stock phrases, remembered this one: "Would you be sorry to die?"

"Ah! very sorry at this moment, but I could never be sorry for having known you."

Julien considered it beneath his dignity not to go back to his room by broad daylight, carelessly.

The sustained attention he gave to his smallest gestures, with the crazy idea in mind of looking like a man of experience, had only one advantage: when he saw Mme. de Rênal again at breakfast, his conduct was a master-piece of circumspection.

As for her, she couldn't look at him without blushing to the whites of her eyes, and couldn't live for a minute without looking at him; she realized the state she was in, and her efforts to conceal it only made matters worse. Julien raised his eyes but once to look at her. At first Mme. de Rênal admired his prudence. But after a while, seeing that this single glance was not repeated, she grew alarmed: "Can it be that he doesn't love me anymore?" she asked herself. "Alas! I am much too old for him; I am ten years older than he."

As they were passing from the drawing room into the garden, she squeezed Julien's hand. Surprised at such an extraordinary token of love, he gazed at her passionately, for she had seemed very pretty to him during breakfast, and with eyes lowered all the while, he had spent the whole time going over her charms, item by item. That look comforted Mme. de Rênal. It did not relieve her of all her anxieties; but her anxieties relieved her almost entirely of the remorse she felt with regard to her husband.

This husband hadn't seen a thing at breakfast. The same did not hold for Mme. Derville. She believed Mme. de Rênal was on the point of succumbing. Out of friendship, she assailed her all day long with bold and incisive hints that were meant to picture for her, in the most hideous colors, the danger she was running.

Mme. de Rênal was dying to be alone with Julien; she wanted to ask him if he still loved her. Despite the unfailing sweetness of her character, she was several times on the point of letting her lady friend know what a bother she was.

That night, in the garden, Mme. Derville arranged things so well that she found herself seated between Mme. de Rênal and Julien. Mme. de Rênal, who had delighted in imagining the pleasure of clasping Julien's hand and of raising it to her lips, couldn't even talk to him.

This hitch added to her anxiety. She was consumed by one misgiving. She had scolded Julien so much for his foolhardiness in coming to her bedroom the night before that she feared he might not come tonight. She left the garden early and went to install herself in her room. But unable to resist her impatience, she went and glued her ear to Julien's door. Despite the doubt and passion that were devouring her, she dared not enter. She considered such behavior the lowest of the low, for it serves as the theme of an old saw in the provinces.

Not all the servants were in bed. Discretion forced her at length to return to her room. Two hours of waiting were two centuries of torment.

But Julien was too faithful to what he called his duty to fail in the execution, step by step, of what he had set himself to do.

When one o'clock struck, he slipped out quietly, made sure the master of the house was soundly asleep, and appeared in Mme. de Rênal's room. That night he found greater happiness in his mistress's company, for he thought less constantly about the role he ought to be playing. He had eyes to see and ears to hear. What Mme. de Rênal said about her age helped to give him confidence.

"Alas! I am ten years older than you! How can you love me!" she kept repeating to him artlessly, because the idea depressed her.

Julien couldn't conceive of this kind of unhappiness, yet he saw that it was real, and he nearly forgot his fear of being ridiculous. The foolish notion that he was regarded as a subaltern lover, because of his humble birth, also vanished. In proportion as Julien's raptures reassured his timid mistress, she recovered a little of her happiness and the faculty to judge her lover. That night, fortunately, he had almost nothing of the borrowed manner which had turned the meeting of the night before into a victory, but not a pleasure. If she had become aware that he was intent on playing a part, this sad discovery would have destroyed her happiness forever. She could not have seen it otherwise than as a sad effect of the difference in their ages. Albeit Mme. de Rênal had never been interested in theories of love, a difference in age is, next to that in fortune, the great commonplace of provincial humor every time the subject is love.

In a few days Julien, having recovered all the ardor of his age, was madly in love. "You have to admit," he told himself, "that she is as good as an angel, and they don't come any prettier."

He had almost completely forgotten the idea of playing a part. In a moment of abandon, he even told her about his nervousness. These confidences carried the passion he inspired to its highest pitch. "So there has never been a happy rival!" Mme. de Rênal told herself delightedly. She ventured to question him about the portrait in which he took such an interest. Julien swore to her that it was of a man.

When she was calm and collected enough to think about it, Mme. de Rênal couldn't get over her amazement that such happiness could be, and that she had never had an inkling of it.

"Ah!" she said to herself, "if only I'd met Julien ten years ago, when I was still considered pretty!"

Julien was a long way from thinking like thoughts. He was still in love with ambition. His was the joy of possessing (he, the poor, the wretched, the despised!) such a noble, such a beautiful woman.

His acts of adoration, his raptures at the sight of his mistress's charms, eventually set her mind somewhat at ease about the difference in their ages. If she had possessed a little of that knowledge of the world which, in the more civilized countries, a woman has already enjoyed for a long while by the time she is thirty, she might have feared for the duration of a love that seemed to be sustained by nothing but surprise and delighted vanity.

At those times when Julien forgot his ambition, he would admire everything about Mme. de Rênal ecstatically—even her hats, her dresses. He couldn't get enough of smelling their perfume. He would open her mirror wardrobe and spend whole hours admiring the beauty and order of everything in it. Leaning on his shoulder, his mistress would gaze at him; he would gaze at all those jewels and frills a husband offers his wife on the eve of their honeymoon.

"I could have married such a man!" Mme. de Rênal would sometimes think; "such a fiery nature! What a marvelous life I should have had with him!"

As for Julien, he had never been so close to those terrible arms of the feminine artillery. "It's not possible," he told himself, "that they have anything finer than this in Paris." At such times, he had no objection whatsoever to his happiness. Often his mistress's sincere admiration and her raptures would cause him to forget the vain theory that had made him so stiff and almost as ridiculous at the beginning of their intimacy. There were moments when, despite his habitual hypocrisy, he found it very sweet to confess his ignorance about a hundred little usages to this great lady who admired him. His mistress's rank seemed to raise him above himself. Mme. de Rênal, on her side, took the sweetest of moral pleasures in educating thus, about a host of little things, a young man of genius who was looked upon by everybody as likely to go so far one day. Even the subprefect and M. Valenod couldn't help admiring him; for which reason they seemed to her less stupid.

As for Mme. Derville, she was far from sharing the same sentiments. In despair over what she thought she had guessed rightly, and seeing that her wise counsel was becoming odious to a woman who had literally lost her head, she left Vergy without giving the explanation for which she had carefully not been asked. Mme. de Rênal shed a few tears over this incident, but before long it seemed to her that she was twice as happy as before. As a result of this departure, she found herself in a tête-à-tête with her lover nearly all day long.

Julien gave himself up to his mistress's sweet society all the more willingly since, every time he was alone too long, Fouqué's proposition would inevitably come back to trouble him. During the first few days of this new life there were moments when he, who had never loved, who had never been loved by anyone, took such an exquisite pleasure in being sincere that he was on the point of telling Mme. de Rênal about the ambition which up to that time had been the very essence of his life. He wished he could talk with her about the strange temptation Fouqué's offer held for him, but a small event put an end to all his frankness.

Chapter XVII

The First Deputy

> O how this spring of love resembleth
> The uncertain glory of an April day;
> Which now shows all the beauty of
>   the sun,
> And by and by a cloud takes all
>   away!
> —*The Two Gentlemen of*
> *Verona*

One evening toward sunset, when Julien was seated by his mistress's side at the end of the orchard and safe from intrusion, he fell into a deep reverie. "Can such sweet moments last forever?" he asked himself. His thoughts were full of the difficulty and the necessity of settling on a career; he deplored the great fit of depression that brings boyhood to a close and spoils the early years of a penniless youth.

"Ah!" he cried, "Napoleon was surely a godsend to the young men of France! Who is there to take his place? How will poor young men get along without him, even those who have more than I: who have just enough money to get a good education, but afterwards, not enough to bribe an official when they reach twenty, so they can launch themselves on a career! No matter what we may do," he added, sighing deeply, "his fatal memory will keep us from ever being happy!"

He suddenly noticed that Mme. de Rênal was frowning; she had assumed a cold and disdainful air; it seemed to her that his manner of thinking was fit for a servant. Brought up on the idea that she was very wealthy, she took it for granted that Julien was too. She loved him a thousand times better than life, would have loved him had he been ungrateful and untrue, even if he had belonged to the opposite party, the Bonapartists . . . and her money meant nothing to her.

Julien was a long way from guessing her thoughts. That frown brought him back to earth. He had enough presence of mind to patch up his remark and give the noble lady, sitting so close beside him on a grassy bank, to understand that what he had just repeated was something he had heard on his trip to see his friend, the wood dealer. It was the talk of godless men.

"Very well! but have nothing more to do with such people," said Mme. de Rênal, still keeping a little of that icy look which had suddenly taken the place of the sweetest and most intimate tenderness.

That frown, or rather, remorse over his rashness, was the first check to the illusion that had been sweeping Julien away. He told himself, "She's kind and gentle, her feeling for me is very strong, but she has been raised in the enemy camp. They must be especially afraid of that class of men of heart who after a good education haven't enough money to start on a career. What would become of those nobles if we were given a chance to do battle with their own arms! If I, for example, as well intentioned and honest as M. de Rênal is at heart, were mayor of Verrières! How quick I'd be to throw out the curé Maslon, M. Valenod, and all their crookedness! How justice would triumph in Verrières! It isn't their talent that would stop me. They're forever groping their way."

On that particular day Julien's bliss came very near to being durable. What our hero lacked was the audacity to be sincere. What he needed was the courage to do battle *on the spot*. Mme. de Rênal was astonished at what Julien had said, for the men in her society kept repeating that Robespierre's return was made possible chiefly by young people from the lower classes who had been too well educated. Mme. de Rênal's cold air lasted quite awhile, and to Julien it seemed pointed. That was because her aversion to improper talk was followed by a fear of having inadvertently said something disagreeable to him. Her distress was sharply defined in her features, otherwise so pure and artless when she was happy and far from bores.

Julien no longer dared to let himself dream aloud. Calmer and less amorous, he decided it would be unwise to go and see Mme. de Rênal in her bedroom. It would be better if she came to him; if a servant caught her running

103

through the house, twenty different reasons might be found to explain her errand.

But this arrangement also had its drawbacks. Julien had received a number of books from Fouqué that he, as a divinity student, could never have asked for at a bookstore. He dared not open them except at night. Many's the time he would have been content not to be interrupted by a visit, the anticipation of which, even the night before this little scene in the orchard, had made reading impossible.

He was in Mme. de Rênal's debt for an entirely new way of understanding books. He had ventured to question her about a host of little things, ignorance about which must bring the comprehension of a young man born out of society to a dead stop, however much native genius may be imputed to him.

This fond education, given by an extremely ignorant woman, was a blessing. It allowed Julien to see society at firsthand, such as it is today. His mind was not confused by accounts of what it was like two thousand years ago, or only sixty, in the time of Voltaire and Louis XV. To his ineffable joy, the veil was rent before his eyes. He finally understood what was going on in Verrières.

The foreground was taken up by the very complicated plots hatched during the past two years in Besançon's prefecture. They were supported by letters from Paris, written by some of the most illustrious names in the land. The issue at stake was to get M. de Moirod, the most pious man in the region, elected first, not second, deputy to the mayor of Verrières.

The candidate running against him was a rich millowner who must, at any cost, be shoved back to the place of second deputy.

Julien finally understood the hints he overheard whenever the local high society came to dine at M. de Rênal's house. This privileged society was deeply concerned over the choice of a first deputy, the possibility of which the rest of the town, especially the Liberals, did not even suspect. What made it important was that, as everyone knew, the east side of Verrières' main street was to be moved back by more than nine feet, for this street had been designated a royal highway.

Now, if M. de Moirod, who had three houses to be moved back, succeeded in becoming first deputy, and afterward mayor, in the event M. de Rênal was elected to Parliament, he would shut his eyes, and it would be possible to make small, imperceptible repairs on the houses that jutted out into the public thoroughfare; thanks to which those houses would last a hundred years. In spite of M. de Moirod's signal piety and his well-known honesty, everyone was sure he would *"go along,"* since he had a big family. Among the houses that were to be set back, nine belonged to the very best people in Verrières.

In Julien's opinion, this intrigue was far more important than the history of the battle of Fontenoy,* a name he saw for the first time in one of the books Fouqué had sent him. There were things Julien had been wondering about for the last five years, ever since he had started going to the curé's house evenings. But discretion and meekness being a divinity student's cardinal virtues, it had been impossible for him to ask questions.

One day Mme. de Rênal was giving an order to her husband's valet, Julien's enemy.

"But madam, today is the last Friday in the month," the man answered in a peculiar way.

"Go, then," said Mme. de Rênal.

"So," said Julien, "he's going to that hay barn that used to be a church and was just recently restored to the Faith; but to do what? There's one of those mysteries I've never been able to fathom."

"It's a very wholesome if rather strange institution," answered Mme. de Rênal. "Women are not allowed; all I know about it is that they all call one another by their first names. For instance, this servant will see M. Valenod there, and that gentleman, proud and stupid as he is, won't be the least offended to hear Saint-Jean address him by his first name, and will answer him in kind. If you really want to know what goes on there, I'll ask M. de Maugiron and M. Valenod for details. We pay twenty francs per servant so that one day they won't cut our throats, if ever the Terror of ninety-three should come back."

Time was flying. The memory of his mistress's charms diverted Julien's thoughts from his black ambition. The necessity of not talking to her about dreary and arguable matters, since they belonged to opposite parties, contributed, without his realizing it, to the happiness he owed her and to the hold she was acquiring over him.

At those times when the presence of too-intelligent children confined them to speak the language of cold reason, Julien would sit perfectly docile and look at her, his eyes aglow with love, and listen to her explain the ways of the world. Often, in the middle of a story about some clever swindle that had amazed her, in connection with a road or a contract for supplies, her attention would suddenly wander in a kind of delirium. Julien was obliged to scold her; she would permit herself the same intimate gestures with him as with her children. She would run her fingers through his hair. This was because there were days when she had the illusion of loving him as her own child. Didn't she have constantly to answer his questions about a thousand simple things that any wellborn child knows by the time he's fifteen? An instant later she would look up to him as her master. Sometimes she was even frightened at his genius; she thought she could see the future great man more distinctly every day in this young priest. She saw him as pope; she saw him as prime minister, like Richelieu. . . .

"Will I live long enough to see you in your glory?" she would say to Julien. "There is a place waiting for a great man; the Throne, the Church, are both in need of one. Our friends are always saying: 'If there isn't another Richelieu to stem the tide of personal opinion, all is lost.' "

Chapter XVIII

A King in Verrières

> Are you good for nothing but to
> be thrown away, like the corpse of
> a people with no soul, and whose
> veins have no blood left in them?
>
> —from The Bishop's Sermon at
> the Chapel of St. Clement

On September 3, at ten o'clock at night, a gendarme
woke up the whole town of Verrières by riding up the
main street at a gallop; he brought the news that his
Majesty the King of ——————— would arrive the following
Sunday, and it was now Tuesday. The prefect authorized,
that is to say, requested, the formation of a guard of
honor; as much pomp as possible should be displayed. A
messenger was dispatched to Vergy. M. de Rênal arrived
in the night and found the whole town in a dither. Everyone had some claim to make; those who had nothing else
to do were renting balconies to watch the king's entrance.

Who should command the honor guard: M. de Rênal
saw right away how important it was, in the interest of
those houses liable to be set back, that M. de Moirod have
this command. It would give him a claim on the office of
first deputy. There was nothing to be said against M. de
Moirod's piety; it was beyond compare, but he had never
mounted a horse. He was a man of thirty-six, timid in
every way, and as much afraid of falling as of being
laughed at.

The mayor sent for him at five o'clock in the morning.
"You see, sir, I am appealing to you for advice, as though
you already held that office in which every decent citizen
desires to see you installed.

"In this unhappy town the factories are prospering, the Liberals are becoming millionaires; they aspire to power, they will use anything for ammunition. Let us consider what is in the best interest of the King, of the monarchy, and above all, of our holy faith. With whom, sir, do you think we may safely entrust the command of the honor guard?"

Despite his horrible fear of a horse, M. de Moirod ended by accepting this honor like a martyr. "Count on me to do it in proper style," he said to the mayor. Barely time enough remained to alter the uniforms that had done service seven years ago, when a prince of the blood passed through.

At seven o'clock, Mme. de Rênal arrived from Vergy with Julien and the children. She found her drawing room filled with the wives of Liberals. They were preaching a union of the two parties and had come to beg her to make her husband promise he would reserve places in the guard of honor for theirs. One claimed that if her husband was not chosen, he would go bankrupt out of grief. Mme. de Rênal got rid of them all in short order. She seemed very busy.

Julien was astonished and even more annoyed at being kept in the dark about whatever she was up to. "I knew it would happen," he told himself bitterly. "Her love has been eclipsed by the delight of entertaining a king in her house. All this fuss has turned her head. She will love me again when her brain is no longer addled by notions about caste."

Surprising thing—he loved her all the more for it.

The decorators were beginning to fill the house; for a long time he kept watching for a chance to have a word with her, but in vain. He finally ran across her coming out of his bedroom, carrying off one of his suits. They were alone. He tried to talk with her. She ran off, refusing to listen to him. "I'm a great fool to love such a woman; ambition is making her as crazy as her husband."

She was more so. One of her fondest wishes, one she had never confessed to Julien for fear of offending him, was to see him put off, if only for a day, his dreary black outfit.

With an adroitness that was truly wonderful in such an artless woman, she prevailed first upon M. de Moirod, and then on the subprefect, M. de Maugiron, to have Julien appointed as a guard of honor in preference to five or six other young men, sons of very well-to-do manufacturers, the piety of at least two of whom was exemplary. M.

Valenod, who counted on lending his calash to the prettiest women in town and on showing off his fine Normans, consented to let Julien, the creature he hated most, have one of his horses. But every guard of honor had, whether owned or borrowed, one of those beautiful sky-blue uniforms, with a pair of colonel's epaulettes in silver, that had been so dashing seven years before. Mme. de Rênal wanted a new outfit, but she had only four days left to order it from Besançon, and to have the uniform, the arms, the hat, etc., everything that makes up a guard of honor, sent back. The amusing thing was that she thought it would be indiscreet to have Julien's outfit made in Verrières. She wanted to surprise him, as well as the town.

Having finished the job of organizing a guard of honor and of rousing public spirit, the mayor had to see about a big religious ceremony; the King of ———— had no intention of passing through Verrières without paying a visit to the famous relic of St. Clement, which is kept at Bray-le-Haut, a short league out of the town. A great number of clergy was desirable; this was the most difficult thing to arrange. M. Maslon, the new curé, was determined to avoid M. Chélan at any price. To no avail, M. de Rênal tried to convince him that this would be unwise. The Marquis de La Mole, whose ancestors were governors of the province for so long, had been appointed to accompany the King of ————. He had known Father Chélan for thirty years. He was certain to ask for news of him on arriving in Verrières, and if he found out that he was in disgrace, he was the kind of man who would go and seek him out in the little house to which he had retired, accompanied by as much of the procession as he could command. What a slap in the face!

"I will be dishonored here and in Besançon," answered the Curé Maslon, "if he shows up among my priests. A Jansenist,* good God!"

"No matter what you say, my dear Abbé," replied M. de Rênal, "I will not expose the administration of Verrières to an affront from M. de La Mole. You don't know the man. He has the right ideas at court; but here in the province he is a malicious joker, satirical and sarcastic, always trying to embarrass people. He is capable, simply to amuse himself, of covering us with ridicule in full view of the Liberals."

It wasn't until late Saturday night, after three days of negotiating, that the Abbé Maslon's pride yielded to the mayor's fear, which turned into courage. The next step was to write a honeyed letter to the Abbé Chélan, begging him to take part in the ceremony of the relic of Bray-le-Haut, if, of course, his great age and his infirmities allowed him to do so.

M. Chélan requested and obtained a letter of invitation for Julien, who was to accompany him in the capacity of subdeacon.

Early Sunday morning thousands of peasants, coming in from the nearby mountains, overflowed the streets of Verrières. The sun was shining brightly. Eventually, around three o'clock, the whole crowd got excited; a bonfire had been sighted on a rock about two leagues from Verrières. This was the signal that the king had just entered the territory of the department. Immediately the ringing of all the bells and the repeated firing of an old Spanish cannon belonging to the town testified to its joy over this great event. Half the population climbed up on the roofs. All the women were on balconies. The guard of honor began to move. Everyone admired their shining uniforms, everyone recognized a relative or a friend. Everyone laughed at M. Moirod's fear: his cautious hand lay ready to grab the saddlebow at any moment. But one observation made them forget everything else; the cavalier at the head of the ninth file was a slim, very good-looking fellow whom no one had recognized at first. Soon a cry of indignation from some and astonished silence on the part of others announced a general reaction. The young man mounted on one of M. Valenod's Norman horses had been identified as the Sorel boy, the carpenter's son. There was an outcry against the mayor, especially from the Liberals. What, just because that little workman dressed up as a priest was his brats' tutor, he had the nerve to make him a guard of honor, to the detriment of Messrs. so-and-so, rich millowners! "Those gentlemen," said a banker's lady, "ought to insult that insolent little man, born on a dung heap."

"He's sneaky and is wearing a saber," replied the gentleman beside her. "He would be vicious enough to cut up their faces."

The talk of the aristocratic society was more dangerous. The ladies were wondering if the mayor alone was responsible for this glaring impropriety. Generally speaking, they did justice to his contempt for a base extraction. While he was the subject of so much discussion, Julien was the happiest of men. Naturally bold, he held himself better on a horse than most of the young people in that mountain town. He could tell from the women's eyes that he was being talked about.

His epaulettes were the shiniest because they were new. His horse kept rearing all the time; his joy was at its peak.

His happiness knew no bounds when, passing close to the old rampart, his horse leaped at the noise of the little cannon and broke ranks. By the greatest good luck he didn't fall; at that moment he felt like a hero. He was Napoleon's aide-de-camp and was charging a battery.

One person was happier than he. First she had watched him pass by from one of the casement windows of the town hall; then, climbing into her calash and swiftly making a wide detour, she arrived in time to shudder when his horse bore him out of the ranks. Finally, leaving the city by another gate, going full gallop in her calash, she succeeded in getting back to the road over which the king was to pass, and was thus able to follow the guard of honor from a distance of twenty paces, amidst a noble cloud of dust.

Ten thousand peasants shouted, "Long live the king!" when the mayor had the honor of haranguing his Majesty. An hour later, after all the speeches had been heard, the king was about to enter the town when the little cannon started shooting again in rapid-fire succession. An accident resulted from this, not to the cannoneers, who had been tried at Leipzig and Montmirail,* but to the future deputy mayor, M. de Moirod. His horse set him down softly in the only mudhole there was in the highway; this caused a commotion, for it was necessary to pull him out so the king's carriage could go on.

His Majesty stopped at the beautiful new church, which had been adorned that day with all its crimson hangings. The king was to dine, and immediately after, get back into his carriage to go and venerate the celebrated relic of St. Clement. The king was barely inside the church when Julien galloped off toward M. de Rênal's house. Once there, and with many a sigh, he took off his handsome sky-blue uniform, his saber, his epaulettes, and dressed again in his threadbare black outfit. He mounted his horse again and in a few minutes was at Bray-le-Haut, which stands on the summit of a very beautiful hill. "Enthusiasm is multiplying these peasants," thought Julien. "You can't move in Verrières, and there are more than ten thousand of them right here, around this old abbey." Half ruined by vandalism during the Revolution, it had been magnificently repaired since the Restoration, and people were beginning to speak of miracles. Julien joined Father Chélan, who gave him a good scolding and handed him a cassock and surplice. He dressed quickly and followed M. Chélan, who was on his way to introduce himself to the young Bishop of Agde. Recently appointed, he was M. de La Mole's nephew, and had been entrusted with showing the relic to the king. But the bishop was not to be found.

The clergy were getting impatient. They were waiting for their leader in the gloomy Gothic cloister of the ancient abbey. Twenty-four curés had been brought together to represent the old chapter of Bray-le-Haut, composed before 1789 of twenty-four canons. After having deplored the bishop's youth for three quarters of an hour, the curés deemed it fitting that the dean should withdraw to advise Monseigneur that the king was about to arrive, and that it was urgent that he repair to the chancel. M. Chélan's great age had made him dean. Despite the ill-temper he had shown Julien, he made him a sign to follow. Julien wore his surplice very well. By means of I don't know what process of ecclesiastical toilet, he had flattened his beautiful curly hair; but by an oversight, which doubled M. Chélan's wrath, his guard-of-honor spurs were visible under the long folds of his cassock.

When they reached the bishop's apartment, a couple of tall lackeys, covered with embroidery, barely condescended to answer the old priest that his Grace was not receiving. They laughed when he tried to explain that as dean of the noble chapter of Bray-le-Haut, he enjoyed the privilege of being admitted at any time into the officiating bishop's presence.

Julien's haughty temperament was shocked at the lackeys' insolence. He set to running through the dormitories of the ancient abbey, shaking every door he came across. A very small one gave way to his efforts, and he found himself in a cell, in the midst of his Grace's valets, all dressed in black with chains around their necks. From his hurried look, they judged he had been summoned by the bishop and let him pass. He took a few steps and found himself in an immense and very somber Gothic hall, paneled entirely in black oak; with the exception of one, the ogive windows had been walled up with bricks. The crudeness of this masonry was not disguised in any way and made a sad contrast with the antique magnificence of the paneling. The two great lateral walls of this room, celebrated among Burgundy's antiquarians and built by Charles the Bold in 1470 in expiation of some sin, were ornamented with richly carved wooden stalls. On them all

112

the mysteries of the Apocalypse were depicted in variegated woods.

This melancholy magnificence, degraded by the view of bare bricks and still-white plaster, moved Julien. He halted in silence. At the other end of the room, close to the only window through which daylight still entered, he saw a portable mirror framed in mahogany. A young man wearing a violet robe and a lace surplice, but bareheaded, had stopped three feet from the mirror. This piece of furniture seemed strangely out of place and had, no doubt, been brought there from town. Julien thought the young man looked irritated; with his right hand he was solemnly making the sign of benediction at the mirror.

"What can this mean?" he asked himself. "Is it a preparatory rite the young priest is performing? Perhaps he is the bishop's secretary. . . . He's probably as insolent as his lackeys. . . . No matter, let's find out."

He went on and covered the length of the hall rather slowly, his eyes turned toward the window and watching the young man, who kept on making the sign of benediction, which he executed slowly but a countless number of times and without resting a second. The closer he came, the better he could distinguish the man's annoyed look. The richness of his surplice trimmed with lace caused Julien to stop involuntarily a few yards from the magnificent mirror.

"It is my duty to speak," Julien told himself at length; but the beauty of the hall had moved him, and he was crushed in advance by the harsh remarks that were about to be directed to him.

The young man saw Julien in the cheval glass, turned around, and suddenly dropping his look of annoyance, said to him in the gentlest of tones, "Very well! Sir, is it fixed at last?"

Julien stood there stupefied. As the young man turned toward him Julien saw the pectoral cross on his chest; it was the Bishop of Agde. "So young," thought Julien, "six or eight years older than I, at the most!"

He felt ashamed of his spurs.

"My Lord," he answered timidly, "I have been sent by the dean of the chapter, M. Chélan."

"Ah! he was highly recommended to me," said the bishop politely, in a tone that doubled Julien's enchantment. "But I beg your pardon, sir; I took you for the person who is supposed to bring back my miter. They packed it badly in Paris; the silver cloth at the top was frightfully damaged. It will make the worst kind of impression,"

113

added the young bishop mournfully, "and still they keep me waiting!"

"My Lord, I will go and look for the miter, with your Lordship's permission."

Julien's fine eyes had their effect.

"Go, sir," answered the bishop with charming civility, "I must have it right now. I am sorry to keep the gentlemen of the chapter waiting."

When Julien reached the middle of the hall, he turned around and saw that the bishop had gone back to giving benedictions. "What can it be?" Julien wondered. "No doubt some kind of ecclesiastical preparation required by the ceremony that is about to take place." When he walked into the cell where the valets stayed, he saw the miter in their hands. Those gentlemen, giving in to Julien's commanding look in spite of themselves, handed over his Lordship's miter.

He felt proud to be carrying it; as he crossed the hall he walked slowly; he held it with respect. He found the bishop seated before the mirror; and from time to time, though weary, his right hand would give the benediction. Julien helped him to put on his miter. The bishop shook his head.

"Ah! it will stay on," he said to Julien with an air of satisfaction. "Will you step back a little, please?" Then the bishop walked rapidly to the center of the room; next, approaching the mirror slowly, he resumed once more his look of annoyance and set gravely to making the sign of benediction.

Julien was motionless with astonishment; he was tempted to understand but didn't dare. The bishop stopped, and giving him a look that suddenly lost its gravity:

"What do you think of my miter, sir; does it look all right?"

"Very well, my Lord."

"It isn't too far back? That would look a bit foolish; but it shouldn't be worn too low on the forehead either—like an officer's shako."

"It seems to me that it sits very well."

"The King of ——— is no doubt used to a venerable and very solemn clergy. I wouldn't want to appear frivolous, especially because of my age."

And the bishop began to walk again and to give his blessing.

"It's clear," said Julien, finally daring to comprehend; "he's practicing his benediction."

After a few minutes the bishop said, "I am ready. Go, sir, and notify the dean and the gentlemen of the chapter."

In a short while M. Chélan, followed by two of the oldest priests, entered through a huge and magnificently carved door, one Julien hadn't noticed. But this time Julien stayed in his place, the last of all, and couldn't see the bishop, except over the shoulders of the ecclesiastics who were crowding around this entrance.

The bishop crossed the room slowly; when he reached the threshold, the curés formed a procession. After a moment's disorder the procession began to move, intoning a psalm.

The bishop brought up the rear, between M. Chélan and another very old curé. Julien slipped in very close to his Grace, as Father Chélan's attaché. They wound their way through the abbey of Bray-le-Haut's long corridors, which despite a blazing sun were damp and gloomy. They eventually reached the portico of the cloister. Julien was stupefied with admiration at such a beautiful ceremony. His ambition roused again by the example of the bishop's youth, Julien couldn't tell which pleased him more, this prelate's sensitivity or his exquisite manners. This politeness was a very different thing from M. de Rênal's, even on his good days. "The closer you get to the highest rank of society," Julien told himself, "the more often you find such charming manners."

They were entering the church by a side door when suddenly an apalling noise reverberated throughout the ancient vaults; Julien thought they were collapsing. It was the little cannon again. Dragged by eight horses at a gallop, it had just arrived, and no more than arrived, had been set up to fire by the Leipzig cannoneers; it was discharging five shots a minute, as if the Prussians were in front of it.

But this wonderful noise no longer impressed Julien. His mind was no longer on Napoleon and the glories of war. "So young," he thought, "to be the Bishop of Agde! But where is Agde? And what does the living come to? Two or three hundred thousand francs, perhaps."

His Grace's lackeys appeared with a magnificent canopy. M. Chélan took one of the poles, but it was in fact Julien who carried it. The bishop took his place under it. He had really succeeded in making himself look old; our hero's admiration knew no bounds. "What can't you do if you're clever!" he thought.

The king entered. Julien had the good luck to see him

115

from very close up. The bishop harangued him unctuously, yet not forgetting to show his Majesty a very polite little hint of nervousness.

We will not repeat any of the accounts of the ceremonies at Bray-le-Haut; for two weeks they filled the columns of all the newspapers in the department. Julien learned, through the bishop's speech, that the king was descended from Charles the Bold.

Afterward, it came within the scope of Julien's duties to audit the accounts of what the ceremony had cost. M. de La Mole, who had procured the bishopric for his nephew, wished to do him the gallant favor of taking all the expense upon himself. The ceremony alone at Bray-le-Haut cost three thousand eight hundred francs.

After the bishop's speech and the king's reply, his Majesty took his place under the canopy; then he kneeled very devoutly on a cushion near the altar. The chancel was surrounded by stalls, and the stalls were elevated two steps above the stone floor. On the higher of these Julien was seated at M. Chélan's feet, very like a trainbearer close to his cardinal at the Sistine Chapel in Rome. There was a *Te Deum*, clouds of incense, and countless rounds fired by the musketry and the artillery; the peasants were drunk with happiness and piety. A day like this can undo the work of a hundred editions of the Jacobin papers.

Julien was six yards from the king, who was really praying with abandon. For the first time, he noticed a small, intelligent-looking man who was wearing a suit with almost no embroidery on it. But he had a sky-blue ribbon over his very simple dress. He was closer to the king than many of the other lords, whose outfits were so heavily embroidered with gold that, as Julien put it, you couldn't see the cloth. A few minutes later Julien learned that this was M. de La Mole. He began to think he had a haughty and even insolent air.

"The marquis can't be as polite as my pretty bishop," he thought. "Ah!" he said to himself, "the priesthood makes a man gentle and wise. But the king has come to venerate the relic, and I don't see any relic. Where can St. Clement be?"

A little clergyman beside him informed him that the venerable relic was in the upper part of the edifice, in a *blazing chapel*.*

"What is a blazing chapel?" Julien wondered. But he was unwilling to ask for an explanation. He paid closer attention.

In the case of a visit from a sovereign prince, etiquette

116

requires that the canons do not accompany the bishop. But as he started walking toward the blazing chapel, my Lord of Agde called to Father Chélan; Julien took the liberty of following him.

After having climbed a long staircase, they reached an extremely small door, the Gothic frame of which was magnificently gilded. This work looked as if it had been done the day before.

In front of the door, twenty-four girls belonging to the most distinguished families in Verrières were assembled on their knees. Before opening the door, the bishop sank to his knees in the midst of all these pretty girls. As he prayed aloud, it seemed they couldn't get enough of admiring his beautiful lace, his gracefulness, his face, so young and gentle. This spectacle caused our young hero to lose whatever of his wits he still possessed. At that instant he would have fought for the Inquisition in good faith. The door opened suddenly. The little chapel seemed to be aflame with light. On the altar, one could see upward of a thousand candles, divided into banks separated by bouquets of flowers. The suave odor of the purest incense came pouring from the sanctuary gate in a swirling cloud. The newly gilded chapel was quite small but very high. Julien noted that some of the candles on the altar were more than fifteen feet tall. The girls could not repress a cry of admiration. None but the twenty-four girls, the two priests, and Julien had been admitted into the vestibule of the chapel.

Shortly afterward the king arrived, followed only by M. de La Mole and by his head chamberlain. The guards themselves remained outside, kneeling and presenting arms.

His Majesty hurled rather than threw himself onto the prayer stool. It was only then that Julien, glued against the gilded door, noticed, from under a girl's bare arm, the charming statue of St. Clement. It stood hidden beneath the altar, in the uniform of a young Roman soldier. He had a gaping wound in his neck from which blood seemed to be flowing; the artist had outdone himself. The moribund yet graceful eyes were half closed. A budding mustache adorned the charming mouth, which, half open, looked as if it were still praying. At the sight of it the girl next to Julien wept copiously; one of her tears fell on his hand.

After a brief prayer in the deepest silence, broken only by the distant sound of all the village bells for ten leagues around, the Bishop of Agde requested the king's permission to speak. He ended a touching little discourse with very simple language, which made it all the more effective:

"Never forget, young Christians, that you have seen one of the greatest kings on earth kneeling before the servants of terrible and almighty God. Those weak servants, persecuted on earth, put to death, as you can see here from St. Clement's still-bleeding wound, those servants triumph in heaven. You will remember this day forever, young Christians, will you not? You will loathe godlessness. You will be forever faithful to that God who is so great, so terrible, yet so good."

On these words, the bishop rose with authority. "Do you promise?" he said, stretching forth his arm with an inspired air.

"We promise," said the girls, bursting into tears.

"I accept your promises in the name of God the terrible!" added the bishop in a voice of thunder. And the ceremony was over.

The king himself was weeping. It was a long while before Julien was collected enough to ask the whereabouts of the saint's bones, sent to Philip the Good, Duke of Burgundy,* from Rome. He was told they were hidden in the charming wax face.

His Majesty deigned to allow the young ladies who had accompanied him into the chapel to wear a red ribbon on which these words were embroidered: HATRED TO GODLESSNESS, PERPETUAL ADORATION.

M. de La Mole had ten thousand bottles of wine distributed to the peasants. That night the Liberals found some excuse for lighting up their houses a hundred times more brightly than the Royalists. Before he left, the king paid a visit to M. de Moirod.

Chapter XIX

To Think Is to Suffer

> The grotesque in everyday events
> conceals from you the real suffering
> caused by the passions.
>
> ——BARNAVE

While he was putting the everyday furniture back into
the bedroom that M. de La Mole had occupied, Julien
found a sheet of tough paper, folded in four. At the
bottom of the first page he read: "To H. E. M. the
Marquis de La Mole, Peer of France, Knight of the
King's Orders," etc., etc. It was a petition, in the big
handwriting of a cook.

Monsieur le Marquis,

I have always lived according to religious principles. I was in Lyons, exposed to the bombs at the
time of the siege, in '93,* of execrable memory. I
take communion; I go to mass every Sunday in the
parish church. I have never missed my Easter duty,
even in '93, of execrable memory. My cook (before
the Revolution I had several servants), my cook
prepares no meat on Friday. I enjoy the general and,
I daresay, well-deserved respect of everyone in Verrières. I walk under the dais in processions, beside
the curé and the mayor. On important occasions I
carry a big taper, paid for out of my own pocket.
For all of which, the certificates are in Paris, at the
Ministry of Finance. I am asking the marquis for the
lottery office in Verrières, which is sure to fall vacant
soon for one reason or another, the incumbent being

very sick, and what's more, voting the wrong way at election time, etc.

De Cholin

In the margin of the petition there was a recommendation signed *De Moirod,* which began with this line: "I had the honor of speaking to you yesterday about the steady fellow who is making this request," etc.

"So even that moron de Cholin can show me the road I ought to take," said Julien to himself.

What survived, a week after the King of ———'s passage through Verrières, of the innumerable lies, stupid interpretations, absurd discussions, etc., etc., the object of which had been, successively, the king, the Bishop of Agde, the Marquis de La Mole, the ten thousand bottles of wine, the spill taken by poor Moirod (who, in hopes of a cross, didn't stir out of his house for a month after his fall)—what survived was the utter indecency of having foisted Julien Sorel, a carpenter's son, on the guard of honor. You should have heard the rich calicó manufacturers on that score, who had made themselves hoarse preaching equality from morning to night in the café. That haughty woman, Mme. de Rênal, was behind this wretched business. The reason? Little Abbé Sorel's fine eyes and fresh, rosy cheeks made it clear enough.

A little after their return to Vergy, Stanislas-Xavier, the youngest child, came down with a fever; all of a sudden Mme. de Rênal fell into a terrible fit of remorse. For the first time, she blamed herself for her love in a consistent way; she seemed to understand, as if by miracle, into what an enormous sin she had allowed herself to be drawn. Though profoundly religious by nature, she had not up to that time given any thought to the magnitude of her crime in the eyes of God.

Long ago, at the Convent of the Sacred Heart, she had loved God passionately; in her present circumstances, she feared him to the same degree. The conflict that rent her soul was all the more frightful in that there was nothing rational about her fear. Julien saw that any attempt at reasoning, far from calming her down, only irritated her; in it she heard the arguments of the devil. Yet since Julien himself was very fond of little Stanislas, he had better luck when he spoke with her about his sickness. It soon took an alarming turn for the worse. Then, continuous remorse made it impossible for her to sleep; she would not come out from behind her fierce silence. Had she opened her mouth, it would have been to avow her crime to God and to man.

"I beseech you," Julien said to her as soon as they were alone, "say nothing to anyone. Let me be the only confidant of your sorrows. If you still love me, say nothing; nothing you can say will cure our little Stanislas' fever."

But his efforts to comfort her had no effect. He didn't know that Mme. de Rênal had got it into her head that in order to appease the wrath of a jealous God, she must hate Julien or see her son die. It was because she realized she could not hate her lover that she felt so miserable.

"Go away, please," she said to Julien one day. "For God's sake, leave this house; it is your presence here that is killing my son.

"God is punishing me," she added in a low voice. "He is just; I adore his equity. My crime is hideous, and I went on living with no sense of guilt. That was the first sign that I had forsaken God; I ought to be punished twice as much."

Julien was deeply touched. He could see neither hypocrisy nor exaggeration in this. "She believes she is killing her son by loving me, and yet this unhappy woman loves me more than her son. That, I am certain, is the regret that is killing her. There's greatness of heart for you! But how could I have inspired such a love—I, so poor, so badly brought up, so ignorant, sometimes so boorish in my ways?"

One night the child was very low. Around two o'clock in the morning, M. de Rênal came to see him. Devoured by fever, the child was extremely red and couldn't recognize his father. Suddenly Mme. de Rênal threw herself at her husband's feet; Julien saw that she was about to tell all and ruin herself forever.

Luckily, this odd behavior annoyed M. de Rênal. "Good-bye! good-bye!" he said, moving away.

"No, listen to me," cried his wife, on her knees before him and trying to hold him back. "Hear the whole truth. It is I who am killing your son. I gave him life and I am taking it away. Heaven is punishing me; in God's eyes I am guilty of murder. I must ruin and humiliate myself; perhaps this sacrifice will appease the Lord."

If M. de Rênal had been a man of imagination, he would have guessed the whole story.

"Romantic notions," he cried out, holding off his wife who was trying to clasp his knees. "Romantic notions, all that! Julien, have the doctor sent for at daybreak."

He went back to bed. Half fainting, Mme. de Rênal fell

121

to her knees, and with a convulsive gesture kept pushing away Julien, who was trying to help her.

Julien was astonished. "So this is adultery!" he said to himself. "Is it possible that those priests, two-faced as they are . . . may be right? Are they who commit so many sins privileged to recognize the true nature of sin? How odd! . . ."

For almost twenty minutes after M. de Rênal retired, Julien watched the woman he loved, motionless and almost unconscious, with her head lying on the child's small bed. "Here is a superior woman brought to the depths of despair for having known me," he said to himself.

"Time is going fast. What can I do for her? I must decide. I no longer count. What do I care about men's opinions and their shabby pretenses? What can I do for her? . . . Leave her? But I would be leaving her alone and a prey to the most awful suffering. That automaton of a husband does her more harm than good. He will say something harsh to her, simply because he is callous; she might go mad, throw herself out the window.

"If I leave her, if I'm not there to keep an eye on her, she will tell him everything. And who knows, perhaps, in spite of the inheritance she is supposed to bring him, he will make a scandal. She might tell everything, good God! to that p—— Abbé Maslon, who is using the illness of a six-year-old child as an excuse not to stir out of this house, and for a good reason. Her grief and her fear of God are making her forget everything she knows about the man; she sees nothing but the priest."

"Go 'way," Mme. de Rênal said to him suddenly, opening her eyes.

"I would give my life a thousand times to know how I could be most useful to you," answered Julien, "never have I loved you so much, dear angel; or rather, only now am I beginning to adore you as you deserve to be. What will become of me away from you, and knowing you are unhappy through my fault! But let's not talk about my suffering. Yes, my love, I will go. But if I leave you, if I stop watching over you, if I am not here to stand between you and your husband every minute of the day, you will tell him all, you will ruin your life. Just remember that he will drive you out of his house in disgrace; all Verrières, all Besançon, will talk about the scandal. All the blame will be laid on you; you will never be able to hold up your head again. . . ."

"That is what I want," she cried, rising to her feet. "I will suffer, so much the better."

"But with this filthy scandal, you will make him miserable too!"

"I will have humiliated myself; I will have thrown myself into the mud; and that way, perhaps, I shall save my son. That kind of humiliation, in everyone's sight, isn't that as good as a public penance? As far as I in my weakness can judge, isn't that the greatest sacrifice I could make to God? . . . Perhaps he will deign to accept my humiliation and leave my son! Point out another, more painful sacrifice, and I will run to make it."

"Let me punish myself. I too am guilty. Do you want me to join the Trappists? The strictness of that life might appease your God. . . . Ah! heavens! If only I could take Stanislas' sickness upon myself. . . ."

"Ah! you love him, you do," said Mme. de Rênal, getting up and throwing herself into his arms.

At the same instant she pushed him away in horror.

"I believe you! I believe you!" she continued, after having kneeled down again. "Oh, my only friend! Oh, why aren't you the father of Stanislas! Then it would not be a horrible sin to love you better than your son."

"Will you allow me to stay and henceforth love you only as a brother? That is the only reasonable expiation; it may appease the wrath of the Almighty."

"And I," she cried out, rising and taking Julien's head between her hands and holding it at a distance before her eyes, "and I, shall I love you like a brother? Is it in my power to love you like a brother?"

Julien burst into tears. "I will obey you," he said, falling at her feet, "I will obey, no matter what you command; that is the only thing left for me to do. My spirit has been struck blind; I cannot see any course to take. If I leave you, you will tell your husband everything; you will ruin yourself and him with you. He will never, after all the ridicule, be sent to Parliament. If I stay, you will believe me to be the cause of your son's death, and you will die of grief. Do you want to see what it would be like if I went away? If you wish, I will punish myself for our sin by leaving you for a week. I will spend it in whatever retreat you wish. At the abbey of Bray-le-Haut, for instance, but swear to me not to reveal a thing to your husband during my absence. Remember that I shall never be able to return if you speak."

She promised, he left, but was recalled at the end of two days.

"Without you, it is impossible for me to keep my oath. I will speak to my husband if you are not here constantly to order me by a look to keep quiet. Every hour of this abominable life seems a day to me."

Heaven at last took pity on the suffering mother. Little by little Stanislas passed out of danger. But the ice was broken; her reason had acknowledged the full extent of her sin; she could never again recover her balance. Remorse stayed with her, and it was all it should have been in a heart so sincere. Her life was heaven and hell: hell when she didn't see Julien, heaven when she was at his feet. "I haven't a single illusion," she would tell him, even at those times when she dared give herself completely to her love. "I am damned, irremissibly damned. You are young; you have succumbed to my seductions; heaven may pardon you. But I am damned. I know it by a sure sign. I am frightened; who wouldn't be frightened at the sight of hell? But deep in my heart, I am not sorry. I would commit my sin again, if it were still uncommitted. If only heaven will not punish me in this world, through my children, I will have more than I deserve. But you, at least, my Julien," she would cry out at other times, "are you happy? Do you think I love you enough?"

Julien's mistrust and his touchy pride, which needed most of all a love inclined to sacrifice, could not resist in the face of a sacrifice so great, so indubitable, and every minute renewed. He adored Mme. de Rênal. "It means nothing to her that she is noble and I a workingman's son; she loves me. . . . For her, I am not a valet who has been assigned the duty of lover." That fear put away, Julien fell into all the extravagances of love, into its deadly uncertainties as well.

"At least," she exclaimed, seeing his doubts about her love, "let me make you very happy during the few days that are ours to spend together. Let us make haste; tomorrow perhaps I shall no longer be yours. If heaven should strike me through my children, it would be useless for me to try to live for your love alone . . . to try not to see that it was my crime that killed them. I could not survive the blow. Even if I wanted to, I couldn't; I would go mad.

"Ah! if only I could take your sin upon myself, as you so generously offered to take on Stanislas' burning fever!"

This great moral crisis changed the quality of the feeling that united Julien and his mistress. His love was no longer based simply on admiration of beauty, on the pride of possessing it.

Their happiness was henceforth of a far superior nature; the flame that devoured them was more intense. They knew raptures filled with madness. Their happiness might have seemed greater than ever in the eyes of the world. But they could never again find the delightful serenity, the unclouded felicity, the easy contentment, of the first stages of their love, when Mme. de Rênal's only fear was that Julien might not love her enough. Sometimes their happiness wore the face of crime.

In her happiest and apparently calmest moments, Mme. de Rênal would cry out all of a sudden, as she squeezed Julien's hand convulsively: "Ah! good God! I can see hell. What horrible tortures! How well I deserve them." Then she would hug him and cling to him like ivy on a wall.

Julien would try in vain to calm her shaken soul. She would take his hand and cover it with kisses. Then, relapsing into a somber reverie, she would say: "Hell would be a blessing for me; I would still have a few days to spend with him on earth; but hell in this world, the death of my children— Yet, perhaps at that price my crime would be pardoned. . . . Ah! good God! Never grant me your pardon at such a price. Those poor children haven't offended you in any way; I, and I alone, am guilty. I love a man who is not my husband."

Afterward Julien would see Mme. de Rênal come into moments of apparent calm. She was trying to bear everything in silence; she didn't want to poison life for the one she loved.

Amidst these alternations between love, remorse, and pleasure, the days passed for them with the speed of lightning. Julien lost the habit of reflection.

Mlle. Elisa went to see about a little lawsuit she had going in Verrières. She found M. Valenod very much out of sorts with Julien. She hated the tutor and often talked with M. Valenod about him.

"You would make me lose my job, sir, if I told the truth. . . . You masters all stick together when it comes to important things. . . . You never forgive us poor servants for talking about certain matters. . . ."

After such timeworn phrases, which M. Valenod, eaten up with curiosity, found a way of cutting short, he learned a few things that were most mortifying to his vanity.

That woman, the most distinguished in the province, on whom he had lavished so much attention for the past six years, unfortunately in the sight of and to the knowledge of everyone; that proud woman, whose scorn had made him blush so many times, had just taken for her lover a little workingman dressed up as a tutor. To add insult to injury, it appeared that Mme. de Rênal adored her lover.

"And," added the chambermaid with a sigh, "M. Julien

didn't have to lift a finger to make this conquest; he didn't even bother to change from his usual cold ways for Madam."

Elisa had not been sure about it until they were in the country, but she thought this affair had been going on for some time.

"That's no doubt the reason," she added spitefully, "that he once refused to marry me. And I, like an idiot, went to ask Mme. de Rênal for advice, begged her to have a talk with the tutor."

That same night, M. de Rênal received from town, along with his newspaper, a long anonymous letter, which informed him in the greatest detail of what was going on in his house. Julien saw him turn pale as he read the letter, written on bluish paper, and cast evil glances at him. Not for the whole evening did the mayor regain his composure; it was to no avail that Julien courted his favor by asking for explanations about the genealogy of the best families in Burgundy.

Chapter XX

Anonymous Letters

> Do not give dalliance
> Too much the rein: the strongest
> oaths are straw
> To the fire i' the blood.
>   —*The Tempest*

As they were leaving the drawing room around midnight, Julien had time to say to his mistress, "Let's not see each other tonight; your husband is suspicious. I could swear that the long letter he read with so much sighing was anonymous."

Luckily, Julien locked himself in his room. Mme. de Rênal had the crazy notion that this warning was only a pretext not to see her. She lost her head completely and came to his door at the usual hour. Julien heard a noise in the corridor and blew out his lamp at once. Someone was trying to open his door; was it Mme. de Rênal; was it a jealous husband?

Very early the next morning the cook, who was shielding Julien, brought him a book, on the cover of which he read these words in Italian: *Guardate alla pagina 130.*

Julien shuddered at her recklessness, searched for page 130, and found pinned to it the following letter, hastily written, bathed with tears, and without any semblance of spelling. Ordinarily Mme. de Rênal handled spelling very well; he was touched by this detail and for the moment forgot about her frightful rashness.

Didn't you want to see me last night? There are moments when I think I have never fathomed the depths of your soul. Your looks frighten me. I am

127

afraid of you. Great God! could it be that you have never loved me? If that is the case, let my husband find out about our love, and let him lock me up forever in a prison, in the country, far from my children. Perhaps God wills it so. I should soon die. But you would be a monster.

Don't you love me? Are you weary of my follies, my remorse, godless man? Do you want to ruin me? I am giving you an easy way to do it. Go, show this letter all over Verrières, or better, show it to M. Valenod alone. Tell him I love you; but no, do not utter such blasphemy; tell him I adore you, that life did not begin for me until the day I first saw you; that in the wildest moments of my youth, I never dreamed of the happiness I owe you; that I have sacrificed my life to you; that I am sacrificing my soul to you. You know that I am sacrificing much more than that for you.

But what does that man know about sacrifice? Tell him, tell him if only to annoy him, that I defy all spiteful men, that there is only one misfortune left to befall me, to see a change in the only man who holds me to life. How happy I should be to lose it, to offer it as a sacrifice, and no longer have to fear for my children!

You may be sure, dear friend, if there was an anonymous letter, it came from that odious creature who has pursued me for six years with his coarse voice, with stories about his leaps on horseback, with his fatuousness, and the endless telling over of all his qualities.

Was there an anonymous letter? Naughty man, that is just what I wanted to discuss with you. No, you did the right thing. Holding you in my arms, for the last time, perhaps, I should never have been able to talk things over calmly, as I can now, being alone. From now on, our happiness will not be so easily come by. Will that be a disappointment for you? Yes, on days when you have not received some entertaining book from M. Fouqué. The sacrifice is made: tomorrow, whether there was an anonymous letter or not, I will tell my husband that I too have received an anonymous letter, and that he must immediately find a way out for you, make some honorable excuse, and send you back to your family without delay.

Alas! my dear, we are going to be separated for two weeks, a month, perhaps! Go. I do you justice; you will suffer as much as I. But after all, this is the only way to parry the effect of that anonymous letter; it isn't the first my husband has received, and on my account at that. Alas! how I used to laugh over them!

My sole purpose in taking this step is to make my husband think the letter comes from M. Valenod; I have no doubt that he is the author. If you leave the house, do not fail to go and locate yourself in Verrières. I will manage things so that my husband will take a notion to spend a couple of weeks there, to prove to the fools that there is nothing amiss between him and me. Once you are in Verrières, make friends with everybody, even the Liberals. I know that all those ladies will be after you.

Do not pick a quarrel with Valenod, or cut off his ears, as you said you would the other day; on the contrary, show him a smiling face. The important thing is that people in Verrière get the impression that you are going into Valenod's house, or someone else's, to educate children.

My husband will never put up with that. Should he resign himself to it, well, then! at least you would be living in Verrières, and I could see you once in a while. My children, who are so fond of you, will come to visit you. Great God! I realize that I love my children more because they love you. Such remorse! how will it all end? . . . I'm getting off the subject. . . . So, you understand what you are to do; be soft-spoken, polite, never contemptuous with those vulgar officials. I am asking you to do this on my knees; they will be the arbiters of our fate. Do not doubt for an instant that, as far as you are concerned, my husband will do whatever *public opinion* may prescribe.

It is you who will furnish me the anonymous letter; arm yourself with patience and a pair of scissors. Cut the words you see below out of a book; then paste them with mouth glue on the sheet of blue paper I am sending you; it came to me from Valenod. Expect your room to be searched; burn the pages of the book you mutilate. If you don't find the words ready-made, have the patience to form them letter by letter. To save you trouble, I made the anonymous letter too short. Alas! if you don't love me anymore, which I fear is true, how long mine must seem!

ANONYMOUS LETTER

Madam,

All your sly carryings-on have been found out; and the persons whose concern it is to put an end to them have been warned. Prompted by what is left of my friendship for you, I urge you to break completely with the little peasant. If you have the good sense to do this, your husband will think he was misled by the advice he received, and we will leave him to his error. Remember that I am in on your secret; tremble, wretched woman; from this hour on, you must walk the straight and narrow, in my sight.

As soon as you have finished pasting on the words that compose this letter (did you recognize the director's way of talking?), leave the house; I will meet you.

I will go into the village, and I will come back looking upset, and, in fact, I will be, very much so. Good God! what a chance I am taking, and all because you *thought you saw* an anonymous letter. Finally, with a stricken look on my face, I will give my husband the letter which a stranger is supposed to have handed me. Meanwhile, you are to go for a walk with the children on the road to the big woods, and don't come back before dinner time.

From the top of the rocks you can see the tower of the dovecote. If all goes well, I will hang a white handkerchief from it; otherwise, there will be nothing.

Ungrateful man, will your heart help you to find a way of letting me know you love me, before you leave for the walk? Whatever happens, be sure of one thing: I couldn't survive our final parting by one day. Ah! wicked mother! Those two words I've just written here mean nothing to me, dear Julien; I can't feel them. I can't think of anything but you at this moment. I wrote them only so as not to hear them from you. Now that I see myself on the point of losing you, what is the use of hiding anything? Yes, let my heart seem abominable to you, but let me not lie to the man I adore! I have already prac-

130

ticed deception too many times in my life. Go. If you no longer love me, I forgive you. I haven't time to reread my letter. It's a small thing, in my estimation, to pay with my life for the happy days I've spent in your arms. You know that they will cost me even more.

Chapter XXI

Dialogue with a Master

> Alas, our frailty is the cause, not
> we:
> For such as we are made of, such
> we be.
>
> —*Twelfth Night*

It was with childish pleasure that Julien spent an hour putting words together. Coming out of his room, he met his pupils and their mother; she took the letter, but so calmly, with such simplicity and courage, that he was frightened.

"Has the glue dried enough?" she asked him.

"Is this the woman whom remorse had almost driven mad?" he wondered. "What are her plans now?" He was too proud to ask, but never, perhaps, had she seemed more attractive to him.

"If this turns out badly," she added in the same cold-blooded way, "I will be deprived of everything. Bury this box somewhere up on the mountain; it may one day be my only resource."

She handed him a case for a glass, covered with red morocco and filled with gold and a few diamonds.

"Go now," she said to him.

She kissed the children, the youngest twice. Julien stood motionless. She walked away briskly, without looking at him.

From the minute he opened the anonymous letter, M. de Rênal's life had been ghastly. He had not been so shaken up since a duel he had almost had to fight in 1816, and to do him justice, at the time, the prospect of stopping a bullet had not made him so miserable. He examined the letter from every angle: "Isn't that a woman's hand?" he asked himself. "In that case, what woman wrote it?" He went over all those he knew in Verrières without being able to pin down his suspicions. "Could a man have dictated this letter? What man?" Uncertainty again; he was envied and no doubt hated by the majority of those he knew. "I must consult my wife," he told himself out of habit, rising from the armchair into which he had collapsed.

Hardly up, "great God!" he said, striking his head. "It's against her especially that I must be on my guard; she is my enemy now." And his eyes filled with tears of rage.

By a just compensation for the hardness of heart that lies at the base of all provincial worldly wisdom, the two men M. de Rênal dreaded most at the moment were his two closest friends.

"Besides those two, I have perhaps ten more friends," and he named them over, estimating as he did the degree of consolation he might expect from each. "All! all of them!" he cried out in a rage, "will take the greatest pleasure in my awful predicament." Fortunately, he believed he was envied, and he had reason enough. In addition to his superb house in town, which the King of ———— had just honored forever by sleeping in it, he had fixed up his château at Vergy very handsomely. The facade was painted white, and the windows were trimmed with smart green shutters. He was comforted for a minute by the idea of such magnificence. The fact is that this château could be seen from a distance of three or four leagues, to the great detriment of all the country houses, or so-called châteaux, in the vicinity, which had been left the humble gray given them by time.

M. de Rênal could count on the tears and pity of one friend, the parish churchwarden, but he was an imbecile who wept over anything. That man was nonetheless his only resource.

"What misfortune is comparable to mine!" he raged; "what loneliness!"

"Is it possible!" said the man, who was truly to be pitied, "is it possible that I haven't one friend I can turn to for advice? For I am losing my mind, I can feel it! Ah! Falcoz! ah! Ducros!" he cried out bitterly. Those were the names of two boyhood friends whom he had alienated by his haughtiness in 1814. They weren't aristocrats, and he had tried to change the terms of equality on which they had been living since childhood.

One of them, a man of mind and heart, a paper dealer,

133

had bought a press in the chief town of the department and started a newspaper. The *Congrégation* had resolved to ruin him: his newspaper was condemned, his printer's license revoked. In these sad circumstances, he tried writing to M. de Rênal for the first time in ten years. The mayor of Verrières considered it his duty to answer like an old Roman: "If the king's minister did me the honor of consulting me, I would say to him: 'Ruin all the printers in the provinces without mercy and make printing a state monopoly, like tobacco.' " Horrified, M. de Rênal recalled the wording of his letter to a close friend, a letter all Verrières had admired in the past. "Who could have guessed that with my rank, my fortune, my crosses, I would one day regret it?" It was in a fit of anger, sometimes against himself, sometimes against everyone in his house, that M. de Rênal spent an awful night; but, fortunately, the idea of spying on his wife never crossed his mind.

"I am used to Louise," he said to himself; "she knows all about my business affairs. If I were free to marry tomorrow, I couldn't replace her." Then he flattered himself with the idea that his wife was innocent; this way of seeing things spared him from showing firmness of character and suited him much better. "How many times have I seen wives slandered!

"What!" he cried out suddenly, as he paced convulsively about the room, "shall I sit by as if I were a nobody, a beggar, while she makes a laughingstock of me with her lover? Am I to let all Verrières gloat over my easygoing nature? What didn't they say about Charmier?" (He was the notorious cuckold of the region.) "When his name comes up, isn't there always a smile on everyone's lips? He's a good lawyer, but who ever talks about his eloquence? 'Ah! Charmier!' they say, 'Bernard's Charmier'; that's how they refer to him, by the name of the man who caused his disgrace.

"Thank heavens," M. de Rênal would say at other times, "I have no daughter, and the way I mean to punish the mother will not hurt my boys' chances for making good matches; I can catch that little peasant with my wife and kill them both; in that case the tragic aspect of the affair may cancel out its ridiculous side." This idea appealed to him; he explored it in detail. "The Penal Code is on my side, but whatever happens, our *Congrégation* and my friends on the jury will save me." He inspected his hunting knife, which was very sharp, but the thought of blood frightened him.

"I could thrash that insolent tutor and kick him out; but what a stir that would make, not only in Verrières but all over the department! After the judgment against Falcoz' newspaper, when his editor-in-chief came out of prison, I helped make him lose his job worth six hundred francs a year. They say that scribbler has dared to show his face again in Besançon; he's clever enough to smear my reputation in such a way that it would be impossible to take him to court! . . . The insolent fellow would insinuate in a thousand ways that what he said was true. A man of good family like me, whose name means something to him, is bound to be hated by plebeians. I can see myself in those awful Paris newspapers; oh, my God! what humiliation! to see the ancient name of Rênal dragged through the mud of ridicule. . . . If ever I traveled, I would have to change my name; what! give up the name that has been my glory and my strength. That would be the height of misery!

"If I don't kill my wife, and I drive her away in disgrace, she has her aunt in Besançon, who will hand over her entire fortune to her without a will. My wife will go and live in Paris with Julien; it will get back to Verrières, and I will still be taken for a dupe." The unhappy man noted then, from the paleness of his lamp, that day was beginning to break. He went out into the garden for a breath of fresh air. At that moment he was almost determined not to make a scandal, especially by the thought that his good friends in Verrières would be overjoyed at a scandal. The walk in the garden calmed him down a bit. "No," he cried out, "I will not deprive myself of my wife; she is too useful." Horrified, he imagined what the house would be like without her; his sole female relative was the Marquise de Rênal . . . old, half-witted, and ill-natured.

An idea of great good sense occurred to him, but the execution of it required a strength of character far superior to what little the poor man possessed. "If I keep my wife," he said, "I know what will happen: one day, at a time when she's provoked me, I will reproach her with her sin. She is proud, we will have a falling-out, and this will all happen before she inherits from her aunt. And how they will laugh at me then! My wife loves her children; in the end, it will all go to them. But I, I will be the talk of Verrières. 'What,' they will say, 'he didn't even know how to get revenge against his wife!' Wouldn't I do better to stick to my suspicions, and not try to prove a thing? In that case, I would tie my hands; afterwards I couldn't accuse her of anything."

An instant later M. de Rênal, goaded once more by his wounded vanity, was trying laboriously to recall the means of verification cited in the billiard room at the Casino or the Noble Circle of Verrières, when some glib talker would interrupt the pool to make merry at the expense of a deluded husband. How cruel those jokes seemed to him now!

"God! if only my wife were dead! Then I would be safe from ridicule. If only I were a widower! I would spend six months in Paris in the best society." After a moment's happiness, granted by the idea of widowerhood, his imagination returned to the problem of ascertaining the truth. Should he, after midnight, when everybody had gone to bed, sprinkle a thin layer of bran in front of the door to Julien's room? The next morning, by daylight, he would see footprints.

"But that trick is no good," he cried out suddenly in a rage, "that hussy Elisa would see it, and soon the whole house would know I'm jealous."

In another story told at the Casino, a husband made sure of his bad luck by sealing his wife and her lover's door with a hair held in place by a bit of wax.

After so many hours of perplexity, this means of clarifying his lot seemed the best by far, and he was thinking about trying it, when at a turn in the path he met the woman he would have liked to see dead.

She was returning from the village. She had been to hear mass at the church of Vergy. A tradition, most unreliable according to the cold historian, but which she credited, would have it that the little church which is in use today was once the chapel of the Lord of Vergy's château. This idea kept haunting Mme. de Rênal the whole time she meant to spend praying in the church. Over and over she pictured her husband killing Julien in the hunt, as though by accident, and then at night making her eat his heart.

"My fate," she told herself, "depends on what he thinks after he has heard me out. After this crucial quarter of an hour, I may not have another chance to talk with him. He is not a wise man, one who is guided by reason. If such were the case, I should be able, with the help of my own weak reason, to foresee whatever he might do or say. He will decide our common fate; he has the power to do so. But that fate lies within the scope of my ingenuity, in the art of directing the thought of that flighty man, whose anger blinds him and keeps him from seeing half of what is going on. Good God! I need talent, a cool head; where to find them?"

Upon entering the garden and seeing her husband at a distance, she recovered her composure as if by magic. His rumpled hair and clothes made it clear that he had not slept.

She handed him a letter, folded but with the seal broken. Without opening it, he glared at his wife with the eyes of a madman.

"Here's a filthy thing," she said to him, "that a sorry-looking man, who claims to know you and to be obliged to you, handed me as I was walking behind the notary's garden. I demand one thing of you: send that M. Julien back to his family, without delay." Mme. de Rênal hurried to pronounce that name, a bit beforehand perhaps, so as to be rid of the awful prospect of having to say it.

She was overcome with joy on seeing what happiness she gave her husband. From the fixity of his look, she knew that Julien had guessed rightly. Instead of being distressed about her present and very real trouble: "What genius," she thought, "such perfect tact, and in a young man without any experience! There is no limit to how far he may go. Alas! success will make him forget me."

This little testimonial of her admiration for the man she adored got her over her commotion. She congratulated herself on the step she had taken. "I have not been unworthy of Julien," she told herself with a sweet and intimate thrill.

Not saying a word, for fear of committing himself, M. de Rênal examined the second anonymous letter, composed, the reader may recall, of printed words pasted on a sheet of bluish paper.

"At any rate someone is doing his best to make a fool of me," thought M. de Rênal, dead with fatigue. "Fresh insults to look into, and always on account of my wife!"

He was on the point of heaping her with the coarsest kind of abuse; the prospect of her inheritance from Besançon barely held him in check. Eaten up by a need to take it out on something, he crumpled the second anonymous letter and set to walking with long strides; he needed to get away from his wife. A few minutes later he returned to her side, somewhat calmer.

"We must make up our minds to turn Julien out," she said to him at once. "After all, he's nothing but the son of a workingman. You can smooth things over with a few écus; besides he knows a good deal and will have no trouble placing himself, at M. Valenod's house, for example, or in the house of the subprefect, Maugiron; both have children. So you won't be doing him any harm...."

"You talk like the fool you are," shouted M. de Rênal in a terrible voice. "How can anyone expect to find good sense in a woman? You never listen to reason; how could you know anything? Weak creatures that we are unfortunate enough to have in our families! ... Your indifference, your idleness, make you good for nothing but to chase butterflies...."

Mme. de Rênal let him go on, and he went on for a long time; he was "passing his anger," as they say in the province.

"Sir," she answered at length, "I speak as a woman who has been outraged in her honor; that is to say, in what is most precious to her."

Mme. de Rênal maintained an unfaltering calm during the whole of this painful conversation, on which depended the possibility of still living with Julien under the same roof. She kept searching for the ideas she thought were best suited to guide her husband's blind wrath. She had been indifferent to all the insulting remarks he had leveled at her; she wasn't listening; she was thinking about Julien at the time. "Will he be pleased with me?"

"That little peasant, whom we've showered with favors and even presents, may be innocent, but he is nonetheless the cause of the first insult I have received. ... Sir! when I read that filthy note, I promised myself that either he or I would leave your house."

"Do you want to make a scandal that will disgrace me, and you too? You will oblige a good many people in Verrières."

"It is true; you are envied by all for the prosperous state to which the wisdom of your administration has brought you, your family, and the town. ... Very well! I will urge Julien to ask you for leave to go and spend a month on the mountain with that wood dealer, a likely friend for a little workingman."

"Do nothing of the sort," replied M. de Rênal calmly enough. "What I insist upon above all is that you do *not* speak with him. You would flare up and he would hold it against me; you know how touchy that little gentleman is."

"That young man has no tact at all," replied Mme. de Rênal. "He may be learned, you are the best judge of that, but at heart he's nothing but a downright peasant. As for me, I've never thought much of him since he refused to marry Elisa; it meant a fortune for him ... and on the pretext that she sometimes makes secret visits to M. Valenod."

"Ah!" said M. de Rênal, raising his eyebrows inordinately, "what, Julien told you that?".

"No, not exactly; with me, he has always talked about the vocation that calls him to the sacred ministry; but believe me, the first vocation of that class of people is to get their bread. He hinted around that he knew something about those secret visits."

"And I, I knew nothing about them!" shouted M. de Rênal, all his fury coming back as he bore down on each word. "Things are going on in my house that I know nothing about. . . . What! there's been something between Elisa and Valenod?"

"Ha! It's ancient history, my dear," said Mme. de Rênal, laughing, "and perhaps nothing bad has come of it. It was at a time when your good friend Valenod would not have been the least put out to have people in Verrières think that a nice little Platonic affair was developing between him and me."

"I had an idea of that once," cried M. de Rênal, striking his head furiously as he paced from one discovery to another; "and you said nothing about it?"

"Was I to come between two friends because of a little puff of vanity in our dear director? Show me the woman in society to whom he has not addressed a few extremely witty and even rather gallant letters."

"Has he written to you?"

"He writes a great deal."

"Show me those letters instantly. That is an order." (And M. de Rênal grew to six feet in his own estimation).

"I will do no such thing," she answered with a gentleness that ran almost to nonchalance. "I will show them to you someday, when you are better behaved."

"This very minute, by God!" shouted M. de Rênal, drunk with rage, and yet happier than he had been for the past twelve hours.

"Will you swear to me," said Mme. de Rênal very gravely, "never to quarrel with the director of the workhouse about those letters?"

"Quarrel or not, I may take his foundlings away from him; but," he went on furiously, "I want those letters this minute; where are they?"

"In the drawer of my desk, but I will most certainly not give you the key to it."

"I will smash it in," he shouted as he ran toward his wife's bedroom.

With an iron pale he did, in effect, smash a valuable secretary made of figured mahogany, which had come from Paris, and which he often rubbed with his coattail whenever he thought he saw a stain on it.

Mme. de Rênal had meanwhile climbed the one hundred and twenty steps of the dovecote at a run; she tied the corner of a white handkerchief to one of the iron bars of the small window. She was the happiest of women. Tears in her eyes, she looked off toward the great wood on the mountainside. "No doubt," she said to herself, "Julien is under one of those thick beeches watching for this happy signal." For a long while she listened closely; then she cursed the cicadas' monotonous sound and the bird songs. Without that tiresome noise, a joyful shout starting from those huge rocks might have reached her. Her hungry eyes devoured the immense slope of dark verdure, even as a meadow, that was formed by the treetops. "How could he lack the wit," she asked herself, on the verge of tears, "to think of some signal to let me know that his happiness is as great as mine?" She didn't leave the dovecote until she began to fear that her husband might come there looking for her.

She found him in a rage. He was skimming M. Valenod's tame sentences, which were hardly accustomed to being read with so much emotion.

Seizing the moment when her husband's shouts left her the possibility of being heard: "I still think my idea is the best," said Mme. de Rênal. "Julien ought to go on a trip. Whatever talent he may have for Latin, he is after all nothing but a peasant, often crude and tactless. Convinced that he is being polite, he pays me compliments every day that are overdone and in bad taste—things he learned by heart from some novel...."

"He never reads them," cried M. de Rênal; "I made sure of that. Do you think I'm blind, the master who doesn't know what's going on under his own roof?"

"Well, then! if he doesn't read those absurd compliments somewhere, he makes them up, and more's the pity! He must have spoken about me in that style in Verrières... but without going so far," said Mme. de Rênal with the air of making a discovery, "he might have talked that way to Elisa, which is about the same thing as speaking in front of M. Valenod."

"Ah!" shouted M. de Rênal, setting the table and the whole apartment to shaking with the hardest blow of the fist that has ever been dealt, "the printed letter and Valenod's letters are written on the same paper."

"At last!" thought Mme. de Rênal. She acted as if she were bowled over by this discovery, and lacking the courage to add a single word, went and sat down at a distance on the divan at the end of the drawing room.

The battle was won; she had much to do to stop M. de Rênal from going and speaking to the supposed author of the anonymous letter.

"How is it you don't realize that to make a scene with M. Valenod, without sufficient proof, would be the worst blunder you could make? You are envied, sir, and who is to blame? Your talents: your wise administration, your tasteful building, the dowry I brought you, and above all, the large inheritance we may expect from my good aunt, an inheritance the size of which is infinitely exaggerated by everyone. All those things have made you the most important person in Verrières."

"You forget my birth," said M. de Rênal, smiling a little.

"You are one of the most distinguished gentlemen in the province," Mme. de Rênal resumed eagerly. "If the king were free and able to give birth its due, you would no doubt figure in the Chamber of Peers, etc. And in such a magnificent position, do you mean to give the town something to gossip about to their heart's content?

"To speak to M. Valenod about his anonymous letter is to proclaim all over Verrières—what am I saying—all over Besançon, throughout the province, that this petty bourgeois, admitted perhaps recklessly into the intimacy *of a Rênal,* has found a way to offend you. If the letters you have just found proved that I responded to M. Valenod's advances, it would be your duty to kill me—I would have deserved it a hundred times over—but not to show your anger in front of him. Remember that all your neighbors are just waiting for an excuse to avenge themselves against your superiority; remember that in 1816 you had a part in certain arrests. That man who took refuge on his roof—"

"I think you neither respect nor like me," M. de Rênal cried out with all the bitterness such a memory roused, "and I was not made peer!"

"I believe, my dear," Mme. de Rênal continued with a smile, "that I will be richer than you, that I have been your companion for twelve years, and that for those reasons I should have a right to my say, above all in today's business. If you prefer a M. Julien to me," she added with ill-concealed spite, "I am ready to go and spend a winter at my aunt's house."

This remark was *felicitous*. It had that firmness which seeks to surround itself with politeness. It decided M. de Rênal. But in keeping with the custom of the province, he kept talking for a long while, went over all his arguments again. His wife let him go on; there was still anger in his voice. Finally, two hours of useless jabbering exhausted the strength of a man who had endured a paroxysm of rage for one whole night. He laid down the line of conduct he meant to follow with regard to M. Valenod, Julien, and even Elisa.

Once or twice during this great scene, Mme. de Rênal was on the verge of feeling some sympathy for the very real unhappiness of this man who had been her friend for the past twelve years. But true passion is selfish. Besides, she was expecting at any moment an avowal of the anonymous letter he had received the night before, and that avowal was not forthcoming. Mme. de Rênal's sense of security suffered for not knowing what ideas that letter might have suggested to the man on whom her fate depended. For in the provinces, husbands are the masters of public opinion. A husband who complains about his wife's conduct covers himself with ridicule (a thing that is becoming less dangerous every day in France); but his wife, if he doesn't give her any money, is reduced to the condition of a working woman, at fifteen sous a day, and even then, virtuous women will hesitate to employ her.

In spite of everything, an odalisk in a harem may love the sultan; he is omnipotent; she can have no hope of escaping his authority by a series of little ruses. The master's vengeance is terrible, bloody, yet military, generous. A blow of the dagger ends all. In the nineteenth century, a husband kills his wife with blows of public scorn; by closing every door to her.

A sense of her danger was sharply awakened in Mme. de Rênal upon her return to her bedroom; she was shocked at the disorder she found there. The locks on all her pretty little chests had been broken. Several pieces of the parquet flooring had been pried up. "He would have shown me no mercy!" she told herself. "To ruin this floor of parti-colored wood that he liked so much; whenever one of his children comes in with wet shoes, he turns red with anger. There it is, spoiled forever!" The sight of such violence instantly removed any feeling of guilt she had about her too-sudden victory.

A little before the dinner bell rang, Julien returned with

142

the children. At dessert, after the servants had withdrawn, Mme. de Rênal said to him very stiffly, "You have expressed a desire to go and spend a few weeks in Verrières; M. de Rênal has been kind enough to grant you a leave. You may depart when you wish. But, so that the children will not waste any time, their themes will be sent to you every day for you to correct."

"I shall certainly not grant you more than a week," added M. de Rênal very sourly.

In his features Julien read the anxiety of a deeply tormented man.

"He has not settled on a course of action yet," he said to his mistress during the minute they were alone in the drawing room.

Mme. de Rênal quickly told him everything she had done since that morning. "Tonight the details," she added, laughing.

"Perversity of woman!" thought Julien. "What pleasure, what instinct, drives them to deceive us?"

"I find you both enlightened and blinded by your love," he said to her rather coldly. "Your conduct today was admirable, but is it advisable for us to try to see each other tonight? This house is swarming with enemies; just think of the passionate hatred Elisa feels for me!"

"Her hatred is very like the passionate indifference you feel for me."

"Indifferent or not, I must save you from the danger to which I have exposed you. If M. de Rênal should happen to speak to Elisa, she might, with one chance remark, tell him everything. What's to prevent him from hiding himself near my room, well armed—"

"What! not even courageous!" said Mme. de Rênal with all the arrogance of a nobleman's daughter.

"I shall never stoop to discussing my courage," said Julien rather coldly; "that is base. Let the world judge after the facts. But," he added, taking her hand, "you can't imagine how fond of you I am, or my joy at being able to say good-bye to you before this cruel absence."

Chapter XXII

Custom and Behavior in 1830

> Speech was given man so that he
> might hide his thoughts.
> —R. P. MALAGRIDA

The minute he arrived in Verrières, Julien began to reproach himself for the injustice he had done Mme. de Rênal. "I should have despised her as a clinging vine if, out of weakness, she had botched her scene with M. de Rênal! She carried it off like a diplomat, and yet I sympathize with her victim, who is my enemy. There is a good deal of bourgeois narrow-mindedness in my makeup; my vanity is shocked because M. de Rênal is a man—illustrious and vast corporation to which I have the honor of belonging. I'm an idiot."

M. Chélan had refused the lodging offered him by the region's most eminent Liberals, vying with one another, when dismissal forced him to leave the rectory. The two rooms he had rented were cluttered with his books. Meaning to show Verrières how a priest ought to be treated, Julien went to his father's mill and took a dozen fir planks, which he carried on his back down the whole length of the main street. He borrowed tools from an old friend of his and in a short time built a kind of bookcase in which he arranged M. Chélan's volumes.

"I thought you had been corrupted by the vanity of the world," said the old man, weeping with joy. "This will more than atone for the childishness of that glittering guard of honor uniform, which has made you so many enemies."

M. de Rênal had ordered Julien to live in his house. No one suspected what had happened. The third day after his arrival, Julien saw a personage no less eminent than the subprefect, M. de Maugiron, climb all the way up to his

144

room. It was only after two long hours of insipid chatter and long jeremiads about the wickedness of men, about the lack of integrity in those trusted with the administration of public funds, about the dangers besetting poor France, etc., etc., that Julien finally saw the purpose of his visit begin to dawn. They were already on the landing of the staircase and, with all due respect, the poor, half-disgraced tutor was showing the future prefect of some lucky department to the door, when it pleased the latter to concern himself about Julien's finances, to praise the moderation of his interest in money matters, etc., etc. At length M. de Maugiron, folding Julien in his arms with a most fatherly air, proposed that he leave M. de Rênal and enter the employ of a civil servant who had children to bring up and who, like King Philip, thanked heaven not so much for having given them to him as for having caused them to be born in M. Julien's vicinity. Their tutor would enjoy emoluments of eight hundred francs, payable, not from month to month, "which is not noble," said M. de Maugiron, but by the quarter, and always in advance.

Now it was Julien's turn to speak; he had been waiting impatiently for an hour and a half. His answer was perfect and, most important, long as a pastoral letter; it let everything be understood yet said nothing clearly. It was filled with respect for M. de Rênal, veneration for the public of Verrières, and gratitude for the illustrious subprefect. This subprefect, amazed to come across someone more Jesuitical than himself, tried in vain to get a precise statement. Delighted, Julien jumped at this opportunity to practice, and began his answer all over again in other terms. Never has an eloquent minister, who wants to use the end of a session when the Chamber looks as though it is about to wake up, said less in so many words. M. de Maugiron had no more than left when Julien began to laugh like a madman. In order to make the most of his Jesuitical high spirits, he wrote a nine-page letter to M. de Rênal, in which he gave an account of everything that had been said to him, and asked him humbly for advice. "The rascal didn't even mention the name of the person who made the offer! It must be M. Valenod, who thinks my exile to Verrières is a result of his anonymous letter."

His dispatch sent off, and happy as the hunter who at six o'clock in the morning on a fine autumn day steps out into a field teeming with game, Julien left the house to go and ask M. Chélan for advice.

But before he reached the good curé's house, heaven showed an inclination to humor his mood and threw M.

Valenod into his way, from whom he made no effort to conceal the fact that his heart was torn in two: a poor boy like himself ought to be dedicated entirely to the vocation heaven has set in his heart, but a vocation is not everything in this vile world. For to labor with dignity in the vineyards of the Lord, and not to be altogether unworthy of one's erudite fellow laborers, one needed instruction; it was necessary to spend two very expensive years at the seminary in Besançon; it was thus indispensable, and one might even say one's duty, to save money, which was much easier to do on a salary of eight hundred francs paid quarterly than with six hundred francs, which were eaten up from month to month. On the other hand, did not heaven, by placing him with the de Rênal children, and above all by inspiring in him a particular fondness for them, seem to be pointing out that it was not right to forsake them to educate other children?

Julien rose to such heights of perfection in this type of eloquence, which has replaced the swiftness of action found in the time of the Empire, that he ended by being bored with the sound of his own voice.

When he returned, he found one of M. Valenod's footmen in full livery; he had been hunting for him all over town with a written invitation to dinner for the same day.

Julien had never been to that man's house; only a few days ago he could think of nothing but how to give him a good cudgeling without ending up in a police court. Although dinner was not until one o'clock, Julien considered it more respectful to present himself at half past noon in the director of the workhouse's office. He found him showing off his importance amidst a host of folders. His big black sideburns, his enormous quantity of hair, his fez set awry on the top of his head, his huge pipe, his embroidered slippers, the big gold chains crossing every which way on his chest, and all that paraphernalia of the provincial financier who thinks he is a lady-killer did not impress Julien the least bit; he thought all the more about the beating he owed him.

He requested the honor of being introduced to Mme. Valenod: she was dressing and was not to be seen. By way of compensation, he enjoyed the advantage of watching the director's preparations. Afterward they went into the apartment occupied by Mme. Valenod, who introduced her children to him with tears in her eyes. This lady, one of the most important in Verrières, had a coarse man's face, to which she had applied rouge for this great occasion. On it she rang all the changes of maternal pathos.

146

Julien thought of Mme. de Rênal. His suspicious nature made him impervious to almost any kind of memory except that which is evoked by contrast, but this time he was caught up to the point of tears. This disposition was increased by the appearance of the director of the workhouse's home. He was shown around. Everything was magnificent and new, and he was told the price of every piece of furniture. But Julien found something shameful about it all that smelled of stolen money. Right down to the servants, everyone in the house looked as if he had set his features against contempt.

The excise-tax collector, the chief of police, and two or three other public officials arrived with their wives. They were followed by several wealthy Liberals. Dinner was announced. Julien, already very ill-disposed, happened to think that on the other side of the dining-room wall there were poor inmates whose portion of meat had perhaps been "trimmed" in order to pay for all these tasteless luxuries, which were supposed to dazzle him.

"They may be hungry at this very moment," he said to himself. His throat tightened. It was impossible for him to eat, almost to talk. It was much worse a quarter of an hour later. From time to time, snatches of a popular song were audible—a rather indecent song, one must admit, that an inmate was singing. M. Valenod looked to one of his servants in full livery, who disappeared, and shortly after, no more singing was to be heard. At the same moment a valet offered Julien some Rhine wine in a green glass, and Mme. Valenod carefully pointed out to him that this wine cost nine francs a bottle at the vineyard. Holding his green glass, Julien said to M. Valenod, "They've stopped singing that nasty song."

"By George! I should think so," answered the director triumphantly. "I've had those beggars silenced."

This was too much for Julien; he had the manner but not yet the heart of his profession. Despite all his hypocrisy, so often called into use, he felt a big tear running down his cheek.

He tried to hide it with the green glass, but it was absolutely impossible for him to appreciate the Rhine wine. "*Stop him from singing!*" he said to himself. "Oh, my God! and you stand for that!"

Luckily, no one noticed his ill-bred pity. The tax collector had burst into a Royalist song. During the uproar of the refrain, sung in chorus, Julien's conscience told him, "This is it, the dirty fortune you will come into, and you will enjoy it only under like conditions, and in like company! You may have a position worth twenty thousand francs, but you will be obliged, while you are stuffing your mouth with meat, to keep some poor prisoner from singing; you will have people in to dine on the money you stole from his wretched pittance, and during your dinner, he will be even more miserable.

"O Napoleon! how sweet it was in your time to rise to wealth through the dangers of battle. But to add basely to the suffering of the wretched!"

I must confess that the weakness Julien has shown in this monologue makes me think poorly of him. He would make a worthy colleague for those conspirators in yellow gloves who would like to change a great country's whole way of life, but are unwilling to have the smallest scratch on their conscience.

Julien was reminded brusquely of his role. It was not to dream and say nothing that he had been invited to dine in such good company.

A retired calico manufacturer, a corresponding member of the academies of Besançon and of Uzès, addressed him from one end of the table to the other, to ask if what everyone was saying about his amazing progress in the study of the New Testament was true.

Immediately there was a deep silence. A New Testament appeared as if by magic in the learned member of two academies' hands. In accordance with Julien's reply, he read half a verse in Latin, chosen at random. Julien recited; his memory was faithful and this prodigious feat was greeted with all the noisy energy of a dinner's close. Julien scrutinized the ladies' flushed faces; several were not bad. He singled out the wife of the fine singer, the tax collector.

"I'm ashamed of myself, really, for speaking Latin for such a long time in front of these ladies," he said, looking at her. "If M. Rubigneau"—he was the member of the two academies—"will be so good as to read a verse in Latin at random, instead of answering him with the Latin text I will attempt to translate impromptu."

This second demonstration crowned his glory.

Several Liberals were there, rich men but happy fathers of children liable to win scholarships and, as such, suddenly converted since the last Mission.* Despite this shrewd political move, M. de Rênal had never been willing to invite them to his house. These worthy people, who knew Julien only by reputation and for having seen him on horseback the day of the King of———'s entrance, were his loudest admirers. "When will the fools get tired of listening to this Biblical language of which they understand nothing?" he wondered. On the contrary, that style amused them by its oddness; they laughed at it. Julien grew weary.

He rose solemnly as six o'clock was striking and spoke of a chapter in Ligorio's new theology that he had to learn, so he could recite it the next day to M. Chélan. "For it is my business," he added jokingly, "to make others recite their lessons and to recite my own."

Everyone laughed a good deal, everyone admired him; such is their idea of wit in Verrières. Julien was already standing; everyone rose, in spite of decorum; such is the power of genius. Mme. Valenod detained him another quarter of an hour; he simply must hear her children recite their catechism. They made the most comical mistakes, which he alone caught. He was careful not to call attention to them. "What ignorance of the first principles of religion!" he thought. He bowed at length and thought he would be able to escape, but he had to endure a fable by La Fontaine.

"That author is very immoral," said Julien to Mme. Valenod. "In a fable about Master Jean Chouart,* he dares to make fun of the most venerable things. . . . He is severely censured by the best commentators."

Before leaving, Julien received four or five invitations to dine. "That young man is an honor to our department," cried all the guests at once in very high spirits. They even went so far as to talk about a pension to be voted against the public funds, which would allow him to carry on his studies in Paris.

While this rash idea was making a stir in the dining room, Julien slipped out by the carriage entrance. "Ah! rabble! rabble!" he shouted three or four times, giving himself the pleasure of filling his lungs with fresh air.

He felt thoroughly aristocratic at the moment, he who had been offended for a long time by the disdainful smile and the haughty superiority that he kept discovering behind every courtesy he had been shown at M. de Rênal's house. He couldn't help but see the vast difference. "Let's forget," he said to himself as he walked away, "even the fact that their money was stolen from poor inmates, who moreover are kept from singing! Would M. de Rênal ever think of telling his guests the price of every bottle of wine he served them? That M. Valenod, whenever he names over his properties, which come up again and again in his conversation, cannot speak of his house, his estate, etcet-

149

era, if his wife is present, without saying *your* house, *your* estate."

This lady, to all appearances very susceptible to the pleasure of ownership, had just made a nasty scene during the dinner with a servant who had dropped a wineglass and *broken up one of her sets*. The servant had answered her with the grossest insolence.

"What a couple!" thought Julien. "They could give me half of what they steal, and I wouldn't live with them. One of these times I'm going to give myself away; I won't be able to hold back the contempt I feel for them."

It was imperative, nonetheless, according to Mme. de Rênal's orders, to attend several dinners of the same kind; Julien was in fashion; he had been pardoned his guard of honor uniform, or rather, that bit of recklessness was the real cause of his popularity. Before long, the only question in Verrières was to see who would bring it off in the struggle to get the learned young man, M. de Rênal or the director of the workhouse. With M. Maslon, those gentlemen formed a triumvirate which had tyrannized over the town for years. People were jealous of the mayor; the Liberals had cause to complain about him. Yet he was, after all, noble and born to a high office; whereas M. Valenod's father had left him no six hundred pounds a year. In this case, people had been obliged to shift from pitying the sorry apple-green outfit that was a familiar sight to everyone in his youth to envying his Norman horses, his gold chains, his suits made in Paris . . . all his current prosperity.

In the flux of this society, which was so new to him, Julien thought he had discovered an honest man; he was a geometrician named Gros and was thought to be a Jacobin. Having vowed never to say anything unless it seemed false to himself, Julien had to be satisfied with what he supposed about M. Gros. From Vergy he received big packages of themes. He was advised to visit his father often, and he conformed to this sad necessity. In other words he was doing a good job of mending his reputation, when one morning he was quite surprised to find himself being wakened by two hands that held his eyes shut.

It was Mme. de Rênal. She had made a trip into town, and by climbing the stairs four at a time and leaving the children to busy themselves with a pet rabbit that was in the party, reached Julien's room a minute before them. This moment was delightful, but short indeed. Mme. de Rênal disappeared when the children came in with the rabbit, which they wanted to show their friend. Julien gave them all a warm welcome, including the rabbit. It seemed to him that he had found his family again; he realized that he loved these children, that he enjoyed chatting with them. He was amazed at the sweetness of their voices, at the simplicity and nobility of their little ways. He felt a need to wash his imagination clean of all the vulgar behavior, of all the disagreeable ideas, in the midst of which he lived and breathed in Verrières. There was always the fear of want in the air; there was always luxury and poverty at one another's throats. The people with whom he dined, speaking confidentially about the roast, would tell him things that were humiliating for them and nauseating for anyone who had to listen.

"You aristocrats have every reason to be proud," he said to Mme. de Rênal. And he told her about all the dinners he had endured.

"So you are in fashion!" She laughed heartily about the rouge Mme. Valenod felt obliged to put on every time she expected to see Julien. "I think she has designs on your heart," she added.

The lunch was delightful. The children's presence, though it might seem a nuisance, in fact added to the general happiness. Those poor children were at a loss to express their joy over seeing Julien again. The servants had not failed to tell them that he had been offered two hundred francs more to educate the little Valenods.

In the middle of the lunch Stanislas-Xavier, still pale from his serious illness, suddenly asked his mother how much the silver service and the goblet from which he was drinking were worth.

"Why do you want to know?"

"I want to sell them and give the money to M. Julien, so he won't be a *fool* for staying with us."

Julien hugged him with tears in his eyes. His mother wept outright, while Julien, who had taken Stanislas on his lap, explained to him that he must not use the word "fool" which, when employed in that sense, was a lackey's way of talking. Seeing how much pleasure this gave Mme. de Rênal, he attempted to explain by means of picturesque examples, which amused the children, what it meant to be a fool.

"I understand," said Stanislas. "It's the crow who is silly enough to let the cheese drop, which is picked up by the fox, who was a flatterer."

Mme. de Rênal, wild with joy, covered her children with kisses, which she could scarcely do without leaning against Julien a little.

151

Suddenly the door opened; it was M. de Rênal. His face, stern and dissatisfied, made a strange contrast with the gentle merriment that his presence was driving away. Mme. de Rênal turned pale; she felt incapable of denying anything. Julien leaped into the breach, and speaking very loudly, proceeded to tell the mayor the story about the silver goblet Stanislas wanted to sell. He was sure this anecdote would be poorly received. The first thing M. de Rênal did was to frown from force of habit at the word "silver." "The mention of that metal," he would say, "is always a preface to some claim on my purse."

But in this instance, more than concern about money was involved; there was an increase of suspicion. The look of happiness that enlivened his family during his absence was not likely to improve matters for a man dominated by such a ticklish vanity. When his wife praised the method—so graceful, so witty!—by which Julien imparted new ideas to his pupils: "Yes! yes! I know; he makes me hateful to my own children. It is easy for him to be a hundred times more likable than I who am, after all, the master. Everything in this century tends to cast odium upon *legitimate* authority. Poor France!"

Mme. de Rênal did not stop to examine the nuances in the welcome her husband had reserved for her. She had just glimpsed a possibility of spending twelve hours with Julien. She had a thousand errands to do in town and declared that she was absolutely set on going to dine at the cabaret; whatever her husband might do or say, she stuck to her idea. The children were delighted by the very word "cabaret," which modern prudishness utters with such great pleasure.

M. de Rênal left his wife at the first dress shop she entered, to go on and make some visits. He returned more surly than in the morning; he was convinced that the whole town was talking about him and Julien. As a matter of fact, no one had yet given him reason to suspect the offensive side of public gossip. What had been repeated to the mayor related only to the question of whether Julien would stay with him at six hundred francs, or accept the eight hundred offered by the director of the workhouse.

This director, who had run across M. de Rênal in society, had "cut him cold." Such behavior was not without a purpose; in the provinces, acts are seldom impulsive; there, strong feelings are so rare that they are suppressed at once.

M. Valenod was what they call, a hundred leagues from Paris, a "show-off"; that is, a creature who is brazen and coarse by nature. His career, a great success since 1815, had confirmed him in his fine ways. He reigned, so to speak, in Verrières under the orders of M. de Rênal; but far more active, blushing at nothing, putting his finger in every pie, tirelessly coming and going, writing, speaking, overlooking affronts, and without any personal pretensions, he had succeeded in counterbalancing his master's prestige in the eyes of the ecclesiastical powers. M. Valenod had said in so many words to the grocers of the region: Give me the two most stupid men among you; to the men of law: Point out the two most ignorant; to the health officers: Designate your two greatest charlatans. When he had assembled the most shameless of each trade, he said to them: "Let us rule together."

The ways of that crowd were distasteful to M. de Rênal. Coarse by nature, Valenod was not offended at anything, not even when the little Abbé Maslon repeatedly gave him the lie in public.

But in the midst of his prosperity, M. Valenod felt a need to fortify himself, by means of insolence in small matters, against the home truths which he realized full well everyone had a right to tell him. His activity doubled after M. Appert's visit had put fear in his heart: he made three trips to Besançon; he wrote several letters for each post; he sent others through strangers who came by his house at nightfall. He was mistaken perhaps in having old Father Chélan removed from office; for that spiteful gesture had caused several devout and wellborn ladies to look upon him as a profoundly wicked man. Besides, this service rendered had made him absolutely dependent upon the Vicar-general de Frilair, who sent him on some very odd errands. Such was the state of his affairs when he indulged himself in the pleasure of writing an anonymous letter. To make matters worse, his wife announced that she meant to have Julien in her house; her vanity was infatuated with the idea.

In this position, M. Valenod foresaw a showdown with his old confederate M. de Rênal. The latter would have some hard things to say, which was pretty much all the same to him; but he might also write to Besançon, or even to Paris. Some minister's cousin might suddenly turn up in Verrières and take over the workhouse. M. Valenod thought of making up to the Liberals; that was why several had been invited to the dinner at which Julien recited. He would be powerfully supported against the mayor. But an election might come up at any time, and it was all too obvious that holding on to the workhouse and a poor showing at the polls were incompatible. The story of these machinations, very accurately surmised by Mme. de Rênal, had been given Julien as he offered her his arm to go from one shop to another, and little by little it drew them toward Fidelity Drive, where they spent several hours almost as peacefully as at Vergy.

Meanwhile M. Valenod kept trying to postpone a decisive scene with his former boss by putting on a bold front. That day his plan worked, but put the mayor in an even worse humor.

Never has vanity at grips with everything that is most sour and meanest about the paltry love of money reduced a man to a sorrier state of mind than that M. de Rênal was in when he entered the cabaret. Never, on the contrary, had his children been more joyful or gayer. The contrast was too much for him.

"I am not wanted in my own family, from what I can see!" he said as he entered, hoping to compel respect by the tone of his voice.

His wife's only response was to take him aside and insist again on the need for sending Julien away. The happy hours she had just spent in his company had given her the ease and firmness she needed to follow a line of conduct she had been contemplating for two weeks. What finally succeeded in jolting the poor mayor of Verrières from top to bottom was the knowledge that everyone in town was joking about his fondness for cash. M. Valenod was generous as a thief, but he himself had behaved cautiously rather than brilliantly with regard to the last five or six collections for the Guild of St. Joseph, for the Congregation of the Virgin, for the Congregation of the Holy Sacrament, etc., etc.

Among the squires of Verrières and the surrounding countryside, shrewdly classified in a register by the collecting friars according to the amount of their donations, M. de Rênal's name was to be seen occupying the last line more than once. It was useless for him to claim that he *earned nothing*. The clergy are not to be trifled with on that score.

Chapter XXIII

The Trials of a Civil Servant

> *Il piacere di alzar la testa tutto*
> *l'anno è ben pagato da certi quarti*
> *d'ora che bisogna passar.*
>
> —CASTI*

Let us leave this petty man to his petty fears. Why did he take a man of heart into his house, when what he wanted was the soul of a lackey? Why didn't he know how to pick his servants? The ordinary course of events in the nineteenth century is that when a powerful aristocrat finds a man of heart in his way, he kills him, exiles him, imprisons him, or so humiliates him that the latter is stupid enough to die of grief. By chance, it is not yet the man of heart who is suffering in this instance. The great misfortune of small towns in France, and of governments by election, like that of New York, is that you are never allowed to forget that fellows like M. de Rênal exist in the world. In the midst of a city of twenty thousand inhabitants such individuals mold public opinion, and public opinion is a terrible thing in a country that has a constitution. A man endowed with a noble and generous mind, and who might have been your friend but lives a hundred leagues away, judges you according to public opinion in your town, which is shaped by the fools whom chance has caused to be born noble, rich, and conservative. Woe to anyone who stands out from the crowd!

Immediately after dinner the family set out again for Vergy; but two days later Julien saw them all returning to Verrières.

Not an hour had gone by when, to his great astonishment, Julien discovered that Mme. de Rênal was making a mystery of something. She would break off her conversations with her husband as soon as he appeared, and almost seemed to wish he would go away. Julien did not have to be told twice. He grew cold and reserved; Mme. de Rênal noticed this but sought no explanation. "Is she about to present me with a successor?" Julien wondered. "So intimate with me only the day before yesterday! But they say that that's the way these great ladies act. They're like kings: No greater courtesy than that shown the minister who, when he reaches home, will find his letter of disgrace."

Julien remarked that in these conversations, which stopped abruptly at his approach, there was often talk of a big house that belonged to the commune of Verrières. Old, but huge and comfortable, it was situated opposite the church, in the busiest part of town. "What might this house and a new lover have in common?" Julien wondered. Out of sorrow he said over those pretty lines by Francis I, which seemed new because it was not a month ago that Mme. de Rênal had taught them to him. By how many oaths, by how many kisses, had not each of those verses been given the lie!

Souvent femme varie,
*Bien fol qui s'y fie.**

M. de Rênal left by stagecoach for Besançon. This trip was decided on in two hours; he seemed very worried. On his return, he threw a big package wrapped in gray paper on the table.

"There's that stupid business," he said to his wife.

An hour later Julien saw a billposter carry off the big package; he followed him eagerly. "I will find out their secret at the first street corner."

He waited impatiently behind the billposter, who with his big brush was smearing the back of the bill. As soon as it was posted, Julien's curiosity read a very detailed announcement of the leasing by public auction of the huge old house that had come up so often in M. de Rênal's conversations with his wife. The allocation of the lease was announced for two o'clock the next day in the town hall, at the extinction of the third candle. Julien was deeply disappointed; he found the notice short indeed; how was there time enough to notify all the prospective bidders? Apart from this the poster, which was dated some two weeks beforehand, and which he reread in its entirety at three different places, taught him nothing.

He went to see the house up for lease. The doorkeeper, who didn't see him coming, was saying mysteriously to a neighbor: "Bah! trouble for nothing. M. Maslon promised him he would get it for three hundred francs; and since the mayor put up a fuss, he's been summoned to the bishop's palace by the Vicar-general de Frilair."

Julien's arrival seemed to bother the two friends a good deal; they didn't say another word.

Julien took care not to miss the sale of the lease. The poorly lighted hall was crowded; people eyed one another strangely. Everyone's attention was focused on a table where Julien saw three small candle ends burning in a pewter plate. The auctioneer called out: "*Three hundred francs, gentlemen!*"

"Three hundred francs! That's a joke," a man said in a low voice to his neighbor. Julien was standing between them. "It's worth more than eight hundred; I'm going to raise the bid."

"You'll be cutting your own throat. What's to be gained if you have M. Maslon, M. Valenod, the bishop, his terrible Vicar-general de Frilair, and the whole clique on your back?"

"Three hundred and twenty francs," shouted the other man.

"Stubborn fool!" commented his neighbor. "Here's one of the mayor's spies right here," he added, pointing to Julien.

Julien turned around sharply to deal with this remark, but the two Francs-Comtois paid no more attention to him. Their coolness helped him to recover his own. At that moment the last candle end went out, and the bailiff's drawling voice awarded the house for nine years to M. de Saint-Giraud, chief clerk in the Prefecture of——, for three hundred and thirty francs.

As soon as the mayor had left the room, the talk started.

"There's thirty francs Grogeot's foolhardiness has brought in for the town," said one.

"But M. de Saint-Giraud," someone answered, "will get even with Grogeot; he'll live to regret it."

"It's scandalous!" said a fat man on Julien's left; "a house I'd have given eight hundred francs for myself, for my factory, and I'd have made a good bargain at that."

"Bah!" a factory owner, a Liberal, answered him, "doesn't M. de Saint-Giraud belong to the *Congrégation*? Don't his four children have scholarships? The poor man!

157

It's simple; the town of Verrières owes him an extra salary of five hundred francs."

"And to think the mayor couldn't stop it!" remarked a third. "He's an Ultra, all right, but he doesn't steal."

"He doesn't steal? No, only magpies steal. It all goes into a common purse, and they split it up at the end of the year. But there's little Sorel; let's get out of here."

Julien came back in a foul mood; he found Mme. de Rênal quite sad.

"You've just come from the auction?" she asked him.

"Yes, madam, where I had the honor of being taken for the mayor's spy."

"If he had listened to me, he would have gone off on a trip."

At that moment M. de Rênal appeared; he was very gloomy. Not a word was spoken at the dinner table. M. de Rênal ordered Julien to go with the children to Vergy; it was a mournful trip.

Mme. de Rênal tried to comfort her husband. "You ought to be used to it by now, dear."

That night they sat in silence around the family hearth; the noise of the blazing beech log was their only distraction. It was one of those melancholy moments that occur in the most united families. One of the children cried out joyously, "Someone's ringing! soneone's ringing!"

"By heavens! if it's M. de Saint-Giraud who's come to gloat, on the pretext of thanking me," cried the mayor, "I'll give him a piece of my mind; that's going too far. It's to Valenod he's obligated, and I am the one who is compromised. What can I say if those damned Jacobin newspapers get ahold of this story, and make a M. Nonantecinq* out of me?"

At that point, a very handsome man with long black sideburns followed the servant into the room.

"M. le Maire, I am il Signor Geronimo. Here is a letter for you that the Chevalier de Beauvaisis, attaché to the embassy in Naples, gave me at my departure only nine days ago." Signor Geronimo added cheerfully, looking at Mme. de Rênal, "The Signor de Beauvaisis, your cousin and my good friend, madam, said that you know Italian."

The Neapolitan's good humor changed this sad evening into a very gay one. Mme. de Rênal insisted that he have supper. She set her whole household in motion; she wanted at all costs to take Julien's mind off the epithet "spy," which he had heard ringing in his ear twice that day. Signor Geronimo was a famous singer, at home in good society and yet a very gay man, qualities which are seldom compatible in France anymore. After supper he sang a little *duettino* with Mme. de Rênal. He told charming stories. At one o'clock in the morning, the children made a great fuss when Julien proposed that they go to bed.

"Just this story," said the eldest.

"It is my own, signorino," replied Signor Geronimo. "Eight years ago, I was like you a pupil at the Conservatory of Naples; I mean, I was your age. But I did not have the honor of being a son of the illustrious mayor of the beautiful city of Verrières."

This compliment moved M. de Rênal to sigh; he looked at his wife.

"Signor Zingarelli," the young singer continued, exaggerating his accent a bit, which made the children burst out laughing, "Signor Zingarelli was an awfully strict master. He is not liked at the conservatory; but he always expects you to act as though you liked him. I sneaked out as often as I could; I would go to the little theater of San Carlino, where I heard the music of the gods; but heavens! how to get eight sous together, the price of a ticket to the pit. An enormous sum," he said, looking at the children and making them laugh. "Signor Giovannone, director of the San Carlino, heard me sing. I was sixteen. 'That child is a treasure,' he said.

" 'Would you like me to engage you, my dear friend?' he came to me and asked.

" 'How much will you pay me?'

" 'Forty ducats a month.' Gentlemen, that is one hundred and sixty francs. I thought I saw heaven opening up.

" 'But how,' I asked Giovannone, 'will you ever get that strict Zingarelli to let me go?'

" '*Lascia fare a me.*' "

"Leave it to me?" cried the eldest child.

"Right you are, my young lord. Signor Giovannone said to me: '*Caro*, a little contract first.' I sign; he gives me three ducats. Never had I seen so much money. Then he told me what I must do.

"The next day I asked to see the terrible Signor Zingarelli. His old valet showed me in.

" 'What do you want from me, rogue?' Zingarelli asked.

" 'Maestro,' I told him, 'I am sorry for my bad conduct. I will never sneak out of the conservatory again by climbing over the iron gate. I am going to work twice as hard.'

" 'If I weren't afraid of spoiling the most beautiful bass

159

voice I have ever heard, I'd put you in prison for two weeks on bread and water, young scamp.'

"'*Maestro*,' I replied, 'I'm going to be a model for the whole school, *credete a me*.* But I ask you one favor; if someone comes asking for me to sing outside, don't let me go. Please say that you cannot.'

"'And who the devil do you think would ask for a good-for-nothing like you? Would I ever let you leave the conservatory? Are you pulling my leg? Get out, get out!' he said, trying to give me a kick in the b——, 'or watch out for dry bread and water.'

"An hour later, Signor Giovannone arrives at the director's house: 'I've come to ask you to make my fortune,' he told him; 'let me have Geronimo. Let him sing in my theater, and this winter I will be able to marry off my daughter.'

"'What do you expect to do with that hoodlum?' Zingarelli asked. 'I won't allow it; you shan't have him. Besides, even if I consented, he would never leave the conservatory; he just swore he wouldn't.'

"'If it's only a question of whether he's willing,' Giovannone said gravely, as he pulled my contract out of his pocket, '*carta canta*! here's his signature.'

"Furious, Zingarelli flung himself on the bell rope: 'Throw Geronimo out of the conservatory,' he screamed, boiling with rage. So they threw me out, I laughing my head off. The same evening I sang the *Aria del Moltiplico*. Punch wants to marry, and counts on his fingers all the things he will need in his house, and he keeps getting mixed up in his calculations."

"Oh, sir, won't you please sing us that aria," said Mme. de Rênal.

Geronimo sang, and everyone cried from laughing so hard. Il Signor Geronimo didn't go to bed until two o'clock in the morning, leaving the family enchanted with his fine manners, his obliging nature, and his gaiety.

The next day M. and Mme. de Rênal gave him the letters he would need at the French court.

"So there is duplicity everywhere," commented Julien to himself. "Here is Signor Geronimo on his way to London with a contract worth sixty thousand francs. If it weren't for the ability of the San Carlino's director, his heavenly voice might not have been recognized and admired for another ten years. . . .

"Faith, I'd rather be a Geronimo that a Rênal. He is less honored in society, but he has never known the grief

160

of making an allocation like the one today, and his life is a gay one."

One thing astonished Julien: the solitary weeks spent in Verrières in M. de Rênal's house had been a time of happiness for him. He had not felt disgusted or had depressing thoughts except at the dinners given for him; in that lonely house, hadn't he been able to read, to write, to think, without being disturbed? He had not been constantly dragged away from his shining dreams by the cruel necessity of studying the impulses of a mean-spirited man, and, what is worse, in order to deceive him by hypocritical words or actions.

"Could happiness be within my reach, then? The price of such a life is next to nothing: I could choose either to marry Mlle. Elisa or to become Fouqué's partner.... Yet, the traveler who has just climbed a steep mountain and sits down at the top finds a perfect pleasure in resting. But would he be happy if he were forced to rest all of the time?"

Mme. de Rênal had begun to entertain gloomy thoughts. Despite her resolution, she had told Julien the whole business about the auction.* "He will make me forget all my vows," she reflected.

She would have sacrificed her life without hesitation to save her husband's had she seen him in danger. Hers was one of those noble and romantic souls for which to be aware of the possibility of doing a generous deed and not do it is a source of regret almost equal to that of a crime committed. Nevertheless, there were ill-fated days when she could not drive away a vision of the inordinate happiness she would taste if, on suddenly becoming a widow, she could marry Julien.

He loved her sons far more than their father did, and in spite of his strict discipline they adored him. She realized full well that by marrying Julien, she would be obliged to leave this Vergy whose shade was so dear to her. She saw herself living in Paris, continuing to give her sons that education which was the admiration of everyone. Her children, herself, Julien, all would be perfectly happy.

An odd effect of marriage, or what the nineteenth century has made of it! The boredom of conjugal life destroys love without fail, when love has preceded marriage. And yet, a philosopher might add, the same boredom soon causes those rich enough not to work to become profoundly bored with all the quiet pleasures. And it is only the frigid souls, among women, whom it does not predispose to fall in love.

161

The philosopher's observation leads me to excuse Mme. de Rênal, but no one in Verrières excused her; and the whole town, without her being aware, talked of nothing but her scandalous passion. Because of this great affair, people were less bored than usual that autumn.

Autumn and part of winter passed very quickly. It was time to leave the woods of Vergy. High society in Verrières was beginning to wax indignant over the fact that its anathemizing made so little impression on M. de Rênal. In less than a week, some of those grave citizens who compensate themselves for their habitual solemnity with the pleasure of fulfilling this kind of mission planted the cruelest suspicions in his mind; but they used the most guarded language.

M. Valenod, who played a close game, had placed Elisa with a noble and highly respectable family in which there were five women.

Elisa, afraid, as she said, of not being able to find a job during the winter, had asked this family for only two thirds of what she had been getting at the mayor's house. On her own initiative, the girl had had the excellent idea of going to the former curé, Father Chélan, for confession as well as to the new one, so she could tell both about Julien's love affair in detail.

The day after his arrival, Father Chélan sent for Julien at six in the morning.

"I am not asking you to explain anything," he said to him. "I beg you, and if need be, order you not to tell me anything. I insist that within three days you leave for the seminary in Besançon or the residence of your friend Fouqué, who is still willing to help you to a magnificent future. I have arranged everything, but you must leave, and not come back to Verrières for a year."

Julien made no reply. He was wondering if he ought to consider his honor offended by the trouble M. Chélan, who was not after all his father, had been to on his account.

"Tomorrow at the same time I shall have the honor of seeing you again," he said to the curé at length.

M. Chélan, who had counted on getting the better of so young a man by force, talked a great deal. Assuming the humblest of attitudes and appearances, Julien did not open his mouth.

He left finally and ran to warn Mme. de Rênal, whom he found in despair. Her husband had just spoken to her with a good deal of frankness. The natural weakness of his character, shored up by the prospective inheritance from

Besançon, had decided him to consider her perfectly innocent. He had just told her that he found public opinion in Verrières in a strange state. The public was wrong; it had been misled by the envious. But still, what was to be done?

For an instant Mme. de Rênal had the illusion that Julien might be able to accept M. Valenod's offer and stay on in Verrières. But she was no longer the timid, simple woman of the year before; her fatal passion, her remorse, had enlightened her. She soon knew the sorrow of proving to herself, as she listened to her husband, that a separation, at least for the time being, was indispensable. "Far from me, Julien will fall back on his ambitious schemes, so natural when one has nothing. And I, great God! I am so rich! and to so little avail for my own happiness! He will forget me. Charming as he is, he will be loved, he will fall in love. Ah! miserable woman. . . . What right have I to complain? Heaven is just; I didn't have the strength to put an end to this crime; it robbed me of my judgment. It depended on me alone to win over Elisa with money; nothing could have been easier. I didn't bother to reflect for one moment; the wild fancies of love took all my time. Now I am ruined."

Julien was struck by one thing: upon informing Mme. de Rênal about the terrible news of his departure, he met with no selfish objection. She was obviously making an effort not to weep.

"We must be brave, my dear." She cut a lock of his hair. "I don't know what will happen to me," she told him, "but if I should die, promise me never to forget my children. Near or far, try to make honest men of them. If there is another revolution, all the aristocrats will be slaughtered; their father will emigrate, perhaps, because of that peasant killed on a roof. Watch over the family. . . . Give me your hand. Farewell, my dear! These are our last moments. Once this great sacrifice has been made, I hope I shall have the heart to think about my reputation in public."

Julien expected despair. The simplicity of her farewell touched him.

"No, I will not take leave of you in this fashion. I will go; they wish it; you wish it yourself. But three days after my departure, I will come back to see you at night."

Mme. de Rênal's whole life was changed. Julien really loved her, then, since it had been his own idea to see her again! Her agony was transformed into one of the keenest impulses of joy she had ever experienced. Everything became easy for her. The certainty of seeing her lover again saved these last moments from being heartrending. From that minute on, Mme. de Rênal's behavior, like her appearance, was noble, firm, and perfectly respectable.

M. de Rênal soon returned; he was beside himself. He finally spoke to his wife about the anonymous letter he had received two months before.

"I mean to take it to the Casino, show everyone that it came from that disreputable Valenod, whom I took out of the gutter and made one of the richest bourgeois in Verrières. I will shame him publicly, then I will fight with him. This is too much."

"I might become a widow, great God!" thought Mme. de Rênal. But in almost the same breath she told herself, "If I don't prevent this duel, as I certainly can, I will be my husband's murderer."

Never had she humored his vanity so skillfully. In less than two hours she made him see, and always for reasons discovered by himself, that he ought to be friendlier than ever with M. Valenod, and even take Elisa back into the house. It took courage on Mme. de Rênal's part to see that girl again, the cause of all her unhappiness. But the idea came from Julien.

Eventually, after having been put on the track three or four times, M. de Rênal arrived all by himself at the financially painful conclusion that it would be most unpleasant for him if Julien, amidst all the effervescence and talk in Verrières, were to stay on there as a tutor for Valenod's children. It was obviously in Julien's interest to accept the director of the workhouse's offer. It was vital, on the contrary, to M. de Rênal's reputation that Julien leave Verrières and enter the seminary in Besançon or the one in Dijon. But how to get him to agree, and then, what would he live on?

M. de Rênal, foreseeing an imminent sacrifice of money, was in even greater despair than his wife. As for her, after this discussion she was like the man of heart who, tired of living, has swallowed a dose of stramonium; he acts by reflex, so to speak, and takes no interest in anything. Thus it occurred to the dying Louis XIV to say: *"When I was king."* Wonderful expression!

Early the next morning M. de Rênal received an anonymous letter. This one was written in the most insulting terms. The most vulgar words applicable to his situation were to be seen in every line of it. It was the work of some jealous subordinate. This letter brought him back to the idea of fighting with M. Valenod. In a while he mustered enough courage to think about action. He left the house alone and went to a gunsmith's shop to buy some pistols, which he had loaded.

"In fact," he told himself, "if the Emperor Napoleon's strict administration came back, I wouldn't have one crooked sou with which to reproach myself. At most I have closed my eyes, but I have some fine letters in my desk authorizing me to do so."

Mme. de Rênal was alarmed by her husband's cold rage; it reminded her of the fatal idea of widowhood, which she had so much trouble thrusting aside. She locked herself in with him. For several hours she talked to him in vain; the new anonymous letter had decided him. Eventually she succeeded in transforming the courage to give M. Valenod a slap in the face into that of offering Julien six hundred francs for a year's board and room in a seminary. Cursing a thousand times the day on which he had had the disastrous idea of taking a tutor into his house, M. de Rênal forgot the anonymous letter.

He was somewhat consoled by a thought which he did not reveal to his wife: by being adroit, and by taking advantage of the young man's romantic notions, he hoped to get him to promise, for a smaller sum, to refuse M. Valenod's offer.

Mme. de Rênal had a much more difficult time proving to Julien that by making a sacrifice, for her husband's convenience, of a position worth eight hundred francs, which the director of the workhouse had offered him publicly, he might honorably accept an indemnification.

"But," Julien kept saying, "I never had, not for a minute, any intention of accepting his offer. You have accustomed me too well to an elegant life; the vulgarity of those people would kill me."

Cruel necessity, with its iron hand, bent Julien's will. His pride held out to him the illusion that he might accept the sum offered by the mayor of Verrières as a loan, and give him his note, promising payment with interest in five years.

Mme. de Rênal still had several thousand francs hidden in the little cave in the mountain. Trembling, she offered them, only too well aware that she might be refused angrily.

"Do you wish," Julien asked her, "to make the memory of our love abominable?"

Eventually Julien left Verrières. M. de Rênal was very happy; when the fateful moment came to accept the money from him, the sacrifice turned out to be too much for Julien. He refused outright. M. de Rênal hugged him with tears in his eyes. Julien had asked him for a letter of reference, and in his enthusiasm he couldn't find terms magnificent enough to praise his conduct. Our hero had five louis saved up and counted on asking Fouqué for a like sum.

He was deeply moved. But by the time he was a league out of Verrières, where he had left so much love, he had nothing on his mind but the delight of seeing a capital, a great fortified city like Besançon.

During this short absence of three days, Mme. de Rênal was beguiled by one of the cruelest deceptions that love has to offer. Her life was bearable; there stood between her and extreme misery this last meeting she was to have with Julien. She counted the hours, the minutes, that kept her from it. At last, during the night of the third day, she heard the signal agreed upon in the distance. After having passed through a thousand dangers, Julien appeared before her.

From that moment on she had but one thought: "I am seeing him for the last time." Far from responding to her lover's eagerness, she was like a cadaver. If she forced herself to say she loved him, she did it with so awkward an air as to prove almost the contrary. Nothing could take her mind off the bitter thought of an eternal separation. Suspicious, Julien believed for an instant that he had already been forgotten. His sharp remarks to this effect were met with tears flowing in silence and an almost convulsive squeezing of his hand.

"But, good God! how do you expect me to believe you?" Julien replied to his mistress's cold declarations; "you would show a hundred times more sincere affection to Mme. Derville, to a simple acquaintance."

Petrified, Mme. de Rênal didn't know what to say. "It is impossible to be more unhappy.... I hope I will die.... I can feel my heart turning to ice...."

Such were the longest answers he could get from her.

When the first light of day made departure necessary, Mme. de Rênal's tears stopped altogether. She watched him tie a knotted rope to the window without saying a word, without returning his kisses. To no avail Julien said to her, "We have, at last, reached that stage which you so desired. Henceforth you may live free of remorse. When your children have the slightest upset, you will no longer see them in the grave."

"I am sorry that you couldn't give Stanislas a kiss," she said coldly.

166

Julien ended by being deeply impressed with the passionless embraces of this living corpse; he could think of nothing else for several leagues. He was cut to the heart, and before passing over the mountain, and as long as he could see Verrières' steeple, he kept looking back.

Chapter XXIV

A Capital

> So much noise, so many busy people! So many thoughts about the future in a twenty-year-old head! What a distraction for love!
>
> ——BARNAVE

He finally caught sight of some black walls on a far-off mountain; it was the citadel of Besançon. "How different it would be," he said with a sigh, "if I were coming to this noble fortified city as a second lieutenant in one of the regiments entrusted with its defense!"

Not only is Besançon one of the prettiest cities in France, it abounds in men of heart and mind as well. But Julien was nothing but a little peasant and had no way of approaching distinguished men.

At Fouqué's house he had put on civilian dress, and in such clothing crossed the drawbridges. His head filled with the siege of 1674, he intended, before he shut himself up in the seminary, to see the ramparts and the citadel. Two or three times he was on the verge of being arrested by the sentinels; he kept going into places the military engineers had forbidden to the public, so they could cut and sell twelve or fifteen francs worth of hay ever year.

The height of the walls, the depth of the moats, the terrible-looking cannons, had been on his mind for several hours when he passed in front of the big café on the boulevard. He stopped, motionless with admiration. It made no difference that he read the word "café" written in big letters above the two huge doors; he couldn't believe his eyes. He made an effort to master his shyness; he dared enter and found himself in a room thirty or forty yards long, the ceiling of which was at least twenty feet high. That day everything seemed magical to him.

Two games of billiards were in progress. The waiters were calling out the scores; the players were running around the billiard tables encumbered with spectators. Billows of tobacco smoke, pouring from every mouth, enveloped them in a blue cloud. The tallness of these men, their round shoulders, their heavy gait, their enormous sideburns, the long frock coats that covered their bodies, everything attracted Julien's attention. These noble sons of ancient Bisontium* spoke only in shouts; they gave themselves the airs of terrible warriors. Julien stood there admiring them; he mused over the immensity and the magnificence of a great capital like Besançon. He felt in no wise up to asking one of the haughty gentlemen, who kept calling out the billiard scores, for a cup of coffee.

But the young lady at the counter had noticed the charming face of this young bourgeois from the country, who, having stopped three feet from the stove with a small bundle under his arm, was contemplating a bust of the king, done in fine white plaster. This young lady, a tall and very shapely Franc-Comtoise, dressed as she should be to give a café the right tone, had already said twice in a small voice meant for Julien's ears alone: "Sir! sir!" Julien's gaze met that of two big blue and most tender eyes, and saw it was he who was being addressed.

He stepped briskly over to the counter and to the pretty girl, as he would have approached an enemy. During this great maneuver, his bundle fell.

What pity our young provincial must inspire in the high-school students of Paris who already know, at fifteen, how to enter a café with so distinguished an air. Yet those children, so sophisticated at fifteen, turn *common* by the time they are eighteen. The impassioned shyness that one encounters in the provinces is sometimes overcome, and in such cases it teaches one how to exercise the will. As he advanced toward the beautiful young girl who had deigned to speak to him, Julien thought: "I must tell her the truth." He was becoming brave by virtue of shyness overcome.

"Madam, I have come to Besançon for the first time in my life; I'd like to have a roll and a cup of coffee; I'll pay for it, of course."

The girl smiled a little, then blushed; for the sake of this good-looking young man, she dreaded the billiard players' ironical attention and their jokes. He might be frightened and never come back.

"Sit here, near me," she said, pointing to a marble table, almost entirely hidden by the enormous mahogany counter that jutted out into the room.

The young woman leaned out over the counter, which gave her a chance to show off a superb figure. Julien noted it; all his ideas changed. The beautiful young lady had just set a cup, a piece of sugar, and a roll before him. She hesitated to call a waiter to pour some coffee, realizing full well that when he came her tête-à-tête with Julien would be finished.

Pensive, Julien was comparing this gay blond beauty with certain memories that stirred him often. The thought of the passion of which he had been the object rid him of nearly all his shyness. The beautiful girl had only a minute to spare; she read Julien's looks.

"That pipe smoke is making you cough; come for breakfast tomorrow before eight; at that hour I am almost alone."

"What is your name?" Julien asked, with the caressing smile of happy shyness.

"Amanda Binet."

"May I send you a little package in an hour, the size of this one?"

The beautiful Amanda thought it over. "I am watched here. What you're asking may get me in trouble; but I will write my address on a card. Put it on your package and you can send it straight to me."

"My name is Julien Sorel," said the young man; "I haven't any family or friends in Besançon."

"Ah! I understand," she said, overjoyed, "you have come for the law school."

"Alas! no," replied Julien, "I am being sent to the seminary."

The most utter discouragement dulled Amanda's features; she called a waiter; she had the heart to do it now. The waiter poured Julien's coffee without looking at him.

Amanda was taking money at the counter. Julien was proud of having dared to speak. There was an argument going on at one of the billiard tables. The shouts and denials of the players, resounding throughout the huge room, made a din that astonished Julien. Amanda was dreaming and her eyes were lowered.

"If you wish, mademoiselle," he said to her with sudden assurance, "I will say I am your cousin."

His little air of authority pleased Amanda. "He's not just anybody," she thought. She said very quickly, without

170

looking at him, for she was keeping an eye out to see if anyone came toward the counter, "I'm from Genlis, near Dijon; say that you're from Genlis too, and my mother's cousin."

"I won't forget."

"Every Thursday at five, in summer, the gentlemen from the seminary pass by the café."

"If you are thinking of me when I pass by, have a bouquet of violets in your hand."

Amanda looked at him in astonishment; this look transformed Julien's courage into rashness; still, he blushed a good deal when he said to her, "I feel the most violent love for you."

"Not so loud, please," she said, looking frightened.

It occurred to Julien to try and recall some sentences from an odd volume of the *Nouvelle Héloise*,* that he had found at Vergy. His memory served him well; for ten minutes he recited the *Nouvelle Héloise* to an entranced Mlle. Amanda. He was feeling happy about his courage, when all of a sudden the beautiful Franc-Comtoise assumed an icy manner. One of her lovers had just appeared in the door of the café.

He walked up to the counter whistling and swaying his shoulders; he looked at Julien. At that instant the latter's imagination, always running to extremes, was filled with notions about dueling. He turned very pale, pushed his cup away, put on a confident air, and looked over his rival most attentively. While this rival bent his head over the counter as he familiarly poured himself a glass of brandy, Amanda, by a glance, ordered Julien to lower his eyes. He obeyed and for two minutes sat motionless in his chair, pale, resolute, thinking only of what was going to happen. He was really very fine at that moment. The rival had been astonished at Julien's eyes. Having tossed off his glass of brandy at one gulp, he said a few words to Amanda, shoved his hands into the side pockets of his big frock coat, and went over to a billiard table, whistling and looking at Julien all the while. The latter jumped to his feet, carried away by rage; but he didn't know how to go about being insolent. He put down his small bundle, and with the most swaggering air he could manage, walked toward the billiard table.

To no avail, prudence kept telling him: "Fight a duel as soon as you get to Besançon, and you put an end to your career in the Church."

"No matter, it won't be said that I stood for an insult."

Amanda saw his courage; it made a pretty contrast with

171

the ingenuousness of his manner; in an instant she liked him better than the tall young man in the frock coat. She rose, and looking as if she were trying to follow someone passing in the street with her eyes, moved quickly to station herself between him and the billiard table: "Careful you don't give that gentleman any dirty looks; he's my brother-in-law."

"What do I care? He looked at me."

"Do you want to make trouble for me? Sure, he looked at you; he may even come over and speak to you. I told him that you are one of my mother's relations, and that you come from Genlis. He is Franc-Comtois and has never been farther than Dôle, on the road to Burgundy, so tell him whatever you please; you don't have to worry."

Julien was still undecided. She added very quickly, her barmaid's imagination supplying her with fibs in abundance, "Sure, he looked at you, but it was at the time he was asking me who you were; he's a man who is gruff with everyone; he didn't mean anything by it."

Julien kept his eye on the so-called brother-in-law. He saw him buy a number in the pool that was being played at the farther of the two billiard tables. Julien heard his coarse voice shout in a threatening tone: *It's my turn.*

Julien passed quickly behind Mlle. Amanda and took a step toward the billiard table. Amanda grabbed him by the arm. "Come and pay me first," she said.

"That's right," thought Julien, "she's afraid I'll leave without paying."

Amanda was just as agitated as he, and very red; she gave him his change as slowly as she could, all the while repeating in a low voice, "Leave the café this minute, or I won't like you anymore; and yet, I like you very much."

Julien did, in effect, go, but slowly. "Isn't it my duty," he kept asking himself, "to go and take a turn at whistling and staring this lout in the face?" Indecision held him back for an hour on the boulevard in front of the café; he watched to see if his man would come out. He didn't, and Julien went away.

He had been in Besançon only a few hours and already had something to regret. The old surgeon major, despite his gout, had given him a few lessons in fencing; such was all the training Julien had at the service of his wrath. But this problem wouldn't have amounted to anything, had he but known how to start a quarrel otherwise than by giving a slap; for if it should lead to a fist fight, his rival, a huge man, would thrash him and walk away.

"For a poor devil like me," Julien thought, "without a

172

protector or money, there won't be much difference between a seminary and a prison; I will have to leave my civilian clothes at some inn, where I will put on my black outfit again. If ever I manage to get away from the seminary for a few hours, in my street clothes I could very well go and see Mlle. Amanda again." This was a fine plan, but though he walked past all the inns in town, Julien dared not enter any of them.

Eventually, as he was passing the Hotel of the Ambassadors for the second time, his anxious eyes encountered those of a stout woman, still rather young, who had a ruddy complexion and a gay and happy look about her. He went over to her and told his story.

"Certainly, my fine little priest," the hostess of the Ambassadors said to him, "I will keep your street clothes for you and even see to it that they are brushed from time to time. In weather like this, it's not safe to put a woolen suit away and never touch it." She took a key and led him herself into a bedroom, where she instructed him to make a note of the things he was leaving.

"God be praised! Don't you look fine dressed that way, Abbé Sorel!" the stout woman said when he came down to the kitchen. "I'm going to serve you a good dinner. And," she added in a whisper, "it won't cost you but twenty sous instead of fifty, which is what everyone else pays; because you have to be careful with your little *nest egg*."

"I have ten louis," replied Julien with a certain pride.

"Ah! for heaven's sake," exclaimed the hostess, alarmed. "Don't talk so loud; there are plenty of hoodlums in Besançon. They will rob you in next to no time. Whatever you do, don't go into the cafés; they are full of hoodlums."

"Really!" said Julien, whom this remark had set to thinking.

"Never go anywhere except to my place; I will make coffee for you. Remember that you will always find a friend here, and a good dinner for twenty sous; that's talking, I hope. Go sit down at the table; I'm going to serve you myself."

"I couldn't eat," Julien told her. "I'm too nervous. I am going into the seminary when I leave your inn."

The good woman wouldn't let him go until she had filled his pockets with provisions. Eventually Julien started off toward the terrible place, the hostess on her doorstep pointing out the way.

Chapter XXV

The Seminary

> Three hundred and thirty-six dinners at eighty-three centimes each, three hundred and thirty-six suppers at thirty-eight centimes, chocolate for those entitled to it; how much there is to be made on the contract!
>
> —THE VALENOD OF BESANÇON*

From a distance he saw the gilded iron cross over the door; he approached it slowly; his legs seemed to be giving way beneath him. "So there it is, that hell on earth I won't be able to leave!"

He finally made up his mind to ring. The sound of the bell echoed as in a lonely place. At the end of ten minutes, a pale man dressed in black came to open the door. Julien looked at him and immediately lowered his gaze. He thought the porter had a peculiar physiognomy. The green, protruding pupils of his eyes were dilated like those of a cat; the still contours of his eyelids suggested a total incapacity for any human feeling; his thin lips were spread out in a circle over projecting teeth. However, this countenance was not the face of crime but rather that of perfect insensibility, which is far more terrifying to the young. The only sentiment that Julien's swift glance could discern on that long, pious face was a profound contempt for everything one might wish to speak with him about that was not concerned with heaven.

Julien raised his eyes with an effort, and in a voice shaky from the beating of his heart he explained that he wished to speak with M. Pirard, the director of the seminary. Not saying a word, the man in black motioned him to follow. They climbed two flights of a wide staircase with a wooden banister. The warped steps sloped sharply away from the wall and seemed ready to collapse. A little door, surmounted by a big cemetery cross made of fir wood and painted black, was opened with difficulty, and the porter showed him into a low, gloomy room, the whitewashed walls of which were decorated with two big pictures darkened by time. There, Julien was left alone. He was stunned, his heart was beating violently; had he dared, he would gladly have wept. A silence of death reigned throughout the house.

At the end of a quarter of an hour, which seemed a day, the porter with the sinister face reappeared in a doorway at the other end of the room, and without bothering to speak, beckoned him to approach. He entered another room, bigger than the first and very poorly lighted. Its walls were whitewashed too, but there was little furniture in it; in passing, Julien saw a pine bed, two straw-bottomed chairs, and a small, cushionless armchair made of pine boards in a corner near the door. At the other end of the room, near a small window with yellowed panes and garnished with untidy vases of flowers, he perceived a man in a shabby cassock seated at a table; he looked angry and kept picking up little squares of paper from a pile, one by one, which he arranged on his table after writing a few words on each. He wasn't aware of Julien's presence. The latter was standing motionless in about the middle of the room, there where he had been left by the porter, who had gone out again, closing the door.

Ten minutes passed thus; the poorly dressed man kept on writing. Julien's shock and terror were such that he felt as if he were about to fall. A philosopher would say, perhaps mistakenly: "This is the violent effect of ugliness on a soul born to love the beautiful."

The man writing looked up; Julien was not aware of this for a moment, but even after seeing him he remained motionless, as though struck dead by the terrible gaze of which he was the object. Julien's troubled sight could barely make out the long face, entirely covered with red blotches except the forehead, which was deadly pale. Between those red cheeks and the white forehead shone two small black eyes that were enough to frighten the bravest. The vast contours of this forehead were defined by thick, flat, jet-black hair.

175

"Are you coming over here, yes or no?" the man said at length impatiently.

Julien approached unsteadily, and at length, ready to fall, and pale, paler than he had ever been in his life, halted three feet from the little pine table covered with squares of paper.

"Closer," said the man.

Julien took a few more steps, stretching out his hand as though looking for something to lean on.

"Your name?"

"Julien Sorel."

"You took your time getting here," he said, fixing him again with his terrible eye.

Julien couldn't endure this look; stretching out his hand, as though to support himself, he fell full length onto the floor.

The man rang. Julien had lost only the use of his eyes and the strength to move; he heard footsteps approaching.

He was lifted up; he was put into the small wooden armchair. He heard the terrible man saying to the porter, "Apparently he has the falling sickness. That's all we needed."

When Julien could open his eyes, the man with the red face had gone back to writing; the porter had disappeared. "I must be brave," our hero told himself, "and above all, hide my feelings"—he was suffering from violent nausea—"if I have an accident, God knows what they will think of me."

In time the man ceased writing, and giving Julien a sidelong glance: "Are you in a condition to answer me?"

"Yes, sir," Julien replied feebly.

"Ah! that's good."

The dark man had half risen and was searching impatiently for a letter in his pine-table drawer, which opened with a screech. He found it, sat down slowly, and staring at Julien again, as though he meant to tear out the little life still left in him: "You have been recommended to me by M. Chélan; he was the best curé in the diocese, a virtuous man if there ever was one, and my friend for the last thirty years."

"Ah! it is M. Pirard to whom I have the honor of speaking," said Julien in a moribund voice.

"Obviously," replied the director of the seminary, looking at him with irritation.

The sparkle in his small eyes doubled and was followed by a twitching of the muscles at the corners of his mouth. It was the look of a tiger relishing his prey in advance.

"The letter from Chélan is short," he said, as though talking to himself. "*Intelligenti pauca*,* in times like these, one can't write too little." He read aloud:

I recommend to you Julien Sorel, of this parish, whom I baptized some twenty years ago; he is the son of a rich carpenter who gives him nothing. Julien will be a remarkable laborer in the vineyard of the Lord. He has a good memory and is intelligent; he is a thinker. Is his vocation durable? Is it sincere?

"*Sincere?*" repeated the Abbé Pirard with an air of astonishment, and looking at Julien; but the abbé's gaze was already a little less devoid of humanity. "*Sincere!*" he repeated, lowering his voice and returning to the letter.

I am asking you for a scholarship for Julien Sorel; he will qualify for it by taking the requisite examinations. I have taught him a little theology, that good old theology of Bossuet, of Arnault, of Fleury.* If this fellow doesn't suit you, send him back to me. The director of the workhouse, whom you know well, has offered him eight hundred francs to be his children's tutor. My spiritual life is peaceful, thank God. I am getting used to the terrible blow. *Vale et me ama.**

The Abbé Pirard, slowing his voice as he read the signature, pronounced the word "Chélan" with a sigh.

"He is at peace," he said. "Indeed, his virtuous life has earned him that reward; may God grant it to me if such should be the case!"

He looked toward the sky and made the sign of the cross. At the sight of this holy sign, Julien felt the profound horror which had frozen him at his entrance into the house begin to diminish.

"In this house I have three hundred and twenty-one candidates for the most sacred profession," said the Abbé Pirard at length, in a severe but not ill-natured tone of voice. "Only seven or eight have been recommended to me by men like Father Chélan; so you are the ninth among those three hundred and twenty-one. But my protection means neither favor nor weakness; it means twice as much exertion against, and punishment of, the vices. Go and lock that door."

Julien made an effort to walk and succeeded in not falling. He noted that one little window, next to the main door, looked out on the countryside. He gazed at the trees; this sight did him good, as if he had caught a glimpse of old friends.

"Loquerisne linguam latinam?" ("Do you speak Latin?") the Abbé Pirard said to him as he was returning.

"Ita, pater optime" ("Yes, excellent father"), answered Julien, coming around a bit. Certainly no man in the world had ever appeared less excellent to him than M. Pirard during the last half hour.

The interview continued in Latin. The expression in the Abbé's eyes was softening; Julien was recovering some of his self-control. "How weak I am," he thought, "to let myself be taken in by this show of virtue. This man is probably just another cheat like M. Maslon"; and Julien congratulated himself for having hidden most of his money in his boots.

The Abbé Pirard examined Julien in theology; he was surprised at the extent of his knowledge. His astonishment increased when he questioned him about particulars of the Holy Scriptures. But when he questioned him about the doctrines of the Fathers, he realized that Julien was barely acquainted even with the names of St. Jerome, St. Augustine, St. Bonaventura, St. Basil, etc., etc.

"In effect," thought the Abbé Pirard, "one can see here that fatal tendency toward Protestantism with which I have always reproached Chélan. A thorough, but too thorough, knowledge of the Holy Scriptures."

(Julien had just spoken to him, without being questioned on this score, about the real time in which Genesis, the Pentateuch, etc., had been written.)

"To what does this endless reasoning about the Holy Scriptures lead," thought the Abbé Pirard, "if not to *free inquiry;* that is to say, the most dreadful Protestantism? And along with that ill-advised study, nothing on the Fathers to offset this inclination."

But the director of the seminary's astonishment knew no bounds when, upon interrogating Julien on the pope's authority, and expecting to hear the maxims of the old Gallican church, the young man recited M. de Maistre's whole book to him.

"An odd man, that Chélan," thought the Abbé Pirard. "Could he have shown him that book in order to teach him to scoff at it?"

It was useless for him to question Julien in an effort to find out whether he believed seriously in M. de Maistre's doctrine. The young man answered only from memory. From that moment on Julien was really very fine; he felt he was master of himself. After a very long examination, it seemed to him that M. Pirard's harshness was now merely affected. To tell the truth, if it weren't for the rule of strict gravity that he had imposed upon himself fifteen years before with regard to his divinity students, the director of the seminary would have embraced Julien in the name of logic: he found such clarity, precision, and incisiveness in his answers.

"Here is a bold and healthy mind," he said to himself, "but *corpus debile*." ("The body is weak.")

"Do you often fall like that?" he asked Julien in French, pointing at the floor.

"That was the first time in my life; the porter's face turned me to ice," added Julien, blushing like a child.

The Abbé Pirard almost smiled. "Such is the effect of worldly vanity; you are obviously accustomed to smiling faces, veritable theaters of falsehood. Truth is stern, sir. But isn't our task here below also a stern thing? You must see to it that your conscience is always on guard against this weakness: *a too great sensitivity to the vain graces of outward appearance*.

"If you had not been recommended to me," said the Abbé Pirard, going back to the Latin tongue with marked pleasure, "if you had not been recommended to me by a man like the Curé Chélan, I would speak to you in the idle tongue of this world, to which, it seems, you are but too well accustomed. The complete scholarship you are asking for is, I should tell you, the hardest thing in the world to come by. But Father Chélan has deserved very little indeed, for his fifty-six years of apostolic labors, if he cannot have one scholarship to the seminary at his disposal."

After these words, the Abbé Pirard instructed Julien not to join any secret society or *Congrégation* without his consent.

"I give you my word of honor," said Julien, from the overflowing heart of an honest man.

The director of the seminary smiled for the first time. "That expression is altogether out of place here," he told him. "It smacks too much of fashionable society's vain idea of honor, which leads them into so many sins, and often to crime. You owe me a saintly obedience by virtue of paragraph seventeen of the bull *Unam Ecclesiam** by St. Pius V. I am your ecclesiastical superior. In this house, my very dear son, to hear is to obey. How much money do you have?"

"Here we are," said Julien to himself. "It's for that, the 'very dear son.'"

"Thirty-five francs, Father."

"Keep a careful record of how you use that money; you will have to account to me for it."

This painful session had lasted three hours; Julien called the porter.

"Put Julien Sorel in cell number one hunded and three," said the Abbé Pirard to the man. As a very special favor, he allowed Julien a room to himself.

"Take his trunk there," he added.

Julien looked down and saw his trunk right in front of him; he had been looking at it for the past three hours and hadn't recognized it.

When he reached number 103—it was a very small room eight feet square, on the top floor of the house— Julien noted that it looked out on the ramparts, and beyond that he could see the beautiful plain which is separated from the city by the Doubs.

"What a lovely view!" Julien exclaimed. While talking to himself in this manner, he did not feel what his words expressed. The violent sensations he had experienced during the short time he had been in Besançon had completely exhausted his strength. He sat down near the window on the only wooden chair in his cell and fell at once into a deep sleep. He didn't hear the bell for supper, nor the one for evening service; he had been forgotten.

When the first rays of the sun woke him the next morning, he found himself lying on the floor.

Chapter XXVI

The World,
or What the Rich Are Lacking

> I am alone in the world; no one
> bothers to think of me. All those
> whom I see making their fortunes
> show a boldness and harshness of
> heart that are not in me. They hate
> me because of my easy-going kind-
> ness. Ah! soon I shall die, either
> from hunger or from the sorrow of
> finding men so hard.
>
> —YOUNG

He hurried to brush his clothes and go downstairs; he
was late. An assistant master scolded him harshly; instead
of trying to justify himself, Julien crossed his arms over
his chest.

"Peccavi, pater optime" ("I have transgressed, I confess
my sin, O my father"), he said with a contrite air.

This beginning was a great success. The clever ones
among the seminarists saw that they had to reckon with a
man who was by no means a novice. The recreation hour
came around. Julien saw that he was an object of general
curiosity. But his only response was reserve and silence.
Following the rules he had laid down for himself, he
considered his three hundred and twenty-one companions
enemies; the most dangerous of all, in his opinion, was the
Abbé Pirard.

A few days later Julien had to choose a confessor; he
was handed a list.

"Eh! good God! who do they take me for?" he said to

himself; "do they think I don't know how to take a hint?" And he chose the Abbé Pirard.

Though he wasn't aware of it, this step was decisive. A little seminarist, a very young native of Verrières who had declared himself his friend on the first day, informed him that if he had picked M. Castanède, the assistant director of the seminary, he might perhaps have acted more wisely.

"Father Castanède is the enemy of M. Pirard, who is suspected of Jansenism," added the little seminarist, whispering in his ear.

Though he thought himself very cautious, all of our hero's first steps, like his choice of a confessor, were blunders. Led astray by the presumptuousness of an imaginative man, he took his intentions for deeds and thought himself an accomplished hypocrite. He pushed his folly so far as to reproach himself for his success in this art of the weak.

"Alas! it is my only weapon! In another age, I would have earned my bread in the face of an enemy, by actions that speak for themselves."

Satisfied with his conduct, Julien took a look around him; everywhere he found an appearance of the purest virtue.

Eight or ten seminarists lived in the odor of sanctity and had visions like St. Theresa's, or that of St. Francis when he received the stigmata on Mt. Verna in the Apennines. But it was a great secret; their friends kept it hidden. Those poor young visionaries were in the infirmary most of the time. Some hundred of the others combined a robust faith with tireless application. They worked to the point of making themselves sick, but without learning much. Two or three stood out by virtue of genuine talent; among others, one named Chazel; but Julien felt an aversion for them, and they for him.

The rest of the three hundred and twenty-one seminarists was made up of nothing but boors, who were never quite sure they understood the Latin words they repeated all day long. Most were peasants' sons; they preferred earning their bread by reciting a few words in Latin to digging up the ground. After making this observation in the first few days, Julien promised himself a quick success. "In every service, there is a need for intelligent men, because, after all, there is work to be done," he told himself. "Under Napoleon, I would have been a sergeant; among these future curés, I will be a vicar-general.

"All of these poor devils," he added, "day laborers from birth, lived on curds and black bread until they came here. In their thatched cottages, they didn't eat meat more than five or six times a year. Like the Roman soldiers who thought of war as a time of rest, these coarse peasants are enchanted with the delights of the seminary."

Julien never read anything in their cheerless eyes after a dinner but physical need satisfied, or the anticipation of physical pleasure before a meal. Such were the types in whose midst he would have to distinguish himself. But what Julien didn't know, and what they were careful not to tell him, was that to be first in the various courses in dogma, in ecclesiastical history, etc., etc., which are studied in a seminary, was in their eyes nothing but a "resplendent" sin. Since Voltaire, since the institution of bicameral government, which is really nothing more than *mistrust and free inquiry* and gives the popular mind that bad habit of *being on its guard,* the Church of France seems to have understood that its real enemies are books. Submission of the heart is everything in its eyes. To succeed at studies, even sacred, is suspect in its opinion, and for good reason. What's to prevent a superior man from going over to the other side, as Sieyès or Gregory did! The trembling Church clings to the pope as its only chance for salvation. Only the pope is in a position to try to paralyze *free inquiry,* and by means of the pious pomp of the ceremonies at his court, make an impression on the bored and sick minds of fashionable society.

Julien, half guessing these various truths, that, nevertheless, every word pronounced in a seminary tends to deny, fell into a profound melancholy. He worked hard and succeeded very quickly in learning things that are very useful to a priest, but in his opinion very false, and in which he took no interest. He thought he had nothing else to do.

"Have I been forgotten by everyone on earth?" he thought. He did not know that M. Pirard had received and thrown into the fire a number of letters postmarked Dijon, in which there shone, despite the perfectly respectable style of expression, the most vivid passion. A profound remorse seemed to be struggling against this love. "So much the better," thought the Abbé Pirard. "At least it was not a godless woman whom this young man loved."

One day the Abbé Pirard opened a letter that seemed to have been half obliterated by tears; it was an eternal farewell. "At last," Julien was told, "heaven has granted me the strength to hate, not the author of my sin—he will always be that which I hold dearest in the world—but my sin itself. The sacrifice has been made, my friend. Not without tears, as you can see. The safety of those to whom I belong, and whom you have loved dearly, has won out. A just but terrible God can no longer avenge himself on them for their mother's crimes. Adieu, Julien, be just to all men."

The end of this letter was almost illegible. The writer gave an address in Dijon, yet hoped that Julien would never answer, or at least that he would use such language as a woman who has returned to a virtuous life might hear without blushing.

Julien's melancholy, abetted by the poor food supplied to the seminary by a contractor at eighty-three centimes a head, was beginning to tell on his health, when one morning Fouqué suddenly appeared in his room.

"I finally got in. Honestly, I've come to Besançon five times to see you. Always the same answer. I posted someone at the seminary door; why the devil don't you ever go out?"

"It's a test I'm putting myself to."

"I find you very changed. Well, in any case, I've finally managed to see you. Two shiny five-franc pieces have just taught me that I was a fool not to have offered them on the first trip."

The conversation between the two friends was endless. Julien's color changed when Fouqué said to him, "By the way, did you know? The mother of your pupils is going in for the most exalted piety?"

And he went on speaking in that detached manner which makes such a strange impression on the passionate soul to whose dearest hopes one has just unwittingly dealt a terrible blow.

"Yes, my friend, the most exemplary piety. They say she makes pilgrimages. But to the everlasting shame of the Curé Maslon, who spied for such a long time on that poor M. Chélan, Madam de Rênal would have nothing to do with him. She goes to confession in Dijon or in Besançon."

"She comes to Besançon," said Julien, his forehead flushing scarlet.

"Quite often," replied Fouqué with a questioning look.

"Do you have any *Constitutionals* on you?"

"What did you say?" replied Fouqué.

"I'm asking you if you have any *Constitutionals*," answered Julien in the calmest tone of voice. "Here they sell for thirty sous a copy."

"What! Liberals, even in the seminary!" exclaimed Fouqué. "Poor France!" he added, mimicking the Abbé
Maslon's hypocritical voice and gentle tone.

This visit might have left a deep impression on our hero
if early the next day a remark addressed to him by the
little seminarist from Verrières, who seemed such a child,
had not led him to make an important discovery. Ever
since he came to the seminary, Julien's conduct had been
nothing but a series of wrong moves. He laughed at
himself bitterly.

The truth of the matter was that the important actions
of his life were well conducted; but he paid no attention
to the details, and the clever ones at the seminary attended to nothing but details. Besides, his companions already
looked upon him as a *freethinker*. He had betrayed himself by a multitude of small gestures.

In their eyes, he stood convicted of an egregious vice:
he thought, he judged for himself, instead of blindly following *authority* and example. The Abbé Pirard had been
no help; he had once spoken to him outside the confessional booth; but even there he listened more than he spoke.
It would have been very much otherwise if he had chosen
the Abbé Castanède.

The moment Julien became aware of his folly, he was
no longer bored. He wanted to know the full extent of the
damage, and to that end, he came out somewhat from
behind the haughty and stubborn silence with which he
had repelled his companions. It was then that they took
their revenge against him. His advances were greeted with
a scorn that was carried to the point of derision. He
realized that, since his entrance into the seminary, there
had not been an hour, especially during the recreation
periods, that had not borne some consequence for or
against himself, that had not added to the number of his
enemies or won him the goodwill of some seminarist who
was sincerely virtuous or a little less loutish than the
others. The damage to be repaired was immense, the task
difficult indeed. Henceforth Julien was constantly on his
guard; it was a matter of shaping an entirely new character for himself.

The movements of his eyes, for example, gave him a
great deal of trouble. It is not without reason that they
are kept lowered in such places. "How presumptuous I
was in Verrières!" Julien told himself. "I thought I was
living; I was only getting ready for life; here I am at last,
out in the world such as I will find it until I've played out
my part, surrounded by real enemies. How immensely

difficult it is," he added, "to keep up this hypocrisy every minute! Hercules' labors were nothing by comparison. The Hercules of modern times is Sixtus V, who, for fifteen years, with his modesty, deceived forty cardinals who had known him as quick-tempered and arrogant all during his youth.

"So learning means nothing here," he told himself resentfully. "Progress in dogma, in sacred history, etcetera, only seem to count. Whatever they say to the contrary is calculated to make fools like me fall into the trap. Alas! the only thing that made me stand out was my quick progress, the way I could grasp that rubbish. Could it be that deep down they value those things at their true worth? Do they judge them as I do? And I was silly enough to be proud of myself! Those first places I always win have served no purpose except to give me bad marks against the real places we will be assigned when we leave the seminary, and in which we will make our money. Chazel, who knows more than I do, always throws a boner into his compositions so he'll be set back to fiftieth place; if he wins the first, it's because of absentmindedness. Ah! what help a word, a single word, from M. Pirard would have been!"

From the moment Julien was disabused, those long exercises in ascetic piety, such as the rosary five times a week, hymns to the Sacred Heart, etc., etc., which had seemed so deadly boring, became his most interesting moments for action. Though judging his conduct severely and trying above all not to overestimate his powers, Julien did not aspire straight off, unlike the seminarists who served as models for the others, to perform a *significant* action every minute; that is to say, one proving a kind of Christian perfection. In a seminary, there is a way of eating a boiled egg which reveals the progress one has made in the life of devotion.

Let the reader, who is perhaps smiling, only deign to remember all the mistakes made by the Abbé Delille while eating an egg when he was invited to lunch at the house of a great lady in Louis XVI's court. Julien sought first to get as far as the *non culpa*; that is, the state of the young seminarist whose bearing, whose way of moving his arms, his eyes, etc., though they have nothing really worldly about them, do not yet suggest a man absorbed in the idea of the afterlife and the *absolute nothingness* of this one.

Julien was constantly finding sentences written in charcoal on the corridor walls, such as this: "What are sixty years of trial weighed against an eternity of bliss or an eternity of boiling oil in hell?" He no longer held them in contempt; he recognized the necessity of having them before one's eyes all the time. "What will I be doing all my life?" he said to himself. "I will be selling a place in heaven to the faithful. How should this place be made visible to them? By the difference between my outward appearance and that of a layman."

After several months of unremitting application, Julien still looked as if he were thinking. His way of moving his eyes and of holding his mouth did not betoken the implicit faith which is ready to believe all and to uphold all, even in martyrdom. It was with anger that Julien saw himself outdone in this line by the coarsest peasants. There were reasons enough why they shouldn't have the look of thinkers.

What trouble he gave himself to achieve that beatific and sanctimonious expression, that countenance of a blind and fervent faith, which is ready to believe everything and to undergo anything, that one finds so frequently in Italian monasteries, and of which, for us laymen, Guercino has left such perfect models in his religious paintings.*

On holidays the seminarists were given sausages and sauerkraut. Those who sat near Julien at the table observed that he was indifferent to this treat; this was one of his first crimes. His companions took it for a despicable sign of the most stupid kind of hypocrisy; nothing made him more enemies. "Look at that bourgeois, look at the fine gentleman," they would say, "pretending he's too good for our best rations, sausages and sauerkraut! Shame on the wretch! the prig! the damned!"

He should have abstained, as a penance, from eating part of it, made a sacrifice of it, and said to some friend, while pointing to the sauerkraut: "What can a mere man offer an almighty Being, except voluntary affliction?" Julien lacked the experience that makes this sort of thing so easy to see.

"Alas! the ignorance of these young peasants, my companions, is an immense advantage to them," Julien would cry out in his moments of discouragement. "When they come to the seminary, the professor doesn't have to rid them of the frightful number of worldly ideas that I brought with me, and which they can read on my face, no matter what I do."

Julien kept studying, with attention bordering on envy, the most boorish of the little peasants who came into the seminary. At the moment when they were stripped of their rateen coats and made to put on black frocks, their whole education was limited to an immense and boundless respect for money, "dry and liquid," as they say in Franche-Comté. That is the sacramental and heroic way of expressing the sublime idea of *cash*.

Happiness for these seminarists, as for the heroes in Voltaire's novels, consisted above all in dining well. Julien discovered in most of them an innate respect for the man who wears a suit of fine cloth. This sentiment shows an appreciation of *distributive justice*, such as it is meted out to us by our courts, for what it is worth—indeed, for less than it is worth. "What chance do you have of winning," they kept telling one another, "if you take one of the *big ones* to court?"

That is the phrase used in the valleys of the Jura to designate a rich man. One can imagine their respect for the richest party of all: the Government!

Not to smile respectfully at the very mention of the prefect's name passes for recklessness in the minds of the peasants of Franche-Comté. Now, recklessness in a poor man is soon punished by a shortage of bread.

After having almost choked on his contempt in the beginning, Julien ended up by pitying them; it had happened more than once that most of his companions' fathers had returned of a winter night to their cottages and found neither bread, nor chestnuts, nor any potatoes in them. "Why is it surprising, then," Julien said to himself, "if, in their opinion, a happy man is first of all one who has just had a good dinner, and next, one who owns a good coat! My comrades have a solid vocation; that is to say, they see the ecclesiastical career as a long continuation of their present good fortune: to dine well and have warm clothing in winter."

Julien overheard a young seminarist, one endowed with imagination, saying to his companion, "Why couldn't I become pope, like Sixtus V, who was a swineherd?"

"Only Italians are made popes," his friend answered, "but they are sure to have us draw lots for the offices of vicar-generals, canons, and perhaps bishops. M.P.——, the Bishop of Châlons, is a cooper's son; that's my father's trade."

One day, in the middle of a dogma lesson, the Abbé Pirard sent for Julien. The poor young man was delighted to escape from the physical and moral atmosphere in which he was immersed.

In the director's office, Julien met with the same reception that had frightened him so the day he entered the seminary.

"Explain to me what is written on this playing card," he said to him, with a look that made Julien wish the earth would open up and swallow him.

Julien read:

Amanda Binet, at the café of the Giraffe, before eight. Say that you come from Genlis and that you're my mother's cousin.

Julien saw the full extent of his danger; the Abbé Castanède's police had stolen the address from him.

"The day I came here," he answered, looking at the abbé's forehead because he couldn't stand his terrible eye, "I was trembling with fear; M. Chélan had told me that this place was rife with informers and all sorts of wickedness; that both spying and denouncing companions are encouraged here. Heaven wills it so, in order to show the young priests what life is really like and fill them with loathing for the world and all its pomp."

"How dare you make fancy speeches to *me*," said the Abbé Pirard in a fury. "You rascal!"

"In Verrières," Julien went on coolly, "my brothers used to beat me whenever they had cause to be jealous. . . ."

"The facts! the facts!" shouted M. Pirard, nearly beside himself.

Not the least bit intimidated, Julien went on with his story.

"On the day of my arrival in Besançon, around noon, I was hungry; I went into a café. My heart was filled with repugnance for such a worldly place, but I thought lunch would cost less there than at an inn. A lady, who appeared to be the mistress of the den, took pity on my look of inexperience. 'Besançon is full of hoodlums,' she said to me. 'I fear for you, sir. If you should get into trouble, call on me; send someone here before eight o'clock. If the porters at the seminary refuse to deliver your message, say you are my cousin, and that Genlis is your hometown. . . .'"

"All this chatter will be verified," shouted the Abbé Pirard, who, unable to stand still, was pacing about the room. "Return to your cell!"

The abbé followed Julien and locked him in. The latter began immediately to inspect his trunk, at the bottom of which the fatal card had been preciously hidden. Nothing else was missing from it, but several things were out of place; yet his key had never left his pocket. "What luck," Julien told himself, "that during the time of my blindness I never took advantage of the permission to go out that M.

189

Castanède offered me so many times, out of a kindness which I can now understand. I might have yielded to the temptation of changing my clothes to go and see the beautiful Amanda; I would have cut my own throat. When they lost all hope of profiting from their information that way, so as not to waste it they used it to denounce me."

Two hours later the director sent for him.

"You were not lying," he said with a less severe look, "but to keep such an address is a piece of rashness the gravity of which you cannot conceive. Poor child! Ten years from now it may do you harm!"

Chapter XXVII

The First Taste of Life

> The present time, good God! It is
> the ark of the Lord. Woe to him who
> touches it.
>
> —DIDEROT

The reader will kindly excuse our giving him so few clear and precise details about this time in Julien's life. Not that we haven't any, far from it; but what he saw in the seminary is perhaps too black for the moderate coloring we have sought to maintain in these pages. Our contemporaries who suffer from certain things cannot be reminded of them without being too horrified to enjoy any pleasure, even that of reading a story.

Julien did poorly in his attempts to apply hypocrisy to his gestures; he lapsed into moments of disgust and even complete discouragement. He was not getting on, and in a wretched career at that. The least outside help would have been enough to keep him steady; the difficulty to be overcome was not so great; but he was alone, like a ship abandoned in mid-ocean. "And if I should succeed," he told himself, "imagine spending a whole life in such bad company! Gluttons who think about nothing but the bacon omelet they will gulp down at dinner, or priests like Castanède, for whom no crime is too black! They will come to power, but at what price, good Lord!

"Man's will is powerful; I read that everywhere; but is it strong enough to rise above disgust like mine? The task of great men used to be easy; however terrible their danger, they thought of it as beautiful. But who, except myself, can grasp the ugliness of all that surrounds me?"

This moment was the most trying in his life. It was so

easy for him to enlist in one of the fine regiments garrisoned in Besançon! He could become a Latin teacher; he needed so little to live on! But then no more career, no future for his imagination to dwell on; it would be death. Such are the details of one of his dreary days.

"Out of conceit, I used to congratulate myself because I was different from the other young peasants! Well, I have lived long enough to see that *difference begets hatred*," he told himself one morning. This great truth had just been demonstrated to him by one of his most stinging reverses. He had worked for a week to ingratitate himself with a student who lived in the odor of sanctity. He was strolling with him in the courtyard, listening submissively to the most incredible nonsense. Suddenly a storm came up, the thunder rumbled. Pushing him away rudely, the holy student shouted: "Listen, every man for himself in this world; I don't want to be blasted by lightning; God might strike you dead as a blasphemer, another Voltaire."

Alone now, his teeth clenched with rage and eyes opened toward a sky furrowed with lightning, Julien cried out: "I'd deserve to be drowned if I let myself rest during this storm! Let's try to make the conquest of some other prig."

The bell rang for Father Castanède's class in sacred history.

That day Father Castanède taught the young peasants, so afraid of hard labor and their fathers' poverty, that the being who seemed so terrible in their eyes, the Government, had no real and legitimate power except that delegated to it by God's vicar on earth.

"Make yourself worthy of the pope's goodness by the holiness of your lives, by your obedience; *be as a staff in his hands*," he added, "and you will obtain a splendid position where you will be master, above any man's control; a lifetime appointment, for which the Government will pay one third of the salary and the faithful, schooled by your preaching, the other two thirds."

After coming out of his class, M. Castanède stopped in the courtyard in the midst of his students, more attentive than usual that day. "It may rightly be said of a parish priest: what the man is worth, the position is worth," he told his students, who had made a circle around him. "I have known, I who am speaking to you, mountain parishes where the incidental income came to more than that of many town parishes. There was just as much money in them, not to mention the fat capons, the eggs, the fresh butter, and a thousand other agreeable particulars; and

192

there the curé comes first in everything; no fine dinner to which he is not invited, made much over," etc.

M. Castanède had no sooner gone up to his room than the students divided into groups. Julien didn't fit into any of them; he was left alone, like a mangy lamb. In each group he saw a student flip a coin, and if he called it right, heads or tails, his companions concluded that he would soon have one of those parishes with a high income.

Then came the anecdotes. Such and such a young priest, ordained less than a year before, having offered a gelt rabbit to an old priest's maidservant, had managed to get the old priest to ask for him as an assistant, and a few months later, for the priest died very quickly, replaced him in the good parish. Another had succeeded in having himself appointed successor to a parish in a big, wealthy market town by being present at all the meals of a paralytic old priest and carving his chickens for him gracefully.

The seminarists, like young people in every career, overestimated the effectiveness of such small maneuvers that, being somewhat extraordinary, strike the imagination.

"I must," Julien told himself, "get used to these conversations." When they were not talking about sausages and good parishes, they discussed the mundane aspects of ecclesiastical doctrine: the contentions between bishops and prefects, between mayors and parish priests. Julien saw the idea of a second God taking shape, but a God much more to be feared and far more powerful than the other; this second God was the pope. They were saying to one another, but lowering their voices, and only when they were sure of not being overheard by M. Pirard, that if the pope did not go to the trouble of appointing all the prefects and mayors in France, it was because he had entrusted this task to the king, by designating him eldest son of the Church.

About this time Julien thought he might be able to turn M. de Maistre's book *Du Pape* to his advantage. To tell the truth, he astonished his companions; but this was another piece of bad luck. He offended them by setting forth their own opinions better than they could. M. Chélan had been as reckless with regard to Julien as he had been on his own account. After having instilled in him the habit of close reasoning and of not allowing himself to be satisfied with idle chatter, he had neglected to tell him that in a person of no consequence this habit is a crime; for sound reasoning always offends.

Julien's gift of gab was, therefore, a fresh crime against him. By dint of thinking about him, his companions succeeded in expressing all the horror he inspired in them with two words; they nicknamed him Martin Luther; "especially," they said, "because of that infernal logic of which he is so proud."

Several young seminarists had rosier complexions and might be considered better looking than Julien; but he had white hands and could not hide certain habits of fastidious cleanliness. This virtue was really not one in the dreary house into which fate had cast him. The dirty peasants in whose midst he lived claimed that he had very lax morals. We fear we may tire the reader if we tell the full story of our hero's thousand misfortunes. For instance, the strongest of his companions meant to make a habit of beating him; Julien was forced to arm himself with a steel compass and let it be known, by signs only, that he would use it. Signs cannot figure so advantageously as words in a spy's report.

Chapter XXVIII

A Procession

> Every heart was moved. The presence of God seemed to have descended into those narrow, Gothic streets, everywhere hung with draperies and strewn deeply with sand by the faithful.
>
> —YOUNG

It was useless for Julien to humble himself and look stupid; he couldn't be liked; he was too different. "Yet," he said to himself, "all those professors are very astute men, chosen among thousands; why don't they like my humility?" Only one seemed to take advantage of his readiness to believe everything and to play the dupe. It was the Abbé Chas-Bernard, director of ceremonies at the cathedral, where for the last fifteen years the hope of a canonry had been dangled before him; while waiting, he taught sacred oratory at the seminary. In the time of his blindness, this was one of the courses in which Julien most regularly found himself at the head of the class. The Abbé Chas had taken that as a reason to show him a friendly disposition, and at the end of his class would gladly take his arm for a few turns around the garden.

"What's at the back of his mind?" Julien kept asking himself. He noted in astonishment that for hours together the Abbé Chas would tell him about the ornaments in the cathedral's possession. It had seventeen vestments trimmed with lace, besides those used for the requiem. He had great expectations of the President de Rubempré's widow; this ninety-year-old lady had kept for at least seventy years her wedding dresses made of superb cloth from

Lyons, brocaded with gold. "Imagine, my friend," said the Abbé Chas, stopping short and opening his eyes wide, "this cloth will stand by itself; there's that much gold in it. It is generally believed in Besançon that, through the widow's will, the cathedral's treasure will be augmented by more than ten chasubles, without counting four or five copes for the holidays. I will go even further," added Father Chas, lowering his voice. "I have good reason to think the widow will leave us eight splendid vermeil candlesticks, which are supposed to have been bought in Italy by the Duke of Burgundy, Charles the Bold; one of her ancestors was his favorite minister."

"But what is the man getting at with all his junk?" Julien wondered. "This sly preparation has been going on for ages, and nothing comes of it. He must be very wary of me! He is slyer than all the others, whose secret aims you can guess easily in two weeks. I understand; he's been suffering from frustrated ambition for the last fifteen years!"

One evening, in the middle of a fencing lesson, Julien was sent for by the Abbé Pirard, who said to him, "Tomorrow is Corpus Domini. (Corpus Christi.) The Abbé Chas-Bernard needs you to help decorate the cathedral; go, and obey."

The Abbé Pirard called him back, and with a commiserating look, added: "It's up to you whether you take advantage of the occasion to wander off into town."

"*Incedo per ignes*,"* Julien answered. (I have hidden enemies.)

The next day, early in the morning, Julien proceeded to the cathedral with eyes downcast. The sight of the streets and of the activity that was beginning to prevail throughout the city did him good. Everywhere people were draping their housefronts for the procession. All the time he had spent in the seminary seemed but an instant to him. His thoughts were at Vergy, and with pretty Amanda Binet, whom he might run into since her café was not very far off. At a distance he caught sight of the Abbé Chas-Bernard in the doorway of his beloved cathedral; he was a fat man with a cheerful face and open look. That day he was triumphant. "I've been waiting for you, my dear son," he called out as soon as he saw Julien from afar, "welcome. This day's labor will be long and hard; let us fortify ourselves with a first breakfast; the second will come at ten o'clock, during high mass."

"I wish, sir," Julien said, looking grave, "not to be left alone for a single minute; please note," he added, pointing

196

to the clock above their heads, "that I got here at one minute to five."

"Ah! you are worried about those wicked boys at the seminary! It is foolish of you to pay them any attention; is a road less beautiful because there are thorns on the hedge that borders it? The traveler goes his way and leaves the nasty thorns to wither on the bush. And now to work, my dear friend, to work!"

The Abbé Chas was right to say the task would be hard. The evening before there had been a big funeral ceremony in the cathedral; it had been impossible to do anything; consequently, all the Gothic pillars that separate the nave from the aisles had to be draped in a single morning with a kind of red damask cloak that rose to a height of thirty feet. The bishop had had four upholsterers sent down from Paris by the mail coach, but those gentlemen could not do everything. Yet, far from encouraging their co-workers from Besançon, they made them twice as clumsy by laughing at them.

Julien saw that he would have to climb the ladders himself; his nimbleness served him well. He took charge of directing the local upholsterers. Delighted, the Abbé Chas watched him flit from ladder to ladder. When all the pillars had been covered with damask, the problem was to set five enormous bouquets of feathers on the great baldaquin above the high altar. A rich crown of gilded wood was supported by eight twisted columns of Italian marble. But to get to the center of the baldaquin, above the tabernacle, it was necessary to walk on an old wooden cornice forty feet above the ground and possibly worm-eaten.

The sight of this arduous path had dampened the Parisian upholsterers' gaiety, so sparkling up to then; they looked up from below, argued a great deal, but made no move to climb. Julien seized the bouquets of feathers and mounted the ladder at a run. He placed them handsomely on the crown-shaped ornament at the center of the baldaquin. When he stepped off the ladder, the Abbé Chas-Bernard clasped him in his arms.

"*Optime*,"* exclaimed the good priest. "I will tell his Grace about this."

The breakfast at ten was very gay. Never had the Abbé Chas seen his church so beautiful.

"Dear disciple," he said to Julien, "my mother used to rent out chairs in this reverend basilica, so you might say I was nurtured in this great edifice. Robespierre's Terror ruined us; I was only eight at the time, but I was already serving at mass in private houses, and on mass days I was given a meal. No one knew how to fold a chasuble better than I; the gold braid was never broken. Since the restoration of the Faith by Napoleon, I have had the good fortune to direct everything that goes on in this venerable mother church. Five times a year my eyes see it adorned with these very beautiful ornaments. But never has it been so resplendent, never have the lengths of damask been so well hung as they are today, or clung so to the pillars."

"At last he's going to tell me his secret," thought Julien. "Here he is telling me all about himself; this is from the heart." But no imprudent remark escaped from this man, who was obviously excited. "And yet he has worked very hard, he is happy," Julien told himself, "and he has not stinted on the wine. What a man! What an example for me! He's way out in front!" (That was one of the crude expressions he had picked up from the old surgeon.)

Since the Sanctus for the high mass was ringing, Julien meant to put on a surplice so he could follow the bishop in the glorious procession.

"What about the thieves, my friend, the thieves!" cried the Abbé Chas. "You haven't thought of that. The procession is starting; the church will be deserted; we will stand guard, you and I. We will be lucky indeed if we aren't missing more than a few yards of that beautiful gold braid around the bottom of the pillars. That is another gift from Mme. de Rubempré; it comes from her great-grandfather, the famous count. It's pure gold, my dear friend," the priest continued, whispering in his ear and obviously excited, "no imitation. I am putting you in charge of the north aisle; don't leave it. I'm keeping the south aisle and the nave for myself. Keep an eye on the confessionals. That's where the thieves have their women spies watch out for the moment our backs are turned."

As he finished speaking the clock struck eleven forty-five; at the same time the great bell began to toll. It was ringing at full peal. These sounds, so full and so solemn, thrilled Julien. His imagination had left earth. The fragrance of incense and of rose leaves, scattered before the Blessed Sacrament by little children dressed up as St. John, brought his exaltation to a pitch.

The bell's deep-toned pealing should have brought nothing more to Julien's mind than the idea of twenty men working at the rate of fifty centimes each, and helped by perhaps fifteen or twenty of the faithful. He should have considered the wear and tear on the ropes, on the framework, the danger from the bell itself, which fell every two centuries, and looked for some way to reduce the bell ringers' wages, or of paying them with indulgences or some other favor drawn on the spiritual treasury of the Church, and which wouldn't flatten her purse.

Instead of these wise reflections, Julien's soul, exalted by the full and virile sounds, was wandering in imaginary space. He would never make a good priest or a great administrator. A soul so moved is good at best for giving birth to an artist. In this matter Julien's presumption shows forth as plainly as can be. Fifty, perhaps, of the seminarists, his companions, made attentive to the realities of life by the power of public hatred and by the Jacobinism which, so they are taught, lies in ambush behind every hedge, upon hearing the great cathedral bell would not have thought of anything but the bell ringers' pay. They would have calculated, with the genius of a Barême,* to see whether the degree of public emotion warranted the money spent on the bell ringers. If Julien had bothered to consider the material interests of the cathedral at all, his imagination, leaping beyond this problem, would have given some thought to economizing forty francs on the vestry and would have let the opportunity to avoid spending twenty-five centimes go by.

While on the finest day in the world the procession was slowly wending its way through Besançon and stopping at all the shining temporary altars erected throughout the city by officials vying with one another, the church stood in a deep silence. A semidarkness and pleasant coolness prevailed throughout; it was still redolent with flowers and incense.

The silence, the deep solitude, the coolness of the long naves, sweetened Julien's reverie. He had no fear of being disturbed by the Abbé Chas, occupied in another part of the building. His soul had all but abandoned its mortal cover, which was walking slowly in the north aisle entrusted to his surveillance. He was all the more tranquil for having made sure there was no one in the confessionals except a few pious women; his eyes gazed without seeing.

However, his fit of distraction was half broken by the sight of two extremely well-dressed women who were both kneeling, one in a confessional, the other close to her on a chair. Though he looked without seeing, nevertheless, either from a vague sense of duty or out of admiration for the noble and simple fashion in which these ladies were dressed, he noted that there was no priest in the booth. "It's odd," he thought, "that these fine ladies aren't on

199

their knees in front of one of the temporary altars, if they are devout; or seated conspicuously in the first row of some balcony, if they are fashionable. How well that dress fits! How charming!" He slowed his pace to get a better look at them.

The one who was kneeling in the confessional turned her head a little on hearing Julien's footsteps in the midst of that great silence. Suddenly she gave a little scream and fainted.

As she lost consciousness the lady who was kneeling fell backward; her friend, who was near, rushed to help her. At the same time Julien had a glimpse of the lady's shoulders as she was falling. A twisted necklace of big pearls, well known to him, caught his eye. Imagine his state when he recognized Mme. de Rênal's hair! It was she. The lady trying to support her head and keep her from falling altogether was Mme. Derville. Beside himself, Julien rushed forward; Mme. de Rênal's fall might have pulled her friend down too if Julien had not caught them. He saw Mme. de Rênal's head wobbling on her shoulder; she was pale and absolutely bereft of sensation. He helped Mme. Derville to place that lovely head against the back of a straw-bottomed chair; he was on his knees.

Mme. Derville turned around and recognized him. "Go away, sir, go!" she said to him in accents of the most livid anger. "Above all, don't let her see you again. Indeed, she will be horrified at the sight of you; she was so happy before you came! Your behavior is atrocious. Go away; leave us alone, if there is any decency left in you."

These words were spoken with such authority, and Julien was so weak at the moment, that he went away. "She has always hated me," he said to himself, thinking about Mme. Derville.

At the same instant the nasal chant of the first rank of priests resounded through the church; the procession was returning. The Abbé Chas-Bernard called out several times for Julien, who didn't hear him at first; eventually he came over to him behind the pillar, where Julien, half dead, had taken refuge, and grasped him by the arm. The priest wanted to present him to the bishop.

"You are faint, my child," the priest said, on seeing him so pale and barely able to walk. "You have worked too hard." The priest offered him his arm. "Come, sit down, here on this little bench for the dispenser of holy water, behind me. I will hide you." They were then to one side of the main door. "Calm down; we still have a good twenty minutes before his Grace appears. Try to pull yourself together; as he comes by I will raise you, for I am still strong and vigorous, in spite of my age."

But when the bishop appeared, Julien was shaking so that the Abbé Chas renounced the idea of presenting him.

"Don't feel too badly," he told him. "I will find another opportunity."

That evening he sent ten pounds of tapers to the seminary chapel—saved, he said, thanks to Julien's carefulness and by his promptness in ordering them to be extinguished. Nothing could have been further from the truth. The poor boy was extinguished himself; not a thought had crossed his mind since he laid eyes on Mme. de Rênal.

Chapter XXIX

His First Advancement

> He understood the times, he knew
> his department, and he is rich.
> —*Le Précurseur*

Julien had not yet come out of the deep reverie into which the incident in the cathedral had plunged him when one morning the stern Abbé Pirard sent for him.

"The Abbé Chas-Bernard has just written me a letter commending you. On the whole, I am fairly well satisfied with your conduct. You are extremely rash and even scatterbrained, without seeming to be; yet, up to now, you have shown a good and even generous heart; you have a superior mind. All things considered, I see in you a spark that must not be neglected.

"After fifteen years of labor, I am on the point of quitting this house: my crime is to have left the seminarists to their own free will, and to have neither protected nor worked against the secret society about which you spoke to me on the tribunal of penance. Before I go, I want to do something for you; I should have acted two months sooner, for you deserve it, if it hadn't been for the accusation based on Amanda Binet's address, found in your room. I am making you assistant master of the New and the Old Testament."

Carried away with gratitude, Julien seriously considered going down on his knees and thanking God; but he gave in to a more genuine impulse. He walked over to the Abbé Pirard and took his hand, which he raised to his lips.

"What's this?" exclaimed the director, looking very cross, but Julien's eyes spoke louder than his action.

The Abbé Pirard gazed at him in astonishment, like a man who, for years, has been unaccustomed to dealing with delicate emotions. This gesture had caught the director off guard; his voice faltered. "Very well, then! Yes, my child, I am fond of you. Heaven knows that this is so in spite of myself. I ought to be just and feel neither love nor hatred for anybody. Your road will be a hard one. There is something about you that offends the common run. Jealousy and slander will hound you. Wheresoever Providence may lead you, your companions will never set eyes on you without hating you. And if they pretend to love you, they will do so to betray you all the more surely. For this there is only one remedy; turn to none but God, who has given you, as a punishment for your presumption, this need for being hated. Let your conduct be flawless; that is the only resource I see for you. If you hold to the truth with an invincible grasp, sooner or later your enemies will be confounded."

It had been so long since Julien had heard a friendly voice that we ought to pardon him for his weakness; he burst into tears. The Abbé Pirard opened his arms to him; this moment was very sweet for both of them.

Julien was wild with joy; this advancement was the first he had ever obtained; the advantages were immense. To conceive of them, one must have been condemned to spend months together without a minute's solitude, and in immediate contact with companions who were at the least importunate, and for the most part unbearable. Their shouting alone would have been enough to create disorder in a delicate constitution. The delight of these well-fed and well-clad peasants was not something they could enjoy for itself, did not seem complete unless they were shouting at the top of their lungs.

Julien would dine alone now, or nearly so, an hour later than the other seminarists. He had a key to the garden and could go walking there during the hours it was deserted.

To his great amazement, Julien observed that he was less hated; he had anticipated, on the contrary, an increase of hatred. His secret desire that no one should speak to him, which was all too obvious and had won him so many enemies, was no longer taken as a sign of absurd arrogance. In the eyes of the coarse creatures who surrounded him, it sprang from a just sense of his own worth. Hatred waned appreciably, especially among the youngest of his companions, now his students, whom he treated with a great deal of courtesy. In due time he even began to have a following; it came to be in bad taste to call him Martin Luther.

But what is the use of telling over his friends, his

enemies? It's an ugly business, and the truer the rendering, the uglier still. Such men as those are, nevertheless, the only teachers of morality the people have, and without them what would the people become? Can the newspaper ever take the place of the parish priest?

Since Julien's promotion, the director of the seminary had taken the habit of never speaking to him except in the presence of witnesses. This line of conduct was a wise one, for the master as well as the disciple; but it was above all a *test*. The invariable rule of the strict Jansenist Pirard was, If, in your opinion, a man is worthy, put an obstacle in the way of everything he desires, of everything he undertakes. If his worth is genuine, he will find a way to knock down the obstacle or get around it.

It was hunting season. Fouqué had the idea of sending a deer and a boar to the seminary, as a gift in the name of Julien's family. The dead animals were set down in the passageway between the kitchen and the refectory. There all the seminarists saw them as they went in to dinner. They were objects of great curiosity. The boar, dead as it was, frightened the youngest; they touched its fangs. There was talk of nothing else for a week.

This gift, which classified Julien's family in that layer of society which commands respect, dealt a mortal blow to envy. His superiority was consecrated by wealth. Chazel and others among the most distinguished seminarists made advances to him, and as much as complained to him for not informing them about his parents' wealth and thus exposing them to a lack of respect for money.

There was a military conscription, from which Julien was exempted in his capacity as a seminarist. This event affected him deeply. "Now I have passed the point forever at which, twenty years ago, a heroic life would have begun for me!"

He was strolling alone in the seminary garden; he overheard some masons at work on the enclosure wall talking among themselves.

"Well, then, you have to go; there's a new conscription."

"In the time of *the other one*, fine and dandy! A mason might become an officer then, a general; it's been known to happen."

"See what it's like now! Nothing but beggars are leaving. The man who can pay stays home."

"If you're born poor you die poor, and that's that."

"Tell me, now, is it true what they're saying, that the other one's dead?" asked a third man.

"It's the big ones who are saying that, don't you see! They are scared of the other one."

"What a difference, there was plenty of work in his time! And to think he was done in by his own generals! It takes a traitor-born to do that."

Their conversation comforted Julien a little. As he moved away he repeated with a sigh: " 'The only King whose people still remember him!' "*

Examination time came around. Julien answered brilliantly; he saw that Chazel himself was trying to show off everything he knew.

On the first day, the examiners appointed by the famous Vicar-general de Frilair were sorely vexed at always being obliged to write "Julien Sorel"—that Julien Sorel who had been pointed out to them as the Abbé Pirard's pet—first, or at least second, on their lists. There was betting in the seminary that on the general list for the examinations Julien would have top place, which carried with it the honor of dining at his Grace the Bishop's palace. But at the end of one session, which had to do with the Church Fathers, a sly examiner, after having quizzed Julien about St. Jerome and his passion for Cicero, happened to speak of Horace, of Virgil, and of other profane authors. Unknown to his companions, Julien had learned a great many passages from those authors by heart. Carried away by his success, he forgot where he was and, at the repeated request of the examiner, gave a fiery recitation and paraphrase of several of Horace's odes. Having let him get farther and farther into the trap for twenty minutes, the examiner suddenly changed his expression and rebuked him harshly for the time he had wasted on such profane studies, and for the useless if not criminal ideas with which he had filled hs head.

"I am a fool, sir, and you are right," Julien said humbly, when he recognized the clever stratagem of which he had been the victim.

The examiner's ruse was considered a dirty trick even in the seminary; this, however, did not stop the Vicar-general de Frilair (the clever man who had so expertly organized the network of the Besançon *Congrégation*, and whose dispatches to Paris struck fear into the hearts of judges, prefects, and right on down to the chief officers of garrisons) from writing in his powerful hand the number 198 after Julien's name. He delighted in thus mortifying his enemy, the Jansenist Pirard.

For ten years his chief aim had been to relieve him of the direction of the seminary. The abbé, himself following the line of conduct he had traced out for Julien, was sincere, pious, free of intrigue, and dedicated to his duties. But heaven, in its wrath, had given him a bilious temperament, made to resent insults and hatred deeply. Not one of the outrages committed against him had been lost on that fiery soul. He would have preferred a hundred times over to hand in his resignation, but he believed he was useful at the post in which Providence had placed him. "I prevent Jesuitism and idolatry from making progress," he kept telling himself.

By the time of the examinations, it had been two months, perhaps, since he had spoken to Julien; yet he was ill for a week when, upon receiving the official letter announcing the results of the competition, he saw the number 198 written after the name of the student whom he regarded as the glory of his house. The only consolation for this austere man was to concentrate on Julien every means of surveillance at his disposal. With unbounded delight he discovered that he was neither angry, nor discouraged, nor planning vengeance.

Some weeks later, Julien shivered with joy at the receipt of a letter; it was postmarked Paris. "At last," he thought, "Mme. de Rênal has remembered to keep her promise." A gentleman who signed himself Paul Sorel, and who claimed to be his relative, was sending him a bill of exchange for five hundred francs. The sender added that if Julien continued to study those fine Latin authors with good results, a like sum would be addressed to him yearly.

"It is she; this is her kindness," said Julien, deeply touched. "She wants to comfort me, but why not a single word of affection?"

He was mistaken about this letter; Mme. de Rênal, directed by her friend Mme. Derville, had surrendered completely to her deep remorse. In spite of herself, she often thought about the strange fellow whose coming into it had upset her whole life, but was careful not to write to him.

If we were using the language of the seminary, we might well recognize a miracle in this remittance of five hundred francs and say that it was from M. de Frilair, of whom heaven had availed itself to bestow this gift on Julien.

Twelve years before, the Abbé de Frilair had arrived in Besançon with the smallest of portmanteaux, which, according to report, contained his whole fortune. Now he was one of the richest landowners in the department. In the course of his prosperity, he had bought half of an estate, the other part of which fell to M. de La Mole by inheritance. Hence a great lawsuit between these illustrious men.

Notwithstanding his brilliant style of life in Paris and the posts he held at court, the Marquis de La Mole realized that it would be dangerous to do battle in Besançon against a vicar-general who had a reputation for making and breaking prefects. But instead of requesting a gratuity of fifty thousand francs, disguised under some heading that would be admissible in the budget, and of abandoning the paltry suit for fifty thousand francs to the Abbé de Frilair, the marquis made it a point of honor. He felt he was in the right; a fine reason!

Now, if I may be allowed to say so: where is the judge who does not have a son or at least a relative to help get on in the world?

A week after he had won the first judgment, to make things clear even to the blindest, the Abbé de Frilair took his Grace the Bishop's coach of state and went in person to deliver a Legion of Honor cross to his lawyer. M. de La Mole, somewhat taken aback by his adversary's boldness, and realizing that his own lawyers were flagging, sought the advice of Father Chélan, who put him in touch with M. Pirard.

At the time of our story, this relationship already dated from several years back. The Abbé Pirard brought all his passionate nature to bear on this matter. By seeing the marquis' lawyers incessantly, he studied his case, and finding it a just one, began to work openly for the marquis against the all-powerful vicar-general. The latter was incensed at such insolence, and on the part of a little Jansenist at that!

"You see what these court nobles, who claim to be so powerful, are really worth!" the Abbé de Frilair would say to his cronies. "M. de La Mole hasn't even sent his agent in Besançon a miserable cross, and he is going to let him be thrown out of office without raising a finger. Yet, so my friends write, this noble peer never lets a week go by without showing off his blue ribbon in the drawing room of the Keeper of the Seals, whoever he may be."

Despite all his activity, and though M. de La Mole was always on the best of terms with the Minister of Justice, and especially with his subordinates, the most the Abbé Pirard had been able to accomplish, after six years of effort, was not to lose the case entirely.

Continually in correspondence with the Abbé Pirard about a matter that both followed up with passionate interest, the marquis came to relish the priest's turn of mind. Gradually, in spite of the vast distance between their social positions, their letters took on the tone of friendship. The Abbé Pirard wrote the marquis that his enemies were trying to force him, by means of repeated affronts, to tender his resignation; and in a fit of anger, provoked by what he called the infamous strategem used against Julien, he told the marquis all about the young man.

Although very rich, this great lord was by no means stingy. Never had he been able to persuade the Abbé Pirard to accept a reimbursement even for the postal fees occasioned by the lawsuit. The marquis seized upon the idea of sending five hundred francs to his favorite student.

M. de La Mole took the trouble of writing the accompanying letter himself. This led him to think about the Abbé's situation.

One day the latter received a short note which, on account of pressing business, urged him to go without delay to an inn on the outskirts of Besançon. There he found M. de La Mole's steward.

"The marquis has instructed me to bring you his calash," the man told him. "He hopes that after reading this letter, you will agree to set out for Paris in four or five days. I am going to use the interim, which you will be so kind as to specify, to have a look at the marquis' estates in Franche-Comté. After which, on the day that suits you, we will set out for Paris."

The letter was short:

Put behind you, dear sir, all the aggravations of the provinces; come breathe the untroubled air of Paris. I am sending you my carriage, with orders to wait for four days on your decision. I myself will await you in Paris until Tuesday. I need only a "Yes" from you, sir, to accept in your name one of the best parishes in the vicinity of Paris. The wealthiest of your future parishioners has never seen you but is more devoted to you than you can imagine. He is the Marquis de La Mole.

Without realizing it, the strict Abbé Pirard loved his seminary, filled with his enemies and to which, for fifteen years, he had consecrated all his thoughts. For him M. de La Mole's letter was like the appearance of the surgeon who has been engaged to perform a cruel and necessary operation. His dismissal was certain. He agreed to meet the steward three days from then.

For forty-eight hours he was in a fever of uncertainty. He finally wrote to M. de La Mole, and for his Grace the Bishop composed a letter that was a masterpiece of ecclesiastical style, if a bit long. It would have been hard to find language more irreproachable and instinct with a more sincere respect. And yet this letter, designed to give M. de Frilair a bad half hour vis-à-vis his superior, articulated all the grounds of his serious charges and descended to the dirty little tricks which, after having been endured with resignation for six years, now forced the Abbé Pirard to leave the diocese. They had stolen the wood from his woodpile; they had poisoned his dog, etc., etc.

This letter finished, he had Julien wakened, who at eight in the evening was already in bed, like all the other seminarists.

"You know where the bishopric is?" he asked Julien in fine Latin style. "Take this letter to his Grace. I will not hide from you the fact that I am sending you into a den of wolves. Be all eyes and all ears. Let there be no falsehood in your answers, but remember that the one who questions you might take a real pleasure in being able to do you harm. I am very glad, child, to be giving you this experience before I leave. For I will not make a secret of it; the letter you are holding is my resignation."

Julien stood motionless; he loved Father Pirard. It was to no avail that personal interest said to him, "After this honest man's departure, the Sacred Heart gang will lower my rank and perhaps drive me away." He couldn't think of himself. What disconcerted, embarrassed him was that he was trying to compose a sentence in a polished form, and really, he couldn't find the wit to do it.

"Well! my friend, aren't you going?"

"They say, sir," said Julien shyly, "that during your long administration, you haven't put anything aside. I have six hundred francs."

Tears kept him from going on.

"*That will be marked down too*," said the ex-director of the seminary coldly. "Go to the bishopric; it's getting late."

As chance would have it, the Abbé de Frilair was on duty that night in the bishop's drawing room; his Grace was dining at the prefecture. So it was to M. de Frilair himself that Julien handed the letter, but he didn't know him.

Julien watched in astonishment as the priest boldly opened the letter addressed to the bishop. The vicar-general's handsome face soon expressed surprise mingled with keen pleasure, then became twice as grave. While he was reading, Julien, struck by his good looks, had time to scrutinize him. This countenance would have appeared more solemn except for the great cunning apparent in certain features, which might have suggested even falseness had the owner of this handsome face stopped being concerned for one moment about this possibility. The very prominent nose formed a single perfectly straight line and, unfortunately, gave this otherwise very distinguished profile an irreparable likeness to that of a fox. Apart from that, the abbé who seemed to be so concerned about M. Pirard's resignation was dressed with an elegance that pleased Julien very much, who had never seen any priest like him.

Julien did not learn until later what the Abbé de Frilair's special talent was. He knew how to entertain his bishop, a likable old man who was cut out to live in Paris and who regarded Besançon as a place of exile. The bishop had very poor eyesight and a passion for fish. Father de Frilair boned the fish that was served to his Grace.

Julien stood silently watching the priest, who was re-reading the resignation, when all of a sudden the door opened with a clatter. A richly dressed footman passed by swiftly. Julien had just time enough to turn toward the door; he caught sight of a small man wearing a pectoral cross. He prostrated himself; the bishop smiled at him benevolently and went on. The handsome priest followed him, and Julien was left alone in the drawing room, the pious magnificence of which he was now free to admire at leisure.

The Bishop of Besançon, a man of spirit, sorely tried but not crushed by the long, hard years of the Emigration, was more than seventy-five years old, and couldn't care less about what might happen in the next ten.

"Who is that seminarist with the sly look, whom I think I saw in passing?" asked the bishop. "According to my rule, shouldn't they all be in bed at this hour?"

"This one is very much awake, your Grace, I swear, and he brings us glad tidings: the resignation of the only Jansenist left in your diocese. That awful Abbé Pirard has finally taken the hint."

"Well, well!" said the bishop with a mischievous smile, "but I defy you to find as good a man to replace him. And to show you how valuable that man is, I am inviting him for dinner tomorrow."

The vicar-general tried to slip in a few words about the choice of a successor. The prelate, not in the least disposed to talk business, said to him, "Before bringing in another one, let's find out a little bit about why this one is leaving. Send that seminarist in to me; the truth is in the mouths of babes."

Julien was sent for. "I will be facing two inquisitors," he thought. He had never felt so brave in his life. When he entered the room two tall valets, better dressed than M. Valenod himself, were undressing his Grace. The prelate thought he should question Julien about his studies before he touched on M. Pirard. He discussed dogma with him for a while and was amazed. Before long he brought up the humanities: Virgil, Horace, Cicero. "Those names," Julien said to himself, "are responsible for my number one hundred and ninety-eight. But I have nothing to lose; let's try to shine." He succeeded; the prelate, an excellent humanist himself, was delighted.

During the dinner at the prefecture a young lady, famous and justly so, had recited a poem called "La Madeleine."* The bishop went on talking literature and soon forgot all about the Abbé Pirard and any other business at hand to debate with the seminarist the question of whether Horace was rich or poor. The prelate quoted several odes, but his memory was sometimes lazy, and with a modest air Julien would recite the ode in its entirety on the spot. What impressed the bishop was that Julien never departed from a conversational tone. He recited his twenty or thirty Latin verses as he might have talked about what was going on in the seminary. They conversed for a long time about Virgil, about Cicero. In the end the prelate could not refrain from paying the young seminarist a compliment.

"It is not possible to be better educated."

"Your Grace," said Julien, "your seminary can show you one hundred and ninety-seven students who are far less unworthy of your distinguished approval."

"How is that?" asked the prelate, astonished at this figure.

"I can back up what I have just had the honor of saying before your Grace with official proof.

"During the annual examination at the seminary, for answering questions on precisely the same subjects that

211

have just won me your Grace's approval, I obtained the number one hundred and ninety-eight."

"Ah! this is the Abbé Pirard's pet," cried the bishop, laughing and looking at M. de Frilair. "We might have known; but it's all in fair play! Isn't it true, my friend," he said, turning to Julien, "that you were roused out of bed to come here?"

"Yes, your Grace. I never left the seminary alone before but once, to go and help the Abbé Chas-Bernard decorate the cathedral on Corpus Christi."

"*Optime,*" said the bishop. "What, was it you, then, who showed such great courage in placing the bouquets of feathers on the baldaquin? They make me shudder every year; I'm always afraid they are going to cost me some man's life. My friend, you will go far, but I don't mean to cut short your career, which will be brilliant, by letting you starve to death."

At the bishop's order, biscuits and Malaga wine were brought in, to which Julien did honor, but not so much as the Abbé de Frilair, who knew that his bishop liked to see people eat merrily and with a hearty appetite.

The prelate, more and more pleased with the end of his evening, spoke for a while about ecclesiastical history. He saw that Julien did not understand. He went on to the moral conditions of the Roman Empire under the emperors in the age of Constantine. The end of paganism was accompanied by the same mood of anxiety and doubt which afflicts the sad and troubled mind in the nineteenth century. His Grace observed that Julien knew nothing about Tacitus, hardly his name.

Julien replied candidly, to the astonishment of his bishop, that this author was not to be found in the seminary's library.

"I am truly very glad of it," said the bishop gaily. "You have helped me out of a dilemma: for ten minutes I have been searching for a way to thank you for the pleasant evening you have provided me, quite unexpectedly to be sure. I never expected to find a doctor in one of my students from the seminary. Although the gift may not be very canonical, I want to give you a Tacitus."

The prelate had eight superlatively bound volumes brought to him and insisted on writing in his own hand, on the title page of the first, a Latin inscription to Julien Sorel. The bishop prided himself on his fine Latin style. He ended by saying to him, in a serious tone that contrasted sharply with the one he had used during the rest of his conversation:

"Young man, *if you behave*, you will one day have the best parish in my diocese, and not a hundred leagues from my episcopal palace either; but *you must behave*."

Julien, loaded down with his volumes, left the bishopric amazed as midnight was striking.

His Grace had not said a word about the Abbé Pirard. Julien was astonished at the bishop's extreme politeness above all else. He had no conception of such urbane manners combined with so natural an air of dignity. Julien was forcibly struck by the contrast upon seeing the somber Abbé Pirard again, who was waiting for him impatiently.

"Quid tibi dixerunt?" ("What did they say to you?") he shouted in a loud voice from as far as he could see him. When Julien got somewhat mixed up in translating the bishop's remarks into Latin: "Speak French, and repeat his Grace's own words, without adding to or cutting anything out," said the ex-director of the seminary with his hard voice and profoundly inelegant manner.

"What an odd present for a bishop to make to a young seminarist!" he observed as he leafed through the superb Tacitus, the gilt edge of which seemed to horrify him.

Two o'clock was striking when, after a very detailed account, he allowed his favorite student to return to his room.

"Leave me the first volume of your Tacitus, the one with the bishop's dedication in it," he told him. "That line of Latin will be your lightning rod in this house after my departure.

"Erit tibi, fili mi, successor meus tanquam leo quaerens quem devoret." ("For you, my son, my successor will be like a raging lion looking for something to devour.")

The next morning Julien thought there was something peculiar about the way his comrades spoke to him. He was all the more reserved for it. "That," he thought, "is the effect of M. Pirard's resignation. Everyone in the house knows about it, and I am considered his favorite. There must be some kind of insult behind their way of acting." But he couldn't see what it was. There was, on the contrary, an absence of hatred in the eyes of everyone he met as he passed through the dormitories. "What can this mean; it's a trap, no doubt; let's watch our step." Eventually the little seminarist from Verrières said to him with a laugh: *"Cornelii Taciti Opera Omnia."* ("The Complete Works of Tacitus.")

At this remark, which was overheard, all of them, as if vying with one another, congratulated Julien, not only for

213

the magnificent gift he had received from his Grace, but also for the two-hour conversation with which he had been honored. They knew everything down to the smallest details. From that moment there was no more jealousy; Julien's favor was basely courted. Father Castanède, who just the evening before had treated him with the utmost insolence, came over, took him by the arm, and invited him to go down to lunch.

Because of a flaw in Julien's character, those crude individuals, insolence had grieved him sorely; their fawning merely disgusted him and gave him not the least pleasure.

Toward noon the Abbé Pirard took leave of his students, but not without having addressed them with a harsh allocution. "Do you desire worldly honors," he said to them, "all the social advantages, the pleasure of commanding, that of scoffing at the law and of being insolent to everyone with impunity? Or else, do you wish your eternal salvation? The dullest among you has only to open his eyes to distinguish the one road from the other."

He had no more than left when the devotees of the Sacred Heart of Jesus went off to chant a *Te Deum* in the chapel. No one in the seminary took the director's speech seriously. "He is in a foul mood because he's been dismissed," everyone was saying. Not one seminarist was naïve enough to believe in a voluntary resignation from a post that gave a man so many connections with the big suppliers.

Father Pirard took a room in Besançon's finest inn; and under the pretext of business affairs, which he didn't have, decided to spend two days there.

The bishop invited him to dine, and by the way of a joke on his Vicar-general de Frilair, tried in every way to make him shine. They were on the dessert when the strange news arrived from Paris that the Abbé Pirard had been appointed to the magnificent parish of N——, four leagues from the capital. The good prelate congratulated him sincerely. He saw this whole affair as a game well played, which put him in a good humor and gave him the highest opinion of the priest's talents. He gave him a splendid certificate of character in Latin and imposed silence on the Abbé de Frilair, who had made so bold as to remonstrate.

That night Monseigneur carried his admiration to the Marquis de Rubempré's house. It was important news for high society in Besançon; the whole company was soon lost in conjecture about this extraordinary favor. They already saw the Abbé Pirard as a bishop. The most astute among them believed M. de La Mole had been appointed minister, and that day they allowed themselves to smile at the imperious airs the Abbé de Frilair wore in public.

The next morning the Abbé Pirard was all but followed in the streets, and merchants came to the doors of their shops when he went to petition the marquis' judges. For the first time they received him courteously. The strict Jansenist, roused to indignation by everything he saw, spent a long time working with the lawyers he had picked for the Marquis de La Mole, then started for Paris. In a moment of weakness, he told two or three college friends who were accompanying him to the calash, the coat of arms on which struck them with admiration, that after having directed the seminary for fifteen years, he was leaving Besançon with only five hundred and twenty francs in savings. These friends embraced him tearfully, and afterward commented to one another: "The good abbé might have spared us that fib; it's really just too ridiculous."

The common man, blinded by his love of money, was not capable of grasping that it was in his sincerity that the Abbé Pirard had found the strength he needed to struggle on alone for six years against Marie Alacoque,* the Sacred Heart of Jesus, the Jesuits, and his bishop.

Chapter XXX

Ambition

> There is only one real nobility
> left; that is the title of *duke*. Mar-
> quis is ridiculous; at the word *duke*,
> people turn their heads.
> —*The Edinburgh Review*

The abbé was astonished at the marquis' noble air and his almost gay tone. Yet this future minister welcomed him without any of those little ways of the great lord, so polished yet so impertinent if one understands them. It would have been time wasted, and the marquis was deeply enough involved in momentous undertakings not to have any to waste.

For six months he had been scheming to make both king and nation accept a certain ministry which, out of gratitude, was to make him duke.

In vain the marquis had kept asking his lawyer in Besançon, over many long years, for a clear and precise explanation of his lawsuits in Franche-Comté. How could the noted lawyer explain them if he didn't understand them himself?

The little square of paper the abbé handed him made everything clear.

"My dear Abbé—" the marquis said to him, after having got all the polite formalities and inquiries about personal matters out of the way in less than five minutes, "my dear Abbé, in the midst of my alleged prosperity, I want the time to concern myself seriously about two small but nonetheless important matters: my family and my affairs. I look after the fortune of my house in noble style; I may take it a long way. I look after my pleasures, and they should come before anything else, at least in my opinion," he added, catching an astonished look on the Abbé Pirard's face. Although a sensible man, the abbé marveled to hear an old man speak so frankly of his pleasures.

"There are no doubt people in Paris who work, but they are perched up on the sixth floor, and if I so much as approach a man, he takes an apartment on the third, and his wife picks a day to be 'at home'; consequently, no more work, no further effort except to be, or appear to be, a gentleman. That's all they care about, once they have bread.

"For my lawsuits, and even for each separate case, I have lawyers who, to put it precisely, kill themselves; just the other day one of them died on me, from consumption. But as for my affairs in general, would you believe it, sir, that I gave up hope three years ago of ever finding a man who, while he is writing for me, will deign to take what he is doing a bit seriously? But that is only half the story.

"I respect you, and I should venture to add, though seeing you for the first time, I like you. Will you be my secretary, at a salary of eight thousand francs, or twice that? I will still have the best of the bargain, I assure you; and I will make it my business to keep your fine parish for you against the day when we no longer suit one another."

The abbé refused; but toward the end of the conversation, the genuine plight in which he saw the marquis suggested an idea to him.

"In the depths of my seminary," he said to the marquis, "I have left a poor young man who, if I'm not mistaken, is going to be dealt with harshly. If he were simply a monk, he would already be *in pace*.

"As of now, the young man knows nothing but Latin and Holy Scripture; but it is not impossible that he will one day display great talents, be it for preaching, be it for the guidance of souls. I don't know what he'll do; but he has the sacred fire, he may go far. I planned to give him to our bishop, if ever one came to us who had something of your way of looking at men and affairs."

"What is your young man's background?" asked the marquis.

"They say he is the son of a carpenter who lives in our mountains, but I am inclined to believe that he is the natural child of some rich man. I saw him receive an anonymous or pseudonymous letter with a bill of exchange for five hundred francs in it."

"Ah! it's Julien Sorel," said the marquis.

217

"How do you know his name?" asked the astonished abbé, and since he blushed at his own question:

"That is something I shan't tell you," answered the marquis.

"Very well!" the abbé continued, "you might try to make a secretary of him; he has energy, intelligence; in short, it's worth a trial."

"Why not?" said the marquis. "But is he the kind of man to let his palm be greased by the chief of police or anybody else and play the spy in my house? That's my only reservation."

After Father Pirard's favorable assurances, the marquis took out a bill for a thousand francs.

"Send this to Julien Sorel for his trip; have him come to see me."

"One can easily tell," said the Abbé Pirard, "that you live in Paris. You have no idea of the tyranny that weighs on us poor provincials, particularly on priests who are not friends of the Jesuits. They won't be willing to let Julien Sorel go; they will know how to cover up with the cleverest excuses; they will tell me he is sick; the post will have lost the letters, etcetera, etcetera."

"Sometime soon, I'll have the minister write a letter to the bishop," said the marquis.

"I forgot to caution you," said the abbé. "Though very lowborn, this young man is high-spirited; he will be of no use in your affairs if you try to curb his pride; you will make him stupid."

"That appeals to me," said the marquis. "I will make him my son's companion; will that do?"

Some time afterward, Julien received a letter in an unknown hand, bearing the postmark Châlons; it contained a draft on a merchant in Besançon and a notice to proceed to Paris without delay. The letter was signed with an assumed name, but on opening it, Julien shuddered; a big ink blot had fallen on the middle of the thirteenth word; this was the signal he and the Abbé Pirard had agreed upon.

Less than an hour later Julien was summoned to the bishop's palace, where he was greeted with an altogether paternal benevolence. Citing Horace all the while, his Grace paid him, with regard to the high destiny that awaited him in Paris, a number of very adroit compliments, which, by way of acknowledgment, required a number of explanations. Julien couldn't tell him anything, primarily because he didn't know anything; and Monseigneur thought all the more highly of him. Some minor priest in the palace sent a note to the mayor, who hurried over in person with a signed passport, on which the space for the traveler's name had been left blank.

The same evening, before midnight, Julien was at the house of Fouqué; that wise soul was more astonished than delighted at the kind of future which seemed to await his friend.

"You will end up," said the Liberal voter, "with a post in the Government which will force you to take some action that will be run down by the newspapers. It is through your disgrace that I shall have news of you.

"Just remember that, even financially speaking, it is better to earn a hundred louis in a sound timber business, where you are your own boss, than to get four thousand francs from any government, be it King Solomon's."

Julien could see nothing in all this talk but the small-mindedness of the provincial middle class. At last he was going to make his appearance on a scene where great events took place. He preferred less certainty and greater opportunities. In his heart there was no longer the least fear of starving to death. The happiness of going to Paris, which he imagined to be filled with clever and continually scheming people, most hypocritical, but polite as the Bishop of Besançon and the Bishop of Agde, blinded him to everything else. He represented himself humbly to his friend as a man deprived of his own free will by the Abbé Pirard's letter.

The next day around noon, he arrived in Verrières the happiest of men; he was counting on seeing Mme. de Rênal again. He went first to the house of his former protector, the good Abbé Chélan. He met with a stern welcome.

"Do you think you have some obligation to me?" M. Chélan said to him, without returning his greeting. "You are going to have lunch with me; meantime, a man will go and hire another horse for you, and you will leave Verrières *without seeing anyone.*"

"To hear is to obey," replied Julien, pulling the face of a seminarist; the talk was henceforth confined to theology and fine Latinity.

He climbed on his horse and rode a league, after which, catching sight of a woods, and no one around to see him enter, he raced into it. At sunset he had a peasant take the horse back to the nearby posting house. Later, he went into the house of a vinedresser, who consented to sell him a ladder and, following Julien, to carry it as far as the little wood that overlooks Fidelity Drive in Verrières.

219

"He's a poor deserter from the army ... or a smuggler," the peasant said to himself as he took leave of Julien. "But what do I care! He paid a good price for my ladder, and I've smuggled a few watches myself in my day."

The night was very dark. Around one o'clock in the morning Julien, loaded down with his ladder, walked into Verrières. As soon as he could, he climbed down into the bed of the torrent that cuts through M. de Rênal's magnificent gardens at a depth of ten feet and is held in by two walls. He climbed out again easily on the ladder. "What kind of welcome will the watchdogs give me?" he wondered. "Everything depends on that." The dogs barked and rushed toward him: but he whistled softly and they came up to be petted. Climbing then from terrace to terrace, though all the gates were shut, he had no difficulty reaching a spot just below Mme. de Rênal's bedroom window, which on the garden side was no more than eight or ten feet above the ground.

In each shutter there was a small heart-shaped opening that Julien knew well. To his great vexation, this small opening was not lighted from within by a night-light.

"Good God!" he said to himself, "Mme. de Rênal is not using that room tonight! Or could the night-light have gone out? Where can she be sleeping? The family is in Verrières, since I found the dogs; but in that room without a light I might run into M. de Rênal himself or a stranger, and then what a scandal!"

The wise thing to do was to go away, but Julien loathed this alternative. "If it's a stranger, I'll run as fast as I can and leave my ladder behind; but if it is she, what kind of reception can I expect? She has fallen into a fit of repentance and high minded piety, of that I can have no doubt; but even so, she still thinks of me, since she wrote not long ago." This argument decided him.

With pounding heart, but nonetheless resolved to see her or perish, he threw some pebbles against the shutters; no answer. He leaned his ladder beside the window, and then he knocked on the shutter, at first gently, then more loudly. "No matter how dark it is, they can still fire at me," Julien observed. This thought reduced his mad undertaking to a question of bravery.

"That bedroom is unoccupied tonight," he thought, "or whoever is sleeping in it is awake by now. So I don't have to worry about that one anymore; now I must try not to let myself be heard by people sleeping in the other rooms."

He climbed down, placed his ladder against one of the shutters, climbed back up, and passing his hand through the heart-shaped opening, had the good luck to find right off the wire attached to the hook that held the shutter closed. He pulled on the wire; to his inexpressible joy, he realized that the shutter was no longer fastened and was yielding to his efforts. "I should open it very slowly and make myself known by my voice." He opened the shutter enough to put his head in, and whispered: *"It's a friend."*

Straining his ear, he made sure that nothing troubled the deep silence of the room. But there had definitely not been any night-light, even burning low, in the fireplace. It was a bad sign.

"Watch out for a rifle shot!" he reflected briefly; then he risked tapping on the pane with one finger. No response; he tapped harder. "Even if it means breaking the window, I must get this over with." While he was knocking quite hard, he thought he caught a glimpse, in the extreme darkness, of something like a phantom crossing the room. Before long he had no doubts; he saw a phantom that seemed to be moving toward him very slowly. Suddenly he saw a cheek leaning against the windowpane to which he had pressed his eye.

He shuddered and drew back a little. But it was so dark that even at this distance he could not tell whether it was Mme. de Rênal. He dreaded an initial cry of alarm; for a while he had been hearing the dogs growling softly and circling around the foot of his ladder. "It is I," he repeated rather loudly, "a friend." No answer. The phantom had disappeared. "Please open; I must speak with you; I am so unhappy!" And he knocked as though he meant to break the glass.

There was a small dry noise; the latch was being opened; he pushed against the casement window and jumped nimbly into the bedroom.

The phantom moved away; he took its arms; it was a woman. All his notions about courage vanished. "If it is she, what will she say?" What was his reaction when he realized, from a little cry, that it was Mme. de Rênal!

He clasped her in his arms; she was trembling and had barely enough strength to push him away.

"Wretch! what are you doing?"

Convulsed as she was, her voice could barely articulate these words. In them Julien heard the most genuine indignation.

"I have come to see you after fourteen months of cruel separation."

"Go, leave me this instant. Ah! M. Chélan, why did you stop me from writing to him? I might have prevented this horror." She pushed him away with truly remarkable strength. "I am repenting for my crime; heaven has deigned to enlighten me," she repeated in a halting voice. "Go! Run!"

"After fourteen months of wretchedness, I shall certainly not leave without having spoken to you. I want to know everything you've done. Ah! I have loved you well enough to deserve your confidence. . . . I want to know everything."

In spite of herself, his tone of authority had some power over her heart.

Julien, who was embracing her passionately and resisting her efforts to free herself, left off pressing her in his arms. This movement reassured Mme. de Rênal somewhat.

"I am going to pull in the ladder," he said, "so that it won't give us away if one of the servants, wakened by the noise, should make the rounds."

"Ah! Go, on the contrary, go," she said to him in unfeigned anger. "What do I care about the opinion of men? It is God who is witnessing this frightful scene you are making and who will punish me for it. You are taking a cowardly advantage of what I once felt for you and feel no longer. Do you hear me, Monsieur Julien?"

He was pulling up the ladder very slowly, so as not to make any noise.

"Is your husband in town?" he asked, not to defy her but carried away by an old habit.

"Don't speak to me so, I beg you, or I will call my husband. I am only too guilty as it is for not having driven you away, no matter what might have happened. I pity you," she said, trying to wound his pride, which she knew to be so touchy.

Her refusal to use the familiar form of address, her abrupt way of breaking so tender a bond, and one on which he was still counting, brought Julien's ecstasy of love to the verge of delirium.

"What! is it possible that you no longer love me?" he said to her in one of those accents from the heart—so difficult to listen to and not be moved.

She made no answer. As for him, he was weeping bitterly. Really, he hadn't the strength to speak.

"So I have been completely forgotten by the only person who has ever loved me. What use is it to go on living?" All his courage deserted him the moment he no longer had to worry about the danger of running into a man; all feeling had vanished from his heart save love.

He wept for a long time in silence; she could hear him sobbing. He took her hand, she tried to withdraw it; and yet, after a few almost convulsive movements, she let him hold it. The darkness was total; they were sitting on Mme. de Rênal's bed.

"How different from the way things were fourteen months ago!" thought Julien, and his tears flowed twice as fast. "It is certain that absence destroys all human feeling! I would do better to leave."

"Tell me at least what has happened to you," said Julien finally, embarrassed by her silence and in a voice almost extinct from suffering.

"There's no doubt," answered Mme. de Rênal in a hard voice, which seemed cold and reproachful to Julien, "that my wrongdoing was well known in town by the time of your departure. Your conduct had been so indiscreet! Some time later, I was desperate then, the respectable M. Chélan came to see me. To no avail, he tried for a long time to make me confess. One day he had the idea of driving me over to that church in Dijon, where I made my first communion. There, he took it upon himself to speak first—" Mme. de Rênal was interrupted by her tears. "How shameful that moment was! I confessed everything. That very good man was kind enough not to crush me with the weight of his indignation, he grieved with me. At that time I was writing to you every day, letters I dared not send. I hid them carefully, and when I was too utterly miserable, I would lock myself in my room and reread my letters.

"In time M. Chélan persuaded me to turn them over to him. . . . Some of them, written with a little more restraint, had been sent to you. You never answered."

"Never, I swear, did I receive any letter from you at the seminary."

"Good God, who could have intercepted them?"

"Imagine how I suffered. Until the day I happened to see you in the cathedral, I didn't know whether you were still alive."

"God in his mercy made me realize how greatly I was sinning against Him, against my children, against my husband," Mme. de Rênal continued. "He has never loved me as I believed, at the time, you loved me. . . ."

Julien threw himself into her arms, really without design and beside himself. But Mme. de Rênal pushed him away and went on with considerable firmness:

"My respectable friend M. Chélan made me understand that in marrying M. de Rênal, I had pledged all my affection to him, even those feelings of which I was ignorant, and which I had never experienced before a fatal acquaintance. . . . Since the great sacrifice of those letters, which were so dear to me, my life has flowed on, if not happily at least calmly enough. Do not trouble it; be a friend to me . . . my best friend." Julien covered her hands with kisses; she could feel that he was weeping again. "Don't cry; you make me feel so badly. . . . Now it's your turn to tell me what you've been doing." Julien couldn't speak. "I want to know what life in the seminary is like," she insisted. "Then you will go away."

Without thinking of what he was saying, Julien told her about the machinations, the countless jealousies he had run into at first, then about his more peaceful life after he had been made assistant master.

"It was at that time," he added, "after a long silence, intended no doubt to make me understand something I see only too clearly now, that you no longer loved me and that I meant nothing to you. . . ." Mme. de Rênal squeezed his hands. "It was at that time that you sent me five hundred francs."

"Never," said Mme. de Rênal.

"The letter was postmarked Paris and signed Paul Sorel, to allay suspicion."

A little debate started as to the possible origin of this letter. The moral climate had changed. Unawares, Mme. de Rênal and Julien had dropped their solemn tone; they had reverted to one of tender affection. They couldn't see each other, the darkness was so deep, but the sound of their voices conveyed everything. Julien put his arm around his mistress's waist; this gesture was fraught with danger. She tried to remove Julien's arm, but at this juncture he cleverly drew her attention to a very interesting detail of his story. As if forgotten, the arm kept the position it had assumed.

After many a conjecture about the origin of the letter with the five hundred francs, Julien had gone back to his story; he gained a little more control of himself as he spoke of his past life, which by comparison with what was happening to him at the moment, interested him so little. His attention was focused entirely on the manner in which his visit was to end. "You must go," she kept saying from time to time in a curt accent.

"What shame for me if I am sent packing! The regret would poison my whole life," he told himself. "She will

224

never write to me. God knows when I'll come back to this part of the country!" In that moment, all that was heavenly about Julien's situation quickly lost its influence over his heart. Seated beside the woman he adored, almost holding her in his arms, in the room where he had been so happy, in the midst of profound darkness, distinguishing clearly that for the last few minutes she had been weeping, realizing, from the heaving of her breast, that she was holding back her sobs, he had the bad luck to become a cold politician, almost as calculating and cold as when, in the courtyard of the seminary, he saw himself exposed to some malicious prank by a companion stronger than he. Julien stretched his story and went on talking about the unhappy life he had led since his departure from Verrières.

"So," said Mme. de Rênal to herself, "after a year's absence, with almost nothing to remind him, and while I was forgetting him myself, all he could think of was the happy days he had known at Vergy." She sobbed twice as hard. Julien saw that his story was a success. He realized that it was time now to play his last card: he came abruptly to the letter he had just received from Paris.

"I have taken leave of his Grace the Bishop."

"What, you're not going back to Besançon? You are leaving us forever?"

"Yes," answered Julien in a resolute voice, "yes, I am leaving the place where I have been forgotten, even by the one I have loved most in my life, and I am leaving it never to return. I'm going to Paris. . . ."

"You* are going to Paris!" cried Mme. de Rênal rather loudly. Her voice was almost smothered by tears and showed how violently agitated she was. Julien needed such encouragement; he was about to take a step that could turn the tide against him; unable to see anything up to then, he had been totally ignorant of the effect he had succeeded in producing. He hesitated no longer; his dread of remorse gave him perfect control over himself. He added coldly as he rose:

"Yes, madam, I am leaving you forever; I hope you will be happy. Farewell."

He took the few steps to the window; he was already opening it. Mme. de Rênal sprang toward him. He felt her head on his shoulder and himself being clasped in her arms as she pressed her cheek against his.

Thus, after three hours of dialogue, Julien obtained

---

* At this point she uses the familiar form *tu*.

that which he had desired so passionately during the first two. Coming a bit sooner, this reversion to tender feelings, the disappearance of Mme. de Rênal's remorse, would have meant divine happiness; thus obtained, by art, it was nothing more than a triumph. Julien insisted, contrary to his mistress's objection, on lighting the night-light.

"Do you wish me, then," he asked her, "to go away without any memory of how you look? Shall the love that is no doubt shining in your eyes be lost to me? Shall the whiteness of this lovely hand remain invisible to me? Remember that I may be leaving you for a very long time."

"How shameful!" thought Mme. de Rênal, yet she could not resist the idea of an eternal separation, which made her burst into tears. In the dawning light the pines were beginning to stand out sharply on the mountain to the east of Verrières. Instead of going away, Julien, drunk with pleasure, asked Mme. de Rênal if he might spend the whole day hidden in her bedroom, and not leave until the following night.

"Why not? This fatal relapse has robbed me of all my self-respect and doomed me to unhappiness forever," she replied, pressing him to her heart ecstatically. "My husband is not the same man; he has suspicions. He thinks I led him by the nose in this whole business and spares me none of his irritation. If he hears the slightest noise, I am lost; he will drive me away like the fallen woman I am."

"Ah! there's one of Father Chélan's expressions," said Julien. "You wouldn't have spoken that way before my cruel departure for the seminary; you loved me then!"

Julien was rewarded for the coldness he had injected into this remark; in a wink he saw his mistress forget the risk she ran from her husband's presence to worry about the much greater danger of seeing Julien doubt her love. Day was coming on apace and lighting up the room brightly. Julien rediscovered all the pleasures of pride when he saw this lovely woman in his arms again, and almost at his feet—the only woman he had ever loved and who, a few hours before, had been totally preoccupied with her fear of a terrible God and her love of duty. Resolutions fortified by a year's constancy had not been able to withstand his courage.

Soon they heard noises in the house; something to which she had not given a thought began to bother Mme. de Rênal. "That spiteful Elisa will be coming to my room; what's to be done with this huge ladder?" She said to her lover. "Where can we hide it? I'm going to take it up to the attic," she cried out suddenly, with a kind of playfulness.

"That's the way you used to look," said Julien, delighted. "But you will have to go through the servant's room."

"I will leave the ladder in the corridor; I will call the servant and send him on an errand."

"Think of something to say in case he passes by the ladder and happens to notice it."

"Yes, angel," said Mme. de Rênal, giving him a kiss. "And you be sure to hide quickly under the bed if Elisa comes in here while I'm away."

Julien was astonished at her sudden gaiety. "So," Julien reflected, "far from troubling her, the approach of real danger restores her good spirits, because it makes her forget her remorse! A truly superior woman! Ah! there is a heart in which it is glorious to reign!" Julien was enchanted.

Mme. de Rênal took the ladder; it was obviously too heavy for her. Julien went to her assistance; he was admiring her elegant figure, which suggested anything but strength, when all of a sudden she seized the ladder and carried it off as she would a chair. She carried it swiftly up to the corridor on the fourth floor, where she set it down alongside the wall. She called the servant, and in order to give him time to dress, climbed to the dovecote. Five minutes later, when she came back down to the corridor, the ladder was gone. What had become of it? If Julien were out of the house, this danger would scarcely have bothered her. But if, at that moment, her husband should see the ladder! The incident could turn out very nastily. Mme. de Rênal ran all over the house. She finally discovered the ladder under the roof, where the servant had carried and even hidden it. This circumstance seemed odd; in the past it would have alarmed her.

"What do I care," she thought, "what happens in the next twenty-four hours, after Julien is gone? What lies in store for me but horror and regret!"

She had some vague idea that she ought to put an end to her life, but what difference would it make! After a separation that she had thought eternal, he had been given back to her; she was seeing him again, and all he had done to find his way to her was proof of so much love!

While relating the incident of the ladder to Julien, she asked, "What shall I tell my husband if the servant reports that he found a ladder?" She mused for an instant. "It will take them twenty-four hours to locate the peasant who sold it to you." And throwing herself into Julien's arms, while she hugged him convulsively, she cried out: "Oh! to die, to die thus!" and covered him with kisses. "But you mustn't die of hunger," she said, laughing.

"Come. First I am going to hide you in Mme. Derville's room, which stays locked all the time." She went to keep a lookout at the end of the corridor, and Julien raced through it. "Be careful not to open if someone knocks," she told him as she locked him in. "In any case, it would only be the children playing jokes on one another."

"Take them out into the garden, under the window," said Julien, "so I may have the pleasure of seeing them. Make them talk."

"Yes, yes," cried Mme. de Rênal, going away.

She returned very shortly with oranges, biscuits, a bottle of Malaga wine; it had been impossible to steal any bread.

"What is your husband doing?" said Julien.

"He is writing out the deals he is going to make with the peasants." But eight o'clock had struck; there was a good deal of noise in the house. If Mme. de Rênal were not seen, she would be looked for everywhere. She was obliged to leave him. Soon she returned, contrary to all good sense, bringing him a cup of coffee. She was worried that he might starve to death. After lunch, she contrived to lead the children out under the window of Mme. Derville's room. He found them much grown, but they had taken on a common look, or else his ideas had changed.

Mme. de Rênal spoke to them about Julien. The eldest responded with affection and regret for their old tutor, but it turned out that the younger ones had almost forgotten him.

M. de Rênal did not stir from the house that morning; he kept going up and downstairs all the time, busy striking bargains with the peasants to whom he was selling his potato crop. Until dinner time, Mme. de Rênal did not have a minute to spare for her prisoner. Dinner announced and served, she had the idea of stealing a bowl of hot soup for him. As she was noiselessly approaching the door of the room he occupied, balancing the plate warily, she came face-to-face with the servant who had hidden the ladder that morning. At the moment, he too was moving silently through the corridor and seemed to be listening. Julien had probably walked carelessly. The servant went away, somewhat embarrassed. Mme. de Rênal turned boldly into Julien's room; this meeting made him shiver.

"You are afraid," she said to him. "Not me; I could face any danger in the world without batting an eyelash. I dread only one thing; that is the moment I will be alone after your departure." And she ran out.

"Ah!" said Julien ecstatically, "remorse is the only danger that sublime soul fears!"

Night came at last. M. de Rênal went to the Casino. His wife had announced a terrible migraine. She retired to her room, made haste to send Elisa away, got up again quickly, and went to open the door for Julien.

It so happened that he really was dying of hunger. Mme. de Rênal went down to the pantry to look for some bread. Julien heard a scream. Mme. de Rênal came back and related to him that after entering the totally dark pantry, going over to the sideboard where the bread was kept, and stretching out her hand, she had touched a woman's arm. It was Elisa who had let out the scream.

"What was she doing there?"

"She was stealing something sweet, or else she was spying on us," said Mme. de Rênal in a tone of utter indifference. "Fortunately, I found a pâté and a loaf of bread."

"Then what do you have in there?" asked Julien, pointing to the pockets of her apron. Mme. de Rênal had forgotten that since dinner time they were stuffed with bread.

Julien clasped her in his arms with the most heartfelt passion; never had she seemed so beautiful to him. "Even in Paris," he told himself confusedly, "I could not find such character." She had all the awkwardness of a woman who is little accustomed to this sort of attention, and at the same time, the true courage of a person who fears nothing but dangers of another order, which are terrifying in a very different way.

While Julien supped heartily and his mistress was teasing him about the simpleness of the meal, since she had a horror of serious talk, the bedroom door was all at once shaken violently. It was M. de Rênal.

"Why have you locked yourself in?" he shouted to her.

Julien had just time to slide under the sofa.

"What! you're all dressed," said M. de Rênal, entering the room. "You're having supper, and you've locked your door."

Any other day this question, posed in all connubial coldness, would have upset Mme. de Rênal, but she realized that her husband had only to slide down a little to catch sight of Julien, for M. de Rênal had flung himself into the chair that Julien had occupied a minute before, opposite the sofa.

The migraine served as an excuse for everything. While her husband, in turn, was narrating to her at great length the details of the pool he had won at the Casino's billiard table, "a pool of nineteen francs, by Jove!" he added, she noticed, on a chair three feet from them, Julien's hat.

More composed than ever, she began to undress, and choosing the right moment, passed swiftly behind her husband and threw her dress over the chair with the hat on it.

M. de Rênal finally left. She begged Julien to begin the story of his life in the seminary all over again. "Last night I wasn't listening. I could think of nothing, the whole time you were talking, but how to find the heart to send you away."

She was recklessness itself. They were talking very loudly, and it might have been two o'clock in the morning, when they were interrupted by a violent blow on the door. It was M. de Rênal again.

"Open the door, quick! There are burglars in the house!" he said. "Saint-Jean found their ladder this morning."

"This is the end," cried Mme. de Rênal, throwing herself into Julien's arms. "He's going to kill both of us. He doesn't think it's burglars. I will die in your arms, happier at my death than I ever was in my life." She made no reply to her husband, who was getting angry; she was kissing Julien passionately.

"Save Stanislas' mother," he said to her with a commanding look. "I am going to jump down into the courtyard from the closet window, and escape through the garden. The dogs remembered me. Make a bundle of my clothes, and throw it down into the garden as soon as you can. Meanwhile, let him break open the door. Above all else, no confession. I forbid it. Better he be suspicious than certain."

"You will kill yourself if you jump," was her only answer and her only concern.

She went with him to the closet window; then she took time to hide his clothes. She finally opened the door to her husband, boiling with rage. He looked around the room, into the closet, without a word, and disappeared. Julien's clothes were thrown to him. He picked them up and ran swiftly toward the lower end of the garden, in the direction of the Doubs.

As he was running he heard a bullet whistle, and at the same time the report of a rifle.

"It can't be M. de Rênal," he thought. "He's too poor

a shot for that." The dogs were running silently at his side. A second shot apparently broke one of the dogs' paws, for it set up the most pitiful yelping. Julien jumped over a terrace wall, made some fifty yards under cover, and started running again in another direction. He heard voices calling to one another and distinctly saw the servant, his enemy, fire a rifle; a farmer had also just taken a wild shot at him from the other side of the garden, but by this time Julien had reached the bank of the Doubs and was getting dressed.

An hour later he was a league out of Verrières, on the road to Geneva. "If they have any suspicions," thought Julien, "they will look for me on the road to Paris."

BOOK TWO

She isn't pretty,
she's not wearing rouge.
—SAINTE-BEUVE

Chapter I

Country Pleasures

O rus quando ego te aspiciam!
—VIRGIL*

"The gentleman must be waiting for the mail coach to Paris?" said the host of the inn where he had stopped for breakfast.

"The one today or the one tomorrow, it makes no difference to me," Julien replied.

The mail coach arrived while he was pretending indifference. There were two empty seats.

"What! it's you, Falcoz old boy," said the traveler coming in from Geneva to the one who climbed into the coach with Julien.

"I thought you had settled down in the vicinity of Lyons, in some delightful valley near the Rhone?" said Falcoz.

"Settled, indeed. I'm running away."

"What! running away? You, Saint-Giraud, with an honest face like that, could you have committed some crime?" said Falcoz, laughing.

"By George, I might as well have. I'm running away from the wretched life a man leads in the country. I love the shady woods and the quiet countryside, as you well know; you have often accused me of being romantic. I have never in my life wanted to hear talk about politics, and politics are driving me away."

"But what party do you belong to?"

"None, and that has been my undoing. Here are my politics: I love music and painting; a good book is an event for me; I'm going on forty-four. How much time do I have left? Fifteen, twenty, thirty years at the most? Very well! I maintain that in thirty years ministers will be a bit shrewder, but just about as honest as they are today. The history of England serves me as a mirror of our future. There will always be a king who wants to increase his prerogative; the eternal ambition to become deputy, the glory and hundreds of thousands of francs amassed by Mirabeau, will keep the rich provincials from going to sleep; they will call that being liberal and loving the people. The desire to become peer or Gentleman of the Chamber will always keep the Ultras on the go. Aboard the ship of state, everyone will want to do the steering, since the job is well paid. So will there ever be a poor little berth on it for the ordinary passenger?"

"The facts, the facts ... which should be very funny, given your quiet nature. Was it the last elections that drove you from your province?"

" 'My hurt has come from farther still.'* Four years ago I was forty years old and had five hundred thousand francs; today I am four years older, and likely poorer by fifty thousand, which I am going to lose on the sale of my Château de Monfleury near the Rhone, a superb site.

"In Paris, I was weary of that never-ending comedy in which one is forced to play a part by what you call nineteenth-century civilization. I craved naturalness and straightforwardness. I bought an estate in the mountains close to the Rhone ... nothing finer under the sun.

"The parish priest and the local squirearchy made up to me for six months. I had them in to dine. 'I forsook Paris,' I told them, 'so I would never have to talk or hear talk about politics. As you see, I have not subscribed to a single newspaper. The fewer letters the mailman brings, the happier I am.'

"That wasn't what the priest was counting on; soon I was subjected to a thousand bothersome requests, annoyances, etcetera. I meant to give two or three hundred francs a year to the poor. Instead, I was asked to give the money to pious organizations: St. Joseph's, The Blessed Virgin's,* and so on. I refused, and then I was insulted in a hundred different ways. I was stupid enough to flare up. After that, I couldn't go out in the morning and enjoy the beauty of our mountains without finding some mischief that would break my train of thought and remind me disagreeably of men and their maliciousness. During the Rogation week processions, for example, the Gregorian chants of which I am fond (it's probably a Greek melody), my fields went unblessed, because the parish priest said they belonged to a godless man. A religious old peasant woman's cow died; she said it was on account of

236

the nearness of a pond that belonged to ungodly me, the sage from Paris, and a week later I discovered all my fish with their bellies in the air, poisoned by lime. I was beset with aggravations of every sort. The justice of the peace, an honest man but worried about his job, always found me in the wrong. The peaceful countryside was a hell for me. Once it was plain that I had been forsaken by the priest, head of the village *Congrégation*, and was not backed up by the retired captain who heads the Liberals, all of them jumped on me, even the mason whom I have kept alive for the past year, even the cartwright, who thought he had a perfect right to cheat me when he mended my plows.

"So as to have some backing and win at least a few of my lawsuits, I became a Liberal; but, as you said, those devilish elections came on; I was asked to vote—"

"For someone you didn't know?"

"No, sir, for a man I knew only too well. I refused; a terrible mistake! From then on, I had the Liberals on my back too; my position was intolerable. I believe that if the parish priest had taken it into his head to accuse me of having murdered my maid, there would have been twenty witnesses from both parties to swear they saw me commit the crime."

"You expect to live in the country and not serve your neighbors' interests, not even listen to their chatter. What an error!"

"It has been corrected at last. Monfleury is up for sale; I am willing to lose fifty thousand francs, if necessary, but I'm happy as I can be; I am leaving that hell of meddling hypocrisy and aggravation. I will look for country peace and solitude in the only place where they exist in France, on a fifth floor overlooking the Champs-Elysées. And I am still debating whether or not to begin my political career in the Roule quarter* by supplying the parish church with bread for consecration."

"All this would not have happened to you under Bonaparte," said Falcoz, his eyes shining with wrath and regret.

"Maybe so, but why didn't he have sense enough to stick to what he knew, your Bonaparte? Everything I have to put up with today is his doing."

Here Julien began to pay the closest attention. He had realized from the first few remarks that the Bonapartist Falcoz was the old childhood friend of M. de Rênal, repudiated by him in 1816, and the philosopher Saint-Giraud must be the brother of the chief clerk in the prefecture of ———, who knew how to go about getting township property knocked down to himself at bargain prices.

"Your Bonaparte is to blame for all that," Saint-Giraud was saying. "An honest man and harmless as they come, who has five hundred thousand francs, and forty years behind him, cannot settle down in the country and find peace there. Bonaparte's priests and nobles drive him away."

"Ah! speak no evil of him. Never was France so highly regarded by other nations as during the thirteen years he reigned. In those days there was a grandeur about everything undertaken."

"Your emperor, may the devil take him," replied the man of forty-four, "was great only on the battlefield, and when he put the finances back on a sound footing, around 1802. But what's the sense of everything he did after that? With his chamberlains, his ceremony, and his receptions in the Tuileries, he gave us a new edition of all the monarchy's tomfoolery. It was a revised edition; it might have lasted a century or two. The nobles and the priests want to go back to the old edition, but they don't have the iron hand it takes to foist it off on the public."

"There's the talk of a one-time printer for you!"

"Who is driving me off my land?" continued the printer angrily. "The priests Napoleon called back with his Concordat, instead of treating them as the state treats doctors, lawyers, astronomers ... as nothing more than citizens, and not lending a hand in the business by which they make their living. Would there be any insolent gentlemen today if your Bonaparte had not created barons and counts? No, they had gone out of fashion. After the priests, it's the little country nobles who have provoked me the most, and forced me to turn Liberal."

The conversation was endless; this text will set France to arguing for the next half century. Since Saint-Giraud kept repeating that it was impossible to live in the provinces, Julien shyly volunteered the example of M. de Rênal.

"By George, young man, you've a good one," exclaimed Falcoz. "That one has turned into a hammer so as not to be the anvil, and a terrible hammer he is. But it seems to me that he has been outflanked by Valenod. Do you know him? A rascal if there ever was one. What will your M. de Rênal say when he finds himself turned out of office some fine day, and Valenod put in his place?"

"He will be left standing face-to-face with his crimes,"

said Saint-Giraud. "Then you know Verrières, young man? Very well! Bonaparte, may heaven confound him, him and his secondhand monarchy, made possible the reign of the Rênals and the Chélans, which has brought on the reign of the Valenods and the Maslons."

This gloomy conversation about politics astonished Julien and distracted him from his voluptuous daydream.

He was not much impressed by his first glimpse of Paris, visible in the distance. The castles in Spain he had built on his future destiny had to compete with his still-present memory of the twenty-four hours he had just spent in Verrières. He swore to himself that he would never forsake his mistress's children and would put everything aside in order to protect them, if priestly arrogance should lead to a new republic and another persecution of the nobility.

What would have become of him the night of his arrival in Verrières if, when he leaned his ladder against Mme. de Rênal's bedroom window, he had found the room occupied by a stranger, or by M. de Rênal?

But then, how delightful those first two hours had been, when his mistress kept trying in all sincerity to send him away and he, seated beside her in the dark, kept pleading his cause! A heart like Julien's is haunted by such memories for a lifetime. The rest of the meeting was already beginning to merge with the first stages of their love, fourteen months earlier.

Julien was wakened from his deep reverie by the carriage's coming to a halt. They had just turned into the courtyard of the posthouse, Rue J. J. Rousseau.

"I want to go to the Malmaison," he said to a cabriolet that was pulling up.

"At this hour, sir? To do what?"

"What's it to you! Drive."

True passion thinks only of itself. That is why, it seems to me, passions are so absurd in Paris, where the other party is always expecting you to think a great deal about him or her. I will refrain from describing Julien's raptures at the Malmaison. He wept. What! in spite of those ugly white walls, put up that year, which cut the park into pieces?

Yes, sir. For Julien, as for posterity, there was no difference between Arcole, Ste.-Hélène, and the Malmaison.*

That evening Julien hesitated a long while before going into a theater; he had strange ideas about that den of iniquity.

A deep mistrust kept him from admiring the Paris of

239

today; nothing interested him except the monuments left by his hero.

"So here I am, at the center of intrigue and hypocrisy! Here reign the Abbé de Frilair's protectors."

By the evening of the third day, curiosity got the better of his plan to see everything before he reported to the Abbé Pirard. This abbé explained in a cold voice the kind of life that awaited him in M. de La Mole's household.

"If at the end of a few months you have not proved useful, you will go back to the seminary, but in good standing. You will live in the marquis' house; he's one of the greatest lords of France. You will wear black, but like a man in mourning, not as a clergyman. I insist that you continue your studies in theology three times a week at a seminary where I will introduce you. Every day at noon you will install yourself in the marquis' library; he means to have you write letters about his lawsuits and other business. In the margin of each letter he receives, the marquis jots down a summary of the answer to be made. I claimed that at the end of three months you would know how to write out those replies, so that out of every twelve letters you presented for the marquis' signature, he might be able to sign eight or nine. At eight o'clock in the evening you will put his desk in order, and at ten you will be free.

"It may happen," continued the Abbé Pirard, "that some old lady or soft-spoken man will hint at immense advantages, or come right out and offer you money for letting him look at the letters received by the marquis—"

"Ah, sir!" cried Julien, blushing.

"It's odd," said the abbé with a bitter smile, "that, poor as you are, and after a year in the seminary, you still have these fits of virtuous indignation. You must have been blind indeed!

"Could it be that blood will tell?" said the abbé in a whisper, and as though talking to himself. "Strangely enough," he added, looking at Julien, "the marquis knows you . . . I don't know how. To start with, he is giving you a salary of one hundred louis. He is a man who acts from caprice alone; that is his defect. He will rival you in childishness. If he is satisfied with you, your salary may later be raised to as much as eight thousand francs.

"But you realize, of course," the abbé went on sourly, "that he is not going to give you all that money for your good looks. You must be useful. If I were in your place, I would speak little and, above all, never talk about anything of which I was ignorant.

"Ah!" said the abbé, "I have gathered some information for you; I forgot to mention M. de La Mole's family. He has two children; a daughter, and a son nineteen years old, elegant par excellence; a madcap who never knows what he will be doing from one minute to the next. He is witty, brave; he fought in the Spanish war.* The marquis hopes, I don't know why, that you will become young Count Norbert's friend. I said that you were a great Latinist; perhaps he expects you to teach his son a few stock phrases about Cicero and Virgil.

"In your place, I would never allow that fine young man to trifle with me; and before responding to his advances, perfectly polite but somewhat spoiled by irony, I would make him repeat them more than once.

"I will not hide from you the fact that the young Count de La Mole is certain to look down on you at first, since you are nothing but a petty bourgeois. One of his ancestors belonged to the court and had the honor of having his head cut off on the Place de Grève,* the twenty-sixth of April, 1574,* for a political conspiracy. Whereas you, you are the son of a carpenter from Verrières, and what's more, in his father's pay. Weigh these differences carefully, and study the family's history in Moreri;* all the flatterers who dine at their house make, from time to time, what they call delicate allusions to it.

"Be careful how you reply to the jokes of M. le comte Norbert de La Mole, major in the Hussars and future peer of France, and don't come complaining to me afterward."

"It seems to me," said Julien, blushing a great deal, "that I shouldn't even answer a man who despises me."

"You have no conception of that kind of contempt; it will appear only in exaggerated compliments. If you were a fool, you might let yourself be taken in; if you wanted to make your fortune, you would let yourself be taken in."

"The day when all that is no longer to my taste," said Julien, "will I be thought ungrateful if I return to my little cell, number one hundred and three?"

"Doubtless," replied the abbé, "all the bootlickers in the house will malign you, but I will step in myself. *Adsum qui feci.* I will say the decision came from me."

Julien was cut to the quick by the bitter and almost nasty tone he discerned in the abbé's speech; this tone completely spoiled his last reply.

The fact is that the abbé had pangs of conscience about liking Julien, and it was with a sort of holy terror that he intervened so directly in the fate of another.

"You will also see," he added in the same begrudging manner, and as though acquitting himself of a painful duty, "you will also see Mme. la Marquise de La Mole. She is a tall blond woman ... devout, haughty, perfectly civil, and even more insignificant. She is the daughter of the old Duke of Chaulnes, so well known for his nobiliary prejudices. That great lady is a kind of scale model, in high relief, of what is most basic to the character of women of her rank. She lets it be known, she does, that to have had ancestors who went on the Crusades is the only distinction she respects. Money comes a long way after; that surprises you? We are no longer in the country, my friend.

"In her drawing room you will hear several great lords talk about our princes in a tone of uncommon levity. As for Mme. de La Mole, she lowers her voice out of respect every time she names a prince, and especially a princess. I would advise you not to say in front of her that Philip II or Henry VIII was a monster. They were *kings,* which gave them imprescriptible rights with regard to all men, and above all with regard to creatures of no birth, such as you and I. However," added M. Pirard, "we are priests, for she will take you for such; under that heading, she thinks of us as valets necessary to her salvation."

"Sir," said Julien, "it seems to me that I will not be in Paris very long."

"As you like, but mark me well: there is no way to fortune for a man of our cloth save through the great lords. Given that indefinable, at least for me, something about your character, if you don't make a fortune you will be hounded. There is no middle course for you. Have no illusions on that score. Men can see that they give you no pleasure when they speak to you; in a sociable country like this, you are doomed to misery if you cannot command respect.

"What would have become of you in Besançon, if it weren't for the Marquis de La Mole's whim? Someday, you will fully appreciate the unusualness of what he has done for you, and if you are not a monster you will feel eternal gratitude toward him and his family. How many poor abbés, more learned than you, have lived in Paris for years on their fifteen sous for a mass and ten sous for their arguments at the Sorbonne! . . . Remember what I told you last winter about the early years of that rogue of a cardinal, Dubois?* Does your pride tell you, perchance, that you are more talented than he?

242

"Take me, for example, a quiet, mediocre man; I planned to die in my seminary; I was childish enough to become attached to it. Well! I was about to be dismissed when I handed in my resignation. Do you know what my assets came to? I had a capital of five hundred and twenty francs, no more, no less; not a friend, scarcely two or three acquaintances. M. de La Mole, whom I had never seen, got me out of that tight corner; he had only to say the word and I was given a parish, the parishioners of which are wealthy, above coarse vices; and the income makes me ashamed, it is so greatly out of proportion to my duties. I have gone on for such a long while only to put a little sense into that head.

"One thing more: I have the bad luck to be quick-tempered; it is possible that one day you and I will stop speaking to one another.

"If the marquise's haughtiness, or her son's disagreeable jokes, should make this house decidedly unbearable for you, I would advise you to finish your studies in some seminary thirty leagues out of Paris, to the north rather than to the south. In the north there is more civilization and less injustice, and," he added, lowering his voice, "I must admit, the proximity of the Paris newspapers frightens petty tyrants.

"If we continue to take pleasure in seeing one another, and the marquis' house does not suit you, I will offer you a place as my assistant, and will give you half of whatever the parish brings in. I owe you that and even more," he added, interrupting Julien's thanks, "for the unusual offer you made me in Besançon. If instead of five hundred and twenty francs I had had nothing, you would have saved me."

The abbé had lost his cruel tone of voice. To his great shame, Julien felt tears in his eyes; he yearned to throw himself into his friend's arms. He could not refrain from telling him, with the most virile air he could muster:

"I have been hated by my father since birth; that is one of my great sorrows; but I will never again complain about my luck. I have found a second father in you, sir."

"That's fine, fine," said the abbé, embarrassed. Then, happening at the right time upon a director-of-the-seminary expression: "You must never say 'luck,' my child, always say 'Providence.'"

The cab stopped. The cabman lifted the bronze knocker on a huge door. It was the Hôtel de La Mole; and so that passersby should have no doubt about it, those words were to be read on a black marble slab above the door.

This affectation annoyed Julien. "They are so afraid of the Jacobins! They see a Robespierre and his tumbril behind every hedge; it's often enough to make you want to die laughing; yet they advertise their house this way so the rabble will know where it is in case of a riot, and loot it." He communicated his thoughts to the Abbé Pirard.

"Ah! my poor child, you will be my assistant very shortly! What an awful thing to think of!"

"Nothing seems plainer to me."

The porter's gravity and, above all, the neatness of the courtyard struck him with admiration. The sun was shining brightly.

"What magnificent architecture!" he said to his friend. He was talking about one of those townhouses with such dull facades in the Faubourg Saint-Germain* which were built around the time of Voltaire's death. Never have fashion and beauty been further apart.

Chapter II

First Taste of High Society

> An absurd and touching memory: the first drawing room in which one appeared at eighteen, alone and with no support! A woman's gaze was enough to intimidate me. The harder I tried to please, the clumsier I became. The notions I formed about everything couldn't have been farther from the mark; either I confided in a person for no reason whatsoever, or I thought a man my enemy because he had given me a solemn look. But then, amid all the frightful anguish my shyness caused me, how fine a fine day was!
>
> —KANT

Julien stopped dumbfounded in the middle of the courtyard.

"Try to look more intelligent," said the Abbé Pirard. "Horrible thoughts occur to you, and then you act like a child! Where is Horace's *nil admirari*? ("Never show enthusiasm.") Remember that this crowd of lackeys, seeing you installed here, will try to make a fool of you; they will look upon you as an equal set above them unfairly. Behind a show of good-naturedness, of good advice, of a desire to be helpful, they will try to lead you into committing some gross blunder."

"I defy them to do it," said Julien, biting his lip, all of his old mistrust returning.

The drawing rooms on the second floor through which these gentlemen passed before reaching the marquis' study would have seemed to you, O reader, as dreary as they were magnificent. If they were given to you just as they were you would refuse to live in them; this is the fatherland of the yawn and of gloomy reasoning. They increased Julien's enchantment twofold. "How could anyone be unhappy," he thought, "living in such a splendid residence!"

Eventually those gentlemen came to the ugliest room in this superb apartment: it was barely light enough to see. There they found a thin little man with a quick eye who was wearing a blond wig. The abbé turned to Julien and introduced him. It was the marquis. Julien had a hard time recognizing him; he was so courteous. This was not the great lord, of such lofty mien, at the Abbey of Bray-le-Haut. It seemed to Julien that his wig had far too much hair on it. Thanks to this observation, he did not feel at all intimidated. It struck him that the descendant of Henry III's friend cut a rather sorry figure. He was very thin and fidgeted a good deal. But Julien soon noted that the marquis' manners were even more agreeable to the interlocutor than those of the Bishop of Besançon himself. The audience lasted less than three minutes. As they were leaving, the abbé said to Julien:

"You looked at the marquis as you might have a portrait. I am no expert in what people here call politeness; soon you will know more about it than I; but still, the boldness of your look seemed hardly polite to me."

They had got back into the cab; the cabman stopped in a street near the boulevard; the abbé led Julien into a suite of large drawing rooms. Julien observed that there was no furniture. He was looking at a magnificent gilded clock, depicting a subject that to his notion was most indecent, when an extremely elegant gentleman approached them cheerfully. Julien made a half bow.

The gentleman smiled and put his hand on Julien's shoulder. Julien shuddered and jumped back. He blushed with anger. The Abbé Pirard, despite his gravity, laughed till he cried. The gentleman was a tailor.

"I am giving you your freedom for two days," the abbé said to him as they left. "You cannot be presented to Mme. de La Mole before then. Anyone else would watch over you like a girl, during these first few days of your stay in this modern Babylon. Ruin yourself right off, if you must go to ruin, and I will be freed of the weakness I have of worrying about you. The day after tomorrow, in the

246

morning, that tailor will bring you two suits. Give five francs to the man who tries them on you. Another thing, don't let these Parisians hear the sound of your voice. If you say a word, they will find a way to make fun of you. They have a talent for that. The day after tomorrow be at my house at noon. . . . Go, ruin yourself. . . . I almost forgot: order some boots, shirts, and a hat from the addresses you see here."

Julien looked at the writing of the addresses.

"It is the marquis' hand," said the abbé. "He is an active man who anticipates everything, and who would rather do a thing himself than give orders. He is taking you into his service so you may spare him that kind of trouble. Will you have the wit to execute creditably all the business that hasty man will no more than hint at? The future will tell; keep your eyes open!"

Julien went into all the shops indicated on the list without saying a word; he noticed that he was treated with respect, and the bootmaker, writing his name in the ledger, put down, "M. Julien de Sorel."

At the cemetery of Père-Lachaise, a most obliging gentleman, who was even more liberal in his speech, volunteered to show Julien Marshal Ney's grave,* which a government's shrewd policy denies the honor of an epitaph. But on parting company with this Liberal, who, with tears in his eyes, all but folded him in his arms, Julien no longer had a watch. It was rich with this experience that two days later he presented himself at noon to the Abbé Pirard, who looked him over carefully.

"Perhaps you will turn into a fop," said the abbé sternly. Julien looked like a very young man in deep mourning; to tell the truth, he looked fine, but the good abbé was too provincial himself to see that Julien still had that sway of the shoulders which in the provinces implies both elegance and importance. On seeing Julien, the marquis judged his graces so differently from the good abbé that he asked the latter:

"Would you have any objection to M. Sorel's taking dancing lessons?"

The abbé was petrified. "No," he answered after a while, "Julien is not a priest."

Climbing a narrow, concealed staircase two steps at a time, the marquis himself showed our hero to a pretty attic room that looked down on the mansion's vast garden. He asked him how many shirts he had brought back from the seamstress.

247

"Two," replied Julien, intimidated to see so great a lord stoop to such details.

"Very good," the marquis replied with a serious air and in a somewhat curt and imperative tone that set Julien to thinking, "very good! Order twenty-two more. Here is the first quarter of your salary."

On his way down from the attic, the marquis called an elderly man to him. "Arsène," he said, "you will look after M. Sorel."

A few minutes later Julien found himself alone in a magnificent library; it was a delightful moment. So as not to be observed in his excited state, he went and hid himself in a gloomy little corner; from there he gazed rapturously at the shining backs of the books. "I will be able to read all of them," he told himself. "How could I help but like it here? M. de Rênal would consider himself disgraced forever and he done a hundredth of what the marquis had done for me.

"But first let's have a look at those letters to be copied."

This job out of the way, Julien ventured over to the books; he almost went mad with joy on finding an edition of Voltaire. He ran and opened the library door so as not to be caught in the act. Next he gave himself the pleasure of opening each of the eighty volumes. They were magnificently bound, the masterpiece of the best binder in London. This was more than enough to carry Julien's admiration to its peak.

An hour later the marquis came in, looked at the copies, and noted to his astonishment that Julien had written *cela* with two *ll*'s, *cella*.* "Could everything the abbé told me about his learning be nothing but a yarn?" Very discouraged, the marquis said to him gently, "You are not very sure of your spelling, are you?"

"That's true," said Julien, giving no thought to the harm he was doing himself. He was touched by the marquis' kindness, which reminded him, by contrast, of M. de Rênal's offensive manner.

"It's a waste of time trying out this little abbé from Franche-Comté," reflected the marquis, "but I needed a man I could count on so badly!

"*Cela* is written with one *l*," the marquis told him. "When your copies are finished, look in the dictionary for the spelling of words you are not sure of."

At six o'clock the marquis sent for him; he looked at Julien's boots with obvious distress. "It's my fault; I neglected to tell you that you are to dress every day at five thirty."

Julien looked at him uncomprehendingly.

"I mean, put on stockings. Arsène will remind you. Today, I will make excuses for you."

As he concluded these remarks, M. de La Mole showed Julien into a drawing room resplendent with gilding. On like occasions, M. de Rênal had never failed to quicken his pace in order to have the advantage of passing through the door first. The thought of his former employer's petty vanity caused Julien to step on the marquis' feet and inflict great pain on him because of his gout. "Ah! he's a clumsy oaf into the bargain," the marquis said to himself. He introduced him to a woman who had a tall figure and an imposing air. It was the marquise. Julien thought she looked impertinent, a little like Mme. de Maugiron, the wife of the subprefect of the borough of Verrières, when she attended the St. Charles Day dinner. Somewhat flustered by the extreme magnificence of the drawing room, Julien did not hear what M. de La Mole was saying. The marquise scarcely bothered to look at him. There were several men in the room, among whom Julien recognized, with ineffable pleasure, the young Bishop of Agde, who had deigned to speak to him some months before at the ceremony in Bray-le-Haut. This young prelate was, no doubt, alarmed by the tender gaze Julien had fixed on him out of shyness, and was not at all eager to recognize this provincial.

To Julien the men assembled in the drawing room seemed somewhat gloomy and constrained; in Paris one speaks in a low voice, and one does not make too much of little things.

A good-looking young man with a mustache, very pale and slim, came in around six thirty; he had a small head.

"You always keep people waiting," said the marquise, whose hand he was kissing.

Julien gathered that it was the Count de La Mole. He thought him charming from the very first.

"Is it possible," he said to himself, "that this is the man whose offensive bantering is supposed to drive me out of the house!"

By dint of scrutinizing Count Norbert, Julien noticed that he was in boots and spurs. "As for me, I must wear shoes, obviously as an inferior."

They sat down to dinner. Julien heard the marquise speak sternly and raise her voice a little. At almost the same instant he caught sight of a young woman, extremely blond and very shapely, who sat down opposite him. She didn't appeal to him at all; yet, after looking at her attentively, he thought he had never seen such beautiful eyes; but they betokened a great coldness of heart. Later on, Julien concluded that they wore the expression of one who is bored and who constantly examines others, yet never forgets her own obligation to be imposing. "Mme. de Rênal had very beautiful eyes too," he said to himself. "Everyone complimented her on them; yet they had nothing in common with these." Julien was too inexperienced to perceive that it was the flash of wit that caused Mlle. Mathilde's eyes to sparkle from time to time. It was thus he heard her named. When Mme. de Rênal's eyes grew animated, it was from the fire of passion, or the effect of a generous indignation at the account of some wicked deed. Toward the end of the meal, Julien found a word to define the beauty of Mlle. de La Mole's eyes: "They are scintillating," he told himself. Otherwise, she bore an awful resemblance to her mother, whom he was beginning to like less and less, and he stopped looking at her. On the other hand, Count Norbert seemed admirable in every way. Julien was so taken with him that he had no idea of being jealous or of hating him because he was wealthier and better born.

Julien thought the marquis looked bored. During the second course, he said to his son:

"Norbert, will you be so kind as to look out for M. Julien Sorel, whom I have just added to my staff, and whom I hope to keep on it, if *cella* is possible.

"He is my secretary," explained the marquis to his neighbor, "and he writes *cela* with two *ll*'s."

Everyone looked at Julien, who bowed his head a bit too emphatically in Norbert's direction, but generally speaking, everyone was satisfied with his appearance.

The marquis must have talked about the kind of education Julien had received, for one of the guests grilled him about Horace. "It was precisely by talking about Horace that I brought it off at the bishop's house," Julien said to himself. "Evidently that's the only author they know." From then on he was master of himself. This change of mood was facilitated by his having just decided that Mlle. de La Mole could never be a woman in his eyes. Since his seminary days he had expected men to do their worst, and was not intimidated easily. He would have enjoyed total self-possession if the dining room had been furnished less sumptuously. It was, in fact, two mirrors, eight feet tall, in which from time to time he caught sight of his interlocutor as he spoke of Horace, that still awed him. His sentences were not too long for a provincial. He had handsome eyes, which a trembling shyness, or happiness when he answered well, made twice as bright. The company thought him agreeable. ... This kind of examination injected a bit of interest into a solemn dinner.

By a sign, the marquis urged Julien's examiner to push him hard. "Can it be that he knows something!" he thought.

Julien discovered his ideas as he answered, and he lost enough of his shyness to show, if not wit (a thing impossible for anyone who does not know the language they speak in Paris), at least fresh insights, though presented neither gracefully nor with good timing, and one could see that he knew his Latin perfectly.

Julien's adversary was an academician from the Inscriptions, who, by chance, knew Latin; he found in Julien a very good humanist and, no longer dreading to see him blush, was making a serious effort to trip him up. In the heat of battle, Julien finally forgot the magnificent furnishings of the dining room and reached a point where he was setting forth ideas about the Latin poets that his interlocutor had not read anywhere. As an honest man, he paid the young secretary the honor due him. Happily someone broached the question as to whether Horace had been rich or poor: a likable, sensual, happy-go-lucky man writing verses to amuse himself, like Chapelle, Molière's and La Fontaine's friend; or a poor devil of a poet laureate, following the court and composing odes for the king's birthday, like Southey, Lord Byron's accuser. There was talk about social conditions under Augustus and under George IV; during both periods the aristocracy was all-powerful; but in Rome it saw its power snatched away by Maecenas, who was nothing but a knight; and in England the aristocracy had reduced George IV almost to the status of a Venetian doge. This discussion seemed to draw the marquis out of the torporous state into which boredom had plunged him at the beginning of the dinner.

Julien knew nothing about all those modern names, such as Southey, Lord Byron, George IV, which he heard mentioned for the first time. But it escaped no one's attention that whenever a question came up about an event that had occurred in Rome, and knowledge about it could be inferred from the works of Horace, or Martial, or Tacitus, etc., he had an undeniable superiority. Julien lay hands boldly on several ideas he had learned from the Bishop of Besançon, in the famous discussion he had had with that prelate; they were by no means the least relished.

251

When the company grew weary of talking about poets, the marquise, who made it a law unto herself to admire anything that entertained her husband, deigned to look at Julien. "The awkward manners of this young abbé may well hide a learned man," said the academician, seated next to the marquise; and Julien heard some of this. Stock phrases suited the mistress of the house's turn of mind very well; she adopted this one about Julien and congratulated herself on having invited the academician to dine. "M. de La Mole finds him amusing," she thought.

Chapter III

First Steps

> That immense valley filled with flashing lights and with so many thousands of men dazzles my sight. Not one knows me, all are superior to me. My head is spinning.
>
> —*Poemi dell'av. Reina*

Early the next morning, Julien was copying letters in the library when Mlle. Mathilde came in through a small private door, cleverly concealed by the backs of books. While Julien was admiring this device, Mlle. Mathilde appeared to be most astonished and quite put out to run into him there. Julien decided that in curlpapers she looked hard, arrogant, and almost masculine.

Mlle. de La Mole had found a way to steal books from her father's library without its showing. Julien's presence made her errand useless that morning, which annoyed her all the more since she had come to get the second volume of Voltaire's *The Princess of Babylon*, a worthy complement to her eminently Royalist and religious education, masterpiece of the Sacred Heart! Already at nineteen this poor girl required the spice of wit if she was to find a novel interesting.

Count Norbert appeared in the library around three o'clock; he had come to study a newspaper so he could talk politics in the evening, and was glad to see Julien, whose existence he had forgotten. He was courtesy itself; he offered to take Julien horseback riding.

"My father has given us leave until dinner time." Julien appreciated the "us" and thought it charming.

"By God! Monsieur le Comte, if it were a matter of

cutting down a tree eighty feet tall, squaring it and sawing it into planks, I'd come off pretty well, I daresay; but ride a horse! that hasn't happened to me more than six times in my whole life."

"Well, this will be the seventh," said Norbert.

Julien had the King of ———'s entrance into Verrières at the back of his mind and really believed he could ride a horse exceptionally well. But coming back from the Bois de Boulogne, right in the middle of the Rue du Bac, he fell as he tried suddenly to avoid a cabriolet, and was covered with mud. He was lucky to have two suits. At dinner the marquis, wishing to converse with him, asked for news about his ride. Norbert hastened to answer for him in general terms.

"Monsieur le Comte is too good to me; I thank him and am deeply appreciative. He was kind enough to give me the gentlest and the best-looking horse; but after all, he couldn't fasten me to it, and for lack of that precaution, I had a fall in the middle of that long street near the bridge."

Mlle. Mathilde tried in vain to smother a burst of laughter; then tactlessly she asked for details. Julien acquitted himself with a good deal of naturalness; he had style without knowing it.

"I augur well of this little priest," said the marquis to the academician: "a provincial who knows how to behave naturally in such circumstances; that's never been seen before and never will be again; and he had to tell his sad story in front of *ladies!*"

Julien set his auditors so much at ease about his mishap that by the end of the dinner, when the general conversation had taken another turn, Mlle. Mathilde was questioning her brother about details of the unlucky incident. Since she persisted in asking questions, and Julien had met her gaze several times, he made so bold as to answer her directly, though he had not been consulted, and all three ended up laughing, like three young people living in a village in the depths of a forest.

The next day Julien attended two courses in divinity and afterward returned to transcribe some twenty letters. In the library he found a young man working close to his own desk; he was dressed with great care, but he cut a mean figure and his countenance was that of envy.

The marquis came in. "What are you doing here, Monsieur Tanbeau?" he asked the newcomer sternly.

"I thought—" replied the young man, smiling basely.

"No, sir, you *thought nothing*. This is a trial, but an ill-fated one."

Furious, young Tanbeau rose and disappeared. He was the nephew of Mme. de La Mole's friend, the academician; he wanted to become a writer. The academician had prevailed upon the marquis to take him on as a secretary. Tanbeau, who was working in a remote room, having learned of the favorable treatment enjoyed by Julien, intended to share it, and had come that morning to set up his desk in the library.

At four o'clock, after hesitating a little, Julien made so bold as to appear in Count Norbert's apartment. The latter was about to go riding and was embarrassed, for he was perfectly polite.

"I think," he said to Julien, "that you will soon be going to the riding school, and in a few weeks I will be delighted to ride with you."

"I wished to have the honor of thanking you for the kindnesses you have shown me; believe me, sir," Julien added very seriously, "that I am fully aware how much I am obliged to you. If your horse was not hurt yesterday by my clumsiness, and if it is free, I should like to mount it today."

"By George, my dear Sorel, it's your neck. Let us assume that I have raised all the objections that prudence demands; the fact is that it's four o'clock, we have no time to waste."

Once on horseback: "What should I do to keep from falling?" Julien asked the young count.

"A lot of things," answered Norbert, as he burst out laughing. "For instance, lean back in your saddle."

Julien broke into a fast trot. They were on the Place Louis XVI.*

"Ah! rash young man," said Norbert, "there are too many carriages here, and driven by reckless drivers at that! Once you're on the ground, their tilburies will run right over you; they won't risk spoiling their horses' mouths by pulling up short."

Twenty times Norbert saw Julien on the point of falling; but the ride came to an end at last without accident. When they returned, the count said to his sister, "I want you to meet a daredevil."

At dinner, addressing his father from one end of the table to the other, he did full justice to Julien's daring; it was the only thing about Julien's style of riding that could be commended. The young count had overheard the men who were grooming the horses in the courtyard that morning take Julien's fall as grounds for making the most outrageous fun of him.

Despite so much kindness, Julien soon felt completely out of things in the midst of this family. All of their ways seemed strange to him, and he was always doing the wrong thing. His blunders were the delight of the footmen.

The Abbé Pirard had left for his parish. "If Julien is a weakling, may he perish; if he is a man of heart, let him manage by himself," he thought.

Chapter IV

The Hôtel de La Mole

> What is he doing here! Does he
> like it here? Does he think he will
> be liked here?
>
> ——RONSARD

If everything about the Hôtel de La Mole's noble drawing room seemed strange to Julien, the pale young man in black likewise struck everyone who bothered to notice him as very odd. Mme. de La Mole proposed to her husband that he send him off on errands those days when they had certain men of note to dinner.

"I mean to push my experiment to the limit," the marquis answered. "The Abbé Pirard maintains that we do wrong to break the pride of people we take into our service. You can't lean on something unless it resists, etcetera. There's nothing wrong with this fellow except that he's an unfamiliar face; otherwise, he is as good as deaf and dumb."

"In order to get my bearings," Julien told himself, "I had better write down the names and a few words about the personalities of the people I see coming into this drawing room."

On the first line he entered five or six friends of the house, who curried his favor on the off chance that he was protected by one of the marquis' whims. They were poor devils, more or less obsequious; but it must be said to the credit of this class of men, such as one finds them today in the aristocracy's drawing rooms, that they were not equally servile with everyone. So and so among them might allow himself to be browbeaten by the marquis, yet would have rebelled against a hard word addressed to him by Mme. de La Mole.

There was too much pride, too much boredom, in the makeup of the mistress and the master of the house; they were too used to insulting, in order to relieve their ennui, to hope for true friends. Yet except on rainy days, and in moments of ferocious boredom, which were rare, they were always perfectly civil.

If the five or six flatterers who evinced such a paternal affection for Julien had deserted the Hôtel de La Mole, the marquise would have been exposed to long moments of solitude; and for women of her rank, solitude is a frightful thing; it is the mark of *disgrace*.

The marquis was perfect for his wife; he always saw to it that her drawing room was adequately stocked: not with peers, for he considered that his new colleagues were not noble enough to visit his house as friends, not entertaining enough to be admitted as inferiors.

Not until very much later did Julien fathom these secrets. Current politics, which are the main subject of conversation in bourgeois households, are not touched on in homes of the marquis' class, except in times of crisis.

Even in this bored century, the need for amusement is still so imperative that even on dinner days the marquis would no more than leave the drawing room when everyone took to his heels. Provided one did not trifle about God, or about priests, or about the king, or about men in high places, or about artists patronized by the court, or about the establishment in general, provided one spoke well neither of Béranger,* nor of the opposition newspapers, nor of Voltaire, nor of Rousseau, nor of anyone who indulged in a bit of plain speaking; provided, especially, one never talked politics, one might discuss any subject freely.

There is no annuity of a hundred thousand écus, no blue sash, that can stand up to such a drawing-room charter. . . . Any idea with the least bit of life in it seemed an indecency. Despite the good tone, perfect politeness, a desire to please, boredom was stamped on every forehead. The young people who came out of a sense of duty, fearful lest they say something that might cause them to be suspected of an idea, or betray their knowledge of some prohibited book, kept silence after a few elegant remarks about Rossini and the weather.

Julien observed that the conversation was usually kept alive by two viscounts and five barons whom M. de La Mole had known during the Emigration. These gentlemen enjoyed incomes of from six to eight thousand pounds; four were partisans of *The Daily*, and three, of the

Gazette of France. Every day, one in particular had an anecdote about the Château to tell, in which the word "wonderful" was not spared. Julien noted that this man had five crosses; most of the others had but three.

By way of compensation, there were ten liveried footmen in the anteroom, and all evening ices or tea was served every quarter of an hour; and at midnight, a kind of supper with champagne.

This is what sometimes prompted Julien to stay on until the end; as a matter of fact, he could scarcely understand how anyone could take the usual conversation of this magnificently gilded drawing room seriously. Sometimes he would look at people conversing to see whether they themselves were not laughing at what they said. 'My M. de Maistre, whose work I know by heart, has said the same things a hundred times better," he thought. "Still, he's boring enough."

Julien was not the only one to be aware of this moral asphyxiation. Some consoled themselves by taking many an ice; others, with the pleasure of saying for the rest of the evening: "I've just come from the Hôtel de La Mole, where I heard that Russia," etc.

Julien learned from one of the flatterers that less than six months ago Mme. de La Mole had rewarded poor Baron Le Bourguignon, subprefect since the Restoration, for his more than twenty years of constant attendance by making him prefect.

This great event had tempered anew the zeal of all those gentlemen; it took very little to make them angry before this; now nothing could make them angry. The hosts' lack of respect was rarely overt, but at table Julien had already overheard two or three short dialogues between the marquis and his wife that were merciless to those seated near them. These aristocrats did not hide their sincere contempt for all who were not descendants of those *privileged to ride in the king's coach.* Julien observed that only the word "Crusade" could impart to their faces an expression of profound seriousness, mingled with respect. Their usual respect always had a shade of self-satisfaction about it.

Amidst all that splendor and all that boredom, Julien took no interest in anything but M. de La Mole. With pleasure, he heard him protest one day that he had had nothing to do with the promotion of poor Le Bourguignon. This was out of consideration for the marquise; Julien had the truth from the Abbé Pirard.

One morning while the abbé was working with Julien in

the marquis' library on the interminable de Frilair suit, Julien asked, all of a sudden: "Sir, is it my duty to dine with Mme. La Marquise every day, or have I been shown a special kindness?"

"It is a signal honor!" replied the abbé, scandalized. "M. N——, the academician, who has paid assiduous court for fifteen years, has never been able to obtain it for his nephew, M. Tanbeau."

"For me, sir, it is the most irksome part of my job. I was less bored in the seminary. Sometimes I see even Mlle. de La Mole yawn, yet she ought to be used to polite attentions from the family friends. I'm afraid of falling asleep. Please get me permission to go and dine for forty sous at some out-of-the-way inn."

The abbé, a true parvenu, was highly appreciative of the honor of dining with a great lord. While he was doing his best to make Julien understand this sentiment, a slight noise caused them to turn their heads. Julien saw Mlle. de La Mole, who had been listening. He blushed. She had come to look for a book and had heard everything; she thought somewhat better of Julien. "That one wasn't born on his knees," she said to herself, "like that old abbé. God! how ugly he is."

At dinner Julien dared not look at Mlle. de La Mole, but she was kind enough to speak to him. A great many people were expected that evening; she urged him to stay on. Parisian girls don't care much for men of a certain age, especially when they are carelessly dressed. Julien didn't need any great store of wisdom to perceive that M. Le Bourguignon's colleagues, who lingered in the drawing room, had the honor of being the usual butt of Mlle. de La Mole's jokes. That evening, whether it was an affectation on her part or not, she was cruel to the bores.

Mlle. de La Mole was the center of a little group that gathered almost nightly behind the marquise's huge armchair. In it were to be found the Marquis de Croisenois, the Count de Caylus, the Viscount de Luz, and two or three other young officers, Norbert's friends or his sister's. These gentlemen were sitting on a large blue sofa. Julien was placed quietly on a small, rather low straw-bottomed chair, at the end of the sofa, opposite the one occupied by the brilliant Mathilde. This modest post was coveted by all the flatterers; Norbert would maintain his father's secretary in it decently by speaking to him occasionally, or by referring to him once or twice each evening. That particular evening, Mlle. de La Mole asked him what might be the height of the mountain on which the citadel of Besançon is situated. For the life of him, Julien couldn't say whether that mountain was higher or lower than Montmartre. Often he laughed heartily over some of the things said in this little group; but he felt incapable of thinking up anything of the sort. It was as if they spoke a foreign tongue which he understood and admired but couldn't speak.

That day Mathilde's friends were in a state of continuous hostility against the guests who kept arriving in this magnificent drawing room. At first the friends of the family were the preferred target, being better known. One may judge whether Julien was attentive; everything interested him, both the victim's background and the manner of poking fun at him.

"Ah! here is M. Descoulis," said Mathilde, "he's not wearing his wig; does he expect to get a prefecture for his genius? He's showing off that bald forehead, which he claims is filled with lofty thoughts."

"There's a man who knows everyone," said the Marquis de Croisenois. "He visits my uncle the cardinal too. He can keep a different lie going with each of his friends, for years on end, and he has two or three hundred friends. He knows how to keep a friendship alive; that is his talent. Just as you see him now, covered with mud, he's already at some friend's door by seven o'clock of a winter morning.

"He has a falling-out from time to time, and he writes seven or eight letters for the tiff. Then he makes up, and he has seven or eight letters for the raptures of friendship. But it is in the frank and sincere outpourings of the honest-man-who-bears-no-grudge that he shines. This maneuver comes into play when he has some favor to ask. One of my uncle's vicar-generals is marvelous when he tells M. Descoulis' life story since the Restoration. I will bring him to see you."

"Bah! I don't believe all that talk, it comes of professional jealousy among grubs," said the Count de Caylus.

"M. Descoulis' name will go down in history," replied the marquis. "He brought about the Restoration, along with the Abbé de Pradt and *MM*. de Talleyrand and Pozzo di Borgo."

"That man has handled millions," said Norbert, "and I can't understand why he comes here to pocket my father's epigrams, often nasty. 'How many times have you done in your friends, my dear Descoulis?' he shouted to him the other day, from one end of the table to the other."

"But is it true, has he betrayed his friends?" asked Mlle. de La Mole. "But then, who hasn't?"

"What!" said the Count de Caylus, "M. Sainclair in your house, the famous Liberal; and what the devil is he doing here? I must go over and talk to him, make him talk; they say he is so witty."

"But what kind of reception will your mother give him?" asked M. de Croisenois. "He has such wild ideas, so generous, so independent. . . ."

"Look," said Mlle. de La Mole, "there's your independent man bowing to the ground before M. Descoulis, and grabbing his hand. For a minute I thought he would raise it to his lips."

"Descoulis must be closer to the Throne than we think," replied M. de Croisenois.

"Sainclair comes here because he wants to get into the academy," said Norbert. "Croisenois, see how he's bowing to Baron L——"

"He couldn't be lower if he went down on his knees," replied M. de Luz.

"My dear Sorel," said Norbert, "you, a man of wit, who has just come down from the mountains, try never to bow the way that great poet does, not even to God the Father."

"Ah! here is the very paragon of wit, M. le baron Bâton," said Mlle. de La Mole, faintly imitating the voice of the footman who had just announced him.

"I think even your servants laugh at him. What a name, Baron Bâton!" (Stick) said M. de Caylus.

" 'What's in a name?' he was saying to us the other day," Mathilde went on. " 'Imagine the Duke de Bouillon (Beef-tea) being announced for the first time. All the public needs, in my case, is to get a bit used to it. . . .' "

Julien left the vicinity of the sofa. Not yet alive to the charming subtleties of light mockery, he required that a witticism be founded on reason if he was to laugh at it. He could see nothing in these young people's remarks but the tone of wholesale denigration, and was shocked. His provincial or English prudery led him so far as to think it was prompted by envy, wherein he was certainly mistaken.

"Count Norbert," he said to himself, "whom I have seen write three rough drafts for a letter of twenty lines to his colonel, would be happy indeed to have written one page in his life like those of M. Sainclair."

Passing unnoticed because of his insignificance, Julien went up to several groups in succession; he had been following Baron Bâton from a distance and wanted to hear him. That great mind looked uneasy, and Julien saw him recover his spirits a little only after having hit upon three or four barbed observations. It struck Julien that his kind of wit required a good deal of room. The baron could not speak in epigrams; he needed at least four sentences of six lines each in order to shine.

"This man doesn't talk, he expatiates," said someone behind Julien. He turned around and blushed with pleasure when he heard someone mention the Count Chalvet. He was the shrewdest man of the day. Julien had come across his name often in the *Mémorial de Sainte-Hélène,* and in the scraps of history dictated by Napoleon. Count Chalvet was terse in his expression; his sallies were bolts of lightning—just, keen, and sometimes profound. If he entered a discussion, it immediately took a step forward. He brought facts to bear; it was a pleasure to hear him. Moreover, in politics, he was a shameless cynic.

"I am an independent myself," he was saying to a gentleman who wore three decorations, and whose leg he was obviously pulling. "Why does everyone expect me to hold the same opinion today as I had six weeks ago? If that were the case, my opinion would be a tyrant."

Four grave young men who were standing around him pulled long faces; those gentlemen did not like flippancy. The count saw that he had gone too far. Fortunately, he caught sight of honest M. Balland, a Tartuffe of respectability. The count began talking to him; people gathered around; everyone sensed that poor Balland was about to be sacrificed. By dint of righteousness and uprightness, though horribly ugly and after an early career that is better left untold, M. Balland had married a very rich woman, who died; after that, another very wealthy woman, who was never seen in society. In all humility, he enjoyed an income of sixty thousand pounds and had his own flatterers. Count Chalvet alluded to all of this mercilessly. Soon there was a circle of thirty persons around them. Everyone was smiling, even the solemn young men, the hope of the age.

"Why does he come to M. de La Mole's house, where he is obviously the butt?" Julien wondered. He went over to the Abbé Pirard to ask him.

M. Balland sneaked away.

"Good!" said Norbert, "there's one less to spy on my father; that leaves only the little cripple Napier."

"Could that be the key to the riddle?" Julien asked

himself. "But in that case, why does the marquis open his door to M. Balland?"

The stern Abbé Pirard, standing in a corner of the drawing room, would make a face every time the footman announced a guest.

"Why, this is a den!" he said, like Basilio.* "I see nothing but shady characters coming here."

Which is to say that the strict abbé had no idea of what makes up high society. But thanks to his Jansenist friends, he had very precise notions about men who gain admission to drawing rooms only by means of their extraordinary wiliness at the service of every party, or by their ill-gotten wealth. For several minutes that evening he answered Julien's eager questions from a full heart, then stopped short, grieved always to be speaking ill of everyone, and putting it down to his own sinful nature. Bilious, Jansenist, and believing in the obligation of Christian charity, his life in society was a conflict.

"What a face that Abbé Pirard has!" Mlle. de La Mole was saying as Julien came back to the sofa.

Julien felt irritated, and yet she was right. M. Pirard was unquestionably the most honest man in the drawing room, but his blotchy face, twitching with pangs of conscience, looked hideous at the moment. "How can you put any stock in physiognomy after that," thought Julien. "It is at those times when the Abbé Pirard's scrupulousness is blaming him for some small slip that he looks utterly wicked; whereas on Napier's face, that of a spy known to everyone, you read nothing but pure and peaceful happiness." The Abbé Pirard had nevertheless made great concessions to this party: he had hired a servant, he was very well dressed.

Julien noted something peculiar going on in the drawing room; all eyes were turned toward the door and there was a sudden hush. The footman was announcing the famous Baron de Tolly, on whom the recent elections had focused everyone's attention. Julien stepped forward and had a good look at him. The baron presided over an electoral college: he had had the bright idea of filching the slips of paper marked with one of the parties' votes. But, by way of compensation, he replaced them with an equal number of small pieces of paper bearing a name that was to his liking. This decisive maneuver had been detected by some of the electors, who had lost no time in paying their respects to Baron de Tolly. The old fellow was still pale from the commotion. A few warped minds had used the word "galleys." M. de La Mole greeted him coldly. The poor baron stole away.

"If he's in such a hurry to leave us, it's because he is going to see M. Comte,"* said Count Chalvet, and everyone laughed.

Amidst a few mute great lords and a number of intriguers, most of them corrupt but all witty men, who kept coming that evening, one after the other, to M. de La Mole's drawing room (there was talk of a ministry for him), little Tanbeau had his first taste of battle. If he did not yet have subtlety of insight, he made up for it, as we shall see, with the energy of his speech.

"Why not sentence that man to ten years in prison?" he was saying when Julien drew near his group. "Snakes should be shut up in the deepest dungeon; they should be left to die in darkness; otherwise their venom rises and becomes more dangerous. What good will it do to fine him a thousand écus. He's poor, granted, and so much the better; but his party will pay for him. He should have had a five-hundred-franc fine and ten years in a dungeon."

"Good Lord! what monster can they be talking about?" thought Julien, who was admiring his colleague's vehement tone and violent gestures. The small, thin, drawn face of the academician's favorite nephew was hideous at the moment. Julien soon learned that the subject under discussion was the greatest poet* of the age.

"Ah, monster!" cried Julien half aloud, as generous tears welled in his eyes. "Ah, you little beggar," he thought, "I'll make you pay for those words."

"And yet," he thought, "such men are the vanguard of the party of which the marquis is a leader. As for that illustrious man he is slandering—how many crosses, how many sinecures he might have accumulated, had he sold himself, I don't say to that servile minister M. de Nerval, but to one of those passably honest ministers whom we have watched follow one another?"

The Abbé Pirard motioned to Julien from afar; M. de La Mole had just spoken a word to him. But when Julien, who at that moment was listening with lowered eyes to a bishop's groaning, was free at last to go over to his friend, he found him saddled with that loathsome little Tanbeau. The little monster detested him as the cause of the preferential treatment Julien enjoyed and so had come to court his favor.

"When will death deliver us from that old corruption?" In such terms and with Biblical vehemence, the little man of letters was holding forth at the moment about the honorable Lord Holland.*

Tanbeau's chief asset was a thorough knowledge of the biographies of living men, and he had just made a quick review of all those who might aspire to influential positions under the new King of England.*

The Abbé Pirard passed into the next drawing room; Julien followed.

"The marquis doesn't like scribblers; I'm warning you; that is his pet aversion. Master Latin, Greek, if you can; the history of the Egyptians, of the Persians, etcetera; he will honor and protect you as a scholar. But don't write a single page in French, especially about weighty matters that are above your station in life, or he will call you scribbler and hold it against you. How is it that, living in a great lord's mansion, you do not know the Duke de Castries' remark about d'Alembert and Rousseau? 'Their kind insist on discussing everything and they haven't a thousand écus a year.'"

"They find out everything," thought Julien, "here as well as in the seminary!" He had written eight or ten rather bombastic pages, a sort of historical eulogy of the old surgeon major, who he said had made a man of him. "And that little notebook," Julien remarked to himself, "has always been locked up!" He went to his quarters, burned the manuscript, and returned to the drawing room. The brilliant rascals had gone; only the men with decorations were left.

Around a table, which the servants had carried in already set, were gathered seven or eight very noble, very devout, very affected women between the ages of thirty and thirty-five. The Field Marshal de Fervaques' dazzling widow entered, apologizing for the lateness of the hour. It was after midnight; she went and took a place beside the marquise. Julien was deeply moved; she had Mme. de Rênal's eyes and her glance.

The group around Mlle. de La Mole was still numerous. She was busy with her friends making fun of poor Count de Thaler.* He was the only son of a renowned Jew, notorious for the wealth he had acquired by lending money to kings to make war on their peoples. The Jew had just died, leaving his son an income of six hundred thousand francs a month and a name, alas! but too well known! This singular position called for unpretentiousness or a vigorous will. Unfortunately, the count was nothing more than a good fellow stuffed with all sorts of pretentions that were roused one after the other by the voices of his flatterers.

M. de Caylus maintained that someone had given him the will to ask for Mlle. de La Mole's hand in marriage (she whom the Marquis de Croisenois, about to become a duke with an income of a hundred thousand crowns, was courting).

"Ah! don't accuse him of having a will," said Norbert piteously.

What this poor Count de Thaler most wanted perhaps was the faculty of volition. With regard to this side of his nature, he would have made a good king. Though he sought counsel from every quarter, he hadn't the courage to follow any piece of advice to the end.

"His face alone would be enough to inspire me with everlasting joy," Mlle. de La Mole was saying. It showed an odd mixture of uneasiness and disappointment; but from time to time, one might clearly discern a swell of self-importance in him, and the peremptory tone in his voice that the richest man in France ought to assume, especially when he is quite good-looking and not yet thirty-six.

"He is timidly insolent," said M. de Croisenois.

The Count de Caylus, Norbert, and two or three young men with mustaches made sport of him, all unawares, to their heart's content, and finally sent him away as one o'clock was striking.

"Are those your famous Arabs waiting in this weather at the door?" Norbert asked.

"No. It's a new team and much cheaper," answered M. de Thaler. "The horse on the left cost me five thousand francs, and the one on the right isn't worth more than a hundred louis; but believe me, he is hitched up only at night. The fact is that his trot matches the other one's perfectly."

Norbert's question reminded the count that it was becoming in a man like himself to have a passion for horses, and that he shouldn't let his own get wet.

He drove off, and those gentlemen took their leave a few minutes later, joking at his expense.

"So," thought Julien, as he listened to them laughing on the staircase, "I have been given a chance to see the opposite extreme of my own situation! I don't make twenty louis a year, and I was rubbing elbows with a man who has an income of twenty louis an hour, and everyone pokes fun at him. . . . A sight like that is a cure for envy."

267

Chapter V

Sensibility and a Great Pious Lady

> Any idea with a bit of life to it
> has the effect of an impropriety
> here, so used are these people to
> colorless remarks. Woe to him who
> invents as he speaks!
>
> —FAUBLAS

After several months' trial, here is how Julien stood on
the day the chief steward of the house handed him his
salary for the third quarter. M. de La Mole had entrusted him with supervising the management of his estates
in Brittany and in Normandy. Julien made frequent trips
to these parts. He was also put in charge of the correspondence relative to that famous lawsuit against the Abbé de
Frilair. M. Pirard had briefed him.

From the short notes the marquis scrawled in the mar-
gins of papers of all kinds that were addressed to him,
Julien composed letters, most of which were signed.

In the divinity school, his professors complained about
his irregular attendance but considered him nonetheless
one of their brightest students. These various labors, into
which he threw himself with all the ardor of frustrated
ambition, soon took away the healthy color he had
brought with him from the provinces. His pallor did him
credit in the eyes of his companions, the young seminarists; he found them far less spiteful, less inclined to bow
down to money, than those in Besançon; they thought he
was consumptive. The marquis had given him a horse.
Fearing he might meet them during his rides, he had told
them that this exercise was prescribed by his doctor. The
Abbé Pirard had taken him to several Jansenist houses.
Julien was astonished; in his mind, the idea of religion was

invincibly linked with that of hypocrisy and the hope of making money. He admired these stern, pious men who gave no thought to the state budget. A number of Jansenists had taken a liking to him and would give him advice. A new world was opening up before him. Among the Jansenists, he made the acquaintance of a Count Altamira, who was almost six feet tall, a Liberal condemned to death in his own country, and a religious man. This strange contrast between piety and a love of liberty impressed Julien.

In the morning he would go riding; in the evening he went to the Jansenist houses. But while he was making himself known in several very commendable drawing rooms, his position at the Hôtel de La Mole deteriorated. There was coolness between him and the young count. Norbert considered that he had replied too sharply to some of his friends' bantering. Julien, furious over having committed a breach of etiquette once or twice, forbade himself ever to speak to Mlle. de La Mole first. Everyone in the Hôtel de La Mole was still perfectly polite, but he felt that he had fallen out of favor. His provincial good sense found an explanation for this state of affairs in the common proverb: "Familiarity breeds contempt."

Perhaps he was a bit more clear-sighted now than when he first arrived, or else his first enchantment with Parisian urbanity had worn off.

As soon as he stopped working, he was a prey to the deadliest boredom. This was the withering effect of the courtesy—so admirable, yet so measured, so carefully graduated according to social rank—that distinguishes high society. A heart the least bit sensitive must see how artificial it is.

One is no doubt justified in criticizing provincials for commonness or lack of polish; but they do show some warmth when they speak to you. Never at the Hôtel de La Mole was there any attempt to wound Julien's pride; and yet, at the end of the day, when he picked up his candle in the anteroom, he felt like weeping. In the provinces, a waiter will take an interest in you if you are the victim of some mishap as you enter his café; but if this accident is in any way damaging to your self-esteem, as he commiserates with you he will repeat ten times over the remark that makes you squirm. In Paris everyone takes care to laugh behind your back, but you are always the outsider.

We will pass over in silence the numerous small incidents that might have made Julien look ridiculous if he were not, so to speak, beneath ridicule. A crazy sensibility led him to commit a thousand blunders. All his pastimes were precautionary measures: he practiced firing a pistol every day; he was one of the good students of the most famous fencing masters. Whenever he had a moment to spare, instead of using it to read, as heretofore, he would rush off to the riding school and ask for the most vicious horses. On his outings with the riding master, he was almost invariably thrown to the ground.

The marquis thought of him as handy, because of his dogged labor, his silence, his intelligence, and little by little entrusted him with all his business matters that were rather difficult to clear up. In those moments when his lofty ambition left him some respite, the marquis conducted his affairs wisely: having the means to find out the latest news, he had good luck at the stock exchange; he bought houses and woods. But he was quick to take umbrage; he gave away hundreds of louis but would go to court over a few hundred francs. Rich men who are high-spirited look for amusement in business affairs, not results. The marquis needed a chief of staff who could put his finances in order and make them clear and easy to grasp.

Mme. de La Mole, though very reserved by nature, would sometimes make fun of Julien. The *unexpected*, arising from sensibility, is the aversion of great ladies; it is the antipode of good breeding. Two or three times the marquis stood up for him: "If he is ridiculous in your drawing room, he excels in my office." Julien, on the other hand, thought he had grasped the marquise's secret. She would condescend to take an interest in everything the minute the Baron de Joumate was announced. He was a cold fellow with an impassive expression. He was small, thin, ugly, very well dressed, spent all of his time at the Château, and usually had nothing to say about anything. That was how his mind worked. Mme. de La Mole would have been passionately happy, for the first time in her life, if she could have married him to her daughter.

Chapter VI

A Manner of Speaking

> Their great mission is to judge
> calmly the minor events in the daily
> life of nations. Their wisdom is sup-
> posed to forestall great anger over
> small causes, or over events that the
> voice of rumor transfigures as it car-
> ries them abroad.
>
> —GRATIUS

For a raw provincial who out of arrogance never asked
questions, Julien didn't make too big a fool of himself.
One morning, after he had been driven into a café on the
Rue Saint-Honoré by a sudden shower, a tall man in a
beaver frock coat, astonished at his gloomy look, stared
back at him in exactly the same way Mlle. Amanda's lover
had done some time ago in Besançon.

Julien had reproached himself too often with having let
that first insult go by to tolerate this look. He demanded
an explanation. The man in the frock coat forthwith
heaped him with the filthiest abuse; everyone in the café
gathered around; passersby stopped at the doorway. Out
of provincial wariness, Julien always carried a brace of
small pistols; his hands squeezed them convulsively in his
pockets. Yet he behaved reasonably and contented himself
with repeating to this man from one minute to the next:
"*Sir, your address? I despise you.*"

The persistence with which he stuck to these six words
eventually made an impression on the crowd.

"Why! the one who is doing all the talking is going to
have to give him his address." After hearing this decision
repeated several times, the man in the frock coat threw five

or six calling cards at Julien's face. Luckily none hit the mark; he had promised himself to use his pistols only if he was touched. The man went away, but not without turning around from time to time to threaten him with his fist and call him names.

Julien found that he was bathed in sweat. "So it is in the power of the lowest of men to rouse me to that point!" he told himself in a rage. "How am I to kill such a humiliating sensibility?"

He wished he could fight at once. But one thing stopped him. Where in all of vast Paris was he to find a second? He hadn't one friend. He had had several acquaintances; but all, unfailingly, at the end of six weeks of his company, had kept their distance. "I am unsociable, and now I'm being harshly punished for it," he thought. Finally, he had the idea of hunting up a former lieutenant of the 96th named Liévin, a poor devil with whom he used often to fence. Julien was frank with him.

"I'm willing to be your second," said Liévin, "but on one condition: if you don't wound your man, you will have a bout with me on the spot."

"Agreed," said Julien, shaking his hand enthusiastically, and they went to look up M. C. de Beauvoisis* at the address shown on his card, in the heart of the Faubourg Saint-Germain.

It was seven in the morning. Only after he had sent in his name did it occur to Julien that this might well be Mme. de Rênal's young relative, once employed in the embassy at Rome or Naples, who had given the singer Geronimo a letter of introduction.

Julien had handed a tall valet one of the cards flung at him the day before and one of his own. He was made to wait, with his second, three long quarters of an hour; finally they were shown into a wonderfully elegant suite. They found a tall young man dressed like a doll; his features displayed the perfection and the insignificance of the Greek ideal. His remarkably narrow head bore a pyramid of the most beautiful blond hair. It was curled with great care; not a single hair was out of place. "It was to have his hair curled like that," thought the lieutenant from the 96th, "that this damned fop made us wait." The striped dressing gown, the morning trousers, everything down to the embroidered slippers, was correct and marvelously tailored. Noble and empty, his countenance bespoke ideas that were both proper and few: the very type of well-bred man, with his horror of the unexpected and of a joke, and with a good deal of gravity.

Julien, to whom his lieutenant of the 96th had explained that to keep a man waiting so long, after having rudely flung his card at his face, was one insult the more, burst into M. de Beauvoisis' apartment. He meant to be insolent, but at the same time he wanted very much to show good form.

He was so impressed by M. de Beauvoisis' gentle manner, by his air at once studied, important, and self-satisfied, by the wonderful elegance of his surroundings, that in a twinkling of an eye he forgot all about being insolent. This was not his man of the day before. His astonishment was such upon meeting so distinguished a person, instead of the coarse creature he had run into at the café, that he could find nothing to say. He presented one of the cards that had been thrown at him.

"That is my name," said the man of fashion, in whom Julien's black outfit, at seven in the morning, inspired little respect, "but I don't understand, to what do I owe the honor. . . ."

His way of pronouncing these last words revived some of Julien's anger.

"I have come to fight with you, sir," and he explained the whole business in one breath. M. Charles de Beauvoisis, after careful consideration, rather approved the cut of Julien's black suit. "It's from Staub, obviously," he said to himself as he listened to him; "that vest is in good taste, those boots are fine; but then, a black suit at this hour of the morning! . . . It's probably to avoid being hit," thought the Chevalier de Beauvoisis.

As soon as he had reached this conclusion, he resumed his tone of perfect politeness and treated Julien almost as an equal. The colloquy was rather long; it was a ticklish business; but in the end Julien could not deny the evidence. The very well-bred young man standing before him had nothing in common with the crude individual who had insulted him the day before.

Julien felt an insuperable reluctance to leave. He dragged out his explanation. He noted the Chevalier de Beauvoisis' self-conceit; that is the name he had used in referring to himself, shocked because Julien had addressed him simply as "Monsieur."

Julien admired his gravity, compounded with a certain modest fatuousness, which never forsook him for an instant. He was astonished at his odd way of working his tongue as he pronounced his words. . . . But still, in all this there wasn't the slightest grounds for starting a quarrel with him.

The young diplomat very graciously offered to do battle with him, but the ex-lieutenant of the 96th, who had been sitting for an hour legs apart, hands on thighs, and arms akimbo, decided that his friend was not the sort to pick a trumped-up quarrel with a man because someone had stolen that man's calling cards.

Julien left in a foul temper. The Chevalier de Beauvoisis' carriage was waiting for him in the courtyard, in front of the steps; by chance, Julien looked up and recognized the driver as his man of the day before.

To see him, grab him by his great jacket, tumble him from his seat, work him over with his riding crop, was only a matter of seconds. Two lackeys came to their comrade's defense; Julien received several punches. At the same instant he cocked one of his small pistols and fired on them; they ran. It was all over in a minute.

The Chevalier de Beauvoisis came down the flight of stairs with the most amusing gravity, repeating in his pronunciation of a great lord: "What have we here? What have we here?" He was obviously very curious, but his diplomat's sense of his own importance would not allow him to show any greater interest. After he had learned what the trouble was, haughtiness still contended in his features with the slightly playful coolness that a diplomat's face should never be without.

The lieutenant of the 96th realized that M. de Beauvoisis wished to fight; the former also wished, diplomatically, to leave the advantage of the initiative to his friend. "This time," shouted the lieutenant, "there are grounds for a duel!"

"I rather think so," replied the diplomat.

"I've fired that rascal," he said to his footmen. "Someone else get up there." The carriage door was opened: the chevalier insisted that Julien and his second get in first. They went to pick up a friend of M. de Beauvoisis, who told them of a quiet spot. The conversation on the way was truly fine. There was nothing unusual about this ride except the diplomat in his dressing gown.

"Though very noble, these gentlemen," thought Julien, "are not boring like the people who come to dine at M. de La Mole's house. And I can see why," he added an instant later; "it's because they allow themselves to be indecent." There was talk about dancers to whom the public had given an ovation for a ballet performed the evening before. These gentlemen kept alluding to spicy anecdotes, about which Julien and his second, the lieutenant from the 96th, were totally ignorant. Julien was not so foolish as to pretend to be in the know; he admitted readily to his ignorance. The chevalier's friend liked his frankness; he told him the stories in the greatest detail, and very well.

One thing astonished Julien no end. A temporary altar, being built in the middle of the street for a Corpus Christi procession, held up the carriage for a short time. The gentlemen indulged themselves in witticisms; the parish priest, according to them, was the son of an archbishop. Never in the house of the Marquis de La Mole, who aspired to be a duke, would anyone have dared to make such a remark.

The duel was over in a minute: Julien had a bullet in his arm. It was bound with handkerchiefs drenched with brandy, and the Chevalier de Beauvoisis very politely urged Julien to allow him to drive him home in the carriage that had brought him. When Julien mentioned the Hôtel de La Mole, there was an exchange of glances between the young diplomat and his friend. Julien's cab was still there, but he found the gentlemen's conversation infinitely more entertaining than that of the good lieutenant from the 96th.

"My God! a duel, is that all there is to it?" thought Julien. "How lucky I was to find that coachman again! How miserable I would have been if I'd had to put up with still another insult in a café!" The amusing conversation had gone on almost uninterrupted. Julien realized then that diplomatic affectation is good for something.

"So boredom is not necessarily inherent," he told himself, "in a conversation between persons of high birth! These men joked about the Corpus Christi procession; they dare tell risqué stories, and in graphic detail. They lack absolutely nothing except sound arguments about politics, and that lack is more than compensated by their graceful tone and the perfect aptness of their expressions." Julien felt very much drawn to them. "How happy I should be to see them often!"

They had barely parted when the Chevalier de Beauvoisis rushed to gather information. It was not reassuring. He was most curious to know his man; could he decently pay him a visit? The little he did find out about him was not encouraging.

"It's perfectly awful!" he said to his second. "It's impossible for me to admit that I fought a duel with one of M. de La Mole's secretaries, and that because my coachman filched my calling cards."

"To be sure, the whole business may well leave you open to ridicule."

The same evening, the Chevalier de Beauvoisis and his friend spread the word that M. Sorel, an impeccable young man otherwise, was the natural son of a close friend of the Marquis de La Mole. This item was readily accepted. Once it was established, the young diplomat and his friend condescended to pay Julien a number of visits during the two weeks he was confined to his bedroom. Julien confessed that he had been to the opera only once in his life.

"Why, that's dreadful," they told him, "it's the only place to go. For your first outing, you must go see *Comte Ory*."*

At the opera, the Chevalier de Beauvoisis introduced him to the famous singer Geronimo, who was enjoying an immense success at the time.

Julien all but courted the chevalier; that mixture of self-respect, mysterious importance, and a young man's fatuousness delighted him. For example, the chevalier stuttered a little because he had the honor of seeing a great lord frequently who had this defect. Never had Julien found united in a single being a ridiculous side that is entertaining and a perfection of manner that a poor provincial ought to try to imitate.

He was seen at the opera with the Chevalier de Beauvoisis; this connection set people to talking about him.

"Well, well!" M. de La Mole said to him one day, "so you are the natural son of a rich nobleman in Franche-Comté, a close friend of mine?"

The marquis cut Julien short when he tried to protest that he had not helped in any way to give credence to that rumor: "M. de Beauvoisis doesn't like the idea of having fought with a carpenter's son."

"I know, I know," said M. de La Mole. "Now it is up to me to give substance to that story, which I fancy. But I have a favor to ask you, one that will cost you but a small half hour of your time: whenever there is a performance at the opera, go to the lobby at half past eleven and watch the exit of the fashionable world. I have observed from time to time that you still have some of your provincial ways; you must get rid of them. Besides, it's not a bad idea to know, at least by sight, the important persons to whom I may one day send you on a mission. Drop in at the box office and make yourself known; you have been given the run of the house."

Chapter VII

An Attack of Gout

> And I was promoted, not because
> I deserved to be but because my
> master had the gout.
>
> —BERTOLOTTI

The reader is perhaps surprised at the marquis' free and almost friendly tone; we forgot to say that he had been confined to his house for the past six weeks by an attack of gout.

Mlle. de La Mole and her mother were at Hyères,* visiting the marquise's mother. Count Norbert saw his father only for brief moments; they were on the best of terms but had nothing to say to one another. Reduced to Julien, M. de La Mole was astonished to find that he had ideas. He had him read the newspapers aloud. Before long the young secretary was capable of singling out the interesting passages. There was a new paper that the marquis abominated; he had sworn never to read it, but talked about it every day. Julien would laugh and marvel at the shabbiness of this duel between power and an idea. Such pettiness on the marquis' part restored all of Julien's self-possession, which he was near to losing as a result of spending his evenings tête-à-tête with so great a lord. The marquis, out of patience with the times, had him read Livy; the translation he improvised on the Latin text amused him.

One day the marquis said in that tone of excessive politeness which often put Julien out of patience: "Allow me, my dear Sorel, to make you a present of a blue suit: when it pleases you to put it on and visit me, in my eyes you will be the Count de Retz's younger brother; that is to say, my friend the old duke's son."

Julien didn't quite understand what it was all about; that same evening he tried a visit in the blue suit. The marquis treated him as an equal. Julien had the heart to recognize true courtesy, but he had no conception of nuances. He would have sworn, before the marquis' whim, that it was impossible to be received more considerately by him. "What a marvelous talent!" Julien said to himself. When he rose to leave, the marquis excused himself for not being able to see him to the door because of his gout.

One thought troubled Julien: "Could he be making fun of me?" He went to consult the Abbé Pirard, who, less polite than the marquis, answered him only by whistling and by talking about something else. The next morning Julien presented himself to the marquis in his black suit, with his portfolio and some letters to be signed. He was received in the old manner. That night, in the blue suit, he found the tone altogether different and absolutely as polite as on the previous evening.

"Since you are not too bored by the visits you are kind enough to pay a poor sick old man," the marquis said to him, "you ought to tell him about all the little incidents in your life, but do it frankly, with no aim in mind but to tell your story clearly and entertainingly. For man must have amusement; that is the only real thing in life. No man can save my life every day in battle, or make me a daily gift of a million; but if I had Rivarol* here beside my chaise longue, he would relieve me of an hour's suffering and boredom every day. I saw a good deal of him in Hamburg during the Emigration." The marquis told Julien Rivarol's anecdotes about the men of Hamburg, who always go about in fours so as to catch the meaning of a joke.

Reduced to the society of this little abbé, M. de La Mole was determined to liven him up. He put Julien's pride on its mettle. Since he had been asked for the truth, Julien resolved to tell all, keeping silence about two things only: his fanatic admiration for a name that always provoked the marquis' wrath, and his total skepticism, which was not very suitable in a future clergyman. His little duel with the Chevalier de Beauvoisis came in handy at this point. The marquis laughed till he cried over the scene in the café on the Rue Saint-Honoré, and the coachman's heaping him with filthy abuse. This was the stage of perfect frankness in the relation between master and protégé.

M. de La Mole took an interest in this strange character. In the beginning, he had played on the absurd side of Julien's nature for his own amusement. Before long he took a greater interest in very gently correcting the young man's false views. "Most provincials who come to Paris admire everything," thought the marquis. "This one detests everything. They are too full of affectation; he hasn't enough. And fools take him for a fool."

The attack of gout was prolonged by the extreme cold and lasted several months.

"One grows quite fond of a fine spaniel," the marquis said to himself. "Why am I so ashamed of becoming attached to this little abbé? He is original. I treat him like a son; well! what is wrong with that! This whim, if it lasts, will cost me a diamond worth five hundred louis in my will."

Once the marquis had realized the steadfastness of his protégé's character, he entrusted him with some new piece of business every day.

It sometimes happened, Julien observed to his terror, that this great lord would give him two contradictory decisions about the same matter. This could get him into serious trouble. From then on, Julien never set to work with the marquis without bringing in a register, in which he would record all the decisions, and the marquis would initial them. Julien hired a clerk to transcribe the decision relative to each transaction into another and private register. This register contained copies of all the letters as well.

At first this idea seemed the height of the ridiculous and of the tedious. But in less than two months the marquis saw its advantage. Julien proposed that he take on a clerk, who had worked for a banker to keep a double-entry account of all the receipts from and expenses of the estates that Julien supervised.

These measures so enlightened the marquis as to the state of his own affairs that he could afford the pleasure of embarking on two or three new speculations without the help of his broker who cheated him regularly.

"Take three thousand francs for yourself," he said one day to his young agent.

"Sir, my doing so could be misrepresented."

"What is it you want, then?" replied the marquis testily.

"Be so kind as to make out an authorization, if you please, and write it down in your own hand on the register; this authorization will give me a sum of three thousand francs. As a matter of fact, all this bookkeeping is the Abbé Pirard's idea." With the bored look of the Marquis de Moncade* when he is listening to the accounts of his intendant, M. Poisson, the marquis wrote out the authorization.

At night, when Julien appeared in the blue suit, business was never mentioned. The marquis' kindness was so flattering to our hero's ever-suffering ego that before long, in spite of himself, he felt a sort of fondness for the likable old man. Not that Julien was tenderhearted, as that word is understood in Paris; but neither was he a monster, and no one, since the death of the old surgeon major, had spoken to him so kindly. He remarked to his astonishment that the marquis had ways of sparing his pride by the most tactful courtesy, the like of which he had never met with in the old surgeon. He realized finally that the surgeon set greater store by his cross than the marquis did by his blue ribbon. The marquis' father had been a great lord.

One day, at the end of a morning session and dressed in his black outfit for business, Julien happened to amuse the marquis, who kept him for two hours and insisted on giving him some banknotes that his broker had just brought him from the stock exchange.

"I hope, my lord, that I will not be wanting in the profound respect I owe you, if I beg your permission to say a word."

"Speak, my friend."

"Will your Lordship please allow me to refuse this gift. It is not to the man in the black suit that it is addressed, and it would altogether spoil the manner you have been kind enough to tolerate in the man in blue." He bowed very respectfully and went out, not looking back.

This gesture diverted the marquis. He told the Abbé Pirard about it that evening.

"There is something I must confess to you at last, my dear Abbé. I know all about Julien's birth, and I authorize you not to keep this confidence a secret."

"His conduct this morning was noble," thought the marquis, "and I am going to ennoble him."

Some time later the marquis was at last able to go out. "Go and spend two months in London," he said to Julien. "Special couriers and other messengers will bring you the letters I receive, with my notations on them. You are to write out the replies and return the letters, each enclosed with its answer. According to my calculations, there will be no more than a five days' delay."

Flying posthaste over the road to Calais, Julien marveled at the futility of the so-called business on which he was being sent.

We will not say with what feeling of hatred and almost of horror he landed on English soil. The reader is acquainted with his wild passion for Bonaparte. In every officer he saw a Sir Hudson Lowe,* in every nobleman a Lord Bathurst,* ordering the infamous measures taken at Ste. Hélène, and for that, being rewarded with ten years in a ministry.

In London he was eventually introduced to high-class foppery. He made friends with some young Russian lords who initiated him.

"You are predestined, my dear Sorel," they told him. "That cold look of being *a thousand leagues away from the present stir*, which we try so hard to assume ourselves, comes naturally to you."

"You haven't understood the age," Prince Korasoff would tell him: "*always do the contrary of what is expected of you*. That, on my honor, is the only religion of our times. Be neither mad nor affected; otherwise, people will expect either madness or affectation from you, and you will not have lived up to the precept."

One day Julien covered himself with glory in the drawing room of the Duke of Fitz-Folke, who had invited him to dinner as well as Prince Korasoff. They had to wait an hour. The way Julien conducted himself in the midst of twenty persons who were also waiting is still cited by the young secretaries at the embassy in London. His expression was priceless.

He insisted, despite his friends the dandies' raillery, on visiting the renowned Philip Vane,* the only philosopher England has had since Locke. He was finishing his seventh year in prison. "The aristocracy is not to be trifled with in this country," thought Julien. "On top of that, Vane has been disgraced, run down, etcetera. . . ."

Julien found him perky; the aristocracy's wrath amused him. "There," Julien told himself as he left the prison, "is the only cheerful man I've met in England." "*For tyrants the most useful idea is that of God*," Vane told him. . . . We will dismiss the rest of his philosophy as being *cynical*.

Upon his return, M. de La Mole said to him: "What amusing idea do you bring me from England?" He remained silent. "What idea have you brought back, amusing or not, that reveals character?" the marquis went on sharply.

"Primo," said Julien, "the soundest Englishman is mad one hour a day; he is visited by the demon of suicide, who is the god of the country.

"Two, wit and genius lose twenty-five percent of their value upon disembarking in England.

"Three, nothing on earth is so lovely, wonderful, moving, as the English landscapes."

"Now it is my turn," said the marquis: "Primo, why did you go and say, at the Russian ambassador's ball, that in France there are three hundred thousand young men of twenty-five who desire war passionately? Do you suppose that kings are pleased to hear such talk?"

"It is hard to know what to say when you are talking to our great diplomats," said Julien. "They have a mania for starting serious discussions. If you stick to the commonplaces of the newspapers, you pass for a fool. If you make so bold as to say something true and original, they are astonished, at a loss for an answer, and they let you know, by the next morning at seven, through the first secretary of the embassy, that you have been improper."

"Not bad," said the marquis, laughing. "Apart from that, Mr. Deep Thinker, I'll wager that you haven't guessed why you went to England."

"I beg your pardon," replied Julien, "I went there to dine once a week with the king's ambassador, who is the politest of men."

"You went to get the cross you see here," the marquis told him. "I don't want to make you put off your black outfit, and I have grown used to the more amusing tone I take with the man in blue. Until further orders, mark this well: when I see this cross, you will be my friend the Duke de Retz's youngest son, who, unawares, has been in the employ of the diplomatic service for the past six months. Observe," added the marquis with a very serious air, and cutting short all of Julien's thanksgiving, "that I have no intention of changing your station in life. That is always a mistake, for the patron as for the protégé. When my lawsuits begin to bore you, or you no longer suit me, I will solicit a good parish for you, like the one our friend the Abbé Pirard has, and *nothing more*," added the marquis very coldly.

The cross set Julien's pride at ease; he talked a great deal more. He considered himself offended less often by, and less often the target of, remarks susceptible of an unflattering interpretation, which, in a lively conversation, might slip from anyone's tongue.

Julien was indebted to this cross for an unusual visit: one from the Baron de Valenod, who had come to Paris to thank the minister for his baronage and reach an understanding with him. He was to be appointed mayor of

Verrières as a replacement for M. de Rênal, after the latter's dismissal.

Julien had a good laugh to himself when M. Valenod informed him that it had just been discovered that M. de Rênal was a Jacobin. The truth of the matter was that, in the general election coming up for the Chamber of Deputies, the newly made baron was the minister's candidate, and in the department's electoral college, extremely Ultra, as a matter of fact, it was M. de Rênal who was being put forward by the Liberals.

Julien tried in vain to get news about Mme. de Rênal; the baron seemed to recall their old rivalry and was impenetrable. He ended by asking Julien for his father's vote in the forthcoming elections. Julien promised to write.

"You ought, Monsieur le Chevalier, to introduce me to the Marquis de La Mole."

"As a matter of fact, *I should,*" thought Julien, "but such a rascal! . . ."

"To tell the truth," he answered, "I don't carry enough weight in the Hôtel de La Mole to take it upon myself to make introductions."

Julien related all of this to the marquis; that evening he told him about Valenod's aspirations, as well as his sayings and doings since 1814.

"Not only," replied M. de La Mole in all seriousness, "will you introduce me to the new baron tomorrow, but I am also inviting him for dinner the day after. He will be one of our new prefects."

"In that case," Julien answered coolly, "I request the office of director of the workhouse for my father."

"Fair enough," said the marquis, resuming his gay manner. "Granted. I was expecting you to moralize. You are learning."

M. de Valenod informed Julien that the holder of the lottery office in Verrières had just died; Julien thought it would be a good joke to give this office to M. de Cholin, that old imbecile whose petition he had picked up a long time ago in M. de La Môle's bedroom. The marquis laughed heartily over the petition, which Julien recited as he gave him a letter to sign, asking the Minister of Finance for that position.

No sooner had M. de Cholin been appointed when Julien learned that this position had been requested by the delegation of the department in the name of M. Gros, the well-known geometrician: that generous man's income amounted to no more than fourteen hundred francs, and every year he had loaned six hundred to the incumbent, who had just died, to help him raise his family.

Julien was dismayed at what he had done. "How will the dead man's family get along now?" The thought wrung his heart. "This is nothing," he told himself. "I will have to commit far worse injustices if I mean to get ahead, and what's more, learn to cover them up with fine, sentimental speeches: poor M. Gros! It is he who deserves the cross; it is I who have it, and it is my duty to act in conformity with the Government that gave it to me."

Chapter VIII

Which Decoration Confers
True Distinction?

> "Your water does not refresh
> me," said the thirsting genie. "And
> yet this is the coolest well in all
> Diar Bekir."
>
> —PELLICO

One day Julien was just returning from the lovely estate
of Villequier, on the banks of the Seine, in which M. de
La Mole took a special interest because, of all his properties, it alone had belonged to the renowned Boniface de
La Mole. In the house he found the marquise and her
daughter, just back from Hyères.

Julien was a dandy now, and understood the art of
living in Paris. His coolness toward Mlle. de La Mole was
perfect. He appeared not to have any recollection of the
time when she had asked him so gaily for details about his
way of falling gracefully off a horse.

Mlle. de La Mole found him taller and paler. His
bearing, his dress, had nothing provincial about them now;
the same did not hold for his conversation. People remarked that it was still too serious, too positive. But in
spite of its reasonableness, thanks to his pride, there was
nothing subservient about it; people felt simply that he
still regarded too many things as important. But they
could see that he was a man to stand back of what he said.

"He wants levity but not wit," said Mlle. de La Mole to
her father, while chaffing him about the cross he had
given Julien. "My brother has been asking for one for the
last eighteen months, and he is a La Mole! . . ."

"Yes, but Julien offers the unexpected; this has never been the case of the La Mole in question."

The Duke de Retz was announced. Mathilde felt an irresistible urge to yawn; the sight of him reminded her of the old-fashioned gilding and the old habitués of the paternal drawing room. She pictured to herself the absolutely boring life she was about to take up again in Paris. And yet at Hyères she longed for Paris. "Here I am nineteen years old!" she thought. "That is supposed to be the age of happiness, according to all those boobies in their gilt-edged tomes." She looked over the eight or ten volumes of new poetry that had piled up on the drawing-room console during her visit in Provence. It was her misfortune to be more intelligent than MM. de Croisenois, de Caylus, de Luz, and her other gentlemen friends. She could imagine everything they would say to her about the beauty of Provencal skies, poetry, the South, etc.

Those beautiful eyes, in which the most profound boredom was visible, and worse yet, despair of finding pleasure anywhere, came to rest on Julien. He, at least, was not exactly like all the others.

"Monsieur Sorel," she asked in a sharp, curt voice that had nothing feminine about it and which is affected by young women of the upper class, "Monsieur Sorel, are you going to M. de Retz's ball tonight?"

"Mademoiselle, I have not had the honor of being introduced to the duke." (One might have thought those words and that title stuck in the arrogant provincial's throat.)

"He has enjoined my brother to bring you to his house, and if you go, you can tell me something about the estate at Villequier; there is some talk of going there in the spring. I should like to know if the château is habitable, and if the countryside is as pretty as they say. There are so many usurped reputations!"

Julien did not answer.

"Come to the ball with my brother," she snapped out.

Julien bowed respectfully. "So even in the midst of a ball I have to account to every member of the family," he thought. "But aren't they paying me to be a businessman?" His bad humor added: "God only knows if what I tell the daughter won't run counter to the father's plans, or the brother's, or the mother's! It's a regular sovereign prince's court. You are expected to conduct yourself like a perfect nonentity, yet never give anyone cause for complaint.

"How I dislike that tall girl!" he thought as he watched

286

Mlle. de La Mole walk away; her mother had called her over to introduce her to several women friends. "She overdoes all the fashions; her dress is falling off her shoulders. ... She is even paler than she was before her trip. ... Her hair is so blond, it's colorless! You might say the light shines through it. Such a haughty way of greeting people, of looking at them! Such queenly airs!"

Mlle. de La Mole had called to her brother just as he was leaving the drawing room. Count Norbert came over to Julien. "My dear Sorel," he said to him, "where would you like me to pick you up at midnight for M. de Retz's ball? He gave me strict orders to bring you along."

"I know very well to whom I am obliged for so much kindness," answered Julien, bowing to the ground.

His bad humor, unable to find any fault in the tone of politeness, even interest, with which Norbert had addressed him, set to mulling over the answer he, Julien, had made to this civil speech. He detected a shade of servility in it.

That night, when he arrived for the ball, he was impressed by the magnificence of the Hôtel de Retz. The front courtyard was covered by a huge awning made of crimson twill spangled with gold stars: nothing could be more elegant. Beneath this awning, the courtyard had been transformed into a grove of orange trees and oleanders in flower. Since care had been taken to bury the tubs sufficiently, the oleanders and orange trees looked as if they were growing in the ground. The drive over which the carriages rolled had been graveled.

To our provincial, the general effect seemed extraordinary. He had no conception of such magnificence; in an instant his excited imagination carried him a thousand leagues away from his bad mood. In the carriage, on the way to the ball, Norbert had been happy, and could see that Julien was in the dumps; they were barely in the courtyard when their roles changed.

Norbert was not interested in anything but a few details, which, in the midst of so much magnificence, had been somewhat neglected. He estimated the cost of each item, and as he worked toward a high figure, Julien observed that he seemed to grow annoyed and almost jealous.

As for Julien, he came fascinated, admiring, and almost shy with excitement to the first of the drawing rooms, where there was dancing. They pressed on toward the door of the second, but the crowd was so big that it was impossible to advance. This second drawing room was decorated to represent the Alhambra at Granada.

"She's queen of the ball, you must agree," said a young man wearing mustaches, whose shoulder was thrust into Julien's chest.

"Mlle. Fourmont, who was the prettiest girl all winter," his neighbor replied, "is aware that she has dropped to second place: see that odd look on her face."

"Really, she's setting all sails to make herself attractive. Look, look at that gracious smile she puts on the minute she's dancing by herself in the quadrille. On my honor, it's priceless!"

"Mlle. de La Mole looks as if she were mistress of the pleasure she takes in her triumph, of which she is well aware. You'd say she's afraid that any man who speaks to her might find her appealing."

"Excellent! There's the art of seduction for you."

Julien tried in vain to catch sight of that alluring woman; seven or eight taller men blocked his view.

"There is a good deal of coquetry in that noble reserve," said the young man wearing the mustaches.

"And those big blue eyes that look down ever so slowly the moment you think they are on the point of giving themselves away," his neighbor added. "My faith, that's as clever as can be."

"See how common the beautiful Fourmont looks beside her," said a third.

"That air of reserve seems to say: 'What great kindness I would show you, if you were the man worthy of me!'"

"And who could be worthy of the sublime Mathilde?" said the first man. "Some ruling prince, handsome, witty, well built, a war hero, and twenty years old at the most."

"The emperor of Russia's natural son ... for whom a sovereign state would be created in honor of this marriage; or simply the Count de Thaler, with his look of a dressed-up peasant. ..."

The doorway was clear now; Julien was free to go through it.

"Since all these stuffed dolls think she is so remarkable, it is worth my while to study her," he thought. "I will find out what those people mean by perfection."

As he stood looking around the room for her, he met Mathilde's gaze. "Duty calls," Julien told himself, but all his irritation was gone, except from his expression. Curiosity urged him forward with a pleasure that Mathilde's dress, cut very low on the shoulders, very quickly heightened in a manner that was not, to tell the truth, flattering to his ego. "Her beauty is young and fresh," he thought. Five or six young men, among whom Julien recognized those he had overheard in the doorway, stood between her and him.

"You, sir, who have been here all winter," she said to him, "isn't it true that this is the prettiest ball of the season?"

He made no answer.

"That quadrille by Coulon strikes me as admirable, and those ladies dance it to perfection."

The young men turned around to see who was the lucky fellow from whom she insisted upon having an answer. It was not an encouraging one.

"I am no judge of that, mademoiselle; I spend all my time writing; this is the first time I have ever seen such a magnificent ball."

The young men with mustaches were scandalized.

"You are a sage, Monsieur Sorel," she replied with a more pointed interest. "You view all of these balls, these entertainments philosophically, like J. J. Rousseau. Such follies astonish without delighting you."

One word had just dampened Julien's imaginings and driven every illusion from his heart. His mouth assumed an expression of disdain, a bit exaggerated, perhaps.

"In my opinion," he answered, "J. J. Rousseau is a fool when he takes it upon himself to judge high society; he didn't understand it, and he brought to it the heart of an upstart lackey."

"He wrote the *Contrat Social*," said Mathilde in a tone of veneration.

"And though he preached a republican form of government and the overthrow of the monarchy, that upstart was drunk with happiness when a duke changed the direction of his after-dinner stroll to accompany one of his friends."

"Ah! yes, the Duke de Luxembourg at Montmorency accompanied a M. Coindet in the direction of Paris. . . ."* replied Mlle. de La Mole with the pleasure and abandon of a first delight in pedantry. She was intoxicated with her learning, much like the academician who discovered the existence of King Feretrius.* Julien's gaze remained piercing and stern. Mathilde had had a moment of enthusiasm; her partner's coldness disconcerted her profoundly. She was all the more surprised since it was she who was used to producing this effect in others.

At that instant the Marquis de Croisenois was making his way eagerly toward Mlle. de La Mole. He halted for a moment ten feet away, unable to reach her because of the crowd. Smiling about the obstacle, he stood gazing at her. The young Marquise de Rouvray was standing beside him; she was Mathilde's cousin. She gave her arm to her husband of two weeks. The Marquis de Rouvray, likewise very young, was full of the foolish kind of love that overtakes a man who, having made a marriage of convenience arranged exclusively by notaries, discoveres that his wife is perfectly beautiful. M. de Rouvray was to become duke upon the death of a very old uncle.

While the Marquis de Croisenois, unable to penetrate the crowd, stood gazing at Mathilde with a smile on his face, her big sky-blue eyes came to bear upon him and his neighbors. "What could be duller," she remarked to herself, "than that whole bunch! There's Croisenois, who is hoping to marry me; he is kind, elegant, and has perfect manners, like M. de Rouvray. If they weren't such bores, those gentlemen would be quite likable. He too will follow me to the ball with the same fatuous look. A year after our marriage, my coach, my horses, my wardrobe, my château twenty leagues from Paris, will all be the best possible, precisely what it takes to make a parvenu like the Countess de Roiville, for example, turn green with envy; and afterward . . .?"

Mathilde was boring herself in advance. The Marquis de Croisenois had managed to reach her and was talking, but she went on musing without listening to him. The sound of his words mingled in her ear with the hum of the ball. Unconsciously she was following Julien with her eyes; he respectfully but with a proud and malcontent air had moved away. In a corner, far from the circulating crowd, she caught sight of Count Altamira, a man condemned to death in his own country, and with whom the reader is already acquainted. Under Louis XIV one of his family had married a Prince de Conti; that historical association gave him some protection from the *Congrégation's* police.

"I see that the death sentence alone confers distinction on a man; it's the only thing that can't be bought.

"Ah! I've just made an epigram! Pity it didn't come when I could have got some credit for it!" Mathilde had too much taste to bring a ready-made witticism into the conversation, but she was also too vain not to be delighted with herself. An air of happiness replaced her bored expression. The Marquis de Croisenois, who was still talking to her, thought he had glimpsed success and waxed twice as eloquent.

"What is there about my epigram that any ill-disposed

person might object to?" Mathilde asked herself. "I should answer the critic: the title of baron, of viscount, can be bought. A cross? It can be had for the asking. My brother just got one; what has he done? A commission is easily come by. Ten years in a garrison, or a Minister of War in the family, and you are a major, like Norbert. A great fortune! ... It is still the hardest thing to achieve, and consequently the most commendable. Funny! That is the opposite of everything the books say. ... Very well, as for a fortune, you may marry M. Rothschild's daughter.

"Really, my observation has depth to it. A death sentence is still the only thing no one has thought of soliciting."

"Do you know Count Altamira?" she asked M. de Croisenois.

She had a look of returning from so far away, and her question bore so little relevance to anything the poor marquis had been saying to her for the past five minutes, that this affable man was disconcerted. Yet he had great presence of mind and was, in fact, noted for it.

"Mathilde is odd," he thought; "that is a nuisance, but she could give her husband such a fine social position! I don't know how that Marquis de La Mole does it; he has close friends among the best men in all the parties of every persuasion; he's a man who can't fail. And besides, this oddness in Mathilde could be taken for genius. When high birth and a huge fortune go with it, genius is not at all ridiculous; it is, in fact, a great distinction! What's more, she knows so well, when she pleases, how to show that mixture of wit, character, and aptness that adds up to perfect civility. ..." Since it is difficult to do two things well at the same time, to think and to reply, the marquis answered Mathilde with a blank look, and as though reciting a lesson. "Who doesn't know poor Altamira?" And he told her the ridiculous, the absurd story of his botched conspiracy.

"Absurd indeed!" said Mathilde, as though talking to herself, "yet he acted. I want to see a man; bring him to me," she said to the deeply shocked marquis.

Count Altamira was one of the most outspoken admirers of the haughty and almost impertinent Mlle. de La Mole; she was, according to him, one of the most beautiful women in Paris.

"How lovely she would be on a throne!" he said to M. de Croisenois; and he let himself be led away without any further ado.

The world is not wanting in people who would like to

establish the idea that nothing is in worst taste than a conspiracy; it smells of Jacobinism. And what is more unseemly than an unsuccessful Jacobin?

The glances Mathilde exchanged with M. de Croisenois mocked at Altamira's liberalism, but she enjoyed listening to the man.

"A conspirator at the ball, what a pretty contrast," she thought. In her opinion this one, with his black mustache, had the air of a lion in repose; but she soon found out that he had but one attitude of mind: *the utilitarian, an admiration for the useful.*

Except whoever might help to give his country a bicameral government, the young count considered that no one was worthy of his attention. He left Mathilde, the most fascinating woman at the ball, with pleasure, because he had seen a Peruvian general come in.

Despairing of Europe, poor Altamira had been reduced to the hope that when the nations of South America became strong and powerful, they might restore to Europe the liberty Mirabeau had sent them.*

A whirlwind of mustached young men had advanced on Mathilde. She saw clearly enough that Altamira had not been charmed, and was piqued over his departure; she saw his black eyes shining as he spoke to the Peruvian general. Mlle. de La Mole surveyed the young Frenchmen with that deep seriousness which none of her rivals could imitate. "Who among them," she was thinking, "is capable of getting himself condemned to death, even supposing that all the odds are in his favor?"

Her peculiar look flattered those who were not very bright but made the others uneasy. They dreaded the explosion of some sharp remark that would be hard to answer.

"High birth bestows a hundred qualities the absence of which is offensive to me; Julien is a case in point," she thought. "But it atrophies those qualities of the heart which cause a man to be condemned to death."

At the same time someone nearby was saying, "That Count Altamira is the second son of the Prince of San Nazaro-Pimentel; it was a Pimentel who tried to save Conradin, beheaded in 1268. Theirs is one of the noblest families in Naples."

"There," said Mathilde to herself, "that proves my maxim very nicely: high birth robs a man of that strength of character without which he can never get himself condemned to death. So I am fated to talk nonsense tonight. Since I'm only a woman, like any other, well! I'd better dance." She gave in to the entreaties of the Marquis de Croisenois, who for the last hour had been begging for a gallopade. To take her mind off her unlucky venture into philosophy, Mathilde chose to be perfectly charming; M. de Croisenois was entranced.

But neither the dance, nor the desire to please one of the handsomest men at court, nor anything else could divert Mathilde. It was impossible to be more popular. She was queen of the ball, which fact she took in coldly.

"What a dull life I shall lead with a fellow like Croisenois!" she said to herself as he led her back to her place an hour later. "Where lies pleasure," she went on sadly, "if, after an absence of six months, I cannot find it in the midst of a ball that is the envy of every woman in Paris? What is more, I am complimented on every side by a society that couldn't be better. None of the middle class is here, excepting a few peers, and one or two Juliens, perhaps. Then too," she added with growing sadness, "what blessings has fate not bestowed upon me: an illustrious name, wealth, youth, everything, alas, but happiness.

"The most dubious of my advantages are precisely those which everyone has been pointing out to me all evening. Wit: I believe them, for it is obvious that they are all afraid of me. If they dare to broach a serious subject with me, at the end of five minutes' conversation I see them, all out of breath and as if making a great discovery, arrive at the conclusion I have been repeating to them for the past hour. I am beautiful: I have that advantage for which Mme. de Staël* would have sacrificed everything, and yet I'm dying of boredom. Is there any reason why I should be less bored if I changed my name for that of the Marquis de Croisenois?

"But, my God!" she added, close to tears, "isn't he a perfect man? He is the masterpiece of the education of this age; you can't look at him but he finds something nice, and even witty, to say to you; he is brave. ... But that Sorel is different," she said to herself, and her eyes put off their sad look for an angry one. "I told him I wanted to talk with him, and he hasn't even bothered to come back."

Chapter IX

The Ball

> The richness of the women's
> dress, the blaze of candlelight, the
> perfumes; so many pretty arms,
> lovely shoulders; bouquets, Ros-
> sini's arias that sweep you away,
> paintings by Ciceri! My senses reel!
> —*Voyages d'Uzeri*

"You are out of sorts," the Marquise de La Mole said to her. "I warn you, that's unbecoming at a ball."

"It's nothing but a headache," answered Mathilde disdainfully. "It's too warm in here."

At that moment, as though to justify Mlle. de La Mole, the old Baron de Tolly fell down in a faint; he had to be carried out. There was talk of apoplexy; it was an unpleasant incident.

Mathilde ignored it. It was a rule with her never to pay any attention to old men, or anyone else known for gloomy observations.

She danced to avoid conversation about the stroke, which was not one, since the baron reappeared two days later.

"M. Sorel hasn't come back," she told herself after she had danced. She was all but hunting with her eyes when she caught sight of him in another drawing room. An astonishing thing, he seemed to have lost that air of cold impassiveness which was so natural to him; he no longer looked English.

"He's chatting with Count Altamira, my condemned man!" Mathilde said to herself. "His eyes are filled with a dark fire; he has the look of a prince in disguise; his gaze is twice as arrogant."

Still talking with Altamira, Julien was drawing near the spot where she stood; she was watching him intently, studying his features in search of those high virtues that make a man worthy of the honor of being condemned to death.

As he was passing close by her, he said to Count Altamira, "Yes, Danton* was a man!"

"O heavens! could he be another Danton?" Mathilde asked herself. "But he has such a noble face, and Danton was so horribly ugly, a butcher, I think." Julien was still fairly close to her; she did not hesitate to call him. She took a conscious pride in asking a question that was quite out of the ordinary for a girl.

"Wasn't Danton a butcher?" she asked him.

"Yes, in the opinion of some," Julien answered with an expression of the most ill-disguised contempt and an eye still ablaze from his conversation with Altamira, "but unfortunately for the wellborn, he was a lawyer in Méry-sur-Seine; that is to say, mademoiselle," he added with a wicked look, "he began like several of the peers I see here. It is true that Danton had one enormous drawback in the eyes of beautiful women; he was extremely ugly."

These last words were spoken rapidly, with an extraordinary and assuredly far from polite air. Julien waited an instant, his torso slightly inclined, his air proudly humble. He seemed to be saying: "I am paid to answer you, and I live on my pay." He did not bother to look at Mathilde directly. She, with her beautiful eyes opened extraordinarily wide and fixed on him, seemed his slave. Eventually, since the silence persisted, he looked up at her as a valet looks to his master, ready to take orders. Although his eyes fully met Mathilde's gaze, still fixed on him in a strange way, he retired with marked eagerness.

"To think that he, who is so genuinely handsome," Mathilde said to herself, coming at length out of her reverie, "would make such a eulogy of ugliness! He's not always thinking of what he's going to say! He is not like Caylus or Croisenois. Sorel has something of that air my father imitates so well when he goes to a ball dressed as Napoleon." She had forgotten all about Danton. "Tonight I'm definitely bored." She seized her brother's arm, and to his great annoyance, forced him to make a tour of the ball. The idea had crossed her mind of following the condemned man's conversation with Julien.

The crowd was huge. She managed, nevertheless, to

rejoin them at the moment when, six feet in front of her, Altamira was going over to a tray for an ice. He was speaking to Julien, his body half turned. He saw an embroidered coat sleeve beside his own also taking an ice. The embroidery seemed to attract his attention; he turned around completely to see the notable to whom the arm belonged. At that instant his black eyes, so noble and guileless, took on a slightly contemptuous expression.

"See that man," he said to Julien in a low voice, "that's Prince d'Araceli, the Ambassador of ——. This morning he asked your Minister of Foreign Affairs, M. de Nerval, for my extradition. Look, there he is over there, playing whist. M. de Nerval is inclined to give me up, since we turned two or three conspirators over to you in 1816. If they send me back to my king, I will be hanged in twenty-four hours. And it will be one of those fine gentlemen with mustaches who will '*make the pinch.*' "

"Infamous!" cried Julien half aloud.

Mathilde didn't miss a syllable of their conversation. Her boredom had vanished.

"Not so infamous," replied Count Altamira. "I told you about myself simply to give you a living example. Watch Prince Araceli; every five minutes he takes a look at his Golden Fleece; he can't get over the pleasure of seeing that trinket on his chest. Poor man, he's nothing but an anachronism. A hundred years ago the Fleece was a signal honor, but then it would have been far out of his reach. Today, among the high-born, you have to be an Araceli to delight in it. He would have hanged a whole town to get it."

"Is that the price he paid?" said Julien anxiously.

"Not exactly," Altamira answered coldly. "He probably had some thirty of the rich landowners in his district, thought to be Liberals, thrown into the river."

"What a monster!" said Julien.

Mlle. de La Mole, leaning toward him out of the most vivid interest, was so close that her beautiful hair almost touched his shoulder.

"You are very young!" replied Altamira. "I was telling you that I have a married sister in Provence; she is still pretty, kind, and gentle; she is an excellent mother, faithful to all her duties, pious yet not sanctimonious."

"What is he driving at?" thought Mlle. de La Mole.

"She is happy now," Count Altamira went on; "she was in 1815. At that time I was hiding in her house, on her estate near Antibes; well, the moment she heard about the execution of Marshal Ney, she started dancing!"

"Is it possible?" said Julien, bowled over.

"That's party spirit for you," replied Altamira. "There are no genuine passions left in the nineteenth century; that is why everyone is so bored in France. People commit the greatest cruelties without cruelty."

"So much the worse!" said Julien. "When they commit a crime they should at least enjoy doing it: that's the only good in crime, and they can't justify themselves even on those grounds."

Forgetting entirely who she was, Mlle. de La Mole was now standing almost directly between Altamira and Julien. Accustomed to obeying her, her brother, upon whose arm she was leaning, was looking elsewhere in the room, and to keep himself in countenance, pretended to have been stopped by the crowd.

"You're right," said Altamira. "Every act is performed without pleasure and without recollection, even crimes. I can show you ten men, perhaps, at this ball who will be damned as murderers. They have forgotten what they are, and so has everyone else.*

"Some of them are moved to tears if their dog breaks a paw. At Père-Lachaise, when their tombs are flowered, as you Parisians put it so quaintly, we are informed that they embodied all the virtues of the valiant knights, and we are told about the great deeds of their ancestors who lived under Henry IV. If, despite the good offices of Prince d'Araceli, I am not hanged, and if ever I am permitted to enjoy my fortune in Paris, I mean to have you to dinner with eight or ten honored and remorseless murderers.

"At this dinner you and I alone will be innocent of bloodshed, yet I will be looked down upon and well-nigh hated as a Jacobin and a bloody monster, whereas you will simply be scorned as a man of the people intruding on well-bred company."

"Nothing could be truer," said Mlle. de La Mole. Altamira stared at her in astonishment; Julien didn't bother to look.

"Note that the revolution at the head of which I happened to be," Count Altamira went on, "did not succeed, solely because I was unwilling to have three heads cut off or distribute to our partisans the seven or eight millions kept in a chest to which I had the key. My king, who today is burning to have me hanged, and who, before the rebellion, was on intimate terms with me, would have given me the great sash of his order, had I cut off those three heads and distributed the money in that chest, for then I should have won a partial victory at least and my

297

country would have had some sort of charter. .... So goes the world; it's a game of chess."

"At that time," replied Julien, his eyes ablaze, "you didn't know the rules; now——"

"I would cut off heads, you mean, and I would not be a Girondist,* as you explained that word to me the other day? ... I will answer you," said Altamira sadly, "when you have killed a man in a duel, which is not nearly so vile a thing as having him executed by a headsman."

"My faith!" said Julien, "the end implies the means; if, instead of being an atom, I had some power, I would have three men hanged to save the lives of four."

His eyes were blazing with a sense of outrage and a contempt for the vain judgments of men; they met Mlle. de La Mole's gaze. She was standing very close to him, yet his contempt, far from changing into a gracious and civil look, seemed to increase.

She was deeply offended, but it was no longer in her power to forget Julien; she walked away resentfully, with her brother in tow.

"I must drink some punch and dance a lot," she told herself. "I mean to pick out the best man to be had here and attract attention at any price. Good, there's that Count de Fervaques, famous for his cheek." She accepted his invitation; they danced. "It's a question of seeing who can be the more impertinent, but if I'm to make a complete fool of him, I will have to make him talk." Soon the other couples in the quadrille were making a mere show of dancing. Nobody wanted to miss any of Mathilde's stinging repartees. M. de Fervaques was getting flustered, and finding nothing to hand but elegant remarks, instead of ideas, began to simper. Mathilde, in a bad mood, was cruel and made an enemy of him. She danced until dawn and went home at last horribly tired. But in the carriage, she used the little strength she had left to make herself even more miserable. She had been scorned by Julien and could not scorn him in return.

Julien was at the peak of happiness. Unawares, he had been enchanted by the music, the flowers, the beautiful women, the general elegance, and, more than anything, by his own imagination, which was filled with dreams of glory for himself and liberty for all.

"What a fine ball!" he said to the count, "nothing is lacking."

"Thought was lacking," replied Altamira.

And his countenance betrayed a contempt that was all

the more stinging since it was plain that courtesy had imposed the obligation of hiding it.

"You are here, Count. Doesn't that make thought present, and conspiring as well?"

"I am here because of my name. But thought is abhorred in your drawing rooms. It must never rise above the level of a vaudeville couplet; then it is rewarded. As for the man who thinks, if there is energy and novelty in his sallies, you call him a *cynic*. Isn't that the name one of your judges gave Courier?* You put him in prison, just as you did Béranger. If any man among you shows his superiority, by virtue of wit, the *Congrégation* drags him off to the police court and well-bred society applauds.

"That is because your antiquated society prizes conformity above everything else. . . . It can never rise above military courage; you will have your Murats* but never a Washington. I see nothing in France but vanity. The man who finds his ideas as he is speaking may very well happen to make an ill-advised remark, but if he does, the master of the house considers himself disgraced."

At these words the count's carriage, taking Julien home, stopped before the Hôtel de La Mole. Julien was in love with his conspirator. Altamira had paid him this fine compliment, which obviously sprang from a deep conviction: "You do not have the Frenchman's levity, and you do understand the principle of utility." Now, it so happened that, just two days before Julien had seen *Marino Faliero,* the tragedy by Casimir Delavigne.

"Hasn't Israel Bertuccio, an ordinary carpenter in a dockyard, more character than all those Venetian nobles?" our plebeian rebel asked himself. "And yet they are men whose proven lineage dates from the year 700, a century before Charlemagne; whereas the very best titles at M. de Retz's ball tonight go back no further than the thirteenth century, and not in a straight line by any means. Very well! in the midst of those noble Venetians, so mighty in name but so effete in character, it is Israel Bertuccio whom one remembers.

"A conspiracy wipes out all the titles conferred by a society's whim. At the very outset of one, a man takes the rank assigned to him by his way of facing death. Intelligence itself loses some of its authority. . . .

"What would Danton be today, in the age of Valenods and Rênals? Not even deputy to the king's prosecutor. . . .

"What am I saying? He would have sold himself to the *Congrégation*; he would be a minister. For after all, the great Danton was a thief. Mirabeau sold himself too.

299

Napoleon stole millions in Italy, and if he hadn't, he would have been cut down by poverty, like Pichegru.* LaFayette alone never stole. Must a man steal, must he sell himself?" Julien wondered. This question stopped him short. He spent the rest of the night reading the history of the Revolution.

The next day, while he was copying letters in the library, he still could think of nothing but his conversation with Count Altamira. "It's a fact," he told himself, after a long reverie, "if those liberal Spaniards really had compromised the people with a few crimes, they could not have been swept out so easily. They were arrogant, prattling children ... like me!" Julien cried all of a sudden, as if wakening with a start.

"What difficult thing have I ever done that gives me a right to judge those poor devils? After all, for once in their lives they dared, they began to act. I am like the man who, as he leaves the table, declares: 'Tomorrow I will not dine, but that will not stop me in the least from feeling just as strong and cheerful as I do today.' Who knows what a man feels when he has gone half the way toward a great deed? For after all, such things are not done in quite the same way you fire a pistol. . . ."

These lofty thoughts were troubled by the unexpected arrival of Mlle. de La Mole, who entered the library. He was so stirred by his admiration for the great virtues of Danton, Mirabeau, Carnot, men who knew how to avoid defeat, that he stared at Mlle. de La Mole without reacting to her, without greeting her, almost without seeing her. When his big eyes opened so wide finally registered her presence, his look grew dull. Mlle. de La Mole noted this bitterly.

To no avail, she asked him for a volume of Vély's *Histoire de France*, perched on the highest shelf, which obliged Julien to go and fetch the taller of two ladders. After Julien had brought the ladder, found the volume, and handed it to her, he was still incapable of paying her any attention. While putting the ladder back, absorbed as he was, he poked one of the glass doors in front of the shelves with his elbow. Splinters crashing to the floor finally roused him. He hastened to apologize to Mlle. de La Mole. He tried to be polite but was no more than that. It was obvious to Mathilde that she had disturbed him, and that he would rather go on thinking about whatever had been on his mind before she came in than talk to her. After having looked at him intently, she went slowly away.

Julien watched her walk. He enjoyed the contrast between the simplicity of her present dress and the magnificent elegance of the one she had been wearing the night before. The difference in her expression was almost as striking. So haughty at the Duke de Retz's ball, this girl wore, at the moment, an almost supplicating look.

"Really," Julien remarked to himself, "that black gown shows off her beautiful figure even better. She carries herself like a queen, but why is she in mourning? If I ask someone the reason for it, I may well commit another blunder." By now Julien had emerged completely from the depths of his enthusiasm. "I will have to reread all the letters I wrote this morning; God knows how many skipped words and stupid mistakes I will find in them." While he was rereading the first of these letters with forced attention, he heard the rustle of a silk dress close by him; he turned around quickly. Mlle. de La Mole was two feet from his table; she was laughing. This second interruption angered Julien.

As for Mathilde, she had just become keenly aware that she meant nothing to this young man; the laugh was an attempt to hide her embarrassment. She succeeded.

"Evidently you have something very interesting on your mind, Monsieur Sorel. Could it be some curious anecdote about the conspiracy that brought Count Altamira to us in Paris? Tell me what it's all about; I'm dying to know. I won't repeat it; I swear." She was astonished at this remark on hearing herself utter it. What! she was pleading with an inferior! Her embarrassment increased; she added in a trifling tone: "What could have turned you, ordinarily so cold, into an inspired individual, into a sort of prophet à la Michelangelo?"

This sharp and prying question, offending Julien deeply, roused all of the wildness in his nature. "Was Danton right to steal?" he asked abruptly, with a look that grew more and more savage. "Ought the revolutionaries of Piedmont, of Spain, to have compromised the people by crimes? have given all the commissions in the army, all the crosses, to undeserving men? Wouldn't the men wearing those crosses have dreaded the king's return? Should the treasury of Turin have been looted? In a word, mademoiselle," he said, advancing toward her with a terrible look in his eye, "oughtn't the man who would drive ignorance and crime from the earth, oughtn't he to move like the whirlwind and do evil as if by chance?"

Mathilde was frightened, could not bear his gaze, and shrank back a little. She looked at him for an instant; then, ashamed of her fear, walked out of the library with a light step.

Chapter X

Queen Marguerite

Love! in what madness do you not
contrive to make us find pleasure.
—*Letters of a Portuguese Nun*

Julien reread his letters. When the bell rang for dinner,
he told himself: "How ridiculous I must have looked to
that Parisian doll! How crazy I was to tell her what I was
really thinking! But maybe not so crazy after all. The
truth on that occasion was worthy of me.

"But why come and question me about personal matters! It was tactless of her. She showed a lack of breeding.
My ideas about Danton are not part of the service for
which her father is paying me."

Upon entering the dining room, Julien was distracted
from his bad mood by Mlle. de La Mole's deep mourning,
which struck him all the more forcibly since no one else in
the family was dressed in black.

After dinner, he found that he was completely rid of
the fit of enthusiasm which had obsessed him all day.
Luckily, the academician who knew Latin was at this
dinner. "There's the man who will make the least fun of
me," Julien said to himself, "if, as I suppose, my question
about Mlle. de La Mole's mourning is a faux pas."

Mathilde kept watching him with a peculiar look on her
face. "That's the way women in these parts flirt, just as
Mme. de Rênal described it to me," Julien told himself. "I
wasn't nice to her this morning; I wouldn't give in to her
whim to chat. She likes me all the better for it. The devil
will have his due, no doubt. Later on, her scornful pride
will find a way to avenge itself. I'm pushing her to do her
worst. How different from the woman I've lost! What a

charming disposition she had! How natural she was! I knew her thoughts before she did; I could see them being born. My only rival in her heart was the fear of her children's death; but that was a natural and reasonable affection, attractive even to me who suffered from it. I've been a fool. My notions about Paris kept me from appreciating that sublime woman.

"What a difference, great God! And what do I find here? Cold and arrogant vanity, every shade of conceit, and nothing more."

They were getting up from the table. "Mustn't let our academician get away," Julien told himself. He stepped up to him as the guests were moving out into the garden, put on a gentle and submissive air, and chimed in with his fury at the success of *Hernani*.*

"If we still lived in the days of the *lettres de cachet!* . . ."* he said.

"Then he wouldn't have dared," cried the academician with a gesture à la *Talma*.*

Apropos of a flower, Julien cited a few lines from Virgil's *Georgics* and declared that nothing could touch the Abbé Delille's poetry.* In a word, he flattered the academician in every way he could. After which, in the most indifferent tone: "I suppose," he said to him, "that Mlle. de La Mole has had a legacy from some uncle, for whom she is in mourning."

"What! you live in the house," said the academician, stopping short, "and you don't know about her mania? To tell the truth, it's strange that her mother allows her to carry on so. But, between you and me, it is not exactly by strength of character that they shine in this house. Mlle. Mathilde has enough for the whole family and leads them by the nose. Today is the thirtieth of April!" The academician paused and gave Julien a knowing look.

Julien smiled as intelligently as he could. "What might be the connection between bossing a whole house, wearing a black dress, and the thirtieth of April?" he wondered. "I must be even slower than I thought."

"I must confess . . ." he said to the academician, and his eyes went on questioning.

"Let's take a turn in the garden," said the academician, delighted at the prospect of making a long, elegant narration. "What! you really don't know what happened on the thirtieth of April, 1574?"

"Where?" asked Julien, astonished.

"On the Place de Grève."

Astonished as he was, this phrase gave Julien no

inkling. His curiosity, his anticipation of a tragic tale, so congenial to his temperament, gave him those shining eyes a storyteller loves to see in his listener. Delighted to find a virgin ear, the academician recounted to Julien at great length how, on the thirtieth of April, 1574, the best-looking boy of his day, Boniface de La Mole, and his friend Annibal de Coconasso, a Piedmontese gentleman, had their heads cut off on the Place de Grève. La Mole was the adored lover of Queen Marguerite de Navarre. "Note," added the academician, "that Mlle. de La Mole is named *Mathilde-Marguerite*. La Mole was, at the same time, the Duke d'Alençon's favorite and the intimate friend of the King of Navarre, afterward Henry IV, his mistress's husband. On Mardi Gras of that year 1574, the court was at Saint-Germain with poor King Charles IX, who was dying. La Mole tried to carry off the princes, his friends, whom the queen, Catherine de' Medici, had detained at court as prisoners. He brought up two hundred horsemen beneath the walls of Saint-Germain; the Duke d'Alençon lost his nerve, and La Mole was thrown to the headsman.*

"But the thing that touches Mlle. Mathilde—she told me so herself, some seven or eight years ago, when she was twelve, for she has a head! a head! . . ." And the academician rolled his eyes heavenward. "The thing that struck her most in this political catastrophe is that Queen Marguerite de Navarre, hidden in a house on the Place de Grève, dared to send someone to ask the executioner for her lover's head. And the following night, at midnight, she took that head in her carriage and went and buried it herself in a chapel situated at the foot of the hill of Montmartre."

"Is it possible?" cried Julien, deeply touched.

"Mlle. de La Mole despises her brother because, as you can see, he doesn't give a rap for all that ancient history and never wears mourning on April thirtieth. It is since that famous execution, and to commemorate the close friendship of La Mole for Coconasso, who, like the Italian he was, had the name of Annibal, that all the men in this family bear that name. And," added the academician, lowering his voice, "according to Charles IX himself, this Coconasso was one of the bloodiest of the murderers on August twenty-fourth, 1572.* But how is it possible, my dear Sorel, that you, a commensal in this house, know nothing of these matters?"

"So that is why Mlle. de La Mole called her brother

'Annibal' twice during dinner. I thought I hadn't heard right."

"That was a reproach. It's odd that the marquise stands for such goings on. ... That tall girl's husband will have his hands full!"

This remark was followed by five or six satirical observations. The joy and malice that shone in the academician's eyes vexed Julien. "Here we are like two servants busy running down our masters," he thought. "But nothing should surprise me on the part of that man from the academy." One day Julien had caught him on his knees before the Marquise de La Mole; he was begging her for a tobacco concession for a nephew in the country.

That night a little chambermaid in Mlle. de La Mole's service, who kept making advances to Julien, as Elisa had once done, made it clear to him that her mistress's mourning had not been put on to attract attention at all. This bizarre notion derived from the very depths of her character. She genuinely loved that La Mole, the adored lover of the most intelligent queen of his time and a man who perished for having tried to liberate his friends. And what friends! The first prince of the blood and Henry IV.

Accustomed to the perfect naturalness that shone through Mme. de Rênal's every action, Julien could see nothing but affectation in all the women of Paris; and whenever he was the least bit disposed to sadness, he could find nothing to say to them. Mlle. de La Mole was the exception.

He was beginning not to take that kind of beauty which is accompanied by a noble bearing for coldness of heart. He had long conversations with Mlle. de La Mole, who, during the fine days of spring, would sometimes stroll with him after dinner in the garden, alongside the open windows of the drawing room. One day she told him that she was reading d'Aubigné's history, and Brantôme. "Strange reading," thought Julien, "and the marquise doesn't allow her to read Walter Scott's novels!"

One day she related to him, her eyes aglow with pleasure, which proved the sincerity of her admiration, the deed of a young woman who lived during the reign of Henry III, about which she had just read in l'Etoile's *Mémoires*. Discovering that her husband was unfaithful, she stabbed him.

Julien's ego was flattered. A person surrounded by so much respect and who, according to the academician, bossed the whole house, was condescending to speak to him in a manner that might almost be taken as friendly.

"I was mistaken," he thought awhile later. "It isn't familiarity—I'm nothing but the confidant in a play. It's her need to talk. I am considered learned in this family. I'm going off to read Brantôme, d'Aubigné, l'Etoile.* I will be able to dispute the truth of a few of those anecdotes Mlle. de La Mole is talking about. I mean to shake off this role of passive confidant."

By degrees his conversations with this girl, whose bearing was so imposing and at the same time so at ease, became more interesting. He forgot his dreary role of plebeian in revolt. He found her well-informed and even reasonable. Her opinions in the garden varied a good deal from those she endorsed in the drawing room. With him she sometimes revealed an enthusiasm and frankness that made a perfect contrast with her usual manner, so proud, lofty, and cold.

"The wars of the League* were the heroic times of France," she said to him one day, her eyes sparkling with intelligence and enthusiasm. "In those days, every man fought for a definite cause, to make his party triumph, and not contemptibly to earn a cross as in the time of your emperor. You must agree that there was less selfishness and pettiness then. I love that period."

"And Boniface de La Mole was its hero," he said to her.

"At least he was loved as it is perhaps sweet to be loved. What woman today would not be horrified to touch her lover's severed head?"

Mme. de La Mole called her daughter. Hypocrisy, if it is to be useful, must be kept hidden; and Julien, as we see, had half confided his admiration for Napoleon to Mlle. de La Mole.

"That's the immense advantage they have over us," thought Julien, now alone in the garden. "The history of their ancestors raises them above vulgar sentiments, and they haven't always to be thinking about their keep! What a miserable position I'm in," he added bitterly. "It is not my place to argue about such momentous questions; I probably see everything in the wrong light. My life is nothing but a series of shams, because I don't have an income of a thousand francs to buy my bread."

"What are you dreaming about, sir?" asked Mathilde, who had come back at a run. There was a note of intimacy in this question, and she had come back running and out of breath to be with him.

Julien was weary of despising himself. Out of pride, he told her frankly what he had been thinking. He blushed a great deal as he spoke of his poverty to one so rich. He tried to convey through his proud manner that he asked nothing. Never had he seemed so good-looking to Mathilde; she discovered in him a sensitivity and frankness that he often lacked.

Less than a month later, Julien was strolling thoughtfully in the Hôtel de La Mole's garden; but his face no longer wore that hard look of intellectual arrogance, stamped on it by a constant feeling of inferiority. He had just left Mlle. de La Mole, after escorting her back to the drawing room door; she claimed to have hurt her foot while running with her brother.

"She leaned on my arm in a very peculiar way!" Julien observed. "Am I a conceited ass, or is it true that she has taken a fancy to me? She listens to me with such a gentle air, even when I tell her how much I suffer because of my pride! She who is so high-handed with everyone else! People in the drawing room would surely be surprised if they could see that expression on her face. She certainly doesn't show that kind and gentle look to anyone else."

Julien tried not to make too much of this odd friendship. He himself compared it with an armed truce. Each time they came together, before resuming the nearly intimate tone of the day before, they would all but ask themselves: "will we be friends or enemies today?" In the first words exchanged, the substance counted for nothing; on either side, they were attentive to form only. Julien had realized that to let himself be offended once with impunity by this very haughty girl was to lose everything. "If I am to have a falling-out, isn't it better to have it right away, defending the just claims of my pride, rather than later while repulsing the show of contempt that must follow the least neglect of what I owe to my own sense of self-respect?"

Several times, on her bad days, Mathilde tried using the tone of the great lady; she brought a rare cunning to bear on these attempts, but Julien repulsed them rudely.

One day he cut her short: "Does Mlle. de La Mole have some order to give her father's secretary?" he asked her. "It is his duty to listen to her orders and to carry them out respectfully; apart from that he has nothing to say to her. He is not being paid to communicate his thoughts."

This kind of behavior and the peculiar doubts Julien entertained soon dissipated the boredom he had experienced regularly during his first months in that magnificent

307

drawing room where everyone was afraid of everything, and where it was improper to treat any subject lightly.

"It would be funny if she were in love with me. But whether she loves me or not," continued Julien, "I have a bright girl for my intimate confidant, one before whom the whole house trembles, the Marquis de Croisenois more than all the rest. That young man who is so polished, kind, brave, who enjoys all the advantages of birth and of fortune, just one of which would set my heart so much at ease! He is madly in love with her; that is to say, as much in love as a Parisian can be. He is supposed to marry her. How many letters M. de La Mole had me write to both lawyers to settle the contract! And I, who see myself as a flunkey, pen in hand in the morning, triumph two hours later, here in the garden, over that very attractive young man; for after all, her preference is striking, undeniable. Perhaps too she hates the future husband in him. She is arrogant enough for that. In which case, I enjoy whatever kindness she shows me by virtue of being a trusted inferior.

"No! Either I am crazy, or she is making up to me; the more I treat her coldly and respectfully, the more she seeks me out. This could be deliberate on her part, an affectation; but I see her eyes light up whenever I appear unexpectedly. Do Parisian women know how to sham to that extent? What do I care! Appearances are for me; let's enjoy the appearances. My God, she's beautiful! How I love those big blue eyes from close up, and looking at me as they often do! What a difference between this and last spring, when I was so miserable living among those three hundred filthy, spiteful hypocrites and kept myself going by strength of character alone! I was almost as nasty as they!"

On his suspicious days, Julien would think, "That girl is laughing at me. She is in cahoots with her brother to keep me guessing. But she seems so contemptuous of that brother's lack of energy! 'He's brave, but then, that's all,' she tells me. 'And brave only when he's facing Spanish swords. In Paris everything frightens him; he sees the danger of ridicule lurking everywhere. He hasn't one thought that dares to deviate from the fashion. It is always I who am obliged to take his defense.' A girl of nineteen! Is it possible at that age to be consistent every minute of the day with the rule of hypocrisy one has prescribed for oneself?

"On the other hand, whenever Mlle. de La Mole fixes her big blue eyes on me with a certain strange expression,

Count Norbert always goes off somewhere. To my mind that's suspect; shouldn't he be indignant to see his sister lavish attention on a *servant* of their house? For I heard the Duke de Chaulnes call me that." At the memory of this, all his other feelings gave way to anger. Did it come from that fussy duke's love of old-fashioned language?

"In any case, she's pretty!" Julien went on, with a tigerish look in his eye. "I will have her; I'll run away afterwards, and woe to him who tries to stop me!"

This project became Julien's only concern. He could think of nothing else. Days went by like hours.

Every time he tried to concentrate on some serious business, his mind would go off into a deep reverie, and he would wake up a quarter of an hour later, his heart throbbing with ambition, his thoughts confused, and mulling over this question: "Does she love me?"

Chapter XI

A Girl's Power

> I admire her beauty, but I fear
> her wit.
>
> —*Mérimée*

If Julien had used the time he spent overrating Mathilde's beauty or working himself into a fury over her family's natural haughtiness, which she was forgetting for his sake, to analyze what went on in the drawing room, he might have understood wherein lay her power over everyone around her. When anyone offended Mlle. de La Mole, she knew how to punish him with a witticism so calculated, so well chosen, so proper in appearance, so timely launched, that the wound kept growing by the minute, the more one thought about it. Little by little it would become agonizing for the offended ego. Since she set little store by many things that were seriously desired by the rest of the family, to them she always seemed cold-blooded. It is pleasant to refer to the drawing rooms of the aristocracy once one has left them, but that is all. The utterly meaningless conversation, the small talk especially, because it goes beyond the demands even of hypocrisy, ends by exhausting the guest's patience with its nauseous sweetness. Civility means nothing in itself, except during the first few visits. So Julien was finding out ... after the first enchantment, the first astonishment. "Civility," he said to himself, "is nothing more than the absence of anger which bad manners might produce." Mathilde was often bored; perhaps she would have been bored anywhere. At such times, it was a distraction and a true pleasure to sharpen an epigram.

Perhaps it was in order to have somewhat more amusing victims than her illustrious kin, or the academician and the five or six other minor officials who curried their favor, that she had raised the hopes of the Marquis de Croisenois, the Count de Caylus, and two or three other young men of the first eminence. For her they were merely fresh subjects for epigrams.

It pains us to confess, for we are fond of Mathilde, that she had received letters from several of them, and had sometimes answered. We hasten to add that this character's behavior is an exception to the rule of the day. In general, it is not a lack of prudence that one might reproach in the pupils of the noble Convent of the Sacred Heart.

One day the Marquis de Croisenois returned to Mathilde a rather compromising letter she had written the day before. He trusted that by this token of the utmost discretion, he would further his suit a good deal. But it was indiscretion that Mathilde liked in her correspondence. Her greatest pleasure was to gamble with her fate. She wouldn't speak to him for six weeks.

She amused herself with those young gentlemen's letters; but according to her, they were all alike. It was always the same most melancholy, most profound passion.

"They are all one and the same perfect man, ready to go off to Palestine," she told her cousin. "Can you imagine anything more insipid? And that's the kind of letter I'm going to receive all my life! Letters like that must not change more than once every twenty years, according to the profession in fashion. They must have been less drab in the time of the Empire. Then, all the young men in high society had seen or taken part in some action that had real greatness to it. The Duke de N——, my uncle, was at Wagram."*

"How much wit does it take to strike a blow with a saber? And when they did, they never stopped talking about it!" said Mlle. de Sainte-Herédité, Mathilde's cousin.

"All the same, I enjoy those stories. To be in a *genuine* battle, one of Napoleon's, where ten thousand soldiers were killed, is proof of courage. Exposing oneself to danger elates the soul, and saves it from the boredom in which my poor adorers seem to be steeped; and that boredom is contagious. Who among them ever thought of doing anything out of the ordinary? They are trying to win my hand, a fine thing! I am rich, and my father will see to it that his son-in-law gets on. Ah! if only he could find one who's a bit amusing!"

Mathilde's sharp, clear, graphic way of seeing things spoiled her speech, as one can see. Often a remark of hers would stand out like a blemish to the eyes of her very polished friends. They would almost have admitted to one another, were she less in fashion, that her language was just a bit too colorful for feminine daintiness.

She, in turn, was very unjust with regard to the good-looking horsemen who people the Bois de Boulogne. She viewed the future not with terror—that would have been a vivid sensation—but with a disgust quite rare at her age.

What was there to wish for? Wealth, noble birth, intelligence, and beauty (so everyone said, and so she believed), all had been lavished on her by the hand of chance.

Such were the thoughts of the most envied heiress in the Faubourg Saint-Germain when she began to enjoy going for walks with Julien. She was astonished at his pride; she admired the petty bourgeois' shrewdness. "He will manage to get himself made bishop, like the Abbé Maury,"* she told herself.

Before long the sincere and unfeigned resistance with which our hero greeted several of her ideas preoccupied her; she kept thinking about him; she would repeat the smallest details of their conversations to her lady friend, and discovered that she could never succeed in conveying their whole character.

Suddenly she was enlightened by a thought. "I have the good luck to be in love," she told herself one day in a rapture of incredible joy. "I'm in love, I'm in love, it's clear as can be! At my age, where can a beautiful, witty girl find excitement if not in love? It's no use; I could never love Croisenois, Caylus, and *tutti quanti*. They are perfect, too perfect, perhaps; in a word, they bore me."

In her thoughts, she went over all the descriptions of passion she had read in *Manon Lescaut*, the *Nouvelle Héloise*, the *Letters of a Portuguese Nun*, etc., etc. There was no question of anything, of course, but the grand passion; trifling love was unworthy of a girl of her age and birth. She reserved the name of love for that heroic sentiment alone which was to be met with in France in the time of Henry III and Bassompierre.* It was a love that never gave way basely in the face of obstacles; far from that, it moved one to do great things. "How unlucky for me that there is no real court, like that of Catherine de' Medici or Louis XIII! I feel that I am equal to the greatest and most daring enterprises. What couldn't I do with a king, a man of heart like Louis XIII, sighing at my feet! I would lead him into Vendée, as the Baron de Tolly says so often, and from there he would win back his kingdom; then, no more charter . . . and

Julien would help me. What does he lack? A name and a fortune. He would make a name for himself, he would acquire a fortune.

"Croisenois lacks nothing, and all his life he will be nothing but a demi-Ultra, demi-Liberal duke, an irresolute fellow who talks when he ought to act, always avoiding extremes, and *consequently finding himself second in command everywhere.*

"What great action is not *an extreme* the moment it is undertaken? Isn't it only after it has been accomplished that it seems possible to the herd? Yes, it is love with all his miracles who will reign in my heart; I can tell by the fire that is stirring in me. Heaven owed me this favor. It will not have lavished every advantage on a single person in vain. My happiness will be worthy of me. Each of my days will not resemble coldly the one that went before. There is already something great and venturesome about daring to love a man so far removed from me by his social position. Will he continue to deserve me? We shall see. At the first sign of weakness, I will drop him. A girl of my birth, with the chivalrous character people so readily ascribe to me [this was her father's observation], ought not to behave like a simpleton.

"Isn't that the role I'd be playing if I loved the Marquis de Croisenois? I should have a new edition of the happiness enjoyed by my female cousins, whom I despise so thoroughly. I know in advance everything the poor marquis would say to me, everything I should say to him. What good is a love that makes you yawn? Might as well turn religious. I should have a signing of the contract, like that of my younger cousin, at which the close relatives would be moved to tears, if they were not already in a bad humor because of one last condition inserted by the other side's notary the day before."

Chapter XII

Could He Be Another Danton?

> *A need for anxiety*, such was the
> disposition of the beautiful Mar-
> guerite de Valois, my aunt who
> eventually married the king of Na-
> varre, whom we now see reigning in
> France under the name of Henry
> IV. A need to gamble was the key
> to that lovable princess's character;
> whence, her continually falling out
> and making up with her brothers,
> from the age of sixteen on. Now,
> what does a young lady have to
> gamble? Her most precious posses-
> sion: her reputation, her good name
> of a lifetime.
>
> —Memoirs of the
> Duc d'Angoulême,
> natural son of Charles IX

"With Julien and me there's no question of signing a
contract, no lawyer at a bourgeois ceremony; with us,
everything is heroic; everything will be the offspring of
chance. Noble birth apart, which he lacks, it is the love of
Marguerite de Valois for the young La Mole, the most
distinguished man of his day. Is it my fault if the young
men at court are such conformists and turn pale at the
idea of any venture that is the least bit unusual? For
them, a little voyage to Greece or Africa is the height of
daring, but even then, they have to go in troops. As soon

as they find themselves alone, they are afraid . . . not of the Bedouin's spear, but of ridicule; and that fear drives them insane.

"My little Julien, on the contrary, prefers to do things by himself. It never enters that privileged being's mind to look to others for moral support or help! He despises other men, and for that reason, I do not despise him.

"If, with his poverty, Julien were noble, my love would be nothing more than a shabby mistake, a vulgar misalliance. I should want none of it; it would lack that which typifies the great passion: the immensity of the obstacle to be surmounted and the dark uncertainty of the outcome."

Mlle. de La Mole was so preoccupied with these fine distinctions that the next day, quite unawares, she sang Julien's praises to the Marquis de Croisenois and her brother. She carried her eloquence so far as to nettle them.

"Watch out for that young man who is so energetic," her brother warned. "If the revolution flares up again, he will have us all guillotined."

She was careful not to answer, and hastened to twit her brother and the Marquis de Croisenois about the fear energy seemed to rouse in them. "It is really nothing but the fear of confronting the unexpected, the dread of losing one's tongue in the presence of the unforeseen. ... Always, always, sirs, that fear of ridicule, a monster which, unfortunately, died in 1816."

"Ridicule cannot survive," M. de La Mole always said, "in a country where there are two parties." His daughter had appropriated this idea.

"Thus, gentlemen," she said to Julien's enemies, "you will have lived in fear all of your lives, and then you will be told: 'It wasn't a wolf, it was only his shadow.' "*

Mathilde soon left them. Her brother's remark had horrified her; she worried over it a great deal; but by the next day, she saw the finest kind of praise in it.

"In this age, when energy is dead, his frightens them. I will tell him what my brother said: I want to see how he will answer. But I will choose a moment when his eyes are shining; at such times it is not in his power to lie.

"This could be another Danton!" she added, after a long and hazy reverie. "Very well! suppose the Revolution did break out again. What part would Croisenois and my brother play? It is written out beforehand: sublime resignation. They would be heroic sheep, letting their throats be cut without saying a word. Even when they were dying, their only fear would be to do something in bad

315

taste. My little Julien would blow out the brains of any Jacobin who came to arrest him, if he had the faintest hope of saving himself. He's not afraid of being in bad taste, not he."

This last observation made her thoughtful; it roused painful memories and took away all her assurance. It made her think of the jibes of *MM.* de Caylus, de Croisenois, de Luz and of her brother. Those gentlemen criticized Julien unanimously for his *priestly* look: meek and hypocritical.

"But," she resumed suddenly, her eyes shining with joy, "the bitterness and frequency of their jibes prove, in spite of themselves, that he is the most distinguished man we have seen this winter. What do his shortcomings matter? or his ridiculous side? He has greatness, and they are offended by it, they who are otherwise so kind and indulgent. There's no denying he's poor, or that he studied to be a priest. They are majors and had no need to study; it's easier that way.

"Despite the disadvantages of his eternal black outfit and of his priestly ways, which he certainly must keep up, poor boy, or risk starving to death, his ability frightens them; nothing could be plainer. As for that priestly look, whenever we are alone together for a few minutes it disappears. And whenever one of those gentlemen says something he considers clever and unexpected, doesn't he always look at Julien first? I've noticed that more than once. Yet they know very well that he will never speak to them, except to reply. I am the only one to whom he addresses a remark; he thinks I have a lofty soul. He answers their objections only insofar as he must in order to be polite. He turns respectful immediately afterward. With me, he will debate for hours on end; he is not sure of his ideas so long as I can raise the least objection to them. In short, we haven't had a falling-out all winter; it's been simply a matter of attracting one another's attention with words. Well, my father, a superior man who will add greatly to the fortune of our house, respects Julien. Everyone else hates him, but no one is contemptuous of him, except my mother's sanctimonious lady friends."

Count de Caylus either had or feigned a great passion for horses; he spent all his time in his stable, often taking lunch there. This great passion, besides his habit of never laughing, earned him a great deal of respect among his friends; he was the "mastermind" of this little circle.

As soon as it had gathered the next evening behind Mme. de La Mole's easy chair, Julien not being present,

M. de Caylus, backed up by Croisenois and Norbert, sharply attacked Mathilde's good opinion of Julien, for no apparent reason and almost the instant he caught sight of Mlle. de La Mole. She saw through this tactic from a mile off and was delighted with it.

"There they are," she said to herself, "all in league against a man of genius whose income doesn't amount to ten louis a year, and who can't speak to them unless he is spoken to. They are afraid of him in his black outfit. How would it be if he wore epaulettes?"

Never had she been more brilliant. With her first assault, she covered Caylus and his allies with droll sarcasm. When the fire of these shining officers' wit had been silenced: "Let some squireen from the mountains of Franche-Comté," she said to M. Caylus, "find out tomorrow that Julien is his natural son, and give him his name and a few thousand francs. In six weeks he will have a mustache like you, gentlemen; in six months he will be an officer of the Hussars like you, gentlemen. Then the greatness of his character will no longer strike you as absurd. I see you, sir, the future duke, about to fall back on that bad old argument: the superiority of court nobility over provincial nobility. But what would you have to say if I should drive you to the wall, if I were naughty enough to give Julien a Spanish duke for a father, a prisoner of war in Besançon during Napoleon's time, who, from a scruple of conscience, acknowledged him on his deathbed?"

All these suppositions about an illegitimate birth were judged to be in rather bad taste by *MM.* de Caylus and de Croisenois. That was all they could see in Mathilde's line of reasoning.

Dominated by her though he was, his sister's language was so plain that Norbert put on a solemn look, which one must admit did not sit very well on his kind and smiling countenance. He risked a few remarks.

"Are you ill, my dear?" Mathilde answered him with a serious little air. "You must be feeling quite ill to answer a joke with a sermon. A sermon, you! Are you trying to get a prefecture, by chance?"

Mathilde very soon forgot the Count de Caylus' annoyed look, Norbert's ill humor, and M. de Croisenois' silent despair. She had to make up her own mind about a fateful idea that had suddenly possessed her.

"Julien is sincere with me," she said to herself. "At his age, in an inferior station, he needs a woman friend. Perhaps I am that friend, but I see no love in him. Given

317

the boldness of his character, he would have told me of it."

This uncertainty, this inner debate which from that minute on filled up Mathilde's day and for which, each time Julien spoke to her, she would find fresh matter, completely dispelled those moments of boredom to which she was so prone.

Daughter of a man of parts who might become a minister and give back the clergy their forests, Mlle. de La Mole had been an object of the most excessive flattery at the Convent of the Sacred Heart. The harm done this way can never be offset. She had been persuaded that with all her advantages of birth, fortune, etc., she ought to be happier than anyone else. This notion is the source of the boredom of princes, and of all their follies.

Mathilde had not escaped the baneful influence of this idea. However intelligent one may be, one cannot at ten be on one's guard against the flattery, apparently so well-founded, of a whole convent.

The moment she decided she was in love with Julien, she was no longer bored. Every day she congratulated herself on having made up her mind to allow herself a great passion. "This amusement has its dangers," she reflected. "So much the better! So very, very much the better! Without a great passion, I was pining away with boredom in the prime of my life, between sixteen and twenty. I have already wasted my best years, obliged, as I was for my only distraction, to listen to the nonsense of my mother's lady friends, who, I have heard, were not altogether so strict at Coblentz* in 1792 as they make out today."

It was during this time, when Mathilde was still plagued with doubts, that Julien did not know what to make of the long looks she would fasten on him. He certainly noted an increase of coldness in Count Norbert's manner, and a fresh outburst of haughtiness in *MM*. de Caylus, de Luz, and de Croisenois. He was used to it. This misfortune sometimes overtook him in the aftermath of an evening during which he had been more brilliant than befitted his place. Without the particular welcome Mathilde reserved for him, and his curiosity about the whole lot, he would have avoided following those brilliant young men with mustaches out into the garden when they accompanied Mlle. de La Mole after dinner.

"Yes, I can't shut my eyes to the fact," Julien told himself, "that Mlle. de La Mole looks at me in a strange way. But even when her fine blue eyes are fixed on me and staring with the utmost abandon, I always see an undercurrent of questioning, of cold-bloodedness, of cruelty, in them. Can that be love? How different from Mme. de Rênal's gaze!"

Once after dinner Julien, who had followed M. de La Mole to his study, hurried down to the garden. As he was walking heedlessly toward Mathilde's group, he overheard a few words pronounced in a loud voice. Mathilde was teasing her brother. Julien distinctly heard his own name pronounced twice. He appeared; abruptly there was a deep silence, and the attempts made to break it were useless. Mlle. de La Mole and her brother were too riled to find another subject of conversation. *MM*. de Caylus, de Croisenois, de Luz, and one of their friends treated Julien with icy coldness. He left.

Chapter XIII

A Plot

> Random remarks, chance encounters, become the most obvious kinds of proof in the eyes of a man of imagination if he has any fire in his heart.
>
> —SCHILLER

The next day he caught Norbert and his sister talking about him again. At his arrival a silence of death set in, as on the night before. His suspicions were boundless. "Could these nice young people be scheming to make a fool of me? That, I must admit, is far more likely, more natural, than Mlle. de La Mole's feigned passion for a poor devil of a secretary. In the first place, do those people have passions? Making a fool of you is what they do best. They are jealous of my poor little superiority in words. Jealousy is another of their weaknesses. Their plan is clear enough. Mlle. de La Mole is trying to convince me that she is interested in me, so she can make a spectacle of me in front of her fiancé."

This cruel suspicion changed Julien's whole outlook. The idea met with a budding love in his heart but had no trouble destroying it. His was a love based on nothing more than Mathilde's rare beauty, or rather, on her queenly manner and marvelous dress. In this respect Julien was still an upstart. A pretty woman in society, so we are told, is that which most astonishes the intelligent peasant when he comes in contact with the highest classes. It was not Mathilde's character that had set Julien to dreaming on days previous. He had enough sense to realize that he

320

knew nothing about her character. What he could see of it might be nothing more than a show.

For example, Mathilde would not have missed a mass on Sunday for anything in the world, and she accompanied her mother to one almost every day. If, in the drawing room of the Hôtel de La Mole, some rash fellow forgot where he was and took the liberty of alluding, however remotely, to some anecdote at the expense of the true or supposed interests of Throne or Altar, Mathilde on the instant became icily serious. Her look, otherwise so lively, would assume all the impassive haughtiness of an old family portrait.

But Julien had found out for certain that she always kept one or two of Voltaire's most philosophical works in her room. He himself would often sneak a few volumes of the fine edition, so magnificently bound. By moving each tome slightly and leaving a gap between it and the next, he was able to conceal the absence of the one he carried off, but he soon noticed that someone else was reading Voltaire. He had recourse to a trick from the seminary: he placed a few bits of horsehair on the volumes that he supposed might interest Mlle. de La Mole. They would disappear for weeks at a time.

Impatient with his bookseller, who sent him all the fake memoirs, M. de La Mole entrusted Julien to buy any new books that were the least bit controversial. But, so the venom should not spread through the house, the secretary had orders to deposit these works in a little bookcase located in the marquis' own bedroom. Shortly afterward he could be sure that if these new volumes were the least bit hostile to Throne or Altar, they would not be long in vanishing. To be sure, it was not Norbert who was reading them.

Julien, making too much of this discovery, imputed to Mlle. de La Mole the duplicity of a Machiavelli. This alleged low cunning of hers was, in his opinion, charming, almost the only moral charm she had. Boredom with hypocrisy and talk about virtue drove him to this excess.

He was being swept away by his imagination more than by his love.

It was only after losing himself in reveries over the elegance of Mlle. de La Mole's figure, her excellent taste in dress, the whiteness of her hand, the beauty of her arm, the *disinvoltura* of all her movements, that he found himself in love. Then, to complete the spell, he imagined her a Catherine de' Medici. Nothing was too deep or too villainous for the character he lent her. It was the ideal of the Maslons, the Frilairs, and the Castanèdes, whom he had admired in his early youth. It was for him, in short, the ideal of Paris.

Could anything be funnier than to suppose depth or villainy in the Parisian character?

"It's possible that this whole trio is making fun of me," thought Julien. The reader knows little about his character if he cannot already see the cold, somber expression his eyes assumed when answering Mathilde's gaze. A bitter irony repulsed the assurances of friendship that an astonished Mlle. de La Mole risked giving him two or three times.

Stung by this odd behavior, the girl's heart, cold by nature, bored, responsive to wit alone, became as passionate as it was in her nature to be. But there was a great deal of pride in Mathilde's makeup too, and the birth of an emotion which made all her happiness dependent upon another was accompanied by a gloomy sadness.

Julien had already profited enough since his arrival in Paris to distinguish this from the cold sadness of boredom. Instead of being avid, as in the past, for evening parties, plays, and entertainments of all sorts, she avoided them.

Music sung by French singers bored her to death, and yet Julien, who made it his duty to watch the crowd coming out of the opera, noted that she had herself taken there as often as possible. He thought he detected that she had lost a little of the perfect restraint that used to shine in all her actions. Sometimes she would answer her friends with witty remarks that offended by reason of their stinging emphasis. It seemed to him that she had it in for the Marquis de Croisenois. "That young man must be awfully fond of money not to drop that girl here and now, no matter how rich she may be!" thought Julien. As for himself, indignant at so many insults offered to the male ego, he was colder to her than ever. Often he went so far as to answer impolitely.

However resolute he was not to be duped by Mathilde's show of interest, it was so obvious on some days, and Julien, who was beginning to open his eyes, found her so pretty, that at times he was embarrassed.

"The skill and abiding patience of these fashionable young people will finally win out over my lack of experience; I ought to go away and put an end to this business." The marquis had just turned over to him the management of several small estates and houses he owned in lower Languedoc.* A trip was necessary; M. de La Mole consented with reluctance. Except in matters of the highest ambition, Julien had become another self to him.

"After all, they haven't had me yet," Julien told himself as he prepared to leave. "Whether the jokes Mlle. de La Mole makes at the expense of those gentlemen are genuine, or intended simply to give me confidence, I have had a good laugh. If there is no plot against the carpenter's son, then Mlle. de La Mole's conduct is a mystery, but at least as much so for the Marquis de Croisenois as for me. Yesterday, for example, her irritation was real enough, and I had the pleasure of seeing a young man, as noble and as rich as I am beggarly and plebeian, put down in favor of me. That's the finest of my triumphs; it will cheer me up in the post chaise as I speed over the plains of Languedoc."

He had kept his departure secret, but Mathilde knew better than he that he was leaving Paris the next day, and for a long time. She had recourse to a splitting headache, which the stuffy air of the drawing room only made worse. She walked a great deal in the garden, and so harried Norbert, the Marquis de Croisenois, de Caylus, de Luz, and other young men who had dined at the Hôtel de La Mole with her sarcasm that she forced them to leave. She kept looking at Julien in a strange way.

"Her look may be an act," thought Julien, "but that quick breathing, all that nervousness! Bah!" he said to himself, "who am I to judge such things? This has to do with one of the sublimest, one of the most cunning women in Paris. Her short breathing nearly had an effect on me; she must have learned that from Léontine Fay,* of whom she is so fond."

They were alone now; the conversation was obviously flagging. "No! Julien doesn't feel anything for me," thought Mathilde, genuinely unhappy.

As he was saying goodbye, she gripped his arm.

"You will receive a letter from me tonight," she said, in a voice so altered that he didn't recognize it. This detail touched Julien directly. "My father," she went on, "thinks highly of your services, as he should. You *must* not leave tomorrow. Find an excuse." And she went away at a run.

Her figure was lovely. It wasn't possible to have a prettier foot; she ran with a grace that bewitched Julien. But can the reader guess what his second thought was, when she was out of sight? He was offended by the imperative tone with which she had pronounced the word "must." Louis XV too, on the point of dying, was sharply

323

annoyed by the word "must," used clumsily by his chief physician, but after all Louis XV was no upstart.

An hour later a lackey handed Julien a letter; it was simply a declaration of love.

"The style is not too affected," Julien told himself, trying by means of literary criticism to contain his joy, which was contracting his cheeks and forcing him to laugh in spite of himself. "At last," he cried out all of a sudden, his passion too strong to be contained, "I, a poor peasant, have had a declaration of love from a great lady!

"As for my own conduct, not bad," he added, suppressing his joy as much as possible. "I have managed to keep my dignity. I have never said I was in love." He fell to studying the writing; Mlle. de La Mole had a pretty little English hand. He had to do something to take his mind off a delight that was turning into delirium.

"Your departure forces me to speak. . . . Not to see you again would be more than I could bear."

A thought struck Julien with the force of a discovery, interrupted his examination of Mathilde's letter, and doubled his joy. "I've won out over the Marquis de Croisenois," he cried, "I, whose talk is always so serious! And he is so good-looking! He has a mustache, a charming uniform; he always finds something witty and subtle to say at just the right time."

Julien had a delightful moment. He wandered aimlessly about the garden, mad with happiness.

A while later he climbed to his office, then had himself announced to the Marquis de La Mole, who, as luck would have it, was not out. Julien had no trouble proving, by showing him a number of stamped papers just in from Normandy, that the care of his Norman lawsuits obliged him to put off his departure for Languedoc.

"I am so glad you are not going," the marquis said to him, when they had finished talking business. *"I enjoy seeing you."* Julien went out; this remark bothered him.

"And I am going to seduce his daughter! make impossible, perhaps, that marriage with the Marquis de Croisenois which is the chief delight of his future; if he were not made duke, at least his daughter would have a folding stool."* Julien had a notion to leave for Languedoc despite Mathilde's letter, despite the explanation given the marquis. This impulse to virtue was short-lived.

"What a fool I am," he told himself, "I, a plebeian, to take pity on a family of that rank! I, whom the Duke de Chaulnes calls a servant! How does the marquis increase his vast fortune? By dumping Government stocks when he

324

learns from the Château that a rumor of a coup d'état is to be set afloat the next day. And I, relegated to the lowest class by a shrewish Providence, I, to whom she has given a noble heart and an income of less than a thousand francs; that is to say, no bread, *practically speaking, no bread;* and I should refuse any pleasure that comes my way! a clear spring that has opened to quench my thirst in the burning desert of mediocrity which I must cross so painfully! By jove! I'm not that stupid; every man for himself in this desert of egoism we call life."

And he remembered some of the disdainful looks directed toward him by Mme. de La Mole, and especially by her friends, the *ladies*.

The pleasure of triumphing over the Marquis de Croisenois completed the rout of his virtuous impulse.

"How I wish he would lose his temper!" said Julien. "With what confidence I should run him through right now." And he made the gesture of the second thrust. "Up to this time I have been an ill-bred pedant, contemptibly abusing my little store of courage. After this letter, I am his equal. Yes," he said to himself with infinite pleasure and speaking slowly, "she has weighed our merits, the marquis' and mine, and the poor carpenter from the Jura has come out on top! Good! now I know how to sign my answer. Don't imagine for a minute, Mademoiselle de La Mole, that I have forgotten my place! I will make you understand and appreciate full well that it is for a carpenter's son you are betraying a descendant of the famed Guy de Croisenois, who followed St. Louis on his Crusade."

Julien could not contain his joy. He was obliged to go down into the garden. His room, where he had locked himself in, seemed too cramped for breathing.

"I, a poor peasant from the Jura," he repeated over and over, "I, condemned to wear this dreary black outfit forever. Alas! twenty years sooner and I would have worn a uniform like them! In those days, a man like me was either killed in battle, or *a general at thirty-six*." The letter, which he held tightly in his hand, gave him the stature and posture of a hero. "Nowadays, it's true, with this black suit a man may have emoluments of one hundred thousand francs and the blue sash at forty, like Monseigneur the Bishop of Beauvais.

"Very well!" he said to himself, laughing like Mephistopheles. "I'm smarter than they are; I've chosen the uniform of my day." And he felt his ambition and his fondness for the ecclesiastical garb increase twofold.

"How many cardinals born poorer than I, who still have governed! My compatriot Granvelle,* for example."

Julien's excitement gradually died down; prudence came to the fore. Like his master Tartuffe, whose role he knew by heart, he said to himself:

> I might well think those words a virtuous ruse.
> And I shall put no stock in talk so sweet
> Until *her* favors, after which I sigh,
> Assure me what I've heard is not a lie.*

"Tartuffe was also done in by a woman, and he was as good as the next man. ... My answer might be shown to someone ... for which event we have this remedy," he added, articulating slowly, and in an accent of restrained ferocity. "We will begin with the most heartfelt expressions in the sublime Mathilde's letter.

"Yes, but supposing four of M. de Croisenois' lackeys jump me and snatch the original?

"No, for I am well armed and have a habit, as everyone knows, of firing on lackeys.

"Very well, but one of them is brave; he rushes at me. He has been promised a hundred napoleons. I kill him or I wound him; fine, that's all they need. They throw me in prison, quite legally; I appear in the police court, and I am sent, with all due justice and equity on the part of the judges, to keep company with *MM*. Fontan and Magalon* in Poissy. Once there, I sleep with four hundred beggars pell-mell. ... And I should have pity on those people!" he shouted, rising impetuously to his feet. "Do they show any to people of the third estate, once they have them in their grip!" This remark was the last gasp of his gratitude for M. de La Mole, the thought of whom had tormented Julien up to now in spite of himself.

"Easy does it, gentlemen; I'm on to that bit of Machiavellianism; the Abbé Maslon or M. Castanède at the seminary couldn't do better. Once you relieve me of the 'provocative' note, I shall become a sequel to the story of Colonel Caron at Colmer.

"One minute, sirs, I am going to send the fatal letter, carefully sealed in a package, to the Abbé Pirard for safekeeping. He is an honest man, a Jansenist, and as such, proof against the charms of the purse. Yes, but he opens letters. ... It is to Fouqué that I shall send this one."

One must admit that Julien's gaze was atrocious, his

face hideous; it was instinct with unalloyed crime. He was the unhappy man at war with all society.

"*To arms!*" cried Julien. And in one bound he cleared the steps in front of the mansion. He went into a public scrivener's stall at the corner of the street; he frightened him. "Copy this," he said, handing him Mlle. de La Mole's letter.

While the scrivener was at work, Julien wrote to Fouqué; he begged him to keep a precious package for him. "But," he said to himself, interrupting his writing, "the censor at the post office will open my letter and give you the one you're looking for. . . . No, gentlemen." He went and bought a huge Bible from a Protestant bookseller, very cunningly hid Mathilde's letter in the cover, had the whole thing wrapped, and his package went on the stagecoach, addressed to one of Fouqué's workmen whose name was unknown to anyone in Paris.

That done, he returned joyous and lighthearted to the Hôtel de La Mole. "*Our turn now!*" he cried, locking himself in his room and throwing off his black coat.

"What! mademoiselle," he wrote to Mathilde, "can it be Mlle. de La Mole, who with the help of Arsène, her father's lackey, has sent a too-charming letter to the carpenter from the Jura, no doubt to make sport of his naïveté. . . ." And he transcribed the most explicit statements from the letter he had just received.

His own would have done credit to the diplomatic caution of M. le Chevalier de Beauvoisis. It was only ten o'clock; Julien, drunk with happiness and a sense of power, so new to the poor devil he was, walked into the Italian opera. He heard his friend Geronimo sing. Never had music exalted him to such heights. He was a god.[1]

[1]*Esprit per. pré. gui.* II.A.30.*

327

Chapter XIV

A Girl's Thoughts

> Such uncertainty! So many sleep-
> less nights! Am I about to make my-
> self contemptible? He himself will
> despise me. But he's leaving, he's
> going away.
>
> —ALFRED DE MUSSET

It had cost Mathilde a struggle to write her letter.
Whatever the beginning of her interest in Julien might
have been, it soon dominated her pride, which, as long as
she had known herself, had reigned absolute in her heart.
This cold, haughty soul was swept away for the first time
in her life by a passionate feeling. But if it dominated her
pride, it was still faithful to the uses of pride. Two months
of conflict and of fresh sensations had renewed, so to
speak, her entire moral being.

Mathilde thought happiness was in sight. This vision,
all-powerful in a brave heart when it is joined to a
superior intellect, had to contend for a long time against
her sense of dignity and all her notions about common
duty. One day she went to her mother's room at seven in
the morning and begged her permission to take refuge at
Villequier. The marquise didn't bother to answer and
advised her to go back to bed. This was her last effort
in the direction of common modesty and deference to conventional ideas.

The dread of doing the wrong thing and of running
counter to ideas held sacred by the Caylus', the de Luzes,
the Croisenois', had little hold over her mind; such fellows, so she thought, couldn't possibly understand her; she
would have consulted them had it been a matter of buying

a calash or an estate. Her real terror was that Julien might be annoyed with her.

"Perhaps too he has nothing but the appearance of a superior man?"

She loathed a want of character; that was her sole objection to the handsome young men who surrounded her. The more they bantered gracefully about everyone who was out of step with the fashion, or followed it awkwardly, under the impression of keeping up with it, the lower they sank in her estimation.

They were brave and that was all. "And yet, brave how?" she asked herself. "In a duel, but nowadays a duel is simply a ritual. Everything about it is known beforehand, even what a man ought to say when he falls. Stretched out on the grass, hand over heart, he is supposed to pardon his opponent generously and say a few words for the fair one, who is often fictitious, or else goes to a ball on the day of his death for fear of rousing suspicion.

"They brave danger at the head of squadrons all shiny with steel ... but solitary, strange, unexpected, and truly ugly danger?

"Alas!" Mathilde said to herself, "at the court of Henry III one found men who were as great by character as by birth! Ah! If only Julien had served at Jarnac or at Moncontour,* I should have no doubts. In those times of might and main, the French were no dolls. The day of battle was almost the least of their worries. Their lives were not bound up like an Egyptian mummy, under a covering that is common to everyone, and always the same. Yes," she added, "it took more true courage to go home alone at eleven o'clock at night, after leaving the Hôtel de Soissons, where Catherine de' Medici lived, than it takes nowadays to run off to Algiers.* A man's life was a game of chance. Civilization and the prefect of police have driven away chance; the unexpected has been banished. Should it appear in ideas, it is epigrammed to death; if it shows up in events, no measure is too cowardly for our fear. No matter what piece of madness fear may lead us to commit, it is excused. Degenerate and boring age! What would Boniface de La Mole have said if, raising his severed head from the grave in 1793, he had seen seventeen of his descendants let themselves be taken like sheep, to be guillotined two days later? Death was certain, yet it would have been bad form to defend oneself and kill a Jacobin or two. Ah! in the heroic age of France, in Boniface de La Mole's day, Julien would have been the major, and my brother the young priest with the right

329

ideas, with caution in his eyes and reason on his tongue."

A few months earlier, Mathilde had despaired of meeting anyone a bit out of the ordinary. She had found some happiness in permitting herself to write to a few young men in society. This boldness, so improper, so reckless in a young lady, might have disgraced her in the eyes of M. de Croisenois, of her grandfather the Duke de Chaulnes, and of the entire Hôtel de Chaulnes, which, seeing the proposed marriage broken off, would want to know why. At that time, on days when she had written one of her letters, Mathilde couldn't sleep. Yet those letters were simply replies.

In the present instance, she had dared to say she loved. She had been the *first* (a terrible word!) to write to a man in the lowest rank of society.

This item, in the event of discovery, insured everlasting dishonor. Which of the women who came to visit her mother would dare to speak up for her? What phrase could they be given to repeat so as to deaden the blow of the awful scorn she would meet with in drawing rooms?

Even to speak was frightful, but to write! "*There are certain things one does not write,*" shouted Napoleon upon learning of the surrender of Baylen.* It was Julien who had told her that story! as if to teach her a lesson in advance.

But all that was as nothing; there were other causes for Mathilde's distress. Forgetting the horrible effect it could have on society, the indelible stain that might result, for she was desecrating her caste, Mathilde was about to write to a man of a very different stamp from the Croisenois', the de Luzes, the Caylus'.

The depth, the *unknown quantity* of Julien's character might have frightened her even if she were establishing an ordinary relation with him. And she was going to make him her lover, perhaps her master!

"Where will his pretentions stop, if ever he has complete power over me? Very well! I will tell myself, like Medea: '*Amidst so many dangers, I still have* ME.' "

She was convinced that Julien felt no veneration for blue blood. Worse, perhaps he felt no love for her.

In these latest moments of awful doubt, notions about feminine pride occurred to her. "Everything about the destiny of a girl like me ought to be unusual," cried Mathilde, all out of patience. Then the pride that had been instilled in her since birth became the adversary of virtue.

330

At this juncture, news of Julien's departure came to quicken the process.

(Such characters are, fortunately, very rare.)

The same night, very late, Julien was malicious enough to have his very heavy trunk carried down to the doorkeeper's lodge; he had called the footman who was courting Mlle. de La Mole's chambermaid to do the carrying. "This maneuver may come to nothing," he told himself, "but if it succeeds, she will think I have left." Very gay, he fell asleep over this prank. Mathilde didn't close her eyes.

Early the next morning, Julien left the house unnoticed, but came back before eight o'clock. He had no more than entered the library when Mlle. de La Mole appeared in the door. He handed her his answer. He considered it his duty to speak to her; at any rate, nothing could be easier, but Mlle. de La Mole would not listen to him and disappeared. Julien was delighted; he hadn't known what to say.

"If this isn't a game agreed upon with Count Norbert, then it's clear that my cold looks have kindled the baroque love this very high-born girl has decided to feel for me. I should be a bit more stupid than is called for if ever I let myself be lured into fancying that tall blond doll." This line of reasoning left him colder and more calculating than ever before in his life.

"In the battle that is preparing," he added, "pride of birth will be like a high hill, forming a tactical position between her and me. It's up there that I'll have to maneuver. I did the wrong thing by staying in Paris; postponing my departure like this will make me look bad and expose me to ridicule, if this is nothing but a game. What did I have to lose by leaving? If they were pulling my leg, I was pulling theirs. If there is anything to her interest in me, I would have increased it a hundred times."

Mlle. de La Mole's letter had given Julien's vanity such keen pleasure that, while laughing over what had happened, he had forgotten to give serious thought to the advisability of departure. It was a flaw in his character to be extremely sensitive to his own omissions. He was sorely vexed by this one, and hardly thought about the incredible victory which had preceded this small reverse. Then, around nine o'clock, Mlle. de La Mole appeared on the threshold of the library, threw a letter at him, and fled.

"It seems that this is to be an epistolary novel!" he said, picking up the letter. "The enemy has made a false move;

as for me, I am going to send coldness and virtue into the field."

He was being asked, with a haughtiness that doubled his secret gaiety, for a decisive answer. He indulged himself for two pages in the pleasure of mystifying those persons who were trying to make a fool of him, and it was still as a joke that he announced, toward the end of his reply, that his departure had been set for the next morning.

His letter concluded: "The garden will do for delivering it," he thought, and went there. He looked up at Mlle. de La Mole's bedroom window.

She was on the second floor, next to her mother's apartment, but there was a high mezzanine. The second floor was so high up that as he walked beneath the alley of sycamores, letter in hand, Julien could not be seen from Mlle. de La Mole's window. The arch formed by the skillfully pruned trees blocked the view. "What!" said Julien to himself irritably, "more carelessness! If they are out to make a fool of me, showing myself with a letter in hand will help my enemies."

Norbert's bedroom was directly over his sister's, and if Julien came out from under the vault formed by the clipped sycamore branches, the count and his friends would be able to follow every move he made.

Mlle. de La Mole appeared behind her window pane; he half showed his letter; she bent her head. Directly Julien started up to his room at a run, and on the main staircase he happened to meet the beautiful Mathilde, who, perfectly at ease and with laughter in her eyes, seized the letter.

"What passion there was in poor Mme. de Rênal's gaze," Julien remarked to himself, "when even after six months of intimacy, she dared to accept a letter from me! Not once, I think, did she look at me with laughing eyes."

He did not state the rest of his comparison so clearly; was he ashamed of the futility of his motives? "But too," he thought, "what a difference in the elegance of Mlle. de La Mole's morning gown, in the elegance of her figure! Catching sight of Mlle. de La Mole at a distance of thirty yards, a man of taste could guess what rank she occupies in society. That is what you might call explicit merit."

Joking all the while, Julien had yet to admit all of his thought to himself: Mme. de Rênal had had no Marquis de Croisenois to sacrifice for him. He had had no rival except that ignoble subprefect Charcot, who took the name de Maugiron because there were no more de Maugirons.

At five o'clock Julien received a third letter; it was tossed at him from the library door. Mlle. de La Mole fled again. "What a mania for writing!" he said to himself, laughing, "when it is so easy for us to talk! The enemy wants to get hold of letters from me, that's clear . . . and several!" He was in no hurry to pen this one. "More elegant sentences," he thought, but he turned pale as he read. There were only eight lines.

I have to speak with you. I must speak with you, tonight. The moment one o'clock strikes, go to the garden. Take the gardener's big ladder by the well; lean it against my window and climb up to my room. There is a full moon, no matter.

Chapter XV

Is It a Plot?

> Ah! how hard it is to bear, the
> time between the conception of a
> great plan and its execution! How
> many vain terrors! What irresolu-
> tion!—Life is at stake.—Much more
> than that is at stake: honor!
>
> —SCHILLER

"This is getting serious," thought Julien, "... and a bit
too obvious," he added, after having thought it over.
"Why! that beautiful young lady can speak to me in the
library with, thank God, perfect freedom; afraid I might
show him the accounts, the marquis never comes here.
Why! M. de La Mole and Count Norbert, the only persons
who set foot in here, are gone almost all day; it's easy
to spot them the moment they come back to the house,
and the sublime Mathilde, for whose hand a sovereign
prince would not be too noble, is asking me to take an
abominable risk!

"It's plain that someone is out to ruin me or, at the very
least, make a fool of me. First they tried to do me in with
my letters, but they were too carefully written. Very well!
What they want now is an action that is clear as day.
Those pretty little gentlemen must think I am either completely stupid or perfectly conceited. The devil! Climb a
ladder to a second floor twenty-five feet above the ground
on the brightest moonlit night in the world! There would
be time to see me, even from the neighboring houses.
Wouldn't I look fine on my ladder!" Julien went to his
room and, whistling the while, packed his trunk. He had
made up his mind to leave and not even answer.

But this wise resolution brought him no peace of mind. "If by chance," he said to himself suddenly, his trunk locked, "Mathilde were acting in good faith! In her opinion, then, I'd be playing the part of a perfect coward. Since I have no birthright, I must have great qualities, ready to show on demand, without benefit of any flattering suppositions, and thoroughly proven by deeds that speak for themselves. . . ."

He spent a quarter of an hour pacing his room. "What use in denying it?" he said finally, "I will be a coward in her eyes. I will lose not only the most dazzling woman in high society, as everyone described her at the Duke de Retz's ball, but also the sublime pleasure of seeing the Marquis de Croisenois sacrificed for my sake. The son of a duke who will be a duke himself. A charming young man who has all the qualities I lack: a sense of what is fitting, birth, fortune. . . .

"Remorse will haunt me all my life—not because of her, there are plenty of mistresses! . . . 'But there is only one honor!' says old Don Diego,* and here I am clearly and unmistakably beating a retreat from the first danger that comes my way; for that duel with M. de Beauvoisis was a joke. This is quite a different matter. I might be shot full of holes by a servant, but that's the least of my worries; I might be dishonored.

"This is getting serious, my boy," he added with a Gascon accent and gaiety. "*Honour* is at stake. Never again will a poor devil, cast down so low by chance, find another such opportunity; there will be other women in my life, but none like this. . . ."

He pondered for a long time; he was walking about hurriedly and stopping short from time to time. A magnificent marble bust of Cardinal Richelieu had been put in his room; in spite of himself, it kept drawing his attention. Lighted up by his lamp, this bust seemed to gaze at him sternly, as if reproaching him for his want of that audacity which ought to come naturally to the French character. "In your time, great man, would I have hesitated?

"At the worst," Julien said to himself finally, "let us suppose that this is a trap; it's quite a dirty business and highly compromising for a girl. They know I'm not the man to keep quiet. So they will have to kill me. That was all right in 1574, in the time of Boniface de La Mole, but the one today would never dare. Those people are not what they used to be. Mlle. de La Mole is so envied! Tomorrow four hundred drawing rooms would echo her shame, and with what pleasure!

335

"The servants gossip among themselves, about the marked preference she keeps showing me; I know, I've heard them. . . .

"On the other hand, her letters! . . . They might think I have them on me. Catching me in her bedroom, they would relieve me of them. I will have to deal with two, three, four men, who knows? Yet, where are they going to get these men? Where can you find close-mouthed hirelings in Paris? They're all afraid of the law. . . . By God! Caylus, Croisenois, de Luz will do it themselves. The hour, and the foolish figure I will cut in their midst, must be what has tempted them. Beware of Abélard's fate,* Mr. Secretary!

"But, to be sure, gentlemen, you will carry my mark; I will aim for your faces, like Caesar's soldiers at Pharsala. . . . As for the letters, I can put them in a safe place."

Julien made copies of the last two, hid them in a volume of the library's handsome Voltaire, and took the originals to the post himself.

When he returned: "Into what mad adventure am I about to throw myself?" he wondered in surprise and terror. He had gone a quarter of an hour without looking straight into the face of his deed for the following night. "But if I refuse, I will despise myself forever after! My refusal will be a great source of doubt for the rest of my life, and for me such a doubt is the bitterest of misfortunes. Wasn't that how I felt in the case of Amanda's lover? I believe I could more easily forgive myself for an out-and-out crime; once it was confessed, I'd stop thinking about it.

"What! an incredibly lucky fate has singled me out of the crowd to set me in rivalry against one of the best names in France, and shall I, out of sheer wantonness, declare myself his inferior! When all's said and done, it would be cowardly not to go. That remark settles it," cried Julien, rising to his feet. . . . "Besides, she's pretty as can be. If this is not a trap, what a crazy risk she is taking! If this is a hoax, by God! gentlemen, it depends on me alone to turn it into a serious matter, and so I shall.

"But if they pin down my arms the moment I enter the bedroom; they might have set up some ingenious contraption!

"It's like a duel," he told himself with a laugh. "There's a parry for every thrust, as my fencing master says, but the good Lord, who wants to get it over with, sees to it that one of the two fencers forgets to parry. In any event, these will answer for me." He pulled out his pocket pistols, and though the primers were in good condition he replaced them.

There were still a good many hours to wait; for something to do, Julien wrote to Fouqué:

My friend, open the enclosed letter only in case of accident, should you hear that something peculiar has happened to me. In which event, rub out the names in the manuscript I am sending you, and make eight copies of it, which you are to send to the newspapers in Marseille, Bordeaux, Lyon, Brussels, etc. Ten days later, have this manuscript printed; send the first copy to the Marquis de La Mole; and two weeks later, throw the other copies by night into the streets of Verrières.

Julien had made this little justificatory record—drawn up in the form of a story, and which Fouqué was not to open except in case of an accident—as little compromising as possible for Mlle. de La Mole, yet it described his own situation very precisely.

Julien was just finishing his package when the dinner bell rang; it made his heart pound. His imagination, engrossed with the account he had just composed, was full of tragic forebodings. He had seen himself seized by the servants, bound, then taken down to the cellar with a gag in his mouth. There a servant kept a close watch on him, and if the noble family's honor required a tragic end to this adventure, it was easily brought to a close with one of those poisons that leave no trace; they would say he had died of a sickness, and would carry him dead up to his room.

Moved by his own story, like a playwright, Julien was really frightened when he entered the dining room. He looked at all those footmen in full livery. He studied their faces. "Which have been chosen for tonight's expedition?" he asked himself. "In this family, memories of Henry III's court are so real, so often recalled, that if they consider themselves insulted they will be quicker to act than other personages of their rank." He looked at Mlle. de La Mole and tried to read the family's plan in her eyes. She was pale, and he thought she had an altogether medieval look. Never had he seen such an air of greatness about her; she was truly beautiful and stately. He almost fell in love with her. *"Pallida morte futura,"** he said to himself. ("Her pallor bespeaks her high purposes.")

To no avail, after dinner, he pretended for a long while to be strolling in the garden; Mlle. de La Mole did not appear. At that moment, talking with her would have freed his heart of a great weight.

Why not admit it? He was afraid. Since he had resolved to act, he gave in to his feelings without shame. "Provided that when the time comes to act I find the courage I need, what difference does it make how I feel right now?" He went to make sure of the location and weight of the ladder.

"It is an instrument," he said to himself, laughing, "of which I have been destined to make use! here as in Verrières! But what a difference! That time," he added with a sigh, "I didn't have to be wary of the person for whom I was exposing myself. What a difference too in the danger! Had I been killed in M. de Rênal's garden, it would have been no dishonor to me. They could easily have found a way to make my death unaccountable. But here, what abominable stories won't they concoct in the drawing rooms of the Hôtel de Chaulnes, the Hôtel de Caylus, the Hôtel de Retz, etcetera, in short, everywhere. Posterity will think I was a monster.

"For two or three years," he went on, laughing at himself. And yet this idea staggered him. "On what grounds will anyone be able to vindicate me? Suppose that Fouqué prints my posthumous pamphlet; it will be but one infamy the more. Why! I was taken into a household, and in return for the hospitality shown me, for all the kindness lavished on me, I print a pamphlet telling what goes on in it! I attack the honor of its women! Ah! rather let us play the dupe a thousand time over!"

It was a ghastly evening.

338

Chapter XVI

One in the Morning

> This garden was very large and
> had been laid out only a few years
> before with perfect taste. But the
> trees had been part of the famous
> Pré-aux-Clercs, so well-known in
> the time of Henry III; they were
> more than a century old. There was
> something rural about the place.
>
> —MASSINGER

He was about to write and countermand his instructions
to Fouqué when eleven o'clock struck. He turned the key
in his bedroom door noisily, as if locking himself in. He
moved throughout the house on cat's feet to observe what
was going on, especially in the fifth-floor dormers, where
the servants lived. There was nothing out of the ordinary.
One of Mme. de La Mole's chambermaids was giving a
party. The servants were gaily drinking punch. "Men who
laugh like that can't be in on tonight's expedition,"
thought Julien. "They would be sober."

Eventually he stationed himself in a dark corner of the
garden. "If they plan to keep everything hidden from the
servants, they will have the men they hired to catch me
come in over the garden wall. If M. de Croisenois has his
wits about him in this business, he must see that it would
be less compromising for the young lady he means to
marry if I were caught just before I stepped into her
bedroom."

He made a very precise and military reconnaissance of
the grounds. "My honor is at stake," he thought. "If I

make a slip, it won't be excuse enough in my own eyes to tell myself: I didn't think of that."

The weather was hopelessly fair. Around eleven the moon had risen; by half past twelve it lit up the entire side of the house that faced the garden.

"She's mad," Julien told himself. When the clock struck one, there was still light in Count Norbert's windows. Never in his life had Julien been so afraid; he saw nothing but the danger of his enterprise and felt no enthusiasm whatsoever.

He went to get the huge ladder, waited five minutes to allow time for a counterorder, and at five past one leaned it against Mathilde's window. He climbed softly, pistol in hand, astonished not to be attacked. As he drew near the window it opened noiselessly.

"There you are, sir," Mathilde said to him nervously. "I've been watching you for the past hour."

Julien was embarrassed; he didn't know how to act; he felt no love at all. In his confusion, he thought he should be forward; he tried to kiss Mathilde.

"Shame on you!" she said, pushing him away.

Well content to be rejected, he cast a hurried glance around him, the moon was so bright that the shadows it made in Mlle. de La Mole's bedroom were perfectly black. "Some men may very well be hidden in here," he thought, "without my being able to see them."

"What do you have in your coat pocket?" Mathilde asked, delighted to find a subject of conversation. She was strangely ill at ease: all her feelings of reserve and shyness, so natural in a well-bred girl, had taken the upper hand again and were putting her to the rack.

"I have all sorts of knives and pistols," answered Julien, no less content to have something to say.

"You will have to let down the ladder."

"It's huge and might break the windows of the drawing room below, or the mezzanine. . . ."

"You mustn't break the windows," Mathilde went on, trying in vain to assume an ordinary conversational tone. "It seems to me that you could lower it with a rope tied to the top rung. I always keep a supply of rope in my room."

"And this is a woman in love!" thought Julien. "She dares to say she loves! So much self-control, so much foresight, shows me clearly enough that I have not triumphed over M. de Croisenois as I so foolishly believed; I have simply taken his place. But does it really matter? Am I in love with her? I have won out over the marquis in the

340

sense that he will be very angry to have a successor, and angrier still because I am that successor. How haughtily he stared at me last night in Tortoni's, when he pretended not to recognize me! How ill-naturedly he greeted me later, when he could no longer avoid it!"

Julien had tied the rope to the highest rung of the ladder; he let it down gently, leaning far out over the balcony to keep it from touching the windows. "A fine time to kill me," he thought, "if someone is hiding in Mathilde's room." But a deep silence prevailed everywhere.

The ladder touched the ground; Julien managed to lay it down in the bed of exotic flowers along the wall.

"What will my mother say when she sees her beautiful plants all crushed! ... You must throw down the rope too," she added with great presence of mind. "If someone saw it hanging from the balcony, that item would be hard to explain."

"And me, how I go 'way?" said Julien jokingly and affecting a Creole accent. (One of the chambermaids in the house came from Santo Domingo.)

"You? You go 'way by door," said Mathilde, enchanted by the idea. "Ah! how worthy is this man of all my love!" she thought.

Julien had just let the rope drop to the ground; Mathilde clasped him in her arms. He thought he had been seized by the enemy and turned around sharply, pulling out his dagger. She thought she heard a window opening. They stood stock-still, not breathing. The moon shone fully on them. The noise was not repeated; there was nothing to worry about.

Embarrassment set in again; it was great on both sides. Julien made sure the door was secured by all of its bolts; he thought seriously of looking under the bed but didn't dare; one or two lackeys might have been posted there. Finally, dreading some future blame from his own sense of prudence, he looked.

Mathilde had fallen prey to all the agonies of extreme shyness. She was horrified at her position.

"What have you done with my letters?" she asked after a time.

"What a fine opportunity to confound those gentlemen if they are eavesdropping, and to avoid the battle!" Julien thought.

"The first is concealed in a big Protestant Bible that last night's stagecoach carried far away from here." He spoke very distinctly as he entered into these details so as to be heard by any persons who might be hiding in the two tall mahogany wardrobes which he had not dared to inspect. "The other two are in the mail and following the same route as the first."

"Good God! why all these precautions?" said Mathilde in astonishment.

"Why should I lie?" thought Julien, and he confessed all of his suspicions.

"That's the reason, then, for the coldness of your letters!" cried Mathilde with more frenzy than tenderness in her voice.

Julien did not catch this nuance. Her use of the familiar address had turned his head, or at least it had laid his suspicions to rest; he had gained stature in his own eyes; he dared to clasp that very beautiful girl who inspired him with so much respect. She only half resisted.

He resorted to his memory, as once before long ago in Besançon with Amanda Binet, and recited several of the most beautiful passages in the *Nouvelle Héloïse*.

"You have a man's heart," she answered, without listening very closely to his recitation. "I meant to test your courage, I admit. Your first suspicions and your determination to see me show that you are even more intrepid than I thought."

Mathilde was making an effort to address him familiarly, and she was obviously more attentive to this odd manner of speech than to the sense of what she was saying. Her use of the familiar form, stripped of all tenderness, ceased to give Julien any pleasure after a few moments. He was astonished at the absence of happiness; finally, in order to feel it, he appealed to his reason. He saw that he was highly esteemed by this proud girl, who never bestowed her praise without reservation; by this line of reasoning, he attained to a happiness based on self-esteem.

True, this was not the soul's ecstasy he had sometimes known in the company of Mme. de Rênal. "Great God, what a difference!" There was nothing tender about his feelings in these first few moments. He felt rather the keenest happiness of crowned ambition, and Julien was above all ambitious. He spoke again about the people he had suspected and of the precautions he had devised. As he spoke, he kept searching for a way to profit from his victory.

Still deeply embarrassed, and looking as if she were horror-stricken at the step she had taken, Mathilde seemed delighted to find a topic of conversation. They talked about ways of meeting again. Julien savored delightedly the fresh proofs of intelligence and bravery which he gave during this discussion. They had to deal with very shrewd people; little Tanbeau was certainly a spy; but he and Mathilde were not exactly slow-witted either.

What could be easier than to meet in the library, and make plans there?

"Without rousing suspicion, I can appear in any part of the house," added Julien, "and almost in Mme. de La Mole's bedroom." It was absolutely necessary to go through it to reach her daughter's room.

If Mathilde preferred that he always come by way of the ladder, it was with a heart drunk with joy that he would expose himself to this slight danger.

As she listened to him talk, Mathilde was offended by his air of triumph. "So he is my master!" She was already a prey to misgivings. Her reason was horrified at the piece of sheer madness she had just committed. Had she been able, she would have annihilated herself and Julien. When, from time to time, by sheer willpower, she was able to quiet her remorse, feelings of shyness and of pained modesty would make her perfectly wretched. She had in no way anticipated the frightful state she was in.

"All the same, I must speak to him," she told herself at length. "It's only proper; one speaks to one's lover." And then, to fulfill her obligation, and with a tenderness that was more apparent in her words than in the sound of her voice, she told him about the various decisions she had reached in the past few days with regard to him.

She had made up her mind that if he dared come to her room, with the help of the gardener's ladder, as stipulated, she would be his. But never have such tender words been spoken in a politer and colder tone of voice. Until now, the meeting had been icy. It was enough to turn love into hatred. What a fine lesson in morality for a rash young woman! Is it worth ruining one's future for such a moment?

After many a doubt, which to the casual observer might seem an effect of the most decided loathing—so great the difficulty her feeling that a woman's duty is to herself had in yielding to even so staunch a will as hers—Mathilde finally became his kind mistress.

To tell the truth, their raptures were a bit forced. For them, passionate love was still a model to be imitated rather than a reality.

Mlle. de La Mole believed that she was performing a duty to herself and to her lover. "The poor boy," she told herself, "has been consummately brave; he must be happy, or it is I who am wanting in character." But she would willingly have paid the price of eternal suffering to redeem the harsh constraint under which she found herself.

Despite the terrible violence she was doing her feelings, she was absolute mistress of her words. Neither regret nor blame came to spoil this night, one that struck Julien as strange rather than happy. How different, good God, from his last stay of twenty-four hours in Verrières! "Those fine Parisian manners have found the way to spoil everything, even love," Julien remarked to himself, quite unfairly.

He indulged in these reflections while standing in one of the tall mahogany wardrobes, into which he had been introduced at the first sounds from the adjoining apartment, which was Mme. de La Mole's. Mathilde followed her mother to mass, the serving women soon left the apartment, and Julien easily made his escape before they returned to finish their work.

He mounted a horse and sought out the most isolated spots in the forest of Meudon. He was far more astonished than happy. The kind of felicity that from time to time welled up in his heart was that of the young second lieutenant who, as a consequence of some amazing action, has been promoted on the spot to colonel by his commanding general; he felt he had been lifted to an immense height. Everything that had been above him the night before was beside him now, or else below. Julien's happiness increased as he rode farther and farther away.

If there was no tenderness in his heart, it was because Mathilde, in all her behavior with him, however strange it may sound, had been fulfilling a duty. There had been nothing unexpected for her in all the events of that night, except the wretchedness and shame she experienced, instead of that heavenly bliss of which the novels speak.

"Could I have been mistaken; is it possible that I don't love him?" she asked herself.

Chapter XVII

An Old Sword

> I now mean to be serious;—it is
>   time,
> Since laughter now-a-days is deem'd
>   too serious.
> A jest at vice by virtue's called a
>   crime.
>
> —*Don Juan*, C. XIII.

She did not appear at dinner time. At night she came to the drawing room for a few minutes but did not look at Julien. This behavior seemed strange; "but," he reflected, "I must confess that, except the things these people do every day and which I have seen them do a hundred times, I know nothing about the ways of high society. She will give me some good reason for all this." Nevertheless, impelled by the liveliest curiosity, he kept studying the expression on Mathilde's features; he couldn't shut his eyes to the fact that she had a cold and ill-natured look about her. Obviously, it was not the same woman who, the night before, had felt or feigned raptures that were too excessive to be true.

The next day, the day after, the same coldness on her side; she never once looked at him, she was not aware of his existence. Devoured by the most intense anxiety, Julien was a thousand leagues from the feeling of triumph which had exhilarated him on the first day. "Could this, by any chance, be a return to virtue?" he wondered. But that idea was far too middle class for the lofty Mathilde.

"Ordinarily she takes very little stock in religion," thought Julien. "She likes it because it serves the interests of her caste. But might she not, out of simple feminine modesty, be reproaching herself harshly for the irreparable error she has committed?" Julien believed he was her first lover.

"But," he would tell himself at other times, "one must admit that there is nothing naïve, simple, or tender about any of her conduct. Never have I seen her looking more like a queen who has just stepped down from her throne. Does she despise me? It would be like her to blame herself for what she has done for me, if only because of my low birth."

While Julien, filled with prejudices drawn from books and from his recollections of Verrières, was pursuing the chimera of a tender mistress who gives no thought to her own existence once she has made her lover happy, Mathilde's vanity was raging against him. Since she had not been bored during the last two months, she no longer dreaded boredom; thus, though he could not have been the least aware of it, Julien had lost his greatest advantage.

"So I have given myself a master!" Mlle. de La Mole kept telling herself as she walked restlessly about her room. "He is the soul of honor, well and good; but if I push his vanity to the limit, he will avenge himself by disclosing the nature of our relations."

Such is the unhappy age in which we live that not even the strangest aberrations are a cure for boredom. Julien was Mathilde's first lover, and in such circumstances, which usually grant a few tender illusions to even the most frigid of hearts, she was a prey to the bitterest speculations.

"He has immense power over me, since he reigns by terror and could inflict a terrible punishment if I pushed him to the limit." This thought alone was enough to drive Mlle. de La Mole into insulting him, for courage was her prime attribute. Nothing could give her a bit of excitement or cure her of a lingering and ever-recurring boredom except the notion that she was playing heads or tails with her whole future.

After dinner, on the third day, since Mlle. de La Mole persisted in ignoring him, Julien followed her, obviously against her will, into the billiard room.

"Very well, sir, so you think you have acquired some great authority over me," she said to him with barely restrained anger, "since in opposition to my clearly expressed will, you claim the right to speak to me? How can you be so cruel and so disloyal? Do you realize that no one has ever presumed so far. . . ?"

Nothing could be funnier than the dialogue between these two young lovers; without realizing it, they were pitted against one another by a feeling of the most intense hatred. Since neither of them was long-suffering by nature, though it must be added that both had the manners of good society, they were soon at the point of notifying one another that they were breaking off forever.

"I swear eternal secrecy," said Julian. "I might even add that I would never speak to you again, were it not that your reputation might suffer from so marked a change." He bowed respectfully and left.

That night he had carried out, with the alacrity of vengeance, what to him seemed a duty: he was a long way from considering himself deeply in love with Mlle. de La Mole. Certainly he had not been in love with her three days before, when she hid him in the tall mahogany wardrobe. But a swift change took place in his heart the moment he saw that he had broken with her forever. His cruel memory began to recall the slightest details of that night, which in reality had left him so cold.

By the second night following their declaration of eternal estrangement, Julien almost went crazy from being forced to admit to himself that he loved Mlle. de La Mole. Terrible struggles ensued from this discovery; all his feelings were thrown into confusion.

A week later, instead of being arrogant with M. de Croisenois, he felt almost like falling upon his neck and bursting into tears.

Getting used to his misery brought him a glimmering of good sense; he made up his mind to leave for Languedoc, packed his trunk, and set out for the posting house.

He felt faint when, after reaching the mail-coach office, he was informed that by an odd chance there was a place for the very next day on the mail for Toulouse. He reserved it and went back to the Hôtel de La Mole to announce his departure to the marquis.

M. de La Mole was out. More dead than alive, Julien went to wait for him in the library. Think how he felt when he discovered Mlle. de La Mole there!

Seeing him come in, she assumed an ill-natured air which he could not possibly mistake.

Carried away by his unhappiness, thrown off by surprise, Julien was foolish enough to say to her, in the tenderest of tones and straight from the heart: "So you don't love me anymore?"

"I am horrified at having given myself to the first man

who came along," said Mathilde as her eyes filled with tears of rage against herself.

"The first man who came along!" Julien shouted, and he leaped toward a medieval sword which hung on the wall as a curiosity.

His suffering, which he thought utmost at the instant he had addressed Mlle. de La Mole, was augmented a hundredfold by the tears of shame he saw her shedding. He would have been the happiest of men if he could have killed her.

At that moment, just when he had drawn the sword, with some difficulty, from its ancient scabbard, Mathilde, delighted at so new a sensation, advanced proudly toward him; her tears had stopped.

The thought of the Marquis de La Mole, his benefactor, suddenly crossed Julien's mind. "I, kill his daughter!" he said to himself, "how horrible!" He made a move to throw away the sword. 'Surely," he thought, "she will burst out laughing at the sight of such a melodramatic gesture"; he was indebted to this thought for the recovery of all his self-control. He inspected the blade of the old sword inquisitively, as if searching for a spot of rust; then he put it back in its scabbard, and with the greatest calm replaced it on the gilded bronze nail from which it hung.

This whole sequence, very slow toward the end, lasted a good minute; Mlle. de La Mole watched him in astonishment. "Well, I've just missed being killed by my lover!" she told herself. This idea carried her back to the finest years in the reign of Charles IX and Henry III.

Looking taller than usual, she was standing motionless in front of Julien, who had just replaced the sword; she gazed at him with eyes from which all hatred had vanished. One must admit that she was very attractive at the moment; certainly no woman ever looked less like a Parisian doll. (That tag summed up Julien's chief objection to the city's women.)

"I am about to relapse into my old weakness for him," thought Mathilde. "If I do, he's bound to think he's my lord and master, especially after a setback and just after I've spoken so harshly to him." She fled.

"My God! how beautiful she is!" said Julien, watching her run. "There's the woman who flung herself so furiously into my arms less than two weeks ago.... And that time will never come back! It's my own fault! At the moment of such an extraordinary gesture, so full of prom-

348

ise for me, I was not even responsive! ... I must admit that I was born with a dull and unlucky nature."

The marquis appeared; Julien hastened to announce his departure.

"For where?" asked M. de La Mole.

"For Languedoc."

"No, if you please, you have been reserved for a higher destiny; if you leave, it will be for the north.... I am, even in the military sense of the word, confining you to the house. You will oblige me by never being absent for more than two or three hours; I may need you from one moment to the next."

Incapable of speech, Julien bowed and withdrew, leaving the marquis highly astonished. He locked himself in his room. There, he was free to exaggerate all the harshness of his lot.

"So," he thought. "I can't even get away! God knows how many days the marquis will keep me in Paris; good God! What is to become of me? And not a friend to give me advice; the Abbé Pirard wouldn't let me finish the first sentence; Count Altamira would offer to affiliate me with some conspiracy, to take my mind off things.

"And yet, I am mad; I feel it; I am mad! Who is there to guide me; what's to become of me?"

Chapter XVIII

Cruel Moments

> And she admits it! She tells me
> all about it in the greatest detail!
> Her beautiful eyes, gazing into
> mine, proclaim the love she felt for
> another.
>
> —SCHILLER

Entranced, Mlle. de La Mole could think of nothing but the happiness of having come so close to being killed. She went so far as to tell herself: "He is worthy of being my master, since he was on the verge of killing me. How many of those good-looking young men in society would have to be fused together to make up one such passionate impulse?

"One must admit that he looked very handsome when he climbed up on the chair to replace the sword in exactly the same quaint position the decorator had given it! I was not so crazy after all to fall in love with him." At that moment, if some decent way of patching things up had presented itself, she would have seized it with pleasure.

Julien, double-locked in his room, was a prey to the most violent despair. Among other wild ideas, he thought of throwing himself at her feet. If instead of keeping out of sight he had wandered down into the garden and through the Hôtel, so as to be within range of any opportunity, he might in an instant perhaps have turned his frightful depression into the most intense happiness.

But artfulness, the absence of which we reproach in him, would have precluded his sublime impulse to grab the sword, which at the time made him seem so handsome in Mlle. de La Mole's eyes. Her caprice, auspicious for Julien, lasted all day; Mathilde envisioned a charming picture of the few great moments during which she had loved him; she missed them.

"In fact," she mused, "in that poor boy's estimate, my passion for him lasted only from one o'clock in the morning, when I saw him arrive by the ladder with all his pistols in the side pockets of his coat, until nine in the morning. It was a quarter of an hour later, while hearing mass at Sainte-Valère, that it first occurred to me that he would think he was my master, and that he might well try to make me obey him, out of terror."

After dinner Mlle. de La Mole, far from shunning him, addressed Julien and invited him, so to speak, to follow her into the garden; he obeyed. This test was her undoing. Though not quite aware of it, Mathilde was yielding to a love for him that was beginning to revive. She found the utmost pleasure in walking at his side; out of curiosity, she kept glancing at those hands which that morning had seized a sword to kill her.

And yet, after all that had happened, there could be no return to their old style of conversation. Little by little Mathilde fell to talking in an intimately confidential tone about the state of her heart. She discovered an uncommon pleasure in that kind of conversation; she went so far as to tell him at great length about the passing fits of enthusiasm she had once felt for M. de Croisenois, and then for M. de Caylus.

"What! M. de Caylus too. . . ." Julien cried out, and all the bitter jealousy of a cast-off lover blazed out in this remark. Mathilde, judging it in that light, was not offended. She went on torturing Julien by detailing her past emotions, which she did most quaintly and in an accent of the most intimate truth. At a turn in the path, Mathilde's arm brushed Julien's. He could see that what she was describing was uppermost in her mind. He noted sorrowfully that as she spoke she made discoveries about her own heart.

The torments of jealousy can go no further. To suspect that a rival is beloved is cruel enough, but to hear about the love he inspires confessed in detail by the woman one adores is perhaps the height of suffering. Oh, how he was punished in that instant for those surges of pride which had led him to set himself above the Caylus' and the Croisenois'! With what deep-seated and heartfelt wretchedness he now exaggerated their smallest advantages! With what burning sincerity he despised himself!

To him, Mathilde seemed a creature more than divine;

words cannot express the extent of his admiration. As he strolled at her side he kept stealing glances at her hands, her arms, her queenly figure. He was ready to fall at her feet, prostrated by love and unhappiness, and cry: "Mercy!"

"This beautiful person, so superior to everyone and who once loved me, will doubtless fall in love with M. de Caylus very soon!"

Julien could have no doubt about Mlle. de La Mole's sincerity; the note of truth was too evident in everything she said. So that absolutely nothing should be wanting to his unhappiness, there were moments when by dint of concentrating on what she had once felt for M. de Caylus, Mathilde came to speak as if she were currently in love with him. To be sure, there was love in her voice; Julien could hear that plainly.

If the hollow of his chest had been flooded with molten lead, he would have suffered less. How, having reached such an extreme of suffering, could the poor boy have guessed that it was only because she was speaking to him that Mlle. de La Mole took such pleasure in recalling a passing fancy she had once felt for M. de Caylus or M. de Croisenois?

Words cannot express Julien's agony. (He observed that his ear had become a confidential servant, in person.) He went on listening to her detailed confessions of a love she had felt for others, in this same alley of sycamores in which a few short days ago he had waited until one o'clock should strike to make his way up to her bedroom. The human being cannot withstand a higher degree of suffering. Mathilde did not leave the garden or Julien until after nine thirty, after her mother had called her three times. . . . "How much worthier is the man I love today than any with whom I was once on the verge of falling in love!" she thought, without being precisely aware of it.

This cruel intimacy lasted for one long week. Mathilde seemed at times to seek out, at others not to avoid, an opportunity to speak with him; and the subject of conversation, to which both seemed to keep returning with a sort of painful pleasure, was the story of what she had felt for other men. She told him about the letters she had written, she recalled her very words, she recited whole sentences to him. Lately, she seemed to contemplate Julien with a sort of malignant joy. His pain was a keen delight for her. In it she saw her tyrant's weakness; she might thus permit herself to love him.

The reader can see that Julien had no experience, that

he had not even read any novels. If he had been a little less clumsy and had he, with some show of composure, said to this girl, whom he worshiped and who confided such odd secrets in him, "Admit that though I can't hold a candle to all those gentlemen, it is nonetheless I whom you love," perhaps she would have been glad to be found out. In any event, success would have depended entirely upon how gracefully Julien expressed this idea, and upon the moment he chose. At any rate, he would have emerged with advantage to himself from a situation that was beginning to seem monotonous to Mathilde.

"So you don't love me anymore, and I adore you!" Julien, mad with love and grief, said to her one day, after a long walk. This was about the worst blunder he could have made.

In the wink of an eye, this statement dashed all the pleasure Mlle. de La Mole had found in speaking to him about the state of her heart. She was beginning to wonder, after what had happened, why he did not take offense at her revelations; she was even beginning to imagine, until he made his stupid remark, that perhaps he no longer loved her. "Pride has no doubt killed his love," she was telling herself. "He's not the man to stand by and watch while fellows like Caylus, de Luz, or Croisenois are chosen over himself, though he admits they are far superior to him. No, I will never see him at my feet again!"

In days previous, out of the ingenuousness of his misery, Julien used often to praise those gentlemen's illustrious qualities in the warmest terms; he went so far as to exaggerate them to her. This nuance did not escape Mlle. de La Mole; she was astonished at it but could not guess the cause. By praising a rival whom he thought enjoyed her love, Julien's frenzied soul was sympathizing with his happiness.

His remark, so frank but so foolish, changed everything in an instant; now sure of his love, Mathilde despised him thoroughly.

She was strolling with him at the time he made his clumsy remark; she left him, and her last look expressed the most awful contempt. Once back in the drawing room, she did not look at him again during the whole evening. By the next day, contempt for him filled her whole heart; there was no room left for that impulse which, for a week, had caused her to take such great pleasure in treating Julien as her most intimate friend; now the sight of him was disagreeable to her. This sensation on Mathilde's part soon turned into disgust; nothing can express the excessive scorn she felt whenever she caught sight of him.

Julien understood nothing of what had gone on in Mathilde's heart, but his clear-sighted vanity made out contempt. He had the good sense to confront her as rarely as possible, and never to look at her.

But it was not without mortal anguish that he denied himself, as it were, her presence. He believed he could feel this cause his unhappiness to grow. "This is the limit of what a man's heart can bear," he told himself. He spent all of his time at a little window in the attic of the mansion; the shutter had been carefully closed, and from there he could at least catch sight of Mlle. de La Mole whenever she appeared in the garden.

Imagine his reaction when, after dinner, he saw her out walking with M. de Caylus, M. de Luz, or such another for whom she had confessed to having once felt a passing fancy.

Julien had had no conception of such intense anguish; he was on the point of screaming; that hypocritical soul, in which hypocrisy had reigned so long, was shaken at last from top to bottom. Any thought that did not bear on Mlle. de La Mole had become odious to him; he was incapable of writing the simplest letters.

"You are mad," the marquis said to him one morning.

Julien, afraid of being found out, spoke of illness and managed to be convincing. Luckily for him, M. de La Mole chaffed him at dinner about his coming trip; Mathilde understood that it might be quite a long one. Julien had already been avoiding her for several days, and the shining young men who had everything that was lacking in this pale, somber fellow, whom she had once loved, no longer had the power to distract her from her musings.

"An ordinary girl," she told herself, "would have picked out the man she preferred from among those young fellows who attract every eye in a drawing room; but one of the characteristics of genius is not to drag one's thoughts through the rut that has been worn by the common run.

"As the companion of a man like Julien, in whom nothing is wanting except wealth, which I have, I should attract attention all the time; I wouldn't go through life unnoticed. Far from living in constant dread of a revolution, like my female cousins who, for fear of the people, dare not scold a postilion who does a bad job of driving their carriage, I would be sure to play a role, and an important role, since the man I have chosen has character and un-

354

limited ambition. What does he lack? Friends, money? I will give him all that." In her thoughts, she was treating Julien somewhat as an inferior whose fortune one intends to make when and how one wishes, and about whose love one does not permit oneself to have the slightest doubt.

Chapter XIX

The Opera Buffa

> O, how this spring of love resem-
> bleth
> The uncertain glory of an April day;
> Which now shows all the beauty of
> the sun,
> And by and by a cloud takes all
> away!
>
> —SHAKESPEARE

Engrossed in the future and in the uncommon role she hoped to play, before long Mathilde began to miss even the arid metaphysical discussions she used often to have with Julien. Wearied by such lofty thoughts, sometimes she would also long for the moments of bliss she had known with him. These latter memories did not occur to her without remorse, and at times it was overwhelming.

"But even if I have slipped," she told herself, "it is still praiseworthy in a girl like me not to have forgotten her duties except for a man of worth; people will not say that it was his handsome mustache or his graceful mount on a horse that attracted me, but rather his deep discussions about the future that lies in store for France, his ideas about the likeness that events about to swoop down on us may bear to the revolution of 1688 in England. I have been seduced," she answered the voice of remorse. "I am a weak woman, but at least I was not led astray like a mindless doll by an outward show; what I loved in his face was the projection of a great soul.

"If there is a revolution, why shouldn't Julien Sorel play the part of Roland,* and I that of Mme. Roland? I

356

prefer that role to Mme. de Staël's; immoral conduct will be a drawback in our century. To be sure, no one will have grounds to blame me for slipping a second time; I should die for shame."

Mathilde's reveries were not all so serious, it must be admitted, as the thoughts we have just transcribed.

She kept watching Julien on the sly; she saw a charming grace in the least thing he did.

"There's no doubt," she said to herself, "I have managed to squelch any notion in his mind that he has even the smallest claim on me.

"Besides, the unhappiness and deep passion in the poor boy's look when he spoke to me so naïvely about his love a week ago in the garden prove it; I must admit that I behaved extraordinarily in getting angry over a statement in which shone so much respect, so much passion. Am I not his wife? What he said was quite natural and, I must admit, very nice. Julien still loved me after those endless conversations during which I spoke of nothing, and cruelly, I admit, but those trifling passing fancies which only boredom with the life I lead had inspired in me for those fashionable young men of whom he is so jealous. Ah! if he but knew how little danger there is from that quarter! How sickly they seem to me, all pale copies of one another compared with him."

While she made these reflections Mathilde, so as not to betray her thoughts to her mother's watchful eye, kept sketching haphazardly on a page of her album. One of the profiles she had just finished amazed, delighted her: it bore a striking resemblance to Julien. "This is the voice of heaven! Here is one of love's miracles," she said to herself ecstatically. "Unwittingly I have drawn his portrait."

She flew to her room, locked herself in, found some colors, applied herself and tried in earnest to draw Julien's portrait, but she could not bring it off. The profile set down by chance was still the best likeness. Mathilde was delighted with it; in it she saw proof positive of a great passion.

She didn't close her album until very late, when the marquise sent for her to go to the Italian opera. She had but one idea, to keep an eye out for Julien and make her mother invite him to go with them.

He did not appear; those ladies had nothing but the run of the mill in their box. During the whole first act of the opera, Mathilde kept dreaming about the man she loved in raptures of the most ardent passion; but in the second act a maxim of love, sung, it must be admitted, to a melody worthy of Cimarosa,* thrilled her to the core. The opera's heroine was singing: "I should be punished for adoring him so; I love him far too much!"

The moment she heard that sublime cantilena, the world and everything in it vanished for Mathilde. People spoke to her; she did not answer. Her mother scolded; she could scarcely bring herself to look at her. Her ecstasy reached a stage of passion and elation comparable to the most violent emotions Julien had felt for her during the past few days. The divinely graceful cantilena to which the maxim was sung, and which seemed to apply so strikingly to her own position, filled every instant when she was not thinking about Julien himself. That night, thanks to her love of music, she was in the state Mme. de Rênal was always in when she thought about Julien. Rational love is doubtless more intelligent than true love, but it knows only brief moments of enthusiasm; it is self-conscious; it judges itself continually; far from leading thought astray, it is built on thought alone.

Back home, whatever Mme. de La Mole might say, Mathilde insisted she had a fever, and spent part of the night playing the cantilena on her piano. Over and over she sang the words to the famous aria that had charmed her:

> "Devo punirmi, devo punirmi,
> Se troppo amai," etc.*

The outcome of this night of folly was that she believed she had succeeded in getting over her love.

(This page will harm the poor author in more ways than one. Frigid hearts will accuse him of indecency. Yet he would not do the young people who shine in Parisian drawing rooms the injustice of supposing that anyone among them is susceptible to the mad impulses that are undermining Mathilde's character. That character is altogether imaginary and, in fact, imagined well outside the pale of those social customs which guarantee so distinguished a place among all the centuries to the civilization of the nineteenth.

It is not prudence that was wanting in the girls who were the ornament of the balls last winter.

Nor do I think one can rightly accuse them of being overly contemptuous of a brilliant fortune, horses, fine estates, and all those things which assure a woman an agreeable position in society. Far from being bored by all those advantages, they generally make them the object of their most constant desires, and if there is any passion in their hearts, it is for such things.

Nor is it love that guides the careers of young men endowed with some talent, like Julien; they fasten themselves to a coterie with an invincible grip, and when the coterie comes into its own, all the good things of society rain down upon them. Woe to the intellectual who is not allied to a clique; even his smallest, most dubious success will attract nothing but blame, and lofty virtue will triumph in the act of robbing him. Well, sir, a novel is a mirror being carried down a highway. Sometimes it reflects the azure heavens to your view; sometimes, the slime in the puddles along the road. And you will accuse the man who carries the mirror on his back of immorality! His mirror shows you slime, and you blame the mirror! Rather, blame the highway where the puddles stand; or rather still, blame the inspector of roads who allows the water to stagnate and the puddles to form.

Now that we are all agreed that Mathilde's character is impossible in our time, an age no less prudent than virtuous, I will be less concerned about provoking the reader as I get on with my story of that lovable girl's follies.)

All the next day she watched for opportunities to confirm her victory over her wild passion. Her chief aim was to be unpleasant to Julien in every way, yet none of his movements escaped her.

Julien was too wretched and above all too disturbed to see through a tactic prompted by so complex a passion as hers; still less could he see how auspicious it was for him. He fell victim to it. Never perhaps had he been so intensely miserable. His wits had so little control over his actions that if some impatient philosopher had said to him: "Give some thought now as to how you may quickly take advantage of a frame of mind that will soon change in your favor; with the kind of rational love that is to be found in Paris, the same sort of behavior cannot persist for more than two days," he would not have understood him. But excitable as he was, Julien had his sense of honor. His first duty was discretion; that he understood. To ask advice, tell the story of his suffering to the first comer, would have been a delight comparable to that of the wretch to whom, as he is crossing a burning desert, heaven sends a mouthful of iced water. He recognized his danger; he dreaded lest he answer the tactless questioner with a stream of tears; he shut himself in his room.

He watched Mathilde strolling for a long while in the

garden; when she finally left, he went down there; he went over to a rose bush from which she had plucked a flower.

The night was dark, he was free to give vent to all his misery with no fear of being seen. It was plain to him that Mlle. de La Mole loved one of those young officers with whom she had just been chatting so gaily. She had loved him too, but she had discovered how unworthy he was.

"And in fact, I'm not worth much!" Julien told himself, fully convinced, "on the whole, I am a very dull fellow, very common, very boring to others, unbearable to myself." He was sick to death of all his good qualities, of everything he had once cared for enthusiastically; and in this state of *inverted imagination,* he undertook to judge life with his imagination. This is the error of a superior man.

The idea of suicide occurred to him several times; it seemed a charming notion; he thought of it as a delightful rest; it was the glass of ice water held out to the wretch in the desert who is dying of thirst and heat.

"My death will make her even more contemptuous of me!" he cried. "What a memory I shall leave!"

Fallen into this last abyss of wretchedness, a human being has no resource but courage. Julien did not have the genius to tell himself, "I should take a chance," but while watching Mathilde's bedroom window that night, through the shutters he saw her put out her lamp; he pictured the charming room he had seen, alas! but once in his life. His imagination stopped there.

One o'clock struck: to hear the sound of the bell and say to himself, "I am going to climb the ladder," took but an instant.

This was a stroke of genius; good reasons came to him in droves. "Could I be more miserable!" he told himself. He ran to the ladder; the gardener had chained it. Filled with superhuman strength, Julien pried open (with the hammer of one of his small pistols, which he broke) a link in the chain that held the ladder. He was master of it in a few minutes and set it against Mathilde's window.

"She's going to be angry, heap scorn on me, what do I care? I will kiss her, one last kiss; then I will go up to my room and kill myself. . . . My lips will have touched her cheek before I die!"

He flew up the ladder, he knocked at the shutter; after a few seconds Mathilde heard him; she tried to open to him; the ladder was against the shutter. Julien hung onto the iron hook used to hold it open, and at the risk of hurling himself downward, gave the ladder a violent shake and shifted it a little. Mathilde was able to open the shutter.

He flung himself into the room, more dead than alive.

"It's you, then!" she said, rushing into his arms. . . .

Who could describe Julien's intense happiness? Mathilde's was almost as great.

She spoke out against herself; she denounced herself. "Punish me for my atrocious pride," she said, clasping him in her arms as if to smother him. "You are my master, I am your slave; I should beg your pardon on bended knees for having tried to rebel." She left his arms to fall at his feet. Still drunk with happiness and love, she told him, "Yes, you are my master. Rule over me forever, punish your slave harshly if she tries to rebel."

Later on she tore away from his arms, lit the candle, and Julien had all he could do to prevent her from cutting off a whole side of her hair.

"I want to remind myself," she told him, "that I am your servant; if ever my abominable pride should lead me astray, show me this hair and tell me: 'It is no longer a question of love, it is no longer a question of what you feel in your heart at this moment; you have sworn to obey; obey on your honor.'"

But it is wiser to leave out a description of such heights of felicity and frenzy.

Julien's valor was equal to his happiness. "I must leave by the ladder now," he said to Mathilde, when he saw dawn breaking over the distant chimneys to the east, beyond the garden. "The sacrifice I am forcing myself to make is worthy of you. I am denying myself a few hours of the most wonderful happiness the human heart can know; I am sacrificing them to your reputation; if you know my heart, you realize what this is costing me. Will you always feel about me as you do now? But your honor has spoken; that is enough. I should tell you that at the time of our first meeting, not all the suspicions pointed to thieves. M. de La Mole has set up a watch in the garden. M. de Croisenois is surrounded by spies; every move he makes at night is reported. . . ."

"The poor boy!" Mathilde exclaimed, and burst out laughing. Her mother and a maid were wakened; suddenly she was being spoken to from behind the door. Julien

361

looked at her; she turned pale as she scolded the maid, but did not even bother to answer her mother.

"But if they think to open the window, they will see the ladder!" Julien said to her.

He clasped her in his arms once more, flung himself onto the ladder, and slid rather than climbed down it; in a moment he was on the ground.

Three seconds later the ladder was under the alley of sycamores, and Mathilde's honor safe. Coming to his senses, Julien found himself all bloodied and almost naked; he had hurt himself by letting go with no thought to what he was doing.

Intense happiness had released all of his native energy; at that moment, if twenty men had shown up, to attack them single-handed would have been but one pleasure the more. Fortunately his military valor was not put to the test. He laid the ladder down in its usual place; he replaced the chain that held it; he did not forget to go back and remove the traces the ladder had left in the bed of exotic flowers under Mathilde's window.

As he was moving his hands over the soft loam in the dark, to make sure the marks were completely effaced, he felt something fall on his hands. It was a whole side of Mathilde's hair, which she had cut off and thrown down to him.

She was at her window. "Look what your servant has sent you," she said to him in a rather loud voice. "It is a token of eternal obedience. I foreswear the exercise of reason; be my master."

Vanquished, Julien was on the point of going to get the ladder and of climbing up to her room again. In the end reason won out.

To get back into the house from the garden was not easy. He succeeded in forcing a cellar door; having got into the house, he was then obliged to break open his own door as quietly as possible. In the confusion, he had left everything behind him in the small bedroom he had just abandoned so hastily, even his key, which was in his coat pocket. "Let's hope," he thought, "that she remembers to hide all those mortal remains!"

Exhaustion eventually got the better of happiness, and as the sun rose he fell into a deep sleep.

The bell for lunch barely managed to waken him; he appeared in the dining room. A little while later Mathilde came in. Julien's pride had a moment's bliss when he saw love shining in the eyes of that very beautiful girl to whom everyone paid homage, but his prudence soon had grounds to be alarmed.

Under the pretext of having had very little time to do her hair, Mathilde had arranged it in such a way that Julien could see at a glance the whole extent of the sacrifice she had made for him in cutting it the night before. If such a beautiful face could have been spoiled by anything, Mathilde might have succeeded in doing so; a whole side of her beautiful ash-blond hair had been sheared unevenly to within half an inch of her head.

At lunch, Mathilde's behavior was wholly in keeping with this first piece of rashness. One would have said that she was doing all she could to let everyone know about her mad passion for Julien. That day, luckily, M. de La Mole and the marquise were deeply engrossed in the list of those who were to be promoted to the *Cordon Bleu,* and on which M. de Chaulnes did not figure. Toward the end of the meal it occurred to Mathilde, while talking with him, to call Julien *"my master."* He blushed to the roots of his hair.

Whether by chance or purposely on Mme. de La Mole's part, Mathilde was never alone for a minute that day. In the evening, as she passed from the dining room into the drawing room, she nevertheless found the right moment to say to Julien, "All my plans have been upset. Do you think this is just a pretext on my part? Mama has decided that one of her maids is to sleep in my apartment."

That day went by like a flash. Julien was at the peak of happiness. By seven o'clock the next morning he was at his desk in the library; he hoped Mlle. de La Mole would be good enough to appear there; he had written her an interminable letter.

He didn't see her until many hours later, at lunch. Her hair was dressed that day with the greatest care; a wonderful art had undertaken to conceal the place where the hair had been cut. She looked at Julien once or twice, but politely, calmly; there was no longer any danger of her calling him *"my master."* Astonishment took Julien's breath away. . . .

Mathilde was taking herself to task for almost everything she had done for him. After mature consideration, she had decided that he was, if not an altogether common fellow, at least not enough above the common to be worth all the strange follies she had committed for his sake. On the whole, she gave scarce a thought to love; that day she was weary of loving.

As for Julien, the commotion in his heart was that of a

sixteen-year-old boy. Terrible doubts, astonishment, despair, assailed him by turn throughout the lunch, which seemed to last forever.

As soon as he could decently rise from the table, he dashed rather than ran to the stable, saddled his horse himself, and rode off at a gallop; he was afraid he might dishonor himself by some show of weakness. "I must kill my feelings through sheer physical exhaustion," he thought as he galloped through the forest of Meudon. "What have I done, what have I said, to fall so out of favor?

"I mustn't do anything, not say anything today," he thought on coming back to the house, "—be as dead physically as I am spiritually. Julien is no more; it is his corpse that moves."

Chapter XX

The Japanese Vase

> At first his heart cannot compre-
> hend the depth of his misery; he is
> more perplexed than moved. But as
> reason returns, he becomes aware of
> the full extent of his misfortune.
> For him, all of life's pleasures lie
> blasted; he can feel nothing but the
> sharp points of despair cutting into
> him. But why speak of physical suf-
> fering? What suffering felt by the
> body alone is comparable to this?
>
> —JEAN PAUL

The dinner bell was ringing; Julien had just time to
dress. He found Mlle. de La Mole in the drawing room.
She was appealing earnestly to her brother and M. de
Croisenois not to go and spend the evening in Suresnes, at
Mme. la Maréchale de Fervaques' house. It would have
been difficult to be more charming or more pleasant to
them. After dinner, *MM.* de Luz, de Caylus, and several
of their friends arrived. One would have said that along
with the cult of sisterly affection, Mlle. de La Mole had
taken up that of the most exact propriety. Although the
weather was delightful that evening, she insisted on staying
out of the garden; she didn't want anyone to leave the
vicinity of the easy chair in which Mme. de La Mole was
stationed. The blue sofa was the center of the group, as in
winter.

Mathilde bore a grudge against the garden, or at any

365

rate it seemed perfectly boring to her: it was linked with memories of Julien.

Unhappiness diminishes intelligence. Our hero was tactless enough to sit down in that little straw-bottomed chair which had once borne witness to such brilliant triumphs. This evening no one spoke to him; his presence went as if unnoticed, or worse. Those of Mlle. de La Mole's friends who were seated near him, at the end of the sofa, pretended in one way or another to turn their backs on him, or at least, so he thought.

"This is an official disgrace," he told himself. He chose to stay awhile and study these people who considered it their right to heap him with disdain.

M. de Luz's uncle held an important post at court, whence it followed that every time a new face joined the circle, that fine officer his nephew would situate the following piquant detail near the beginning of his conversation: his uncle had set out for St. Cloud at seven o'clock, and he counted on sleeping there that same night. The conversation would be brought around to this item with every appearance of unpretentiousness, but it never failed to come up.

While observing M. de Croisenois with the stern eye of unhappiness, Julien noted the very great influence this kind and likable young man assigned to occult causes, to a point where he would become gloomy and irritable if anyone ascribed an event of any importance to a simple and quite natural cause. "This is the first stage of madness," Julien said to himself. "His character bears a striking resemblance to the Emperor Alexander's, such as Prince Korasoff described it to me." During the first year of his stay in Paris, poor Julien, just out of the seminary and dazzled by the accomplishments, so new to him, of all those pleasant young people, could do nothing but admire them. Their true character was only beginning to stand out to his sight.

"I am playing a shameful role here," he thought suddenly. The problem was to leave his straw-bottomed chair in some not-too-awkward way. He hunted for an excuse, but he was making new demands on an imagination that was totally occupied elsewhere. He was obliged to fall back on the memory, but his, it must be admitted, was not rich in that kind of resource. The poor boy was still quite raw, so he was perfectly clumsy and everyone noticed when he rose to leave the drawing room. Misery was too apparent in all his behavior. For three quarters of an hour he had been playing the part of the importunate inferior, for whom no one goes to the trouble of hiding what he thinks.

The critical observations he had just made to himself about his rivals kept him, however, from taking his misfortune too tragically. He had the recollection of what had happened two nights before to sustain his ego. "Regardless of the thousand advantages they have over me," he told himself as he entered the garden alone, "Mathilde has never been to any of them what she deigned to be twice in my life for me."

That was the extent of his wisdom. By no means did he understand the character of that unusual person whom chance had recently made mistress absolute of his happiness.

He did nothing the next day but ride his horse and himself to death. That evening he made no further attempt to draw near the sofa, to which Mathilde remained so loyal. He noted that Count Norbert did not even bother to look at him when he met him in the house. "He must be doing himself a strange violence ..." thought Julien, "he, who is by nature so polite."

For Julien, sleep would have been happiness. But in spite of his physical exhaustion, all-too-alluring memories would begin to invade his whole imagination. He hadn't the wit to see that with his long rides in the woods around Paris, acting only upon himself and in no wise upon Mathilde's heart or mind, he was leaving the disposition of his fate to chance.

It seemed to him that one thing might bring infinite relief to his pain: that was to speak with Mathilde. And yet, what did he dare say to her?

He was brooding over this question at seven o'clock in the morning, when all of a sudden he saw her walk into the library.

"I know, sir, that you wish to speak with me."

"Good God! who told you?"

"I know, what difference does it make? If you have no honor you may ruin me, or at least try to do so; but that danger, which is not, I think, a real one, will certainly not keep me from being sincere. I no longer love you, sir; my wild imagination played me false. . . ."

At this terrible blow, mad with love and grief, Julien tried to justify himself. Nothing could be more absurd. Can one justify oneself for being disliked? But reason no longer had any power over his actions. A blind instinct pushed him to delay her decision about his fate. It seemed to him that so long as he kept talking, all was not lost.

Mathilde was not listening to what he had to say; the sound of his voice irritated her; she could not conceive how he had the audacity to interrupt.

That morning, the remorse of virtue and that of pride made her equally miserable. She was, as it were, dumbfounded at the thought of having given certain rights over herself to a little abbé, a peasant's son. "It is almost," she would tell herself when she exaggerated her misfortune, "as if after having dreamed about the power, the qualities, and the distinctions of the man whom I should love, I had to reproach myself with a weakness for one of the lackeys."

In bold, proud natures, it is only one step from anger with oneself to wrath against others; in such cases, a fit of rage is a keen pleasure.

In an instant, Mlle. de La Mole had reached the point of showering Julien with tokens of the most withering scorn. She was infinitely witty, and her wit excelled in the art of torturing a person's vanity and of inflicting the cruelest wounds on it.

For the first time in his life, Julien found himself subjected to the onslaught of a superior mind, set against him by the most violent hatred. Far from having the least idea in the world of defending himself at the moment, he came to despise himself. As he listened to her overwhelm him with such cruel marks of scorn, calculated with so much wit to destroy any good opinion he might have of himself, he began to think that Mathilde was right and that she couldn't say enough.

As for her, she took a delightfully arrogant pleasure in thus punishing herself and him for the devotion she had felt a few days earlier.

She had no need to invent or consider for the first time the cruel things she was telling him with such great satisfaction. She merely repeated what the counsel in her heart for the party opposed to love had been telling her all week long.

Each remark increased Julien's frightful wretchedness a hundredfold. He tried to run away; Mlle. de La Mole held him by the arm in an authoritative grip.

"Please observe," he said to her, "that you are speaking very loudly; they can hear you in the next room."

"What of it!" replied Mlle. de La Mole haughtily. "Who will dare to say he has heard me? I mean to cure your conceited little self forever of any notions it may have entertained with regard to me."

When Julien was able to leave the library, he was so

astonished that he felt less miserable. "Well! she doesn't love me anymore," he kept repeating aloud, as if to let himself know where he stood. "It seems that she loved me for a week or ten days; but I, I will love her all my life.

"Is it really possible that she meant nothing to me! that I felt nothing for her, just a few short days ago!"

The pleasures of pride were flooding in upon Mathilde's heart. So she had been able to break off forever; to triumph so completely over such a powerful inclination made her perfectly happy. "Now that little gentleman will understand, once and for all, that he has not and never will have any hold over me." She was so happy that, for the moment, she really did not feel any love.

After so atrocious, so humiliating a scene, love for anyone less passionate than Julien would have been impossible. Without forgetting for a single instant who she was, Mlle. de La Mole had so directed her unpleasant remarks to him and so calculated them that they must seem true, even when recalled with a cool and collected mind.

The conclusion Julien drew from the first moment of such an astonishing scene was that Mathilde's pride was boundless. He firmly believed that it was all over between them forever, and yet, the next day at lunch, he was awkward and shy in her presence. This is a fault with which we could not have taxed him up to now. In small as in important matters, he had always known precisely what he ought and wanted to do and did it.

That day, after lunch, after Mme. de La Mole asked him to get a seditious yet quite rare tract that her curé had brought her secretly that morning, Julien, as he took it from the console, knocked over an old blue porcelain vase, ugly as it could be.

Uttering a cry of distress, Mme. de La Mole rose and came over to consider the ruins of her cherished vase at close range. "It was old Japanese porcelain," she said. "It came to me from my great-aunt, the Abbess de Chelles; it was a gift from the Dutch to the regent Duke of Orléans, who gave it to his daughter. . . ."

Mathilde had followed her mother and was delighted to see the blue vase broken; she thought it horribly ugly. Julien was silent and not too upset; he saw Mlle. de La Mole standing very close to him.

"That vase," he told her, "is destroyed forever; so it is with a feeling that was once master of my heart. I beg you to accept my apologies for all the foolish things it made me do." And he went out.

"Actually, you'd think," commented Mme. de La Mole as he was leaving, "that M. Sorel is glad, and proud of what he has just done."

Her words fell directly on Mathilde's heart. "It's true," she told herself, "my mother has guessed rightly. Those are his sentiments." Only then did her joy over the scene she had made the day before come to an end. "Very well, it's all over," she said to herself with apparent calm, "I have learned a great lesson; my error is frightful, humiliating! It's enough to make me behave for the rest of my life."

"Isn't what I said the truth?" Julien was thinking. "Then why does the love I once felt for that mad woman still torment me?"

That love, far from dying, as he had hoped, made rapid progress. "She's mad, it's true," he told himself; "is she less adorable for that? Can a girl be prettier? Haven't all the keen pleasures that the most elegant civilization has to offer been united, as if in a competition with one another, in the person of Mlle. de La Mole?" Memories of past happiness took hold of Julien and soon demolished all the work of his reason. Reason must struggle in vain against memories of that sort; its stern efforts do nothing but enhance their charm.

Twenty-four hours after the destruction of the old Japanese vase, Julien was decidedly one of the unhappiest of men.

Chapter XXI

The Secret Note

> Everything I am telling you, I
> saw; and though I might have been
> deceived while seeing it, rest assured
> that I am not deceiving you as I
> tell it.
> —From a letter to the author

The marquis sent for him; M. de La Mole seemed rejuvenated, his eyes glittered. "Let us talk a bit about your memory; I'm told it's prodigious! Could you learn four pages by heart and go and recite them in London? but without changing a word! . . ."

The marquis crumpled the latest *Daily* ill-temperedly and tried in vain to dissimulate his very concerned look, one Julien had never seen him wear, not even when it was a question of the de Frilair suit.

Julien was already experienced enough to sense that he should appear to be completely taken in by the playful tone in which he was being addressed. "That edition of the *Daily* may not be very entertaining, but with my Lord's permission I shall have the honor of reciting the whole thing to him tomorrow morning."

"What! even the advertisements?"

"Accurately, and without a single omission."

"Can you give me your word on that?" replied the marquis, suddenly grave.

"Yes, sir. Nothing but the fear of breaking it could trouble my memory."

"As a matter of fact, I meant to put that question to you yesterday; I am not asking you to swear never to repeat what you will hear; I know you too well to do you that injustice. I have answered for you; I am going to take you to a drawing room where twelve persons will be gathered; you will make notes of what each one says.

"Don't worry, it won't be a jumbled conversation; each man will speak in turn. I don't mean to say in an orderly fashion," added the marquis, resuming the playful, knowing air that was so natural to him. "While we are speaking, you will write some twenty pages; you will return here with me; we will boil down those twenty pages to four. It is those four pages that you will recite to me tomorrow morning instead of the whole edition of the *Daily*. You will set out immediately afterward; you must go posthaste, like a young man who is traveling for his pleasure. Your aim will be to go unnoticed by everyone. You will come into the presence of a very eminent man. Then, you will have to be more clever. It's a question of outwitting his whole entourage; for among his secretaries, his servants, there are men who have sold out to our enemies and who lie in wait to intercept our agents.

"You will carry an ordinary letter of introduction. The moment his Excellency looks at you, pull out my watch, this one, which I am lending you for the voyage. Take it. There, that much is done. Give me yours.

"The duke himself will be pleased, at your dictation, to write out the four pages you will have learned by heart. That done, but no sooner, mark me well, you may, if his Excellency should question you, tell him about the meeting which you are going to attend.

"Here is something to keep you from getting bored between Paris and the minister's residence: the fact is that there are people who would like nothing better than to take a potshot at the Abbé Sorel. In that event, his mission would be finished. And I foresee a long delay, for, my dear fellow, how should we learn of your death? Your zeal could not carry so far as to break the news to us.

"Now run out and buy a suit of clothes," continued the marquis with a serious air. "Dress in the style of two years ago. Tonight you ought to look shabby. During the trip, on the contrary, you will be your usual self. Does that surprise you, or have your suspicions hit the mark? Yes, my friend, one of the venerable worthies whom you will hear holding forth tonight is quite capable of sending out a description, thanks to which someone may well give you opium, at the least, one night in some good inn where you will have called for supper."

"It would be better," said Julien, "to do thirty leagues

extra and not take the direct route. I'm going to Rome, I suppose. . . ."

The marquis assumed an air of haughty displeasure the like of which Julien had not seen on his face since Bray-le-Haut. "That is what you will find out, sir, when I think fit to tell you. I don't like questions."

"That wasn't meant for one," Julien answered effusively. "I swear to you, sir, that I was thinking out loud; I was searching my mind for the safest route."

"Yes, your mind seems to have been very far away. Never forget that an ambassador, especially one of your age, ought not to give the impression of forcing one's confidence."

Julien was deeply mortified, he was in the wrong. His self-esteem kept hunting for an excuse and found none.

"Observe, then," added M. de La Mole, "that people always appeal from the heart when they have done something foolish."

An hour later Julien was in the marquis' waiting room, looking like a subaltern, wearing out-of-date clothes, a cravat of dubious whiteness, and with something of the flunkey about his whole appearance.

On seeing him, the marquis burst out laughing, and then only was Julien completely pardoned.

"If that young man betrays me," thought the marquis, "whom shall I trust? And yet, when a man acts, he has to trust someone. My son and his illustrious friends of the same kidney have heart and loyalty enough for a hundred thousand; if it came to fighting, they would perish on the steps of the throne; they know how to do everything . . . except that for which there is a present need. The devil if I see one among them who could learn four pages by heart and go a hundred leagues without being tracked down. Norbert would know how to get himself killed, like his forefathers; a raw recruit can do as much. . . ."

The marquis lapsed into a profound reverie. "As for getting himself killed," he said with a sigh, "perhaps Sorel will know how to do that as well as he. . . .

"Let's get into the carriage," said the marquis, as though to drive away an importunate idea.

"Sir," said Julien, "while they were altering this outfit for me, I memorized the first page of today's *Daily*."

The marquis took the newspaper. Julien recited without mistaking a single word. "Good," thought the marquis, very much the diplomat that evening, "all this time the young man hasn't noticed the streets we have taken."

They walked into a large and rather gloomy drawing

room, partly paneled and partly hung with green velvet. In the middle of the room, a glum lackey was finishing setting up a long dinner table, which he then transformed into a worktable by means of a vast green cover all spotted with ink, left over from some ministry.

The master of the house was an enormous man whose name was not pronounced; Julien decided that he had the physiognomy and eloquence of a man who is digesting.

At a sign from the marquis, Julien had stayed at the lower end of the table. To give himself something to do, he set to trimming quills. Out of the corner of his eye he counted seven men in conversation, but Julien saw them only from the back. Two of them appeared to address M. de La Mole as equals; the others seemed more or less deferential.

Another notable entered without being announced. "This is strange," thought Julien, "no one is announced in this drawing room. Is this a precaution that has been taken in my honor?" All rose to greet the newcomer. He was wearing the same extremely distinguished decoration as three other men who were already in the drawing room. Everyone spoke rather low. In sizing up the newcomer, Julien was limited to whatever he might learn of him from his features and appearance. He was short and thickset, with a ruddy complexion and a glittering eye void of any expression other than the viciousness of a boar.

Julien's attention was sharply distracted by the almost immediate arrival of an altogether different individual. He was a tall, very thin man who wore three or four vests. His gaze was affectionate, his gestures polished.

"It's the very look of the old Bishop of Besançon," thought Julien. This man obviously belonged to the Church; he looked to be no more than fifty or fifty-five. It was impossible to have a more paternal air.

The young Bishop of Agde appeared; he seemed astounded when, as he reviewed those present, his eye fell on Julien. He hadn't spoken a word to him since the ceremony at Bray-le-Haut. His surprised look embarrassed and irritated Julien. "What!" the latter asked himself, "will knowing a man always turn into a bad thing for me? All those great lords, whom I have never seen before, do not intimidate me in the least, but that young bishop's look chills me to the bone! I must say, I am a very odd and unlucky fellow."

An extremely dark little man came bursting in a while later, and began speaking at the door; he had a yellow complexion and a rather mad look. Upon the arrival of

374

this merciless talker, groups formed, apparently to avoid the nuisance of having to listen to him.

As they turned away from the fireplace, they drew near the lower end of the table, occupied by Julien. He felt more and more abashed, for in the end, try as he would, he could not help but overhear them, and inexperienced as he was, he fully understood the importance of the matters being discussed with no attempt at concealment; and how much the eminent persons whom he had so conspicuously before his eyes must count on their being kept secret!

Already, though as slowly as possible, Julien had trimmed some twenty quills; that resource would soon fail him. To no avail he sought an order in M. de La Mole's eyes: the marquis had forgotten him.

"What I'm doing is ridiculous," Julien said to himself as he trimmed his quills; "but such mediocre-looking men, entrusted by others or by themselves with such important affairs, are likely to be very touchy. My unfortunate way of looking at people has something inquisitive and not very respectful about it, which would no doubt nettle them. If I definitely look down, I will seem to be gathering in their words."

His embarrassment was very great; he was hearing strange things.

Chapter XXII

The Discussion

> The republic—for every man, to-
> day, who is willing to sacrifice all
> for the good of the nation, there are
> thousands, millions, who are con-
> cerned about nothing but their plea-
> sures, their vanity. In Paris, a man
> is esteemed for his carriage, not for
> his virtue.
>
> —Napoleon, *Mémorial*

The footman rushed in, saying: "His Excellency, the Duke of ———."

"Shut up, you fool!" said the duke as he came in. He said this so well, so majestically, that in spite of himself Julien thought that to know how to show his temper to a lackey must be this great man's sole accomplishment. Julien looked up, then lowered his eyes at once. He had so well guessed the importance of the new arrival that he feared his glance might be an indiscretion.

This duke was a man of fifty, dressed like a dandy, who walked on springs. He had a narrow head with a big nose and a curved face, all thrust forward. It would have been difficult to look nobler or more insignificant. His arrival determined the opening of the meeting.

Julien was suddenly interrupted in his physiognomical observations by M. de La Mole's voice. "Allow me to introduce to you the Abbé Sorel," the marquis was saying. "He is endowed with an astonishing memory; it was only an hour ago that I told him about the mission with which he may be honored, and to give a proof of his memory, he has learned the first page of the *Daily* by heart."

"Ah, the news from abroad about that poor N——," said the master of the house. He took up the paper eagerly, and giving him a look that was comical in its attempt to seem important, said to Julien: "Speak, sir."

There was a deep silence; all eyes were fixed on Julien. He recited so well that at the end of twenty lines the duke said, "That will do." The little man with the look of a boar sat down. He was the chairman since, scarcely in his place, he pointed out a card table to Julien and made him a sign to bring it over. Julien sat down at it with everything he needed for writing. He counted twelve persons seated around the green baize.

"Monsieur Sorel," said the duke, "retire to the next room; you will be sent for."

The master of the house assumed a very anxious air and muttered to his neighbor, "The shutters aren't closed. It's no use looking through the window," he shouted stupidly to Julien.

"Here I am up to my neck in what is a conspiracy at the very least," thought the latter. "Luckily it is not the kind that leads to the Place de Grève. Even if there were some danger, I owe that much and more to the marquis. It would be a blessing if I were given a chance to make up for all the sorrow my follies may one day cause him!"

All the while he was thinking about his follies and his bad luck, he kept looking over the place, so as never to forget it. Only then did it occur to him that he had not heard the marquis tell the cabman the name of the street, and the marquis had ordered a hackney, something he never did.

Julien was left to his reflections for a long while. He was in a drawing room hung with a red velvet with wide gold braids. On the console there was a big ivory crucifix, and on the mantlepiece, the book *du Pape*, by M. de Maistre, gilt-edged and magnificently bound. Julien opened it so as not to appear to be listening. From time to time they spoke very loudly in the next room. Finally the door opened; he was called in.

"Consider, gentlemen," the chairman was saying, "that from now on we will be speaking in the Duke of ——'s presence. This gentleman," he said, pointing to Julien, "is a young Levite, who is devoted to our holy cause, and who will be able to repeat with ease, thanks to his astonishing memory, even our most inconsequential talk.

"That gentleman has the floor," he said, indicating the paternal-looking individual who wore three or four vests. Julien thought it would be more natural to refer to him as the gentleman with the vests. He took some paper and wrote a great deal.

(Here the author wanted to insert a page of dots. "That would be in bad taste," said the editor, "and in a piece of writing as frivolous as this, bad taste is death."

"Politics," replied the author, "are a millstone around the neck of literature and will sink it in less than six months. Politics in the midst of imaginary concerns is like a pistol shot in the middle of a concert. The noise is ear-splitting without being energetic. It does not harmonize with the sound of any instrument. The politics here will mortally offend one half of the readers and bore the other, who will have found them far more convincing and energetic in the morning paper."

"If your characters don't talk politics," the editor rejoined, "they are not Frenchmen of 1830, and your book is not the mirror you claim it to be. . . .")

Julien's minutes were twenty-six pages long; here is a pale extract of them; for it was necessary, as usual, to delete the absurdities, the excess of which would have seemed odious or unrealistic to the reader (e.g., *The Police Gazette*).

The man in the vests with the fatherly look (he might have been a bishop) smiled often, and his eyes, surrounded by baggy lids, would assume an odd brilliance and a less irresolute expression than usual. This worthy, who had been asked to speak first before the duke ("but what duke?" Julien asked himself), apparently to set forth the various views and act as solicitor general, seemed to Julien to lapse into the uncertainty and inconclusiveness for which those magistrates are so often blamed. During the course of the exposition, the duke even went so far as to reproach him for this.

After several moral and indulgently philosophical observations, the man in the vests said, "Noble England, led by a great man, the immortal Pitt, spent forty billion francs to thwart the Revolution. If this assembly will permit me, I shall broach a gloomy idea with a certain frankness. England never really understood that with a man like Bonaparte, especially since there was only a collection of good intentions to oppose him, nothing could be decisive but an attempt on his person. . . ."

"Ah! still singing the praises of murder!" said the master of the house with a worried look.

"Spare us your sentimental homilies," shouted the chairman ill-humoredly; his boar's eye shone with a fierce luster. "Continue," he said to the man in the vests. The chairman's cheeks and forehead had turned crimson.

"Today, noble England," the speaker went on, "is crushed; for every Englishman, before he can buy his bread, is obliged to pay the interest on the forty billion francs that were used against the Jacobins. She no longer has a Pitt—"

"She has the Duke of Wellington," said a military man, assuming a most important air.

"Silence, if you please, gentlemen," shouted the chairman. "If we start arguing again, it will have been useless to call in M. Sorel."

"We all know that the gentleman has many ideas," said the duke with a nettled air and looking at the interrupter, formerly one of Napoleon's generals. Julien could see that this remark was an allusion to something personal and most offensive. Everybody smiled; the turncoat general seemed beside himself with rage.

"Pitt is no more, gentlemen," the speaker went on, with the discouraged look of a man who has given up hope of making his audience listen to reason. "Even if there were a new Pitt in England, you can't hoodwink a nation twice in the same way—"

"That's why a victorious general, a Bonaparte, could never come to power again," shouted the military heckler.

This time neither the chairman nor the duke dared to flare up, though Julien thought he saw in their eyes that they were itching to do so. They looked down, and the duke was satisfied to sigh loudly enough to be heard by all.

But the speaker had grown short-tempered. "Someone is in a hurry to see me finish," he said heatedly, and altogether putting aside that smiling politeness and carefully guarded language that Julien had taken for the expression of his character: "—someone is in a hurry to see me finish; someone has not taken the least account of the effort I have been making not to offend anybody's ears, however long they may be. Very well, gentlemen, I will be brief.

"And I will put it to you in plain language: England hasn't a sou to spare for the good cause. If Pitt himself came back, for all his genius he couldn't manage to hoax the small English landowners again, for they know that the short campaign of Waterloo alone cost them a billion francs. Since you want plain speaking," added the speaker, growing more and more excited, "I say to you: *Help yourselves,* for England hasn't a guinea for your cause, and if England doesn't pay, Austria, Russia, Prussia, who have courage but no money, cannot mount more than one or two campaigns against France.

"One may hope that the young soldiers rallied by Jacobinism will be beaten in the first campaign, in the second perhaps; but in the third—even at the risk of sounding like a revolutionary to you who know me, I say—in the third you will have to face the soldiers of 1794, who were not the regimented peasants of 1792."

Here the interruption came from three or four points at once.

"Sir," said the chairman to Julien, "go into the next room and make a fair copy of the opening minutes you have taken down." Julien left the room, to his great regret. The speaker had just begun to deal with various probabilities that were the subject of his usual meditations.

"They are afraid I will laugh at them," he thought. When he was called back, M. de La Mole was saying with a seriousness that to Julien, who knew him, seemed very funny: "... Yes, gentlemen, it is about this unfortunate nation in particular that one might ask: 'Shall it be a god, a table, or a bowl?'*

" '*It shall be a god!*' cried the fabulist. It is to you, gentlemen, that his reply, so noble and so profound, seems to belong. Act on your own initiative and noble France will reappear almost as our ancestors made her and as our eyes still saw her before the death of Louis XVI.

"England, her noble lords at least, loathes vile Jacobinism as much as we do: without English gold, Austria, Russia, and Prussia cannot fight more than two or three battles. Will that be enough to bring about a happy occupation, like the one M. de Richelieu wasted so stupidly in 1817? I think not."

Here there was an interruption, but smothered by everyone's *ssh.* Again it came from the old imperial general, who wanted a blue sash and was trying to make himself conspicuous among the drafters of the secret note.

"I think not," resumed M. de La Mole, after the tumult. He insisted on the "*I*" with an insolence that delighted Julien. "Well played," he said to himself, all the while making his pen fly nearly as fast as the marquis' speech. "With a well-turned phrase, M. de La Mole has wiped out that turncoat's twenty campaigns."

"It is not to foreign nations alone," continued the marquis in the most restrained tone, "that we may be obliged for another military occupation. All those young people who write inflammatory articles for the *Globe* will furnish you three or four thousand young captains, among whom may be found another Kléber, a Hoche, a Jourdan, a Pichegru, but not so well intentioned."

"We didn't have the sense to glorify *him*," said the chairman. "We ought to have kept his legend alive."

"In short, there must be two parties in France," M. de La Mole went on, ". . . two parties, not in name only, but two distinct, sharply divided parties. Let us be clear about who is to be crushed. On the one hand journalists, voters, public opinion: in a word, youth and all who admire it. While youth is being deafened by the sound of its own idle talk, we, we have the certain advantage of consuming the state budget."

Here another interruption.

"You, sir," said M. de La Mole to the heckler, with wonderful arrogance and ease, "you do not consume, if the word offends you, you devour forty thousand francs, put down to the state budget, and the eighty thousand you receive from the civil list.

"Very well, sir, since you force me to do it, I will go ahead and take you as an example. Like your noble ancestors who followed St. Louis on the Crusades, you ought, for those one hundred and twenty thousand francs, to have at least a regiment to show us, or a company. What am I saying! half a company, were it only fifty men, but ready to·fight and devoted to the good cause, in life as in death. You have nothing but lackeys, of whom, in the event of a revolution, you yourself would be afraid.

"The Throne, the Altar, the aristocracy, may perish tomorrow, gentlemen, so long as you have not created a force of five hundred *devoted* men in each department; I mean devoted not merely with all the bravery of the French, but with Spanish steadfastness as well.

"Half of that troop should be made up of our own children, of our nephews, in short, of true gentlemen. Each of them should have at his side, not a chattering petty bourgeois, ready to don the tricolored cockade if 1815 should repeat itself, but a good, simple, frank peasant like Cathelineau;* our gentleman will indoctrinate him; he should be his foster brother if possible. Let each of us sacrifice a *fifth* of his income to form this devoted little troop of five hundred men in every department. Then you may count on a foreign occupation. The foreign soldier will never advance even so far as Dijon until he is sure of finding five hundred friendly soldiers in each department.

381

"Foreign kings will not listen to you unless you can tell them that twenty thousand gentlemen are ready to take up arms and open the gates of France to them. That is a hard service, you say. Gentlemen, it is the price of our heads. Between the liberty of the press and our life as gentlemen, there is a war to the death. Turn manufacturer, peasant, or take up your gun. Be timid if you will, but don't be stupid. Open your eyes.

"In the words of the Jacobin song, I say to you, *'Form your battalions'*; then some noble Gustavus Adolphus* will appear, who, moved by the imminent danger to the monarchical principle, will dash three hundred leagues away from his own country and do for you what Gustav did for the Protestant princes. Do you mean to go on talking without acting? In fifty years there will be nothing but presidents of republics in Europe, and not one king. And with those four letters, K–I–N–G, priest and gentleman will vanish. I foresee nothing but *candidates* paying court to mud-bespattered *majorities*.

"It is pointless for you to say that at this moment France hasn't a single general of any standing, known to and loved by all, that the army has been organized solely in the interest of Throne and Altar, that all the veteran troops have been dismissed from it, whereas every Prussian and Austrian Regiment can count fifty noncommissioned officers who have been under fire.

"Two hundred thousand young men in the lower middle class are in love with the idea of war. . . ."

"Enough of these unpleasant truths," said a grave dignitary in a pompous voice, a man who must have been high up in the ecclesiastical hierarchy, for M. de La Mole smiled pleasantly instead of getting angry, which seemed significant to Julien.

"Enough of these unpleasant truths; now let us summarize, gentlemen. The man who stands in need of having a gangrenous leg cut off would be ill-advised to tell his surgeon: 'That diseased leg is quite healthy.' If you will pardon the expression, gentlemen, the noble Duke of ————* is our surgeon."

"There, at last, the cat is out of the bag," said Julien to himself. "It is toward ———— that I shall gallop tonight."

382

Chapter XXIII

The Clergy, Forests, Liberty

> The first law of every creature is self-preservation; that is, survival. You sow hemlock and expect to see grain ripen.
>
> —MACHIAVELLI

The grave worthy spoke on. One could see that he knew what he was talking about. With a gentle and temperate eloquence that pleased Julien no end, he set forth the following great truths:

"One, England hasn't a guinea for our cause; economy and Hume are all the fashion there. Not even the *Saints** will give us money, and Mr. Brougham* would laugh at us.

"Two, it is impossible to get more than two campaigns from the kings of Europe without English gold; and two campaigns against the petty bourgeoisie will not suffice.

"Three, the necessity of forming an armed party in France, without which the monarchies of Europe will not risk even two campaigns.

"The fourth point, which I will make so bold as to propose to you as obvious, is this:

"*The impossibility of forming an armed party in France without the clergy.*

"I say this to you boldly, gentlemen, because I am going to prove it. We must give everything to the clergy.

"For, busy day and night with its affairs and guided by men of great ability, domiciled far from political storms, three hundred leagues beyond your frontier—"

"Ah! Rome, Rome!" cried the master of the house."

"Yes, sir, *Rome!*" replied the cardinal proudly. "Regardless of the witticisms, more or less clever, that were in fashion when you were young, I say straight out that in 1830 only the clergy led by Rome, can reach the masses.

"Fifty thousand priests will repeat the same words on a day designated by their leaders, and the people, who, after all, supply the soldiers, will be more deeply touched by the voice of its priests than by all the light verse* in the world. . . ." (This personal allusion provoked a murmur.)

"The clergy's intelligence is superior to yours," the cardinal went on, raising his voice. "Every step you have taken toward realizing that essential condition, *an armed party in France,* has been taken by us." Here facts were brought to bear. "Who sent eighty thousand rifles into Vendée?" etc., etc.

"So long as the clergy is not in possession of its forests, it has nothing. At the first sign of war, the Minister of Finance writes to his agents that no one has any money except the clergy. At heart, France is not devout; she loves war. Whoever gives her one will be doubly popular: for to wage war is to starve the Jesuits, as the common people put it; to wage a war is to deliver those monsters of pride, the French, from the threat of foreign intervention."

The cardinal was listened to favorably. . . . "M. de Nerval," he said, "must quit the government; his name irritates the public uselessly."

On that remark, everyone rose and spoke at once. "They are going to send me out again," thought Julien, but even the cautious president had forgotten Julien's presence and existence. Every eye was searching for a man whom Julien recognized. It was M. de Nerval, the Prime Minister, whom he had glimpsed at the Duke de Retz's ball.

The disorder was at its height, as the newspapers say when they talk about the Chamber. By the end of a good quarter of an hour, things had quieted down a bit.

Then M. de Nerval rose to his feet, and assuming the tone of an apostle: "I would not swear to you under oath," he said in a queer voice, "that the ministry means nothing to me.

"It has been made clear to me, gentlemen, that my name swells the ranks of the Jacobins by turning a great many moderates against us. I should therefore resign voluntarily, but the ways of the Lord are visible to a small number. And," he added, looking at the cardinal, "I have a mission. Heaven has told me: either you shall bear your head to the scaffold, or reestablish the monarchy in France, and reduce the chambers to what the parliament was under Louis XV, and *that*, gentlemen, *I will do*."

He left off speaking, sat down, and there was a long silence.

"There's a good actor," thought Julien. He always made the mistake, in this instance as well, of imputing too much wit to men. Stirred by the debates of such a lively evening and above all by the sincerity of the discussion, M. de Nerval at that moment believed in his mission. For all his courage, the man had no sense.

Midnight struck during the silence that followed upon the ringing declaration, "*that I will do*." To Julien's ear, the sound of the clock had something stately and baleful about it. He was deeply affected.

The discussion resumed in a short while with growing energy, and above all, with incredible ingenuousness. "These people will have me poisoned," thought Julien at certain times. "How can they say such things in front of a plebeian?"

Two o'clock was striking and they were still talking. The master of the house had fallen asleep long ago; M. de La Mole was obliged to ring for fresh candles. M. de Nerval, the minister, had left at a quarter to two, but not without having studied Julien's face often in a mirror close by him. His departure seemed to have set everyone at ease.

While the candles were being changed: "God knows what that man is going to tell the king!" whispered the man in vests to his neighbor. "He could make us look ridiculous and spoil our future."

"You must admit that he has an extraordinary sense of his own importance, even cheek, to show his face here. He used to come to this house before he got the ministry; but a portfolio changes everything, overrides all a man's other interests; he should have sensed that."

The minister had no more than left when Napoleon's general closed his eyes. Next he spoke of his health, his wounds, consulted his watch, and went away.

"I'll bet," said the man in vests, "that the general is running after the minister; he's going to make excuses for being here and will claim that he's leading us on."

When the servants, half asleep, had finished changing the candles: "Let us now take counsel," said the chairman, "let us have done with trying to convince one another. Let us turn our thoughts to the contents of the note which will be in the hands of our friends abroad within

385

forty-eight hours. There has been talk about ministers. Now that M. de Nerval has left us, we can say it: what do we care about ministers? We will tell them what to do."

The cardinal showed his approval with a sly smile.

"Nothing is easier, it seems to me, than to sum up our position," said the young Bishop of Agde, with the concentrated and restrained zeal of the most exalted fanaticism. Until then he had kept silent; his eyes, which Julien had been observing, at first gentle and calm, were ablaze after the first hour of discussion. Now his heart brimmed over like lava from Vesuvius.

"From 1806 to 1814, England made but one mistake," he said, "that was, not to act directly and personally against Napoleon. Once that man had created dukes and chamberlains, once he had restored the Throne, the mission God had entrusted to him was over; he was good for nothing but to be sacrificed. The Holy Scriptures teach us in more than one place how to put an end to tyrants." (Here there were several citations in Latin.)

"Today, sirs, it is not one man who must be sacrificed; it is Paris. All France copies Paris. What use is it to arm your five hundred men to a department? A risky undertaking with which you will never have done. What use to drag France into an affair that concerns only Paris? Paris alone, with its newspapers and drawing rooms, has done the harm. May the new Babylon perish.

"We must settle this difference between the Altar and Paris once and for all. Such a catastrophe is essential even to the worldly interests of the Throne. Why did Paris under Napoleon not dare to breathe? Ask the artillery at St. Roch."

It wasn't until three in the morning that Julien left with M. de La Mole.

The marquis was ashamed and tired. For the first time, when he spoke to Julien, there was a note of entreaty in his voice. He asked him on his word never to reveal the overzealousness, that was his expression, to which chance had made him a witness. "Don't mention it to our friend abroad, unless he insists a good deal, in order to find out who our young hotheads are. What do they care if the state is overthrown? They will be cardinals and will fly to Rome. The rest of us will be slaughtered in our châteaux by the peasants."

The secret note, which the marquis drafted from the twenty-six pages of minutes recorded by Julien, was not ready until a quarter to five.

"I'm dead tired," said the marquis, "and it shows in this note, which is not very clear toward the end; I am more dissatisfied with it than with anything I have ever done in my life. Come, my friend," he added, "go rest for a few hours, and lest someone kidnap you, I'm going to lock you in your room."

The next day the marquis drove Julien to an isolated château a good distance from Paris. There, they were greeted by strange hosts, whom Julien judged to be priests. Someone handed him a passport that bore a fictitious name but stated the real destination of his trip, which he had always pretended not to know. He climbed alone into a calash.

The marquis wasn't in the least worried about his memory; Julien had recited the secret note to him several times; but he was very much afraid that he might be intercepted.

"Above all, try to look like a fop, who is traveling to kill time," he said to him in a friendly way as they left the drawing room. "There may have been more than one false brother at last night's meeting."

The trip was swift and cheerless. Julien was hardly out of the marquis' sight when he had put the secret note and mission out of his mind and was mulling over Mathilde's scorn.

In a village a few leagues beyond Metz, the postmaster came out to tell him that there were no more horses. It was ten o'clock at night; Julien, deeply annoyed, called for supper. He set to strolling in front of the door and eventually, without being noticed, slipped into the stable yard. He saw no horses.

"All the same, there was something peculiar about that man," Julien said to himself. "He kept studying me with his big coarse eyes."

As you can see, he was beginning not to believe exactly everything he was told. He was thinking of slipping away after supper; so as to learn more about the region, he left his room and went down to warm himself at the kitchen fire. What was his joy when he found il Signor Geronimo the singer there.

Settled in an armchair that he had had moved close to the fire, the Neapolitan was groaning loudly and doing more talking by himself than the twenty German peasants together who stood around him gaping.

"These people are ruining me," he cried to Julien. "I have promised to sing tomorrow in Mainz. Seven sovereign princes have come running to hear me. Let's get a breath of air," he added with a significant look.

When they had gone a hundred paces down the road and out of hearing, he said to Julien, "Do you know what's going on? That postmaster's a crook. While I was out walking, I gave a little scamp twenty sous and he told me all about him. There are more than a dozen horses in a stable at the other end of the village. They are trying to delay some courier."

"Really?" said Julien, looking innocent.

Discovering the ruse was only half of it; they still had to get away; that is what Geronimo and his friend couldn't bring off. "Let's wait until dawn," said the singer eventually; "they are suspicious of us. Perhaps they have designs on you or on me, who knows. Tomorrow morning we will order a good breakfast; while they are fixing it we'll go for a walk, we'll make our escape; we'll rent horses and go on to the next post."

"And your baggage?" said Julien, thinking that perhaps Geronimo himself might have been sent to stop him. There was nothing for it but to have supper and go to bed. Julien was still in his first sleep when he woke with a start at the sound of two men talking in his room, and not bothering much to keep their voices down.

He recognized the postmaster, armed with a bull's-eye lantern. His light was aimed at the trunk of the calash, which Julien had had carried up to his room. A man at the postmaster's side was rummaging calmly in the open trunk. Julien couldn't make out anything of him but his coat-sleeves, which were black and very tight.

"That's a cassock," he told himself, and reached quietly for the little pistols he had slipped under his pillow.

"No need to worry about waking him up, father," the postmaster was saying. "The bottle of wine they were served is the one you fixed yourself."

"I don't see any sign of papers," replied the priest. "Lots of linen, perfumes, pomades, trifles; he's a modern young man bent on his pleasures. The agent is more likely the other one, who puts on an Italian accent."

The men drew closer to Julien in order to search the pockets of his traveling clothes. He was very much tempted to kill them for thieves. He wouldn't have to worry about the consequences. He had a good mind to do it. "I would be a downright fool," he thought, "I would jeopardize my mission." His clothes searched—"This is no diplomat," said the priest. He moved away, and it was lucky for him.

388

"If he touches me in bed, woe to him!" Julien was saying to himself. "He might very well come over and stab me, and that's one thing I won't tolerate."

The priest turned his head, Julien half opened his eyes. What was his astonishment! It was the Abbé Castanède! As a matter of fact, although the two men made an effort to speak rather softly, it had seemed to Julien from the first that he recognized one of the voices. He was seized by an inordinate desire to rid the world of its most cowardly knave.

"But my mission!" he said to himself.

The priest and his acolyte went out. A quarter of an hour later Julien pretended to waken. He called out and woke up the whole house.

"I've been poisoned," he shouted, "I'm suffering horribly!" He needed a pretext to go and help Geronimo. He found him half asphyxiated by the laudanum contained in the wine.

Wary of some prank of this sort, Julien had supped on the chocolate he had brought with him from Paris. He couldn't contrive to rouse Geronimo enough to persuade him to leave.

"They could give me the whole kingdom of Naples this minute," the singer kept saying, "and I would not give up the voluptuous pleasure of sleep."

"But the seven sovereign princes!"

"They can wait."

Julien started out alone, and without further incident reached the vicinity of the great man. He wasted a whole morning soliciting an audience. Luckily, around four o'clock the duke wanted some fresh air. Julien saw him come out on foot; he was quick to approach him and ask for alms. Standing six feet away from the great man, he pulled out the Marquis de La Mole's watch and showed it off affectedly. *"Follow me at a distance,"* the notable said without looking at him.

A quarter of a league from there, the duke turned abruptly into a little café-hauss. In a bedroom of this lowest-class inn, Julien had the honor of reciting his four pages to the duke. When he had finished, he was told, *"Begin again and go slower."*

The prince took notes. *"Make your way on foot to the next posting house,"* he told Julien. *"Leave your baggage and your calash here. Get to Strasbourg as best you can, and on the twenty-second of the month [it was now the tenth], be in this same coffeehouse at half past noon. Don't leave for another half hour. Silence!"*

Such were the only words Julien was to hear. They were enough to fill him with the greatest admiration. "This is the way," he told himself, "important matters are handled; what would this great statesman say if he had heard those wild chatter-boxes three days ago?"

Julien spent two days getting to Strasbourg; he thought he would have nothing to do once he got there. He made a wide detour. "If that devil of an Abbé Castanède recognized me, he's not the kind to lose track of me easily. . . . And how he would enjoy making a fool of me and ruining my mission!"

The Abbé Castanède, the *Congrégation*'s chief of police for the whole northern frontier, had fortunately not recognized him. And it never once occurred to the Jesuits of Strasbourg, though very zealous, to keep an eye on Julien, who with his cross and blue frock coat looked like any young officer who is very much preoccupied with his own person.

Chapter XXIV

Strasbourg

> Infatuation! You have all of love's
> energy, all its capacity to know suf-
> fering. Only its enchanting plea-
> sures, its sweet delights, are beyond
> your sphere. I could not say as I
> watched her sleeping: "She is mine
> alone, with her angelic beauty and
> sweet frailties! There she is, deliv-
> ered into my power, such as heaven,
> in its mercy, made her to enchant
> the heart of a man."
>
> —SCHILLER

Forced to spend a week in Strasbourg, Julien sought to
divert himself by turning his thoughts to military fame and
patriotic devotion. Was he really in love? He couldn't say.
All he could find in his tormented soul was Mathilde,
mistress absolute of his happiness as of his imagination.
He needed all of his native energy to keep from sinking
into despair. To put his mind to anything not connected
with Mlle. de La Mole was beyond his power. Ambition,
small successes that gratified his vanity, were once enough
to distract him from the feelings Mme. de Rênal inspired in him. Mathilde had absorbed his whole life; he
found her everywhere in his future.

Wherever he looked in that future, Julien saw failure.
The fellow we knew in Verrières—so presumptuous, so
arrogant—had fallen into a fit of ridiculous modesty.

Three days ago, he could have killed the Abbé
Castanède with pleasure; yet, in Strasbourg, if a child had

picked a quarrel with him, he would have said the child was in the right. As he thought over the rivals, the enemies he had run across in his lifetime, he found in every case that he, Julien, had been wrong.

This was so because that powerful imagination, which had once been ceaselessly occupied with painting a future of brilliant successes for him, was now his implacable enemy. The absolute solitude of a traveler's life increased the power of his gloomy imagination. What a treasure a friend would have been! "But," Julien asked himself, "is there one heart that beats for me? Even if I had a friend, am I not honor bound to eternal silence?"

He was riding sadly around the outskirts of Kehl. It is a market town on the banks of the Rhine, immortalized by Desaix and Gouvion Saint-Cyr. A German peasant was showing him the little streams, the roads, the islets in the Rhine which the courage of those great generals has made famous. Guiding his horse with his left hand, Julien held unfolded in his right the superb map that embellishes the *Mémoirs* of Field Marshal Saint-Cyr. A gay shout caused him to look up.

It was Prince Korasoff, that London friend who, several months ago, had initiated him into the fundamentals of high-class foppery. Faithful to that great art, Korasoff, having arrived the day before in Strasbourg, an hour ago in Kehl, and who had never in his life read a line about the siege of 1796, proceeded to tell Julien all about it. The German peasant stared at him in amazement, for he knew enough French to make out the enormous blunders the prince was committing. Julien's thoughts were a thousand leagues removed from the peasant's; he kept gazing in astonishment at this handsome young man; he admired the graceful way he rode his horse.

"A happy nature!" he said to himself. "How well his pants fit; how elegantly his hair is cut. Alas! if I had looked like that, perhaps after having loved me for three days, she wouldn't have taken a dislike to me."

When the prince had finished his siege of Kehl, he said to Julien: "You have the face of a Trappist; you are overdoing the rule of gravity which I explained to you in London. A gloomy air is not in good form; it's the bored look you want. If you are sad, it can only mean that you are lacking something; something didn't work out for you.

"*It is to show oneself inferior.* If you are bored, on the contrary, it is because whatever has tried in vain to please

392

you is in itself inferior. You can see then, my dear friend, how seriously you are mistaken."

Julien threw an écu to the peasant, who was listening to them open-mouthed.

"Well done," said the prince, "a graceful gesture, a noble disdain! very good!" And he started off at a gallop. Julien followed him, filled with stupid admiration.

"Ah! if I were like that, she wouldn't have preferred Croisenois to me!" The more his reason was offended by the prince's absurd ways, the more he despised himself for not admiring them, and reckoned himself unfortunate not to possess them. "That is the way to be," he told himself. Self-disgust can go no further.

The prince, finding him decidedly woe-begone, said as they were riding back to Strasbourg, "See here, my friend, you are poor company. Have you lost all your money, or could you be in love with some little actress?"

The Russians copy French ways, but always fifty years behind the times. At present they are up to the reign of Louis XV.

This bantering about love brought tears to Julien's eyes. "Why not consult this very likable man?" he asked himself suddenly.

"Well, yes, my dear friend," he said to the prince, "you see me here in Strasbourg deeply enamored and even cast off. A charming woman, who lives in a nearby town, has dropped me after three days of passion, and the change is killing me."

He described to the prince, under assumed names, Mathilde's character and behavior.

"Stop there," said Korasoff. "To give you confidence in your doctor, I'm putting an end to your confidences. This young woman's husband enjoys an enormous fortune, or what is more likely, she herself belongs to the highest nobility in the region. She has to have something to be proud about."

Julien nodded; he hadn't the heart to speak.

"Very well," said the prince, "here are three rather bitter pills for you to take without delay:

"One. Once a day you are to go and call on Mme. — what do you call her?"

"Mme. de Dubois."

"What a name!" said the prince, bursting out laughing. "Ah, pardon me; for you, it is sublime. To see Mme. de Dubois daily is essential. But above all, do not go and let her see you looking cold and out of sorts. Remember the golden rule of the age: be the contrary of what is expected. Be exactly as you were a week before she honored you with her favors."

"Ah! I was at peace then," cried Julien despairingly, "I thought I was taking pity on her. . . ."

"The moth gets burned by the candle," continued the prince, "a comparison old as the hills.

"One. You are to see her every day.

"Two. You must court some woman in her circle, but without making any show of passion, do you understand? I will be frank to say that your role is a difficult one; you will be playing a part in a comedy, but if anyone guesses that you are acting, you are done for."

"She is so clever, and I am not! I'm done for," said Julien mournfully.

"No, only you are more in love than I thought. Mme. de Dubois is very much wrapped up in herself, like all women upon whom heaven has bestowed either too much nobility or too much money. She is always looking at herself, instead of you; consequently, she doesn't know you. During those two or three fits of love she permitted herself in your favor, by a great effort of the imagination, she saw you as the hero of her dreams, and not as you really are. . . .

"But what the devil, all of this is elementary, my dear Sorel; are you a downright schoolboy?

"By Jove! let's go into this shop; look at that charming black cravat; I'd say it was made by John Anderson, on Burlington Street. Do me the pleasure of buying it, and of throwing away that wretched black rope you have around your neck.

"Now, then," said the prince, coming out of the best haberdashery in Strasbourg, "what kind of company does Mme. de Dubois keep? Good god! what a name! Don't be offended, my dear Sorel, it's just too much for me. . . . To whom shall you make love?"

"To an exemplary prude, the daughter of an immensely rich stocking merchant. She has the most beautiful eyes in the world, which I find ever so attractive; she no doubt enjoys the highest social position in the region; but in the midst of all her grandeur, she blushes to the point of getting flustered, if anyone so much as mentions trade or the shop. Unfortunately, her father was one of the best-known tradesmen in Strasbourg."

"So, if someone is talking about *industry*," said the prince laughing, "you can be sure then that your beauty will be thinking about herself and taking no account of you. That ridiculous side of her nature is divine and most helpful; it will keep you from ever losing your head the least bit when you are in the presence of those beautiful eyes. Success is certain."

Julien had in mind the Field Marshal de Fervaques' widow, who came to the Hôtel de La Mole a good deal. She was a beautiful foreigner who had married the Field Marshal a year before his death. She seemed to have no other aim in life than to make everyone forget that she was the daughter of a tradesman, and in order to be someone in Paris, she had set herself at the head of the ranks of virtue.

Julien sincerely admired the prince. What wouldn't he have given to have his absurd ways! The conversation between the two friends was endless; Korasoff was overjoyed; never had a Frenchman listened to him for such a long time. "So," the delighted prince told himself, "at last I have found the way to make myself heard, by giving lessons to my masters!"

"It's understood, then," he repeated to Julien for the tenth time, "not a hint of passion when you are talking to the young beauty, the Strasbourg stocking dealer's daughter, in Mme. de Dubois' presence. On the contrary, burning passion when you write. To read a well-written love letter is the supreme pleasure for a prude; it's a moment's respite. She is not playing a part in a comedy, she dares listen to her heart. Therefore, two letters a day."

"Never, never!" said Julien, discouraged. "I'd rather be ground up in a mortar than put three sentences together. I'm a corpse, my dear friend; hope nothing further of me. Leave me to die by the side of the road."

"Who's talking about putting sentences together? In my dressing case I have six volumes of love letters in manuscript. There are some for every type of woman; I have some for the most highly virtuous. Didn't Kalisky make love at Richmond Terrace—you know it, three leagues out of London—to the prettiest Quakeress in all England?"

Julien felt less miserable when he left his friend at two o'clock in the morning.

The next day the prince sent for a copyist, and two days later Julien had fifty-three carefully numbered love letters, all intended for the most sublimely and most cruelly virtuous.

"If there aren't fifty-four," said the Prince, "it's because Kalisky was sent packing; but what does it matter to you if you are ill used by the stocking dealer's daughter, since all you want is to work on Mme. de Dubois' feelings?"

Every day they went horseback riding; the prince was crazy about Julien. Not knowing how to show him his sudden affection, he ended by offering him the hand of one of his cousins, a rich heiress in Moscow. "And once married," he added, "my influence and that cross you have there will make you colonel in two years."

"But this cross wasn't given by Napoleon, far from it."

"What does that matter," said the prince, "didn't he invent it? It's still the most important one in Europe, by a long shot."

Julien was on the point of accepting, but his duty kept calling him back to the great man; on taking leave of Korasoff, he promised to write. He received an answer to the secret note he had brought and sped toward Paris. But he had been alone scarcely two days in a row when the thought of leaving France and Mathilde seemed to him a punishment worse than death. "I won't marry the millions Korasoff is offering me," he told himself, "but I will follow his advice. After all, the art of seduction is his specialty; he has had nothing else on his mind for the last fifteen years, since he's thirty now. You can't say he lacks wit; he's subtle and cunning; but enthusiasm and poetry are impossible in that kind of nature. He's a pander; all the more reason why he should know what he's doing.

"It has to be done; I'm going to court Mme. de Fervaques. She may bore me a little, perhaps, but I will gaze into those beautiful eyes which are so like those that have loved me best in the world.

"She's a foreigner; that means a new character to observe.

"I'm crazy; I'm going to ruin myself; I must follow my friend's advice and not listen to myself."

Chapter XXV

The Ministry of Virtue

> But if I indulge in that pleasure
> with so much caution and circum-
> spection, it will no longer be a plea-
> sure for me.
>
> —LOPE DE VEGA

He had no more than returned to Paris when, upon
leaving the study of the Marquis de La Mole, who seemed
most disconcerted by the dispatches presented to him, our
hero rushed off to see Count Altamira. To the distinction
of being under a death sentence, that handsome foreigner
joined a good deal of gravity and had the good luck to be
religious. These two merits and, more than anything else,
the count's illustrious name, were quite acceptable to
Mme. de Fervaques, who saw a great deal of him.

Julien confessed to him solemnly that he was smitten
with her.

"Her virtue is of the purest and loftiest kind, albeit a bit
Jesuitical and high-flown. There are days when I understand every word she uses, but I can't make out a whole
sentence. She often gives me the impression that I don't
know French as well as they say I do. There's an acquaintance that will cause your name to be bandied about;
it will give you weight in society. But let's go and pay a
visit to Bustos," said Count Altamira, who was a stickler
for method. "He once courted the field marshal's
widow."

Don Diego Bustos had the matter explained to him at
great length without saying a word, like a lawyer in his
office. He had a big monkish face, a black mustache,

matchless gravity, and was, moreover, a good Carbonaro.*

"I understand," he said to Julien eventually. "Has the widow had any lovers, or hasn't she? And, consequently, can you have any hope of succeeding? That is the question. Which is to say that I, for my part, have failed. Since I got over being offended, I have reached the following conclusions: she is often out of temper, and as you will see shortly, she's quite vindictive. In her I do not find the choleric temperament, which is that of genius and casts as it were a gloss of passion over all its actions. On the contrary, it is to the phlegmatic and calm temperament of the Dutch that she owes her rare beauty and fresh complexion."

Julien was growing impatient with the Spaniard's slowness and imperturbable phlegm; from time to time, in spite of himself, a few monosyllables escaped him.

"Do you want to hear what I have to say?" Don Diego Bustos asked him gravely.

"Excuse my *furia francese;* I am all ears," said Julien.

"The widow de Fervaques is consequently much addicted to hating; she persecutes people she has never seen mercilessly: lawyers, and poor devils of writers who have made up songs, like Collé, you know?

> *J'ai la marotte
> D'aimer Marotte,"* etc.*

Julien was obliged to sit through a whole recitation. The Spaniard was delighted to sing in French. No one ever heard out that divine song more impatiently. When it was ended: "The widow," said Don Diego Bustos, "had the author of this one sacked: *'Un jour l'amant au cabaret . . .'* " *

Julien dreaded lest he sing this song too. Bustos was satisfied to analyze it. It was really blasphemous and quite indecent.

"When the widow flew into a temper over that song," said Don Diego, "I pointed out that a woman of her rank ought not to read all the trash that is printed. Whatever progress piety and gravity may be making in France, there will always be a literature of the tavern. When Mme. de Fervaques had the author's job at eighteen hundred francs taken away from him, a poor devil on half-pension, I told her: 'Take care; you have attacked that rhymester with your weapons; he may well answer you with his rhymes: he will make up a song about virtue.

398

The gilded drawing rooms will be on your side, but people who like to laugh will repeat his epigrams.' Do you know, sir, what the widow said to me? 'For the Lord's sake, all Paris might see me walk to martyrdom; that would be a novel sight in France. The people would learn to respect the quality. It would be the happiest day of my life.' Never were her eyes more beautiful."

"And they are magnificent," cried Julien.

"I can see you're in love. . . . So," continued Don Diego Bustos solemnly, "she hasn't the choleric disposition, which runs to vengeance. If she enjoys doing harm to others, therefore, it is because she is unhappy herself. I suspect some *inner woe*. Could this be the prude who has tired of her game?"

The Spaniard gazed at him in silence for a good minute.

"That's the whole question," he added gravely, "and therein you may find some grounds for hope. I gave it a good deal of thought during the two years I offered myself as her very humble servant. Your whole future, you who are in love, sir, hinges on that great problem: Is this a prude who is weary of her trade, and ill-natured because she is unhappy?"

"Or else," said Altamira, finally coming out of his deep silence, "could it be, as I have told you twenty times, purely and simply a case of French vanity? It is her father's memory, the well-known cloth merchant, that is the source of unhappiness for this naturally cold and gloomy character. Only one thing could make her happy; that is, to live in Toledo and be tormented every day by a confessor who would show her hell gaping wide."

As Julien was taking his leave: "Altamira tells me that you are one of us," said Don Diego, still more gravely. "One day you will help us to win back our liberty, so I mean to help you in this little diversion. It would be a good thing if you knew the widow's style; here are four letters in her hand."

"I'm going to copy them," cried Julien, "and bring them back to you."

"And you will never breathe a word about what we have said?"

"Never, on my honor!" cried Julien.

"May God help you, then!" added the Spaniard, and he accompanied Julien and Altamira in silence as far as the staircase.

This scene cheered up our hero somewhat; he was on

the verge of smiling. "Here is the devout Altamira," he said to himself, "helping me in an adulterous scheme."

Throughout all of Don Diego Bustos' solemn conversation, Julien had been attentive to the hours struck by the Hôtel d'Aligre's clock.

Dinner time was nearing; so he was going to see Mathilde again! He went home and dressed with great care.

"First blunder," he told himself as he went down the stairs. "The prince's prescription must be followed to the letter." He went back to his room and put on the plainest kind of traveling suit.

"Now," he said to himself, "we must concentrate on our looks." It was only half past five, and dinner was at six. He took a notion to go down to the drawing room, which he found empty. At the sight of the blue sofa, he fell to his knees and kissed the spot where Mathilde rested her arm; he shed tears, his cheeks were burning. "I must wear out this stupid sensibility," he told himself angrily. "It will give me away." He picked up a newspaper, for appearances' sake, and went three or four times from the drawing room into the garden.

Trembling, and only when he was well hidden by a huge oak, did Julien dare to look up at Mlle. de La Mole's window. It was hermetically sealed. He was on the point of fainting and stood leaning against the oak for a long while; then, with faltering steps, he went to have a look at the gardener's ladder.

The link he had once forced, under circumstances, alas! so different, had not been repaired. Carried away by a mad impulse, Julien pressed it to his lips.

After having wandered for a long while between drawing room and garden, Julien felt horribly tired; this was an initial success that pleased him greatly. "My eyes will look dull and not give me away!" Gradually, the guests arrived in the drawing room; never once did the door open without throwing Julien's heart into a state of deadly commotion.

They sat down to table. Eventually Mlle. de La Mole appeared, still faithful to her habit of making people wait. She blushed a great deal when she saw Julien; she hadn't been informed of his arrival. Following Prince Korasoff's recommendation, Julien looked at her hands; they were trembling. More troubled himself by this discovery than words can say, he was rather glad to seem merely tired.

M. de La Mole sang his praises. The marquise addressed him an instant later to inquire about his tired look. Julien kept telling himself every minute: "I mustn't stare at Mlle. de La Mole, but I shouldn't avoid her eyes either. I should appear to be as I really was a week before things went wrong...." He had reason to be satisfied with his success and stayed on in the drawing room. Attentive for the first time to the mistress of the house, he made every effort to make the men in her circle talk and keep the conversation alive.

His courtesy was rewarded: around eight o'clock Mme. de Fervaques was announced. Julien stole away and soon reappeared, dressed with the greatest care. Mme. de La Mole was infinitely grateful to him for this mark of respect, and tried to show how pleased she was by telling Mme. de Fervaques about his trip. Julien situated himself close to the widow, in such a way that Mathilde should not catch sight of his eyes. Seated thus, and following all the rules of the art, he treated Mme. de Fervaques as an object of the most dumbfounded admiration. The first of the fifty-three letters of which the Prince Korasoff had made him a gift opened with a tirade about that very sentiment.

The widow announced that she was going to the opera buffa. Julien rushed to it; he found the Chevalier de Beauvoisis there, who took him into the Gentlemen of the Privy Chamber's box, right next to that of Mme. de Fervaques. Julien gazed at her constantly. "It is essential," he told himself as he returned to the house, "that I keep a diary of this siege; otherwise I will forget my attacks." He forced himself to write two or three pages on this boring subject, and while doing so (marvelous to say) almost succeeded in not thinking about Mlle. de La Mole.

Mathilde had all but forgotten him during his trip. "After all, he is nothing but a common fellow," she kept thinking. "His name will always remind me of the greatest stain on my life. I must return in good faith to conventional notions about modesty and honor; a woman has everything to lose if she forgets them." She let it be known that she was at last willing to allow the arrangement with the Marquis de Croisenois, ready for such a long time, to be concluded. He was wild with joy. He would have been astonished, indeed, if anyone had told him that resignation was at the base of Mathilde's change of heart, which had made him so proud.

Mlle. de La Mole's ideas changed completely when she saw Julien. "In truth, that man is my husband," she kept telling herself. "If I am to return in good faith to common notions about chastity, it is obviously he whom I should marry."

She expected importunate advances, woebegone looks on Julien's part; she was preparing her answer, for he would no doubt on rising from the dinner table try to say a few words to her. Far from that, he remained staunchly behind in the drawing room; not even his eyes turned toward the garden; God knows what it cost him! "It's better to have this out right away," thought Mlle. de La Mole. She went into the garden alone; Julien did not appear. Mathilde happened to walk close by the French windows; she saw him very busily engaged in describing to Mme. de Fervaques the ruined old castles that crown the sloping banks of the Rhine and give them such character. He was beginning to handle the kind of sentimental and picturesque language that passes for *wit* in certain drawing rooms pretty well.

Prince Korasoff would have been proud of him had he been in Paris: that evening went exactly as he had predicted. He would have approved the line of conduct Julien held to in the days following.

As the result of an intrigue among the members of the inner sanctum of the Government, several blue sashes were to be distributed; Mme. de Fervaques was insistent that her great-uncle be made a knight of the order. The Marquis de La Mole was making the same claim for his father-in-law; they joined forces, and the widow came almost daily to the Hôtel de La Mole. It was from her Julien learned that the marquis was about to become a minister; he had offered the *Camarilla** a most ingenious plan for wrecking the Charter, without any repercussions, in three years' time.

Julien might hope for a diocese if M. de La Mole got a ministry; but to his eyes all of those momentous concerns were as if covered with a veil. His imagination was no longer capable of perceiving them, except vaguely and, so to speak, in the distance. The terrible wretchedness that was making an obsessed man of him showed him all of life's concerns in the light of his relationship with Mlle. de La Mole. He calculated that after five or six years of careful attention he would succeed in making her love him again.

This very cool head had fallen, as we can see, into a state of total irrationality. Of all the qualities that had distinguished him before, nothing remained but a little firmness. Faithful to the letter about observing the line of conduct laid down by Prince Korasoff, he would post himself close to Mme. de Fervaques' armchair every evening, but he couldn't find a word to say.

The demands he made upon himself to appear cured in Mathilde's sight used up all his strength of his soul; he sat in the widow's presence like a creature barely alive; even his eyes, as in cases of extreme physical suffering, had lost all their fire.

Since Mme. de La Mole's way of seeing things was never more than a pale copy of the views of a husband who might well make her duchess, for several days she had been praising Julien's talent to the skies.

Chapter XXVI

Platonic Love

> There also was of course in Adeline
> That calm patrician polish in the
> address,
> Which ne'er can pass the equinoctial
> line
> Of anything which Nature would
> express:
> Just as a Mandarin finds nothing
> fine,
> At least this manner suffers not
> to guess
> That anything he views can greatly
> please.
> —*Don Juan*, C. XIII, st. 34

"This whole family's way of looking at things is a bit mad," the widow said to herself. "They are crazy about their young abbé, and he doesn't know how to do anything but listen; true, he has fine eyes."

Julien, for his part, found the widow's comportment a nearly perfect example of that "patrician calm" which is instinct with an exact politeness and, even more, the impossiblity of any strong emotion. Any impulsive movement, a lack of self-possession, would have scandalized Mme. de Fervaques almost as much as a want of majesty in one's attitude toward one's inferiors. To her, the least show of sensibility seemed a kind of *mental intoxication*, for which one ought to blush, and very prejudicial to everything a woman of high rank owes to herself. Her great delight was to talk about the king's last hunt; her

404

favorite book, the *Mémoires du duc de Saint-Simon,** especially the genealogical part.

Julien knew which spot in the drawing room, according to the disposition of the lights, best suited Mme. de Fervaques' type of beauty. He was always there early, but always took great care to turn his chair in such a way as not to catch sight of Mathilde. Astonished at his constancy in hiding from her, she left the blue sofa one evening and came to work at a little table next to the widow's armchair. Julien saw her fairly close up, from under Mme. de Fervaques' hat. Those eyes upon which his fate depended frightened him at first at such close range, then jolted him out of his usual listlessness; he talked, and very well.

He was addressing the widow, but his sole aim was to work on Mathilde's feelings. He became so excited that at a certain point Mme. de Fervaques could no longer understand what he was saying.

This was all to the good. If it had occurred to Julien to add a few phrases from German mysticity, or high religiosity, or Jesuitism, the widow would have ranked him then and there among the superior men called upon to regenerate the age.

"Since he has the bad taste," Mlle. de La Mole said to herself, "to talk to Mme. de Fervaques for such a long time, and so fervently, I will not listen to him anymore." She kept her word for the rest of the evening, though it was not easy.

At midnight, when she took the candlestick from her mother to accompany her to her bedroom, Mme. de La Mole stopped on the staircase to deliver a long eulogy of Julien. In the end Mathilde was thoroughly irritated; she couldn't sleep. One thought calmed her: "A fellow I despise can still pass for a man of great worth in the widow's estimation."

As for Julien, he had acted, he was less miserable; his gaze happened to fall on the Russia leather portfolio wherein Prince Korasoff had enclosed the fifty-three love letters of which he had made him a present. Julien saw a note at the bottom of the first: *"Letter No. 1 is to be sent a week after the first meeting."*

"I'm late!" cried Julien. "It's a long time since I started seeing Mme. de Fervaques." Immediately he set about transcribing this first love letter; it was a homily filled with stock phrases about virtue, and a deadly bore. Julien had the good luck to fall asleep over the second page.

Several hours later, the broad sun caught him sound asleep at his table. One of the most painful moments in his life was that during which, every morning, upon wakening, he *informed* himself of his wretchedness. That day he was almost laughing by the time he finished copying his letter. "Is it possible," he asked himself, "that there really was a young man who wrote like that!" He counted several sentences that ran to nine lines. At the bottom of the original he saw a penciled note.

These letters are to be delivered personally: on horseback, black ruff, blue frock coat. One should hand the letter to the porter with a contrite air, deep melancholy in one's gaze. If one happens to see a chambermaid, one wipes one's eyes furtively. Say a few words to the chambermaid.

This was all carried out to the letter.

"What I am doing is bold, indeed," thought Julien as he left the Hôtel de Fervaques, "but so much the worse for Korasoff. Daring to write to such a famous prude! I will be treated to the utmost contempt, and nothing could amuse me more. That is, after all, the only comedy to which I can still respond. Yes, to cover that hateful creature I call *me* with ridicule would be amusing. . . . If I followed my own inclination, I would commit some crime, just to take my mind off things."

For a month, the happiest moments in Julien's life had been those during which he put his horse back in the stable. Korasoff had expressly forbidden him, under any pretext whatsoever, to look at the mistress who had forsaken him. But the hoofbeat of the horse she knew so well, Julien's way of knocking on the stable door with his crop to call a groom, would sometimes attract Mathilde behind her window curtain. The muslin was so thin that Julien could see through it. By looking in a certain way from under the brim of his hat, he could catch a glimpse of Mathilde's figure without seeing her eyes. "It follows," he said to himself, "that she can't see mine, and that is not the same thing as looking at her."

That evening Mme. de Fervaques behaved toward him exactly as if she had not received the mystical and religious philosophical dissertation that, in the morning, he had handed her porter so melancholically. The evening before, chance had revealed to Julien the means of being eloquent; so he again situated himself in such a way as to see Mathilde's eyes. She, on the other hand, a minute after the widow's arrival, left the blue sofa; that is, deserted her circle. M. de Croisenois appeared to be dismayed at this latest caprice. His visible anguish took the sting out of Julien's own suffering.

This unforeseen event made Julien talk like an angel; and, as self-conceit will slip even into hearts that serve as a temple for the most august virtue, the widow said to herself, as she climbed back into her carriage: "Mme. de La Mole is right; that young priest *is* distinguished. During the first few days, my presence must have made him shy. To tell the truth, the people one meets in that house are decidedly frivolous; I see nothing there but virtues helped along by old age, and that once stood very much in need of time's chilling hand. That young man must have seen the difference. He writes well, but I greatly fear that the request he makes in his letter, for me to enlighten him with my counsel, may be, after all, prompted by a feeling of which he is unaware.

"Yet, how many conversions have begun in the same way! What makes me hopeful about this one is the difference between his style and that of other young men whose letters I have had occasion to see. It is impossible not to recognize that there is unction, deep seriousness, and a great deal of conviction in this young Levite's prose; he must have Massillon's gentle virtue."*

Chapter XXVII

The Best Positions in the Church

Service! . . . Ability! . . . Worth!
Nonsense! Join a clique!
—*Télémaque*

Thus, for the first time, the idea of a diocese was
associated with Julien in the mind of a woman who,
sooner or later, was to distribute the finest positions in the
Church of France. This advantage would scarcely have
interested Julien; at that moment his thoughts could not
have risen to anything beyond his present misery. Everything added to it; for example, the sight of his bedroom
had become unbearable. At night, when he returned to it
with his candlestick, every piece of furniture, every small
ornament, seemed to take on a voice for the purpose of
informing him acidly of some new detail of his misfortune.

"Today I've been sentenced to hard labor," he told
himself as he entered his room, with a sprightliness he had
not felt for a long time. "Let's hope the second letter will
be as boring as the first."

It was, even more so. What he was copying seemed so
ridiculous that he was soon transcribing it line by line,
without a thought to the sense of it.

"It is even more turgid than the documents for the
Treaty of Münster* that my professor of diplomacy had
me copy in London."

It was only then that he remembered Mme. de Fervaques' letters, the originals of which he had forgotten to
return to the grave Spaniard, Don Diego Bustos. He got
them out; they were really almost as amphigoric as those

of the young Russian lord. Their vagueness was total. The intention was to say everything and nothing. "This is the Aeolian harp of style," thought Julien. "Amidst all these lofty thoughts about nonbeing, death, the infinite, etcetera, I see nothing genuine except a disgusting fear of ridicule."

The above monologue, which we have abridged, occurred daily for two weeks in a row. Falling asleep while copying a sort of commentary on Revelations, delivering his letter the next day with a melancholy look, putting the horse back in the stable in hopes of catching sight of Mathilde's dress, working, putting in an appearance at the opera in the evening whenever Mme. de Fervaques didn't come to the Hôtel de La Mole; such were the monotonous events of Julien's life. It was more interesting when Mme. de Fervaques came to see the marquise; then he could catch a glimpse of Mathilde's eyes from under the brim of the widow's hat, and he would wax eloquent. His quaint and sentimental periods were beginning to take a turn that was both more striking and more elegant.

He realized full well that what he was saying must seem absurd to Mathilde, but he was trying to impress her with elegant diction. "The more what I say is false, the more I ought to please her," Julien thought; and then, with really abominable cheek, he overdid certain aspects of nature. He very soon became aware that if he was not to appear common in the widow's eyes, he must above all refrain from simple and reasonable ideas. He went on in this vein or cut short his amplifications according to whether he read success or indifference in the eyes of the two great ladies whom it was essential to please.

On the whole his life was less horrible now than when his days had been spent in idleness.

"Well," he said to himself one night, "here I am transcribing the fifteenth of these abominable dissertations; the first fourteen have been faithfully delivered to the widow's Swiss guard. I shall have the honor of filling all the pigeonholes in her desk. And yet she treats me exactly as if I were not writing! What is her object? Could it be that my perseverance bores her as much as it does me? I must say, that Russian, Korasoff's friend, who was in love with the beautiful Richmond Quakeress, was a devil of a fellow in his day; he's as tiresome as they come."

Like all ordinary mortals whom chance has placed in full view of a great general's maneuvers, Julien understood nothing of the attack executed by the young Russian against the stern English girl's heart. The first forty letters were designed merely to win pardon for making so bold as to write. It was necessary first to have that sweet person, who was perhaps infinitely bored, contract the habit of receiving letters which were a little less insipid perhaps than her daily life.

One morning Julien was handed a letter; he recognized Mme. de Fervaques' coat of arms and broke the seal with an eagerness that would have seemed quite impossible for him a few days earlier. It was simply an invitation to dinner.

Julien hurried to look at Prince Korasoff's instructions. Unfortunately, the young Russian had tried to imitate Dorat's light touch* where he should have been simple and intelligible; Julien could not guess what pose he was to assume at the widow's dinner.

The drawing room was of the greatest magnificence, gilded like the Gallery of Diana in the Tuileries, with pictures painted in oil in the paneling. There were light spots in those paintings. Later Julien was informed that the mistress of the house thought the subjects indecent and had had the pictures corrected. *"This moral century!"* he thought.

In the drawing room he noticed three of the notables who had been at the drafting of the secret note. One of them, the Lord Bishop of ———, the widow's uncle, had all the Church positions at his disposal and, so everyone said, he couldn't say "no" to his niece. "What a big step I have taken," Julien said to himself with a melancholy smile, "and how little it means to me! Here I am dining with the famous Bishop of ———."

The dinner was mediocre and the conversation trying. "It's the dinner table of a bad novel," thought Julien. "Here, all the greatest questions to which men have turned their thoughts are boldly attacked. And after you have listened for three minutes you wonder which will win out, the speaker's bombast or his disgusting ignorance."

The reader has no doubt forgotten that little man of letters named Tanbeau, the academician's nephew and a future professor, who, with his base slander, seemed to have been hired to poison the Hôtel de La Mole's drawing room.

From this little man, Julien had his first inkling that it might very well be that Mme. de Fervaques, though not answering his letters, looked indulgently upon the sentiment that dictated them. M. Tanbeau's black soul was torn in two whenever he thought about Julien's success; "but on the other hand, since a worthy man cannot, any more than a fool, be in two places at once, if Sorel becomes the sublime widow's lover," the future professor kept telling himself, "she will find some advantageous position for him in the Church, and I shall be rid of him at the Hôtel de La Mole."

The Abbé Pirard also treated Julien to long sermons about his popularity at the Hôtel de Fervaques. There was *sectarian jealousy* between the austere Jansenist and the virtuous widow's Jesuitical drawing room, where all were regenerative and monarchist.

Chapter XXVIII

Manon Lescaut

> Now, once he was fully convinced
> of the prior's stupidity, of his asi-
> ninity, he got on quite well by call-
> ing black white and white black.
>
> —LICHTENBERG

The Russian's instructions forbade imperatively that one
ever contradict by word of mouth the lady to whom one
was writing. One was not for any reason whatsoever to
depart from the role of ecstatic admirer; the letters always
started from that assumption.

One evening at the opera, in Mme. de Fervaques' loge,
Julien praised the ballet *Manon Lescaut** to the skies.
His only reason for going on so was that he found it per-
fectly insignificant.

The widow said the ballet was much inferior to the
Abbé Prévost's novel.

"What!" thought Julien, astonished and amused, "a
woman of such lofty virtue can speak highly of a novel!"
Two or three times a week Mme. de Fervaques made a
profession of the most thorough contempt for writers
who, by means of their shabby works, tried to corrupt a
younger generation that was, alas! only too prone to
errors of the senses.

"In that category of the immoral and dangerous,
Manon Lescaut," pursued the widow, "occupies, so they
say, one of the first ranks. In it the weaknesses and
well-deserved agonies of a very criminal heart are, so they
say, depicted with a truthfulness of some depth; which did
not prevent your Napoleon from declaring at Ste. Hélène
that it is a novel written for lackeys."

That remark roused Julien to all his old alertness. "Someone has been trying to harm me in the widow's estimation; someone must have told her about my enthusiasm for Napoleon. That information has nettled her enough to make her give in to the temptation of letting me know it." This discovery entertained him all evening and made him entertaining.

As he was taking leave of the widow in the lobby of the opera: "Remember, sir," she said to him, "that one must not love Bonaparte when one loves me; one may, at the most, accept him as a necessary evil imposed by Providence. Besides, that man did not have a mind flexible enough to appreciate the masterpieces."

"When one loves me!" Julien repeated to himself. "That means nothing, or it means everything. Such are the secrets of language in which we poor provincials are deficient." He thought a great deal about Mme. de Rênal as he copied an endless letter destined for the widow.

"How does it happen," she asked him the next day, with an air of indifference, which he found poorly played, "that you speak to me of *London* and of *Richmond* in a letter you wrote last night, so it seems, after coming out of the opera?"

Julien was quite embarrassed; he had copied line for line without a thought to what he was writing, and had obviously forgotten to substitute *Paris* and *St. Cloud* for *London* and *Richmond* in the original. He began two or three sentences but with no possibility of finishing them; he felt himself on the verge of giving in to a giggle. At last, while hunting for his words, he came upon this idea: "Uplifted by the most sublime of discussions about the greatest concerns of the human soul, my mind, as I wrote you, may well have wandered."

"I am making an impression," he told himself, "that will allow me to forgo the boredom of the rest of the evening." He left the Hôtel de Fervaques at a run. That night, when he had another look at the original of the letter copied the night before, he came very quickly to the fateful lines where the young Russian spoke of London and Richmond. Julien was astonished indeed to find this letter almost tender.

It was the contrast between the apparent frivolity of his conversation and the sublime and almost apocalyptic depth of his letters that had distinguished him. The widow especially liked the length of his sentences; "this isn't the choppy style made fashionable by Voltaire, that immoral man!" Although our hero did all in his power to

413

banish every kind of good sense from his conversation, it still had an anti-Royalist and impious coloring that did not escape Mme. de Fervaques. Surrounded by personages who were eminently moral, but who often didn't have one idea in an evening, the lady was deeply impressed by anything that looked like a novelty, but at the same time, she thought she owed it to herself to take offense at it. She called any failure to do so, *keeping the imprint of a frivolous age.*

But such drawing rooms are not worth the visit unless one is soliciting something. All the boredom of the dull life Julien was leading is no doubt shared by the reader. These are the wastelands of our journey. During the time usurped from Julien's life by the Fervaques episode, Mlle. de La Mole had to force herself not to think about him. Her heart was a prey to the most violent conflicts; sometimes she flattered herself that she despised the gloomy young man; but for all that, his conversation captivated her. What astonished her most was his perfect falseness; he never said a word to the widow but it was a lie, or at least an abominable disguise for his true opinion, which Mathilde knew perfectly well on almost every subject. His Machiavellianism impressed her. "Such depth!" she would tell herself. "What a difference between him and the pompous boobies or common crooks, such as M. Tanbeau, who talk the same language!"

Nevertheless, Julien had some awful days. It was only to fulfill the most painful of duties that he appeared daily in the widow's drawing room. His effort to play a part used up whatever strength of soul remained to him. Many times, at night, as he crossed the huge courtyard of the Hôtel de Fervaques, he managed to keep from sinking into despair only by force of character and by reasoning with himself.

"I conquered despair in the seminary," he would tell himself, "and yet, what an awful prospect I had before me then! I was either making or marring my fortune; but in any case, I saw myself obliged to live on intimate terms for a whole lifetime with the most despicable and disgusting company on earth. The following spring, just eleven short months afterwards, I was probably the happiest young man of my age."

But all too often these fine arguments were unavailing against the terrible reality. Every day he saw Mathilde at lunch and at dinner. From the numerous letters M. de La Mole dictated to him, he knew that she was on the eve of marrying M. de Croisenois. That amiable young man was already showing up twice a day at the Hôtel de La Mole; the jealous eye of a forsaken lover did not miss a single move he made.

When he thought he had seen Mlle. de La Mole treating her intended kindly, upon returning to his room, Julien could not help but gaze at his pistols lovingly.

"Ah! wouldn't I be better off," he kept telling himself, "to pick the initials out of my linen and go into some lonely forest twenty leagues from Paris and put an end to this abominable life! Since I would be a stranger, in the vicinity, my death would go unreported for two weeks, and who would give a thought to me after that!"

This argument was quite reasonable. But the next day Mathilde's arm, glimpsed between the sleeve of her dress and her glove, was enough to plunge our young philosopher into memories which, though cruel, nevertheless bound him to life. "Very well!" he would say to himself at those times, "I will follow that Russian policy to the hilt. How will it all end?

"As for the widow, once I have copied out those fifty-three letters, I won't, to be sure, write her any more. As for Mathilde, either these painful six weeks of shamming will not have the least effect on her anger, or they will win me a moment's reconciliation. Good God! I should die of happiness!" He was powerless to finish his thought.

When, after a long reverie, he managed to pick up the thread of this thought again, he would say to himself, "So, I should win one day of happiness, after which her harsh treatment, founded, alas, on my inability to please her, would begin all over again, and I would have nothing to fall back on; I would be lost, ruined forever. . . .

"With the character she has, what guarantee can she give me? Alas! my want of talent explains everything. My manners must be very inelegant; my way of speaking, heavy and monotonous. Good God! Why am I, I?"

Chapter XXIX

Boredom

> To sacrifice oneself to one's passions, granted; but to passions one doesn't feel! O dreary nineteenth century!
>
> —GIRODET

After reading Julien's long letters with no pleasure at first, Mme. de Fervaques began to take an interest in them; but one thing distressed her: "What a pity M. Sorel is not a full-fledged priest! It would be possible to admit him into a kind of intimacy. What with that cross and those almost civilian clothes, a woman would be exposed to cruel questions, and what could she say?" She left her thought unfinished: "Some malicious lady friend might suppose and even spread the story that he was some little second cousin, my father's relation, some shopkeeper decorated by the National Guard."

Until she met Julien, Mme. de Fervaques' greatest pleasure had been to write the word "Maréchale"* before her name. After that, a sickly parvenu vanity, which took offense at everything, fought against her initial interest.

"It would be so easy for me," the widow kept telling herself, "to make him vicar-general of some diocese near Paris! But M. Sorel with nothing after it, and M. de La Mole's secretary at that! It's discouraging."

For the first time this soul, *which dreaded everything*, was touched by an interest that had nothing to do with her pretensions to rank and social superiority. Her old doorkeeper noted that whenever he brought a letter from that handsome young man who looked so sad, the distracted and annoyed look the widow was always careful to put on when any of her household came near her was sure to vanish.

The boredom inherent in a way of life whose only aim is to make an impression on the public, when at the bottom of her heart the person takes no real pleasure in that kind of success, became so intolerable since she had begun to think about Julien, that if the chambermaids were not to be ill used all day long, it was enough if the widow had spent an hour with that unusual young man the evening before. His growing prestige was able to withstand anonymous and very adroitly composed letters. In vain, little Tanbeau furnished *MM*. de Luz, de Croisenous, de Caylus, with two or three astute pieces of slander which those gentlemen took pleasure in spreading about without concerning themselves overly much about the truth of the accusations. The widow, whose temperament was not made to bear up against such unrefined methods, would tell Mathilde about her misgivings, and was always reassured.

One day, after having asked three times if there were any letters, Mme. de Fervaques suddenly resolved to answer Julien. It was a victory for boredom. At the second letter, the widow was almost stopped by the unseemliness of writing such a commonplace address in her own hand: *To M. Sorel, care of the Marquis de La Mole.*

That evening she told Julien very coldly, "You must bring some envelopes with your address on them."

"Here I am, set up as her lover and valet," thought Julien, and he bowed, amusing himself by imitating Arsène, the marquis' old valet.

The same evening he brought her some envelopes, and the next day, very early, he received a third letter: he read five or six lines at the beginning and two or three near the end. There were four pages in a small, closely written hand.

Little by little she took the pleasant habit of writing almost every day. Julien would answer with faithful copies of the Russian letters and, such is the advantage of the high-flown style, Mme. de Fervaques was not in the least surprised that there was so little connection between his replies and her letters.

How her pride would have been irritated if little Tanbeau, who had appointed himself the voluntary spy of Julien's proceedings, had been in a position to inform her that all those letters, unopened, were thrown haphazardly into Julien's drawer.

One morning the doorkeeper, paying no attention to the

417

widow's coat of arms, brought one of her letters to him in the library; Mathilde ran into the man and saw the letter with its address in Julien's hand. She entered the library as the doorkeeper was leaving. The letter was still on the edge of the table. Busy writing, Julien had not put it in his drawer.

"This is something I will not endure," cried Mathilde, seizing the letter. "You have forgotten me altogether, I who am your wife. Your conduct is atrocious, sir."

At these words her pride, astonished at the frightful impropriety of the step she had just taken, made her choke; she burst into tears, and before long it appeared to Julien that she couldn't breathe.

Surprised, confused, Julien was hardly in a way to make out everything wonderful and lucky that this scene implied for him. He helped Mathilde to sit down; she all but abandoned herself in his arms.

The first instant he noticed this impulse was one of extreme joy. In the second, he thought of Korasoff. "I may ruin everything by a single word."

His arms grew stiff, so painful was the effort his policy forced him to make. "I must not even allow myself to press that lovely, supple body against my heart, or she will scorn and abuse me. What a horrible character she has!"

As he cursed Mathilde's character, he loved her a hundred times the more for it; it seemed to him that he held a queen in his arms.

Julien's impassive coldness doubled the pangs of wounded pride that were rending Mlle. de La Mole's heart. She was far from having the self-control necessary to try and guess from his eyes what he felt about her at the moment. She could not bring herself to look at him; she trembled lest she meet with an expression of contempt.

Sitting motionless on the library sofa, her head turned away from Julien, she was a prey to the keenest suffering that pride and love can inflict on a human heart. What an atrocious situation she had got herself into!

"It was reserved for me, wretch that I am, to see my most indecent advances repulsed! And repulsed by whom?" added her pride, wild with suffering, "repulsed by one of my father's servants."

"This is something I will not tolerate," she said aloud. Rising to her feet furiously, she opened the drawer of Julien's table, which was two paces away. She stood as if frozen with horror upon finding eight or ten unopened letters in it, each in every respect like the one the doorkeeper had just brought up. In all the addresses she recognized Julien's writing more or less disguised.

"So," she shouted, beside herself, "not only are you on good terms with her, you despise her as well. You, a nobody, to scorn the Field Marshal de Fervaques' widow!

"Ah! Forgive me, my dear," she added, throwing herself at his knees. "Scorn me if you wish, but love me; I cannot live any longer without your love." And she fell to the floor in a dead faint.

"There she is at my feet, that haughty woman!" Julien said to himself.

Chapter XXX

A Box at the Opera

As the blackest sky
Foretells the heaviest tempest.
—*Don Juan,* C. I, st. 73

Amidst all these intense emotions, Julien was more astonished than happy. Mathilde's abuse brought home to him the wisdom of the Russian's policy. "*Speak little, act little*: therein lies my only salvation."

He picked up Mathilde, and, without a word, put her back on the sofa. Gradually tears got the better of her. To keep herself in countenance, she took Mme. de Fervaques' letters in her hands; she broke the seals slowly. She gave a nervous, quite noticeable start when she recognized the widow's writing. She kept turning over the sheets of these letters without reading them; most were six pages long.

"At least answer me," said Mathilde at length, in the most supplicating voice, but not daring to look at Julien. "You know very well that I am proud; that misfortune is due to my position, and even to my nature, I admit. So Mme. de Fervaques has stolen your heart from me. . . . Has she made all the sacrifices for you to which this fatal love betrayed me?"

A gloomy silence was Julien's only response. "By what right," he thought, "is she asking me to commit an indiscretion unworthy an honorable man?"

Mathilde tried to read the letters; tearful eyes made this impossible.

She had been wretched for a month, but that haughty soul was still far from admitting her feelings to herself. Chance alone had brought about this explosion. For a moment, jealousy and love had got the best of pride. She was seated on the divan, very close to Julien. He looked at her hair and her alabaster neck; for a moment he forgot everything he owed himself; he put his arm around her waist and almost clasped her to his chest.

She turned her head toward him slowly; he was astonished at the great suffering in her eyes, such that he could find no trace of their usual expression.

Julien felt his strength ebbing away, so mortally painful was the act of courage which he was imposing upon himself.

"In a little while those eyes will show nothing but the coldest disdain," Julien said to himself, "if I let myself be swept away by the happiness of loving her." Meanwhile, in a faint voice and in sentences that she had barely the strength to finish, she kept assuring him how sorry she was for a behavior that had been prompted by overweening pride.

"I have my pride, too," Julien said to her in a barely distinct voice, and his features showed the extreme limit of physical exhaustion.

Mathilde turned toward him sharply. To hear his voice was a bliss the hope of which she had all but forgone. In that moment she remembered her haughtiness only to curse it; she would have liked to find some unusual, some incredible way of proving the extent to which she adored him and detested herself.

"It is probably because of your pride," Julien went on, "that you honored me briefly; it is certainly because of my brave firmness, which is fitting in a man, that you respect me at the moment. I could be in love with the field marshal's widow. . . ."

Mathilde shuddered; her eyes took on a strange expression. She was about to hear her sentence pronounced. This reaction was by no means lost on Julien; he felt his courage weakening.

"Ah!" he said to himself, listening to the sound of the empty words his mouth was shaping as he would to a strange noise, "if only I could cover those pale cheeks with kisses, and you not feel them!"

"I might be in love with the widow . . ." he continued, and his voice kept getting feebler, "but certainly, I have had no proof positive of her interest in me. . . ."

Mathilde stared at him; he bore up under her look; he hoped at least that his expression had not betrayed him. He felt pierced with love to the heart's core. Never had he worshiped her to that point; he was nearly as much out of

421

his head as Mathilde. If she had had enough self-possession and the heart to manipulate him, he would have fallen at her feet, forswearing all his foolish comedy. He still had enough strength to go on talking. "Ah! Korasoff," he cried inwardly, "you should be here; how I need a word of advice to guide me!" During that time, his voice was saying:

"For want of any other sentiment, gratitude alone would be enough to make me feel an attachment for the widow; she has been kind to me, she has comforted me when I was despised. . . . I am free, of course, not to have unlimited faith in certain appearances, extremely flattering, no doubt, but perhaps, too, not very durable."

"Ah! great God!" cried Mathilde.

"Well, then! what guarantee will you give me?" replied Julien in a sharp, firm tone of voice, and seeming for an instant to drop the careful forms of diplomacy, "what guarantee, what god will assure me that the position to which you seem willing to restore me at the moment will hold for more than two days?"

"My boundless love, and unhappiness if you no longer love me," she said to him, taking his hands and turning to face him.

The violent movement she made had shifted her cape a little; Julien caught a glimpse of her lovely shoulders. Her slightly mussed hair brought back a delightful memory. . . .

He was about to give in. "A careless word," he told himself, "and that long succession of days spent in despair will begin all over again. Mme. de Rênal used to find reasons for following the dictates of her heart; this girl from high society will not let her heart be moved until she has proven to herself with good reasons that it ought to be."

He perceived this truth in a wink, and in the wink of an eye he also recovered his courage.

He withdrew his hands, which Mathilde held clasped in her own, and with pointed respect moved a little way from her. A man's courage can do no more. Next, he busied himself with gathering up all of Mme. de Fervaques' letters, which were scattered over the divan, and with an appearance of the utmost courtesy, cruel at such a moment, he added: "Mlle. de La Mole will please be so good as to allow me to consider this matter further." He left the room quickly and she heard him closing all the doors in succession.

"The monster wasn't the least bit upset," she said to herself. "But what am I saying, monster! He is wise, prudent, kind; it is I who have done more wrong than anyone could imagine."

This frame of mind persisted. Mathilde was almost happy that day, for she was all love; one would have thought that her heart had never been shaken by pride, and such pride!

She shuddered with horror when, that evening in the drawing room, a footman announced Mme. de Fervaques; to her ear, the man's voice was sinister. She couldn't bear the sight of the widow and moved away from her very shortly. Julien, anything but elated by his painful victory, dreaded that his own looks might give him away, and had not dined at the Hôtel de La Mole.

His love and his happiness increased as rapidly as the moment of battle receded; he was already at the stage of blaming himself. "How could I have resisted her," he said to himself; "what if she no longer loves me! That proud heart could change in a minute, and there's no denying that I treated her horribly."

That evening he realized that he must absolutely show up in Mme. de Fervaques' loge at the opera buffa. She had invited him expressly; Mathilde would not fail to hear about his presence or his impolite absence. Notwithstanding the obviousness of this argument, he didn't have the strength, at the beginning of the evening, to plunge into society. By talking, he would lose half of his bliss.

Ten o'clock was striking; he simply had to make an appearance.

Fortunately, he found the widow's box full of women. He was relegated to a seat near the door, where he was completely hidden by hats. This position saved him from making a fool of himself; the divine accents of Caroline's despair in the *Matrimonio Segreto** set his tears to flowing. Mme. de Fervaques saw those tears; they made such a contrast with the virile steadiness of his usual expression that the great lady's soul, surfeited a long time before with everything that is most corrosive about *upstart* pride, was touched. What little remained to her of a womanly heart prompted her to speak. She wanted to enjoy the sound of her own voice at the moment.

"Have you seen the de La Mole ladies?" she asked him. "They are in the third tier." At that instant Julien leaned, impolitely enough, out of the box; he saw Mathilde; her eyes were glistening with tears.

"But this isn't their day for the opera," thought Julien; "such eagerness!"

Mathilde had induced her mother to go to the opera buffa, despite the unsuitableness of the location of the box, which one of the household flatterers had pressed upon them. She wanted to see if Julien would spend the evening with the widow.

Chapter XXXI

Frighten Her

> That, then, is the great miracle of
> your civilization! You have turned
> love into a routine affair.
>
> ——BARNAVE

Julien rushed to Mme. de La Mole's box. The first thing
that crossed his sight was Mathilde's tear-filled eyes; she
was weeping without stint. There was no one there but
inconsequential people, the lady friend who had lent the
box and some men of her acquaintance. Mathilde put her
hand on Julien's; she seemed to have lost all fear of her
mother. Almost choked with weeping, she said but one
word to him: "*Guarantees!*"

"Let me at least keep from talking to her," thought
Julien, deeply moved himself and hiding his eyes as best he
could with his hand, under the pretext that in the third
tier of boxes the chandelier was blinding. "If I speak she
can no longer have any doubts about the depth of my
feelings; my voice will betray me; all may yet be lost."

His conflict was far more painful than in the morning;
his heart had had time enough to be affected. He was
afraid he might give Mathilde reason to think that she had
triumphed; so, drunk with love and pleasure, he took it
upon himself not to speak.

That, in my opinion, is one of his finest traits; a fellow
capable of such self-control may go far, *si fata sinant.**

Mlle. de La Mole insisted on bringing Julien back to the
house. Fortunately it was pouring. But the marquise made
him sit facing her, spoke to him constantly, and prevented
him from saying a word to her daughter. One might have
thought that the marquise was looking out for Julien's

425

happiness; no longer afraid of ruining everything through the violence of his emotion, he gave in to it extravagantly.

Dare I mention that upon returning to his room, Julien threw himself down on his knees and covered the love letters Prince Korasoff had given him with kisses?

"O great man! how can I ever repay you?" he shouted in his folly.

Little by little some of his composure returned. He compared himself with a general who has just half won a great battle. "My advantage is certain, immense," he told himself, "but what will tomorrow bring? All may be lost in a moment."

On a passionate impulse, he opened the *Mémoires dictées à Sainte-Hélène* by Napoleon, and for two long hours forced himself to read; but only his eyes read; no matter, he kept forcing himself. Throughout this odd session his head and heart, having risen to the level of the loftiest considerations, worked on unbeknownst to him. "Her heart is very different from Mme. de Rênal's," he kept telling himself, but he went no further.

"Frighten her!" he shouted all of a sudden, throwing away the book. "The enemy will obey you only insomuch as he is afraid of you, and after that will not dare to show contempt."

Drunk with joy, he set to pacing his little room. To tell the truth, his present happiness owed more to pride than to love.

"Frighten her!" he went on repeating proudly, and he had reason to be proud. "Even in her happiest moments, Mme. de Rênal always doubted that my love was as great as hers. But in this case there is a demon to be subdued, and *subdue* I must."

He knew very well that by eight the next morning Mathilde would be in the library; he did not appear until nine o'clock, and though he was burning with love, his head commanded his heart. Hardly a minute went by without his saying to himself: "Always keep her preoccupied with that great doubt: 'Does he love me?' Her brilliant position, the flattery of all who speak to her, incline her to reassure herself *a bit too quickly*."

He found her pale, calm, seated on the divan, but to all appearances incapable of a single movement. She held out her hand to him.

"Dear, I have offended you, it's true; are you angry with me? . . ."

Julien was not prepared for such simplicity in her tone. He was on the verge of betraying himself.

"You want guarantees, my dear," she added after a silence that she hoped would be broken. "That is only right. Carry me off; let us set out for London. . . . I will be ruined forever, dishonored. . . ." She had the courage to take her hand out of Julien's to cover her eyes with it. All of her sentiments about feminine modesty and reserve had returned to that heart. . . . "Very well! dishonor me," she said at length with a sigh; "that is a *guarantee*."

"Yesterday I was happy because I had the courage to be strict with myself," thought Julien. After a brief silence, he was enough master of his heart to say icily, "Once on the road to London, once you are dishonored, as you put it, what assurance have I that you will love me? That my presence in the post chaise will not seem a nuisance to you? I am not a monster; to ruin your reputation would be just one calamity the more for me. It is not your position in society that stands in our way; it is, unfortunately, your character. Can you yourself be sure that you will love me for one whole week?"

("Ah! let her love me for a week, only a week," Julien murmured to himself, "and I will die of happiness. What does the future matter to me, what does life matter? And that divine happiness could begin this instant if I wished; it depends on me alone!")

Mathilde saw he was thoughtful.

"So, I am altogether unworthy of you," she said, taking his hand.

Julien kissed her, but in that instant the iron hand of duty clutched his heart. "If she sees how much I adore her, I will lose her." And before he stepped out of her arms, he had again assumed all the stern dignity that becomes a man.

On that day and the days following, he was able to hide his immense happiness; there were moments when he even went so far as to refuse himself the pleasure of folding her in his arms. At other times he would be carried away by a delirious joy, no matter what his better judgment might say.

It was in the garden, near a bower of honeysuckle, arranged to screen the ladder, that he had been accustomed to post himself in order to watch Mathilde's shutter and weep over her fickleness. A huge oak grew close by, and its trunk hid him from prying eyes.

As he strolled with Mathilde by this same spot, which reminded him so vividly of his great unhappiness, the

427

contrast between his past despair and his present felicity was too much for him. Tears flooded his eyes, and raising his beloved's hand to his lips: "This is the spot where I kept alive by thinking of you; from here I watched those shutters; I waited hours on end for the happy moment when I should see this hand open them. . . ."

His moment of weakness was total. He painted for her in the truest colors, such as one does not invent, the depths of his despair at the time. Short interjections bore witness to the present happiness which had put an end to his atrocious suffering. . . .

"Good God! what am I doing," Julien said to himself, coming around all of a sudden. "I'm ruining everything."

Greatly alarmed, he thought he already saw love beginning to fade in Mlle. de La Mole's eyes. This was an illusion, but Julien's color changed rapidly; his whole face turned deadly pale. His eyes grew dull for an instant, then a haughtiness tinged with malice succeeded an expression of the truest and most unreserved love.

"What is the matter with you, my dear?" asked Mathilde, tenderly and anxiously.

"I'm lying," said Julien angrily, "and I'm lying to you. I hate myself for it, and yet, God knows, I think highly enough of you not to lie. You love me, you are devoted to me, and I have no need of making pretty speeches to please you."

"Great God! were all those charming things you have been telling me for the past two minutes nothing but pretty speeches?"

"I blame myself bitterly for it, dear friend. I made all that up for a woman who was once in love with me and who bored me. . . . It's the flaw in my character. I am the first to condemn myself for it; forgive me. . . ."

Bitter tears flowed down Mathilde's cheeks.

"Whenever I am forced to reflect for a moment, by some little thing that has offended me," Julien went on, "my execrable memory, which I am cursing right now, offers me a way out and I abuse it."

"Without knowing it, then, could I have done something to displease you?" said Mathilde with charming simplicity.

"One day, I remember, as you passed by this honeysuckle, you picked a flower. M. de Luz took it from you, and you let him keep it. I was two feet away."

"M. de Luz? That's impossible," replied Mathilde, with

the haughty air that was so natural to her, "I don't do that sort of thing."

"I am certain," Julien retorted sharply.

"Very well! it's true, my dear," said Mathilde, looking down sadly. She knew positively that for many months now she had not permitted M. de Luz any such liberty.

Julien gazed at her with ineffable tenderness. "No," he told himself, "she doesn't love me any the *less*."

She reproached him that evening, laughingly, with his taste for Mme. de Fervaques. "A bourgeois in love with a social climber! Hearts of that kind are probably the only ones my Julien can't drive crazy. She has made a regular dandy out of you," she said, toying with his hair.

During the time he thought Mathilde despised him, Julien had become one of the best-dressed men in Paris. Yet he had an advantage over other men of that type; once his dress was complete, he gave it no further thought.

One thing galled Mathilde: Julien went right on copying the Russian's letters and sending them to the widow.

Chapter XXXII

The Tiger

> Alas! why these things and not others?
>
> ——BEAUMARCHAIS

An English traveler tells a story about living on familiar terms with a tiger; he had raised it and would fondle it, but on his table he always kept a loaded pistol.

Julien never gave in to his inordinate happiness except at those times when Mathilde could not read the expression of it in his eyes. Conscientiously he fulfilled his duty of saying something harsh to her every now and then.

Whenever Mathilde's gentleness, which he noted with astonishment, and her extravagant devotion were about to deprive him of his self-control, he had the heart to leave her abruptly.

For the first time Mathilde loved. Life, which had always dragged on at a snail's pace for her, now flew. Nevertheless, since pride had inevitably to show itself in some way, she insisted on exposing herself boldly to all the risks love might make her run. It was Julien who was the careful one; and it was only when danger was involved that she would not yield to his will. Yet submissive and almost humble with him, she was all the more arrogant toward everyone in the house who came near her, family or valets.

In the drawing room at night, in the midst of sixty people, she would call Julien over to talk with him in particular, and for a long while.

One evening as little Tanbeau was settling down beside them she asked him to go to the library and fetch the volume of Smollett in which the revolution of 1688 is discussed; and since he hesitated:

"There's no hurry," she added with an expression of insulting arrogance that did Julien's heart good.

"Did you see the look on that little monster's face?" he asked her.

"His uncle has ten or twelve years' service in this drawing room; otherwise I'd have him turned out this minute."

Her behavior toward *MM*. de Croisenois, de Luz, etc., though perfectly polite as to form, was scarcely less provoking. Mathilde reproached herself keenly for all the confidences she had once made to Julien, and all the more since she didn't dare confess to him that she had exaggerated the almost entirely innocent tokens of interest of which those gentlemen had been the object.

Despite her finest resolutions, her womanly pride stopped her every day from telling Julien: "It is only because I was talking to you that I enjoyed describing my momentary weakness when M. de Croisenois, putting his hand on the marble table, happened to brush mine and I didn't take it away."

Now, one of those gentlemen had only to speak to her for a few minutes, and she would discover that she had a question to ask Julien, and would use that as a pretext to keep him close by her.

She discovered that she was pregnant and informed Julien delightedly.

"Now can you doubt me? Isn't this a guarantee? I am your wife forever."

This announcement left Julien astounded. He was on the verge of forgetting his first rule of conduct. "How could I be deliberately cold and offensive to this poor girl who is ruining herself for me?" If she looked a bit unwell, even on days when the awful voice of wisdom made itself heard, he could no longer find the heart to address her with one of those cruel remarks, so indispensable, according to his experience, if their love was to last.

"I mean to write to my father," Mathilde said to him one day. "He is more than a father to me; he's a friend. As such I consider it unworthy of you and of me to try to deceive him, even for a minute."

"Good God! What are you going to do?" said Julien, alarmed.

"My duty," she answered, her eyes shining with joy. She considered herself more high-minded than her lover.

"But he will drive me away in disgrace!"

431

"That is his right; we must respect it. I will take your arm and we will leave by the main gate, in broad daylight!"

Amazed, Julien begged her to put off doing anything for a week.

"I must," she replied; "honor speaks. I have seen my duty, I must follow it, this very instant."

"Well, then! I order you to put it off," said Julien finally. "Your honor is safe; I am your husband. The situation will be altered for both of us by this momentous step. What's more, I am within my rights. Today is Tuesday; next Tuesday is the Duke de Retz's day at home; that night, when M. de La Mole returns, the doorkeeper will hand him the fatal letter. . . . He thinks of nothing but making a duchess of you, I'm certain; imagine how wretched he will be!"

"You mean to say, imagine his revenge?"

"I am capable of taking pity on my benefactor, of feeling awfully sorry to hurt him; but I am not afraid, and never shall be, of anyone."

Mathilde submitted. This was the first time since she had announced her condition to Julien that he had spoken to her with authority; never had he loved her so much. It was with happiness that the tender side of his nature seized upon the pretext of Mathilde's state to excuse himself from making cruel remarks to her. The thought of the avowal to be made to M. de La Mole disturbed him profoundly. Would he be separated from Mathilde? However sorrowful she might be to see him go, a month after his departure would she give a thought to him?

He was almost equally horrified to think of the just reproaches the marquis might level at him.

That night he confessed to Mathilde this second cause of his distress, and later, led astray by love, he made an avowal of the first as well.

She changed color. "Really," she said to him, "six months away from me would be a calamity for you?"

"Immense . . . the only one in the world that I look upon with terror."

Mathilde was happy indeed. Julien had played his part with such application that he had succeeded in making her think that, of the two, she was the more loving.

The fateful Tuesday came around very quickly. Returning home at midnight, the marquis found the letter, which was addressed in such a way that he would open it himself, and only when there were no witnesses about.

432

Father:

All the social ties that bound us have been broken; none remain but those of nature. After my husband, you are and always will be the person dearest to me. My eyes keep filling with tears, I keep thinking of the pain I am causing you, but if my shame is not to become public, and if I am to leave you time enough to deliberate and to act, I cannot defer the confession I owe you any longer. If your affection for me, which I know to be very great, will grant me a small pension, I will go and settle down wherever you wish, in Switzerland, for example, with my husband. His name is so humble that no one will recognize Mme. Sorel as your daughter, the daughter-in-law of a carpenter in Verrières. There, you have the name that has been so hard for me to write. For Julien's sake I dread your wrath, to all appearances so well justified! I will never be a duchess, Father, but I knew that when I gave him my love; for it is I who loved first, it is I who seduced him. From you and from our ancestors I have inherited too lofty a soul for my attention to be attracted by anything that is or strikes me as vulgar. It was to no avail that, with an aim to please you, I considered M. de Croisenois. Why did you set true worth before my eyes? You yourself said to me, when I returned from Hyères, "That young Sorel is the only person who knows how to amuse me." The poor boy is just as sorry as I am, if that is possible, for the distress this letter is causing you. I cannot prevent your being angry, as a father; but love me always, as a friend.

Julien has always respected me. If he talked with me from time to time, it was only because of his profound gratitude to you; for his natural loftiness would incline him never to reply, except formally, to anyone who is so far above him. He has a keen and innate sense of the difference between social positions. It was I, I confess it blushingly to my best friend—and never shall such a confession be made to anyone else—it was I who one day in the garden squeezed his arm.

After twenty-four hours, why should you be angry with him? My offense is irreparable. If you insist, assurances of his deep respect and of his sorrow over having displeased you will be conveyed to you through me. You would never see him, but I would go and join him wherever he wished. That is his right; that is my duty; he is the father of my child. If your generosity will grant us an income of six thousand francs to live on, I will accept it gratefully. Otherwise, Julien plans to settle in Besançon, where he will take up the profession of teaching Latin and literature. However lowly the position from which he starts, I am certain he will rise. With him I have no fear of remaining unknown. If there is a revolution, I am sure he will play an important part. Can you say as much for any of those who have asked for my hand? They have fine estates! I cannot see in that circumstance alone cause for admiration. My Julien could achieve a high position even under the present regime, if he had a million and my father's patronage. . . .

Mathilde, knowing the marquis was a man who acted on first impulses, had written eight pages.

"What is to be done?" Julien asked himself as he walked in the garden at midnight while M. de La Mole read the letter. "Where lies, first, my duty, second, my interest? My debt to him is immense; without him I would have been a conniving subaltern, but not conniving enough to escape being hated and persecuted by the others. He made me a man of the world. As a result the crooked deals I shall have to pull will be, one, fewer; two, less ignoble. That is worth more than if he had given me a million. I am obliged to him for this cross and the semblance of diplomatic service which have set me apart from the crowd.

"If he took up his pen to prescribe my conduct, what would he write? . . ."

Julien was suddenly interrupted by M. de La Mole's old valet. "The marquis wants to see you at once, dressed or not." The valet added in a low voice as he walked at Julien's side: "The marquis is furious; watch your step."

434

Chapter XXXIII

The Torments of Weakness

> In cutting this diamond, a bun-
> gling workman robbed it of some of
> its brightest sparkle. In the Middle
> Ages—what am I saying?—even
> under Richelieu, a Frenchman had
> the *strength to will.*
>
> —MIRABEAU

Julien found the marquis in a rage; for the first time in
his life, perhaps, that lord behaved vulgarly. He heaped
Julien with all the abuse that came to his mouth. Our hero
was astonished, angered, but his gratitude was not shaken
in the least. "Think how many fine plans, long cherished in
his most private thoughts, the poor man has seen come to
nothing, ruined in an instant! But I owe him an answer;
my silence will only increase his wrath." The answer was
supplied by the role of Tartuffe.

"*I am no angel.* . . . I have served you well; you have
paid me generously. I was grateful, but I am twenty-two
years old. . . . No one in this house understood me but
you, you and that kind person. . . ."

"Monster!" shouted the marquis. "Kind! Kind! The day
you discovered she was kind, you should have fled from
the house."

"I tried to. At the time I asked your permission to go to
Languedoc."

Weary of pacing furiously about and broken by sorrow,
the marquis flung himself into an armchair. Julien heard
him murmuring to himself, "This is not a wicked man."

"No, I have never been so with you," cried Julien,

435

falling to his knees. But he was extremely ashamed of this gesture and rose quickly.

The marquis was really unhinged. At the sight of this movement, he began again to heap Julien with atrocious insults, worthy of a cabman. Perhaps the novelty of these curses was a relief to him.

"What! my daughter's name will be Mme. Sorel! What! my daughter won't be a duchess!" Every time those two thoughts presented themselves so clearly, M. de La Mole was in torment and had no control over his feelings. Julien feared a beating.

In his intervals of lucidity, when the marquis was beginning to get used to his calamity, the reproaches he addressed to Julien were reasonable enough. "You should have left the house, sir," he kept telling him. "It was your duty to leave.... You are the lowest of the low...."

Julien went over to the table and wrote:

> For a long time, my life has been unbearable to me; I am putting an end to it. I beg the marquis to accept, please, these assurances of my boundless gratitude, and my apology for the inconvenience my death in his house may cause him.

"Will the marquis be pleased to glance at this paper.... Kill me," said Julien, "or have me killed by your valet. It is one o'clock in the morning: I am going for a walk in the garden, toward the back wall."

"Go to the devil," the marquis shouted to him as he was going out.

"I understand," thought Julien, "he wouldn't mind if I spared his valet the trouble of my death. Let him kill me himself, fair enough; that is the satisfaction I am offering him.... But, by Jove, as for me, I enjoy living.... I have obligations to my son."

This idea, appearing distinctly to his imagination for the first time, engrossed him entirely after the first few minutes of the walk, which had been given over to a sense of danger.

This altogether new concern made a careful man of him. "I need advice as to how I should act with that impetuous man.... He's out of his senses; no telling what he might do. Fouqué is too far off; besides, he could never understand the feelings of a man like the marquis.

"Count Altamira.... Can I be sure of his eternal silence? My asking for advice must not be a step that will only make matters worse. Alas! there is no one left but

436

that gloomy Abbé Pirard. . . . His mind has been shrunken by Jansenism. . . . A rascally Jesuit would know the ways of the world and be more help to me. . . . M. Pirard is apt to beat me at the mere mention of the crime."

The spirit of Tartuffe came to Julien's rescue: "Very well, I will go and confess myself to him." Such was the last resolution he made in the garden, after having walked two full hours. He had stopped thinking about the possibility of being surprised by a shot; sleep was getting the best of him.

Very early next morning, Julien was several leagues out of Paris and knocking at the stern Jansenist's door. To his great astonishment, he found that the abbé was not overly surprised at his secret.

"Perhaps I am somewhat to blame," the abbé remarked to himself, more worried than irritated. "I thought I had guessed that affair. My affection for you, unhappy child, kept me from warning her father. . . ."

"What is he going to do?" Julien asked him sharply. He loved the abbé at that moment, and a scene would have been very painful to him.

"I see three alternatives," Julien went on. "One, M. de La Mole may have me put to death"—and he told the abbé about the suicide note he had left with the marquis—"two, have me filled with holes by Count Norbert, who would challenge me to a duel."

"You would accept?" said the abbé, furious and rising to his feet.

"You don't let me finish. Certainly, I would never fire on my benefactor's son.

"Three, he could send me away. If he tells me: Go to Edinburgh, to New York, I will obey. Then they would be able to hide Mlle. de La Mole's condition, but I would never stand for their doing away with my son."

"Have no doubts about it, that's the first thing that corrupt man will think of. . . ." abortion

Back in Paris, Mathilde was desperate. She had seen her father around seven o'clock. He had shown her Julien's letter; she dreaded lest he consider it noble to put an end to his life. "And without my permission?" she said to herself in an agony born of rage.

"If he is dead, I shall die," she told her father. "It is you who would be the cause of his death. You would rejoice over it, perhaps. . . . But I swear by his shade that I would first put on mourning, and then I would go out in public as the *widow Sorel*; I would send out my own death

437

notices; you may count on that. . . . You will find me neither irresolute nor cowardly."

Her love was turning into madness. For his part, M. de La Mole was dumbfounded. He began to take a more rational view of things. At lunch time, Mathilde did not appear at all. The marquis was relieved of an immense weight and, above all, flattered when he realized that she had said nothing to her mother.

Around noon Julien arrived. One could hear his horse's hooves ringing in the courtyard. He dismounted. Mathilde sent for him and threw herself into his arms, almost in sight of her chambermaid. Julien was not very grateful for this outburst of feeling; he had emerged from his long conference with the Abbé Pirard very diplomatic and calculating. His imagination had been dampened by a reckoning of possibilities. Tears in her eyes, Mathilde informed him that she had seen his suicide note.

"My father might change his mind; do me the pleasure of leaving this instant for Villequier. Get back on your horse; leave the house before they get up from the table."

Since Julien did not alter his cold, astonished look one jot, she had a fit of weeping. "Let me manage our affairs," she cried out in a passion, as she hugged him. "You know very well that I do not part from you willingly. Write to me under cover of my chambermaid; make sure the address is in a strange hand. I will write you volumes. Farewell! Flee."

Her last words hurt Julien's pride; he obeyed nonetheless. "It's inevitable," he was thinking, "that even in their best moments those people find some way to offend me."

M. de La Mole did not have the heart to behave like a typical father. Mathilde firmly resisted all of his wise schemes. She would never consent to enter into negotiations on any basis other than the following: She would be Mme. Sorel, and would live in poverty with her husband in Switzerland, or in her father's house in Paris. She thrust the idea of a clandestine delivery violently aside.

"Thence would arise the possibility of slander and of disgrace for me. Two months after our marriage, I will go on a trip with my husband, and it will be easy for us to imply that my son was born at the proper time."

Greeted at first by outbursts of rage, her firmness eventually caused the marquis some misgivings.

In a moment of compassion, he said to his daughter, "Here! this is a certificate for an annuity of ten thousand

438

francs; send it to your Julien, and let him be quick to make it impossible for me to take it back."

To *obey* Mathilde, with whose love of command he was well acquainted, Julien had ridden forty useless leagues: he was in Villequier, settling accounts with the tenant farmers; the marquis' gift was the occasion of his return. He went to ask sanctuary of the Abbé Pirard, who, during his absence, had become Mathilde's most useful ally. Every time the abbé was questioned by the marquis, he would prove to him that any course other than a public marriage would be a crime in the eyes of God.

"And happily," the abbé would add, "worldly wisdom is in agreement with religion on this point. Could one count for a minute, given Mlle. de La Mole's impetuous character, on a secrecy she had not imposed upon herself? If the straightforward course of a public marriage is not followed, society will busy itself with this strange misalliance for a much longer time. Everything should be spelled out at once, without the least mystery, real or apparent."

"It's true," said the marquis, pensive. "If that plan were followed, after three days any talk about the marriage would sound like the ruminations of a man who has no ideas of his own. They could take advantage of some sweeping anti-Jacobin decree by the Government and slip away incognito afterwards."

Two or three of M. de La Mole's friends thought as the Abbé Pirard did. In their opinion the great obstacle was Mathilde's resolute character. But despite so many fine arguments, in his heart the marquis could not get used to the idea of renouncing all hope of a *stool* for his daughter.

His memory and his imagination were stocked with all sorts of tricks and duplicity that had been possible in his youth. To yield to necessity, to stand in fear of the law, seemed to him absurd, and dishonorable for a man of his rank. He was paying dearly for all those bewitching dreams about his cherished daughter's future in which he had indulged himself for the past ten years.

"Who could have foreseen it?" he said to himself. "A girl with such a lofty character, so intelligent, prouder than I of the name she bears! whose hand was requested of me in advance by the most illustrious names in France!

"Better throw caution to the wind. This is an age that confounds all distinctions! We are marching toward chaos."

Chapter XXXIV

A Man of Spirit

> The prefect plodding along on his horse said to himself: "Why shouldn't I become a minister, president of the council, a duke? Here's how I'd wage war. . . . By that means I would put all the innovators in irons.
>
> —*The Globe*

No argument can break the hold of ten years of pleasant dreaming. The marquis felt that it was unreasonable to be angry, yet could not bring himself to pardon. "If this Julien could only die by accident," he sometimes said to himself. It was thus that his afflicted imagination found some relief by pursuing the most absurd chimeras. They paralyzed the influence of the Abbé Pirard's sound reasoning. A month went by without the negotiations advancing a single step.

In this family matter, as in politics, the marquis kept having brilliant insights, over which he would be enthusiastic for three days on end. At such times, a plan of action would displease him because it was backed by sound arguments; but no argument whatsoever could find favor in his eyes unless it supported his pet plan to some degree. For three days he would labor with all the fire and enthusiasm of a poet to bring things to a certain pass; next day he would be totally indifferent.

At first Julien was disconcerted by the marquis' delay; but after a few weeks, he began to guess that M. de La Mole had, in this matter, no fixed plan. Mme. de La Mole and the whole house believed that Julien was traveling in the provinces for the management of the estates; he was hidden in the Abbé Pirard's rectory and saw Mathilde almost daily; as for her, every morning she would go and spend an hour with her father, but sometimes they went whole weeks without a word about that which was uppermost in their thoughts.

"I have no desire to know where that man is," the marquis said to her one day. "Send him this· letter." Mathilde read:

> The estates in Languedoc bring in 20,600 francs yearly. I am giving 10,600 francs of this to my daughter, and 10,000 to M. Julien Sorel. I am, of course, deeding the estates themselves. Tell the notary to draw up two separate deeds of gift and to bring them to me tomorrow; after which, no further relations between us. Ah, sir, is this what I should have expected?
>
> The Marquis de La Mole

"I thank you very much," said Mathilde gaily. "We are going to move into the Château d'Aiguillon, between Agen and Marmande. They say the country there is as beautiful as Italy."

This gift surprised Julien extremely. He was no longer the stern, cold man we have known. His son's future took up all of his thoughts in advance. This fortune, unexpected and quite considerable for one so poor, made him an ambitious man. He saw himself with thirty-six thousand francs a year, as much his wife's as his own. As for Mathilde, all her feelings were concentrated on her adoration of her husband, for it was thus in her pride that she always referred to Julien. Her great, her sole ambition was to have her marriage recognized. She spent all her time congratulating herself on the great wisdom she had shown in casting her lot with a superior man. Personal worth was all the fashion in her mind.

Almost continual absence, a multiplicity of business affairs, little time to talk about love, all helped to consummate the good effect of the wise policy Julien had contrived some time ago.

Mathilde finally grew impatient at seeing so little of the man she had come to love genuinely. In a moment of ill humor she wrote to her father, and began her letter as in *Othello*:*

That I preferred Julien to the enjoyments society has to offer the Marquis de La Mole's daughter is clear enough from my choice. Those pleasures of attention and petty gratifications of vanity mean nothing to me. It is almost six weeks now that I have been separated from my husband. That is long enough to show you my respect. Sometime before next Thursday, I will leave the paternal roof. Your kindness has made us rich. No one but the honorable Abbé Pirard knows my secret. I will go to his house; he will marry us, and an hour after the ceremony, we will be on our way to Languedoc, never to set foot in Paris again, except by your order. But what cuts me to the heart is that all this will be turned into a racy anecdote about me, about you. Might not the silly public's epigrams force our excellent Norbert to pick a quarrel with Julien? In that event, I'd have no power over him . . . I know. We should see the insurgent plebeian in him come to the fore. I beseech you on bended knees, oh father! come to my wedding in M. Pirard's church next Thursday. The point of the malicious anecdote will be blunted; the life of your only son and that of my husband will be safe, etc., etc.

The marquis was thrown into a strange state of perplexity by this letter. So, at last, he was going to have *to take a stand*. All his little habits, all of his everyday friends, had lost their influence over him.

In these strange circumstances his main character traits, stamped upon him by the events of his youth, reasserted all their power. The trials of the Emigration had made him a man of imagination. After having enjoyed a huge fortune and all the distinctions of the court for two years, he had been subjected by 1790 to the frightful ordeals of the Emigration. That hard school had worked a change in the heart of the twenty-two-year-old man. The truth is that he had merely pitched his tent in the midst of his present riches; he was not dominated by them. But the very imagination which preserved his heart from the gangrene of gold had made him a prey to an insane passion to see his daughter embellished with a fine title.

During the six weeks just elapsed, impelled at one point by a whim, the marquis had decided to make Julien rich. Poverty seemed disgraceful, a dishonor to himself, M. de La Mole, and unthinkable in his daughter's husband. He

442

poured out his money. The next day, his imagination taking another tack, it seemed to him that Julien was about to understand the mute language of his generosity with money, would change his name, exile himself to America, write Mathilde that he was dead to her. M. de La Mole supposed the letter written, studied the effect on his daughter's personality. . . .

The day on which he was roused from these short-lived dreams by Mathilde's *real* letter, and after having thought for a long time about killing Julien, or of having him put out of the way, he was dreaming of building a brilliant fortune for him. He had him taking the name of one of his estates; and why shouldn't he pass on his own peerage to Julien? The Duke de Chaulnes, his father-in-law, had spoken to him several times, since his only son had been killed in Spain, of his desire to make over his own title to Norbert. . . .

"There's no denying that Julien has an uncommon aptitude for business, daring, and perhaps even *brilliance,*" the marquis was saying to himself. "But deep down in that character, I see something appalling. That is the impression he makes on everyone, so there is something to it." (The harder it was to put his finger on this real thing, the more the old marquis' fanciful mind was appalled.)

"My daughter put it very shrewdly the other day (in a letter omitted here): 'Julien hasn't affiliated himself with a single drawing room, with any coterie.' He has not tried to line up any backing against me, not the smallest resource, in the event I forsake him. . . . But is this due to his ignorance of the present state of society? . . . Two or three times I have told him; 'there is no *real* and profitable candidacy except that of the drawing rooms. . . .'

"No, he hasn't the adroit and wily talent of an attorney general, who wastes not a minute nor an opportunity. . . . His character is not at all in the style of Louis XI.* And yet I have heard him utter the harshest maxims against generosity. . . . I can't make him out. . . . Could it be that he repeats those maxims to himself as a *dam* against his own strong feelings?

"In any case, one thing is clear: he can't bear contempt. That is the hold I have over him.

"He has no religious awe of high birth; he doesn't respect us instinctively. . . . That's a fault. But still, the soul of a seminarist ought not to find anything unbearable except the want of pleasures and of money. Very different, he can't stand contempt at any price."

Hard pressed by his daughter's letter, M. de La Mole saw the necessity of making up his mind.

"In short, here is the great question: Did Julien's audacity push him so far as to undertake to woo my daughter because he knows I love her more than anything else in the world, and that I have an income of three hundred thousand francs?

"Mathilde maintains the contrary.... No, my Julien, this is a score on which I will not allow myself to have any illusions.

"Was there true love in all this ... unforeseen? Or else a vulgar desire to rise to a fine position? Mathilde is farsighted; she sensed right off that this suspicion could ruin him in my estimation; whence, her avowal that it was she who took it upon herself to fall in love with him first. . . .

"But how could a girl with such a haughty character forget herself so far as to make physical advances! . . . Squeeze his arm in the garden one evening . . . disgusting! As if she didn't have a hundred less indecent ways of letting him know that she meant to distinguish him.

"*He who excuses himself accuses himself;* I mistrust Mathilde. . . ." That day the marquis' reasoning was more conclusive than usual. Nevertheless, habit won out; he resolved to bide his time and write to his daughter. For they wrote from one side of the house to the other. M. de La Mole dared not talk things over with his daughter and stand up to her. He was afraid of bringing the whole matter to a close with a hasty decision.

Take care not to commit some new piece of folly; here is a lieutenant's commission in the Hussars for the Chevalier Julien Sorel da La Vernaye. You see what I am doing for him. Do not oppose me; do not question me. Be sure that he leaves within twenty-four hours and makes himself known in Strasbourg, where his regiment is. Here is a draft on my banker. I expect obedience.

Mathilde's love and joy were boundless. She meant to profit from her victory and so answered on the spot.

"M. de La Vernaye would be at your feet, overcome with gratitude, if he were aware of everything you have been pleased to do for him. But, in the midst of this generosity, my father has forgotten me;

444

your daughter's honor is in danger. The wrong step might cause an eternal blotch, one that an income of sixty thousand francs could never erase. I will not send the commission to M. de La Vernaye unless you give me your word that, sometime within the next month, my marriage will be celebrated in public, at Villequier. Shortly after that period, which I beg you not to exceed, your daughter will be unable to appear in public, except under the name of Mme. de La Vernaye. How I thank you, Papa dear, for saving me from the name Sorel, etc., etc."

The answer was unexpected.

Obey, or I will retract everything. Tremble, rash girl. I don't know yet what manner of man your Julien may be, and you know less about him than I. See that he leaves for Strasbourg, and that he toes the line. I shall let my will be known in two weeks.

So firm a reply astonished Mathilde. *"I don't know Julien."* That statement plunged her into a reverie, which ended very shortly in the most charming suppositions; but she took them for the truth. "My Julien's spirit has not put on the shabby little *uniform* of the drawing rooms, and my father doesn't believe in his superiority precisely because of that which proves it. . . .

"In any event, if I don't obey this crotchet, I foresee the possibility of a public scene; a scandal will lower my position in society and might make me less attractive to Julien. After the scandal . . . poverty for ten years; and the folly of choosing a husband for his worth cannot escape ridicule except through the most brilliant opulence. If I live far away from my father, at his age he may forget me. . . . Norbert will marry a clever, likable woman; the old Louis XIV was captivated by the Duchess of Burgundy. . . ."

She decided to obey but was careful not to impart her father's letter to Julien; that wild nature might decide to do something rash.

That night, when she told Julien that he was a lieutenant in the Hussars, his joy knew no bounds. The reader can judge it from the ambition he had shown all of his life, and from the passionate fondness he now felt for his son. The change in his name struck him with astonishment.

445

"After all," he thought, "my novel is finished, and the credit is due to me alone. I was able to make that monster of pride fall in love with me," he added, looking at Mathilde. "Her father can't live without her, nor she without me."

Chapter XXXV

A Storm

> O Lord, grant me mediocrity!
> —MIRABEAU

His thoughts were elsewhere; he but half responded to the lavish tenderness she showed him. He remained mute and gloomy. Never had he seemed so great, so adorable, in Mathilde's eyes. She was apprehensive lest some nicety of his pride should prompt him to spoil everything.

Every morning almost, she would see the Abbé Pirard arriving at the house. Could Julien have made out something of her father's intentions through him? Might not the marquis himself have written to him on the spur of the moment? After such great good luck, how was she to explain Julien's stern look? She dared not question him.

She *dared not!* She, Mathilde! From that moment on there was something undefinable, something unforeseen, something like terror in the way she felt about Julien. This frigid heart felt all the passion an individual can know who has been raised amidst that excessive civilization which Paris admires.

Early the next morning, Julien was at the Abbé Pirard's rectory. Post horses pulled into the courtyard with a dilapidated chaise, rented from the nearby post.

"That kind of setup will no longer do," said the stern abbé to him grudgingly. "Here are twenty thousand francs, of which M. de La Mole is making you a present; he stipulates that you spend it within the year, but taking care to expose yourself to as little ridicule as possible." In such a big sum, tossed to a young man, the priest could see nothing but an opportunity to sin.

"The marquis adds: 'M. Julien de La Vernaye will have

447

received this money from his father, whom it is unnecessary to designate otherwise. M. de La Vernaye will perhaps deem it fitting to make a gift to M. Sorel, the carpenter in Verrières, who looked after him during his childhood. . . .' I can take care of that part of the bargain," the priest added. "I have finally persuaded M. de La Mole to come to terms with that Abbé de Frilair, such a Jesuit. His influence is definitely too much for us. Implicit recognition of your high birth by that man who governs Besançon will be one of the unstated conditions of the agreement."

Julien could not contain his joy any longer; he embraced the abbé; he considered himself acknowledged.

"For shame!" said M. Pirard, pushing him away, "what means this worldly vanity? . . . As for Sorel and his sons, I will offer them an annual pension of five hundred francs in my name, to be paid to each of them, so long as I am satisfied with their conduct."

Julien had already turned cold and distant. He gave thanks, but in very vague terms that committed him to nothing. "Is it really possible that I am the natural son of some great lord exiled to our mountains by that terrible Napoleon?" This idea seemed to him less and less far-fetched by the minute. . . . "My hatred for my father must be a proof. . . . I am no longer a monster!"

A few days after this monologue, the Fifteenth Regiment of Hussars, one of the most splendid in the army, was drawn up in battle order on Strasbourg's parade ground. The Chevalier de La Vernaye was mounted on the finest horse in Alsace, one that had cost him six thousand francs. He had qualified as a lieutenant without ever having been a second lieutenant, except on the muster roll of some regiment he had never heard of.

His impassive air, his severe and almost wicked look, his pallor, his unalterable coolness, made a reputation for him at the outset. A while later, his impeccable courtesy and reserve, his skill with pistol and sword, which he demonstrated without too much affectation, discouraged any idea of joking aloud at his expense. After wavering for five or six days, public opinion in the regiment declared itself in his favor. "That young man has everything," said the facetious old officers, "except youth."

From Strasbourg, Julien wrote to M. Chélan, the former parish priest of Verrières, who was now on the verge of extreme old age:

By now you will have learned, with joy I am cer-

448

tain, about the events that have disposed my family to make me rich. Here are five hundred francs, which I beg you to distribute, without any fuss or mention of my name, to those who are so wretchedly poor as I was in the past, and whom you are doubtlessly helping now as you once helped me.

Julien was drunk with ambition, not with vanity; nevertheless, he paid a good deal of attention to appearances. His horses, his uniforms, his servants' livery, were all kept up with a correctness that would have done credit to the punctiliousness of a great English lord. Lieutenant for barely two days, and through a favor, he had already calculated that in order to be commander-in-chief of an army by thirty, at the latest, like all the great generals, he would have to be more than lieutenant at twenty-three. He had thoughts for nothing but glory and his son.

It was in the middle of a rapture of the most unbridled ambition that he was taken aback by a young footman from the Hôtel de La Mole, who came as a messenger.

All is lost [Mathilde wrote]; hurry back as fast as you can. Give up everything. Desert if you have to. As soon as you get here, wait for me in a hackney, near the little garden door, at number —— in —— Street. I will come out and talk to you. Perhaps I can take you into the garden. All is lost, irretrievably, I fear. Count on me; you will find me staunch and devoted in adversity. I love you.

In a few minutes Julien had obtained a leave from his colonel and left Strasbourg at a gallop; but the terrible anxiety that was devouring him made it impossible to continue traveling by this means beyond Metz. He flung himself into a post chaise; and with almost incredible speed, he arrived at the designated spot, near the little garden door of the Hôtel de La Mole. That door opened, and in the same instant Mathilde, forgetting what people might say, rushed into his arms. Fortunately it was only five in the morning and the street was still deserted.

"All is lost; my father, dreading my tears, left Thursday night. For where? No one knows. Here is his letter; read it." And she climbed into the hackney with Julien.

I could pardon him everything, except his scheme to seduce you because you are rich. That, unlucky girl, is the awful truth. I give you my word of honor

449

that I will never consent to your marrying that man. I will guarantee him an income of ten thousand pounds if he is willing to live far away, beyond the frontiers of France, or better still, in America. Read the letter I have received in reply to my request for information. The shameless man himself urged me to write to Mme. de Rênal. I will never read a line from you concerning that fellow. I have a horror of Paris and of you. I advise you to cover up that which must happen with the greatest secrecy. Sincerely disavow a base man and you will win back a father.

"Where is the letter from Mme. de Rênal?" Julien asked coldly.

"Here. I didn't mean to show it to you until I had prepared you for it."

What I owe to the sacred cause of religion and morality obliges me, sir, to take the painful step of addressing you. A law which cannot be ignored commands me to harm my fellow man, but only to the end of avoiding a greater wrong. The anguish I feel must give way to my sense of duty. It is only too true, sir, that the conduct of the person in question, about which you have asked for the whole truth, may well have seemed inexplicable or even honorable. The party in question may have considered it proper to hide or disguise some of the facts; prudence as well as religion called for this. But that conduct, with which you desire to be acquainted, was, in fact, most blameworthy, and more so than I can say. Poor and covetous, it was by means of the most consummate hypocrisy and through the seduction of a weak, unhappy woman that that man sought to further himself and become somebody. It is part of my painful duty to add that I am forced to think that Monsier J. has no religious principles whatsoever. In all good conscience, I am constrained to believe that one of his methods for getting on in a household is to attempt to seduce the woman who has the most influence in it. Clothed in an appearance of disinterestedness and with phrases taken from novels, his great and sole object is to gain control over the master of the house and his fortune. He leaves behind him misery and everlasting regret, etc., etc.

This extremely long letter, half obliterated by tears, was

certainly in Mme. de Rênal's hand; it was even written with more care than usual.

"I can't blame M. de La Mole," said Julien, after having finished it; "he is just and wise. What father would give his cherished daughter to such a man! Good-bye!"

Julien jumped down from the hackney and ran to his post chaise, waiting at the end of the street. Mathilde, whom he seemed to have forgotten, took a few steps to follow him, but the staring merchants who kept coming to the doors of their shops and to whom she was known, forced her to dash back into the garden.

Julien set out for Verrières. During the fast trip he couldn't write to Mathilde as he had planned; his hand on the paper could do nothing but scrawl.

He reached Verrières on a Sunday morning. He went into the shop of the local gunsmith, who heaped him with congratulations on his recent good fortune. It was the talk of the region.

Julien had a hard time making him understand that he wanted a brace of pistols. At his request, the gunsmith loaded them.

The *three bells* was sounding; that is a well-known signal in French villages which, after the various morning chimes, announces that mass is about to begin.

Julien entered Verrières' new church. All the high windows in the edifice were veiled with crimson hangings. Julien stood a few paces behind Mme. de Rênal's pew. She appeared to be praying fervently. The sight of that woman who had loved him so made Julien's arm tremble to such an extent that at first it was impossible for him to carry out his plan. " I can't do it," he kept telling himself, "I am physically unable."

At that moment, the young priest who was officiating at the mass rang the bell for the *Elevation*. Mme. de Rênal lowered her head, which for an instant was almost entirely hidden by the folds of her shawl. Now Julien could not recognize her so easily. He fired a shot and missed; he fired a second shot; she fell.

Chapter XXXVI

Sordid Details

> Expect no show of weakness on my part. I have avenged myself. I deserve to die, and here I am. Pray for my soul.
>
> —SCHILLER

Julien stood motionless; he saw nothing. When he had somewhat recovered his senses, he noted that all the faithful were running out of the church; the priest had left the altar. Slowly Julien began to follow some of the women, who screamed as they went. One, trying to get out faster than the others, pushed him roughly. He fell. His feet got tangled in chair overturned by the crowd. As he rose he felt his neck being squeezed; a gendarme in full uniform was arresting him. Automatically Julien tried to reach for his small pistols, but a second gendarme pinned his arms.

He was led off to prison. He was taken into a room, his wrists were shackled, he was left alone. The door was double-locked behind him. All this was done very quickly, and he was unconscious of it.

"By George! the game's up," he said aloud as he came to. "Yes, in two weeks the guillotine . . . or else, kill myself between now and then."

He could reason no further; his head felt as if it had been pressed violently. He looked to see whether someone was holding it. A few moments later he fell into a deep sleep.

Mme. de Rênal was not fatally wounded. The first bullet had pierced her hat; as she was turning around, the second shot went off. The bullet hit her shoulder but, amazingly enough, had ricocheted off the shoulder blade (which it nevertheless broke) toward a Gothic pillar, from which it chipped a huge splinter.

When, after a long and painful bandaging, the surgeon, a solemn man, said to Mme. de Rênal, "I am as sure of your life as I am of my own," she was deeply grieved.

For a long time she had sincerely wished to die. The letter she had written to M. de La Mole, a duty imposed upon her by her present confessor, came as the final blow to this creature weakened by a too-constant affliction. That affliction was Julien's absence. She herself called it *remorse*. The director of her conscience, a virtuous and fervent young clergyman newly arrived from Dijon, was not deceived.

"To die thus, and not by my own hand, isn't a sin," thought Mme. de Rênal. "Perhaps God will pardon me for rejoicing over my death." She didn't dare to add: "And to die by Julien's hand is the height of bliss."

She was no more than rid of the surgeon's presence and of the crowd of friends who had come running, when she called for Elisa, her maid.

"The jailer," she said to her, blushing a great deal, "is a cruel man. He will no doubt mistreat him, supposing that he will be doing me a favor.... I can't bear the thought of it. Couldn't you go, as if on your own account, and hand the jailer this little package, which contains a few louis? You are to say that religion does not allow him to mistreat him.... Above all, he must not go and talk about this gift of money."

Julien was indebted to the circumstance to which we have just alluded for the jailer of Verrières' humanity; it was still M. Noiraud,* that perfect officer of the law, who, as we have seen, had been thrown into such a funk by M. Appert's presence.

A judge appeared in the prison.

"I have committed murder with premeditation," Julien said to him. "I bought two pistols and had them loaded at such and such a gunsmith's shop. Article 1342 of the Penal Code is explicit; I deserve the death penalty and I expect it." Incapable of understanding such frankness, the mean-spirited judge tried to cross-examine him, in the hopes of making the accused "cut his own throat."

"But can't you see," Julien said to him, with a smile, "that I am incriminating myself, as much as you wish? Go, sir, you will not lose the game you are stalking. You will have the pleasure of convicting me. Spare me your presence."

"I still have one tiresome duty to perform," thought Julien. "I must write to Mlle. de La Mole."

I have had my revenge [he wrote her]. Unfortunately, my name will appear in the papers, and I cannot slip out of this world incognito; I beg your pardon. I shall die in two months. My revenge was atrocious as the pain of being separated from you. From this moment on I forbid myself to write or to pronounce your name. Never speak of me, not even to my son; silence is the only way to honor me. For the herd, I will be a common murderer. . . . Allow me to speak the truth in this hour of death: you will forget me. This great catastrophe, about which I advise you never to breathe a word to a living soul, will exhaust for several years everything I see in your character that is romantic and overly adventurous. You were born to live with the heroes of the middle ages; at this juncture, show their strength of character. See to it that what must come to pass is done in secret and without compromising you. You must use an assumed name and not confide in anyone. If you absolutely must have a friend's help, I bequeath you the Abbé Pirard.

Speak to no one else, especially not to people of your own class: the de Luzes, the Caylus'.

A year after my death, marry M. de Croisenois; I beg you, as your husband I order you, to do it. Never write to me, I will not reply. Far less evil than Iago, so it seems to me, like him I say: *'From this time forth, I never will speak word.'*

Henceforth I will neither speak nor write; you have had my last words as well as the last of my adoration.

J. S.

It was after sending off this letter that Julien, somewhat recovered, felt thoroughly wretched for the first time. One by one each of his ambitious hopes was to be uprooted from his heart by that great phrase: "I must die." Death in itself did not seem horrible to him. His life had been one long preparation for calamity, and he had never tried to put out of mind that which is considered the worst of all.

"What, then," he said to himself, "if in sixty days I had to fight a duel with a man who was an expert fencer; would I be so pusillanimous as to think about it all the time, my heart filled with terror?"

He spent more than an hour examining himself in this light. When he had seen clearly into his soul, and the truth appeared before his eyes as solidly as one of the pillars in his prison, he gave some thought to remorse.

"Why should I have any? I have been abominably insulted; I have killed, I deserve to die, but that's all. I will die after having settled my account with humanity. I leave no unsatisfied obligations behind me; I am not owing to anyone. There is nothing shameful about my death except the means; that alone, it's true, will more than suffice to disgrace me in the eyes of Verrières bourgeoisie. But from an intellectual point of view, what could be more despicable than their attitude! I still have one way to win their respect: that is to throw gold pieces to the crowd as I go to my execution. My memory, associated in their minds with gold, will glitter."

After this spell of reasoning, the truth of which seemed obvious in a minute, Julien said to himself, "I have nothing left to do on earth," and fell into a deep sleep.

Around nine o'clock in the evening, the jailer, bringing in his supper, woke him up.

"What are they saying in Verrières?"

"Monsieur Julien, the oath I took before the crucifix at the royal court, the day I was sworn into office, obliges me to keep silent."

He said nothing more but stayed on. The spectacle of such vulgar hypocrisy amused Julien. "I should," he thought, "make him wait a long time for the five francs he's asking for his conscience."

When the jailer saw the meal finished with no attempt at bribery forthcoming: "The friendship I bear you, Monsieur Julien," he said, with a false, gentle air, "forces me to speak, even though they say it's contrary to the interests of justice, since it could help you to set up your defense. . . . Monsieur Julien, who is a decent fellow, will be glad to know that Mme. de Rênal is better."

"What! she isn't dead!" cried Julien, rising from the table, beside himself.

"What! You didn't know!" said the jailer with a stupid look, which soon turned into one of happy greed. "It would be only right if monsieur gave something to the surgeon, who, according to law and justice, ought not to have talked. But to please monsieur, I went to his house and he told me everything—"

"So the wound was not fatal," said Julien, out of patience and advancing toward him. "You will swear to that on your life?"

455

The jailer, a giant six feet tall, was frightened and shrank back toward the door. Julien saw that he had taken the wrong road to reach the truth; he sat down again and threw a napoleon to M. Noiraud.

As the man's story proved to Julien that Mme. de Rênal's wound was not mortal, he felt himself being overcome by tears.

"Get out!" he said to him brusquely.

The jailer obeyed. The door was scarcely closed when Julien cried: "Great God! she's not dead!" And weeping hot tears, he fell to his knees.

In that supreme moment he was a believer. What did the hypocrisy of priests matter? Could it take anything away from the truth and sublimity of the idea of God?

Only then did Julien begin to repent for the crime committed. By a coincidence that saved him from despair, in the very same instant, the state of physical irritation and near madness into which he had been plunged ever since his departure from Paris for Verrières came to an end.

His tears were prompted by a generous impulse; he had no illusions about the sentence that awaited him.

"She will live, then!" he kept telling himself. "She will live to pardon me and to love me. . . ."

Very late the next morning, the jailer woke him and said, "You must be a tough one, Monsieur Julien. I've been here twice but didn't have the heart to waken you. Here are two bottles of first-rate wine sent by M. Maslon, our parish priest."

"What? is that rascal still here?" asked Julien.

"Yes, monsieur," replied the jailer, lowering his voice, "but don't talk so loud. It might do you harm."

Julien laughed heartily. "As matters stand, my friend, you're the only one who could do me harm, if you stopped being kind and humane. . . . You will be well paid," said Julien, breaking off and resuming his lordly air. This manner was instantly justified by the gift of a coin.

M. Noiraud recounted anew and in the greatest detail everything he had learned about Mme. de Rênal, but he didn't so much as mention Mlle. Elisa's visit.

The man was as low and obsequious as he could be. An idea crossed Julien's mind: "This shapeless giant probably earns no more than three or four hundred francs a year, since his prison is far from crowded. I can guarantee him ten thousand if he is willing to escape with me to Switzerland. . . . The hard part of it is to convince him of my good faith." The thought of the long confabulation he

456

would have to have with such a vile creature filled Julien with disgust; he thought about something else.

That night it was already too late. A post chaise came to get him at midnight. He enjoyed the company of the gendarmes, his traveling companions. In the morning, when he arrived at the prison of Besançon, the authorities were kind enough to quarter him in the upper story of a Gothic donjon. He judged the architecture to be early fourteenth century; he admired its grace and piquant lightness. Through a narrow gap between two walls at the end of a deep courtyard, he had a view of a superb landscape.

The next day there was an interrogation, after which he was left alone for several days. His heart was at peace. To him his case was simple as it could be: "I meant to kill, I deserve to be killed."

He did not brood over this conclusion. The trial, the nuisance of appearing in public, the defense . . . he considered all of these so many petty inconveniences, boring rituals; it would be time enough to think about them on the day itself. The idea of the moment of death scarcely gave him pause either: "I will think about it after the trial." Life was not boring for him; he saw everything from a new angle. His ambition was gone. He rarely thought about Mlle. de La Mole. Remorse preoccupied him a great deal and often showed him a vision of Mme. de Rênal, especially during the silence of the night . . . in that high donjon, broken only by the shriek of the osprey!

He thanked heaven that he had not wounded her fatally. "An astonishing thing!" he said to himself. "I thought that with her letter to M. de La Mole she had ruined my future happiness forever; yet, less than two weeks from the date of that letter, I don't give a hang for anything that concerned me then. . . . An income of two or three thousand francs to live quietly in a mountain country like Vergy. . . . I was happy then. . . . I wasn't aware of my own happiness!"

At other times he would rise from his chair with a start. "If I had wounded Mme. de Rênal fatally, I would have killed myself. . . . I need to be certain I would have, so as not to loathe myself.

"To kill myself! That is the great question," he thought. "Those judges are such sticklers for form, so dead set against the poor defendant; they would hang the best citizen in town to get a cross. . . . I could escape from

457

their clutches, their insults in bad French, which the local papers will call eloquence. . . .

"But I may have five or six weeks, more or less, to live. Kill myself! by George, no," he said to himself a few days later. "Napoleon went on living. . . .

"Besides, life is pleasant; this place is quiet; there are no bores here," he added, laughing, "not one." And he set to making a note of the books he wished to have sent down from Paris.

Chapter XXXVII

A Donjon

> The tomb of a friend.
> ——STERNE

He heard a racket in the corridor; usually no one came up to his cell at that hour. The osprey flew off with a shriek, the door opened, and the venerable Father Chélan, trembling all over and leaning on a cane, threw himself into his arms.

"Ah! good God! is it possible, my child.... Monster! I should say."

The good old man couldn't utter another word. Julien was afraid he might fall. He was obliged to lead him over to a chair. The hand of time had lain heavily on this man who was once so energetic. To Julien he seemed no more than a shadow of himself.

When he had caught his breath: "I received your letter from Strasbourg only the day before yesterday, with your five hundred francs for the poor of Verrières; it was brought to me up on the mountain at Liveru, where I have retired to my nephew Jean's house. Yesterday, I heard about the catastrophe.... O heavens! is it possible!" The old man had stopped weeping; he looked as if he were void of thought, and added mechanically: "You will need your five hundred francs; I've brought them back to you."

"I need to see you, father!" cried Julien, deeply moved. "Besides, I have money."

But he couldn't get another sensible remark out of him. From time to time M. Chélan shed a few tears, which rolled silently down his cheeks; then he would gaze at Julien, and seemed to be stunned at seeing him take his hands and raise them to his lips. That countenance, so lively before, which had once expressed the most noble sentiments so energetically, did not again put by its apathetic look. After a while some sort of peasant came to get the old man. "You mustn't make him talk too much and tire him out," he said to Julien, who gathered that this was the nephew. This apparition left Julien plunged in a mood of bitter unhappiness that checked his tears. The world seemed sad and comfortless to him; he felt that his heart was frozen in his chest.

That instant was the bitterest he had known since his crime. He had just seen death in all its ugliness. Every one of his illusions about generosity and greatness of soul was dissipated like a cloud before a storm.

This frightful mood lasted several hours. After mental poisoning, physical antidotes are in order, and champagne. But Julien would have considered himself cowardly to have recourse to it. Toward the end of a horrible day, all of it spent pacing his narrow turret, he cried out: "What a fool I am! The sight of that poor old man shouldn't have thrown me into this awful fit of depression unless I was to die of old age like everyone else; but a quick death in the prime of life will save me from that same pitiful decrepitude."

Yet, whatever arguments he might advance, Julien was moved, like a fainthearted creature, and consequently miserable over the visit. All the roughness and grandeur of his character, his Roman virtue, had left him; death loomed at him from a greater height, and seemed less easy.

"That will be my thermometer," he said to himself. "Tonight I am ten degrees below the courage I need to make me equal to the guillotine. This morning I had that courage. But what does that matter! Provided it comes back at the right time." This idea of a thermometer amused him and in the end diverted his thoughts.

The next morning, when he woke up, he felt ashamed of the previous day. "My happiness, my peace of mind, are at stake." He was almost resolved to write the attorney general and request that no one be allowed to see him. "What about Fouqué?" he thought. "If he should take it upon himself to come to Besançon, how hurt he would be!"

It was two months perhaps since he had thought of Fouqué. "I was a great fool in Strasbourg; I never thought further than the collar of my suit." Memories of Fouqué preoccupied him a good deal and left him more deeply affected than ever. He paced nervously. "Now I am

460

definitely twenty degrees below the death level. . . . If this weakness gets worse, I will do better to kill myself. What joy for the Abbé Maslons and the Valenods if I die like a cur!"

Fouqué arrived; that good, simple man was wild with grief. His only idea, if it could be called that, was to sell everything he owned, bribe the jailer, and rescue Julien. He talked to him for a long time about M. de Lavalette's escape.*

"You have hurt my feelings," Julien said to him. "M. de Lavalette was innocent, I am guilty; unintentionally, you have reminded me of the difference. . . .

"But do you mean it? What? you would sell everything?" said Julien, suddenly becoming watchful and mistrustful again.

Delighted to see his friend responding at last to the idea uppermost in his mind, Fouqué gave him a detailed account, within a hundred francs more or less, of what he could get for each of his properties.

"What a sublime gesture for a provincial landowner!" thought Julien. "How much saving, the result of how much petty haggling, that used to make me blush when I watched him do it, he is willing to sacrifice for me. None of those handsome young men I saw at the Hôtel de La Mole who read *René** would ever do anything so ridiculous. Excepting those who are very young, whose wealth is inherited, and who above all do not know the value of money, which of those fine Parisians would be capable of such a sacrifice?"

All of Fouqué's mistakes in French, all his low-class ways, vanished; Julien threw himself into his arms. Never have the provinces, when compared with Paris, received a finer tribute. Overjoyed at the momentary enthusiasm he saw in his friend's eyes, Fouqué took it as an assent to escape.

This glimpse of the *sublime* restored to Julien all the strength that M. Chélan's apparition had taken from him. He was still quite young, but, in my opinion, this was a fine plant. Instead of progressing from softheartedness to wiliness, like the majority of men, with age he would have come into an easily touched benevolence. He would have got over his crazy mistrustfulness. . . . But what good are these vain predictions?

The interrogations were becoming more frequent, despite the efforts Julien made, all of which were meant to shorten the process. He kept repeating every day: "I took

a life, or in any case I tried to, and with premeditation."
But the judge was a stickler for form. Julien's statements
did not shorten the interrogations in the least. The judge
was put on his mettle. Julien didn't know that they had
meant to transfer him to an awful dungeon, and that it
was thanks to Fouqué's efforts that he was left in his
pretty room one hundred and eighty steps above the
ground.

The Abbé de Frilair was one among several important
men who had commissioned Fouqué to supply them with
firewood. The good merchant had managed to see the
all-powerful vicar-general himself. To his ineffable delight,
M. de Frilair informed him that, touched by Julien's good
qualities and the services he had once rendered the seminary, he planned to commend him to the judges. Fouqué
glimpsed a hope of saving his friend, and as he left, bowing to the ground, begged the vicar-general to dole out a
sum of ten louis in masses to be said for the accused's acquittal.

Fouqué was strangely mistaken. M. de Frilair was not
another Valenod. He refused, and even sought to make
the good peasant understand that he would do better to
keep his money. Seeing that it would be impossible to
make himself clear without being imprudent, he advised
him to give that sum in alms for the poor prisoners, who,
in fact, wanted for everything.

"That Julien is a strange fellow; what he did is inexplicable," thought M. de Frilair, "and nothing should be so
for me.... It might be possible to make a martyr of
him.... In any case, I mean to get to the *bottom* of this
affair and I may perhaps find an opportunity to frighten
that Mme. de Rênal, who has no respect for us and in
her heart detests me. . . . I may even happen upon the
means, through this affair, for a splendid reconciliation
with M. de La Mole, who has a weakness for the little
seminarist."

The settlement of the lawsuit had been signed a few
weeks earlier, and the Abbé Pirard had left Besançon,
but not without having spoken of Julien's mysterious birth,
on the very day the wretch had attempted to kill Mme. de
Rênal in Verrières' church.

Julien saw but one more disagreeable event standing
between him and death; it was his father's visit. He consulted Fouqué about the idea of writing to the attorney
general in order to be spared all visits. This horror of the
sight of a father, and at such a time, shocked the honest

bourgeois wood dealer's heart profoundly. He believed he understood why so many people hated his friend with a passion. Out of respect for his misfortune, he kept his feelings hidden.

"At any rate," he answered coldly, "the regulations for solitary confinement would not apply to your father."

Chapter XXXVIII

A Powerful Man

> There is such mystery about her
> ways, such elegance in her figure!
> Who can she be?
>
> ——SCHILLER

The doors of the donjon were opened very early the next day. Julien awoke with a start.

"Ah! good God," he thought, "here's my father. What a disagreeable scene!"

At the same instant, a woman dressed as a peasant rushed into his arms and hugged him convulsively; he could hardly recognize her. It was Mlle. de La Mole.

"Naughty man, it's only from your letter that I learned where you were. Until I reached Verrières, I knew nothing about what you call your crime, which is no more than a noble vengeance and reveals the loftiness of the heart beating in this breast."

Despite his bias against Mlle. de La Mole, which, it must be added, he did not clearly acknowledge to himself, Julien found her pretty indeed. How was it possible not to see a noble and disinterested sentiment in all her conduct and speech, far superior to anything a mean and common soul would have dared? He believed he had fallen in love again with a queen and gave in to his enchantment. After a short while, he said to her with rare nobility of locution and of thought:

"The future stood out quite clearly to my view. After my death, I had you remarried to M. de Croisenois, who would have married a widow. That charming widow's noble but somewhat romantic heart, astonished and converted to the cult of vulgar prudence by a singular, tragic and,

464

for her, momentous event, had deigned to recognize the very real worth of the young marquis. You would resign yourself to the kind of happiness everyone knows: respect, wealth, high position.... But, dear Mathilde, your coming to Besançon, if anyone suspects it, will deal a mortal blow to M. de La Mole, and that is something for which I could never pardon myself. I have already caused him so much grief! The academician will say that he has warmed a serpent in his bosom."

"I must admit that I hardly expected so much cold logic, so much worry about the future," said Mlle. de La Mole half angrily. "My chambermaid, who is almost as cautious as you are, got a passport for herself, and I came down here posthaste under the name of Mme. Michelet."

"Mme. Michelet was able to get in to see me as easily as all that?"

"Ah! you are still the superior man, he whom I have singled out! First, I offered a hundred francs to a judge's secretary, who maintained that I couldn't possibly get into the turret. After pocketing the money, the good man made me wait, raised objections; I thought he meant to cheat me.... " She paused.

"Well?" said Julien.

"Don't be angry, Julien dear," she said, kissing him. "I was obliged to give my name to the secretary, who took me for a young working girl from Paris in love with handsome Julien.... In fact, those are his words. I swore to him that I am your wife, and I will have permission to visit you every day."

"That does it," thought Julien. "I couldn't stop her. But after all, M. de La Mole is such a great lord that public opinion will have no trouble finding an excuse for the young colonel who is going to marry this lovely widow. My death will smooth over everything." And he abandoned himself joyously to his love for Mathilde. It was madness, greatness of soul, everything that is most uncommon. She seriously proposed committing suicide with him.

After these first raptures, and when she had surfeited herself with the happiness of seeing Julien, a lively curiosity seized her all of a sudden. She was studying her lover, whom she found very superior to anything she had imagined. Boniface de La Mole seemed to have returned from the dead, but more heroic.

Mathilde saw the best lawyers in the region, whom she offended by offering them gold too bluntly; but in the end they accepted it.

She promptly came to the conclusion that in cases that were doubtful or of far-reaching consequence, everything depended in Besançon upon the Abbé de Frilair.

Under the humble name of Mme. Michelet, she at first met with insurmountable difficulties in her efforts to see the all-powerful Congreganist. But rumors about a beautiful young milliner, who was madly in love and had come to Besançon from Paris to comfort the young Abbé Julien Sorel, spread throughout the town.

Mathilde went about the streets of Besançon on foot, alone; she was hoping not to be recognized. In any case, she did not think it would be entirely unavailing to her cause if she made a great impression on the common people. In her folly, she dreamed of inciting them to revolt and rescue Julien as he walked to his death. Mlle. de La Mole believed she was dressed simply and as a sorrowful woman ought to be; she was, and attracted everyone's notice.

In Besançon she had become the object of everyone's attention, when, after a week of soliciting, she obtained an audience with M. de Frilair.

However great her courage, the idea of an influential Congreganist and that of profound and circumspect villainy were so closely linked in her mind, she trembled as she rang the bell at the bishopric. She was hardly able to walk by the time she reached the staircase leading to the first vicar-general's apartment. The solitude of the episcopal palace gave her a chill. "If I sit down in an armchair, that chair might seize my arms; I would vanish. To whom could my maid go to inquire about me? The captain of the police would take good care to do nothing. . . . I am all alone in this city!"

After her first look at the apartment, Mlle. de La Mole felt reassured. In the first place, it was a footman in very elegant livery who had opened to her. The drawing room in which she was left to wait displayed that subtle and delicate luxury—so different from gross magnificence—which is not to be found even in Paris except in the best houses. As soon as she caught sight of M. de Frilair, who was coming toward her and looking paternal, all her notions about horrible crimes vanished. In his handsome face she did not find even a trace of that energetic and rather savage virtue to which Parisian society has such an aversion. The half smile that animated the features of this priest, who had all Besançon under his thumb, betokened a man of good society, a learned prelate, a skillful administrator. Mathilde thought she was in Paris.

It took M. de Frilair no more than a few minutes to bring Mathilde around to admitting that she was the daughter of his powerful adversary, the Marquis de La Mole.

"I am not, in fact, Mme. Michelet," she said, assuming again all of her haughty bearing, "and I don't very much mind admitting it, since I have come to consult you, sir, about the possibility of arranging M. de La Vernaye's escape. In the first place, he is guilty of nothing more than rashness; the woman he fired upon is in good health. In the second place, for the purpose of bribing the subalterns, I can put up fifty thousand francs at once and pledge my word for twice as much. And finally, there is no limit to what I and my family will do out of gratitude for the man who saves M. de La Vernaye."

M. de Frilair seemed astonished at the name. Mathilde showed him several letters from the Minister of War addressed to M. Julien Sorel de La Vernaye.

"You can see, sir, that my father has taken charge of his career. It's a very simple matter. I married him secretly, and my father wanted him to be a high-ranking officer before he announced the marriage, which is a rather odd one for a La Mole."

Mathilde noted that his expression of kindness and of gentle gaiety vanished quickly as M. de Frilair came upon these important discoveries. Shrewdness mixed with profound guile showed in his face.

The abbé had his doubts; he reread the official documents slowly. "How am I to make use of these strange confidences?" he wondered. "Here I am, suddenly on an intimate footing with a friend of the famous Field Marshal de Fervaques' widow, almighty niece of the Lord Bishop of————, by whom one is made bishop in France.

"An opportunity I always thought of as far in the future has presented itself without warning. This business could lead me to the object of all my desires."

At first Mathilde was frightened by the rapid change in the countenance of this very powerful man with whom she found herself alone in an isolated apartment. "But after all!" she said to herself shortly, "wouldn't it have been the worst luck not to have made any impression at all on this cold egoist, this priest sated with power and pleasure?"

Dazzled by the short and unforeseen path to the episcopate which was opening up before his eyes, and astonished at Mathilde's genius, M. de Frilair was thrown off his guard momentarily. Mlle. de La Mole saw him, ambi-

467

tious and eager to the point of nervous trembling, almost at her feet.

"It's all clear now," she thought. "He thinks that nothing is impossible for Mme. de Fervaques' lady friend." Despite a still quite painful feeling of jealousy, she had the courage to explain that Julien was the widow's intimate friend and used to see Monseigneur the Bishop of —————— at her house almost every day.

"If they made up the jury panel of thirty-six from among the notable inhabitants of the department by drawing lots four or five times," said the vicar-general with the keen look of ambition, and stressing his words, "I should consider myself unlucky indeed if I couldn't count eight or ten friends in each list, and the most intelligent of the bunch. I would almost always have the majority on my side, and even more than that if I wanted a conviction; you see, Mademoiselle, it's the easiest thing in the world for me to grant absolution. . . ."

The abbé broke off suddenly, as if astonished at the sound of his own words; he was admitting things the laity should never hear.

But Mathilde was dumbfounded in turn when he informed her that what astonished and most interested Besançon society about Julien's strange case was that he had once inspired a great passion in Mme. de Rênal, and had for a long time shared it. M. de Frilair could easily perceive the extreme agitation his account was producing.

"I have my revenge" he thought. "Here at last is the way to lead this determined little woman by the nose. I was shaking for fear I couldn't bring it off." Her look of distinction and of not being easy to manage doubled the charm of the rare beauty he saw almost supplicant before him. He recovered all his self-possession and did not hesitate a second to twist the dagger in her heart.

"I wouldn't be at all surprised," he said to her in a light tone, "if we should learn that M. Sorel fired the two shots at that woman, once so beloved, out of jealousy. She is far from unattractive, and lately she had been seeing a good deal of a certain Abbé Marquinot from Dijon, a kind of Jansenist, without any morals, like all of them."

Leisurely, voluptuously, M. de Frilair tortured the pretty girl's heart, whose secret he had stumbled on.

"Why," he asked, fixing his hot eyes on Mathilde, "would M. Sorel have chosen the church, if not because at that very moment his rival was celebrating mass in it? Everyone allows that the lucky man whom you are protecting is ever so intelligent and even more farsighted.

What could have been easier than to hide himself in M. de Rênal's garden, which he knows so well? There, almost certain of not being seen, caught, or suspected, he could have done away with the woman of whom he was jealous."

This line of reasoning, apparently so well founded, was all it took to drive Mathilde frantic. That spirit, lofty yet imbued with the cold cautiousness which in polite circles passes for a true expression of the human heart, was not capable of readily understanding the kind of joy that may come of throwing caution to the wind, one that can be so keen for a passionate nature. In the upper classes of Parisian society, in which Mathilde lived, passion is rarely able to slough off prudence; it's from the sixth floor that people throw themselves out the window.

At last the Abbé de Frilair was sure of his hold. He gave Mathilde to understand (he was, no doubt, lying) that he could do as he pleased with the district attorney in charge of prosecuting the case against Julien.

Once the thirty-six jurors for the session had been designated by lots, he would approach at least thirty of them directly and personally.

If Mathilde had not seemed so pretty to M. de Frilair, he would not have spoken so plainly until the fifth or sixth interview.

Chapter XXXIX

Intrigue

> March 31, 1676. He that endea-
> voured to kill his sister in our house,
> had before killed a man, and it had
> cost his father five hundred écus to
> get him off; by their secret distribu-
> tion, gaining the favour of the coun-
> sellors.
>
> —LOCKE, *Journey Through
> France**

On leaving the bishopric, Mathilde rushed to dispatch a messenger to Mme. de Fervaques; the fear of compromising herself did not hold her back for a second. She implored her rival to obtain a letter for M. de Frilair, written entirely in the Lord Bishop of ———'s hand. She went so far as to beg her to hurry down to Besançon herself. Coming from a proud, jealous soul, this gesture was heroic.

Taking Fouqué's advice, she had the good sense not to say anything to Julien about her activities. Her presence upset him enough without that. A more decent man at the approach of death than he had been in the course of his life, he felt guilty not only about M. de La Mole but with regard to Mathilde as well.

"What!" he would say to himself, "at times I am absent-minded and even bored in her presence. She is ruining herself for me, and this is how I reward her! Could it be that I really am a wicked man?" This question would have troubled him very little when he was ambitious; in those days, failure was the only shame in his opinion.

His bad conscience with regard to Mathilde was all the more pronounced since, at the moment, he inspired her with the most extraordinary, the wildest passion. She could talk of nothing but the strange sacrifices she would make in order to save him.

Elated by feelings of which she was proud and that had prevailed over her arrogance, she was unwilling to let an *instant* of her life go by without using it for some extraordinary effort. The oddest schemes, the riskiest for herself, filled up her long talks with Julien. Well paid, the jailers let her have the run of the prison. Mathilde's notions did not stop at the sacrifice of her reputation; it mattered little to her if she let all society know about her condition. To fling herself on her knees in front of the king's carriage going at a gallop, to attract the sovereign's attention at the risk of being run over a thousand times, and beg for Julien's pardon, was among the lesser chimeras entertained by this inflamed and courageous imagination. With friends who stood close to the throne, she was sure of being admitted to the reserved areas of the park of St. Cloud.

Julien felt that he was hardly worth such devotion; to tell the truth, he was weary of heroism. He would have responded to a simple, naïve, and almost shy affection, whereas Mathilde's haughty spirit could never forgo the idea of a public.

Amidst all her anguish, all her fears for the life of this lover, whom she did not wish to survive, she had, so Julien felt, a secret need to astonish the public by the immoderateness of her love and the sublimity of her undertakings.

Julien was annoyed with himself for not feeling touched by all this heroism. What would have been his reaction had he known of all the mad schemes with which Mathilde had overwhelmed the good Fouqué's devoted but eminently rational and narrow mind?

Fouqué couldn't quite say what was wrong with Mathilde's devotion, for he too would have sacrificed his whole fortune and exposed his life to the greatest danger to save Julien. He was stupefied at the quantity of gold Mathilde tossed around. In the first few days, the sums spent in this manner filled him with respect, for he had all of the provincial's veneration for money.

Before long he discovered that Mlle. de La Mole's plans changed frequently, and, to his great relief, found the word to censure a disposition he found so tiresome; she was *changeable*. From this epithet to *stubborn*, the greatest anathema in the provinces, is but a step.

"It's odd," Julien said to himself one day as Mathilde was leaving the prison, "that a passion so strong, and of which I am the object, should leave me so indifferent. I adored her two months ago! I read somewhere that as death approaches a man loses all interest; but it's terrible to feel ungrateful and not be able to change. Does that make me an egoist?" He took himself to task on that score in the most humiliating terms.

In his heart ambition was dead; another passion had risen from its ashes. He called it remorse for having attacked Mme. de Rênal. He was, in fact, head over heels in love with her. He felt a strange happiness when, left absolutely alone and with no fear of being interrupted, he could give himself up entirely to the memory of happy days he had spent in Verrières or at Vergy. The slightest incidents of those days, too quickly flown, held an irresistible charm and freshness for him. He never thought about his successes in Paris; they bored him.

Out of jealousy, Mathilde half guessed his state of mind, which was becoming more pronounced every day. She was fully aware that she had to compete against his love of solitude. Sometimes she would utter Mme. de Rênal's name in terror. She would see Julien shiver. Henceforth her passion knew no bounds or restraint.

"If he dies, I die after him," she kept telling herself in all possible good faith. "What would the Paris drawing rooms say if they saw a lover condemned to die worshiped to that extent by a girl of my rank? To find like sentiments, you have to go back to the age of heroes; it was love affairs of this kind that set hearts to beating in the reign of Charles IX and of Henry III."

In the midst of her most intense raptures, when she was holding Julien's head against her heart: "What!" she would say to herself in horror, "can this charming head be doomed to fall! Very well!" she would add, inflamed with a heroism that was not devoid of happiness, "these lips which are pressed against this beautiful hair will be cold less than twenty-four hours later."

Memories of those moments of heroism and of terrible delight held her in an invincible grasp. The notion of suicide, so engrossing in itself, but up to now so remote from that lofty mind, made its way into her thoughts, soon to reign there with absolute power. "No, my ancestors' blood did not cool off as it came down to me," Mathilde told herself proudly.

"I have a favor to ask," her lover said to her one day:

"put your child out to nurse in Verrières. Mme. de Rênal will keep an eye on the nurse."

"What you are asking me is hard, indeed. . . ." And
Mathilde turned pale.

"Yes, it is, and I beg your pardon a thousand times,"
cried Julien, coming out of his reverie and folding her in
his arms.

After having dried her tears, he returned to his idea,
but more adroitly this time. He first gave the conversation a gloomy, philosophical turn. He spoke of that future
which would so soon be closed to him.

"You must agree, my dear, that a passion is accidental
in life, but an accident that happens only to superior
souls. . . . The death of my son would, in fact, be a
blessing to your family's pride; that is the conclusion your
servants will draw. Neglect will be the lot of this child of
sorrow and shame. . . . I hope that at a time which I do
not wish to specify, but which, nevertheless, I have the
courage to foresee, you will obey my last instructions: you
will marry the Marquis de Croisenois."

"What, dishonored as I am!"

"Dishonor cannot fix itself to a name like yours. You
will be thought of as a widow, a madman's widow, and
that is all. I will go so far as to say that, not having money
for its motive, my crime will not be considered in the
least dishonorable. Perhaps by then some philosophical
legislator will have persuaded his prejudiced contemporaries to abolish capital punishment. Then some friendly
voice will mention me as an example: 'Look, Mlle. de La
Mole's first husband was mad, but not evil; he was not a
criminal. It was absurd to cut off his head. . . .' Then my
memory will be infamous no more; that is, not after a
certain time. . . . Your position in society, your fortune,
and if I may say so, your genius, will make it possible for
M. de Croisenois, once he's your husband, to play a part
to which he could not have aspired all by himself. He
has nothing but birth and bravery, and those qualities by
themselves, which made up the accomplished man in
1729, are out of date a century later, and lead to nothing
but pretensions. It takes more than that if a man is to
set himself at the head of French youth.

"Whatever the political party into which you push your
husband, you will bring to it the benefit of a strong and
enterprising character. You may take the place once held
by the Chevreuses and the Longuevilles during the Fronde.
. . .* But by that time, my dear, the heavenly fire that
burns in you now will have waned a bit.

473

"If you will allow me to say so," he added, after a good many other preparatory remarks, "fifteen years from now you will look back on the love you felt for me as a folly—pardonable, but nonetheless a folly. . . ."

He stopped suddenly and began to muse. He found himself face-to-face again with an idea that was very offensive to Mathilde: "In fifteen years Mme. de Rênal will worship my son, and you will have forgotten him."

Chapter XL

Peace

> It is because I was mad then that I am wise now. O philosopher, you who see only the immediate, how short are your views! Your eye is incapable of following the subterranean work of the passions.
>
> —GOETHE

Their talk was cut short by an interrogation, followed by a conference with the lawyer in charge of the defense. Those were the only absolutely disagreeable moments in a life full of negligence and tender dreaming.

"It was murder, and murder with premeditation," said Julien to the judge as well as the lawyer. "I'm sorry, gentlemen," he added with a smile, "but this reduces your task to almost nothing.

"After all," Julien reflected, when he had succeeded in ridding himself of those two creatures, "I must be brave, and conspicuously braver than those two. They think of this ill-fated duel as the crowning evil, as the *king of frights,* but I shall not concern myself seriously about it until the day of the trial.

"That is because I have known a greater misfortune," continued Julien, philosophizing to himself. "I suffered far more during my first trip to Strasbourg, when I thought Mathilde had thrown me over.... And to think how passionately I desired this total intimacy which leaves me so cold today! ... In fact, I am happier alone than when that beautiful girl is sharing my solitude...."

His lawyer, a man of rules and formalities, thought he was crazy and, like the public, was convinced that jealousy had shoved the gun into his hand. One day he ventured to let Julien know that this allegation, true or false, would make an excellent plea for the defense. But in the wink of an eye, the accused became his incisive and passionate self once more.

"On your life, sir," shouted Julien furiously, "remember never to utter that abominable lie again." For a moment the cautious lawyer was afraid of being murdered.

He was getting his plea for the defense ready, since the decisive moment was rapidly drawing near. Besançon and the whole department talked of nothing but the famous case. Julien was ignorant of this detail; he had requested that no one speak to him ever about that sort of thing.

The same day, at their first remark, Julien had silenced Fouqué and Mathilde, who had tried to inform him of certain public rumors very liable, they felt, to give grounds for hope.

"Leave me to my ideal existence. Your pestering, your little accounts of real life, all more or less offensive to me, would pull me down from the heavens. A man dies as best he can; as for me, I want to face death in my own way. What do I care what the public thinks? My connection with it will be cut off sharply enough. For pity's sake, say no more about those people; it's bad enough to be exposed to such rabble as the prosecutor and my lawyer."

"So," he said to himself, "it appears that I am destined to die dreaming. A nobody like myself, sure of being forgotten after two weeks, would be a fool, indeed, to go along with this farce. . . .

"It's odd all the same that I never learned the art of enjoying life until I saw the end of it so close."

He spent these last days out walking on the narrow, flat roof of the donjon, smoking the excellent cigars for which Mathilde had sent a courier to Holland, and unaware that his appearance was awaited daily by all the telescopes in the city. His mind was at Vergy. He never spoke of Mme. de Rênal to Fouqué, but two or three times his friend told him that she was recovering rapidly, and those words resounded in his heart.

Though Julien's mind was almost always in the land of ideas, Mathilde, concerned with realities, as befits an aristocratic heart, had been able to further the intimacy of the direct correspondence between Mme. de Fervaques and M. de Frilair to such a point that already the great word "diocese" had been pronounced.

The venerable prelate in charge of church appointments

had added in a postil to one of his nieces's letter: *"That poor Sorel is impulsive and nothing worse; I hope he will be restored to us."*

At the sight of these lines, M. de Frilair was beside himself with joy. He had no doubts about saving Julien.

"Without that Jacobin law which requires an endless list of jurors on the panel, and which has no real aim other than to strip the wellborn of all their influence," he was saying to Mathilde on the eve of the drawing for the session's thirty-six jurors, "I could answer for the verdict. I got the Curé N—— acquitted."

It was with pleasure the next day that M. de Frilair recognized five Congreganists from Besançon among the names drawn from the urn, and, among the out-of-towners, those of *MM.* Valenod, de Moirod, de Cholin. "I can answer right now for those eight jurors," he told Mathilde. "The first five are tools; Valenod is my agent; Moirod owes me everything; de Cholin is an imbecile who is afraid of his own shadow."

The newspaper spread the jurors' names throughout the department, and Mme. de Rênal, to her husband's ineffable terror, resolved to go to Besançon. The best M. de Rênal could do was to extract a promise from her that she would keep to her bed, and so avoid the unpleasantness of being called as a witness.

"You don't understand my position," the ex-mayor of Verrières kept telling her. "I am now a Liberal *by defection,* as they say. There's no doubt but that rascal Valenod and M. de Frilair can easily get the attorney general and the judges to do anything they please that will go against me."

Mme. de Rênal submitted to her husband's order willingly. "If I appeared at the assize court," she told herself, "it would look as if I were asking for revenge."

Despite all the promises of discretion she made to her confessor and to her husband, she had no more than arrived in Besançon when she wrote to each of the thirty-six jurors in her own hand:

I will not appear at all on the day of the trial, sir, because my presence might be prejudicial to M. Sorel's case. I desire only one thing in the world, and passionately, that he be saved. Have no doubts about it, the horrible thought that an innocent man had been led to his death because of me would poison the rest of my life and no doubt shorten it. How could you condemn him to death when I am still alive? No, without a doubt, society has no right to take a life, especially that of an individual like Julien Sorel. Everyone in Verrières has known him to have moments of aberration. That poor young man has powerful enemies; yet even among his enemies (and how many he has!), who questions his wonderful talents and his profound learning? This is no ordinary fellow you are about to judge, sir. For close to eighteen months, we all knew him to be pious, well-behaved, diligent; but two or three times a year he was seized by a fit of melancholy that verged on derangement. The whole town of Verrières, all our neighbors at Vergy, where we spend the summer months, my whole family, the subprefect himself, will do justice to his exemplary piety; he knows all of the Holy Bible by heart. Would an ungodly man have applied himself for years to learn the Holy Book? My sons will have the honor of presenting you with this letter. They are children: be so good as to examine them, sir. They will give you any details about the poor young man that might still be needed to convince you that it would be barbarous to condemn him. Far from avenging me, you would be signing my death warrant.

What argument can his enemies oppose to this fact: My wound, which was a result of one of those moments of derangement that even my children used to notice in their tutor, is so far from dangerous that after less than two months it has allowed me to post from Verrières to Besançon. If I learn, sir, that you feel a moment's hesitation about saving a man whose guilt is so slight from the barbarity of the law, I will leave my bed, to which I am confined solely by my husband's orders, and go and throw myself at your feet.

Find that premeditation was not established, sir, and you will not have the blood of an innocent man on your conscience, etc., etc.

Chapter XLI

The Verdict

> The district will long remember
> that famous trial. Interest in the
> defendant caused a general stir, be-
> cause his crime was astonishing yet
> not atrocious. And even if it had
> been, he was such a handsome
> young man! His great good fortune,
> so soon ended, aroused even more
> pity. "Would they convict him?"
> asked the women of their male ac-
> quaintances; and one saw them turn
> pale as they waited for the answer.
>
> —SAINTE-BEUVE

Finally dawned the day so much dreaded by Mme. de
Rênal and Mathilde.

The strange look of the city increased their terror
twofold and left not even Fouqué's staunch heart un-
touched. The whole province had come running to Besançon to see the outcome of this romantic trial.

As of several days ago,.no rooms were to be had in the
inns. The presiding judge of the assize court was beset
with requests for tickets: every lady in the city wanted to
attend the trial; Julien's portrait was being hawked about
the streets, etc., etc.

Mathilde had kept in reserve for this supreme moment
a letter written entirely in the hand of his Lordship the
Bishop of ———. That prelate, who directed the Church
of France and made bishops, had deigned to ask for Ju-

lien's acquittal. On the eve of the trial, Mathilde took this letter to the almighty vicar-general.

At the end of the interview, when she burst into tears as she was leaving: "I can answer for the jury's verdict," M. de Frilair, almost moved himself and coming out from behind his diplomatic reserve at last, said to her. "Among the twelve persons in charge of determining whether your protégé's crime has been established, and especially whether it was premeditated, I can count on six friends who are devoted to my career, and I made it plain that it is up to them to put me in the bishop's·palace. Baron Valenod, the mayor of Verrières, who owes me his office, can do what he likes with two of his subordinates, MM. de Moirod and de Cholin. To tell the truth, the drawing has given us two very unorthodox jurors for this business; yet, though ultra-Liberal, they abide by my orders on important occasions, and they have been urged to vote like M. de Valenod. I have learned that a sixth juror, a manufacturer, an immensely rich and talkative Liberal, aspires secretly to a contract for supplying the War Ministry, and would not, I daresay, want to offend me. He has been told that M. de Valenod has my last word on the matter."

"And who is this M. Valenod?" Mathilde asked uneasily.

"If you knew him, you could have no doubts about our success. He is an audacious, impudent, coarse speaker, a born leader of fools. Eighteen hundred and fourteen took him out of the gutter, and I am going to make a prefect of him. He's likely to beat the other jurors if they won't vote his way."

Mathilde felt somewhat reassured.

Another discussion lay ahead of her that evening. So as not to prolong a disagreeable scene, the outcome of which, in his opinion, was already decided, Julien had made up his mind not to take the floor.

"My lawyer will do the talking; that's more than enough," he told Mathilde. "I will be made a spectacle before my enemies only too long as it is. Those provincials were offended by my sudden wealth, for which I am obliged to you, and believe me, there is not one among them who does not wish for my conviction, though he may blubber like a fool when they take me out to die."

"They want to see you humiliated, that is only too true," answered Mathilde, "but I don't think they are in the least cruel. My presence in Besançon and the sight of my suffering have aroused the interest of all the women;

your good looks will do the rest. If you speak a few words before the judges, the whole audience will be on your side," etc., etc.

The next morning at nine, when Julien came down from his prison to go into the trial room of the courthouse, the gendarmes had a great deal of trouble making a way through the huge crowd that had crammed into the courtyard. Julien had slept well, he was quite calm, and felt nothing more than a philosophical pity for the envious crowd which, without cruelty, would soon be applauding his death sentence. He was surprised indeed when, held up for a quarter of an hour in the midst of the crowd, he was forced to acknowledge that his presence evoked a feeling of tender pity in the public. He did not hear a single disparaging remark. "These provincials are not so spiteful as I thought," he said to himself.

Upon entering the courtroom, he was struck by the elegance of the architecture. It was true Gothic, with a host of small, pretty columns carved in the stone with the greatest care. He thought he was in England.

But his attention was soon engrossed by a dozen or fifteen pretty women who, sitting opposite the dock, filled up the three balconies over the judges and the jury. On turning around toward the public, he saw that the circular gallery which projects out over the amphitheater was filled with women; most of them were young and seemed to him very pretty; their eyes were shining and full of concern. In the rest of the room, the crowd was huge; people were struggling at the doors, and the guards could not obtain silence.

When all the eyes that had been searching for Julien remarked his presence, then saw him take the slightly elevated seat reserved for the accused, he was greeted with a murmur of astonishment and tender interest.

That day you would have said that he wasn't twenty years old; he was dressed simply but with perfect grace; his hair and forehead were charming; Mathilde had insisted on presiding over his toilet herself. Julien's pallor was extreme. Hardly seated on the bench, from all sides he heard: "God! how young he is! ... But he's only a boy. ... He's much better looking than his picture."

"Defendant," the gendarme seated on his right said to him, "see those six ladies sitting in that balcony?" The gendarme pointed to a small gallery jutting out over that part of the amphitheater where the jurors sit. "That one is the prefect's wife," continued the gendarme. "Beside her, the Marquise de M——, that one likes you; I heard her talking with the examining magistrate. Next comes Mme. Derville—"

"Mme. Derville!" exclaimed Julién, and his forehead flushed a vivid red. "When she leaves here, she will write to Mme. de Rênal," he thought. He knew nothing of Mme. de Rênal's arrival in Besançon.

The witnesses were examined. This took several hours. At the first words of the case for the prosecution, pronounced by the district attorney, two of those ladies seated in the little balcony, directly facing Julien, burst into tears. "Mme. Derville is not so easily moved," thought Julien. Yet he noted that she was very red.

The advocate general was running to pathos in bad French over the barbarity of the crime committed; Julien noted that Mme. Derville's neighbors looked as if they disapproved of him thoroughly. Several jurors, obviously acquaintances of these ladies, spoke to them and seemed to reassure them. "That can only be taken as a good omen," thought Julien.

Up to then he had felt nothing but unalloyed contempt for all the men at the trial. The district attorney's shabby eloquence increased his feeling of disgust. But Julien's coldness gradually gave way before such marked interest, the object of which was plainly himself.

He was pleased with his lawyer's resolute bearing. "No fancy speeches," he whispered to him as he was about to take the floor.

"All the bombast pilfered from Bossuet that has been trotted out and used against you has helped your cause," said the lawyer. In effect, he spoke barely five minutes before most of the women had their handkerchiefs out. Encouraged, the lawyer addressed the jury in extremely bold terms. Julien shivered, he felt that he was on the point of tears. "Great God! what would my enemies say?"

He was about to give in to feelings that were getting the best of him, when, fortunately, he happened to catch an insolent stare from the Baron de Valenod.

"The cur's eyes are blazing," he said to himself. "What a triumph for that base soul! If my crime had led to nothing but this, I should curse it. God knows what he'll say to Mme. de Rênal about me at parties next winter!"

This idea canceled all others. Not long after, his train of thought was broken by the public's murmur of approval. His lawyer had just finished his plea for the defense. Julien remembered that it was proper to shake his hand. Time had passed swiftly.

Refreshments were brought in for the lawyer and the accused. It was only then that Julien was struck by one detail: Not a single woman had left the hearing to go to dinner.

"By George, I'm dying of hunger," said the lawyer, "and you?"

"So am I," answered Julien.

"Look, there's the prefect's wife having her dinner too," the lawyer said, pointing to the small balcony. "Buck up! it's going fine." The session resumed.

While the presiding judge was summing up, midnight struck. He was forced to break off; amidst the silence of universal anxiety, the clock bell's reverberation filled the room.

"Here begins the last of my days," thought Julien. Before long he was ablaze with the idea of duty. Up to then he had dominated his feelings and kept his resolution not to speak, but when the presiding judge of the assize court asked him if he had anything to say, he rose. Before him he saw Mme. Derville's eyes, which in that light seemed very shiny. "Could she, by chance, be weeping?" he wondered.

"Gentlemen of the jury, a horror of contempt, which I thought I might defy at the moment of death, prompts me to speak. Gentlemen, I do not have the honor of belonging to your class; in me you see a peasant in revolt against the baseness of his lot.

"I am not asking for mercy," Julien went on, steadying his voice. "I have no illusions, death awaits me; it will be just. I had the heart to make an attempt on the life of a woman who is worthy of every kind of respect and homage. Mme. de Rênal had been like a mother to me. My crime is abominable, and it was *premeditated*. So, Gentlemen of the Jury, I deserve to die. Yet even if I were less guilty, I see men here who, not to be stopped by any consideration of mercy that my youth might deserve, would like to punish through me and discourage forever a whole class of young men who, born to an inferior position in society and, so to speak, oppressed by poverty, have had the luck to obtain a good education and the audacity to mingle with what the rich in their pride call society.

"That, gentlemen, is my crime, and it will be punished all the more severely because I am not, in fact, being judged by my peers. In the jury box I see no wealthy peasant . . . only outraged burghers. . . ."

For twenty minutes Julien went on in this vein; he said

everything he had on his chest; the district attorney, who aspired to the aristocracy's favor, kept jumping up in his chair, but in spite of the somewhat abstract turn Julien had given the discussion, all the women were bursting into tears. Mme. Derville herself had a handkerchief over her eyes. Before closing, Julien returned to the idea of premeditation, to his repentance, to his respect, to the filial and boundless adoration that, in happier times, he had felt for Mme. de Rênal. . . . Mme. Derville gave a scream and fainted.

One o'clock was striking when the jurors retired to their room. Not a single woman had given up her place; several men had tears in their eyes. The conversations were at first very lively; but little by little, the jurors' decision being slow to come, the general weariness began to cast a calm over the assembly. It was a solemn moment; the lights sparkled brilliantly. Very tired, Julien heard people near him debating as to whether this delay was a good or a bad sign. He noted with pleasure that everyone was for him; the jury did not come in and yet no woman had left the room.

Two o'clock had just struck when a great stirring became audible. The little door to the jury room opened. The Baron de Valenod advanced at a grave and theatrical pace; he was followed by all the jurors. He coughed, then declared that by his soul and conscience, the unanimous finding of the jury was that Julien Sorel was guilty of murder, and of murder with premeditation: this verdict carried the death penalty. It was pronounced a minute later. Julien looked at his watch and remembered M. de Lavalette; it was a quarter past two. "Today is Friday," he thought.

"Yes, but this is a happy day for Valenod, who condemned me. . . . I am too closely watched for Mathilde to be able to save me as Mme. de Lavalette did. . . . So in three days, at this same hour, I will know what to believe about the 'great perhaps.' "

At that moment he heard a scream, and was called back to the things of this world. The women around him were sobbing; he saw that every face was turned toward a little gallery contrived in the capital of a Gothic pilaster. Later he learned that Mathilde had been hiding there. Since the scream was not repeated, everyone went back to looking at Julien, for whom the gendarmes were trying to make a way through the crowd.

"Let's try not to give that crook Valenod anything to laugh about," thought Julien. "With what a grieved and humbugging look he pronounced the verdict, which carries a death sentence! While that poor man presiding over the assize, even though he's been a judge for years, had tears in his eyes when he sentenced me. What joy for Valenod to have his revenge for our old rivalry over Mme. de Rênal. . . . So I will never see her again! It's all over. A last farewell is impossible for us, I'm sure. . . . How happy I would have been to tell her how much I detest my crime!"

He spoke only these words: "I find I have been justly condemned."

Chapter XLII*

After bringing Julien back to the prison, the guards put him in a cell reserved for the condemned.

He, who usually noted even the smallest details, was totally unaware that he had not been made to climb back up to his donjon. He was imagining what he would say to Mme. de Rênal, if, at the last minute, he had the good luck to see her. He expected her to interrupt him, and with his first remark he meant to make clear to her the full extent of his contrition. "After such a deed, how could I convince her that I love her alone? After all I did try to kill her, whether out of ambition or out of love for Mathilde."

Getting into bed, he discovered that the sheets were made of coarse linen. The scales fell from his eyes. "Ah! I'm in the dungeon," he told himself, "as a condemned man. It's only right.

"Count Altamira was telling me that on the eve of his death Danton said in his gruff voice: 'It's odd, but the verb "to guillotine" cannot be conjugated in all its tenses. You can say: "I will be guillotined, you shall be guillotined"; but you cannot say: "I have been guillotined." '

"Why not," Julien went on, "if there is another life? My faith, if I meet the God of the Christians, I'm done for; he's a despot, and as such, filled with thoughts of vengeance. His Bible speaks of nothing but terrible punishments. I have never loved him; I have never been willing to believe that anyone could love him sincerely. He is merciless." (And Julien recalled several passages in the Bible.) "He will punish me in some horrible way. . . .

"But if I should see Fénelon's God! Perhaps he would say to me: 'A great deal will be forgiven you, for you have loved a great deal. . . .'

"Have I loved such a great deal? Ah! I loved Mme. de

*Stendhal left the last four chapters untitled.

Rênal, but my conduct was atrocious. In her case, as in others, I forsook simple and modest worth for all that glitters. . . .

"And yet, what prospects I had! . . . Colonel in the Hussars, had we gone to war; secretary of a legation in peacetime; after that, ambassador . . . for I would soon know the ropes, and even if I were a downright fool, would the Marquis de La Mole's son-in-law have to worry about competition? All my blunders would be pardoned, or rather, set down as accomplishments. A man of accomplishments, enjoying the best life has to offer, in Vienna or in London. . . .

" 'Not quite, sir—you are to be guillotined in three days.' "

Julien laughed heartily over this flash of his own wit. "Really, a man has two persons in him," he reflected. "Who the devil thought up that sly remark?

"As a matter of fact, yes, my friend . . . to be guillotined in three days," he answered his interrupter. "M. de Cholin will rent a window, going halves with the Abbé Maslon. Well, then, which of those two worthies will cheat the other out of the price of that window?"

This passage from Rotrou's *Venceslas* came to him all of a sudden.

Ladislas: . . . My soul is ready.
The King (Ladislas' father): So is the scaffold; betake your head there.

"Fine answer!" he thought, and fell asleep. Someone woke him in the morning by holding him tightly.

"What! already!" said Julien, opening a haggard eye. He thought he was in the executioner's hands.

It was Mathilde. "Luckily, she didn't understand me." This observation restored his self-possession. He found Mathilde changed, as if by six months of illness: really, she was not recognizable.

"That unspeakable Frilair has betrayed me," she said, wringing her hands. Rage kept her from weeping.

"Wasn't I fine yesterday when I took the floor?" replied Julien. "I was improvising, and for the first time in my life! True, it may well be the last."

At that moment Julien was playing on Mathilde's character with all the coolness of a skillful pianist at the keyboard. "I lack the advantage of an illustrious birth, it's true," he added, "but Mathilde's great heart has raised her

487

lover to her own level. Do you think Boniface de La Mole handled himself any better in front of his judges?"

That day Mathilde was tender without affectation, like a poor girl who lives on the sixth floor; but she couldn't get him to speak in less high-flown language. He was paying her back, unwittingly, for the torment she had often inflicted on him.

"No one knows the source of the Nile," Julien was saying to himself. "It has never been granted the eye of man to see the king of rivers in the state of a simple stream; and so no human eye shall see Julien weak, because in the first place he is not. But my heart is easily moved; the most commonplace remark, if it rings true, can affect my voice and even cause my tears to flow. How many times have the hardhearted despised me for that flaw! They thought I was begging for mercy; that is something I must never allow.

"They say that at the foot of the gallows, Danton was moved to tears by the memory of his wife; but Danton had put strength into a nation of idlers, and kept the enemy from reaching Paris. . . . I alone know what I might have done. . . . In the eyes of the world, I am at best a *might-have-been*.

"If Mme. de Rênal were here in my dungeon instead of Mathilde, would I be able to control myself? The excessiveness of my contrition and of my despair would be taken by Valenod and all the patricians of the region for an ignoble fear of death; they are so proud, those faint hearts whose wealth sets them above temptation! 'You see what it means,' *MM*. de Moirod and de Cholin, who have just sentenced me to death, would say, 'to be born a carpenter's son. A man may become educated, clever, but the heart! . . . one cannot learn to have a stout heart.' That holds for even this poor Mathilde, who is weeping now, or rather who cannot weep anymore," he said, looking at her reddened eyes. And he clasped her in his arms: the sight of genuine suffering made him forget his syllogism. "She may have wept all night," he told himself, "but with what shame she will look back on all this one day! She will think of herself as having been led astray, in her tender youth, by a plebeian's lowly way of thinking. . . . Croisenois is weak enough to marry her and, by Jove, he will do well. She will make him play a role.

> By that right a spirit firm and farseeing in its
> plans
> Has over the dull spirit of vulgar humans.*

488

"Here's a funny thing! Now that I must die, all the verses I ever learned in my life keep coming back to me. That must be a sign of decadence. . . ."

Mathilde kept repeating to him in a dull voice, "He's there in the next room." Finally Julien paid attention to what she was saying. "Her voice is feeble," he thought, "but all of that domineering character is still in her tone. She's lowered her voice to keep from getting angry."

"Who is in there?" he asked her gently.

"The lawyer, to have you sign your appeal."

"I will not appeal."

"What! you won't appeal," she said, getting to her feet, her eyes sparkling with anger, "and why not, if you please?"

"Because at this moment, I feel I have the courage to die without making too big a fool of myself. And who can say whether in two months, after a long stay in this damp dungeon, I will be so well-disposed? I foresee visits from priests, from my father. Nothing on earth could be more disagreeable. I'd rather die."

This unexpected contrariness roused all the haughtiness in Mathilde's character. She had not been able to see the Abbé de Frilair before the hour when the cells in Besançon's prison were unlocked; her fury came down on Julien. She adored him, and for a full quarter of an hour he recognized in her imprecations against his character, in her misgiving about having loved him, all of that haughty spirit which had once heaped him with such cutting abuse in the library at the Hôtel de La Mole.

"Heaven owed it to the glory of your house to see to it that you were born a man," he said to her.

"But as for me," he thought, "I would be a great fool to go on living two more months in this disgusting hole, a butt for every infamous and humiliating insult the aristocratic faction can think up,* and for my sole comfort the curses of this madwoman. . . . Well, the morning after next, I shall fight a duel with a man known for his coolness and his remarkable skill. . . ." " 'Remarkable indeed,' " said his Mephistophelian voice. " 'He never misses.'

"Good enough, so be it, fine and dandy!" (Mathilde was still carrying on.) "By George, no," he said to himself, "I will not appeal."

This resolution taken, he lapsed into a reverie. "The postman will bring the newspaper at six as usual when he makes his rounds; at eight o'clock, after M. de Rênal has read it, Elisa will come in on tiptoes and lay it on her bed.

Later she will wake up. All of a sudden, as she reads, she will be upset; her pretty hand will tremble; she will read down to these words: '*At five past ten he was no more.*'

"She will weep bitterly, I know her; the fact that I meant to kill her will count for nothing; she will forget everything. And the person whose life I tried to take will be the only one who will weep sincerely over my death.

"Ah! this is the antithesis!" he thought, and for the quarter of an hour more that the scene Mathilde was making endured, he thought only of Mme. de Rênal. In spite of himself, and though often replying to what Mathilde said to him, he couldn't take his mind off his memory of the bedroom in Verrières. He saw the *Besançon Gazette* on the orange taffeta coverlet. He saw that very white hand clutching it convulsively; he saw Mme. de Rênal weeping. . . . He followed the course of each tear down that lovely face.

Unable to do anything herself, Mlle. de La Mole called in the lawyer. As luck would have it, he had been a captain in the Italian campaign of 1796, during which he had fought at Manuel's side.*

For form's sake, he opposed the condemned man's resolution vigorously. Julien, wishing to treat him respectfully, enumerated all his reasons.

"By Jove, that's one way of looking at it," M. Félix Vaneau, the lawyer, ended by telling him. "But you have three full days to appeal, and it is my duty to come back every day. If a volcano should erupt under this prison within the next two months, you would be saved. You could die of a sickness," he said, looking Julien in the eye.

Julien shook his head. "I thank you, you are a good man. I will think it over."

And when Mathilde finally left with the lawyer, he felt much more affection for the latter than for her.

Chapter XLIII

An hour later, when he was sleeping soundly, he was roused by tears he felt running over his hand.

"Ah! it's Mathilde again," he thought half wakefully. "True to her strategy, she has come to attack my resolution with tender sentiments." Bored by the prospect of a new scene in the pathetic style, he kept his eyes closed. Belphegor's lines,* when he is running away from his wife, crossed his mind.

He heard a strange sigh; he opened his eyes; it was Mme. de Rênal.

"Ah! I see you once more before I die; is this an illusion?" he cried, throwing himself at her feet.

"Forgive me, madam, I am nothing but a murderer in your eyes," he said immediately upon recovering himself.

"Sir ... I have come to beg you to appeal. I know you don't want to—" Her sobs were choking her; she couldn't speak.

"Be so good as to pardon me."

"If you wish me to pardon you," she said, rising and throwing herself into his arms, "appeal your death sentence right away."

Julien was covering her with kisses. "Will you come to see me every day during these two months?"

"I swear I will. Every day, unless my husband forbids it."

"I'll sign!" cried Julien. "What! You forgive me! Is it possible!" He clasped her in his arms; he was wild. She gave a little scream.

"It's nothing," she told him. "You hurt me."

"Your shoulder," Julien cried, bursting into tears. He stood off a little and covered her hand with kisses of flame. "Who could have guessed it would be like this the last time I saw you, in your room in Verrières?"

"Who could have guessed at the time that I would write that unspeakable letter to M. de La Mole?"

"You know that I have always loved you, that I have never loved anyone but you."

"Is it really possible!" cried Mme. de Rênal, ecstatic in turn. She bent over Julien, who was at her knees, and for a long time they wept in silence.

Never before in his life had Julien known such a moment.

A good while later, when they were able to speak, Mme. de Rênal said: "And young Mme. Michelet, or rather Mlle. de La Mole, for I am really beginning to believe that strange story?"

"It's true only in appearance," answered Julien. "She is my wife but she does not rule in my heart."

Though interrupting one another a hundred times, they managed with great difficulty to tell one another what each did not know. The letter sent to M. de La Mole had been written by the young priest who directed Mme. de Rênal's conscience, and afterward copied by her.

"What a horrible thing religion has made me do!" she said. "And even then, I softened the most awful passages in that letter. . . ."

Julien's raptures and his happiness proved to her how fully he pardoned her. Never had he been so madly in love.

"I think I am pious," Mme. de Rênal said to him in the course of the conversation. "I sincerely believe in God; I believe too, and it has even been proved to me, that the crime I am committing is horrible, and yet as soon as I saw you, even after you had fired at me twice with a pistol—" And at this point, in spite of her, Julien covered her with kisses.

"Let me be," she continued, "I want to discuss this with you, lest I forget. . . . As soon as I see you, all thought of duty vanishes; I am nothing but love for you; or rather—the word 'love' is too feeble—I feel for you what I ought to feel for God alone: a mixture of respect, love, obedience. . . . To tell the truth, I don't know what it is you inspire in me. Should you tell me to stab the jailer, the crime would be committed before I had thought about it. Explain that to me distinctly before I leave you; I want to see clearly into my own soul, for in two months we must part. . . . By the way, must we part?" she said to him with a smile.

"I take back my promise," cried Julien, getting up. "I will not appeal my death sentence if by poison, knife, pistol, carbon gas, or by any other means whatsoever, you attempt to end or shorten your life."

Mme. de Rênal's expression changed all at once; the most vivid tenderness gave way to a deep reverie.

"If we should die right now?" she said to him at length.

"Who knows what we may find in the other life?" replied Julien, "perhaps torment, perhaps nothing at all. Can't we spend two months together in some delightful way? Two months, that's a good many days. Shall I ever have been so happy?"

"No, you shall never have been so happy!"

"Never," repeated Julien rapturously, "and I am talking to you as I talk to myself. God keep me from exaggerating."

"To speak so is to command me," she said with a timid and melancholy smile.

"Very well, then! you swear by the love you bear me never to make an attempt on your life by any means, whether direct or indirect.... Remember," he added, "that you must live for my son, whom Mathilde will turn over to lackeys once she is the Marquise de Croisenois."

"I swear," she replied coldly, "but I insist on leaving with your appeal, written in your own hand and signed. I myself will go to the attorney general."

"Take care, you will compromise yourself."

"After having gone so far as to visit you in prison, I will always be, in Besançon and in all Franche-Comté, a heroine of anecdotes," she said, looking deeply grieved. "The limits of strict modesty have been crossed. . . . I am a woman without honor. True, it was for you. . . ."

Her voice was so sad that Julien embraced her, with a happiness entirely new to him. It was no longer the intoxication of love; it was utmost gratitude he felt. He had just become aware, for the first time, of the full extent of the sacrifice she had made for him.

Some charitable soul, no doubt, informed M. de Rênal about the long visits his wife was making to Julien's prison; for, at the end of three days, he sent her his carriage with the express order to return at once to Verrières.

This cruel separation started the day off badly for Julien. Two or three hours later he was advised that a certain priest, a schemer who had, nevertheless, not been able to make his way among the Jesuits of Besançon, had stationed himself that morning in the street, outside the prison gate. It was raining heavily, and this man was trying to play the martyr. Julien was in a bad mood and this bit of nonsense depressed him.

He had already refused to see the priest that morning, but the man had taken it into his head to confess Julien and make a reputation for himself among the young women of Besançon with all the confidences he would claim to have received.

He kept declaring in a loud voice that he was going to spend the day and the night at the prison gate. "God has sent me to move the heart of this new apostate...." The common people, always interested in a scene, were beginning to flock.

"Yes, my brethren," he was telling them, "I will spend the day here, and the night, as well as every day and every night following. The Holy Ghost has spoken to me, I have a mission from on high; it is my duty to save young Sorel's soul. Join with me in prayer," etc., etc.

Julien had a horror of scandal and of anything that might draw attention to himself. He thought of seizing the moment to make his escape from the world incognito; yet he still had some hope of seeing Mme. de Rênal again, and he was hopelessly in love.

The prison gate was situated on one of the busiest streets. The thought of that muddy priest, drawing a crowd and making a scandal, tortured his soul. "No doubt about it, he repeats my name every minute!" That moment was more painful than death.

He called two or three times, at hourly intervals, for the turnkey, who was devoted to him, and sent him out to see if the priest was still at the prison gate.

"Sir, he's on both knees in the mud," the turnkey told him every time; "he's praying out loud and saying litanies for your soul...."

"Impertinent man!" thought Julien. At that moment, in effect, he heard a muffled humming; it was the people responding to the litanies. To crown his annoyance, he saw the turnkey himself move his lips, repeating the Latin phrases.

"People are beginning to say," added the turnkey, "that you must be hard hearted indeed to refuse the help of that holy man."

"O my native land! how barbaric you still are!" cried Julien, drunk with rage. And he went on thinking out loud and taking no account of the turnkey's presence.

"That man wants an article in the newspaper, and now he's sure to get it. Ah! damned provincials! In Paris I wouldn't be subjected to all these harassments. There, the charlatanism is more subtle."

"Show in that holy priest," he said eventually to the turnkey, sweat pouring down his forehead. The turnkey made the sign of the cross and went out joyfully.

That holy priest turned out to be horribly ugly; he was even dirtier. The cold rain increased the gloom and dampness of the dungeon. The priest tried to embrace Julien, and began to work up his emotion as he spoke to him. The lowest kind of hypocrisy was all too obvious; never in his life had Julien been so angry.

A quarter of an hour after the priest's entrance, Julien considered himself an absolute coward. For the first time death seemed horrible to him. He kept thinking about the state of putrefaction his body would be in two days after the execution, etc., etc.

He was about to give himself away by some sign of weakness or throw himself on the priest and strangle him with his chain, when it occurred to him to ask the holy man to go and say a good forty-franc mass for him that same day.

Since it was close to noon, the priest took off.

Chapter XLIV

As soon as he was gone, Julien wept a good deal, and wept about dying. He told himself eventually that if Mme. de Rênal were in Besançon, he would confess this weakness to her. . . .

At the moment he most regretted that adored woman's absence, he heard Mathilde's footstep. "The worst thing about being in prison," he thought, "is that you can't shut your door to anyone." No matter what Mathilde said, it only irritated him.

She told him that on the day of the trial M. de Valenod, having his appointment as prefect in his pocket, had dared to defy M. de Frilair and indulge himself in the pleasure of condemning Julien to death.

"Whatever did your friend have in mind," M. de Frilair had just said to her, "to arouse and then attack the petty pride of that *bourgeois aristocracy!* Why talk about *caste?* He showed them what they had to do in their own political interest: those boobies hadn't given it a thought and were ready to weep. That business about caste blinded them to the horror of condemning a man to death. You must admit that M. Sorel is very green in such matters. If we don't manage to save him by an appeal for mercy, his death will be a kind of suicide. . . ."

Mathilde took no pains to conceal from Julien what she herself did not yet suspect: namely, that the Abbé de Frilair, seeing Julien as a lost man, believed it would further his own ends if he aspired to become his successor.

Almost beside himself with impotent rage and vexation, Julien said to Mathilde: "Go hear a mass for me, and leave me a minute's peace." Already very jealous of Mme. de Rênal's visits, and having just learned about her departure, Mathilde understood the cause of Julien's ill-temper and burst into tears.

Her suffering was real; Julien could see that but was all

the more irritated. He felt a crying need for solitude, and how was he to get it?

After having tried every argument to soften him, Mathilde finally left, but in almost the same instant Fouqué appeared.

"I need to be alone," he told his faithful friend. And, since he saw him hesitating: "I'm drawing up my appeal for mercy. . . . Another thing . . . do me a favor, never talk to me about death. If I need to have some particular thing done that day, let me be the first to mention it."

When Julien had at last obtained the solitude he wanted, he felt lower in spirits and more cowardly than ever. The little strength remaining to that enfeebled soul had been exhausted by the effort to hide his state from Mlle. de La Mole and Fouqué.

Toward nightfall, a thought comforted him: "If this morning, when death looked so ugly to me, I had been notified for the execution, *the public's eye would have been a goad to glory*; perhaps my bearing would have been somewhat stiff, like that of a timid fop entering a drawing room. A few discerning individuals, if there are any among these provincials, might have guessed my faint-heartedness . . . but no one *would have seen it*."

He felt delivered to some extent from his wretchedness. "I am a coward right now," he kept chanting to himself, "but no one will ever know it."

An event almost more unpleasant awaited him the next morning. For a long time his father had been promising a visit; that day, before Julien woke, the white-haired old carpenter showed up in his cell.

Julien felt weak, he was expecting the most disagreeable kind of reproaches. To make this painful sensation complete, that morning he was feeling keenly remorseful about not loving his father.

"Chance has set us close together on earth," he was saying to himself, while the turnkey was tidying up the cell, "and we have done one another just about as much harm as possible. He's come here at the time of my death to give me the last blow."

The old man's harsh reproaches began as soon as they were alone.

Julien couldn't hold back his tears. "What a shameful weakness!" he told himself in a rage. "Everywhere he goes he'll exaggerate my want of courage; what a triumph for the Valenods and all those shabby hypocrites who rule over Verrières. They are mighty big in France; they enjoy all the social advantages. Up to now I could at least tell myself: 'They get the money, it's true, and all the honors are heaped on them, but I, I have nobility of heart.'

"But here is a witness everyone will believe, and one who will assure the whole town of Verrières, exaggerating all the while, that I was weak in the face of death. I will be made out to have been cowardly in the face of an ordeal that anyone can understand!"

Julien was close to despair. He didn't know how to get rid of his father. And to sham in such a way as to deceive the shrewd old man was, for the moment, altogether beyond his powers.

His mind was running swiftly over all the possibilities.

"*I've saved up money!*" he cried out suddenly.

This inspired remark transformed both the old man's countenance and Julien's position.

"What shall I do with it?" Julien went on more calmly. The effect he had produced took away all his feeling of inferiority.

The old carpenter was burning with a desire not to let this money, part of which, it appeared, Julien meant to leave to his brothers, get away from him. He spoke for a long time and vehemently. Julien chose to be facetious.

"Very well! since the Lord has inspired me to make my will, I will leave a thousand francs to each of my brothers and the rest to you."

"Good, good," said the old man, "what's left is due me; but since God in his mercy has touched your heart, and if you mean to die like a good Christian, you ought to pay your debts. There's still the cost of your food and your education, which I advanced, and to which you haven't given a thought. . . ."

"That's a father's love for you!" Julien kept repeating, heartsick, when he was finally alone. Soon the jailer appeared.

"Sir, after the grandparents' visit I always bring my guests a bottle of champagne. It comes a little high, six francs a bottle, but it cheers the heart."

"Bring three glasses," Julien told him with childish eagerness, "and show in two of those prisoners I hear walking in the corridor."

The jailer led in two repeaters who were waiting to go back to the penitentiary. They were two gay scoundrels and really quite remarkable for their cunning, courage, and self-possession.

"If you give me twenty francs," one of them said to Julien, "I will tell you my life story, in detail. It's first-rate."

"Are you going to tell me a pack of lies?" said Julien.

"Not at all," he answered. "My friend here, who's jealous of my twenty francs, will peach on me if I don't tell the truth."

His story was abominable. It showed a brave heart with one abiding passion left, the love of money.

After they were gone, Julien was not the same man. All his anger against himself had vanished. His cruel suffering, envenomed by faintheartedness, to which he had been a prey since Mme. de Rênal's departure, had turned into melancholy.

"If I had been less the dupe of appearances, I would have seen that the drawing rooms of Paris are filled with respectable men like my father or clever rascals like these convicts. They're right; the men who frequent those drawing rooms never waken in the morning to that agonizing thought: 'How will I get my dinner?' They boast about their honesty! And, if called upon for jury duty, proudly convict the man who stole a silver fork and spoon because he was faint with hunger. But where there's a court, and once it's a question of losing or winning a portfolio, my upright gentlemen from the drawing room will stoop to crimes that are identical with those which the necessity of dining inspired these two convicts to commit.

"There is no such thing as *natural rights*; that idea is a piece of time-honored nonsense well worthy of the prosecutor who went after me the other day and whose ancestor got rich on one of Louis XIV's confiscations. A *right* does not exist unless there is a law to forbid one's doing such and such a thing under penalty. Before there were laws nothing was *natural* except the lion's strength, or the need of the creature who was hungry, who was cold, in a word, *need*. . . . No, the men society honors are nothing but crooks lucky enough not to get caught red-handed. The prosecutor unleashed by society against me owes his wealth to a swindle. . . . I attempted murder, and I have been justly condemned, but with the exception of that one act, Valenod, who convicted me, is a hundred times more harmful to society.

"Well, then!" Julien went on sadly, but without anger, "in spite of his greed, my father is better than all those men. He never loved me. And I have just filled his cup to overflowing by shaming him with a dishonorable death. That dread of wanting for money, that exaggerated view of man's wickedness which is called *avarice*, makes him see a prodigious source of comfort and security in the sum of three or four hundred louis that I may leave him. Some

499

Sunday after dinner, he will show off his gold to all the envious in Verrières. 'At that price,' his look will say, 'who among you would not be delighted to have a son guillotined?' "

This philosophy might be true, but was such as to make a man wish for death. So passed five long days. He was courteous and gentle with Mathilde, who he could see was exasperated by the most intense jealousy. One night, Julien was thinking seriously of doing away with himself. His mind was unstrung by the deep depression into which Mme. de Rênal's departure had plunged him. Nothing gave him pleasure anymore, neither in real life or in his imagination. Want of exercise was beginning to tell on his health and to give him the weak, excitable character of a young German student. He was losing that male arrogance which, with an energetic oath, repulses certain indecent thoughts by which the minds of the unhappy are assailed.

"I have loved truth. Where is it? Hypocrisy is everywhere, or at least charlatanism, even in the most virtuous, even in the greatest men"—and his lips took on an expression of disgust—"no, man cannot trust in man.

"While she was taking up a collection for her poor orphans, Mme. de —————— told me that such and such a prince had just given ten louis: a lie. But what am I saying? Napoleon at Ste. Hélène! . . . His proclamation in favor of the King of Rome,* pure charlatanism.

"Great God! if such a man, and what's more at a time when misfortune ought to have reminded him sternly of his duty, can lower himself to charlatanism, what can you expect from the rest of the species? . . .

"Where lies truth? In religion. . . . Yes," he added with a bitter smile of the most utter contempt, "in the mouths of the Maslons, the de Frilairs, the Castanèdes. . . . Perhaps in true Christianity, where the priests would not be paid, any more than the apostles were? . . . But Saint Paul was paid with the pleasure of commanding, of speaking, of being talked about. . . .

"Ah! if only there were a true religion! . . . Fool that I am! I see a Gothic cathedral, venerable windows, and my feeble heart conjures up the priest in those windows. . . . My soul would understand him, my soul needs him. . . . But all I ever find is a conceited ass with dirty hair . . . another Chevalier de Beauvoisis, excepting the good manners.

"But a true priest, a Massillon, a Fénelon—Massillon consecrated Dubois. The *Mémoires de Saint Simon* have

spoiled Fénelon for me; but, in short, a true priest. . . .
Then all loving souls would have a rallying point in the
world. . . . We would not be isolated. . . . That good priest
would talk to us about God. But what God? Not the one
in the Bible, a cruel little despot thirsty for vengeance . . .
but the God of Voltaire, just, good, infinite. . . ."

He was shaken by his memories of that Bible which he
knew by heart. . . . "But how could anyone, *where two or
three are gathered together*, believe in the great name
God, seeing the frightful abuse our priests make of it?

"To live in isolation! . . . What torment!

"I'm losing my mind, and being unjust," Julien said to
himself, striking his forehead. "I am isolated here in this
dungeon; but I didn't *live in isolation* on the earth; I held
to the powerful idea of *duty*. The duty I prescribed for
myself, whether wrongly or rightly, has been like the
trunk of a stout tree which I could cling to during the
storm. I wavered, I was shaken—after all, I am only a
man—but I was not swept away.

"It's the damp air in this dungeon that makes me think
about isolation.

"But why be hypocritical while I'm damning hypocrisy?
It isn't death, nor the dungeon, nor the damp air; it's
Mme. de Rênal's absence that is getting me down. If, to
see her in Verrières, I was forced to live for weeks on
end hidden in the cellar of her house, would I complain?

"The influence of my contemporaries has won out," he
said aloud with a bitter laugh. "Even when I am talking to
myself alone, and two steps from death, I am still hypocritical. . . . O nineteenth century!

". . . a hunter fires his rifle in a forest, his prey falls, he
rushes to seize it. His boot runs into an anthill two feet
high, destroys the ants' habitation, scatters the ants and
their eggs far and wide. . . . The most philosophical among
those ants will never be able to comprehend that huge
black appalling body: the hunter's boot, which has pene-
trated their abode with incredible speed, and which was
preceded by a dreadful noise accompanied by a sheaf of
reddish fire. . . .

"So life, death, eternity, are simple matters for anyone
who has faculties huge enough to comprehend them. . . .

"A dayfly is born at nine in the morning, during the
long summer days, to die at five in the evening; how could
it understand the word 'night'?

"Give it five hours more; it will see and understand
what night is.

"Likewise, I shall die at twenty-three. Give me five more years of life, to live with Mme. de Rênal."

And he set to laughing like Mephistopheles. "What madness to go on discussing these great questions!

"One. I am as hypocritical as if there were someone here to listen to me.

"Two. I am forgetting to live and to love, when I have so few days left to live. . . . Alas! Mme. de Rênal is absent; perhaps her husband will not let her come back to Besançon and go on disgracing herself.

"That is what isolates me, and not the absence of a just, good, omnipotent God, who is not wicked and thirsty for vengeance.

"Ah! if only He existed. . . . Alas! I would fall at his feet. I deserved to die, I would tell him; but, great God, good God, long-suffering God, give me back the one I love!"

The night was far advanced. After Julien had had an hour or two of peaceful sleep, Fouqué arrived.

Julien felt strong and resolute, like a man who sees clearly into his soul.

Chapter XLV

"I won't play poor Father Chas-Bernard the dirty trick of sending for him," he said to Fouqué. "He wouldn't be able to eat for three days. But try to find me a Jansenist, some friend of M. Pirard, who is above intrigue."

Fouqué had been waiting impatiently for this opening. Julien acquitted himself decently of all that is owing to public opinion in the provinces. Thanks to the Abbé de Frilair, and despite his poor choice of a confessor, Julien in his cell was the protégé of the *Congrégation;* if he had been more politic, he might have managed his escape. But the bad air in the cell was having its effect; his reasoning power was falling off. Yet this made him all the happier about Mme. de Rênal's return.

"My first duty is to you," she said, kissing him. "I ran away from Verrières. . . ."

Julien had no false pride where she was concerned; he told her all about his moments of weakness. She was kind and charming.

No sooner had she left the prison that evening than she sent for the priest who had fastened himself to Julien as to a prey, to come to her aunt's house; since all he wanted was to get himself accredited among the young women in Besançon's high society, Mme. de Rênal had no trouble persuading him to go and make a novena at the Abbey of Bray-le-Haut.

Words cannot describe the madness and extravagance of Julien's love.

By dint of gold and by using and abusing the influence of her aunt, a rich woman well-known for her piety, Mme. de Rênal got permission to see him twice a day.

Hearing of this excited Mathilde's jealousy to the point of frenzy. M. de Frilair had admitted to her that for all his influence he could not flout convention so far as to obtain permission for her to visit her friend more than once daily. Mathilde had Mme. de Rênal followed in order to know every move she made.

M. de Frilair exhausted all the resources of a very astute mind trying to prove that Julien was unworthy of her. Amidst all these torments, she loved him but the more and made a horrible scene almost every day.

Julien wished with all his might to behave honorably, right to the end, toward this poor girl whom he had compromised so strangely; but his unbridled love for Mme. de Rênal would win out every time. When by means of unconvincing arguments he was not able to persuade Mathilde that her rival's visits were innocent, he told himself: "The end of the play must be very near; that's an excuse for not being able to hide my feelings any better."

Mlle. de La Mole learned of the Marquis de Croisenois' death. M. de Thaler, that very rich man, had taken the liberty of making some unpleasant remarks about Mathilde's disappearance; M. de Croisenois went to his house to persuade him to retract them. M. de Thaler showed him anonymous letters, addressed to himself and filled with details arranged in such a way that it was impossible for the marquis not to have an inkling of the truth.

M. de Thaler went so far as to make a number of indelicate jokes. Drunk with rage and despair, M. de Croisenois exacted reparations so heavy that the millionaire preferred a duel. Stupidity triumphed; and one of the men in Paris most worthy of being loved met his death at less than twenty-four years of age.

This death made a strange and sickly impression on Julien's weakened spirit. "Poor Croisenois," he said to Mathilde, "was really quite a reasonable man and behaved very decently toward us; he must have hated me that time you behaved so recklessly in your mother's drawing room and had every right to pick a quarrel with me; for the hatred that follows upon a woman's scorn is usually furious. . . ."

M. de Croisenois' death altered all of Julien's plans for Mathilde's future; he spent several days proving to her that she ought to accept M. de Luz's hand. "He's a timid, not overly Jesuitic man," he kept telling her, "who will, no doubt, present himself as a candidate. More sullenly ambitious and steadier than poor Croisenois, and with no dukedom in his family, he won't scruple to marry Julien Sorel's widow."

"A widow who despises the grand passion," replied Mathilde coldly, "for she has lived to see her lover prefer another woman to her after only six months ... and a woman who is the cause of all their misery."

"You are unfair; Mme. de Rênal's visits will provide the lawyer in Paris who's handling my appeal for mercy with an unusual angle: he will picture the murderer as honored by the kind attentions of his victim. That might have a good effect, and one day you may see me as the hero in some melodrama," etc., etc.

A raging jealousy impossible to avenge, unremittent and hopeless misery (for, even supposing Julien was saved, how was she to win back his heart?), and the shame and pain of loving this unfaithful man more than ever had plunged Mlle. de La Mole into a dejected silence; nor could M. de Frilair's eager attention, any more than Fouqué's rough frankness, avail to bring her out of it.

As for Julien, excepting those moments usurped by Mathilde's presence, he lived on love and gave scarce a thought to the future. By a strange effect of that passion, when it is very great and nothing feigned, Mme. de Rênal all but shared his jauntiness and gentle gaiety.

"In the old days," Julien said to her, "when I might have been so happy during our walks in the wood at Vergy, a wild ambition would drag my soul off to imaginary countries. Instead of pressing this lovely arm against my heart, when it lay so close to my lips, I would let the future steal me away from you; I was too busy with the countless battles I would have to wage in order to build a colossal fortune. ... Yes, I might have died without knowing what happiness is had you not come to see me in this prison."

Two incidents came to trouble this quiet life. Julien's confessor, albeit a thoroughgoing Jansenist, was not proof against one of the Jesuits' schemes, and unwittingly became their tool.

He came to tell Julien one day that lest he fall into the dreadful sin of suicide, he should do everything possible to win a pardon. Now, since the clergy had a great deal of influence at the Ministry of Justice in Paris, an easy way offered itself: he should have a spectacular conversion. ...

"Spectacular!" repeated Julien. "Ah! I've caught you at it too, father, playing the game like a missionary. ..."

"Your age," the Jansenist went on gravely, "the appealing face with which Providence has favored you, even the motive of your crime, which remains inexplicable, the heroic efforts Mlle. de La Mole has lavished on your cause ... in a word, everything, including the amazing

505

friendship your victim has shown you, has contributed to make you the hero of Besançon's young women. They have neglected everything for you, even politics. . . .

"Your conversion would resound in their hearts and leave a deep impression. You have it in your power to render a major service to religion. And I, should I hesitate for the frivolous reason that the Jesuits would follow the same path on a like occasion? If I did, then, even through this particular case, which has escaped their rapacity, they would still be doing harm. Let it not be so. . . . The tears your conversion will cause to flow will wipe out the corrosive effect of ten editions of Voltaire's godless works."

"And what shall I have left," Julien answered coldly, "if I despise myself? I used to be ambitious, I don't blame myself for that; I acted then according to the standards of the time. Now I just live from day to day. But, generally speaking, I know I'd be thoroughly miserable if I lent myself to some piece of cowardice."

The other incident, which was painful to Julien in quite a different way, was created by Mme. de Rênal. I don't know which scheming lady friend had succeeded in convincing that very timid, naïve soul that it was her duty to go to Saint-Cloud and throw herself at King Charles X's feet.*

In her imagination, she had already made the sacrifice of parting from Julien, and after such an effort, the unpleasantness of making a spectacle of herself, which at any other time would have seemed worse than death, was as nothing in her eyes.

"I will go to the king, I will admit openly that you are my lover; the life of a man and of a man like Julien ought to prevail over every other consideration. I will say it was out of jealousy that you made an attempt on my life. There are many examples of poor young people who have been saved in similar cases by the humanity of the jury, or that of the king—"

"I will stop seeing you, I will have my door closed to you, and I will surely kill myself the next day, out of despair, unless you swear not to take any step that will make a public spectacle of both of us. This idea of going to Paris isn't yours. Tell me the name of the scheming woman who suggested it. . . .

"Let us be happy during the few days of this short life. Let us hide our existence; my crime is only too obvious. Mlle. de La Mole has all kinds of influence in Paris; believe me, she is doing everything humanly possible. Here in this province, I have all the rich and influential citizens against me. Your gesture would sour even more those wealthy and, above all, conservative men, for whom life is so easy. . . . Let us not make laughingstocks of ourselves for the Maslons, the Valenods, and a thousand better men."

The bad air of the dungeon was becoming unbearable to Julien. Luckily, on the day it was announced to him that he must die, a brilliant sun gladdened all nature, and Julien was in a brave mood. For him, to walk in the open air was a delightful sensation, like a stroll ashore for the voyager who has been at sea for a long time. "Come now, everything is going fine," he told himself, "I don't feel the slightest want of courage."

Never had that head been more poetical than at the moment it was about to fall. The sweetest times he had known in the woods at Vergy came crowding back into his mind, and with an extreme vividness.

Everything went smoothly, decently, and without the least affectation on Julien's part.

Two days before, he had said to Fouqué: "What state I'll be in, I can't say; this dungeon, so damp, so ugly, gives me such bouts of fever that sometimes I don't know where I am; but as for fear, no; they won't see me turn pale."

He had made arrangements in advance so that on the morning of the last day, Fouqué would carry off Mathilde and Mme. de Rênal. "Take them away in the same carriage," he had told him. "See to it that the post horses keep moving at a gallop. Either they will fall into one another's arms or show a deadly hatred for one another. In either case, those poor women will be somewhat distracted from their terrible grief."

Julien had exacted from Mme. de Rênal an oath that she would live to care for Mathilde's son.

"Who knows? Perhaps we still have sensations after death," he said to Fouqué one day. "I should rather like to rest, since rest is the word, in that small cave on the tall mountain that looks down on Verrières. Many's the time—I've told you about it—when I had withdrawn at night into that cave, and was looking out over the richest provinces of France in the distance, that ambition would fire my heart. In those days it was my only passion. . . . In short, that cave is dear to me, and there's no denying that the way it is situated is enough to make a philosopher envious. . . . Very well! those good Congreganists of Besançon will do anything for money; if you go about it

507

the right way, they will sell you my mortal remains. . . ."

Fouqué succeeded in this mournful transaction. He was spending the night alone in his room with his friend's body when, to his great surprise, he saw Mathilde enter. A few hours earlier he had left her ten leagues out of Besançon. Her look and her eyes were wild.

"I want to see him," she said.

Fouqué hadn't the heart to speak or to rise. He pointed to a big blue cloak on the floor; what remained of Julien was wrapped up in it.

She dropped to her knees. The memory of Boniface de La Mole and Marguerite de Navarre gave her, no doubt, a superhuman courage. Her trembling hands undid the cloak. Fouqué turned his head.

He heard Mathilde walk hurriedly about the room. She lit several candles. By the time Fouqué had the strength to look at her, she had set Julien's head on a little marble table and was kissing it on the brow.

Mathilde followed her lover to the tomb he had chosen for himself. A great number of priests escorted the coffin, and unbeknownst to everyone, alone in her carriage draped with black, she bore on her lap the head of the man she had loved so dearly.

Having thus arrived at a spot near the peak of one of the tall mountains in the Jura range in the middle of the night, twenty priests said a mass for the dead in the small cave, magnificently illuminated by countless tapers. All the inhabitants of the small mountain villages through which the procession passed had followed it, attracted by the strangeness of this ceremony.

Mathilde appeared in their midst in a long mourning dress, and at the end of the service had several thousand five-franc pieces thrown to them.

Having stayed behind with Fouqué, she insisted on burying her lover's head with her own hands. Fouqué nearly went mad with grief over this.

Through Mathilde's good offices, the rough cave was ornamented at great expense with marbles carved in Italy.

Mme. de Rênal kept her promise. She made no attempt whatsoever on her life; but three days after Julien, she died while embracing her children.

* * *

The bad thing about the reign of public opinion, which, it must be added, procures *liberty*, is that it meddles with

508

that which is none of its business: for instance, private life. Hence, America's and England's gloominess. To avoid infringing upon any private life, the author has invented a small town, Verrières, and when he needed a bishop, a jury, an assize court, he situated them all in Besançon, where he has never been.

Notes

(The numbers in parentheses refer to pages.)

BOOK ONE

(13) *Verrières:* Several towns in France bear this name, but Stendhal's description does not fit any of them. It seems rather a composite of his birthplace, Grenoble, which he hated, and some of the towns near it.

Franche-Comté: A province in eastern France on the Swiss border.

Doubs: Chief river of Franche-Comté.

Verra's jagged peaks: An imaginary mountain chain.

(14) *1815:* The year of Waterloo, Napoleon's banishment to Ste. Hélène, and the restoration of the monarchy.

(18) *Saint-Germain-en-Laye:* A town near Paris famed for its terrace designed by Le Nôtre, Louis XIV's great gardener.

Italy: In Napoleon's Italian campaign, 1796.

Jacobin: Most extreme of the revolutionary parties, it was responsible for the Reign of Terror.

(19) *Château:* Familiar way of referring to Charles X's residence and court at St. Cloud.

M. Appert: Benjamin Appert, well-known philanthropist and prison reformer.

keeps us from doing good: Historical fact. (Stendhal's note.)

(22) *Buonaparte's campaigns:* The legitimists insisted on the Italian pronunciation to imply that Napoleon was a foreigner, hence a usurper.

(24) *Palais-Royal:* The names above evoke the frivolous and elegant life-style of the *Ancien Régime*.

(25) *Machiavelli:* "And am I to blame if that's the way things are?"

Abbé: Every priest is an abbé, but not every abbé is a priest, the chief difference being that the priest is ordained and has certain privileges not extended to the abbé, such as saying mass, hearing confession, etc. As used by Stendhal, the term is honorific and applied to any ecclesiastic below the rank of bishop.

(27) *Mémorial de Sainte-Hélène:* First edition, 1823. It is a record of Napoleon's conversations with Las Cases, who shared his exile for eighteen months.

(29) *Ennius:* Roman poet (239–169 B.C.). "By delaying, he saved the day."

(30) *M. de Maistre:* Published in 1819 and profoundly reactionary, *Du Pape* is an apology for papal absolutism.

(31) *thirty-six francs:* That is, six crowns worth six francs apiece.

(33) *Congrégation:* A religious organization that included all of the social classes and had a good deal of political influence, since it was favored by the government and numbered several powerful Royalists in its ranks.

Constitutional: The liberal newspaper of the middle class. Anti-Bourbon and anticlerical, it was read by old soldiers, students, and shopkeepers. Its watchword was "Revolution."

Mme. de Beauharnais: Josephine, Napoleon's first wife.

(36) *Figaro:* "I no longer know what I am,/ What I'm doing." *The Marriage of Figaro,* I, 5.

(46) *Gymnase:* A theater in Paris built in 1820.

(49) *The Daily:* A Royalist and reactionary newspaper.

(57) *Vergy:* A town near Dijon in Burgundy. Gabriella is the heroine of a thirteenth-century metrical romance, *Châtelaine de Vergy.* In the eighteenth century dramatization of the legend by Du Belloy, *Gabrielle de Vergy,* the heroine is forced by her jealous husband to eat her lover's heart. Stendhal seems to have Du Belloy's version in mind when he alludes to the legend on page 136.

(61) *Strombeck:* The reference is to Pierre Guérin's painting, "Aeneas Relating to Dido the Disasters of Troy," which hangs in the Louvre.

(63) *Charles the Bold:* Duke of Burgundy (1433–1477).

(93) *Blason d'Amour:* Love in Latin is *amor;*

And so from love comes death,
But, before that, care that gnaws,
Grief, tears, traps, crimes, remorse.

(105) *battle of Fontenoy:* An important French victory on May 11, 1745, over the English allied with the Austrians.

(109) *Jansenist:* Member of a rigorous seventeenth-century Catholic sect that had more in common with Calvinism than with Roman Catholicism. Though the movement was all but spent by the nineteenth century, Stendhal associates his good priests (Pirard, Chélan) with it and his bad priests (Frilair, Castanède) with Jesuitism.

(111) *Leipzig and Montmirail:* Locales of two of Napoleon's victories against the sixth coalition.

(116) *blazing chapel: Chapelle ardente,* a mortuary chapel lighted by numerous candles.

(118) *Philip the Good, Duke of Burgundy:* (1396–1467). Father of Charles the Bold.

(119) *'93:* Year of the Reign of Terror.

(148) *Mission:* Refers to the Society of Missions, a Jesuit organization that by 1822 had the full support of the ultra-conservative government. Its aim was to revive the faith throughout France, and its methods were often dramatic (sermons in cemeteries, processions, setting up crosses, etc.). When a Mission came to town, the Liberals would sometimes counter it with a production of *Tartuffe.*

(149) *A fable about Master Jean Chouart:* "The Curé and the Corpse."

(155) *Casti:* "The pleasure of holding one's head high all year is dearly paid for by certain quarters of an hour one must live through."

(156) *fie:* "Woman is often fickle,/ Mad is he who trusts her."

(158) *M. Nonantecinq:* Name applied derisively to a judge in Marseille who in 1830 condemned a Liberal pamphleteer. During the trial, the judge used the regional term *nonantecinq* for the number ninety-five instead of the standard *quatre-vingt-quinze.*

(160) *credete a me:* Believe me.

(161) *the auction:* M. de Rênal has compromised himself by participating, under pressure, in a fake auction, staged to give an air of legality to the leasing of communal

513

property to a political favorite at an outrageously low price.

(169) *Bisontium:* Latin for Besançon.

(171) *Nouvelle Héloise: Julie ou la Nouvelle Héloise,* romantic novel by Jean-Jacques Rousseau, published in 1761.

(174) *The Valenod of Besançon:* This epigraph implies that every workhouse has an unscrupulous Valenod at its head.

(177) *Intelligenti pauca:* A word to the wise.

Bossuet, Arnault, Fleury: Theologians of the seventeenth century. All three were Gallicans; the last two, Jansenists.

Vale et me ama: Farewell and love me.

(179) *Unam Ecclesiam:* This bull is Stendhal's invention.

(187) *paintings:* See, in the Louvre, Francis, Duke of Aquitaine, laying aside his armor and putting on a monk's habit, No. 1130. (Stendhal's note.)

(196) *Incedo per ignes:* "I walk through fire," Horace, *Odes,* II, i. 7.

(197) *optime:* Excellent.

(199) *Barême:* Seventeenth-century mathematician and author of a book on accounting.

(205) *him!:* This line is taken from Brenellerie's *Eloge de Voltaire* and refers to Henry IV, not to Napoleon.

(211) *"La Madeleine":* By Delphine Gay (1804–1855).

(215) *Marie Alacoque:* Saint and mystic (1647–1690) who did much to spread the cult of devotion to the Sacred Heart of Jesus. This order was vigorously opposed by the Jansenists.

BOOK TWO

(235) *Virgil:* "O countryside, when shall I see you again!" This quotation is not from Virgil but from Horace, *Satires,* II, iv, 60.

(236) *still: Phèdre,* I, 3.

St. Joseph's, The Blessed Virgin's: Religious associations directed by the *Congrégation.*

(237) *Roule quarter:* Now in the eighth *arrondissement* of Paris.

(239) *Arcole, Ste. Hélène, Malmaison:* One of Napoleon's significant victories (November 17, 1796); the island to which Napoleon was exiled after Waterloo; the house where he lived with Josephine when he was First Consul.

(241) *Spanish war:* In 1823, a French expeditionary force defeated the Spanish liberals and restored Ferdinand VII to the throne.

Place de Grève: Now the Place de l'Hôtel de Ville.

the twenty-sixth of April, 1574: The abbé is alluding to the decapitation of Boniface de La Mole, which occurred on April 30, 1574. Stendhal gives the correct date on p. 303 and after.

Moreri: Biographer (1643–1680), who wrote a *Grand Dictionnaire Historique.*

(243) *Dubois:* Cardinal Guillaume Dubois (1656–1723). Born a druggist's son, he rose to become cardinal and prime minister. Perhaps his anti-Jansenism explains the Abbé Pirard's disapproval of him.

(244) *Faubourg Saint-Germain:* The aristocratic quarter of Paris since the time of Louis XV.

(247) *grave:* Marshal Ney (1769–1851). A victim of ultra-Royalist reaction, he was executed for having rejoined Napoleon during the Hundred Days.

(248) *cella:* Stendhal made the same error, as a clerk at the Ministry of War, a job his cousin Pierre Daru found for him when he first came to Paris at eighteen.

(255) *Place Louis XVI:* Now Place de la Concorde.

(258) *Béranger:* Bonapartist and anti-Royalist (1780–1857). He was imprisoned twice for his satirical verse.

(264) *Basilio:* Not in Beaumarchais' *The Barber of Seville.* This speech is probably Stendhal's invention.

(265) *M. Comte:* A famous sleight-of-hand artist.

poet: Béranger, sentenced December, 1828, to nine months in prison and fined ten thousand francs.

(266) *Lord Holland:* An English liberal (1772–1840), who had protested against Napoleon's exile to Ste. Hélène.

King of England: William IV (1830–1837).

Count de Thaler: Stendhal has the Baron de Rothschild in mind.

(272) *M. C. de Beauvoisis:* It is never made clear whether this really is Mme. de Rênal's cousin, whose name is spelled "Beauvaisis" when he is first mentioned on p. 158.

(276) *Comte Ory:* An opera by Rossini.

(277) *Hyères:* A town on the southern coast of France.

(278) *Rivarol:* (1753–1801). Famous for his caustic maxims and witty conversation.

(279) *Marquis de Moncade:* A character in *L'école des Bourgeois* (1728), a comedy by L. Soulas d'Allainval.

(281) *Sir Hudson Lowe:* Napoleon's custodian during his exile on Ste. Hélène. His treatment of Napoleon has been criticized generally as excessively restrictive.

Lord Bathurst: Henry, 3rd earl (1762–1834). Secretary for War and the Colonies during Napoleon's exile. Lowe was under his orders.

Philip Vane: A fictitious name.

(289) *Paris:* Rousseau describes this incident in *Les Confessions* (Book X).

King Feretrius: The academician translated Jupiter Feretrius ("he who strikes,") as "Jupiter and King Feretrius." See Stendhal, *Promenades dans Rome,* "*Jupiter et le roi Feretrius.*"

(292) *them:* This page, written on July 25, 1830, was printed on August 4th. (Stendhal's note.) On July 25, 1830, Charles X signed four unconstitutional decrees that provoked the revolution that forced his abdication.

(293) *Mme. de Staël:* Writer (1766–1817), best known as a theorist of romanticism. She had many lovers in her lifetime.

(295) *Danton:* (1759–1794). A leader of the French Revolution.

(297) *else:* It is a malcontent who is speaking. (This "Note," which Stendhal ascribes to Molière's *Tartuffe,* is, of course, his own.)

(298) *Girondist:* A member of a moderate political party during the French Revolution that took its name from Gironde, the department from which its leaders came.

(299) *Courier:* Paul-Louis (1772–1825), political writer and friend of Stendhal. The king's attorney had labeled him "cynic."

516

Murats: Refers to Joachim Murat (1767–1815), one of Napoleon's marshals. Of him Napoleon said, "The bravest of men in the face of the enemy, incomparable on the battlefield, but a fool in his actions everywhere else."

(300) *Pichegru:* Charles (1761–1804), a heroic French general of the revolutionary army who went over to the Bourbons in 1795.

(303) *Hernani:* A romantic play by Victor Hugo (presented February 25, 1830), which caused a violent antagonism between classicists and romanticists.

lettres de cachet: Letters under the king's seal ordering imprisonment without trial.

Talma: (1763–1826). Napoleon's favorite actor and the greatest tragedian of his day.

Abbé Delille's poetry: Jacques Delille (1738–1813). Enormously popular during his lifetime, his nature poetry was thoroughly discredited after his death by Rivarol and Ste. Beuve among others.

(304) *headsman:* This part of Stendhal's account is based on historical fact. Joseph de Boniface seigneur de La Mole and Annibal Coconasso were executed on the Place de Grève on April 30, 1574, for trying to liberate Henry of Navarre and the Duke d'Alençon. The rest of the account derives from legend.

August twenty-fourth, 1572: Date of the Saint Bartholomew's Day Massacre. Instigated by Marie de' Medici, it began in Paris and resulted in the death of three thousand Hugenots.

(306) *Brantôme, d'Aubigné, l'Étoile:* All three were historians and chroniclers of the sixteenth century.

League: The League was a sixteenth-century organization of Catholic nobles whose aim was to keep France from becoming Protestant. Henry IV's conversion to Catholicism marks the end of the wars it waged against the monarchy.

(311) *Wagram:* Place of Napoleon's great victory (July 6, 1809) over the Austrians.

(312) *Abbé Maury:* Jean Siffrey Maury (1746–1817), a cobbler's son who became a cardinal.

Bassompierre: A knight (1579–1646), who was made marshal of France by Henry IV and later imprisoned for conspiracy by Richelieu. He wrote his famous *Mémoires* in prison.

(315) *shadow:* La Fontaine, *Fables,* "The Shepherd and his Flock."

(318) *Coblentz:* German city on the Rhine to which the *émigrés* fled and from which they launched an invasion of France.

(322) *Languedoc:* A province in southern France.

(323) *Léontine Fay:* A famous actress of the day.

(324) *folding stool:* The rank of duchess conferred the privilege of sitting on a stool (*tabouret*) in the king's or queen's presence on certain occasions.

(326) *Granvelle:* Antoine Perrenot de Granvelle (1517-1586). Born at Ornans and by no means poor, he was made cardinal and eventually succeeded his father as minister to the Emperor Charles V and later served Philip II of Spain in the same capacity.

lie: Tartuffe, IV, 5.

Magalon: Fontan and Magalon were sent to prison by Charles X's Government for satirizing it in their periodical *The Album.*

(327) *Esprit per. pré. gui. II.A.30:* (Note by Stendhal.) Deciphered by M. Maurice Parturier ("L'aventure Mary-Grasset et le Rouge et le Noir," *Bulletin du Bibliophile,* 20 mai 1932), the note reads: "Esprit perd préfecture Guizot 11 aout, 1830." Stendhal here alludes to the government's refusal to give him the prefecture he had asked for after the July revolution. He blames the minister Guizot's mistrust of men of wit.

(329) *Jarnac, Moncontour:* Both battles occurred in 1569 and were victories for the Catholic forces, led by Henry III, over the Protestants.

Algiers: Taken by the French in 1830.

(330) *Baylen:* (July 22, 1808). The defeated general admitted in writing that his army had stolen some sacred vases.

(335) *Don Diego:* Corneille, *Le Cid,* III, 6.

(336) *Abelard's fate:* Abelard was castrated by the Canon Fulbert, Héloïse's uncle.

(338) *futura:* "Pale with her coming death," Virgil, *Aeneid,* IV, 644.

(356) *Roland:* during the Revolution, Mme. Roland directed her husband's career so skillfully that he was twice made

Minister of the Interior. When she was guillotined, he committed suicide.

(358) *Cimarosa:* Italian composer (1749–1801), much admired by Stendhal.

amai, etc.: "I should punish myself, punish myself/ If I have loved too much," etc.

(380) *bowl:* La Fontaine, *Fables*, "The Sculptor and the Statue of Jupiter."

(381) *Cathelineau:* The Catholic and Royalist peasant leader (1759–1793) of the Vendean insurrection against the revolutionary government.

(382) *Gustavus Adolphus:* Swedish king (1594–1652), who led his army into Germany in support of the Protestant princes during the Thirty Years' War.

Duke of ———: The Duke of Wellington, in charge of the army of occupation at the beginning of the Restoration.

(383) *Saints:* Nonconformist, liberal Whigs.

Brougham: Liberal politician and reformer (1778–1868), warmly admired by Stendhal.

(384) *verse:* Probably an allusion to Béranger's anti-Royalist and anticlerical songs.

(398) *Carbonaro:* One of the Carbonari, a revolutionary organization that was first anti-Napoleon, then anti-Bourbon.

Marotte, etc.: I've fallen into the folly (*marotte*)
Of being in love with Marotte.

cabaret: "One day the lover in the cabaret . . ."

(402) *Camarilla:* A clique of those closest to Charles X and sympathetic to his desire for absolute power.

(405) *Saint-Simon:* The chronicler of the court of Louis XIV.

(407) *Massillon's gentle virtue:* (1663–1742). Bishop of Clermont, he was noted for his gentle yet effective sermons.

(408) *Treaty of Münster:* Signed at the end of the Thirty Years' War (1648).

(410) *Dorat's light touch:* Allusion to Claude Dorat (1734–1780). His writing is notable for its facility, affection, and elegant frivolity.

(412) *Manon Lescaut:* Produced May 3, 1830. The libretto for the ballet was written by Scribe, the music by Halévy.

(416) *Maréchale:* The wife of a *maréchal* or marshal of France.

(423) *Matrimonio Segreto:* Cimarosa's masterpiece.

(425) *si fata sinant:* If the fates are willing.

(441) *Othello:* A paraphrase of Desdemona's speech (I, 3.):

> "That I did love the Moor to live with him,
> My downright violence and storms of fortunes
> May trumpet to the world."

(443) *Louis XI:* (1423–1483). Called "the spider," he was famous for his wiliness in political affairs and his cruelty toward his enemies.

(453) *M. Noiraud:* This character was introduced as "M. Noiroud" on p. 21.

(454) *word: Othello,* V, 2.

(461) *M. de Lavalette's escape:* Victim of the White Terror, Lavalette was condemned to death for having joined Napoleon during the hundred days. He escaped from prison by disguising himself in his wife's clothes.

René: A novel by Chateaubriand, published in 1805. It might be called the French *Werther.*

(470) *Journey Through France:* From Peter King, *Life of John Locke, with extracts from his Correspondence, Journals and Commonplace Books.* 1676.

(473) *Fronde:* A civil war (1648–1653) waged by the aristocracy during the minority of Louis XIV against the queen, Anne of Austria, and her minister, Mazarin.

(488) *humans:* Voltaire, *Mahomet,* II, 5.

(489) *up:* A Jacobin is talking. (Stendhal's note.)

(490) *Manuel's side:* Allusion to Jacques-Antoine Manuel. Famous as a Liberal deputy, he was expelled from the Chamber in 1823 for his opposition to the Spanish expedition and restoration of Ferdinand VII.

(491) *Belphegor's lines:* Allusion to "Belphegor," a story by La Fontaine.

(500) *King of Rome:* Title conferred on Napoleon's son (1811–1832) at birth.

(506) *King Charles X's feet:* The action of the novel takes place during his reign (1824–1830), which ended in revolution.

AFTERWORD

Not the least surprising thing about *The Red and the Black* is that its author wrote it and had it published in 1830. Henri Beyle, whom we know better by his pseudonym Stendhal, was forty-seven years old. Though fond of writing from his early teens, he had set his heart on being a poet or a comic dramatist; his previous books dealt mainly with musicians and travel; his one earlier novel, *Armance* (1827), was deservedly a failure. He never regarded himself as a professional man of letters; love, he wrote, was the one great affair of his life. The novel was in rather poor health and low repute in 1830, and Stendhal, who declares that "this novel is not one," defines it in his subtitle as a "chronicle."

Moreover, 1830 is the year when Romanticism triumphed in France, with major achievements by Berlioz, Delacroix, and Victor Hugo at the "battle of *Hernani*," his first great dramatic success. Stendhal, though he praised the relevance of Romanticism in *Racine and Shakspeare*, loathed the inflamed rhetoric of the Romantics and claimed to model his style, especially in *The Red and the Black*, on the dry clarity of the Napoleonic Code. Probably his greatest contribution to the development of the novel was his rigorous psychological realism. Despite Goethe and Balzac, *The Red and the Black* attracted relatively little notice in its day, and Stendhal combined wishful thinking with foresight when he appealed to the judgment of his readers of 1880, 1900, or 1935.

Stendhal himself was a man of many contrasts and paradoxes. In a life devoted to the pursuit of happiness through love affairs, he more than once missed happiness by his concern for conquest. Holding a military view of sexual encounters as victories or defeats for the aggressive male, he planned his campaigns with calculating care—only to show himself often, when the chips were down, a trembling or occasionally impotent lover, a Werther masquerading as a Don Juan, a sheep in wolf's clothing. In his writings he combines his *espagnolisme,* or Spanish passion for glory, with the cold logic that he owes to his eighteenth-century roots and particularly to the "ideologues" Cabanis and Destutt de Tracy, and with an ironic view of human folly that shows not only in his comments but also in his swift dry style. One critic has called him "the least a poet, and the most poetic, of men." Finally, although disdainful of the meretricious vices he found in most novels, he was at the same time extremely diffident about the merits of his own.

Henri Beyle was born to Chérubin and Henriette (Gagnon) Beyle, a well-to-do bourgeois couple, in Grenoble on January 23, 1783. His father was a lawyer who liked to dabble in real estate and agricultural experiments. He loved and adored his mother, who died when he was only seven; his father he abhorred, often writing of him as "the bastard." Among others he liked were his mother's father and aunt; others he hated were his aunt Séraphie, who had charge of his early upbringing, and a later private tutor, the Jesuit Abbé Raillane, a main source of his lifelong anticlericalism. He so loathed the conservatives who ruled his young life that he rejoiced in the execution of Louis XVI as he did in the death of his aunt Séraphie. Self-willed and rebellious, he was, even by his own account, no model child; but his was a miserable childhood.

His fifty-nine-year life spanned the French Revolution, the Napoleonic Wars, the Directory, the Consulate, the Empire, the Hundred Days, the Bourbon Restoration, the July Revoluton (1830), and a dozen years of the Monarchy of July. He hated the money-motivated bourgeois class into which he was born and found himself an aristocrat in taste; but his sympathy lay with the underdog people against the oppressive French class system. Napoleon was his early hero, but when he brought back the priesthood and nobility and established the Empire, Beyle felt that he betrayed the Revolution. From that time on, though he served several governments rather well, it was without a sense of full commitment.

He never married. His restless pursuit of happiness led him into many travels, many loves, and many employments centering in military and civilian administration. His early success in school mathematics took him from Grenoble to Paris for the entrance examination for the Ecole Polytechnique; but apparently feeling no vocation, he never presented himself for this. Friends and distant relatives of his family who served Napoleon with distinction, the Darus, took him under their wing, found him a job, took him with them to work with the armies in Italy, and got him a commission in the 6th Dragoons, which he soon resigned in disgust with the drabness of barracks life. Back in Paris from 1802 on, Beyle devoted his main energies to a devious and unsuccessful courtship and to preparing to write plays, preferably comedies. He fell in love with an actress, Mélanie Guilbert, followed her to Marseilles in 1805, became her lover, and worked for a clothing company there for about a year. After returning to Paris and government service, he was sent to Brunswick for two years in army administration and later to Vienna, where he elaborated a vain plan to seduce Mme. Daru. In Paris again, he rose in his profession and found a new mistress; and on a holiday in Milan in 1811 he declared his love to an earlier *princesse lointaine* (as he thought), Angela ("Gina") Pietragrua, and was admitted into the ranks of her lovers, in which he remained for four years. Dispatched to Moscow in 1812 with messages for Napoleon and others, he saw the city burn and took part in the dismal retreat. He spent a while in Dresden on a new army assignment, a sick leave in Italy, and a busy time in Dauphiné directing defensive preparations against the threatened Allied invasion. He saw this come, however, with some relief, and transferred his allegiance to the restored Bourbon government; but his career was shattered, he was deeply in debt, and he retired to Milan in 1814 for a seven-year stay.

In this same year he started publishing with his largely borrowed *Lives of Haydn, Mozart, and Metastasio*, followed in 1817 by the *History of Painting in Italy* and *Rome, Naples, and Florence in 1817*. He at last broke off with Angela Pietragrua and fell into a hopeless four-year love for Mme. Mathilde ("Méthilde") Dembowski. In 1820 he learned that liberals around Milan suspected him of being a French royalist secret agent, while the Austrian authorities there thought him a republican *carbonaro*. In a suicidal mood he returned to Paris, where, with occasional side trips to England and Italy, he spent nine financially precarious but fruitful years as a free-lance writer. He frequented the salons of Mme. Destutt de Tracy and Mme. Ancelot, contracted successive *liaisons* with Countess Clémentine ("Menti") Curial, Mme. Alberthe ("Mme. Azur") de Rubempré, and a rejuvenating young Italian girl, Giulia Rinieri, who boldly declared her love to him when he was forty-seven. His perceptive deterministic treatise *On Love* (1822) went almost unsold, but he continued undaunted to write. *Racine and Shakspeare* (1823, 1825), which rejected the Frenchman and hailed the Englishman as the master of the modern sensibility, established him as a spokesman for Romanticism. Also of this period are his *Life of Rossini*; his first novel, *Armance*; his first real success, a high-grade guidebook called *Walks in Rome* (1829); and the first of his two great novels, *The Red and the Black* (1830). He was reading proof for this in Paris during the July Revolution.

Under the new government of Louis-Philippe a career opened up again for Henri Beyle. He hoped for a prefecture, but had to settle for a consulate, first briefly at Trieste, and then, again suspected of liberalism by the Austrian authorities, in the Papal town of Civitavecchia not far from Rome, where he spent most of the rest of his life. He served the state with bored efficiency; even to be in Italy was not enough. He had one long sick leave (1836–1839) in Paris where he worked for Foreign Minister Molé, and a shorter one from 1841 until his death a year later. He wrote many works, several of them incomplete, including *Souvenirs of Egotism, Lucien Leuwen*, the autobiographical *Life of Henri Brulard, Memoirs of a Tourist, Trip in the Midi*, and *Lamiel*. His finest achievement was his other great novel—his best in the eyes of many—*The Charterhouse of Parma*, written in less than eight weeks in Paris late in 1838; and he lived to rejoice in Balzac's generous praise of it. A paralytic stroke in March, 1841, warned him that death was near; it came a year later, after another such stroke in a Paris street, on March 23, 1842.

Coming to the novel, as we have seen, diffidently and only in his forties, Stendhal completed three (*Armance*, 1827; *The Red and the Black*, 1830; *The Charterhouse of Parma*, 1839), wrote much but not all of two others (*Lucien Leuwen*, 1834–1835; *Lamiel*, 1839–1842), and made many false starts. *Armance* studies the doomed love for Armance of the impotent young Octave de Malivert; *Lucien Leuwen* shows the growth, sexual education, and gradual emancipation of a rich banker's son, the unheroic hero of the title. *The Charterhouse of Parma* is the history of a charming young Italian noble, his bewildering experience at Waterloo, his life amid the political machinations of Parma, his love for his jailor's daughter, Clélia Conti, and the love that his passionate young aunt, the Duchess Gina Sanseverina, devotes to him and his welfare. *Lamiel* relates the worldly education and amorous career of a young girl foundling of great energy and thirst for experience. Diverse as they are, Stendhal's five novels have much in common. Each centers completely on a single hero (or heroine), usually from late adolescence on; each includes many autobiographical touches; each hero reveals much of Stendhal's temperament; each is presented with much the same blend of sympathy and irony that is so striking in *The Red and the Black*.

Stendhal found little in the novel of his day to emulate or admire. In his letter of 1832 to Count Salvagnoli seeking to promote *The Red and the Black* he speaks of three popular types: that written for chambermaids and devoured in the provinces, full of perfect protagonists and wildly romanesque episodes; the dull type written for the salons of Paris; and, on a higher level, those of Walter Scott. These last, he writes, have made long descriptions so popular that an author is sure to succeed if he spends two pages on the view from the hero's room, two more on his costume, and another two on the chair he is sitting in. He himself, weary of Scott's medievalry, has dared "to narrate an adventure that took place in 1830 and to leave the reader in complete ignorance about the form of the dresses worn by Mme. de Rênal and Mlle. de La Mole . . ." For, as he tells us elsewhere, "to write anything but the analysis of the human heart bores me." Another statement shows his eagerness to involve the reader and his concern about how to do so: "A novel," he writes, "is like a bow; the violin casing that renders the sounds is the reader."

Although a prefatory "notice by the editor" suggests that *The Red and the Black* was written in 1827, and although Stendhal himself several times assigns its composition to Marseilles in 1828, the plan clearly originated on the night of October 25–26, 1829, in Marseilles. Some time earlier Stendhal had read in the *Gazette des Tribunaux* of the trial in Bagnères and condemnation to five years in prison of a young cabinet maker named Lafargue for killing and decapitating his mistress. In his *Walks in Rome* he points to Lafargue as an example of the energy that the French so badly need, and Lafargue's behavior at many points suggests that of Julien Sorel. Much closer to the plot of *The Red and the Black* is an earlier story in the same *Gazette* (December 28–31, 1827) of the trial and execution of Antoine Berthet of Brangues, a twenty-five-year-old attempted murderer. Born of poor, honest working parents, physically frail but studious and intelligent, Berthet was adopted by the curate of Brangues, taught the rudiments, and sent to a seminary in Grenoble. Illness made him abandon his studies, but the well-to-do Michoud family engaged him as tutor to one of their children. Julien's affair with Mme. de Rênal is foreshadowed in vague terms:

> Did Mme. Michoud, an amiable and intelligent woman, then aged thirty-six and with a blameless reputation, think that without danger she could lavish signs of kindness upon a young man of twenty whose delicate health required special care? Did a precocious immorality in Berthet make him misunderstand the nature of this care? However all this may be, before a year was up M. Michoud had to think of setting a term to the young seminarian's stay in his house.

Berthet then entered the Belley seminary to go on with his studies. Later, leaving the Church, he became a preceptor with M. de Cordon, but after a year Cordon dismissed him "for reasons not perfectly known and that seem to be connected with a new intrigue." (In an 1830 account in another journal Berthet claimed that a letter from Mme. Michoud to M. de Cordon led to his dismissal.) Disappointed in his ambition, he went to Lyon, bought two pistols, stationed himself in the church near Mme. Michoud's pew, waited for communion, and fired two shots which did not kill her. His execution followed a long "antisocial" harangue to his judges.

Stendhal had many great gifts as a novelist, but not, as one critic has remarked, that of Scheherazade. He could not put his best into his dialogue if he had at the same time to be thinking of plot. His two great novels—*The Charterhouse of Parma* less, to be sure, than *The Red and the Black*—depend on borrowed plots. Yet what he takes remains the framework; what he makes of it is fully his own.

Just when he read the accounts of the Berthet case we do not know; but after his return to Paris late in 1829 from Marseilles, where the idea of the book had crystallized, his devoted cousin Romain Colomb tells of seeing on his table a mysterious dossier labeled "Julien." It was by this name that he thought of his book for some time; the final title came to him as an inspiration only after the first proofs. In January, 1830, he thought of making his hero a disciple of Plutarch and Napoleon. He recognized that his Marseilles manuscript was too skeletal and must be filled out. In April he signed a contract with Levavasseur to publish the book: fifteen hundred copies in two editions of different formats for 1,500 francs. By May the novel was well blocked out; but Stendhal—as he was to do later for *The Charterhouse of Parma*—continued working on the later chapters even as he corrected proofs, right through the July Revolution and into the fall, of the earlier ones. The book was published just after he left in early November, 1830, for his consulate in Trieste.

The title has been interpreted in various ways: as the colors of roulette, suggesting the play of chance; as the black of the priest and the *Congrégation* and the red of a host of candidates: the executioner, Jacobinism, the robes of the magistrates who condemn Julien to death, the curtains that adorn the church, and so on. The likeliest and most widely accepted explanation—and of course Stendhal may well have had more than one meaning in mind—is that the black indeed represents the clergy, which Julien chooses as being the only way in his time for a workman's son to rise in the world, while the red represents the soldier's uniform that Julien would have chosen if he had been born twenty-five years earlier.

Twice in his book Stendhal uses a famous metaphor (which he first attributes whimsically to Saint-Réal) when he calls the novel a mirror moving along a road. This tells part of what he is trying to do, for he subtitles his novel "A Chronicle of 1830" and takes justifiable pride in its value as a social document. However, the context in which he discusses this metaphor as his own (II:19) shows that it is mainly a defense for representing unedifying thoughts and actions. To his prospective prudish reader of the 1830's—and there were to be many of these—he protests: the mirror merely shows the mire, and you accuse the mirror. Mirrors, however, are passive; Stendhal's realism is neither passive nor photographic.

The style is dry, understated, crisp, ironic, full of unexpected twists and turns. It requires agility of the reader; one critic has compared reading Stendhal to riding a surfboard. This seems a bit excessive; but the reader, remembering the bow and the violin casing, must do his share; he must not nod. An example or two will illustrate.

Julien, arriving at Besançon but not yet at the seminary, wanders into a café and meets its hospitable young hostess, Amanda Binet (I:24):

> The young woman leaned out over the counter, which gave her a chance to show off a superb figure. Julien noted it; all his ideas changed.

For detached and ironic—though sympathetic—analysis, here is Julien's seduction of Mme. de Rênal (I:15). Having promised himself to do so and told her he would, he enters her room at two in the morning and is greeted with solemn reproach:

> There was a moment's confusion. Julien forgot his useless plan and reverted to his natural self. Not to find favor in the eyes of such a lovely woman seemed to him the worst of misfortunes. His only answer to her reproaches was to throw himself at her feet and clasp her knees. Since she said some very harsh things to him, he burst into tears.
>
> When Julien left Mme. de Rênal's bedroom some hours later, it might be said, in the style of the novel, that he had nothing more to desire. He was, in fact, obliged to the love he had inspired, and to the unexpected impression her seductive charms had made on him, for a conquest that all his clumsy maneuvering could never have brought off.
>
> Yet, victim of a bizarre pride, even in the sweetest moments, he still aspired to the role of a man who is used to subjugating women. He applied himself with incredible effort to spoil whatever was likable about him. . . . In a word, what made Julien a superior person was precisely what kept him from relishing the happiness that lay at his feet.

As these samples show, Stendhal the narrator is rarely absent for long. He is glad to tell us what he thinks—and what we should think—about many subjects: the weaknesses of the French, notably the bourgeoisie, provincials and Parisians alike; the desiccating oppressiveness of the Restoration; and, above all, about his protagonists: what they feel, why they feel so, and why they are acting well or badly, wisely or—more often—foolishly. A generation later, Flaubert's reaction against Romantic effusiveness will lead him to seek—not too successfully—to keep himself out of his books. Stendhal's reaction is found not in self-exclusion but in his dry ironic tone. He likes to talk to his reader, quietly, urbanely, as a man of the world. Again and again, as in the seduction scene just quoted, he comments on the actions of his heroes: "How fine—and how foolish!" His admirers, the "happy few" who are now legion, enjoy him as one of the wittiest and most perceptive of moralists.

As many critics have noted, Stendhal is the founder of the modern realism that shows man working out his destiny amid the economic, political, and social forces that shape his time. The France of 1830 is always there in all these aspects, both as a whole and in its two parts, Paris and *la province*. Much of that France is symbolized in Valenod, the man on the make, one-time would-be lover of Mme. de Rênal and would-be employer of Julien, who by cheating the poor and affecting the right politico-religious attitudes rises from his position as director of the poorhouse to supplant Rênal as mayor of Verrières and become a baron and future prefect. Julien is shown (II:13) as "the unhappy man at war with all society"; and it is his disgust with society, as represented by Valenod, that leads him at his trial to make the bitter speech that transforms his sentence, as one critic has put it, from a condemnation into a stoic suicide.

Yet firmly as *The Red and the Black* is rooted in the social, economic, and political climate of the time, its real subject is simply Julien Sorel, his life and above all his loves.[1]

The two loves are the first and only ones for Julien, and each is the first for each woman. The women are sharply contrasted. Mme. de Rênal, just under thirty, rich, noble, and thoroughly pious, married and with three young sons, has never presumed to judge her pompous husband or to admit to herself that he bored her, never supposed that conjugal relations could be sweeter and happier than theirs. Her deep affection for her children makes her fear that their new tutor will be harsh; her relief at Julien's youth and timidity makes her grateful and kind; bit by bit she falls in love with him. He, for his part, though drawn to her, regards her successive favors—letting him hold her hand, keep her hand, enter her room at night, make love to her—as steps in the war that he owes himself to wage against the upper classes.

[1]Stendhal was fond of comparing the intrusion of politics into the imaginary world of the novel with a pistol shot in the middle of a concert; see II:22 and *Armance, Walks in Rome*, and *The Charterhouse of Parma*.

Only after making love to her—as with Mathilde later—does he come to love her. The only obstacle to her love for him is religious remorse; this leads her finally to respond to M. de La Mole's inquiry by her letter denouncing Julien; but later her love again prevails; she casts aside remorse and false shame, stays with Julien openly all she can in his prison, and dies three days after his execution. Stendhal himself remarks several times that here is true love, uncalculating and complete; and it is this love that prevails in Julien's heart.

Mathilde de La Mole is more controversial. Stendhal at one point (II:11) says that he, the author, loves her (or likes her), and elsewhere refers to her and Mme. de Rênal as his pair of heroines; some critics have thought that he admired her as much as her rival, since even her final romanesque act is in defiance of bourgeois mores. I think he is far more detached than that. A count's daughter, rather beautiful, cutting if not clearly witty, she is the idol of Paris high society at nineteen; but this society, with its stereotyped young nobles, courageous and polite but unimaginative and afraid of ridicule, bores her to tears. The life she craves is that of 1574, when her idolized ancestor Boniface de La Mole was decapitated for his part in a plot against Charles IX. Mathilde cherishes the legend that Queen Margaret of Valois was La Mole's mistress and after his execution embalmed and preserved his head. The only love Mathilde is capable of is romanesque, theoretical, an *amour de tête*—and a release from boredom. Since Julien seems to despise all those around him—as in part he does, and as does she—she marks him as a man not to be despised himself. When he seems indifferent to her, as Stendhal points out in his letter to Salvagnoli, she falls in love out of piqued vanity and presently gives herself to him "solely to give herself the pleasure of thinking she has a grand passion."

Julien for his part gains this love of hers by chance and pride. His aim once again is to win a battle against society; when she first declares herself to him he resolves to have her and get out. The only time he clearly loves her—despite occasional later declarations that seem forced—is when she turns against him after their first night together. As long as he shows that he is still in love with her his cause is hopeless; as he soon learns, the only way to win her back is to be cold to her and pursue another woman. She is fated to love him best when he loves, or seems to love, her least; her criterion of merit seems to be capacity for disdain. To be sure, when she becomes pregnant with his child, tells her father, and resolves to marry Julien, he looks forward to a future with her—but mainly because of his prospective career as a noble army officer and for the sake of his future son, not for her sake; he still thinks of her (II:34) as "that monster of pride." In prison he is bored with her, weary of her heroics and need for spectators, happier alone, fully happy only with Mme. de Rênal. Mathilde resolves to kill herself within twenty-four hours of Julien's death; but she still plays out her grisly romanesque act with his decapitated head, still alive, while within three days and without heroics, obviously out of love and grief for Julien, Mme. de Rênal is dead. There are indeed two heroines; but I think there is no question which one Stendhal prefers, invites us to prefer, and considers capable of genuine love.

Julien of course is the center of our interest and attention. An unfortunate young man at war with society, he is also a very particular one. Worshiping Rousseau and above all Napoleon, he is primarily ambitious not, like his society, for money and pleasure, but for power and, especially, for glory, for a clear sense of his own superiority. To achieve this end hypocrisy is often needed, and —above all—strict obedience to his sense of duty, which often denies him happiness and constantly demands difficult, often heroic, actions to raise him up in his own eyes and those of others. Calculating in affairs of love, he aspires to the role of worldly seducer.

Yet he is often only a would-be egoist; his heart, as he recognizes (II:42), is easily touched. Despite his hard principles, he is capable of love—for Mme. de Rênal, for her children, for Abbé Pirard, for his devoted friend Fouqué, even—for a time and in his way—for Mathilde. Mme. de Rênal is not deluded in seeing tenderness and great idealism in him. Stendhal makes it abundantly clear that if Julien is at war with his society, one reason is that that society is corrupt.

What most disarms the reader in Julien is, I think, a kind of innocence, of which he is charmingly unaware. He thinks he knows at every point what others are thinking of him, but again and again he is wrong. As we have seen, he wins Mme. de Rênal in spite of the role he is earnestly trying to play. Determined that he must be a Tartuffe to succeed in this world, he is often an Alceste. What Stendhal most admires in him is his energy and unpredictability.

This unpredictability has led to wide differences of opinion about one episode: his attempt to kill Mme. de Rênal, which Stendhal in effect refuses to explain, describing his trip from Paris to Verrières and the two shots fired at her in one terse page. Some critics, overlooking Julien's frequent spontaneity, have seen this action as completely inconsistent with his calculating side. Some have inferred that he was in a kind of shock that allowed him no thoughts at all; and indeed Stendhal speaks three times in the next few pages of Julien's coming back to himself. However, I think it is truer to the text, and certainly to Stendhal's own comments in his letter to Salvagnoli, to see this as primarily an act of vengeance which will prove that he is no common *arriviste*. As the father of Mathilde's unborn child, he has attained the pinnacle of success: ennobled, rich, with a brilliant military career in prospect. Suddenly he feels himself betrayed by the person he has loved best—and unjustly at that, since Mme. de Rênal's letter to the Count de La Mole has portrayed him as a vulgar climber. Once earlier he had started to kill Mathilde (II:17), when she told him of her shame at having given herself to the first man who came along; though he held back then, he can act violently when his honor is wounded. And, probably to show himself incapable of sly self-seeking, he chooses to shoot his betrayer in a public, sacred place, the church. He clearly plans to kill her and to pay for it with his life.

Few characters if any in fiction can keep us believing but—even after many readings—also guessing as does Julien. And to a considerable extent the other major characters share this *imprévu,* this unpredictability. It is one of the great achievements of *The Red and the Black,* for here, as not always in life, it carries conviction. For this the reader may well be grateful.

—Donald M. Frame

SELECTED BIBLIOGRAPHY

Works by Stendhal (Henri Beyle)

Published During His Life

Vies de Haydn, de Mozart, et de Métastase (Lives of Haydn, Mozart, and Metastasio), 1814 Music Biography and Criticism

Histoire de la peinture en Italie (History of Painting in Italy), 1817 Study

Rome, Naples et Florence, 1817; revised 1826 Travel Book

De l'amour (On Love), 1822 Study

Racine et Shakespeare, I, 1823; II, 1825 Study of Romanticism

Armance, 1827 Novella

Promenades dans Rome (A Roman Journal), 1829 Travel Journal

Le Rouge et le Noir (The Red and the Black), 1830 Novel (0451-517938)

Memoires d'un touriste (Memoirs of a Tourist), 1838 Travel Journal

La Chartreuse de Parme (The Charterhouse of Parma), 1839 Novel (0451-518586)

L'Abbesse de Castro (includes *Vittoria Accoramboni* and *Les Cenci*), 1839 Novellas

Published After His Death

Journal (covers his years 1801–1818), 1888 Journal

Lamiel, wirtten 1839; published 1889 Unfinished Novel

Vie de Henri Brulard (The Life of Henri Brulard), written 1835–1836; published 1890 Autobiography

Souvenirs d'égotisme (Memoirs of Egotism), written 1832; published 1892 Autobiography

Lucien Leuwen, written 1834–1835; published 1894 Unfinished Novel Trilogy

Le Chasseur Vert (The Green Huntsman)

Le Télégraphe (The Telegraph)

Biography and Criticism

Adams, Robert M. *Stendhal: Notes on a Novelist.* New York: Noonday Press, 1959.

Alter, Robert, in collaboration with Carol Cosman. *A Lion for Love: A Critical Biography of Stendhal.* New York: Basic Books, 1979.

Auerbach, Erich. "In the Hôtel de la Mole." In his *Mimesis: The Representation of Reality in Western Literature*. Trans. Willard R. Trask. Princeton: Princeton Univ. Press, 1953, pp. 454-492.

Bersani, Leo. "The Paranoid Hero in Stendhal." In his *A Future for Astyanax: Character and Desire in Literature*. Boston and Toronto: Little, Brown, 1976, pp. 106-127.

Brombart, Victor, ed. *Stendhal: A Collection of Critical Essays*. Englewood Cliffs, N.J.: Prentice-Hall, 1962.

————. *Stendhal: Fiction and the Themes of Freedom*. New York: Random House, 1968.

Giraud, Raymond. *The Unheroic Hero in the Novels of Stendhal, Balzac and Flaubert*. New Brunswick, N.J.: Rutgers Univ. Press, 1957.

Green, F. C. *Stendhal*. Cambridge: Cambridge Univ. Press, 1939.

Hemmings, F. W. J. *Stendhal: A Study of His Novels*. Oxford: Clarendon Press, 1964.

Howe, Irving. "Stendhal: The Politics of Survival." In his *Politics and the Novel*. New York: Horizon Books, 1957.

Levin, Harry. "Stendhal." In his *The Gates of Horn: A Study of Five French Realists*. New York: Oxford Univ. Press, 1963, pp. 84-149.

Lukács, Georg. "Balzac and Stendhal." In his *Studies in European Realism*. London: Hillway, 1950, pp. 65-84.

Ortega y Gasset, José. "Love in Stendhal." In his *On Love: Aspects of a Single Theme*. Trans. Toby Talbot. New York: New American Library, 1957, pp. 19-78.

Turnell, Martin. "Stendhal." In his *The Novel in France*. New York: New Directions, 1959, pp. 123-208.

————. "Stendhal's First Novel." In his *The Art of French Fiction*. New York: New Directions, 1959, pp. 61-90.

————. "Stendhal's Last Novel." In his *The Rise of the French Novel*. New York: New Directions, 1978, pp. 147-168.

Wood, Michael. *Stendhal*. Ithaca, N.Y.: Cornell Univ. Press, 1971.

READ THE TOP 20
SIGNET CLASSICS